P9-DTQ-124

ALSO BY BEVERLY BYRNE

Women's Rites

A
MATTER
OF
TIME

Beverly Byrne

A MATTER OF TIME

VILLARD BOOKS
NEW YORK
1987

Copyright © 1987 by Beverly Byrne

All rights reserved under International and Pan-American Copyright Conventions. Published in the United States by Villard Books, a division of Random House, Inc., New York, and simultaneously in Canada by Random House of Canada Limited, Toronto.

Grateful acknowledgment to reprint excerpts from the poem "Burnt Norton" in *Four Quartets* by T. S. Eliot is made to Harcourt Brace Jovanovich, Inc., and to Faber and Faber Ltd. Copyright 1943 by T. S. Eliot; renewed 1971 by Esmé Valerie Eliot.

ISBN: 0-394-56287-9

Library of Congress Catalogue
Card Number: 87-40180

Manufactured in the United States of America

9 8 7 6 5 4 3 2

First Edition

BOOK DESIGN: JESSICA SHATAN

FOR BILL,
AS ALWAYS

Time present and time past

Are both perhaps present in time future

And time future contained in time past.

If all time is eternally present

All time is unredeemable.

What might have been is an abstraction

Remaining a perpetual possibility

Only in a world of speculation.

What might have been and what has been

Point to one end, which is always present.

Footfalls echo in the memory

Down the passage which we did not take

Towards the door we never opened

Into the rose-garden. My words echo

Thus, in your mind.

—T. S. ELIOT, "Burnt Norton"

A
MATTER
OF
TIME

Prologue

1964: IPSWICH, MASSACHUSETTS, AND ROME, ITALY

In the silence and the stillness was the music. The child sought the silence often; head bent, rapt, listening to the four notes echoing within. She sought it now, perched on a swing descending from the gnarled branch of an apple tree, one small, sneakered foot dug into the scuffed grass, anchoring the sturdy little body to the earth. The mother watched and knew.

"I wish Sarah was more outgoing," Rita Myles said.

The neighbor woman followed Rita's glance out the kitchen door to the swing. "She's only five, don't worry. Next year, when she goes to school, it will be different."

Rita sliced more cake, poured more coffee. Her eyes kept straying to the child on the swing and her gestures bespoke agitation.

"Stop worrying," the neighbor said. She spoke of other things in hope of distracting the mother.

Minutes passed and the child didn't move. The wind rose and ruffled her dark curls and clouds blew in over the marshlands that ringed this northeastern corner of Massachusetts, and still she remained motionless.

Rita went to the door. "Sarah, come in, honey. It's going to rain. Come have some cake."

The little girl's head rose; to Rita it seemed as if she had summoned her daughter back from a far place. Dutifully Sarah clambered off the swing and came, stopping to pick up a stuffed doll lying in the grass. Rita held open the screen and waited, closing it firmly once Sarah was inside. "Say hello to Mrs. Katz," she prompted.

"Hello. Is it going to thunder?"

"Maybe," Milly Katz admitted. She ruffled the dark curls and kissed the plump cheek, smelling the special smell of childhood on the soft, fresh skin. Her own children were older, past the time of cuddling. "What do you care? You're safe in here with Mommy and me." One woman poured the child's milk, the other gave her cake.

"When it thunders, the music gets louder," the child said.

"Sarah! You promised to stop telling that fib. It's a sin. The baby Jesus doesn't like fibbing." Rita turned to Milly. "She's made up this crazy story about a song she hears."

"So? Sarah's got a good imagination. What's wrong with that?"

"It makes me nervous," Rita said. "Frank and I keep telling her, but you know how she is. Stubborn."

They spoke as if the child could not hear or understand, but of course she could. "I do hear the music," she insisted. "It's not a fib. I can hear it now. Listen." She hummed a simple melody, repeated it. Just four notes.

"Catchy," Milly said. "Maybe you'll be a songwriter when you grow up."

A few minutes later Milly left the Myleses' house and returned to her own across the street, entering through the kitchen at the back and absentmindedly pausing to put her fingers to her lips and touch them to the mezuzah that hung on the doorpost. They put it here when they bought the house five years ago, not in front because they did not wish to be ostentatious about Jewish things the neighbors would not understand.

There was a piano in the living room, bought when a child now grown and uninterested had shown a hint of musical talent. Milly could play a little, just by ear, and she insisted on keeping the piano tuned. Now she turned back the cover and exposed the keys and hummed the tune Sarah had hummed. With one finger she picked out the notes. Do-sol-la-fa. And again. Do-sol-la-fa.

She returned to the kitchen and stood on a chair and took a notebook from its hiding place in the cupboard above the refrigerator, behind the teapot she only used at Passover. She flicked through all the pages with writing on them until she came to a blank one. Then she wrote the date and the time and the words, "Sarah says she hears music. The notes are do-sol-la-fa."

The bishop was not comfortable with his new rank or its titles. Called to Rome and raised to the purple a year before, he still preferred to be addressed as a Benedictine monk. His associates were instructed to call him Dom Malachy. The young American priest knew that, but not much else. "I'm not sure I understand, Dom Malachy."

"Because I'm saying things it's not now fashionable to say." The bishop was tall and slim; the aristocratic heritage showed, but so too the asceticism and the holy fire of belief behind his dark eyes. "These days the Holy Father feels he must make public apologies and the Church takes on herself the guilt of the Jews."

Father Larry Donovan searched for a proper response. This interview could secure for him a post with the bishop's office and he wanted that. He was not particularly interested in the work of overseeing the scriptural courses in the seminaries of Rome, but he had been four years a student in the city, and he hoped to remain. Besides, a Vatican posting would help his career, even if eventually he returned to Boston. "You believe the Jews really are guilty?"

"In a sense, yes. We cannot ignore the history, Father Donovan."

"But it's often confused, perhaps even distorted, wouldn't you say?"

"Sometimes. Often by the Jews themselves." The bishop turned in his chair and looked at the shelves of books behind him. He was above all else a formidable scholar, which had precipitated the call to Rome. "I could, for instance, tell you of a document no one has seen, but to which there are tantalizing references. Supposedly it was written soon after the death of our Lord, a revisionist tale of the relations between the synagogue and the infant Church. They call it the Alexandria Testament."

Donovan was confused. "And . . ."

"And if by chance the Jews should find it, they would use it to harm the Church. You can rely on that, Father."

"If I were to be asked to join your staff, Dom Malachy, would my duties involve looking for this Alexandria Testament?"

The older man laughed softly. "No, it's merely an interest of mine. I only mentioned it to illustrate my point. Things are often not what they seem, that's what I want you to realize. Particularly not where Jews are concerned."

Donovan felt sweat drip beneath his cassock. "I see. I would try to be alert to that, of course."

"I hope so. You Americans are often so pragmatic. That can be a mistake. Tell me, Father, are you familiar with the writings of Carl Jung?"

"No, sir, I can't say I am."

The bishop reached behind him and withdrew a thick volume. "This has recently been published. *Memories, Dreams, Reflections,* a distillation of Dr. Jung's thought and work. One idea of his interests me particularly, racial memory, the collective unconscious. Suppose, for example, the descendants of the writer of the Alexandria Testament had some deeply hidden memory of it. Some vestigial knowledge of what it contained, perhaps even where the document itself could be found. That might explain these references that keep cropping up century after century."

"Fascinating," Donovan said. He didn't know what to add.

"Yes. And whatever you're thinking, not farfetched. I know it for a fact." The bishop rose, signaling the end of the interview. "I shall think about our talk, Father, and let you know my decision."

The following week the American priest was invited to become part of the bishop's staff. And that put all the pieces in place for what was to follow, though neither Father Donovan nor Dom Malachy had ever heard of little Sarah Myles.

Book One

APRIL 1983–
NOVEMBER 1984

O_{ne}

On a Sunday morning in April of 1983, when she was twenty-four years old, Sarah Myles lost her faith. More correctly, she admitted it was gone. The realization came while she was at the ten o'clock Mass in Holy Trinity Church on Beacon Street in Brookline, Massachusetts.

"Let us offer each other a sign of Christ's peace," the young priest said. Sarah turned dutifully to the man on her left and the little girl on her right and shook their hands. She knew neither of her fellow parishioners and they didn't know her, but they smiled at each other and attempted to put some genuine warmth in the gesture.

The priest elevated the consecrated host. "This is the Lamb of God. This is Jesus, who takes away our sins and the sins of the world."

And that's when it happened.

I don't believe any of this . . . as if a voice were speaking the words slowly and clearly inside her head . . . I haven't believed it for months, for over a year. So what am I doing sitting here going through the motions? Being an outrageous hypocrite, that's what.

She remained where she was a few moments more, examining the taste and the shape of such an extraordinary revelation, trying to understand what she felt. Except that she didn't really feel anything. Truth was not, in this case, a place in the heart; it was an intellectual certitude, a realization that her universe had turned upside down—and that however much she might wish it to be different, she couldn't ignore the fact that she was standing on her head.

The congregation began moving in the pews, spilling out into the aisle to form the line that would take them to the altar for Holy Communion. Sarah rose and followed them, but she didn't approach the altar; instead she turned and slipped out the door to the street.

For a few moments she stood on the red-brick steps, looking at the world which should be so suddenly changed, and was not. The only remarkable thing was that in twenty-four hours winter had given way to spring. It was a glorious morning, bright and sunny and almost warm. There were crowds of people milling about enjoying the event. Taking a deep breath, Sarah turned her back on Holy Trinity Church and stepped into the throng.

She was largely unaware of it, but though she was not quite five feet tall, most people noticed Sarah. It wasn't her unusually deep-set green eyes or her dark, curly hair, today tied back with a red cotton bandanna. It wasn't the chunky fisherman's knit sweater worn over faded cords from which the Calvin Klein label hung by a thread, or the voluptuous figure the casual clothes didn't conceal. The secret of Sarah Myles's appeal was her vibrancy, the quality of unbridled life she conveyed. Sarah was a mover. Her bounce and her energy showed in the way she carried herself, the way she walked; it was in the swing of her hips and the unconscious toss of her head. It was her exuberance that was so attractive; the good looks were a bonus. Sarah Myles stood out, even among this crowd of affluent, energetic young.

Though legally a separate city, Brookline was an overflow of Boston. The eighties had seen a renaissance of that great city, it was no longer the staid bastion of the legendary Brahmins, the nation's slightly shabby, albeit genteel, maiden aunt. Boston had

entered the world of trendy today, and the glitz had spread. Brookline too jived to a contemporary beat. Sarah's route home was lined
with small shops filled with artful displays of boiler suits and running gear and patchwork pillows and Aztec-inspired jewelry.
Gourmet groceries displayed cheeses from every corner of the
globe and liquor stores filled their windows with wine, not scotch.
Porsches and BMWs jostled for space on the road, and the drivers
had to watch for joggers and cyclists. Normally Sarah enjoyed the
scene; today she ignored it.

What had happened to a lifetime's training? To a complete set of
values? To an integrated way of looking at the world? Where had
it all gone? And when? She hadn't made some labored decision to
leave the Church. It had left her. Somehow it had moved itself
intact out of her orbit, taking with it the rituals and rubrics, the
formulae that stood for beliefs and convictions. And she'd refused
to notice what was happening until the separation was complete,
until she was transformed into an outsider who no longer read or
wrote the shorthand. She could see the marks, but they were obscure scrawls, without sense or meaning.

There was a bakery on the corner of her block. The earthy smell
of humped pumpernickel loaves mingled with that of overblown
buttery croissants. She usually bought something wonderful here
after Mass on Sundays. She stopped automatically, but the crowd
at the bakery counter was three deep. And she wasn't hungry.
Sarah moved on.

When she turned the corner, she was on West Street. It had never
been part of the golden ghetto, that fabled Brookline enclave of
fantasy-Hollywood homes inhabited by Jewish millionaires. This
block was lined with two- and three-story structures built in the
forties for those who served them and sold to them, the Poles and
the Irish who in the postwar boom were able to move out of
crowded Boston tenements. On West Street the boasts were nice
setbacks and big comfortable porches. In its heyday it had been
blue-collar heaven. Now that *gentrification* and the *singles life-style*
were the favored buzzwords, the street had changed. Sarah's apartment was typical. It had been converted from the attic of a
two-family house. You added a picture window and an exterior
staircase and presto, rental income.

Sarah loved the place. The first thing she did when she moved in three years ago was to paint the stairway bright blue and set a terra-cotta pot on each step. Today green tips were newly emerged from the earth in the pots. The white jonquils she'd planted would be in flower soon. And she'd already decided to have slashes of color during the summer. Acid red geraniums and purple petunias. Not a traditional combination, but Sarah had majored in art history and she worked at Boston's prestigious Grimes Museum as assistant to the assistant director. She knew the colors would work.

Before she climbed the stairs, she could hear Bruce Springsteen telling the whole neighborhood he was born in the U.S.A. When she opened the door of the flat, the music was deafening. Pinkie, of course; she adored Springsteen. And it wasn't unlike Penelope Lee Arbuckle, fugitive from Virginia, to go out and leave the stereo playing. "Looks like it's just you and me, Brucie. We've got to stop meeting like this." Sarah turned down the volume.

Then she realized she wasn't alone. The smell of coffee wafted from the tiny kitchen under the eaves, and she could hear the sound of the shower. So her roommate was still home.

There was a red lace half-cup bra hanging from a corner of Sarah's favorite picture. She had long ago accepted Pinkie's habit of trailing her belongings all over the small apartment. Sarah just went behind her, restoring order to their shared universe. She crossed the room and removed the bra. So she couldn't avoid look-ing at the picture.

It was her most prized possession, a Chagall print from the Bible series. This one was of Daniel, an old, flint-gray, hard-edged man set against a blue background. Daniel the seer, the prophet who alone in his time could decipher the handwriting on the wall. The print was one of a limited edition of two thousand, bought with five hundred hard-earned dollars when she first left her parents' Ipswich house. A declaration that Sarah was grown up, had both taste and money of her own. And now? Could she still love Daniel if she thought him a prophet without a God? Crazy. Of course she could. Millions of nonbelievers were art lovers.

"Hi, you're back early." Wrapped in a turquoise kimono that displayed the long legs Sarah openly envied, and toweling her short blond hair, Pinkie emerged from the bathroom. "Coffee's ready."

She loped into the kitchen, as usual bumping her head and swearing. "Fuck these picturesque rafters. What'd y'all bring from the bakery?" Five years in the North hadn't affected Pinkie's southern drawl.

"Nothing."

"Nothing? What do I send you to church for, sugar? You think it has something to do with religion? We're reduced to the buttermilk lemon cake your mama sent yesterday. Not exactly penance. That lady must be the best baker on the planet."

"Probably. Listen, I've decided not to go to church anymore. And you just gave me the best explanation. That's what it's been about, religion. But not belief."

Pinkie came out of the kitchen carrying a tray with two mugs of coffee and two enormous slices of cake. She tilted her head and studied Sarah. "Do I detect a serious crisis?"

"Is there some other kind of crisis?"

Pinkie sighed. "If you don't want to talk about it, that's okay. But just tell me to mind my own business, don't correct my English."

"Sorry." Sarah took a mug of coffee and ignored the cake. She curled into the corner of the sofa. It was covered in a muted purple madras plaid and she'd upholstered it herself. Springsteen was still singing in the background. She opened her mouth to say something to Pinkie. And it happened again, the phenomenon she'd lived with all her life, that she had to accept because it wouldn't go away. She heard other music, four repeated notes, *do, sol, la, fa.* . . .

Sarah put her head back and closed her eyes. When it came, the interior song drowned out everything else, it pulled at her, summoned her. But to where? She didn't want to know. That way lay chaos. She pushed the sound away, tried to struggle back into the present. There were a few seconds when she teetered on the edge, when the music might have won. But it didn't. Sarah did.

Pinkie was accustomed to that brief and silent battle. She knew something was happening in Sarah's head, but not exactly what. They'd talked about it a few times, but it was always Sarah who raised the subject. Pinkie found the whole thing incomprehensible. She just told herself it was one of Sarah's peculiarities, like wanting everything neat and tidy. She turned off the stereo and dropped into a burgundy twill chair, also upholstered by Sarah. "You want to talk, sugar? About this church thing, I mean." Gently, because for all her superficial brashness, Pinkie cared.

"Nothing to talk about. I just realized I'm not a Catholic anymore, that's all."

"Oh, okay." The blonde took a big bite of the lemon cake. "Maybe I'll stop being FFV too. You're right, all this cultural heritage crap is a pain in the ass."

Sarah grinned. "I don't think being descended from one of Virginia's first families is exactly the same thing. Anyway, you work so hard at trashing southern womanhood they've probably drummed you out of the corps in absentia."

Pinkie finished the cake and licked her fingers. "We're talking about you, not me. Mind telling me how you came to make this momentous decision?"

Sarah pulled the bandanna from her head. The long dark curls spilled free, and she ran her fingers through them. "I got almost to the end of Mass this morning and I realized I was just going through the motions. No belief anymore, no conviction."

"Know what I think? I think it's something to do with that ass Hal Watkins. I mean the Church is always telling you sex is only for married folks and making babies, and here you are sleeping with that schnook and getting nothing out of it, and certainly not intending to make a baby."

Sarah shook her head. "Not here I am, there I was. I haven't seen Hal in three months. Anyway, that's not it. Did I ever tell you about Charlie Ryan?" Pinkie shook her head. "Okay, forget it," Sarah said. "It's not important now. But take my word for it, Catholics are used to sinning and believing at the same time. We're good at it. It's not about being perfect, just about trying to be."

"So?"

"So it's not guilt that's bothering me. That's an easy out, but it doesn't apply." She looked into the mug of coffee and avoided Pinkie's eyes. "You know about my music, the four notes I've always heard in my head?"

"I know what you've told me. And sometimes I see you fighting it, like just now. But I don't pretend I understand."

14

"That's just it," Sarah said softly. "Neither do I. All my life I've lived with that music and with my religion. Only the two things have never come together. That's crazy. Religion is about the unknown; being a Catholic should have made me able to deal with the music in a rational way. But it never did."

"You ever talk to a priest about it, sugar?"

"Sure, a couple of them, when I was a kid. They always told me to forget about it, that it was my imagination." Sarah hummed the four notes aloud. "It's not my imagination, Pinkie; it never has been. And if priests really had some pipeline to another world, another reality, they should know that."

"You really hear this music, like we can hear Springsteen if we turn on the stereo?"

"No. I've told you, it's not like that. It's inside my head, not outside. But not the way you remember a melody or hum it to yourself either." She spread her hands in a helpless gesture. "Different, but real."

Pinkie sighed. "Okay, if you say so."

"Do you realize you're the only person I've talked to about it since I was twelve? Even my mother always refused to discuss it. When I was little, I tried to make her understand, but I could see she was scared to death. She insisted I was lying, fibbing she called it, because that's what she needed to believe. I got over being angry with her about it. But outside the confessional I never told another soul until you. Maybe because you're such a nut nothing seems crazy to you."

"Not true. I'll tell you what I think is crazy. This celibate life you've been living since you got rid of Watkins. One swallow doesn't make a spring, sugar. And one lousy lover doesn't knock the entire male sex out of the running. Find a new man, Sarah. Get yourself properly laid. It will cure whatever ails you." Pinkie stretched luxuriously. "I guarantee it, and I should know."

Sarah laughed and stood up. "Now that you mention it, you should, so I'll take your advice under consideration. Meanwhile you'd better get dressed. You said Max would be here around noon. It's ten of."

"Puttin' on clothes is a waste of time." Pinkie uncurled herself

15

from the chair and headed for the bedroom. "We'll just rush back to his place and tear 'em all off."

"I'm going to dye your wedding gown scarlet," Sarah called after her.

"Better not. Anybody marrying Mrs. Schwartz's little Maxie has to do it in white satin with all the trimmings. She'll boil you in chicken soup if you mess that up."

Which was true, though probably the last female on earth Mrs. Schwartz would have chosen for her son was Penelope Lee Arbuckle, FFV. And on the surface of it Pinkie should have agreed. Max Schwartz was a dentist with an apartment on India Wharf and a practice near his parents' home in Newton. He was thirty-two, balding, stood barely five feet five and weighed perhaps one-forty with his clothes on. Pinkie went out with him the first time because she lost a bet at her office. She didn't arrive home until six the next morning. And she came and woke Sarah up.

"Listen, I have to tell somebody . . . I've never been so thoroughly, wonderfully, completely fucked in my twenty-seven promiscuous years. That's the world's most amazing little Jewish firecracker, sugar. I just may marry the bastard." Three weeks later they were engaged.

At noon the bell rang. Sarah let Max in. He kissed her cheek. "Hi, doll. Where's my big, beautiful, blond shiksa?"

"Getting dressed. Max, listen, I want to ask you something. Why are you getting married by a rabbi?"

"Why? Because I don't want my father to cut me out of his will and my mother to have a stroke."

Sarah narrowed her eyes and studied him. "Is that it, Max? The rabbi is just for your folks? Nothing to do with you?"

Pinkie came in before he could answer. "No, you don't. You're not getting Maxie embroiled in your theological problems. We have to see the caterers at one, and I've got plans for the rest of the afternoon. C'mon, lover, your southern belle is ringing, and horny as hell."

They were on their way out the door when Pinkie paused by a table piled high with magazines. They were all Sarah's, mostly serious journals of contemporary Catholic thought. "Under the new dispensation you better figure out what you're going to do with all this," she said.

Sarah waited until they'd left, then walked to the table and flipped through the magazines. Hidden in the folds of one was a letter. Something Pinkie didn't know about, something that lent more importance than she realized to her parting comment.

Sarah held the letter in her hand for a moment, tapping it against her palm. It was from the Sister Provincial of the Franciscan Missionaries of Mary. She'd been corresponding with the convent since she broke up with Hal. And trying to decide if she was serious. She'd never been in love with Hal, so it wasn't a rebound choice. Not in the usual way. It was just that the whole thing had been such a letdown. Her first affair, and it had been a big nothing that left her empty and unsatisfied. So maybe she wasn't ever going to fall in love, maybe she needed something bigger, grander. Maybe she should be a nun. Maybe that's what the four notes in her head were all about. A call from God. Despite her mother and the unsympathetic priests.

She moved to the picture window and stared at the street, the letter still in her hands. A bunch of neighborhood kids were skating in the sunshine. Sarah watched them for a while. Finally she opened the envelope and read the letter again.

". . . I appreciate your interest in working with our sisters in Central and South America. We're convinced that if the option for the poor means anything, it must be that congregations like ours, founded to bear apostolic witness to the gospel in faraway lands, have a primary obligation to the third world. On the other hand, that alone is not a sufficient reason to become a member of our community. I hope you will pray and think deeply about this, Sarah. If after doing so you believe our Lord is calling you to join us, please complete the enclosed application form. . . ."

The form was three pages long and very detailed. It included a request for a copy of her baptismal certificate and the name of her pastor. It had, however, no space for explaining about four notes of recurrent music heard since childhood. Sarah took a deep breath, then she carefully tore the contents of the envelope to shreds.

The kids were still skating in the street. And it was still a gorgeous day. She dropped the scraps of paper into the wastebasket and went out. She knew the little girl who lived downstairs. "Hey, Jill, lend me your skates and I'll show you why I was the number one roller skater in all of Ipswich." She was a little nervous while she put them on, but in ten seconds she knew she could still do it. Sarah was a mover.

Father Tom Lasky was chaplain of St. Joseph's College for Girls in Topsfield. Sarah had known him all during her four years at St. Joseph's, and she saw him occasionally after she graduated in 1980. Not for sacramental reasons, she never went to confession to Father Lasky. He was just a good friend. And two months ago, when she conceived the notion of becoming a Franciscan missionary and going off to El Salvador or Nicaragua, he'd seemed a logical confidant. So now she had to tell him that she'd changed her mind.

"I'm not surprised," the priest said. "I've never thought it was right for you."

"Why?" Funny to bridle at that now, when she'd decided the same thing. But she did. "Why?" she repeated. "And don't tell me I'm not the type."

"I don't really know why. But it's true, you're not the type."

"What is the type, for God's sake?"

"I don't know that either. Only that people called to the religious life go at it differently from you. They're responding to *someone,* not something. What you are is a compulsive liberal. You feel guilty because you're white and middle-class and talented. That's not a good enough set of reasons to enter the convent."

"A knee-jerk liberal is the phrase. And artists are talented. Knowing a lot about the history of art just makes me educated."

"Okay, educated then. What were you planning, lectures on the German Impressionists for the Sandinistas?"

"I wasn't planning anything. Presumably one is trained to be of use."

Father Lasky grinned. "Do you mind telling me why we're arguing about this if, as you say, you tore up the entry form and don't plan to go?"

"No reason. I guess I'm just bad-tempered this evening. It's Friday, I'm tired."

He cocked his head. "You're going home for the weekend from here, right?"

18

"Right. And I'm leaving before you subject me to any more of your cut-rate analysis. *Ciao,* Dr. Freud."

In good weather the drive from Topsfield to Ipswich took exactly twenty-six minutes. Sarah knew every bend of the road. When she agreed to commute to St. Joseph's, her father had bought her the 1977 Honda Civic she still owned. It suited her, and she swore the car could find its own way to the home of Rita and Frank Myles. Which was a good thing, because she wasn't thinking about her driving. She hadn't told Father Lasky about her apostasy, for the same reasons she'd never told him about her music. It just seemed too difficult to explain. But seeing him tonight inevitably made her focus on the whole thing again.

What does it mean, not believing? How do you get a "big bang" without some intelligence creating the elements that go into it? Okay, but that's more fundamental, it's not what the Church is really about. She found herself whispering words aloud in the car, snatches of the Creed. ". . . and I believe in Jesus Christ, our Lord. For our sake He came down from heaven . . . conceived of the Holy Spirit, born of the Virgin Mary . . . God from God, light from light . . . true God and true Man. . . ."

That was the problem, that's the part that sounded like pie in the sky. A personal, caring God. Jesus, our brother. Jesus who promises us life everlasting. Tremendous if it was true, but she didn't really think it was. She wasn't interested in building a life on self-delusion. And the music? Is that a delusion? No, it's real. But the Church never offered any explanation for that, it was uncomfortable with it. Like her mother, the lifelong devoted Catholic, was uncomfortable with it. So no Church and no convent. And as far as the four notes went, she'd keep on doing what she'd done for years, ignore them. She was damned good at it.

And by the time she got that far she was there, at the big white colonial house on the edge of the salt marsh. Sarah took a deep breath, got out of the car, and walked up the path with her customary jaunty step. The door was always unlocked. "Hi, anybody home? It's me."

"You're late." Rita Myles came out of the kitchen to meet her daughter in the front hall. "I was worried, honey."

"I'm sorry." Sarah put her small overnight bag down on the

19

braided rug, next to a pine dry sink filled with dried silver-white ovoids of honesty. "I brought you some daffodils, first of the season. How about my changing this arrangement?" She picked up the vase and followed her mother to the kitchen.

"What kept you?" Rita was cooking, taking something from the refrigerator. It was concealed behind a door painted in dull colonial red and fitted with irregular handmade arrow hinges. "Daddy waited for a while, but he's sleeping now."

"He'll be down for dinner, won't he?"

"Yes, probably. I think he's planning to go back to the factory tonight."

"He works too hard, it's silly. No wonder he's tired."

"He's getting on," Rita said gently. "But he doesn't like to admit it." She touched her carefully arranged blond hair with one hand, reminding herself she was still twenty years younger than her husband.

"I can't stay the whole weekend," Sarah said. "Something's come up. I have to go back tomorrow night." That would work, it would get her out of the necessity of accompanying her parents to Mass on Sunday morning.

She expected a protest, but Rita had something else on her mind. "Listen, honey, a man from New York wrote me last week. He had one of my cakes while he was on vacation in Rockport. Burnt Sugar Almond. The large loaf. He said it was the best he ever tasted and I should market it all over the country."

Sarah went on arranging the flowers and watched her mother slice onions and add them to the beans and molasses in the Crock-pot on the pine counter. Rita scored the rind of a piece of salt pork and laid it on top of the mélange. Her Boston baked beans were almost as famous as her cakes. These would be ready for dinner tomorrow night.

"Exactly when do you add the grape jelly?" Sarah asked. That was Rita's secret ingredient, two tablespoons of Welch's grape jelly in every pot of beans.

"Four hours before they're ready to serve. Just the other day Milly Katz was saying I should market the beans right across the country too. But like I told Milly, I couldn't take on something like that without you." Rita's smile was tremulous and there was the hint of a sob in her voice.

20

"Mom, I'm sorry, but we've been all over this."

"I know. I won't mention it again. But do you think I should write to the man in New York?"

"Sure, if he's got concrete ideas, not just praise."

"I couldn't judge that. Would you write him for me? Make the first contact."

Sarah turned her back. "I'm very busy, my job's demanding. You know that."

"Yes, sure. Forget it." The two women were silent for a few moments, pretending to be absorbed with their separate tasks. Rita spoke first. "You never told me what made you late."

"I stopped to see Father Lasky."

"Oh." Reproach was in the single sound. There was little to be gained by spending one's time with a celibate priest. Sarah should be looking for a husband if she wouldn't consent to working with her mother and making her small bakery, Cakes, Etc., a nation-wide miracle like Sara Lee. "Seen Hal lately?" Rita asked.

Sarah put the last yellow flower in place. "No. We broke up months ago. I told you that."

"Yes, I guess you did. Only I hoped . . ."

She turned from the vase and put her arm around her mother's shoulders and felt some of the stiffness go out of them. "Listen," she said softly, "how about my coming into the shop tomorrow afternoon? It will give you a few hours off."

It was a peace offering eagerly accepted. "That would be swell, honey. The parish council is having a meeting about whether to sell some of the old vestments. I'd like to go."

"Who in hell wants to buy old vestments?"

"Some company in Chicago. They have antique value now."

Sarah remembered when the parish council was called the Altar and Rosary Society. She was giggling as she carried the daffodils back to the hall.

Cakes, Etc. was located in a storefront next to Frank Myles's big commercial bakery. Sarah's father produced sliced packaged bread for supermarkets. Everything in his factory was automated, from the first weighing out of the ingredients to the final sealing of the plastic wrappers. Next door his wife made by hand luscious cakes and pies and cookies. They sold briskly at astronomical prices.

The shop had yellow and white checked gingham curtains at the window, there were always bouquets of fresh or dried flowers in evidence, the counter was hand-rubbed pine, and the work area behind it was entirely open to the view of the customers. Cakes, Etc. looked exactly like a picture out of *Yankee* magazine, everybody's New England dream come to life.

Rita did all the baking herself. She condescended to employ two salesclerks, but she absented herself from her business only if her daughter was present. When the bakery opened fifteen years ago, Sarah had enjoyed donning a yellow smock and helping her mother. She began hating it after she was in college, when Rita launched the campaign to take them as a double act into the world of nationwide marketing and high finance. She put on a smock with reluctance Saturday morning and forced herself to smile when her mother waved good-bye.

Whatever her emotional reactions, Sarah had to admit that the bakery was a tribute to her mother's intestinal fortitude. Rita was entirely self-taught. She'd always been a good baker, but when she decided to open the shop, she went out and acquired a small library of *haut monde* cookbooks and worked her way through them until she was as comfortable in the world of *les pâtés brisées et feuilletées* as she was with blueberry muffins and apple pies. And Sarah had picked up almost as much knowledge, simply by osmosis.

Today Rita had refrained from giving her any instructions. Part of the plan to make Sarah aware of the confidence reposed in her, and the challenge involved in seeing that the Black Beauty chocolate cakes weren't overbaked for even a minute. They were Rita's specialty, made with an unbelievably large quantity of chocolate and a stupefyingly small amount of flour. Black Beauties defied all the rules of cake making, but as long as the timing was followed precisely, they sent chocolate lovers into ecstasy. If not, their extraordinary moist and fudgy quality would be lost.

Sarah pulled down the door of one of the bank of ovens and cast a critical eye on the cakes. The centers were still wobbly and the hissing sounds made by the baking batter were exactly right, muted but not yet stilled. Sarah took them from the oven with a repressed shudder. For reasons she preferred not to think about, she never ate chocolate cake.

· · ·

"Jesus, I can't believe it!" Pinkie snapped shut the final suitcase. "By this time tomorrow night I'll be a married lady."

Sarah grinned. "Well, at least married."

"Y'all are lucky, runt, I'm going to ignore that." She cast a final look around the living room. "That's it, isn't it? I haven't forgotten anything?"

"Not that I can see. All the evidence of a part-time bordello is gone. Chez Sarah is returned to pristine normalcy."

"And it's only two. The Widow Arbuckle doesn't land until three-thirty. Sugar, your well-hinged habits are getting to me. I've never been early for anything in my life."

"Just as I planned it," Sarah said. "There's time for my little surprise." She disappeared into the kitchen and returned with a frosted bottle of Taittinger and an enormous bowl of crimson strawberries.

Pinkie yelped with delight. "Ah, the glamour of it. Marvelous!"

Sarah popped the cork on the champagne with dramatic abandon. The wine fizzed over her hand and onto the table, but she ignored the spill and poured two glasses to the rims. "Here's to your wonderful future, darling. And to the last six months. They've been fun." Her voice gentled. "I mean it, thanks for being you."

Pinkie took the glass she was offered, but instead of drinking she put it down and hugged Sarah hard. "I'm going to miss you so much. You're my lucky charm, sugar. Everything in my life's gotten better and better since I wandered into that damned museum."

That was where they met, in the women's room at the museum on a blistering hot September day. Sarah had gone in expecting to encounter the usual assortment of staff and dowager visitors. Instead there was only Pinkie, dressed in a skintight red satin sheath and pulling on purple panty hose. "Came here to change 'cause it's quiet and sort of private," the blonde had drawled. "I've been living at the Y. I don't think they'd take kindly to my going out in an outfit like this. And a coat in this heat was more than I could bear. Y'all don't mind, I hope."

Sarah had stared in fascination and said no, she didn't mind. And they'd started to talk and she discovered that the blonde was on her way to her first night's work as a go-go dancer in a bar in Boston's notorious Combat Zone.

"Can't stand my so-called career anymore," Pinkie explained. "I'm a special education teacher, work with retarded kids. Only my ability to handle the pain evaporated a few weeks ago. And I'm broke. And what the hell, this is a job without emotional commitment, right?"

"You might say that." Sarah kept staring at the other woman, the purple stockings were decorated with sequined flowers. "Special education must be very demanding. How did you get into it?"

"Had a baby sister died of Down's syndrome and complications when she was eleven. While I was in college. So it seemed like a good idea."

"I see. It doesn't sound like go-go dancing is going to be a satisfying second career."

"True, but after you wag your tits and your ass around for six hours, they give you cash money. Thirty-five dollars and no deductions."

"That broke?" Sarah asked.

"That broke."

"Got time for a hamburger? On me, you can pay me back when your finances improve."

Pinkie had the time. And the two women discovered that they laughed a lot together, that they liked each other. Two weeks later the blonde took a job with a publisher of textbooks, and a month after that she was sharing Sarah's apartment. And that had been good for both of them.

Sarah finished her champagne and glanced at her watch. "Drink up, it's time to go to the airport and meet your mother."

Pinkie groaned and popped a final strawberry into her mouth. "You're a doll to drive me. I need moral support, but Mama absolutely forbade Max to come. She made me swear I wouldn't see him today. Bad luck according to her. The Widow Arbuckle is originally from Georgia; if you knew the South, that would explain it."

"Not necessary," Sarah said. "My New England mother would say the same thing. A universal taboo. And for God's sake, don't let on you left Max's place in the small hours of the morning. I'm sure the prohibition was supposed to start from midnight last night."

24

Pinkie giggled. "I'd never last that long."

They put the last of the suitcases into the Honda, and Sarah climbed behind the wheel. "Hey, I just thought of something. If your mother is from Georgia, it must be your father who was FFV."

"Sometimes you're so smart it's scary. Yup. The Widow Arbuckle's only basking in reflected glory. But I hasten to add she's DAR in her own right. Maxie's getting a genuine, pure-blooded flower of southern womanhood, no mistake. If I'd let Mama have her way and come up north a couple of weeks ago to be with me in 'my time of need,' you'd have seen just what that means."

"Tell me something," Sarah said. "All your smart-mouth cracks, do you really have such complete disdain for the whole thing?"

"Serious-talk time? No, not complete disdain. For a lot of people it serves a need, creates a framework. Women like my mother, who never had any role except wife and homemaker, it gives them something outside themselves to relate to. But I was always the oddball who didn't fit in. And I've had hot pants since I was sixteen. That's probably very southern, too, only I wasn't willing to let the fires smolder in secret." Pinkie twisted in the passenger seat, so she was facing Sarah. "Maybe that explains you. Maybe you're frigid because you're a Yankee."

"Wrong on both assumptions. I'm not frigid, just not like you, able to divorce sex from feeling."

"Who's divorcing? I feel plenty. And it's great. At least it can be. That's what I keep trying to tell you."

Sarah flashed her a smile. "You know what I mean. And since this is such a special day, I'll let you in on a big secret. I'm not a real Yankee. I'm adopted. I wasn't born in the North. As a matter of fact, I was born in Georgia."

Adopted. A chosen child. When she was little, Sarah used to lie in bed and say the word over and over. Adopted. Not truly Rita and Frank Myleses' only child.

Probably she was a princess and her real mother put her here in Ipswich with the commoners to protect her from the evil king who

25

didn't want Sarah to grow up and inherit the kingdom. Or maybe she'd been born in Hollywood. Her mother was a movie star. Someday soon she'd be sorry she gave away her little girl. Then she'd come and get Sarah and take her to California. Once, when she was seven, she heard a man on television talking about children's adoption fantasies. She didn't understand very much, just that he said all kids made up such stories. She'd wanted to shout, "Not me! I really am adopted. My mother told me so. . . ."

She was nine when she started asking probing questions. No longer content with just her imaginings, she pressed Rita and Frank for explanations. How old was she when they got her? What orphanage was she in? What did they know of her real parents? At first they found excuses not to answer. The bakery was busy, it took all their time, especially now that Rita had opened Cakes, Etc. next to Frank's big commercial facility. But Sarah persisted.

"St. Jude found you for me," Rita said at last. "Daddy's a lot older than me, you know that. So when God didn't send us a baby of our own, we decided we'd adopt one. Only none of the regular adoption agencies would allow it. Because of Daddy's age. Then we went to the Holy Land with a pilgrimage group and I prayed to St. Jude. He's the patron saint of hopeless cases. Sister told you that at school, didn't she?"

Sarah had nodded, but she was frustrated and angry because Rita wouldn't say more. She wanted to know exactly how St. Jude had answered Rita's prayers. Sometimes prayers got answered in funny ways. Even Father said so.

"Georgia," her mother replied one day when Sarah would not be silenced. Rita was melting chocolate in an enormous double boiler that lived permanently on the rear of the black gas range in the back of her shop. She stirred the chocolate and sniffed it, then she took it from the stove and poured it into a waiting bowl. "We got you in Georgia. A girl there . . . she wasn't married."

Rita's voice was low, her hands busy delicately folding the melted chocolate into the batter. "The laws weren't so strict in Georgia, at least not then in 1959."

Sarah didn't look at her mother. She stared at the cake batter instead; first it was marbled with mahogany brown, then the whole mass turned a lighter nutty color. Lighter still when Rita deftly

26

folded in the beaten egg whites. Georgia. A girl who wasn't married. Not a princess. Not even a movie star. Just a girl who was bad and did things that were a sin if you weren't married.

She never ate chocolate cake after that. Pies and tarts and lemon cakes and butterscotch brownies, and a dozen other things that Rita made, but never chocolate cake.

Sarah was thirteen when her secret idol, fifteen-year-old Charlie Ryan, invited her to go fishing. When they were little, they'd played together a lot, but Charlie had ignored her for the last few years. Now he'd asked her for a real date. Sarah was convinced it was a date. That's why she didn't tell Rita about it. She wasn't allowed to date; neither were any of her girlfriends. They'd just die when she told them about going fishing with Charlie Ryan.

Only nothing worked out as she expected. Instead there was that awful business behind the barn where they'd gone to dig worms for bait. And she blacked Charlie's eye and got in big trouble for that, and they never got to go fishing at all, and she never told anybody what had happened. Except Father Martin, of course, in confession. And all he said was to tell God she was sorry and not do it again. Only she hadn't really done anything; Charlie had. But Father Martin seemed to think it was her fault. His last words were that she must fight against impulses to sin. He'd said the same thing when she tried to tell him about the music she heard. She must resolve to be a good girl and forget anything that would separate her from the love of the Lord. Only she couldn't forget about Charlie or about the music, especially not the music. And somehow both things served to make the Georgia story more detailed in her mind.

A cheap, stupid girl who must have let some boy pull down her pants and do it. And then she was pregnant and her family were ashamed of her and the boy said maybe it wasn't even his kid and why didn't she just give it away? Like a show she'd seen on television. And probably some priest got the idea that there must be somebody in the North who wouldn't mind a bastard baby if they wanted one bad enough, and no doubt he wrote to a priest in Boston.

Maybe that's what it meant that the Church was "one, holy, Catholic and apostolic," the way they said. Priests and nuns could talk to each other anywhere in the world and get people to do whatever they wanted. So Rita and Frank Myles, who weren't good enough to get a baby from a real adoption agency, went to Georgia and got Sarah.

She'd thought she was special and been disavowed of that, but all the while she was growing up, Sarah was different. Her parents were both fair and she was dark; but not just her looks separated her from Rita and Frank. Sarah was artistic, truly talented according to her teachers, and often stubborn and defiant over some trivial thing. There was no dealing with her then. They said that Sarah would argue with the pope himself, given a chance. And she was good at it; a precocious, bright little girl brimming with energy, but a difficult child. And not surprising, considering. They said that too.

Another thing they said was that she was pretty. Rita kept Sarah's cloud of curly brown hair long, and everybody was always commenting on her big green eyes. But Sarah didn't feel pretty, just peculiar. She heard an aunt say, "Well, you can't expect Sarah to look like a Myles," and after that she prayed every night to wake up blond and not so skinny, and at least a little bit like Rita.

By the time she was in high school, Sarah knew that was impossible, but she'd also learned something of the argument about heredity versus environment. In sociology class she argued vehemently for the latter. She didn't dream about being a princess anymore. She just wanted to be accepted by the people around her.

When she was graduated and offered a scholarship to an art school in Boston, she turned it down. Neither did she choose some expensive secular university. Sarah enrolled in St. Joseph's Girls' College in neighboring Topsfield. She would major in art history; she would also remain with her mother and father, safe in the bosom of the Church.

For once the Myleses' circle thoroughly approved of Sarah, who'd always been so different. The changeling child whose origins were slightly sordid had proved herself worthy of their long years of tolerance and Rita and Frank's devotion.

Pinkie had declined to convert to Judaism. "It's not that I've got anything against it in particular, but I can't see myself in any religion," she'd confided to Sarah. "So poor Max is having a hell of a time finding a rabbi to marry us. Seems like they don't approve of mixed marriages. Not even when it's something mixed with nothing."

But Max was determined, and in the end he found a man sympathetic to his plight. The rabbi insisted that the ceremony be private. It took place in his home, with only the immediate family present. Afterwards Sarah and a couple of hundred others were invited to a reception at the Ritz. Max's mother had suggested one of Boston's newer hotels, but Mrs. Arbuckle was picking up the bill. The old landmark was her choice and her style.

Pinkie looked gorgeous in white satin complete with a veil and a train; she even managed to look delicate and virginal. Max gazed at her adoringly throughout the proceedings, but still succeeded in appearing dignified. The mothers were a study in contrasts. Mrs. Schwartz was chic in a kind of hard-edged way Sarah didn't associate with having a stroke if her son wasn't married by a rabbi. She wondered if Max had more personal reasons for insisting on the religious ceremony. The Widow Arbuckle—thanks to Pinkie she could never think of the woman in any other terms—was all fluttering aqua chiffon and tinkling laughter. She dripped southern charm and made it seem sincere.

Fascinating as all this was, Sarah didn't spend a lot of time observing it. The band was great and she was hardly off the dance floor. Until she got a hastily scrawled note asking her to come to the room set aside for the bride to change. She found Pinkie there alone. "What's up, sweetie? I was told you needed me."

Pinkie had changed into a blue silk dress and she was carefully touching up her makeup. "Just wanted to tell you I made sure the photographer got a picture of the two mamas together. I'm going to frame it and hang it in the living room. So Maxie and I can know what we have to live up to."

Sarah choked with laughter. "You're wicked," she sputtered. "But I can't wait to see it." The two women hugged. "Have a fantastic honeymoon. Don't wear Max out."

Pinkie opened her eyes wide. "You mustn't say such things to me when I'm so nervous about my wedding night. Sarah, do you think it's true? Do boys really put their thing—"

"Shut up!" She pushed Pinkie toward the door. "Get out of here, call me the minute you get back to town."

"Oh, I surely will. Just to tell you if it's true."

With Pinkie gone the apartment seemed empty. And she had more time to think—about the hole where her religion had been, for instance. But on balance, it wasn't difficult to defect. She slept late most Sunday mornings. Once she invited the local chapter of her network, the Boston Museum Women, to brunch. Seven sharp, committed females accustomed to fighting their way up in what was still very much a man's field certainly filled the little place on West Street.

And being among them, on her turf as it were, made Sarah think about her job in a new way. Okay, she told herself after they left, if you're not going to run off and take the veil, what are you going to do? She looked at herself in the mirror over the bathroom sink and swept her hair out of her face. Maybe she should cut it; short would make her look older. Maybe she should really go after a CAREER. Why not sharpen her skills and her nails? Claw her way to the top? Aim at something terrific like a directorship? She could go back to school nights, get a master's degree. . . .

She let the heavy hair fall back to her shoulders and grimaced. Maybe, but not quite yet.

She turned from the mirror, and the music surfaced once more. *Do, sol, la, fa* . . . The underlying theme of her life, the mystery she no longer acknowledged as a mystery, the barrier that stood between her and some thing, some place she could neither define nor locate. *Do, sol, la, fa* . . . Sarah grabbed a tissue and blew her nose hard. Stupid to cry over something that probably wasn't ever going to go away. C'mon, girl, wash your face and go out for a walk. Doing something physical always helped to still the music, she'd learned the trick years before.

By the end of May all the Catholic magazines had ceased appearing in her mailbox, and she'd managed to find excuses not to be in Ipswich any weekend. That part hadn't been hard. The Grimes was soon to mount a major show, a Klee retrospective. Sarah had charge of the catalog. It was an important, difficult job, and she devoted long hours to it, and knew she was doing good work. There was only one hitch. Her boss uncovered a few widely disparate sources that commented on religious ethos as the motivation for the artist's sense of fantasy. "Work on that, Sarah, expand it. It's a great new insight, and you're religious, you'll do a great job."

"Not these days. I'm not doing the religious scene anymore. Besides, it's never seemed to me to have much to do with a sense of fantasy."

Her boss shrugged. "A debatable idea. I still think the theme ought to be explored in the catalog."

She felt desperate. "Can't you write that part?"

He hesitated. "I suppose I can, if you insist."

Sarah watched him walk away. So much for working harder at her career.

In mid-June the catalog went to the printers and her work load lightened considerably. Sarah made the mistake of saying that during a phone conversation with her mother.

"That's good, honey. Can you come home this weekend, then? We haven't seen you for ages."

She made some excuse and hung up quickly. An hour later her father called. He almost never did that. "Look. I don't like to pressure you, Sarah, but your mother's very upset. Couldn't you come up for a day or two?"

"Yes, of course." There was nothing else she could say. "I can't stay long, but I'll come up Friday evening."

"That's great, sweetie. We'll look forward to it."

The storm was just getting started when she left the museum on Friday. God, it was terrible weather. Maybe she should wait and go to Ipswich tomorrow. But if she did, she'd have to stay until Sunday. And go to church with her parents. She wished for the raincoat that was in her suitcase in the car, pulled up the collar of her white linen blazer, and made a dash for the Honda.

And that decision changed everything.

The rain lashed down in oblique sheets angled by the howling wind. Sarah clung to the wheel with both hands, struggling to keep the car on the highway she could barely see. Her fingers were numb; the car's door didn't fit properly; she was freezing to death. It was June, for God's sake; she'd figured she needn't fix the door until the fall. But this damned storm had a wintry fierceness about it. The wind buffeted its way inside and swirled in the small interior. Sarah tried to ignore it and drove on.

She spotted the golden arches of a McDonald's on her right, so she must be level with Peabody. Halfway home. Maybe she should stop for coffee and a Big Mac; the storm might let up in half an hour or so. By the time she made up her mind, McDonald's was behind her. Too difficult to turn around on Route 1 in a driving rain. She kept going.

There was an odd thumping noise from the back seat, and she panicked and turned her head for an instant. No, nothing. Just her sketchbook jouncing up and down. She'd put it in the car before she went to work this morning, thinking she might try some drawings of the marsh birds. She hadn't done any in years. But she should have put the damned thing in the trunk. Too late for that now; besides, she was almost there.

Sarah turned her eyes back to the highway, squinting into the rain to distinguish the black strip rolling out ahead of her. A vicious gust of wind shook the Honda, it almost wrenched the wheel from her hands. She felt the back end skid, and for one terrible moment she could see nothing at all. And suddenly there was something in front of her face, something pressing against her nose and her cheeks, plastering itself to her forehead.

The cover that had been ripped off the sketchbook molded itself to her features for two or three seconds longer, then the wind subsided suddenly, the paper dropped to her lap. Sarah tried to push it away with her arms and still keep her hands on the wheel. Her foot trembled on the accelerator; fright was gagging nausea and cold sweat pouring down her back. She couldn't see the road.

"Hail, Mary, full of grace . . ." The prayer surged up, dragged from some inchoate instinct seated in her belly, and froze on her lips.

She leaned into the windshield, trying to recapture the vision of narrow black ribbon she'd been following, but it wasn't there. There was something horizontal instead, something coming up to meet her. The double metal bars of the highway guard. And she was driving straight into them.

Then she wasn't driving at all . . . just flying free, sailing out over the earth, oddly suspended on sheets of rain. Her last remembered impulse was laughter.

"We've been very lucky, Mrs. Myles. There doesn't seem to be any damage to the brain. All the tests are okay. Considering the state of the car, a broken arm and leg and a fractured pelvis are minor injuries. They'll heal. Very lucky."

"But why doesn't she speak? I keep talking to her, but she doesn't answer, doesn't open her eyes."

Rita's voice. And the doctor's. Sarah could hear them talking. She wanted to turn her head, to say, "It's okay, Mom. I'm all right." She couldn't. Nothing would move when she told it to, not even her eyelids.

"Be patient, Mrs. Myles. She's concussed. But that will pass. I really do think there's been no serious damage. And like I said, that's a miracle."

A miracle. She used to wonder if the music was a miracle. Not the way it was now. It was a curse. Louder and louder. Pounding in her head. And she was less able to control it; because she was so ill, so weak. The four notes punctuated this time out of time, went on and on. How long? She didn't know and she still couldn't ask. There were only variations of sleep to fill the minutes. Deep sleep when she heard nothing at all, half sleep when she heard *do, sol, la, fa* . . . Over and over again. And something more. Something she'd never experienced before.

Sarah, Sarah, Sarah . . . Her name was being called; she could sense people around her. Crowds of people, but not the nurses and doctors. She didn't know who the shadowy figures were, only that they were somehow both here and not here. And she was sad; a terrible, overwhelming grief twisted her heart, but she didn't know what she was sad about. Once she felt a nurse gently wipe her cheeks and heard her whisper, "Don't cry, Miss Myles, you're going to be okay. Really."

Sarah wanted to explain that she wasn't weeping because of the accident. But try as she might, she still couldn't speak.

Oh, Alexandria! Great city of the fertile, fruitful plain, watered by the Nile, embracing the *Mare Internum* with your mighty harbor and wharves along which a man could not walk from end to end in even one day. Alexandria, where Egyptians, Greeks, Jews, Romans, Phoenicians, Persians, Cilicians, indeed every known race, foregather. They come to see and be seen; to learn in your fabled library and university, to marvel at your colonnades and arcades, to gaze avariciously at the vast array of goods in your countless markets, to taste pleasure sweeter even than the honey which within his glass shroud embalms the corpse of your founder, Alexander the Great. Oh, Alexandria, nearly four hundred years young on this day of infamy.

"Sarah bas Michael, you are *herem,* an abomination to the Lord."

The man spoke the words solemnly, but apparently without feeling. Hard dark eyes glinted above a carefully tended gray beard; the lines life had marked on his face seemed etched in granite.

He stood in the eastern corner of that small room in his home which served as a synagogue, where on this day there met a *beth din,* a court of Jewish law. In compliance with that already ancient law there were three judges, all men of wisdom and learning. Two of them now rose and turned from the watchers and opened the Ark. The Torah scrolls could be seen within, robed in velvet and silk, beautifully and richly decorated. For this, after all, was noble Alexandria.

The man who had spoken lifted a ram's horn to his mouth and looked for a moment at the woman standing before him. Then thrice he blew the shofar. The wailing notes echoed from the rafters, reverberated from the carved wooden walls. When the echo died, he spoke again. "You are *herem* and your child is *herem,* but in its mercy this court has decreed that you shall be neither stoned nor put to the sword. You may live."

The eyes of the girl squeezed tightly shut, as if to hold back tears. She clutched the child to her more tightly. From behind a curtain a woman was heard to sob; the mother, no doubt. The men in the small synagogue shuffled their feet uneasily, but he who pronounced the anathema did not falter.

"Go from this place. Do not return. Henceforth we will not speak to you. No Jew will speak to you. You will be given no bread, no shelter, no comfort. When your physical body dies, you will be cast into the place below the earth where the accursed weep and wail in eternal flames. Already your soul is dead, for you have killed it. We will mourn you for seven days; then your name will pass from our memory and our speech. Go, Sarah bas Michael. Take your accursed child and go."

He crossed the room and opened the door. The street was silent because it was the Sabbath. In that reverent stillness they stared at each other a moment more, the girl and the old man. She stretched out her hand. "Please . . . " The whisper was a plea for mercy— and something more, a plea for love. The man's lips quivered a moment. It was the only sign of feeling, but he suppressed it almost instantly. He turned away and closed the door. She was shut out of all she knew and cherished.

The gray-bearded rabbi faced the assembled men. His glance strayed once to the curtain behind which were the women, among them his wife. He took a deep breath, then reached up and tore the right shoulder of his garment. The sound was obliterated by his wail of grief. "Aagh! My daughter is dead. The Holy One gives and the Holy One takes away. Blessed be His name."

Now sounds of weeping and sorrow filled the room. Reb Michael was mourning his daughter, that same Sarah whom he'd pronounced anathema. His only daughter. Sarah the beautiful, perhaps the dearest of his five children. Sarah, who made music that would shame angels, who always seemed to know what he thought, what he wanted or needed. Sarah, whom he loved.

A long time she walked the quiet, all but empty streets. Terrified, sometimes blinded by tears, holding the child, sometimes pausing in the shelter of a doorway to give it suck. No one could be seen to look at her, though Sarah sensed eyes peering from behind the shutters. They all knew what had happened and why. They had expected it. Only she had believed her father would relent when he saw the child, his granddaughter whom she'd named Rachel, but the others had known he would not. Reb Michael would abide by the law, they said, and on this spring day they were proved right.

Sarah continued walking; sometimes the weight of her anguish and her fear caused her to stagger, especially when she passed the great colonnaded temple. It was almost a rival in magnificence to

37

Herod's temple in Jerusalem, and it was the oldest in the Diaspora. And it was her heritage, Rachel's heritage. But they had been turned out, sent to wander the street like stray dogs, to beg crusts of bread from strangers. Was any grief like unto her grief?

Eventually she left the section of the Jews behind and came to those three-fifths of the city inhabited by the others, they who neither honored the Sabbath nor kept it holy. She was in the marketplace of the Gentiles, where there was the noise of rolling carts, the braying of beasts of burden, the smell of birds roasting on charcoal braziers, and of wine being poured from great jugs into smaller. There was loud talk and much gesturing as trade was done in half a hundred different stalls.

Among them was the stall of Farak el Fidha; behind it was his house. It was larger than her father's house, grander. It had marble gates, and the smell of peach blossoms wafted from the courtyard. It was a rich man's house. Sarah lifted her hand to knock, lost her courage, finally found it again. A few seconds passed, and nothing happened; she knocked again, louder and more urgently this time.

At last a servant came and opened the door, and she saw six tumbling fountains spilling water from the mouths of silver fish fashioned by Farak's own hand. It was the hand of the finest silversmith in the city, and this should have been the house she came to as a bride, not a beggar. "Please, I must speak to the master."

The servant knew who she was; he knew too her shame. He averted his eyes from the child, but he took pity on her and did not send her away. "Wait here."

A few moments later Farak came. He was a small man, smaller than Reb Michael, with dark skin and pale, close-set eyes. He looked nothing like Anwar, his son. That thought stabbed Sarah's heart with new pain. She could not bear to think of Anwar. If he were here . . . But he was not, and she and the child must survive. She held out the infant. "Here is Rachel, your granddaughter. Anwar's daughter."

Farak shook his head. "So you say, but I don't know that it is true. Go home to your own people, Sarah bas Michael."

"I have no people," she whispered. "My father has declared me anathema. Because I bore your son's child, because we are not married, because you do not follow our laws, and neither you nor your son are circumcised. Rachel and I"—she dropped her eyes and looked at the infant—"we have nowhere to go." She wanted to say more, to beg for mercy, but her throat was constricted with tears, and she could not.

"Anwar is away." She knew that, of course. Seven months past he went to Persia to buy jewels, and he would not return until midsummer. "When my son comes home," Farak continued, "he can say whether this child is his."

"She is. You know she is. Everyone knows. I have been with no man but Anwar."

The sound of the closing door silenced Sarah's words. "Farak!" she screamed. "Farak, you cannot turn us away. Our Lord Jesus, think of what he said—" But if the silversmith heard her words, her appeal to that authority they both recognized as ultimate, he did not reply. At last, still sobbing, Sarah walked on.

By nightfall she had reached the outskirts of the city; beyond were only the Roman garrison and the open fields. There was a camp of sorts here, and many women. They served the soldiers, cooked and weaved for them, lay with them, sometimes bore their children, but they were not wives. They were outcasts as she was an outcast. Exhausted and without hope, Sarah found a sheltered place between a camel shed and a wall. She sat down on the ground and wedged the child beside her; then she took from beneath her cloak the only thing she had taken from her father's house. It was a lyre of ten strings, and she began to strum them softly because her music was all the comfort left to her on this blackest of days.

The moon rose, a pearly white sliver in the black sky. It was time to eat and she was hungry, but she had no food. In her father's house there was always food, sustenance for both body and spirit. At this hour the entire household would be at the Lord's Supper.

Indeed, they were. Though this was a day of pain and mourning,

Reb Michael sat with his students and colleagues. To mark the close of the Sabbath, the women had brought them bread and beans and roasted meats. And of course, there was wine. Reb Michael took the bread into his hands and looked around the table. He blessed the bread first in the old way, "Blessed art thou . . . who has given us bread to eat," and then in the new way that the Lord Jesus has commanded: "This is my body, take thou and eat."

The blessed bread passed from hand to hand, and all ate. The last one, the youngest son of the rabbi, took his share and rose and passed it to his mother, waiting in the doorway. She would share it with the women in the next room.

"This is the cup of my blood of the new and eternal covenant," Reb Michael said as he lifted the goblet. When he had pronounced the words, he sipped the wine and gave it to the others to drink. As with the sacred bread, what was left was given to the women to share among themselves. Thus did they all obey the Master's words "Do this in commemoration of me."

The most important part of the meal was now over; they had done as the crucified and risen Jesus had commanded them to do. They had fed their souls; now they would fill their bellies with ordinary food. Later they would tell over and over the stories of the Master, what Jesus said, what he did, how he died and rose again. But none of them would mention Sarah or Rachel, or wonder aloud if they had food or shelter from the dark. Both were dead according to the Law. Did not Jesus say that he had not come to change the Law?

Beside the camel shed Sarah continued to strum the lyre. A woman approached. "You play well," she said.

Sarah looked up. The woman's voice was rough, her accent untutored, and her features thickened and coarse. But her shawl was neatly arranged around her head, and her eyes were clear. And kind. "Thank you," Sarah said. "I'm sorry if I disturbed you."

"You didn't. I like your music." The woman bent forward and peered more closely at the girl and the infant. "Is the child dead?"

Sarah dropped the lyre and snatched Rachel into her arms, as if to protect her, as if the woman's saying it could make it so. "No, no! Only sleeping." Just then the baby began to cry and Sarah fumbled with the fastenings of her dress that she might give her suck.

"Not here," the woman said. "It's cold and there are wild dogs. Come inside."

Sarah hesitated only a moment. Then she rose, and carrying Rachel and the lyre, she followed Darai the Whore into her home.

$\mathcal{T}_{wo}$

After a week Sarah could stay awake and talk and focus on the people around her, but the sense of another presence and of grieving didn't go away.

"You seem a little depressed," the orthopedist said. "It's natural enough, but there's no reason. Everything's going to be okay. Promise."

"It's not that." She wondered how much she dare say or if she wanted to say anything at all. Not talking about it was a lesson she'd learned well, the habit of a lifetime. But that applied only to the music; this was so much more. An invasion. "Prepare to repel boarders," she murmured. "Time to call in the troops."

"Huh?" The doctor was young and nice-looking and obviously very puzzled. "I'm not sure I understand."

"Neither do I exactly. Look, since it happened, I've had this weird sense of"—she hesitated—"of something or someone being in my head. Somebody very upset about something."

"You mean as if you're two people, one who's lying here in not very good shape and another one watching?"

"Not quite." The second one isn't me. She almost said that, but she didn't dare. "I really can't be very clear about it."

"Okay, an accident like yours is bound to cause trauma of all sorts. Don't worry about it, I'll get the neurologist to have another look. Just to be sure."

The tests were comprehensive; they took three days. And when they were finally finished, the neurologist said there was no physical damage to the brain or the nervous system. Nothing to explain what Sarah said she felt.

"I don't feel it," she corrected. "I experience it. Do you understand what I mean?"

"Not exactly. But that kind of thing's not my field. Let's have you talk to someone else, shall we?"

"I thought you guys gave up the third person and the royal *we* these days," Sarah said. The neurologist looked as if he had no idea what she was talking about and fled the room.

"Why do you need a psychiatrist?" Rita demanded. "If you're depressed I'll get Father Martin to come."

"I'm not depressed and Father Martin's the last one I need. Mom, remember how when I was a kid, I used to say I heard music?"

"I remember. It was your imagination, honey. All kids do things like that."

Rita was a little too determined, as if she'd always known that was a fiction between them, and Sarah was suddenly tired of the whole charade. "Not my imagination, not then and not now. I'm going to talk to their shrink."

Unfortunately she disliked the psychiatrist on sight. She was an attenuated woman, tall and angular, a few years older than Sarah, with pale eyes and mousy hair. Still, Sarah wanted to cooperate. She smiled as brightly as she could and tried to explain.

The psychiatrist produced a child's keyboard, one of those electronic toys meant to foster creativity. "Can you play the four notes for me?"

"Sure." Sarah picked them out. *Do-sol-la-fa.* "I've heard them forever; that's not the problem now. It's this sense of somebody trying to get my attention, to get into my head. Somebody who's desperately unhappy."

"The somebody is yourself," the woman said. "Trying to make you deal with things you've apparently blocked out." She quizzed Sarah about her childhood, raising her eyebrows when she learned about the adoption. She looked sanguine when Sarah said her first period had been uneventful and that no, she wasn't a virgin, but there was no special man right now.

"And how do you manage your sexual needs when there's not what you're calling a 'special man'?"

"This really isn't getting us anywhere." The conversation seemed both classically Freudian and silly. "I need help dealing with something that's happening here and now." She gestured to the casts that held her practically immobile. "Sex isn't my big problem at the moment."

Of course her childhood shaped her; the adoption, Catholicism, Charlie Ryan, all of it was part of who she was. That's how life was. Sarah knew that; she didn't need to discuss it. It would cast no light on the peculiar symptoms from which she was suffering now.

The psychiatrist gave up after three visits. "Yes, I agree, you're whatever laymen mean by sane. But there are problems. If you don't want to begin a long-term analysis, Sarah, to dig into your true feelings about being adopted, I can only suggest you ignore this music and the presence you say you feel. It came as a result of trauma. Maybe it will go away when you take up your normal life again."

But normal life, the life she'd been living, was suddenly snatched from her grasp. Until two weeks ago she'd had an excellent job with career potential and her own home, independence she'd fought hard for. Now her boss wrote, a letter full of sympathy and excuses, to say they couldn't hold her job open longer than a month, and the orthopedist told her it would be at least three months before the casts came off. So she couldn't go back to work for many weeks, and she certainly couldn't live alone until she was more mobile. Moreover, she couldn't afford to keep the apartment if she wasn't working. So it was back to Ipswich and Rita and Frank, and her girlhood bedroom looking over the salt marsh.

Her parents went to Brookline and packed up everything in Sarah's apartment and hired a van to bring it all home and stored it

45

in the attic. Rita suggested that Sarah unpack a few things, like her favorite Chagall print, for instance, and put them in her room, but she refused. I don't want to make this a permanent place, she told herself, I'm not going to be here long. Still, the sense of having been thrust back into dependence was painful and paralyzing.

She might have fought harder to avoid the trap she saw opening in front of her, but her strength was sapped by almost constant pain. It wasn't the result of her injuries, at least not directly. It was wrenching, debilitating, sick-making headaches.

They began before she left the hospital, but Sarah didn't mention them to the doctors. She didn't want to give them any excuse to keep her longer. She couldn't hide the awful agony from her mother, however. Rita called their family GP, and he prescribed painkillers; but they made Sarah sleepy and nauseated, and as soon as they wore off, the headaches returned. "Migraine is often emotional in origin," the GP said. And Sarah grimaced and didn't discuss it with him further.

At the end of June Pinkie drove up to Ipswich to see her. "I waited until now to come. I'm not any good with real sickies. Bringing joy and laughter to convalescents, that's my forte."

"So make with the jokes," Sarah said. "I sure could use some, y'all."

"How many psychiatrists does it take to change a light bulb?" Pinkie asked. And without waiting for an answer: "Only one, but the light bulb really has to want to change. What's the matter? You're not laughing."

"Wrong joke," Sarah said. "I've had a bellyful of Freudian gobbledygook lately. Are you willing to listen to a weird story?"

"Nothing I'd rather do. And in this setting a little weirdness is welcome."

They were in the backyard under the apple tree. Sarah sat in the carefully cushioned and supported chair that Frank had rigged to accommodate her casts. Pinkie sprawled on the grass; gorgeous, glowing with health and happiness. Rita had provided lemonade and peanut butter crunch cookies. "America is safe. Normalcy thy name is Rita and Frank Myles," Sarah said. "But that kid of theirs, well, she's not so normal at all. . . . "

She told Pinkie all about it: the increased decibel level of the music, the voice calling her name, the presence, and the grief.

"How come I can tell you everything? I have a hell of a time explaining to anyone else."

Pinkie helped herself to another cookie. "Well, sugar, explaining you are not. Telling, yes. But if there was an explanation buried in there, I sure did let it pass me by."

"Because there isn't one. The damn thing just *is*." She lowered her voice and looked away. "And it's getting worse. Yesterday I got . . . sort of flashes. Like a speeded-up picture frame. A scroll of some kind and candles."

"Jesus!" Pinkie breathed. "Look, what you need is to get out of here. We've rented a cottage on Nantucket for the week of the Fourth. You come on down there with us. No, don't shake your head, that's not an invitation, it's an order." She got up and brushed the grass from her jeans. Her rear end was spreading, Sarah noticed. Married life was agreeing so well with Pinkie she was getting fat. But the blonde seemed unconcerned. "Where's your mama? I'm going to set it all up with her."

The cottage turned out to be not the old seafarer's place Sarah had expected; it was an ultramodern structure of glass walls and redwood decks, hanging over the ocean and filled with people. "Just what the doctor ordered," Pinkie told her. "If anybody ever needed to loosen up, it's you. And these dentist types Maxie hangs out with get real good stuff. Put away the aspirins and have a drag of this."

She passed a lit joint, and Sarah took a deep toke, holding the smoke in for a moment before she exhaled. Below them Max and three others waved from the beach. "Go on," Sarah said. "You're not going to make me feel rotten by sitting up here with me, are you? Go have a swim. I'm perfectly content."

Pinkie went, and Sarah sat alone on the deck, looking at the crazy contrast of her casts and her green bikini, staring at the novel in her lap, but unable to concentrate long enough to read. Pinkie had left the joint behind. It was almost burned out. Sarah studied it, then took one more drag before extinguishing it. She didn't usually do any kind of drugs, not even grass. It just wasn't her scene, but any solace was welcome these days.

Sarah! Sarah! Listen. . . . Sounds of weeping and wailing. Shouts

47

in some language she didn't understand. Candles and some kind of curved horn that made a piercing, unmelodic shriek.

Oh, God! Sarah struggled to rise, fumbling with her crutches, letting the book fall unnoticed to the floor. She wanted to run. Where? Anywhere. Away from the voices and the horn and the endlessly repetitive four notes.

"What's up?" Max appeared from the room behind her, toweling his short, wiry body, alerted by the suddenness of her movements perhaps, by the wild look she suspected was on her face. "Something wrong, doll?"

Sarah shook her head. "No, nothing. Pinkie gave me a joint, 'specially good, she said. I guess it didn't agree with me."

Max laughed. "Sarah the pure. Don't let Pinkie corrupt you, doll. You're fine just the way you are. C'mon in out of the sun. I'm going to make you one of Dr. Schwartz's all-time terrific never-beaten banana maple milk shakes."

He was nice and fun and well meaning, they all were. Pinkie had even provided an extra man. Another dentist, they didn't seem to have any friends who weren't dentists. This one was cute and red-headed and freckled and, according to Pinkie, "particularly well hung. Just take a look at the bulge in his bathing suit. You could manage, sugar. Even with the casts. Why not? He's a sweetie. He'd be gentle. And"—she stretched languidly—"you'd feel so, so good. I absolutely guarantee it."

"Pinkie, I can't and I don't want to. It's just too casual and contrived for me."

"Has to be one or the other, if we're speaking the same language. Casual or contrived, not both."

"You know what I mean."

"Yes, I do. Okay. I only hope you don't wither away before this paragon you're saving yourself for appears."

She smoked no more dope, and there were no repeats of the experience she'd had the first day. No more shouts or horns. Just the headache, the music, and the sense of otherness she'd almost learned to live with. The rest of the weekend passed calmly, and if the other guests thought Sarah Myles a little dull and not the exciting woman Pinkie had promised, they were too polite to say so, and too busy having their own good time to worry about it.

"I'm sorry it wasn't better for you," Pinkie said when she drove Sarah back to Ipswich.

"I'm sorry I was such a drag on the party. Forgive me, honey. And don't give up on me. I'm going to lick this thing yet."

"Sure you are," Pinkie agreed. "Call you next week for a progress report."

Sarah determined simply to ignore the whole thing, concentrate on getting her physical health back. "The headaches aren't so terrible," she told her mother. "They're sure to pass."

But Rita continued to worry. "Sarah, listen," she said one day. "Don't get mad. I called Father Lasky. I mean, I figured you're closer to him than to Father Martin."

"What did you call him for?"

"To talk to you. Just talk. It can't hurt, can it?"

"There's nothing for us to talk about," Sarah insisted.

"I just thought he might be able to help, honey."

"My mother thinks you should exorcise me," Sarah told the priest when he came. "She's told you about my mysterious voice and the presence and this damned music?"

"Yeah. And the headaches, too."

"Well, what do you think? Am I possessed?"

Lasky grinned. "I rather doubt it." He held up his empty hands. "Look, no bell, no book, and no candle."

She laughed, and after that he came about once a week and Sarah enjoyed talking to him, but it didn't affect either the mysterious voice or the headaches. Both occurred with greater frequency and more intensity.

In late August the casts were removed from her arm and her leg; she could walk with the help of a cane. The physical therapist recommended swimming, and Sarah went to the beach; but after twenty minutes she had to go home. The pain in her head was unbearable in the hot summer sun. And the voice wouldn't leave her alone. She imagined it was shouting at her, calling her name, over and over again. *Sarah! Sarah! Sarah!* And the music was so loud she wanted to clap her hands over her ears and scream to drown it out. She forced herself to resist the urge.

·   ·   ·

In Paris it was evening. Hot, humid, still. August was the hottest month of the year, and the most somnolent. The city was on vacation. The Israeli called Dov Levi was among the few who had nowhere to go. He slept fitfully in the same cheap hotel room on the Rue du Bac which he'd occupied for ten years; tossing, drenched in sweat. He'd staggered in during the morning, after he didn't know how many bottles of wine, and slept all day. Many of his days passed thus. And his nights. Wine and sleep produced oblivion.

Sarah! Listen to the music, Sarah!

He woke with a muttered curse and sat bolt upright. He'd actually heard it. He could swear he had. The four notes, the music that had once been the center of his world. But how? After all these years, it wasn't possible. Besides, she was dead. They were both dead. Trembling, he lay back down and closed his eyes; but sleep wouldn't return, and eventually he got up and went out to look for a bar, one that was open despite the fact that it was August.

"Look," Father Lasky said the next time Sarah saw him. "I have a friend, a parapsychologist. He's tops in his field. I think you should talk to him."

"I don't want to talk to any more shrinks. I'm not nuts, so they don't know what to do with me."

"I know you're not nuts. And my friend isn't a psychiatrist. A parapsychologist specializes in investigating unusual physical and mental phenomena."

"A ghost chaser?"

"Sometimes. Go talk to him, Sarah. He teaches at Harvard, but he's taking a year off at the moment. Writing a book. He lives nearby. What can you lose?"

She didn't agree at first. She kept telling herself she'd get over the whole thing on her own. Lick it with sheer determination, the way she had her fear of driving after the accident.

It was Frank who bought her another car. "You've got to get back up on the horse, honey," her father insisted. Sarah knew he was right.

The car was a bright red Pinto, and Frank took her for one ride around the block, then parked it in the driveway and handed her the keys. Two days later Sarah made herself drive it, and after a few moments the panic subsided and confidence returned. She felt triumphant about that; moreover, she knew that, except for the headaches, her body was also healing. So she should think about finding another job in Boston and another apartment, and taking up her interrupted life.

But she couldn't concentrate on reading help wanted ads, or preparing a résumé, or going on interviews because the voice and the music and the pain in her head just wouldn't go away.

The first Tuesday in October she telephoned Father Lasky. "I'm getting desperate," she admitted. "I'll see your spook detective. What's his name and address?"

"Dr. Jarib Baraak. Not a medical doctor, remember, a professor. And I'm sure you're doing the right thing; Jarib specializes in cases like yours."

She sighed. "Just what I've always wanted to be, a case. Where do I find him?"

"In Rowley, number seven Willard Lane. I'll call and make an appointment." He rang back half an hour later and said that Jarib Baraak would see her the following afternoon.

Rowley was less than ten miles away, she'd been there often. It was the archetypical small New England town: saltbox houses with pitched roofs and strictly symmetrical doors and windows, a little white church with a steeple, and a road lined with maples just beginning to turn. If ever there was sanity and order in the world, it must be here. Sarah inhaled the scents of autumn and took a deep breath. Then she resolutely marched up to the door of Number 7 Willard Lane and rang the bell.

"Come in. You're Miss Myles, of course. I've been expecting you."

The front hall of Jarib Baraak's house was minute, barely room for the two of them. He immediately opened the door on the right and waited for her to precede him. "This is a very old house, built in 1759. It's too small to boast anything so grand as a study. Since I live alone, it doesn't matter. I do most of my work in here."

The living room was square and perfectly proportioned; the walls were lined with bookshelves, and there was a big desk in one corner. Two comfortable chairs covered in dark wine-colored leather were pulled up in front of a glowing log fire. He gestured at the chair nearest the window. "Will you be comfortable here? Not too hot, I hope."

"No, this is fine. It's a chilly afternoon. I love a fire."

She sat down, conscious of the room's quiet charm, wondering whether he was a bachelor or divorced, feeling incongruous because her clothes were deliberately assertive. She wore Guess jeans, a black cashmere turtleneck, a red velvet jacket, and red suede boots. The outfit seemed out of place in the relaxed atmosphere. It put her on the defensive. She tried to sound cool and controlled. "Thank you for seeing me, Dr. Baraak, and I'm sorry I think it's going to turn out such a bust."

"Please don't bother with the title. I'm not a medical doctor, you realize that? Just a professor on sabbatical."

"Yes, that's what Father Lasky said. You've known him a long time, haven't you?"

"About sixteen years. We were students together at Harvard. That was before Tom became a priest. I'm glad to say he's kept an open mind. He still tolerates agnostics like me. What can I get you to drink?"

"Whatever you're having will be fine."

"White wine then. It's what the English call 'plonk' and the French, *vin ordinaire*. In any language it's innocuous and refreshing." Baraak busied himself across the room with the drinks, and she really had a chance to look at him.

He was a big man, something over six feet probably, and broad. Not flabby, though, not fat. Sarah noted the fit of his navy twill trousers, and that he had straight dark hair, brushed back and a little on the long side, very professorial. A bit more of the dark hair showed above the open collar of a white shirt and V-necked blue sweater. His eyes were blue, too, and he was clean-shaven. She'd imagined he would have a beard. Instead he had a nice cleft chin and a slightly too big nose that countermanded the academic impression. It made him look a little tough. But nicely so. Father Lasky was thirty-five; if they'd been students together, Jarib Baarak must be the same age.

"Your name is very unusual." She took the glass of wine from his hands, noting that they were square, the fingers blunt. Competent-looking hands.

"My parents came from Egypt. Which explains Baraak. I was always told that Jarib was a family name. When I discovered that it's Hebrew in origin and means 'to strive,' it made sense. We're Jews, though I don't think anyone's been religious for the last few generations. Sarah is also Hebrew, by the way. It means 'princess.' Did you know that?"

"No." She shook her head, pushing her heavy mane of hair off her forehead with the back of her wrist. "I knew it was biblical, not what it meant."

"Then I've been able to add a bit of enlightenment to the afternoon." He smiled a big, slow, gentle smile. Instantly appealing. "Now, tell me why you're so sure our visit is going to be a bust, as you put it."

Sarah stared into her glass. "You study weird happenings, isn't that right? I don't think I'm very weird. At least I don't want to be. It's just that since the accident I have a crazy fantasy that keeps recurring."

"According to Tom, a voice that calls your name and four notes of music. An accurate description?"

"As far as it goes. But there's nothing new about the music. I've heard that since I was a kid."

"Really? I didn't realize that. Tom didn't say."

"He didn't know. I've never talked about it. I learned at an early age that it made people very nervous."

"But not you?"

She shrugged. "Sometimes, but mostly I just lived with it because it was always there."

"And now, since the accident?"

"Now I'm getting fierce headaches that are literally driving me 'round the bend. And there's more. I sense a presence, as if someone were trying to reach me. . . . God, I know how that sounds. Séances and mediums and all that bullshit."

"Not to me," he said softly. "It doesn't sound exactly like that for one thing; for another, sometimes it isn't bullshit."

Her head jerked up, and her green eyes narrowed. "You believe in séances, getting in touch with the dead?"

"Not the way you mean. Look, let's leave that for a while, shall we? I promise I'll explain myself, but first I'd like to hear more about your experience. Do you have any sense of what you call the presence as male or female? Does it speak to you?"

"I think the voice that calls my name is a woman. The presence is more confused. Sometimes it's as if it were one person, again I think a woman; other times it's more as if a whole group of people are . . . struggling to get in. I can't put it any other way." She shivered.

"You're frightened," he said. "Relax, it's only scary because you don't understand it. But more of that later, too. Is that it? Anything else to report?"

"Sometimes I get what I call flashes. Like bits of film playing in my head. I see things. But they come and go very quickly. I can't make out any detail."

"What have you seen?"

"A kind of scroll, and candles. And once it was as if a lot of people were crying and wailing and there was a curved kind of horn that made a terrible piercing noise. I didn't recognize it at the time, but since then I've decided it was an animal horn, the kind of thing primitive peoples blow."

For the first time Jarib looked startled. "Not just primitives. Jews still use a ram's horn as part of their worship. It's called a *shofar*. But that's not what's important, do you both see and hear simultaneously? Words *and* pictures?"

"Sometimes, yes. You sound surprised."

"I am. That's unusual. I'll have to do some research before I say more about it." He rose and fetched the wine bottle and refilled their glasses. "Listen, can I call you Sarah and will you call me Jarib? If we're going to work together, it's a lot easier."

She nodded. Jarib was a nice name; he was a nice guy. She sipped the wine and settled more comfortably into the chair.

"I'd like to bring up one more preliminary topic. Tom told me you were reluctant to come here, a hostile witness. Care to comment on that?"

Sarah's smile was rueful. "Father Lasky lets it all hang out, doesn't he? Okay. I'm not too thrilled about this whole thing. Not what's happening to me and not getting involved with somebody who makes a specialty of studying weirdos. If it weren't for the headaches, I probably wouldn't have agreed to see you."

"Parapsychology isn't necessarily about weirdos; a lot of very normal people, whatever that means, have extraordinary experiences that are difficult to explain. Think about the Greek root of the word. *Para* means 'beside,' so *paranormal* phenomena are 'beside the normal.' And since such phenomena exist, witness yourself, it stands to reason that people are going to want to investigate them. In the world of science parapsychology is a stepchild, but a member of the family nonetheless. Does that give you a bit more confidence?"

She looked down at her hands, folded in her lap. "A little. But the truth is I'm desperate enough to talk to anyone. The headaches are literally destroying me. I want to take up my life, go back to work, move out of my folks' house. I can't do anything until the damned pain goes away."

"That part should be easy."

Sarah's eyes widened. "You mean that?"

"Yes. The doctors say there's no physical reason for the headaches, right?"

"Right. And I've even had a psychiatrist admit I'm relatively sane."

"Okay, then you're getting the headaches because you're fighting the paranormal experience. Well, we're not going to fight it; we're going to explore it and find out what it's all about. Once you start doing that, presto!" He snapped his fingers. "No more headaches."

She downed the rest of her wine in one gulp. "You're sure?"

"Reasonably so. Game to give it a try?"

Sarah didn't hesitate. "Yes, but I can't say I'm a convert. I still think séances and ghosts are a crock."

He chuckled. "Your skepticism is a good thing. Being gullible is the mark of a fool. But if you're going to know the difference between what I do and what makes the occasional headline, I've got to give you some background. Ever hear of J. B. Rhine?"

She shook her head and he continued. "In 1930 at Duke University Rhine started a laboratory to study paranormal phenomena. In those days it was part of the psychology department. He concentrated on what's called ESP, extrasensory perception. Receiving information in some manner other than through the five senses we ordinarily use to tell us about the world."

She pushed her hair back with an impatient gesture. "To me that doesn't sound any better than the séances and the mediums."

"You're a tough case," Jarib said, grinning. "But you're a Catholic. Sounds a little inconsistent to me. Doesn't a large part of your faith have to do with the unseen and the unexplainable?"

Sarah studied her fingertips, these days she had time to keep them perfectly manicured. "I was raised in the Catholic Church; at the moment I'm not a paid-up member of the club."

"Fair enough," he said easily. "It was an impertinent question anyway. Sorry. But for my purposes it's important to know you're a goat."

Sarah raised her eyebrows.

"That's not an insult," he said. "To tell you what it means, I have to back up a bit. The classic test of ESP is done with twenty-five cards. Five of them are marked with a wave, five with a cross, five with a circle, five with a star, and five with a square. The backs of all the cards are blank. Ever study any math?"

"Not since high school. And I was terrible."

"You'll have to take my word for it then. Given the distribution I've described, if someone tried to guess the design on the cards looking only at the blank sides, he'd be right an average of five out of twenty-five times. Just on the law of probability. So any score above five is better than average. Below is worse than average. From a scientist's point of view, both results would be significant."

"How does that make me a goat?"

He stood up and poked at the fire. A log at the back caught and flamed. Outside it was dusk and the room was dim. Jarib switched on a lamp and bathed them in a warm golden light. It was strangely intimate. Sarah found herself staring at him, hanging on to his every word.

"I'm getting to the goats and the sheep." He stood leaning on the mantel, watching her. "In 1942, at Radcliffe, Dr. Gertrude Schmeidler conducted a now-famous experiment. She was using the cards to test a group of students for ESP. Before she began, she asked them to say whether or not they believed in the existence of

ESP. Those that said they did she categorized as sheep; the ones who denied believing in it she put down as goats. When the tests were completed, she found that the sheep had scored significantly above average. That was important. But more important was that the goats had scored markedly below."

He leaned forward slightly, pinning her with his forthright stare. "Don't you see, Sarah? The goats had used reverse ESP; they deliberately, if unconsciously, cheated to make sure they wouldn't get high scores. They ignored their genuine hunches, that modicum of ESP we all have and use every day. In so doing, they controlled the outcome of the test because they willed to do so. The goats proved more about ESP than the sheep. And you are a goat. We're going to have to remember that in all our work."

He stood up and so did she. It had been a long session, and apparently it wasn't quite over. "There are two things I want you to do," Jarib said. "First, whenever you feel one of these experiences coming on, don't fight it."

Sarah tensed. "Just give in? I can't do that!"

"Why not? Look, nothing bad has happened to you so far, nothing attributable to the voice or the music or anything else." He laid a hand on her shoulder. "Listen, for all your cynicism I think you've got some subliminal ideas about diabolical possession and evil spirits. This has nothing to do with that, none of the signs point to it. It's too early to say, but I suspect what we've got here is a kind of time warp. You're picking up signals. Rather like a radio antenna. Does that make any sense?"

"Sort of. But the possibilities it raises are very confusing."

"I know. So we won't deal with them just yet. But trust me, let the experience happen and just roll with it. Go with the flow, as they say nowadays. Okay?"

"I'll try."

"Fine. Once you start doing that, I'm fairly certain the headaches will go away. And I want you to keep a notebook, a kind of journal. Immediately after any experience write down the date, time, place, what you were doing when it happened, and exactly what you saw and heard. We'll go over it together when we meet."

But for their next three meetings there was little to go over. Sarah had only repeats of previous experiences: the music, the sense of a presence, sadness; she saw the scroll once and the horn another time. There was nothing new, and Jarib wasn't ready to say more about what he thought it meant. Instead they talked. Not idly. Jarib Baraak had set out to alter the way Sarah saw the universe.

He spoke about the stupidity of ignoring facts because they don't fit preconceived ideas. "The best-educated people, particularly scientists, can be the worst," he said vehemently. "In September of 1768 the peasants of the French town of Luce heard what they took to be a violent clap of thunder. Immediately afterward they saw an enormous boulder half buried in one of their fields. They declared that a giant rock had fallen from the sky and because of all the brouhaha, the French Academy of Sciences sent Lavoisier, the famous chemist, to investigate. His conclusion was that all the peasants were fools or liars. The stone had tumbled from the back of some wagon. Everybody knows rocks don't fall from the sky."

"A meteorite?" Sarah asked tentatively.

Jarib smiled. "You're learning. A meteorite that had the temerity to call attention to itself before we'd investigated such phenomena. Before science had cataloged meteorites and admitted them to the list of things we're entitled to credit."

He smoked a pipe filled with a sweetly pungent mixture he said was Egyptian. "My concession to roots or racial memory or some such." The smoke curled in the air and hovered over their heads; it mingled with the scent of burning applewood in the fireplace. They were drinking fresh-pressed cider that Sarah had impulsively purchased on her way to Rowley. There was a sensual pleasure in the sweet taste, the good smells, the feel of the leather chair. There was nothing unreal in the atmosphere, nothing threatening.

"We need the world to be stable," Jarib said. "It's our innermost imperative. We all know we're going to die eventually, but we act as if we expect to live forever. Because to say we 'know' it is a mistake. We have been told about it, we've seen it happen over and over again, but we don't really assimilate it because the concept of ceasing to exist, of nonexistence, isn't part of our personal experience. We go to sleep, in a way that's like dying, but inevitably we wake up. And we constantly tell ourselves that the world is a logical, sane place. No matter what the evidence to the contrary."

Sarah sipped her cider and watched him over the rim of the glass.

His face was so mobile and strong. It never ceased to fascinate her. She wondered if he'd let her sketch him sometime. She had to force herself to concentrate on what he'd been saying. He was silent, waiting for her to speak. "It's all very confusing," she said hesitantly.

"Only if you refuse to let go of your preconceptions. Hysteria and obsession are the result of a narrowing of consciousness, an *idée fixe* of whatever form. When we are truly open-minded—*wide-minded* might be a better term—we don't have to be afraid." He put the pipe down and clasped his hands behind his head, looking not at her but at the fire.

"Let me regale you with another classic experiment. Twenty years ago at Innsbruck University Dr. Anton Hajos constructed a pair of glasses that made everything look distorted. Straight lines became curved, angles were twisted, outlines were fuzzy. He inveigled a group of students into wearing his glasses constantly for a week. At first they were nauseated and dizzy and thoroughly disoriented. But those that persevered soon reported that the sensations passed. They became accustomed to the world seen through the glasses. It looked completely normal to them. When the test period was over and they took the glasses off, they experienced the same trouble. The world you and I insist is ordinary looked topsy-turvy and frightening. They were physically sickened by it."

She stood up and walked to the window. It was divided by delicate wood mullions; the glass was old and splintered the light into an infinity of prisms. The street outside looked odd seen through that particular window. The aptness of the vision struck her with sudden force, and she caught her breath.

"Exactly," Jarib said softly. "I bought this place for an unconscionable price as soon as I looked out that window. It makes the point so well."

Sarah turned to face him. "Okay. I see what you're getting at. How is all this going to help me?"

"How many headaches did you have this past week?"

She opened her mouth, then closed it again. "Only one," she whispered. "I've been getting them almost every other day, but since I saw you last, only one."

"Because the conflict engendered by your attempt simply to

push the whole thing away is what caused the headaches. Now, by letting the experience happen, by conquering your fear, you're in control. So you're ready to look at the thing itself. Exactly what is happening to you?" He stood up and approached her. "Sarah, I'm suggesting we try to find out, push it to its limits."

"The time warp?"

"Yes, if that's what it is."

"You're not sure, is that what you're saying?"

He shrugged. "It's the hypothesis that makes the most sense, so it's what I'm buying for the moment. But as I've been saying, an open mind is everything in work like this."

Sarah grimaced and turned away. "Just another experiment to you, Dr. Baraak. Meanwhile it's my head that's being tampered with."

"No!" He spit out the word and took her by the shoulders and spun her 'round to face him. "That's not what's going on here and I want you to get that idea right out of your mind. This is much more interesting, Sarah, much more exciting. You just might be getting a chance to investigate something that people have been trying to get a handle on for years. You're a rarity, my girl. Words and pictures, concrete images with sound. Do you really want just to bury that?"

She moved away from his grip and stood silent for a moment. "Let me ask you a question," she said finally. "How did you get into this field? Why?"

"I got in by accident. I heard a lecture in my sophomore year and I was hooked. But I was predisposed to succumb. My parents are both science types. Chemists. I was brought up on the idea of cause and effect, that two and two equal four. But it seemed, I don't know exactly how to put it, like a cold kind of world. And an isolated one. When my parents emigrated to America, they came alone. So there was no family, no grandparents, no aunts or uncles or cousins. And not a lot of friends. My folks aren't the type who make close friends. To cap it, I'm an only child. So I found an escape in science fiction. I read it all, the good stuff and the junk. It seemed like a way to combine the world my parents insisted was real with the make-believe I longed for. Make sense?"

"Yes." She had a vision of Jarib as a lonely kid, filling his life with books, and was ashamed of herself for feeling so self-pitying a moment earlier. "How come you didn't join NASA?"

"That was another route to go. For a while I considered it. I was going to be a physicist. But when I discovered the byway of parapsychology, I was entranced. I'm not a pure science type, and this isn't a pure science." He shook his head ruefully. "Mind telling me why we're talking about me?"

"Just stalling till I can give you an answer," she admitted.

"And?"

"And I think I'll do it, go on a little further anyway." He looked very relieved. "Tell me one thing more," Sarah said. "Eventually will I know why I hear the voice and the music?"

"You'll know *about* them," Jarib said. "That's all science is capable of telling us, Sarah. The whys of things are the province of philosophers and theologians. Look, what chemistry has demonstrated is that a molecule of water is composed of two hydrogen atoms bonded to one oxygen atom. Why that configuration and not some other produces what we call water, what chemist would claim to know that?"

He paused for a moment, lighting his pipe again. "The nature of your experience so far is something like a tape recorder: You can press the play button at will. Just by relaxing and drifting the tiniest bit below conscious control. Right?"

"Yes. I find I always hear it just when I'm falling asleep. So now I've learned to read until I actually am asleep. I wake up every morning with a book still in my hands and the reading light on."

"Okay, but that's a ploy, a stall. We're going to see if you can get the recorder to stop repeating the same words. We'll try to make the tape move on. If we succeed, you'll know a lot more about your experience. I can't say that you'll have any greater understanding of why it happens or what, in any sense, it means." He stood up. "Is that going to be enough, Sarah? It's all I can offer."

Sarah bit her lip and stared at the backs of her hands. Finally she looked up and smiled. "It beats the alternatives. I guess it will have to be enough."

"Very well, let's begin." He put down the pipe and rose. "Ever sit in the lotus position?"

"Not the true lotus. I used to be able to do what I think is called the false lotus. With my feet under my thighs. I don't think I could now. I'm still pretty stiff."

He remembered about the accident and looked embarrassed. "Sorry, that was thoughtless of me. Anyway, it doesn't matter. It's not strictly necessary, it just helps sometimes. We're discovering that a lot of what Eastern religion has taught for centuries is absolutely true. Mind and body are connected. One of the salient Zen instructions is that the spine should be absolutely straight. You can stay in the chair and achieve that. Put your feet flat on the floor and your hands in your lap."

He moved behind her where she couldn't see him, only hear his voice. "What we're trying to do is get you totally relaxed. Take a deep breath. Now let it out." He waited until she'd done as he said. "Good. Again. Be conscious of the breath. Be aware of its sinking down into the pit of your belly, then rising again. No, don't breathe through your mouth. Just your nose."

He spoke in a low, steady voice, a kind of rhythm shaped his words. "Imagine an empty space at the top of your head. Sarah. Feel it expand and fill your neck and your shoulders. The space is spreading down your right arm now. It's going into your elbow and your wrist . . . now into your thumb and your index finger. . . ."

Sarah! Listen to the music. Sarah! Do-sol-la-fa. Do-sol-la-fa. . . . So much pain, such a terrible sadness. I want to die; if I die, it will all be over. No, it will not end. After death the eternal fires. Do-sol-la-fa. So much pain and sadness. Has ever there been any grief like this grief? . . .

"No. I can't bear it. Jarib, I want to stop."

He was with her instantly, his hands beneath her arms, lifting her gently to her feet. "Okay, Sarah. I'm right here, it's okay. What happened?"

"The grief, the woman is grieving terribly. I felt all her pain. It was awful."

"Sarah, think carefully, did she tell you about it, was she saying she was in pain?"

"Yes, but not to me exactly. It was as if she were thinking her own thoughts, feeling them; only I could feel them, too." She shuddered. "It was awful."

"Okay, calm down. Here, drink this." He poured a brandy and waited until she drank it. "Look, what you've got to realize is that you aren't the cause of her grief, whatever it is, and it isn't happening to you. You're an observer, Sarah. You're somehow there inside her head, or she's inside yours. You mustn't let it upset you."

"That's easy to say, you're not feeling it."

"I know. I only wish I were. But if you stick with it, if you don't give up, I think we'll come out on the other side." He ran his fingers through his hair; she'd noticed he did that a lot. "It's so exciting, so remarkable, I get a little carried away. But it's up to you whether or not you go on. I don't want to push you."

"You think I'll—how did you put it?—come out on the other side?"

"Yes, I do. And I don't think you'd be content just to let this thing hang around in your life, the way the music has always done. Even without the headaches. So I'm not being wholly selfish in encouraging you to go on."

She spoke in a small whisper. "The truth is, I'm scared."

"Here, look at me." He put his fingers under her chin and tilted her face to his. "I'm not going to let you go on this journey alone, and I'm not going to let anything bad happen to you. Trust me."

She looked into his eyes. They were dark blue, smoky, intense. And she was feeling . . . what? Strange things. "Okay," she said at last. It was an affirmation of much she didn't yet understand. Did he know that?

"A gutsy girl," he said, and walked to the desk and began making notes and the special mood was broken. Sarah wondered if he'd felt strange things, too, but all he said was: "I'd better see you again in a couple of days. Saturday morning all right?"

"Yes."

Then, when they were standing on the front step saying good-bye, he suddenly asked. "Do you always wear jeans?"

Sarah glanced down. Levi's today, and a plaid lumber jacket. L.L.Bean rather than *Vogue*. She'd wanted to come on a little less strong. "Don't you like jeans?"

"I'm old-fashioned enough to want to see a girl's legs once in a while."

He grinned at her, and she carried that grin in her mind all the way back to Ipswich.

"Holy shit, sugar! A time warp? And you're going to 'push it all the way.' You're going along with that? What kind of a flake is this Egyptian anyway?"

They were in an Indian restaurant, the table crowded with the remains of Tandoori chicken and half-eaten nan. "He's not Egyptian, he came here when he was an infant, and he's a Harvard professor, hardly a flake." Sarah gestured with a piece of the Indian flat bread, waving it at Pinkie. "What are you so upset about? You're the one who listened to all my crazy stories and shrugged them off. Why the sudden switch?"

Pinkie leaned forward, agitated and earnest. "The thing is all along you had crazy things happening to you, but you weren't crazy. So all I needed to do was listen. Now you're letting this professor conduct an experiment with you as the guinea pig. That's different."

"If I don't, I'll never understand what's happening and why."

"So what? You said the headaches are gone. Okay, he's done it. Now get on with your life." She reached over and covered Sarah's hand with her own. "Come back to Boston, sugar. You can stay with me and Max until you find a job. It'll be fun."

Sarah shook her head. Her hair was up today, accentuating the small, chiseled features, the big green eyes. She looked very vulnerable. "I can't. Not yet. C'mon, this is my one day in the big city, I want to do some Christmas shopping."

Pinkie grabbed the check and insisted on paying it. Then, just as they were shrugging into their coats: "Say, it couldn't be that you're going along with this pharaoh type because you've got the hots for him, could it?" She sounded hopeful.

"Don't be ridiculous," Sarah said firmly.

Milly Katz leaned over the sink and watched Sarah Myles turn her red Pinto into the garage across the street. She kept watching until the girl got out of the car, gathered up her bundles, and went into the house. Sarah was walking much better now. She didn't need the cane anymore; today there was even a spring to her step. And she looked happy. Milly was glad about that; she hadn't seen Sarah look happy since the accident, not until she started visiting that man in Rowley.

Milly made herself a cup of tea and sat at her kitchen table to drink it. It was a nice kitchen. Pleasant and cheerful with a lovely view of the marsh. And of the Myleses' house. They hadn't bought it for that reason. Harry and she decided to live in Ipswich in '57, three years before Milly took on what she thought of as her project.

Ipswich didn't have more than a handful of Jews; they'd worried about that, and the fact that they had to drive all the way to Beverly to attend synagogue. But they decided it was worth it. They could get so much more house for their money in Ipswich. And the schools were good, so the kids would be all right. Harry said he actually enjoyed the commute to his hardware store in Beverly, and Milly didn't mind driving ten miles to get to her Hadassah meetings. Her other social engagements weren't related to religion. She was past president of the PTA and an active member of the Ipswich Early Americana Society. The latter had proved particularly convenient. Rita Myles was a member, too.

Milly took a notebook from its place at the rear of the kitchen counter. She had filled three pages with information and she read it over slowly. Then decided. She'd drive to the Peabody shopping center and call Paris. Normally she only did it once or twice a year and she'd done so in June, right after the accident. Anything unusual, that's what she'd been asked to watch for and report. A major accident was unusual, she'd realized. And now? Well, maybe or maybe not. But she decided to err on the side of too many rather than too few reports.

Carefully she underlined the salient points of her investigations. Jarib Baraak. A professor from Harvard. On sabbatical. Living in Rowley. Seeing Sarah once a week. And his specialty was something weird. She'd copied it from the Harvard register, then had to look up the meaning of the word. Parapsychology. Well, the old man in Paris would doubtless know what that meant. After twenty-four years she'd decided he knew just about everything.

· · ·

Forty miles south, on Lake Street in Brighton, a meeting was taking place—apparently unrelated. Bishop Thomas Crown, one of the archdiocese's four auxiliary bishops, was staring pensively at the seminary professor he'd summoned to his office in the chancery. "Well, Monsignor, what do you think?"

Monsignor Larry Donovan cocked his head and studied his questioner. "It's an intriguing proposition, but why me? I'm not a Scripture scholar."

In his young days the bishop had been. That gave his comment added poignancy. "Precisely. Most of my colleagues can't see the forest for the trees. They've been staring at the damn thing too long. And they love convoluted arguments about periods and commas."

"With respect, Your Excellency, your thesis is exactly that, a convoluted argument."

"Only on first blush, son, only on first blush. Here, let me give you a simple example." The old man was nearing eighty, and he was never going to have a diocese of his own, much less a red hat. He reached for two small leather-bound missals from the shelf behind his desk. He had Parkinson's disease, and his hands trembled as he flicked through the pages and ran his finger down the lines of text. But his voice was firm, and his mind obviously unclouded. "The Passion of our Lord Jesus Christ according to St. John. Chapter eighteen. I quote from the authorized Jerusalem Bible version of 1966. Very current as these things go."

He cleared his throat. "Our Lord is being questioned by Annas, the high priest. Jesus answers him, 'I have spoken openly for all the world to hear; I have always taught in the synagogue and the Temple where all the Jews meet together.' Now, Monsignor, do you know what's odd about that statement?"

Donovan thought for a moment. "Given your thesis, the use of the article. Why does he say 'the' Jews?"

"Yes. This is a Jew being questioned by a Jew, the current leader of the religion he has followed all his life. He would say, 'where all *we* Jews meet together,' or just 'all Jews.' But putting in *the* distances him from his coreligionists."

"Subtle," Donovan said. He bent over the text. He had coppery orange-red hair that appeared to have been colored by a child with a crayon. It was thinning, but there was no trace of gray. His hair glittered in the light from the reading lamp. "I never really thought of it before, but you're right. And the other translations?"

Bishop Crown opened the second missal. "Here's Knox. '. . . where all the Jews foregather.' Same thing. And later, Jesus speaking to Pilate, '. . . if my kingdom . . . belonged to this world my servants would be fighting to prevent my falling into the hands of the Jews. . . .' Is this logical? A man is talking about his own people, his mother and foster father, his closest friends, the multitudes who have followed him—Jews all. But suddenly he is separating himself, making no distinction between those who have connived to bring him down and the others, the ones who followed him everywhere shouting hosannas. Good God, man, it's as plain as the nose on your face!" Monsignor Donovan's nose was enormous, and the bishop colored slightly and looked away. "I mean, it's obvious. The text has been doctored by somebody with an ax to grind."

"The original writer, according to you."

"Yes, that's what I think. Here we are, it's some sixty years since it all happened, the eyewitnesses are dead, and for the first time those following the new religion are beginning to write the tale. And now they see themselves as having a mission to the whole world. They're desperate to prove that they're not just a Jewish sect."

"If you're right, it's more than that. John is positively vitriolic. The Jews wanted to put him to death . . . for fear of the Jews they did such and so."

The old man had incipient cataracts in both eyes. These days any reading made them water. He took a large handkerchief from the pocket of his cassock and wiped them carefully. "Exactly." There was a lot of feeling in the single word.

"Your Excellency, can I ask something? How did you happen to get involved in this?"

"That's simple. My mother." He turned a small, framed photograph of a woman so that his guest could see it. It was merely a snapshot, blurred and indistinct, of an ordinary-looking middle-aged woman. The dress and the hairstyle marked the period as the twenties. "She was Jewish," Crown said. "A convert when she married my father. Her family never forgave her. They went through a period of mourning, as if she were dead, and never spoke to her again. But she always considered herself a Jew as well as a Christian; to her it was a continuous line. She raised me to prize what there was of Jew in me."

Donovan nodded. "I see. That brings me back to my original question. Why me? Why a professor of moral theology to head up your committee?"

The bishop laughed. "No particularly profound reason. I like you. I liked your style at that ethics conference in Chicago last year. And you have the respect of the left and the right. That will be useful." He passed a piece of paper across the desk. "Here's the list of the people who've agreed to serve. I've consulted them all, by the way. There's complete agreement on your appointment as chairman, if you'll take it."

Each of the names was known to Donovan, by reputation if not personally. Scripture specialists all, many were celebrated scholars. A quick analysis yielded seven men and two women. All but three were Americans; the foreigners were a Dutchman, a German, and one British nun. "Has Rome approved this?"

Crown laughed. "The best way. They said nothing. I wrote and told them what I proposed, an ad hoc committee to study special aspects of Jews and the Scriptures. With the famous tag line 'If I don't hear from you by such and such a date, I'll presume we are free to proceed.' I didn't hear."

"So if they don't like what we come up with, they'll just say it was a bureaucratic oversight. They never approved our going ahead."

"Exactly," the bishop said again. "Your ten years at the Vatican trained you well."

"In gamesmanship, yes. Your Excellency, what do you know of Bishop Malachy Fanti?"

"The Swiss Scripture scholar? I've met him only once or twice. Can't say I liked him." Crown was wary, wondering if perhaps the monsignor had some allegiances of which he was unaware. "I don't think he should be on our team."

"Hardly," Donovan said dryly. "Once upon a time I knew him well. A brilliant and a holy man. But . . ." He hesitated, then made up his mind to continue. "He's violently anti-Semitic. It's a mania with him. Like some insane aberration."

"I've presumed as much from some of his published work. Any idea why?"

"None. I often wondered about it, but never found out. May I venture another question?" The older man made an acquiescent gesture. "Does something called the Alexandria Testament mean anything to you?"

Crown pursed his lips and thought for a moment before answering. "I've a vague memory of having heard of it, but when or in what context escapes me."

"Supposedly it's some apocryphal document written during the apostolic period. It's supposed to tell a different version of the relations between the synagogue and the early Church. One in which some of the gospel accounts are contradicted. And the Jews come out looking much better than they do in your examples there." He pointed to the missals still on the bishop's desk.

"You think this document exists? That we could find it?"

"I haven't any idea. The point is Fanti. He's spent his life searching for the Testament; it's like some reverse kind of holy grail to him. He's convinced he has a mission to find and suppress it. And don't ask me why, because I don't know that either."

"All right, I won't ask. But I don't see what this has to do with your accepting the chairmanship of the committee."

"I'm not sure. It just seems a little odd. As a young man I ran into Fanti and heard his theories. By the way, he insists that descendants of whoever wrote it have a racial memory about it. So if you find one of them, you can find the Alexandria Testament."

Donovan held up his hand to forestall Crown's comment. "I know. But when he talks about it, you believe it; he's very convinced and very persuasive. Anyway, what I was starting to say was that first I learn about all that, then twenty years later you invite me to be part of a project involving a rethink of Jews and the early Church, which just doesn't happen to be remotely related to my own field. Does that sound like fate?"

"Divine Providence, more likely. Knowing Fanti's hidden agenda, you can make sure he doesn't sabotage ours."

Donovan leaned back in his chair. He was fifty-six, but he looked younger, a slight man, almost effeminate except for the outsize nose. "I grew up with more than the usual share of preju-

69

dices," he said. "My father was a dental technician; he made false teeth. Most of the dentists he worked for were Jews. He was always complaining that they didn't pay him enough. And Jewish dentists had a lot more money than we did. When I was about ten, a Jewish family moved into the neighborhood. The father was a tailor. Barely making ends meet, like the rest of us. We harassed them unmercifully. I remember I once chalked 'Christ killer' on the front door."

"You'll do it then," the bishop said quietly. "To atone a little."

"I'm not at all sure that's why," Donovan said, laughing softly. "But yes, I'll do it."

The bishop saw him to the door, then returned to his desk. He allowed himself two small whiskeys per day. The first one was due just about now, and he took a bottle from his drawer and poured carefully. Palsy was a damned nuisance. Almost worse than his failing vision. He should retire to some convent in the country. Dodder in the sun and leave the problems to younger men. Well, maybe he would now. Snagging Larry Donovan for his committee was the coup he'd prayed for.

The man was a bird dog; once he took the scent, he didn't give up. And he wasn't interested in how many angels could dance on the head of a pin. Right and wrong and how to choose between them, that was Donovan's forte. He'd see things through. The scholars on the committee would argue and carp and disagree—despite the fact that he'd chosen them all because they supported his main thesis—but Donovan would keep them from getting lost in minutiae. So it had been a good day. He turned to the picture of his mother and raised his glass in salute.

Deep in the Vatican there occurred an apparently unrelated incident: Two other churchmen met. Both were Italians, both nearing seventy. They were unlike Crown and Donovan. Perhaps equally devoted to their Church and their God, but crusted with a heavy layer of European cynicism, with a pragmatism bred by centuries and supported by the complex structure of the institution they served. Neither was interested in theology, and neither had any knowledge of the committee being formed in America.

"Pawn to king's bishop four," Cardinal Bellini said. "Your queen is *en prise*."

"Yes, so I see." Bishop Longo hesitated with his hand over the white queen. "Have you heard what he's planning?"

The cardinal did not raise his glance from the board. He did not need to ask; he knew his companion referred to His Holiness the pope. "Every day I hear something new he's planning. But he's old and ill. Most of the plans will never see fruition."

"This one will. He's giving Fanti the red hat."

Bellini's head snapped up. "He can't!"

"Why not? The pope makes cardinals as he chooses."

"But it's insane. Fanti's a fanatic."

"He's holy," Bishop Longo said. "Unworldly, not like the rest of us. For some, for the Holy Father, that sort of thing has enormous appeal."

"It's insane," Bellini insisted. "The pope is dying. There's going to be an election. Can you see Fanti locked up with the rest of us trying to choose a pope? You could argue for six months and not get him to negotiate."

"I know. And I'll tell you something more. There are those already mentioning Fanti as His Holiness's successor. They say that's what's intended." His large hand grasped the threatened queen and swept her to the extreme right of the board. "Your move."

"I can't believe it." The cardinal ignored the game. "Why would anyone want to make a man like Fanti pope?"

"The Holy Father because of Fanti's saintliness. For the rest of us his fanaticism is perhaps more important. Ultimately both could make him malleable." The bishop removed an imported French cigarette from a solid gold case. When he lit it, the harsh, acrid tobacco scented the room. "A practical man like yourself, for instance. You could keep a Fanti interested in his prayers and his cause, and manage everything else."

"You mean, he goes on raving against Jews and chasing his mysterious Alexandria Testament, while the Church is run by those with her best interests at heart?"

"Something like that." Longo drew deep on the cigarette and let the smoke filter out his nostrils. "It's still your move, my friend."

71

Bellini quickly moved his rook.

Longo gave him no time to reconsider. His hand swooped down over the queen and swiftly pushed her back into the attack. "Check. And mate in three."

The cardinal peered at the board for long seconds; then he sighed. "You win as usual." He tipped over the black king. It lay emasculated and ineffectual among the lesser pieces that had caused its downfall. The two men stared first at it, then at each other. Eventually they smiled.

The next day was Saturday. Sarah put on a dark green skirt with a matching jacket and a blue and green print blouse with a bow at the neck. Rita had bought her the outfit; it was nothing like the clothes Sarah chose for herself. Demure, sweet, her mother's idea of feminine, not hers. She started for the door of her room, then changed her mind. Swiftly she stripped off the suit and the blouse and dropped them in a heap on the bed. She pulled on the same things she'd worn last week. Jarib Baraak would have to take her as she was.

He didn't comment on her clothes. "We're going to begin with an experiment today. It's not vital, Sarah. The outcome isn't terribly important. I just want a record of the results at this early stage of our work."

He seated her at the desk in the living room and indicated a small console in one corner. "An intercom," he said, switching it on. "It connects with the dining room across the hall. I'll be in there turning over these cards." He spread them in front of her.

"The ESP cards you talked about. The ones that separated the sheep from the goats."

"The same. As you can see, the symbols are quite straightforward. This squiggly line is called the wave. The others are self-evident."

Sarah looked at the crosses, circles, squares, and stars and nodded. "Okay, but why the intercom?"

"A nod to proper scientific method, even though we're not trying to prove anything. It can be argued that the investigator influences the results if the subject can see him. Unconsciously tips the answer by some movement. Being in separate rooms helps to eliminate that possibility. Ready?"

"Ready."

He left her alone, and a few seconds later she heard his voice coming through the speaker on the desk. "Now," he said.

"A square," Sarah answered at once. She was amazed that she didn't have to think about her reply. It just came out, as quickly as that.

Jarib's voice: "Now."

"Another square."

"Now."

"A circle . . . no, it's a star."

They did the run of twenty-five cards three consecutive times. Sarah got six right the first two times and five the third.

"Interesting," Jarib said.

"That doesn't sound encouraging. Your buzzword is significant."

He didn't smile. "Nothing is significant so early in an investigation."

"Sorry."

The tone of her voice alerted him, and he looked up. "No, I'm sorry. Like most scientists, I tend to take myself too seriously. It's a bad habit. Don't ever hesitate to slap me down when it happens."

She felt strangely spent, as if the card calling had exhausted her, though she'd been conscious of no special effort while it was going on. She put her fingers to her temples and leaned back. The desk chair was big, Jarib would need a big chair, and it tilted. Her feet didn't reach the floor.

"Tired?" Jarib asked.

"Yes, all of a sudden. I don't know why."

"Forgive what sounds like a crank statement, you've been expending psychic energy."

"I keep wanting to ask you about cranks. All your talk about having an open mind. Do you believe in UFOs and little green men from Mars?"

He laughed his rich, full laugh. "Hell, no. Most of the sightings are invented by poor slobs who desperately need attention. But I don't disallow the possibility that such things as UFOs could exist."

"No little green men?"

"Not from Mars. On the basis of current evidence, it's unlikely in the extreme." He put the cards away. "Come see my kitchen. We can make a pot of coffee."

The kitchen was a surprise. Immaculately neat and very modern. No concessions to the age of the house and its environs. There were a bank of cabinets finished in mat white plastic, stainless steel counters, a black glass cook top, and a wall oven. "It's not what I expected," Sarah said.

"I like things to be functional, to work. When I bought the house, I could see that every room but the kitchen would work for me as it was. So this was the only thing I changed."

"It isn't the age of the house that attracted you then, it's history?"

Jarib paused, as if he had not before considered the idea. "I guess not in the way you mean. I expect you see things I don't. I've never been interested in art, never studied it. Maybe sometime you can teach me a little. We'll visit a museum and you can tell me what I should be seeing. They always seem like dusty old tombs to me."

"You're on."

He poured mugs of coffee and rummaged in a cabinet. "I had some cookies in here awhile back."

"Thanks, but no cookies."

"You're not on one of these crash diets, I hope."

Sarah laughed. "Never. I eat like a horse. I'm just not hungry now." She leaned against the refrigerator and sipped her coffee. "Jarib," she said finally. "You haven't asked about my headaches."

"Okay, consider yourself asked."

"None. Not a twinge all week."

He grinned.

"My parents think you're a miracle worker," she said.

Unaccountably her face was hot. She was remembering Rita's comment. "That's one thing you have to say for Jews, they're usually smart." She'd wanted to protest, but she hadn't. Rita would be unable to see that it was an anti-Semitic remark. She'd deny any prejudice at all, point out that she quite liked Milly Katz, who lived across the street. Only some of them . . .

Sarah pushed the memory away. Besides, it was Rita who'd suggested she invite Jarib to the party. "My folks would like you to come to our open house on New Year's Day. We have it every year, it's a family tradition."

"Does the invitation come from you as well as your parents?"

"Yes, of course."

Not wholly true. Rita had to insist. And Sarah didn't know why the notion of Jarib in the Ipswich house had bothered her then, bothered her now. "Please come," she said despite that.

"I'd love to," Jarib said.

Baraak stood for a moment outside the Myleses' house. It was three in the afternoon and snowing gently. Large flakes drifted down and settled on the four-inch carpet of snow left by a Christmas Eve storm. The beautifully balanced white colonial facade was accentuated by two tall pines flanking the front door. The snow enhanced the charm. The house was at its best in such a setting. Despite the lack of interest in art he'd professed, he was reminded of a Currier and Ives print.

"Yes," Sarah agreed when he mentioned it. "Thought about in your terms, they shaped our vision of New England. Now we're all busy making the reality conform to that image."

"You certainly learn fast," Jarib said with a grin.

She hung his coat in the crowded closet by the stairs. "Come say hello to Mother and Dad."

He found himself studying her, as if seeing Sarah for the first time. She wore a dress of scarlet velvet that fitted her torso and swirled around her hips and legs. He hadn't realized what a superb figure she had. Like a tiny but perfect sculpture. Another art image. Sarah Myles was affecting his thought process. "Before we go in," he said, "I want to say you look lovely."

He saw her flush with pleasure. The color in her cheeks accentuated the cloud of dark hair that fell almost to her shoulders.

"Thank you. It's not exactly an occasion for jeans."

Rita Myles was a round woman. She had on a ruffled pink silk dress that accentuated her plump, round body. Her gray-streaked blond hair was shaped into something he remembered from years ago. A beehive he thought it was called. It made a halo around her round face; even her wide blue eyes were round. "Dr. Baraak, I'm pleased to meet you at last. You've been so good for Sarah."

"Sarah is helping herself," he said. "I'm just a guide."

"Now don't be modest. You've worked a miracle, a positive miracle. All the doctors in that hospital couldn't help, but you have."

He wondered if she thought he was a physician, but there wasn't time to pursue the question. "There's Frank over by the bar." Rita spoke quickly, jumping from one sentence to another without a pause in between. "You must have a drink, Doctor; just go on over and meet Sarah's dad. He'll fix you up."

Sarah took his hand and led him through the crowded room, stopping for an introduction occasionally. The guests were all local people, men and women who knew each other and chatted happily about families and business and the doings of the town meeting.

Baraak wondered what he could say to them if Sarah disappeared, and what, if anything, they knew of his work. People like this had been running people like him out of town on rails for centuries. And nothing had changed. He knew that better than most. He shivered, and reminded himself that he didn't dwell on any of that. Not anymore. It was pointless.

"Daddy, this is Jarib Baraak."

A surprise. Frank Myles was a good deal older than his wife. In fact, Sarah's father was an old man. "Delighted to meet you, sir," Baraak said. He noted that Myles's hand felt fragile and insubstantial, that he was stooped and gray, his thin face lined. Not just old, unwell.

But his voice was firm. "Glad you could come, Doctor. We're very grateful for what you've done for Sarah. Those headaches were getting the best of her until she started seeing you."

He tried again to explain that he wasn't a medical doctor, but Myles was distracted by another guest. Jarib wondered what, if anything, Sarah had told her parents about what they were really doing. Nothing, he decided. Rita and Frank Myles were unlikely to understand the notion of the time warp—or approve. Sarah interrupted his thoughts. "What would you like to drink?"

"White wine if it's available."

She produced the bottle with a flourish. "Provided in your honor. Most of this crowd tend to rye and ginger, or scotch and soda if they feel daring. I'd hoped Pinkie and Max would be here, but they couldn't make it. Too bad, they'd have lightened the atmosphere."

"Pinkie's your friend from the South, isn't she?"

"Yup. Penelope Lee Arbuckle Schwartz, FFV. And just as improbable as that sounds. I wanted you to meet her."

"I've a hidden prejudice," Jarib said. "I don't get on with southerners; all that sweetness makes me sour."

Sarah shot him a quick glance; there was a shade of seriousness behind the quip. She decided to ignore it because just then he took a sip of the wine and toasted her with his incredible, wonderful eyes.

Rita Myles appeared at their side. "Sarah, honey, will you go see if you can help old Mrs. Grant find her coat? Come have something from the buffet, Dr. Baraak."

It was in the dining room. A bounteous spread on a pine trestle table covered with a homespun cloth. On the floor was a braided carpet which Rita said she'd made herself. "I'm president of the Ipswich Early Americana Society," she said. "I helped found it years ago. There was a Historical Society, but they only let in people who'd been in town since the *Mayflower*. That's silly, don't you think? Any American can be interested in the colonial period. Why, even Milly Katz belongs and she's—" She broke off, remembering, and blushed and turned away. "Now what will it be? Turkey or ham? Maybe a little of both, and some of my homemade baked beans."

She mounded an enormous quantity of food on his plate, her atonement for the slip of the tongue. Baraak knew better than to try to stop her. Once she'd done that, she drifted away.

He found his way to a corner where he could observe the crush. The people around him weren't exactly as he'd thought on first glance, or as Sarah had implied. With the expansion of the highway system and the burgeoning of Boston, Ipswich had ceased to be a wholly insular and rural town. He spotted a few women in designer dresses and men with blow-dried hair. The yuppies had arrived. Doubtless that helped to make Rita Myles's bakery such a success. Probably the ones here were favored customers. But they seemed undigested lumps in this celebration of the way things used to be.

What he could see of the house fascinated him. It was a perfect reproduction of colonial New England, not a false note anywhere. Undeniably attractive and, in its way, chic. But the total effect struck him as sad and artificial, lacking any touch of originality. What was astounding was that this background had produced Sarah. The sensitive girl with her flashes of defiance seemed totally out of sync with her home and her parents. It was an important insight; he'd have to think a lot more about it.

"Well, Frank, what did you think of Sarah's Dr. Baraak?" Rita leaned up on one elbow, looking at her husband in the twin bed across from hers.

"Seemed a nice enough guy. I didn't have much chance to talk to him. And I don't think you ought to call him Sarah's that way, honey. Don't get yourself all upset the way you always do."

"I'm not upset. I'm the one who insisted on asking him. I mean, we had to get a look at him, didn't we, Frank? And he is Jewish, I'm not prejudiced, but there's no denying the fact."

"Just concentrate on how much he's helped her. Anyway, there's no reason to think she's interested in him that way."

"That's what I hoped until I saw her looking at him tonight. A nice boy like that Hal Watkins she drops for no reason. Now this. It couldn't be because . . ." She swallowed the rest of the sentence, unable to say the words.

"Don't!" Frank said instantly. "Don't think about that, Rita."

"I mustn't, I know. But Dr. Baraak's awfully good-looking, Frank, you have to admit it. He has a house right in Rowley, too. That's only a few minutes from here."

Frank Myles sighed. There was no taming Rita's enthusiasms or her worries. When she got an idea, that was it. At least he always found it so. Sarah usually managed to stand up to her mother, but it was never easy. Except, Rita was absolutely nuts about the girl, so sometimes she gave in. Or seemed to.

Rita looked soft and easy, but Frank knew better. She had a will of iron. Of course, if she hadn't, they wouldn't have Sarah. It would have all turned out so differently. Involuntarily he shuddered. But he was here in their pretty house. His wife was curled up comfortably in the next bed. Sarah was in her room down the hall. None of the terrible things he'd feared had ever happened. They wouldn't now. It was too late. It was all behind them. "It was a lovely party, honey," he whispered. "Just terrific. Good night."

"Good night, Frank."

Rita switched off the lamp and lay thinking of the party. Lovely, just as Frank said. And Sarah looked so beautiful. Funny, to her Sarah didn't look at all like— She clamped a damper over the thought. Don't let on you know anything, she'd told herself years ago. Never, not even in your own mind. Rita had followed the rule with absolute devotion.

Three

"Listen, Sarah, we've got to talk a bit about your background. I'm not prying, it may be important."

Sarah stretched her arms over her head and wiggled her toes above the fire. Her sweater rode up and exposed the bare, taut skin of her midriff. She seemed unconscious of it. Jarib was not. He averted his eyes. "Pay attention," he said brusquely. "I'm serious."

"Ask away. Anything you want. You've met my folks, seen my house, you know where I went to school and what I do for a living. At least what I did. What else is there?"

"Sarah, you're being deliberately obtuse. Tom Lasky says you're adopted."

"Oh, that."

"Yes, that."

"I don't know much about it." She stood and walked to the bookshelves, then moved her finger idly across the titles. "You have eclectic taste. Not just scientific goodies, you like poetry, I see."

"Yes, I do. Please, Sarah. I think it may really be important."

"Jarib, let me ask you a question for once. When you first mentioned a time warp, I thought I understood what you meant. But the more I think about it, the less sure I am."

"It's a shorthand phrase that covers a lot of territory," he said. "Most of it's only suspected and largely unexplored. You know Einstein's theory, that time is a river, all of it existing always, but we can see only the stretch we're on, not around the bends."

"And the past and the future are what's around the bends?"

"Much oversimplified, but yes."

"And I'm seeing around one of the bends?"

"Maybe. It's one explanation for what's happening."

"The past," she said firmly. "The woman and the others, they're in the past."

Jarib leaned forward, his body newly tense. "You're sure of that? Why?"

"I can't say exactly. But I am. That's just how it feels."

"A scroll and a candle could give that impression, but it could be erroneous."

Sarah was adamant. "It's not only that. There's something about the . . . I can only call it the syntax of the thing. But not in the purely semantic sense." She spread her hands in a gesture of frustration. "I can't explain any better than that."

"Okay, you don't have to. You're the one who is living it. If that's what you think, you're ninety percent certain to be right. Which reinforces a parallel theory I've been toying with. Parallel to Einstein and certainly not original with me. I'd never presume to be so smart. But Jung speaks of something he calls racial memory. That could be an explanation of your experience, too. And that's one reason I want to know what you know about your background."

She'd moved to the other side of the room, putting distance between them, trying to appear casual, but her small frame was rigid. "Please tell me what you know." His probing was gentle but insistent. "Tell me about the adoption, the circumstances."

After a few seconds she began. "They were married for five years and Mother didn't get pregnant. It was in the fifties, they didn't know the things they do now about infertility. The doctors just told them it was unlikely they'd ever have a child. They went to the Catholic adoption bureau. But Dad's twenty years older than Mother, he was fifty then. The social workers said they weren't eligible to adopt. They tried everything, even a pilgrimage to the Holy Land to pray for a child. Eventually Mother went down South. To Georgia. The adoption law was much looser there. She got in touch with some shyster. In those days unwed mothers were pariahs."

Sarah put her hands to her head, gripping her temples as if another headache were beginning. "God, can't you just see it? Some poor kid desperate because she was pregnant . . ."

Jarib wanted to get up and go to her, put his arms around her, ease her pain. He made himself stay in the chair. "And she got you then? Is that it?"

"A little later, I think. Mother hates to talk about it. I don't blame her. She never lied to me; they both told me from the first that I was adopted. A chosen child, that was the preferred phrase. I was three months old when they got me; my birthday's the twentieth of August. They brought me home to Ipswich the twenty-third of November, 1959. When I was a kid, we used to celebrate the day, a sort of second birthday." Finally she faced him. Her skin was pale and drawn; her green eyes looked enormous. "That's it, that's all there is to it."

He rose and poured a glass of wine. She drank it down in one quick swallow. Jarib touched her cheek, then quickly withdrew his hand. "Are you curious about the part you don't know? Who your real mother and father were?"

Sarah's eyes flashed. Emerald sparks. "Listen, don't use that phrase. I hate it. Real mother, real father. What does it mean? Screwing in the back of some jalopy with no thought for the future, you think that makes you a parent? Well, it doesn't. Rita and Frank Myles *are* my mother and father. I don't give a damn about that poor fool girl in Georgia. Or her probably half-wit boyfriend. It's the in thing to want to know, but I don't. I'm just grateful I was so lucky."

Jarib took the empty wineglass from her hand. "Thank you for trusting me. We won't talk about it again."

82

"Okay." She smiled, and the merry gamin look returned. "I need a cup of coffee. Let's visit your lab that pretends it's a kitchen."

Sarah made the coffee, a routine they'd drifted into. He liked to watch her work; her hands were swift and graceful. She'd shown him some of her sketches, and he often imagined her drawing. Quick, sure strokes, he was sure of it.

"Black, no sugar." She passed him the mug. "Ugh. How do you stand it?"

"A habit from student days. It sounded tough and sophisticated, I guess."

She doctored her own cup liberally and stirred, looking at him with her head cocked. "You are a great question asker, Dr. Baraak, but not so good with the answers. You know all about me, but I know damn little about you."

"Like what, for instance?"

"Like exactly how old are you? When's your birthday?"

"Born March fifteenth, 1948. I'll be thirty-six this year. An old man."

"A nice old man." She hesitated, took a sip of the coffee, then: "Jarib, are you married?"

"I was."

"And now?"

"No, I'm not married now."

Silence invaded the kitchen.

Jarib turned away and closed his eyes. A woman danced behind them. Lovely, blond, icy, terrifying. He knew Sarah was watching him. He pushed his mug away and nodded toward the window. "It's time for you to go. Looks like snow, you don't want to get caught in a storm."

All week she told herself he wasn't married now. It was a present she hugged close, a knowledge that made her gay and full of laughter. She found herself dreaming about Jarib's big hands, imagining them touching her. As for how grim he'd looked when he said it, she'd deal with that. If he gives me a chance, I can, Sarah thought. Jarib worries about the past too much; I'll make him concentrate on the future.

She had a more pressing worry: how to move the relationship

83

on. Jarib seemed to be holding back, and she wasn't a natural flirt, she'd never consciously gone after a man; Hal Watkins, for instance, had pursued her. It was time to use her secret weapon; she phoned Pinkie Monday morning, after ten so Max was sure to be gone and Pinkie would be alone. "Listen," she said, "I need advice, but no smart-ass cracks please. This is for real."

"Don't scare me half to death, sugar. Spill it. I'll be good, I promise."

"It's Jarib. I want him, Pinkie."

"Is that all! Jesus, I thought you were going to start in on time warps and all that shit. Well, praise the Lord, Sister, you've seen the light. Glory, hallelujah!"

"Pinkie! You promised."

"Yeah, okay. I'm sorry." Her voice gentled. "You want Mama to tell you how to get him, is that it?"

"Something like that, only it's not Mama I'm asking, God forbid. It's you."

"Right. Sarah, do you think the feeling is mutual?"

She hesitated only a moment. "Yes. Nothing definite, but I do."

"Then there's nothing to worry about and nothing I need to tell you. Just let it flow, sugar, and do what comes naturally."

"That's it? That's your gold-plated, FFV, southern bombshell advice? Do what comes naturally?"

Pinkie giggled. "It surely is. And don't knock it. The trick is to let the wanting show. Just let those barriers down in your own head; Mother Nature will do the rest."

Sarah didn't feel particularly enlightened when they hung up. But she was laughing. Pinkie could always make her laugh. Lately, she realized, she felt like laughing much of the time. Considering what else was going on in her life, that was remarkable, but it was true. When the music and the voice and the presence called out to her, she relaxed and let the experience hold sway. It seldom lasted more than a minute or two. Then she'd carefully write down the details so that she could discuss them with Jarib. They hadn't changed in months, not since last summer when she saw the horn and heard its single piercing note. And in between times, when the time warp or whatever it was left her alone, she ignored it. Because thinking about Jarib was much nicer.

On Tuesday, the day after she'd talked to Pinkie, Sarah ran into Tom Lasky on the street in Ipswich. She had a swift and sudden intuition that he'd contrived the meeting, but no evidence, only an unsubstantiated hunch.

"You're looking well, Sarah. Much better than at any time since the accident. Can I assume Jarib's helping you?"

"Yes. Jarib's marvelous, Father. I owe you a lot for sending me to him." Somehow she didn't want to say more, and she dashed off with a gay wave.

Tom Lasky watched her retreating form and frowned. Jarib is marvelous. He'd heard those words before. A lifetime ago.

Saturday mornings and Wednesday afternoons, those were the times of their appointments. The first Wednesday in February was bitterly cold. Sarah turned the Pinto into the driveway next to the saltbox and hurried up the walk. A bit jerkily because her leg was stiff on days like this. She rang the bell three impatient times. "Hurry up, Jarib! I'm freezing."

"Come in. Sorry to say the furnace has packed up, but there's a fire."

The room was chilled despite it. And Jarib looked preoccupied as well as cold. "Why so solemn?" she asked, feeling a little tinge of fear because she was so sensitized to his moods.

"You've been stalled in one place too long. We have to move to the next step. I'm worried that I haven't prepared you as well as I might. The most important thing is that you mustn't be afraid."

"I'm not," she said softly. "Not with you. You said we'd make the journey together, remember?"

"I remember. And it's true. But you have to do a lot of it alone. There's no other way. It's your will that's all important, Sarah. You can control the entire process as long as you will to do so." He put his hands on her shoulders. His blue eyes bored into hers. "A hell of a lot of what we normally think of as inexplicable is simply the will at work. Shamans, voodoo, faith healing. The function of the human will, all of it. Ready?"

She nodded. "Don't worry, I'll be fine, I want to do it." Because it will please you, darling Jarib, who isn't married now. "Just tell me what happens next."

"Sit down." He indicated her usual chair. "You'd better be warm." He spread an old plaid lap rug over her knees. "Okay?"

Sarah squirmed for a moment, adjusting her position. "Perfect. I may fall asleep."

"That's all right, too. What matters is that you relax and concentrate."

"Both at the same time?"

"Yes. That's the trick." He stood behind her again, his voice floating in the air over her head. "Relax, Sarah. Remember all the relaxation and breathing exercises we've done. But this time I want you to concentrate deliberately on the presence and the music, think about it, really listen. Try to ask the woman why she's so sad. You've been wholly a passive observer, unwilling at first, then receptive. Now I want you to go beyond that and solicit an active role in whatever drama's being played. Will yourself into the picture so you can see more. Do you think you can do that?"

"Yes." She closed her eyes, breathed deeply, and followed the breath as he'd taught her to do. Down deep into her belly, out through her lungs and her nose. Deep, deep, deep. *Do-sol-la-fa . . .* A liquid, limpid sound with a resonance all its own, an instrument she couldn't identify. *Alone, so alone, so frightened, so much grief.*

"Why? Why are you grieving?" Sarah whispered the words aloud. There was no answer, only the sensation of loss, of heartbreak. No others present, the woman alone, and no scroll or candle or horn, but something new. Sand. Blowing all around her. A terrible wind. Her body jerked forward as if to shield herself from its force.

"What is it?" Jarib demanded. "What's happening?"

"Wind and sand. Blowing. A storm."

"What else, Sarah?" He placed the tips of his fingers on her shoulders and moved his thumbs to the nape of her neck, holding her, giving her a link to here and now so there was no danger of her being lost forever in the otherness she explored. "Don't give up, go deeper."

But she couldn't. After a few seconds she jerked away from his touch. "That's it, there's nothing more."

Sarah held out the package. "Take it, it's a birthday present."

"My birthday isn't until tomorrow," Jarib said. Then: "I mean, thank you. I didn't expect you to remember."

"March fifteenth, of course I remember. And I won't see you tomorrow. Saturday mornings and Wednesday afternoons. As far as I know, that's when you're born and die. Except for the New Year's party, it's the only time I see you."

"I'm writing a book. I've got to be disciplined about it." Disciplined about not seeing you more, my sweet, adorable Sarah.

"Okay. Aren't you going to open your present?"

He undid the wrappings. It was a book, not new, old and worn with a well-read look. The Faber & Faber edition of Eliot's *Four Quartets*. Jarib caught his breath.

"You said you liked poetry. I looked on your shelves and you didn't seem to have this one."

"I love poetry. And I used to have this, but somehow it disappeared. Thank you, it's a perfect choice."

"I think so." She took it from his hands. "Look, this bit from 'Burnt Norton.' '. . . the still point, there the dance is . . . and there is only the dance.' That's what we're reaching for, isn't it? The still point. If I could get there and hold it, then I'd see everything."

"Yes." His voice choked and he turned away.

"What is it? Have I done something wrong?"

"No. Please don't think that." Only the dance. Lenore dancing. Her blond head thrown back, her artful body arched in tune with rhythms discernible only to her. "Please, Sarah, you mustn't be upset. I love your present."

She saw in his face that somehow her gift wakened memories of another woman. The wife he no longer had. The wife he'd never mentioned except that one time. She'd convinced herself he didn't care about her anymore. Apparently she was wrong. Sarah hated herself for it, but she started to cry.

"Oh, God, don't. Please, Sarah, don't."

He took a step nearer, tentatively reached out a hand to wipe away her tears. Then the restraints gave way. She was in his arms and he was tasting her mouth and the salt of her tears, and all the months of telling himself this must not happen were as if they'd never been.

Their mouths parted, and she repeated his name again and again. "Jarib, Jarib, Jarib." It was a benediction. "I love you, Jarib. I love you."

So tiny. She was such a tiny, precious thing. She barely came to his shoulder. He had to lift her from the floor to kiss her, and she weighed almost nothing at all. He held her a long time, swaying with her in his arms, and she clung to him as if he were life itself. Finally he gently set her down. "Listen to me, my dearest Sarah. This is a very dangerous development. I'm not quite sure how to handle it."

She looked at him without flinching. "Do you love me, Jarib?"

"Yes."

"Then nothing else matters. I love you and you love me. Nothing else is important."

He turned away, running his fingers through his hair, wanting instead to put his fist through the nearest wall. "I only wish it were that simple. It's not; it's complicated, Sarah. There's so much I can't tell you."

"Then don't. Don't tell me anything yet. Not until you're ready."

Whence came this wisdom, this certain knowledge that to question would be to lose him, this understanding that she must be patient, then he would be hers? And why Jarib Baraak? When Hal Watkins had been tried and proved wanting, when so many men she might have cared for had been shadowed with the memory of Charlie Ryan, he of the slobbering mouth, blue-veined penis, and devastating taunts. "Go tell whoever you want, Sarah Myles. And I'll tell what an ugly cunt you have. It's big and hairy and it stinks like old socks."

But dutiful sex agreed to because she needed to prove to herself that she was normal was no part of this; neither was an ugly childhood memory. She had come of age at last; she understood fifteen-year-old Charlie's motive, he'd been as terrified as she. And she could intuit Jarib's need now. "We'll just go on as we are, Jarib.

Until you work it out. Until you're ready to talk to me about whatever it is."

But of course, it wasn't quite like that.

The appointments increased in frequency. Only Sundays were forbidden. Jarib didn't explain, just said he couldn't see her on Sundays. Other than that, they spent as much time as possible together. It was necessary, they told each other. The investigation must proceed, and there wasn't much time now. It was Jarib who said that. Soon she'd be well enough to take up her life where the accident interrupted it. She'd move back to Boston.

Sarah didn't contradict him, though she knew she wouldn't do it. How could she leave Jarib, her love? She lived for the hours they spent together, for the opportunity to see him, study the way his thick hair waved back from his forehead, the way he carried his broad shoulders. Always she longed to touch him, but Jarib exercised strict control and Sarah knew she must respect it. After that one time in the kitchen, he did not kiss her again. He didn't take her hand anymore, or put his fingertips on her neck when she was trying to concentrate on the voice. Jarib needed to maintain such physical distance. Sarah understood. She bided her time. But it was hard. The worst of it was she knew so little.

In April she decided to talk to Father Lasky. They'd been students together, known each other for years, Jarib had said so. She made an appointment to see the chaplain.

"Sit down, Sarah. I'm delighted. I thought I wasn't on your preferred list any longer."

"I'm sorry. I've been very busy."

"Are you looking for another job?"

"No, not yet." She hesitated, jammed her hands into her pockets, and didn't look at him. There was so much she wanted to say, but she was afraid.

"But you're planning to go back to work, aren't you, Sarah?"

"Of course. I'm just not ready yet. I haven't had time to start job hunting."

"Okay. But you don't look very relaxed to me. It's Dr. Baraak, isn't it? Jarib's taking all your time and attention."

She took a deep breath. "Yes." Only the merest hesitation, then she plunged. "Father, I love him. And he loves me. But he's holding back. I don't know why and he won't tell me. I thought you might."

The priest toyed with a letter opener on his desk, thought for a few seconds before he spoke. "Sarah, he's eleven years older than you. Are you sure his feelings are what you imagine them to be? Forgive me, but it's a logical question. Mightn't you be misreading some things?"

"No. I'm not. Jarib has told me he loves me."

Lasky's head snapped up. "Jarib's done that?"

"Yes. You look shocked. Am I so unlovable?"

"Of course not. It's just . . . Sarah, why have you come to me with this now?"

"I told you, Jarib won't discuss whatever it is that bothers him about us. And it's not the age difference. It's more than that. He did tell me that you two were students together at Harvard. So you've known him a long time, and maybe you can explain." She took another breath. "And look, I know he was married before. That's part of it, but it's not the whole story."

He passed a hand over his eyes, as if in pain. "I'm sorry. I can't tell you. It's a long, sad, and complicated tale, Sarah. But it belongs to Jarib, it's not mine to pass on."

"I'm not surprised. I wouldn't expect you to betray a confidence. But"—she bit her lip and leaned forward—"I could make him happy, Father. I don't think Jarib's had much happiness."

"No, you're right. A lot of recognition, but not much happiness. In his field he's the best there is. Jarib can make people understand the inexplicable, not be afraid of it. Some years back he did a television series for Public Broadcasting; it was picked up and carried nationwide. Harvard hired him then, for a big salary and a lot of perks. They don't really have a parapsychology department, but they're covering their flanks." He smiled a little sadly. "Just in case. Personally I think that's why they still have a department of theology. But that's not the point, is it? The thing is you'd destroy Jarib, not save him. I can't tell you why, only that it's true. And you'd separate yourself from God because one thing I can tell you, you couldn't ever marry him in the Church."

"I don't care about that." She said the words quietly but firmly. "I don't consider myself a Catholic any longer."

Lasky didn't look surprised. "Your mother told me a few months ago that you've stopped going to Mass."

"And?"

"And I told her that was your affair. It's a personal decision, Sarah. We've given up burning people at the stake if they don't toe the party line."

"Then you agree that Jarib's being divorced has nothing to do with it?"

He looked at her, and it seemed as if he were carefully choosing his words. "I didn't say anything about divorce. And I don't think you've changed so dramatically. I think you're undergoing a crisis of faith, and in the end you won't want to be separated from your God or your Church."

"You have it all figured out, don't you?" she said bitterly. "Poor Sarah's been through a bad time; now she's hearing voices and she's in love with an 'older' man. If we're just patient, she'll come 'round and be a good girl again."

"I never said any of that. You know I don't spout platitudes. And I'm not a hellfire-and-brimstone type. If I were, I wouldn't have sent you to Jarib in the first place. But I did, and it seems I made a terrible mistake. Headaches are better than this, Sarah. Better than destroying two lives."

She clenched her hands in her lap until the knuckles were white. She wanted to put them over her ears and scream, anything to block out his words. "I'm sorry I ever came here," she whispered hoarsely. "You don't understand at all. Please, forget everything I said. Don't mention it to Jarib. You mustn't."

He avoided responding to that. "You're going to go on with it then?"

"I don't think that's any of your business," she said as she left his office.

She saw Jarib later that same day. He knew something was wrong as soon as she walked into the house. "What is it? You're tight as a drum."

"Nothing. Just some silly business with an old friend. Please, let's get started." Hold me, she wanted to say. Please, hold me. But she couldn't do that. She'd taken enough risks today.

"All right, sit down." Lately he'd started darkening the room, hoping that might help her concentrate. Now he drew the drapes and turned on a small lamp. He could barely see her in the shadows, but still he sensed her anxiety. "Sarah, nothing's going to work when you're like this. Don't you want to tell me what happened? Maybe you'll relax if you just get it out of your system."

"No. I'm okay. Really."

"Very well, but let me talk a bit before you start. I've been thinking of examples for you. Things that illustrate the willpower which is so vital to your breaking through. For instance, do you know that four people using one finger each can lift any person, no matter how heavy? Don't shake your head. They can.

"The thing's practically a parlor trick. The subject is seated in a straight chair. Then the four lifters each place a finger under his knees and arms. When they try to lift him, they probably won't succeed. So they each place their hands on top of the subject's head, making certain that none of them has his two hands next to each other, and concentrate for sixty seconds. They immediately resume their attempt at a one-finger lift, and the subject rises into the air as if he weighed nothing."

Despite her mood, she giggled. "You're making it up."

"No, I'm not. It's been done over and over again. It almost never fails, even if the lifters are skeptics. The only requirement is that they must truly concentrate during the one minute. The will is an extraordinary thing, Sarah. It's been called faculty X, the element of ourselves we least understand. It's why Hindu fakirs can lie on nails or walk over hot coals. It's what you must bring to bear on this problem."

She stared at him for a moment. Yes. But not just the problem he meant. "Let's begin, Jarib." He switched off the lamp. She was there almost instantly.

Sarah, listen to the music. The most beautiful music in the world, Sarah.

A pause, waiting, reaching. Concentrate on the notes. *Do-sol-la-fa.* But not exactly that. Strange notes. What instrument? Try to see the instrument. Reach deep inside where the voice is and see what's making the music. See it, Sarah. You must. For Jarib. A curved thing. With strings. Long fingers are plucking the strings.

A fleeting image. Gone. Bring it back. Concentrate. Bring it back. The instrument is of pale wood, U-shaped. The fingers attached to delicate wrists. Yes.

"I see it. . . ."

But only for seconds. She couldn't hold it. Sarah slumped in her chair, and Jarib turned on the light.

"Okay, okay, little one. That's enough. Don't try to do more."

Soothing, gentle. Sweet Jarib. Sarah's eyes remained closed. Touch me, Jarib. The way you used to before you became afraid. Touch me. I'm willing it.

He crossed to where she sat and knelt before her. Almost of their own accord his hands took hers. "You achieved something special, didn't you?"

She smiled at him. "Yes. I think so."

"You said, 'I see it.' What did you see?"

"The instrument. The one making the music. Give me a sheet of paper. I'll sketch it for you."

He handed her a pad and left her bent over the drawing while he went to make coffee. When he returned, she gave him the sketch.

"It's a lyre, isn't it?" Jarib asked.

"Yes, one of the oldest instruments in the world. Extremely simple. The sounding board is a bent frame, usually of wood, and the strings are plucked by hand. It owes a lot to the bow and arrow, it's that old."

"You've drawn ten strings. Isn't that unusual?"

Sarah bent forward and studied her drawing. "Yes, it is. I didn't realize, and I didn't count them when I was seeing it. The whole thing happened too fast. But I'm sure that's exactly what it looked like."

"Great. That's wonderful, Sarah. Aren't you pleased?"

"Yes." She smiled and sipped her coffee, then put down the mug. "Give me back the paper. There's something else."

A few moments later she handed him the finished drawing. She'd added a pair of hands holding the lyre. With slim fingers and delicate wrists. On the left wrist was a wide bangle inset with three stones. "They were blue," she explained. "Turquoises, I think."

93

**ALEXANDRIA:
A.D. 60**

The sliver of moon that saw Sarah bas Michael join Darai the whore waxed and waned and waxed yet again. The child Rachel throve, unaware that her birthright had been made forfeit. To earn enough to keep them both alive, Sarah lay with the Roman soldiers and others who came here to the edge of the desert to buy love. But though she was beautiful, there were never many who paid to possess the Jewess. The sadness in her was pervasive; men sensed it and shied away.

Among her own kind, in what had once been her world, no one

spoke of Sarah or of Rachel. And into this silence came Anwar, the son of Farak el Fidha, returned from Persia. He had bought well and his father was delighted with him. The silversmith had already created many designs that waited only for these jewels to be complete. He knew that Anwar would create others, perhaps more exquisite than his father's. Farak's fame was not based on his ability to create beauty. He was renowned from Alexandria to Rome for the hiding places he could conceal in any ornament. It was well known that Farak kept an enormous Nubian bodyguard to protect him from former clients who wished to murder him, so that the secret he had created would be known only to them.

But Farak wasn't thinking of that threat now. "Tonight there will be a banquet to celebrate your return," he told his son.

Anwar paid little attention to that promise. "What of Sarah bas Michael?" he asked eagerly. "Do you have news of her? Is the wedding arranged?"

The father turned away and didn't answer, and soon afterward Anwar left and went to the house of Reb Michael.

"My daughter is dead," the rabbi told him. "And you have killed her."

For many minutes Anwar didn't understand. He was so distraught he grabbed the old man's shoulders and shook him and demanded the truth. "She is dead," Reb Michael insisted. "Go away. I never want to see you again." And when he turned from the young man, his cheeks were wet with tears.

Anwar ran from the house, half crazed with fury and grief, but a woman waited for him beneath an olive tree at the end of the road. She was Leah, Sarah's mother, and she told him the story of Rachel's birth and the anathema her husband had pronounced.

"But why?" Anwar demanded. "We are betrothed. We planned to marry as soon as I returned. Everyone knows that."

Leah nodded. "Yes, but my husband would not permit such a marriage. You and your family do not follow our laws."

"We are followers of Jesus. Just as you are."

"But you break the Law," Leah insisted. "To be truly a disciple of the Lord Jesus, you must do as he did. When the betrothal took place, you promised to be circumcised and give up unclean food and keep the Sabbath. Now you refuse."

Stubbornly Anwar shook his head. "Paulos of Tarsus said it was unnecessary. We heard him preach three years ago at Caesarea on his way to Rome. And you too are a follower of the Nazarene; why must you cling to the old ways?"

Leah spit on the ground at his feet. He'd never seen a woman do such a thing. Anwar took a step back.

"Paulos of Tarsus," she said. "He is to blame for everything. Even for what my daughter and my granddaughter now suffer."

"Now . . . but where are they? Your husband told me Sarah was dead!"

"To us they both are, Sarah and Rachel, the child. It is our Law." She didn't try to explain further. Only said, "They live with Darai the Whore."

"How do you know this?"

She laughed at him, but it was not a pleasant sound. "Women always know such things," she said. And she turned and walked away.

When Anwar found Sarah, she looked much older to him, and so sad, but still beautiful. "Go away," she told him. "You shouldn't have come here. It's too late."

"No! I love you, I want to see my daughter."

That at least was his right. Sarah brought Rachel to him, and she could not help smiling when he held the child and marveled at each tiny perfect toe and finger. "She has your features," Anwar pronounced, "but my eyes."

It was true. Already at three months Rachel's eyes had changed from blue to green. "Yes," Sarah agreed. She reached out and took the baby from him and said, "But she is a whore's child now; you will want no part of her."

97

Anwar turned away. "It's true then, what they say here, you are a whore for the Roman soldiers?"

"It's true," Sarah admitted. "If I were not, neither Rachel nor I would have food to eat or a place to sleep."

Anwar was silent and a few moments later he left.

Sarah never expected to see him again, but five days later he returned. "I don't care," he told her. "I have thought and prayed and I don't care. I love you. I want you and my child."

"Where can you take us?" she asked. "Your father would not have us in his house before any of this." She looked around at Darai's home, and the gesture included all that her presence in it implied. "He won't accept us now."

"We will go to a home of our own," Anwar insisted. "I do not need my father. I am a better craftsman than he is. I will find customers who will gladly pay for my work."

At first Sarah rejected this insane scheme, but by the time autumn came and the harvest was beginning she had agreed. Because she loved Anwar and she longed for Rachel to know her father. Having made up her mind to defy both his family and hers, she never looked back. Not even when she saw the hovel which was the only place Anwar had been able to find for them to live.

"No one will sell to me," he said. "None of our own kind, that is. My father forbade it." He did not need to explain to Sarah that

Farak was a wealthy and powerful man. "This place belongs to a foreigner, a Cilician. I have made him a set of goblets, and in payment we're allowed to live here for a year."

"It doesn't matter," she told him. "We can manage. Later, when we have more money, we will find something better."

But more money was inordinately difficult to come by. Anwar had taken from his father's house a share of the jewels he'd brought back from Persia and some silver and some gold. They were his due, payment for the years he'd labored on Farak's behalf, and angry as he was, the man did not deny his son this small patrimony. But he saw to it that no one of the wealthy and powerful who were his clients would buy from the younger man.

Anwar was reduced to selling to the outcasts and fringe groups who clustered in the same part of the city where he and Sarah lived. And they, knowing his straits, always managed to argue down the price. Soon his original store of materials was gone, and what little he was paid had to be spent to buy more, which in turn was sold for barely enough to replenish the supply.

And that was not their only problem. Sarah and Anwar wished to be married, but no one would perform the service for them. The Gentile Christians were all afraid to offend Farak, and the Jews could have nothing to do with Sarah, who was anathema.

"We must go to Jerusalem," Sarah told Anwar. "To the elders of the Church. They will marry us."

"The Church in Jerusalem agrees with your father," Anwar said sullenly. "They are Judaizers, just as he is. They say we must follow Jewish Law if we would also follow Jesus."

"But they are honorable men," Sarah insisted. "And they have no part in the quarrel between our families. They will take pity on us."

Secretly she knew that Anwar was right; the Church in Jerusalem kept strictly to Jewish Law and insisted that all others who followed Jesus must do likewise. But secretly, too, she hoped that the leaders in Jerusalem would convince Anwar of the truth. Indeed, she herself still kept the laws, and she wished Anwar to keep them too. He must be made to see that Paulos of Tarsus was wrong. And a man who had never personally known the Lord Jesus, as had the leaders in Jerusalem.

"It doesn't matter anyway," Anwar said. "We cannot pay to join a caravan traveling to Jerusalem."

"I know a way." Sarah felt his eyes on her. She wondered if he imagined she was suggesting that she'd once again lie with the soldiers. "My music," she added quickly. "If I will play and sing in the inn where the soldiers gather, I will be paid."

Anwar would not permit it. Not until he had no money to buy

oil or grain, or materials with which to fashion things to sell. Not until he had begged his father for help and been told that unless he left Sarah and her child, no help would be forthcoming.

Finally he gave in. "But I myself will bring you to the inn," he told Sarah. "And I'll wait and bring you home again. Only for a little time, until I can make more things and sell them."

The first night Sarah went to the soldiers' inn, Anwar did exactly as he promised. He brought her to the door and he watched while she walked the long tunnel that led to the wine cellars where she would entertain the soldiers. Finally she turned to look at him one last time; then she disappeared behind the blue curtain that covered the entrance.

Anwar's heart wrenched with pain. "Sarah!" he shouted after her. "Sarah, no!"

He ran after her, but by the time he pushed his way past the curtain she was already playing her lyre. The melody was one which she herself had composed, a four-note theme that was known to all who had ever heard her. The soldiers were listening in silence. For a long time Anwar watched, and he listened.

When it was over and they'd come home again, he kissed her gently. "You are the strongest, most courageous woman in the world," he told her. "I've made you a present."

Secretly, when Sarah couldn't see, he'd fashioned a bracelet; a wide bangle, copper because these days he could not afford any-thing more precious, inset with three beautiful turquoises. The stones were the last of his share of the jewels brought back from Persia. "But you must sell this!" Sarah said. "It's beautiful, Anwar. The workmanship is perfect."

"I didn't make it to sell. I made it for you." He would not be dissuaded, and ever afterward, night and day, Sarah wore the bracelet.

Four

"Let her go. Jarib. There's been enough tragedy. Don't make more." Lasky kept his fingers around the glass of whiskey, but didn't drink. They were in Baraak's living room. It was nearly midnight. The priest had waited three weeks to come. Since he'd talked to Sarah, he'd battled his conscience, tried to decide what to do. In the end he knew he couldn't just stay silent. Not and live with himself afterward.

"We're investigating an extraordinary paranormal phenomenon, Tom. We're making real progress. Sarah's unique in experiences of this kind. There's nothing quite like it in any of the records."

"And that's what this is all about? The glory of science? And Sarah's just the subject."

"I didn't say that. You're twisting my meaning. But Sarah herself wants to go on. She has to live with this thing; you can't blame her for wanting to know more about it. If we stopped now, she'd have no peace. I'm not just making excuses. It's true."

"Yes, I believe you. You've always been an honorable man,

Jarib. That's your cross, isn't it? And my salvation. Because of your sense of honor, I've been able to leave all the worry and remorse to you."

Baraak reached for the bottle of scotch and refilled his glass. "Don't make me responsible for your salvation, Tom. That's too damn big a load to carry. We've been all over that. And *honor*'s your word; I just call it 'facing responsibility.' It was my fault. We both know that."

Lasky leaned back in his chair and studied his old friend with a sense of infinite sadness. So much guilt and pain, so little faith to assuage it. "I'll never understand how you can do what you do, know what you know, and yet not believe."

"I do believe. Just not in your terms. Tom, why did you suddenly come here? All these months and you've said nothing, indicated no disapproval. Why now?"

"Sarah's in love with you."

Jarib looked into his glass. "She's been under a great deal of strain. And we've been working together very closely. It's rather like people falling in love with their analysts. Anyway, I expect she'll get a new job fairly soon and move away. She'll forget all about me."

"Maybe." The silence was palpable. "She talked to me awhile ago. Wanted to know what was holding you back, since she's sure you love her."

"She shouldn't have done that."

Lasky bent forward. "She's desperate, Jarib. She tried to make me promise I wouldn't tell you about our conversation. I didn't promise. And you haven't said anything. Do you love her?"

A long pause. Outside an owl hooted. The first one he'd heard this year. A harbinger of spring, the mating time. "Yes. I never expected to. Not any woman ever again. But yes, I love her."

"And are you lovers?"

Jarib shook his head. "That's not really any of your business, but no, we're not."

"Your reliable sense of honor again." The priest drained his glass. "Whatever she says now, I believe Sarah is a deeply committed Catholic."

"Perhaps," Jarib said. "That's just one of the complications."

Lasky rose. "I have to go."

They walked together to the front door. Jarib opened it. They were washed in the cold air of the April night. Lasky took a step forward, then stopped. He turned back. The expression on his friend's face made him want to weep. Still. "Give her up," he repeated. "You're married, Jarib."

"Married? You call what I am married?"

Without warning mid-May turned mild and summery. The grass greened and flowers bloomed in quick, kaleidoscopic progression; daffodils still nodded yellow heads while apple trees were misted in blossom, and the buds of a few early roses began to swell. "The times are out of joint," Jarib said one afternoon.

"Yes. And it's just too beautiful to be indoors. Can't we skip our session today?" Sarah pleaded. "Let's play hooky, Jarib. Let's go for a long walk."

They went to Crane's Beach. A long expanse of creamy sand and humped dunes hugging the Atlantic along Ipswich Bay. She wore a cotton dress in a tiny Laura Ashley print, stylized red tulips on a white field. Bought because she knew Jarib would like it. She hardly ever wore jeans anymore. The skirt swirled around her bare legs. Her hair was caught up in a tortoiseshell clip, and the wind plucked at a few curls and caused them to dance around her sun-flushed face and the nape of her neck. They walked side by side, not touching. Until Jarib grabbed her hand. "You're beautiful. I'm breaking the rules, but I have to say it."

"Your rules." She held tight to his hand. "Not mine. But I've played by them."

"Yes, you have. Thank you, Sarah."

There was no one else on the beach. May was too early, despite the weather. Gulls swooped and soared, and Sarah took a candy bar from her shoulder bag and broke it into pieces, throwing morsels into the air for the gulls to catch, stopping occasionally to pop one into Jarib's mouth. "You're a scavenger, just like they are."

"Of course. And I prey on innocent maidens." Suddenly he put his hand behind her head and drew her to him. Sarah raised her face to his and they kissed. When they broke apart, he moved away and stood staring at the sea. "This was a bad idea. We'd better go."

"No. Not yet, please. Come, we'll walk some more. Just walk, that's all."

The sun moved to the edge of the horizon. Still it wasn't cold. "It will be dark soon," Jarib said. "Better get you home."

"I don't turn into a frog when it gets dark. And I'm completely well now, Jarib. There's no one expecting me at home."

She always went home. Her parents worried if she wasn't there for dinner. She'd told him so. "What about your folks?" he asked.

She laughed softly. "I'm a big girl, you know. Twenty-five next August. Besides, they're away for the weekend. Gone to see Dad's sister in New Hampshire."

Gone despite Rita's objections and fussing about leaving Sarah alone. Gone because for once Frank Myles insisted on having his way. Sarah was practically well now, wasn't she? he'd said. Rita had to agree that she was.

"I'm free as a bird for two days," Sarah said.

Jarib shook his head ruefully. "Sarah, Sarah. What am I going to do with you?"

"Feed me for one thing. Take me to dinner, Jarib. That's not a crime, is it? We both have to eat."

They had Sarah's car, but Jarib drove. They went to an old place on the edge of town, a colonial house that had been made into a restaurant. The rooms were small, and only two or three tables could be accommodated in each. It lent an air of intimacy, though Jarib had intended just the opposite. A restaurant is safe, he'd thought. Plenty of people.

Instead they were as if alone, and Sarah drank a lot of wine with her dinner and insisted he keep up with her, laughing and refilling his glass the moment it was empty. Before he realized it, they'd got through two bottles. She insisted he taste one of her shrimps and give her a bite of his lobster. There was intimacy, too, in the simple gesture of passing the fork back and forth, watching her mouth open and close on the morsel of food.

When they finished dinner, a full moon rode low in the sky. "How beautiful," Sarah murmured. "Please, let's drive back to the beach. I want to see the moon on the water."

He could refuse her nothing. Beautiful Sarah, who had freshened springs of feeling he'd long since thought dry.

The night was August balmy, the air caressingly soft. "The times are out of joint," Jarib said again.

"No, they aren't, they're perfect."

She jumped from the car and ran down to the beach, flinging her shoes away as she did so, running along the shore and letting the water lap at her toes. "See, I told you I was completely cured," she called back to him. "Come with me, Jarib! Come!"

He joined her, laughing, taking her hand, feeling the wine in his belly and the rising tide of desire. When she pulled his head down to hers, he didn't try to resist. They kissed a long time, devouring each other, tasting, sucking breath from one body to another. Then Sarah started for the dunes, pulling him after her. When they came to a sheltered place, she stopped. Her breath came hard and he could see her breasts rise and fall. He reached out to touch them, and she put her hands over his, pressing them into her flesh. Together they sank onto sand still warm from the sun. "Make love to me, Jarib." Not a whisper or a plea, a fierce demand uttered while she stared into his eyes. "Make love to me."

He groaned. "I can't. It's wrong."

"No, it's right. Whatever happens afterward. I want you, my darling Jarib. Make love to me."

She wore white cotton panties. He drew them over her hips and down her legs, and she kicked them away impatiently. He kissed her again, gently this time. Not hurrying. There was no need now. They both knew what must follow. They were committed. "I love you." He spoke the words against her cheek, and while he said them, he entered her.

"I'm sorry," he said afterward.

She took his head in her hands and pushed him slightly away, so she could look into his eyes in the moonlight. "No, you mustn't be. It was wonderful, perfect. We're perfect together."

Jarib kissed her and held her, and still she could feel his unease. "Listen, my darling," she whispered. "You mustn't imagine you've seduced an innocent. I wanted this. All my life I've wanted it."

He grinned. "All your life? Waiting just for me?"

"Yes," she said, laughing. "Just like in the storybooks." Sarah flipped onto her side and picked up a handful of sand and let it sift through her fingers. "Well maybe not exactly. Once, when I was a kid, there was a boy. We got involved in something too exploratory to be called sex, but pretty ugly. I blacked his eye."

Jarib hooted with laughter.

"It's true," Sarah insisted. "And I got into trouble for that. Nobody bothered to ask what he did, not that I'd have told them. In my mind it became associated with my music, with what made me different, strange. It was . . . something more about myself I had to protect. Do you understand?"

Her hair had come loose, and he pulled his fingers through it, loving the feel of the silky curls. "I think so. And that's why you say you're not an innocent?"

She grinned at him. "Professor, are you prying? No, don't answer. I'll tell you anyway. There was someone else awhile ago. It was still really just exploration. I decided a twenty-four-year-old virgin was a joke."

"Did it make you happy?"

"No, it bored me. You make me happy." She grabbed his hand and pressed it to her lips. "You make me whole, Jarib. You bring all the pieces together."

Jarib pulled her back into his arms. "Sarah. My adorable, wonderful Sarah. I love you so damned much."

The private chapel of the pope was a few steps from his bedroom. Under this pontiff it was a thing totally removed from the splendor of St. Peter's and the Vatican, austerely simple and now hushed.

The frail old man moved very slowly. The eyes of the small group privy to this intimate ceremony watched him lift the traditional red hat with its three silk tassels. "The mark of a prince of the Church," His Holiness said softly. "A prince to serve, not be served. We have chosen you, Dom Malachy Fanti, because you understand such things." He was ill. His voice was barely audible, and despite thirty years in Rome, his Italian was still marked by the clipped accents of the North.

"We wish you to be a reminder to your fellow cardinals, to all of us, of what we are to be, how we are to spend our brief time on this earth. Do not fail us, Dom Malachy. Make us all remember that we are priests of God first, and men of this world second."

Contrary to custom, Dom Malachy had arranged no great party to follow the ceremony. The pope had heard of this, and received the news with satisfaction. "Come," he said as they left the chapel. "Come to my rooms. There are some simple refreshments, I have invited a few others. Friends."

There were five men in His Holiness's sitting room. "You know everyone, I think," the old man said. "Except perhaps Cardinal Bellini."

The pope took Malachy's arm and led him to the corner where Bellini waited. "A sly old fox," he whispered in the Benedictine's ear. "But useful. I think you and he will be good for each other. And ultimately, perhaps in spite of both of you, that will be good for the Church."

The two men shook hands, and the pontiff watched them exchange pleasantries. Please, God, I am right, he prayed silently. Please, God, this Bellini and his conniving can give us a saint as the next pope.

"Sarah, I want you to go back to Boston."

"Jarib, no! How can you say such a thing? How can you think it?" A joke, it had to be. Sarah turned and pummeled her small fists against his bare chest.

He caught her hands, holding them motionless in his strong grip. "Listen to me, it would be the best thing. We need time, a little distance. You need that, Sarah. I think the reason it's so tough to break through lately is that the whole thing's just too intense."

She grew suddenly calm and loosed her hands and sat up in the bed. It was late afternoon; the times of their meetings hadn't changed, only the content. These days they spent a frustrating hour downstairs while Sarah tried unsuccessfully to duplicate what she'd achieved the day she saw the bracelet, then came up here.

The dormered ceiling of Jarib's bedroom was so low she could almost reach up and touch it. It was painted palest cream, and years before someone had stenciled a crude design of leaves along the line where the ceiling met the walls. Sarah stared at the faded tracery of green. "It's not the paranormal phenomenon you're worried about. Jarib, don't pretend it is. It's you and me. But time doesn't always erase things. It won't change the fact that I love you."

"And I you." He sat up and put his hand under her chin and turned her face to his. "I love you. And I believe in your love for me. But I've been married before, and you're a Catholic."

"Was. I was a Catholic."

"You've never said what changed your mind."

She looked out the window and tried to organize her thoughts. "Originally, the dichotomy in my life. Here's this whole religion thing with promises of life everlasting, but my hearing four notes of music all my life is pushed away, and I'm told I'm not really having the experience when I know I am. On a more cerebral level, it's a structure that's perfectly logical in itself, very well thought out and sophisticated, that's what separates Catholicism from all the *nouveau* fundamentalists. Anti-intellectual it definitely is not. But despite that, you have to grant a set of premises. If you don't, the whole thing is nonsense."

"And you don't?"

"Not anymore."

"Okay, but it's not just that. I'm eleven years older than you. And I've a complex, worrisome past."

"Which you won't tell me about. Even now. You make demands, Jarib, but without explanations. That's not fair."

"I know. That's part of why I want you to go away for a while. I have to put things in order, think my way through all the implications. Then I'll tell you the whole story, and what you want to do about it will be up to you. That's probably not much, but it's all I can offer."

She decided to try another tack, be practical. "I can't hope to get another job with a museum right away. They don't grow on trees. And art is the only thing I know."

"I thought of that. I called a friend. She owns an antique shop, she's looking for an assistant, and she'd be delighted to hire you."

Sarah felt panic rise in her throat. "Jarib, I don't know anything about antiques. Besides . . ."

"You know art history and you have an eye for line and design. Ivy will train you. She's good, you'll learn a lot."

Jealousy joined the panic. "Do you know her very well?"

He chuckled. "Not the way you mean. I met her years ago. I was buying a gift for . . . someone. I know damn all about antiques, and Ivy was that rarity, an honest dealer. As a matter of fact, she whetted my taste for old things, and she's the one that found this house when I wanted a place to get away and write. Enough information, Miss Green Eyes?"

"No. How old is she? Is she pretty? Is she married?"

"She's in her thirties, I guess. And she is pretty if you like them large-sized and tough. I think she's divorced, but we've never talked about it. Sarah, we're evading the real issue. Will you go? For me?"

"Don't! That's emotional blackmail, Jarib. You're taking the decision out of my hands and putting it on another plane entirely. To prove my love, I have to do something I think is wrong for both of us."

Saying nothing, he got out of the bed and put on a short robe of royal blue velour. Sarah loved the robe; it made his eyes an even brighter shade of blue.

"Sometimes you're a lot wiser than I give you credit for," he said finally. "You're right. I am pressuring you in ways that are despicable. That's what's wrong with this whole thing. I can't seem to do anything else."

She'd gone too far, launched them both into even more dangerous waters. "Jarib." Her voice was soft, and she was proud because it didn't tremble. "If I go, will I see you? Are you proposing to take a sabbatical from me?"

"No, of course not. I'll come down once a week at least."

"Just not on Sundays. Never on a Sunday, like the song."

He looked hard at her. "No," he said finally. "Never on a Sunday." He started for the door. "I'm going down for some coffee. Make up your own mind, Sarah."

When she joined him in the kitchen, he was still angry. She could see it in the tense set of his shoulders, the way he gripped his pipe, and the tight look of his mouth. Maybe not angry, just disturbed.

She poured herself a cup of coffee and pulled a stool up to the counter. She could see her image reflected in the stainless steel, distorted and out of proportion. "Okay, I'll give it a try. If your buddy Ivy really wants to hire me, I'll go."

He looked so relieved she wanted to cry. Relieved because he was getting rid of her. "Can I ask one more thing? Without your getting mad."

"Don't make me sound like such an ogre. Ask anything you want." Bright now, even gay. Because he'd gotten his own way.

"All along you've said it would be bad for me to stop probing the voice and the rest. If I'm only going to see you once a week, what happens then?"

"I thought a lot about that. As a matter of fact, it seems like a good time to take a short break."

Short. Her heart leaped when she heard the word. He wasn't intending purgatory to continue for long. She'd been afraid to ask.

Jarib didn't notice her reaction. "You haven't made any progress since you identified the lyre and saw the hands, none of my research has turned up anything new to go on, and you haven't had a headache in months. So I don't think it's a bad idea for us to cool it for a while. If there are any new developments, or bad effects, I'm only a phone call away. Speaking of which, let's call Ivy now and tell her it's a go."

Jarib had everything worked out.

For three weeks they made plans by phone. Sarah kept finding excuses not to go to Boston until she started the job. As if her physical appearance forty miles away would somehow effect a break with Jarib she only yet imagined. Ivy was prepared to accept this; apparently she trusted Jarib.

"You can bunk with me for a while, if you don't mind living over the store," she said. Sarah agreed.

"Why ever for?" Pinkie demanded. "Come stay with Max and me. This Ivy dame's a stranger; maybe you'll hate each other on sight. Maybe she doesn't wash her underwear, or lives on instant coffee and frozen dinners."

Sarah clutched the receiver tighter. These days she was deciding her life by messages winging along telephone wires, mysteriously propelled through the ether. Which seemed apt. "I don't think so, she sounds nice. And she's a friend of Jarib's. Besides, it will be convenient. No commuting time." A friend of Jarib's, that was the real reason. A link with him when so many of them were being stretched and broken.

Maybe Pinkie realized that; she didn't insist. "Okay, if you're sure. But remember, we're always here. And there's a key under the mat if we're not."

She was to move into Ivy's on Monday, July 10. "Can we see each other Sunday night?" she asked Jarib. "Just this once, considering."

He got a tense look around the mouth. "Sunday's no good, you know that."

"Yes. I just thought—"

He pulled her into his arms. "Forgive me. Please. I promise I'm trying to make sense out of it all. Saturday. Then I'll pick you up at your folks' place Monday morning."

The weekend produced lousy weather. On Saturday morning she drove to Rowley with exaggerated care, because driving in the rain still made her nervous. As soon as she walked into the house, she could see that Jarib hadn't prepared the living room for a work session; he wasn't pretending this day was like all those past. She turned to him, her eyes wet with tears, wanting to say so much, not knowing how to begin. But he didn't let her speak, just kissed her and led her upstairs, and they spent hours in his bed, making sweet, slow, forgiving love; trying to assuage the pain each of them knew the other felt.

It was nearly 2:00 A.M. when she got home. A sliver of light showed under the door of her parents' bedroom, and she was grateful that even Rita realized you couldn't ask a woman soon to be twenty-five where she'd been or why she was so late.

Monday turned bright and sunny, warm but not humid, dream weather. Jarib arrived at nine. Sarah already had her suitcases packed and in the hall. He exchanged pleasantries with Frank, and with Rita, who had stayed home from her bakery to see Sarah off. Once, while he was loading the car, Sarah followed him out with some art supplies she'd nearly forgotten, and Jarib commented that her folks didn't seem to mind her leaving again.

"They've expected it right along," she explained. What she didn't say was that she knew Rita was delighted that at least this meant Sarah would see less of Jarib. It was her consolation prize, a distancing between her beloved daughter and the man she always referred to as "that Jewish doctor."

It was nearly ten when they drove away from the big white house. They hadn't been able to leave until they had coffee and crisp waffles with cream and fresh strawberries, Rita's contribution to making this seem a happy occasion. And when they were on the highway, just the two of them alone again, Sarah found that she couldn't say any of the serious things that perhaps should be said. Instead she felt compelled to work at being bright and gay. Because Jarib was obviously tense, and somehow it seemed important that he didn't guess how nervous she was.

For weeks she'd tried to imagine what Ivy and her home and her business would really be like. None of the speculation prepared her for the real thing. The building was in one of the oldest parts of the city, on Bromfield Street. It dated from the turn of the century; three stories high, dwarfed either side by newer, taller structures. Which meant that most of the windows looked out on brick walls and narrow, dark alleys. In the shop it didn't matter. On the two top floors, where Ivy lived, the problem had been solved by locating the living room, dining room, and kitchen on the third floor and lighting them with huge glass skylights. They let in the sun by day and framed a vivid starry panorama by night.

The rooms deserved this brilliant illumination. The floors were of polished parquet covered in Chinese carpets of subtle design and softest color; the windows were hung with rich, glowing damask, which blocked out the ugly views, as well as provided a foil for the exquisite decor. Sarah recognized an original Boucher hanging on the wall, and guessed that much of the furniture was both antique and priceless. "Wow!" she whispered to Jarib. "Why didn't you warn me?"

"Didn't know," he said smugly. "Never been up here before. I told you, Ivy and I aren't that kind of friendly."

Ivy returned from the kitchen, bearing a tray of drinks, so Sarah couldn't comment. But she was enormously pleased and reassured.

It wasn't in the same order of being, but Sarah was pleased by her bedroom, too. It was on the second floor, looking out on the narrow, pedestrian street. A smallish room, but with big front windows that let in light and air. The walls were papered in toile de Jouy, the stylized pastoral scenes worked in rich wine red on a pale cream background. The curtains and the spreads on the two twin beds were of off-white linen, and the wall-to-wall carpet echoed the dark red of the wallpaper. The total effect was restful and pleasing. There was a small bathroom, also red and white, and enough closet space.

Sarah thought of Ivy's crack about living over the store and giggled. Ivy's bedroom occupied the entire remainder of the floor, an enormous, palatial expanse of shimmering silver-embossed walls and white carpet. Her bed was the largest Sarah had ever seen, with a peaked canopy of woven silver fabric that drifted to the floor in iridescent ripples. She wondered if Ivy had a lover. Many lovers perhaps. But Jarib wasn't one of them and never had been, so it mattered very little.

The shop was called Bell, Book, and Candle. An obvious kind of pun, but clever. "I had a nutty idea at first," Ivy Bell said. "I figured I'd stock only bells, books, and candles, but of course that soon went by the board. Genuine antiques of any type are hard to come by these days. A dealer has to carry a wide range to survive."

She did have a representative sampling of bells and books, even a few candles; but the long, narrow store on Bromfield Street was crammed with china, furniture, and pictures as well. "My periods are only mildly eclectic," Ivy explained. "A little Americana, but mostly European things of the seventeenth and eighteenth centuries. That's what sells best here."

"Why is that?" Sarah asked.

"The place is in such a weird location for one thing. I'm not over near Quincy Market with the trendies, or in the Back Bay with the old guard. This is just workaday, ordinary Boston. My customers seek me out because I have a reputation for finding a certain kind of very solid value. The sort of thing that can qualify as an investment as well as a decoration."

"How did you come to locate here? And why doesn't Americana qualify as solid value?"

"Second question first. Some kinds of early colonial pieces are superb value. But there's a hell of a lot of kitsch within the category, not to mention endless reproductions. And if people are serious collectors in the field, they expect to acquire things up in your neck of the woods. Out there in rural heaven the things look right."

Sarah laughed. "You sound as if the country is some kind of torture chamber."

"It is to me. City born and city bred, and too much smog-free air makes me dizzy. Besides, I look god-awful in jeans. My ass is too big."

Sarah didn't think Ivy's ass was too big. It was round and full, like her breasts, and she could carry both because she was tall and had a slender waist. She also had dark red hair she wore slicked back from her face in a severe chignon, and slanty brown eyes behind large, chic, horn-rimmed glasses. Ivy wasn't pretty in the conventional sense of the word, she was simply terrific-looking.

"Jarib tells me you're bright and talented," Ivy said. "And you're certainly adorable. All my life I've secretly wanted to be a little China doll. . . . Oh, well, it would be a waste of time hating you. Bad for the complexion." She grinned. "Besides, Jarib has charged me with looking after you. He'll tar and feather me if I don't."

"You're very kind to take me on, Ivy. But whatever Jarib says, I don't need looking after. I hope I start earning my salary pretty quickly."

"The problems of tiny women," Ivy said. "Men think you're perpetually a child."

"And women that you're a China doll," Sarah said quietly.

For a second neither of them said anything; then Ivy laughed. "Click," she said. "Sorry, I won't make the same mistake again. And don't worry about earning your pay. I'll see that you do. But since you're getting all the boring jobs around here, I should tell you why we're buried in the dullest part of town. My father owned this business and the site. When he died, my brother got everything except the business and this building. The business wasn't worth much then, Dad had been semiretired for years, but I could have sold the building for what's usually called a tidy sum. Only I'm perverse enough to prefer running the shop and living upstairs. The only problem is that it's practically on the street. The dust is a constant hassle." She pushed her glasses down on her nose and looked at Sarah over the rims. "I feel ridiculous asking you to do the dusting, but I did warn you."

"Yes, you did. And I agreed, so stop worrying about it." She picked up a dustcloth and began. "A little salsa music and I can make this into an aerobics workout."

"No salsa," Ivy said firmly.

Sarah shrugged.

A few days later Ivy explained more. "Look, I can't offer you interesting work. The business is small, and I do all the important buying and selling myself. But I genuinely need someone smart and trustworthy who can be here when I'm not, and take care of any drop-in customers that appear."

"And keep the place dusted and tidy," Sarah added.

"It's going to be awfully dull, isn't it?"

Sarah cocked her head. "Maybe not. How would you feel about teaching me the antique business? Not so I could do your job," Sarah added hastily. "Just so I could be more useful."

Ivy grinned. "I'm not worried about competition, and obviously you're accustomed to responsibility. Okay, why not?"

"Starting when?" Sarah asked.

"Right now." Ivy disappeared into her office and returned with an armload of books. "Have a look at these."

They were all specialized studies of narrow elements of the world of collectibles: *French Commodes in the Sixteenth Century, The Art of Sheraton,* and *Bavarian Painted Bedsteads.*

"For openers," Ivy said.

"For openers," Sarah agreed.

She had plenty of opportunity to read. The shop's important customers always came by appointment. To see Ivy. They'd have been furious if they'd been shunted off to an assistant. And drop-in trade was rare. A tiny table costing fifteen hundred dollars was not an impulse buy. So after spending about an hour and a half each morning dusting all the precious things, Sarah studied. The balance of her time she spent thinking about Jarib.

She saw him once a week, as promised; on Mondays when the shop was closed. Usually he arrived by ten, and they'd go to a little café for coffee while they planned their time together.

"Any headaches?" That was always his first question.

"No. And I haven't been hearing the woman's voice or even sensing her presence. She's still there, I know she is. But I don't want to hear her, so I don't."

"Is that a strain, holding her off? I don't think pushing too hard is a good idea."

"I don't have to push. Somehow I seem to be in control again. Rather the way I was before the accident. Of course, then I only had the music to deal with."

Jarib reached out and stroked her cheek with one finger. "Okay, that's good for now. Later, when you're ready, we'll invite her back and see what she has to tell you."

"When you're ready, darling." She didn't want Jarib to forget that this whole thing, the enforced separation and the pause in the investigation, was his idea.

"When I'm ready," he agreed. He didn't quite meet her eyes.

Sarah covered his hand with her own. "It's okay, Jarib. I'm not pushing you either."

He lifted her fingers to his lips. "Thank you for that. Now, what shall we do with our day?"

They never had any difficulty deciding; there were many things to do in Boston. And Sarah was determined that these interludes would be relaxed. So once they went to the Quincy Market and spent hours poking around and buying silly inconsequentials: a set of nesting Russian dolls for her, bayberry-scented aftershave for him. That evening they finished up with steamed clams and scrod in the Union Oyster House near North Station. Another day they divided between the swan boats in the Public Garden and the Arnold Arboretum. "Fun things," Sarah told Pinkie. "Because each Monday, when he arrives, he looks so worried and unhappy."

"Don't forget to look out for Sarah's happiness, too," Pinkie said gently.

"That's just it," Sarah admitted. "He's all my happiness. As long as I'm with him, it doesn't matter where we go or what we do."

"Listen, you can tell me to mind my own business, but do Jarib's rules include no screwing?"

"Mind your own business," Sarah said. And added, "Yes, they do."

"Jesus, how can you stand it?"

118

"He needs this break. And somehow it's important to him that we're not lovers during the interim. I think he sees that as being fair to me."

"Crazy," Pinkie said.

"Yes, but that's okay, too. For a while."

Sarah's own doubts were stifled by Jarib's repeated promise, "It won't be long now, darling. I really am trying." He always ended their time together with those words. For the moment that was enough; but it didn't mean she wasn't puzzled, or desperate to understand what had happened to create Jarib's mysterious problem.

"Ivy, how did you first meet Jarib?"

They were having tea in Ivy's cramped little office behind the showroom. The older woman had kicked off her shoes, and her stockinged feet were propped on a museum-quality eighteenth-century English desk. Ivy seemed cavalier about the precious things she bought and sold, but Sarah now knew her well enough to realize she'd never put her feet on the desk if she were wearing shoes.

Ivy wiggled her toes. "Nobody ever warned me that the antique business was hell on the feet and the backside. I'm either walking for hours looking for something to buy or sitting on some god-awful metal chair waiting for an opportunity to bid on it." She sipped her tea; it was Earl Grey, blended with the pungent essence of bergamot oil. The flowery scent filled the small office. "When did I first meet Jarib Baraak? Let's see . . . 1970, I think. Right after I opened up. Back when I was still trying to do the thing with the books and the bells and the candles. He came in off the street looking for a first edition. Yes, around March 1970. He was still at Harvard. A senior."

"I never knew Jarib collected first editions. He has a lot of books, but none of them seems particularly rare or special."

Ivy chuckled. "Jarib's not a collector of anything but weirdos and their weird stories, present company excepted." She had been told nothing of Sarah's voice or her song, and she grinned innocently at her. "It was to be a gift. He wanted a first edition of Isadora Duncan's autobiography. See, right in character, old Isadora was as nutty as they come."

"She was a dancer, wasn't she?" Sarah had a half-formed intuition that this was important. Some kind of insight was picking at the back of her mind. Jarib getting so upset when she quoted the Eliot lines about "only the dance."

"Yes. And not really so crazy, not by today's standards. Isadora pioneered modern dance and free love and was a scandal back in the early part of the century. She'd probably look damn tame now."

"Did you have the book?"

"No, but I started a hunt. Jarib was one of my first serious customers, and I was determined to succeed. I found it after two months. He'd been checking with me once a week, so we got to know each other a bit. I was ecstatic about getting him what he wanted. Felt like a real pro. And he was absurdly grateful."

"Do you know who he gave the book to?"

Ivy made a point of pouring herself another cup of tea, deliberately avoiding Sarah's eyes. "His then girlfriend, Lenore Lasky, the dancer. The girl he married."

Sarah took a deep, startled breath. Lasky, as in Father Tom Lasky. She wanted time to consider that, but she couldn't stop now when she was so close to yet more vital information. "What happened to her? Jarib has never said. He doesn't like to talk about it."

Ivy was silent for a few seconds. When she spoke, her voice was kind. "You're really in love with him, aren't you? It isn't just a casual fling."

"Yes." What else was there to say? How could she explain what she felt to Ivy or anyone else?

"What about Jarib? Is it reciprocal?"

Again the simple one-word answer. "Yes."

"I see. And he's a closed-mouthed bastard, isn't he? Well, I'm sorry, pet. I'm not going to be very enlightening. I heard he'd married her soon after he bought the book. Read it in the paper, I think. But I didn't see Jarib again for five or six years. Then I ran into him at a party. I was having a mad affair with a mathematics professor, if you can imagine it. How to do it by the numbers. Anyway, there was Jarib, the same beautiful hunk of man, only a little older. With a lot more lines in his face than he should have had. But very successful. He'd just finished the television series where he slammed all the kooks and charlatans and convinced a lot of people that parapsychology could be respectable. And come back to Harvard as local boy makes good.

" 'Congratulations, and where's your wife?' say I, the eternal fool. 'Gone,' he tells me. 'Lenore's gone.' And he never said another word about her. Even though we took up our friendship again. We've had drinks or dinner together a few times a year for ages, but Jarib has never explained whether *gone* meant 'dead' or 'disappeared' or something else. Sorry, Sarah. Not very enlightening, like I said."

"You're sure her maiden name was Lasky?"

"Oh, yes. I met her a couple of times. And I had her name engraved on the bookplate. Jarib asked me to. I'm sure."

"Then that tells me something. Thanks, Ivy."

She didn't explain about the name. Ivy probably wouldn't care that Jarib must be somehow related by marriage to a priest with whom he was still friendly. Only Sarah cared, because it was another piece in the puzzle which filled her life.

The next night she had dinner with Pinkie and Max in their superslick apartment on India Wharf. She sat on their black leather sofa with her feet on a black-and-white hand-loomed rug and drank the spritzers Max made, with Perrier water and this season's favored California white zinfandel, and tried to tell them about it.

"Okay, sugar," Pinkie said. "I see the connection, but why does it matter? Even Catholic priests have families, I'm told. It's okay long as they don't beget them."

And Sarah couldn't really explain. "It's just odd that neither of them ever told me," she said lamely.

Max grimaced. "I agree. Sarah, why don't you just cut this guy loose? I've got a friend I'd love you to meet. Nice, sensitive, good-looking, makes a lot of bread—"

"A dentist," Sarah said.

"Yeah, a specialist, only does root canal. Four hundred a tooth, but he's an artist. What's wrong with that?"

"Nothing, Max, darling. Nothing. But I'm too wrapped up in Jarib to care."

Pinkie rolled her eyes toward the carefully installed track lighting. "Lawsy! Lawsy! The girl's got the true religion; she's in love."

But in the end they were kind and supportive, and Sarah knew they were genuinely concerned.

"Look," Pinkie said just before Sarah left, "why don't you simply ask Jarib what the connection is?"

Sarah debated doing that, but decided against it. Later she would wonder if anything would have been different if she had.

Timothy Durant appeared for the first time on a sweltering day in August. The air conditioner was trying, but the shop was over eighty. Perversely a number of people had come in off the street today. Why should people want to browse among antiques in the blistering heat? Why did people do anything? Sarah tried to be philosophical, but all the opening and shutting of the door made the air conditioner even less effective.

Her blue dress was of the thinnest possible Indian cotton, but even that weighed her down and stuck to her skin. She longed to go upstairs and spend hours in a tub of cold water. Or better yet, swim in the ocean off Crane's Beach. With Jarib. But it was only Tuesday; endless hours must pass before she would see him. When the bell of the front door rang yet again, signaling another visitor, Sarah sighed in frustration.

"Afternoon," the man said. His English accent was apparent in the single word. "Is Ivy here?"

"No, I'm sorry. Was she expecting you?"

"Should have been. I wrote from London."

"She didn't say anything. Hang on a minute and I'll check her diary."

When Sarah returned from the office, he was studying the inlaid marquetry frame of a hand mirror, holding it to the light of the door. His profile was arresting. A well-modeled head on a tall, slim body. Thick, curly blond hair that betrayed careful cutting in its apparently artless shape. A high forehead and thin, high-bridged nose, narrow but well-formed chin. She was reminded of Bellini's fifteenth-century monks; a strange combination of carnality and otherworldliness.

When he turned to face her, his eyes heightened the impression. Hazel, with absurdly long lashes. Innocent eyes that nonetheless seemed to look through her. "Any joy?"

"What?"

He smiled. "Sorry, a bit of British slang. Any luck? Did you discover my name in Ivy's diary?"

He unnerved her somehow. "No. I don't know your name."

"So you don't. Timothy Durant. And you are . . .?"

"Sarah Myles. I'm Ivy's assistant."

"Delighted. Ivy always has exquisite taste. Now, when shall I see the mistress of this fabled establishment?"

"I don't know. There's no appointment listed in her diary, and she didn't say when she'd be back."

"Very naughty, but perhaps it's the post. Nothing in our uncertain world is less sure than the Royal Mail. Not to worry, I'm in town for a while. I shall beard the lioness in her den tomorrow. Meanwhile, maybe you can tell me a bit about this interesting mirror."

Sarah felt horribly inadequate. His looks, his foreign accent and mannerisms, his obvious sophistication—they all combined to make Timothy Durant formidable. And she suspected he knew more about the mirror than she did. People who had appointments with Ivy Bell were always walking encyclopedias as far as antiques were concerned. Nonetheless, she had to try, that was her job. "It's French. Nineteenth century. Part of a set made for a gentleman's dressing table."

He smiled. "Elementary, my dear Watson. DeFel's work, I suspect. A minor god in the pantheon of cabinetmakers. Have you the rest of the set?"

Sarah shook her head. She was right. He'd forgotten more than she was ever likely to learn. "No. Just the mirror. The price is on the back. Two hundred and twenty-five dollars."

The Englishman hooted with laughter. "Not to me, my sweet. I'm in the trade, as they say. Never mind. I might have this as a gift for dear old Dad. I'll haggle with Ivy later." He put the mirror back on a mellow mahogany gateleg table, the top of which was a selection of artful clutter, and started for the door. Then he turned back. "Look, shouldn't you do the right thing by a poor foreigner? What about that famous American hospitality? Come have a drink. We can find some place where the air conditioning works."

"Thank you, but I'm sorry. I can't leave the shop and I'm not due to close it for a couple of hours."

"A responsible employee. My bad luck. Well, ta, Sarah Myles. Tell Her Highness I'll call tomorrow at nine sharp. And any conflicting appointments are to be canceled."

Ivy was upset at having missed Timothy Durant. "I never got his damned letter. Maybe he's never heard of the telephone. Typically English. He did seem certain he'd come back, didn't he?"

"Absolutely. Nine tomorrow morning. Is he very rich? He seems young for it."

"Mid-twenties, I guess. And it isn't that he's rich, though I think the family Durant have a few shekels put by. He's Hamish Durant's son and heir." Ivy smiled at Sarah and pushed a damp curl from her cheek. "You look as if you've been in an oven all afternoon. We'll have to get someone to look at that air conditioner. Go on up and have a shower. I'll close up."

"First tell me who Hamish Durant is; you sound as if you're curtsying when you say his name."

Ivy's laugh was a rising tremolo of pleasure. "Oh, I like that. And I suppose it's true. Durant's sole owner of one of the most respected auction houses in Europe. They're much smaller than Sotheby's or Christie's, but in their field, the best there is. And sharks. Young Tim is worse than his father. But if he's come all this way to see me, it signals a profit opportunity in the offing. I'll curtsy for that any day."

Timothy came the next morning as promised. He and Ivy spent a long time closeted in her office. Then they went upstairs into the private quarters.

Sarah had a sudden vision of Timothy's slim and elegant body enveloped in Ivy's voluptuousness, the two of them writhing in the great silver bed. She flushed. She was being prurient. There was no reason to suppose that they'd gone upstairs to make love. The picture wouldn't go away, however. And when the pair returned, Ivy was pink with emotion. Excitement perhaps? Satiety? Sarah was absurdly jealous. Not of Timothy, of the imagined act of love. Damn you, Jarib Baraak. Sort out your life and let's get on with ours.

"Sarah, you're a million miles away." Ivy's voice interrupted Sarah's thoughts. "I said that we're going to close the shop for an hour or so. Timothy's taking us to lunch at the Ritz. I wanted to keep you at the grindstone, but he insists that I can't go unless you do too." Ivy's smile was utterly friendly and open. Sarah felt ashamed.

In the following days Timothy Durant was a frequent visitor. He and Ivy had a business deal in the making. Ivy confided that it was going to net her a fortune. "In Britain it's illegal for auctioneers to buy outright. They might put the things back in their own sales, and that's a no-no. But they always know what's being offered everywhere. Timothy's going to keep his eyes open and let me know when there are sales worth going to. If I can, I'll go over and buy; otherwise he'll find a way to do it. He'll take care of shipping the stuff to America and I'll sell it here."

"Sounds perfect," Sarah said.

"Well, almost. He wanted to split the profits down the middle, but I talked him into taking a percentage of the price I pay. What I make on it after that is my affair."

Sarah eyed her speculatively. "You have a real head for business, don't you? Not just an eye for beauty. And you seem to handle Tim Durant very well. So he can't be such a fierce shark after all."

"Oh, yes, he is. But he's hungry for what he calls 'a little lolly on the side.' I think the old man keeps him on a short leash. Anyway, be nice to him, Sarah. He likes you. And we haven't reached a final agreement yet. I need him softened up for the kill."

Sarah found it easy to be nice to Tim. He didn't intimidate her anymore. He was amusing and easy to be with, and his accent and dry English wit were charming. Two weeks later, when he returned to London, she was sorry. Tim had helped to fill the empty hours until she'd be with Jarib again.

In the ensuing months things seemed to stagnate. Sarah longed to pressure Jarib, to hurry him, but she didn't dare. "You've got to get out of yourself," Pinkie said. "You can't just moon around waiting for Mondays, sugar."

She was right, of course. Sarah did try. The antiques business was fascinating, and slowly she was succumbing to its lure. In this world, unlike that of museums, it wasn't simply a matter of beauty or lasting value, there was the element of commercialism to give it an edge. The first time Sarah sold an important piece on her own, a rare nineteenth-century German clock, she was elated.

The buyer wasn't one of Ivy's regulars; he simply appeared one day, looked around, and inquired about the clock. Sarah had been reading about it only the previous week. She could speak knowledgeably and she did. "How much?" the man asked finally. Sarah referred to the little stick-on label and told him.

"I'll take it if you come down five hundred," the man said.

The clock was priced at two thousand dollars. Sarah knew Ivy always had a twenty percent margin for haggling. "I could let it go for eighteen hundred," she said. "But not a penny less." She still had two hundred dollars to bargain with.

The man hesitated, looked at his watch. Thin and gold and obviously very expensive. "Oh, what the hell. She'll love it. Okay, eighteen hundred."

Whoever "she" might be, Sarah blessed her.

That evening Sarah and Ivy went out to dinner and shared a bottle of champagne to celebrate. "You learn fast," Ivy said. "But I always knew you would. It's time you started taking a little more responsibility."

After that she took Sarah with her to a couple of private sales, and customers who didn't ask for Ivy personally were sometimes referred to Sarah.

She told Jarib, and he was complimentary and supportive. It felt good. She loved him no less, wanted him as much as ever. But thanks to her own common sense, Pinkie's carping, and Ivy's encouragement, she wasn't quite so disconnected from any reality that wasn't him. So she could bear his stalling a bit better. That's how she thought of it now: Jarib was stalling. Whatever he had to face, he couldn't yet do so. Soon she'd have to insist. But the risk that posed was still beyond her ability to take. She waited.

Tim Durant wrote frequently, business letters to Ivy that usually included a brief personal note for Sarah, but as yet he hadn't found a sufficient number of sales occurring in a short enough time span to justify the major buying spree for which Ivy hoped.

On Halloween that changed. A few days previously Sarah had gone to Ipswich and brought back half a dozen enormous orange pumpkins. She carved clever faces into them, and Ivy put them around the shop. They were witty and amusing, and both women were delighted with the effect.

"I wish some of my oldest, fogiest customers could see the place," Ivy said. "They'd love it."

The shop bell jangled, and she turned expectantly, but it was only the mailman. Except "only" was not exactly correct. He brought the letter from Tim she'd been waiting for. "Two important furniture sales, one in England and one in France. Both in the same week! Tim says there's stuff worth having in each one."

"Great!" Sarah enthused. "And you'll get a vacation abroad out of it. With a tax write-off no less."

"Mmm." Ivy cocked her head. "I've been thinking about that. I hate England. Particularly this time of year. It's cold and wet. I've been considering an alternative. How about your going as my agent?"

"Me?" Sarah was aghast. "I don't know enough to buy for you."

"Yes, you do. I'll have the catalogs in advance anyway; Tim's already sent them. I'll know what I want and how much I'm prepared to pay. All you have to do is nod your head and bid. Besides, Tim will be there to guide you."

"I couldn't," Sarah insisted.

"Why not? Jarib? You'll be gone only a week or ten days; it won't kill him."

Sarah shook her head. "It's not that. I just don't feel adequate."

"That's crazy. If I say you are, that's it. It's my money you'll be spending. Besides"—Ivy slid her glasses down her nose and tapped the letter from England against one palm—"Tim suggested it be you. He's not just looking for a little something on the side; he has a point. I'm fairly well known as a dealer, even abroad. It will affect the price; the competition is always prepared to bid higher when a dealer seems interested. But nobody's ever seen you. They'll figure you're just a rich American buyer Tim's squiring around."

In the end it was agreed. Sarah would go to England on Monday, November 19.

"You aren't going to fall madly in love with some English lord and stay, are you?" Jarib said wistfully.

"That's not my plan," Sarah said. Then, seeing the look in his eyes: "I can't imagine loving anybody but you."

They were sitting in his car, in the garage at the Prudential Center, going home after a movie, and he leaned over and kissed her with more urgency than he usually permitted himself. Then pulled away abruptly.

"Darling," she whispered, "how much longer is this going to go on?"

He put both hands on the wheel and stared straight ahead. "I'm trying. I've been speaking to people. It could be settled soon."

What? What was he going to settle? How? It was on the tip of her tongue to ask him, but she didn't. Later, she promised herself. When she returned from the European trip. She'd force it all out into the open then.

Rowley on the night of Sunday, November 18. Jarib worked late, tried to concentrate. Instead he kept thinking that tomorrow he'd see Sarah, they'd be together until he took her to the airport to catch her flight to London. He glanced at his watch. It was gold, a Gucci. An indulgence he'd permitted himself a couple of years ago. Something to mitigate the sterility of his life. His life before Sarah. The hands pointed straight up. Midnight. He'd better get some sleep if he were going to get an early start for Boston in the morning.

He put an extra quilt on the bed before crawling in. It was bitter cold. There'd be a hard frost by dawn. He'd taken to noticing such things since moving to this area. He wondered if the market gardeners next door had harvested all their pumpkins.

Jarib wondered other things as well. How was he going to straighten out his life? When would he find the courage to tell Sarah the truth, try to explain the terrible burden of guilt he carried? Not yet, after she came back from London. And while she was gone, he'd sit down and sort it all out. In his head first, the kind of vacillating he'd been doing sickened him. Either he had a right to a life with Sarah or he didn't. He owed it to both of them to come to a decision about that. Then there was the law. It could be made to set him free, if he wanted it to. But he needed to talk to another lawyer. Maybe somebody younger than the old geezer he always used, sharper. Somebody who could make him feel more confident about airtight financial arrangements, help soothe his bad conscience.

Baraak groaned and tried to relax. Thoughts of Sarah intruded between him and sleep, made him tumescent. Damn! He ought to have more control at his age. Sarah, lovely Sarah. His. But by what right? He was trying to have his cake and eat it, too. He groaned again.

The doorbell rang. He wasn't sure of it at first. Who would be ringing his bell at this hour? It was 2:00 A.M. according to the luminous clock on the dresser. It rang again. Repeatedly. An urgency to the sound, somehow doorbells always sounded urgent in the middle of the night. He grabbed his robe and fumbled it on while he ran down the stairs. When he snapped on the hall light, he had to pause a second to let his eyes adjust.

"Jarib, are you there? It's Tom." Lasky's voice was a harsh whisper designed to alert Baraak without disturbing the neighbors.

"Tom, what the hell . . ." Jarib opened the door, then closed it swiftly. An atavistic need to hide from the strangers outside the walls.

The tiny hall was freezing, the overhead light unnaturally bright in the surrounding dark. "Come into the living room. What's the matter? You look like death."

"Your phone's out of order. Did you know? I reported it." Lasky heard his own voice in amazement. The silliness of the statement struck him with force. As if he could make it up to Jarib by doing him that small service.

Jarib's heart was pounding. The fright of the nighttime summons. But the fear wasn't faceless anymore. He was looking at his longtime friend, his brother-in-law. He began to feel a little calmer. "Sit down, Tom. We both need a drink. Then you can tell me whatever it is."

He poured two brandies and drank his, grateful for the burning sensation of the liquor, conscious of the fact that his hands had stopped shaking. Tom hadn't touched his glass. "Drink up, you'll feel better."

Obediently the priest sipped the brandy. He wore his black suit and white dog collar. It occurred to Jarib that since Tom's ordination he'd not seen him in other clothes. That must be unusual. Surely priests wore civvies sometimes. This certainly wasn't the time to ask. He waited for the other man to speak.

"It's Lenore, Jarib. She's out."

The words hung in the air between them. For long seconds neither said anything else.

"How . . ." Jarib couldn't finish the question. His tongue had become a thick, unresponsive thing in his mouth.

Lasky made a despairing gesture, then put his head in his hands. His voice was so low Jarib had to strain to hear him. "They tried to tell me how it happened. I couldn't concentrate. What difference does it make? She's out."

"When? Why didn't they call me?"

"A few hours ago. I told you, your phone's out of order. They didn't realize at first. Just thought you weren't in. Eventually they called me. I came straight here."

They talked a few moments more, neither able to concentrate on the other's words, each lost in his private pain. Lasky left. Jarib had offered him a bed for the night, but been refused. And he was grateful for it; he needed to be alone.

For some seconds he stood staring at the door that had closed behind the priest, hearing the echo of his departing car. Then he went into the living room and sat at his desk. An hour passed. More. Jarib remained silent and motionless. At last he took a sheet of paper and began to write. The note was short; it took only a few minutes to compose. When it was finished, he put it in an envelope. His fingers trembled when he wrote Sarah's name and address, but he did it.

When the envelope was sealed, he went upstairs and got dressed. Then, just before he left the house, he unlocked the bottom drawer of his desk and removed the small handgun he kept there. He loaded it carefully before putting it in his pocket.

It was seven when he left the house. The tardy November dawn was just breaking. A rooster crowed; birds sang. A lovely country morning. He looked toward his neighbor's fields. They had harvested all the pumpkins. He was glad.

Not much traffic on the road at this hour, he'd be in Boston before eight. Neither Sarah nor Ivy was likely to be up. They wouldn't see him in any case. He'd just drop the letter through the mail slot in the shop door. He had to do that if Sarah was to have it this morning. And she must. It was Monday; she'd be expecting him. A pain cramped Jarib's gut. Grief and guilt were a bad combination. He'd known that for a long time, but it didn't make the emotions go away.

$\mathcal{B}ook$
$\mathcal{T}wo$

TWO WEEKS IN
NOVEMBER 1984

$\mathcal{F}ive$

MONDAY,
NOVEMBER 19

Sarah got the letter when she was full of the excitement of seeing Jarib in an hour. She found it in the kitchen, next to the carton of orange juice. She had a premonition of disaster the moment she recognized Jarib's handwriting.

She read it through quickly at first. Then again. The words weren't getting through to her. She must be misunderstanding them somehow. But each time the same sentence of death stared at her from the page. "... gone away. Forgive me ... never see you again ... be happy, find someone else ... forgive me. ..."

At last she crumpled the paper into a ball in her fist and sat shivering at the marble-topped ice cream parlor table in Ivy Bell's sunny kitchen.

Hours later she was still in shock. "You've got to snap out of it," Ivy said. She sat down on the side of the bed. "Listen to me, no, don't turn away. You are not the first woman to be dumped, and God help us, you sure won't be the last. It hurts like hell. I know that. But you've been lying in bed wallowing in your pain all morning. You're not doing yourself any good, and if you don't mind my saying so, you're not much good to me. You're supposed to go to London tonight. You're acting as my agent, spending my money, remember?

"Of course, I remember." Sarah put her hands over her eyes, as if shutting out the light could shut out the pain. "Stop worrying, I'll be fine in a little while."

"Sure you will, you and Jesus Christ, resurrection a specialty." Her voice softened. "Still no answer at Jarib's?"

"None, I've been phoning every fifteen minutes. It just rings and rings."

"What about that priest, the one who's supposed to be an old friend of Jarib's and has the same last name as Lenore? Have you gotten hold of him?"

"No. They say he's gone on retreat and can't be disturbed. Won't even say when he'll be back at the college."

Ivy sighed. "Typical. No man's ever around when you need him."

The phone rang. Sarah started and half rose. Hope was a shining thing in her eyes. Ivy picked up the extension by the bed. "Yes, Mrs. Myles, she's right here."

Sarah shook her head vehemently; Ivy continued to hold out the receiver. Finally Sarah took it, and listened to a replay of a conversation she'd had three times today. Which was her own fault, she never should have blurted out the story when Rita called the first time. But she'd just finished reading Jarib's letter. And Pinkie was in Virginia, visiting her mother. And Ivy wasn't someone you turned to for sympathy. And God knows she wanted sympathy. So she told Rita that Jarib had left her, and Rita said she should have expected it. "They're so clannish, honey. All Jews are. They never really trust anybody but their own kind. . . ."

This time the call was to say that Rita was driving into Boston to pick her up. "Come home, honey. So I can look after you."

It took Sarah five minutes to convince her mother she didn't need looking after. Besides, she was going to London in a few hours.

"Now? You're going all that way when you feel so rotten?"

"It's my job, Mom. Stop fussing, I'm fine. Come see me off at the airport, okay?" She hung up. Ivy was staring at her.

134

"Look," the redhead said finally. "If you want me to go in your place, I will. I don't think it's a good idea for either of us, but I'll do it."

Sarah pressed her fingers to her temples. "I don't know. I can't think straight. I just can't believe Jarib would do this. I keep telling myself he's done it, but I can't believe it. I expect him to call any minute and explain." Two tears escaped the control she was trying so hard to maintain. They rolled down her cheeks. Sarah was almost unaware of them. In the course of five hours tears had become part of her life; like breathing, like feeling the terrible weight of betrayal pressing in on her.

"Listen to me," Ivy said firmly. "I can't make everything wonderful for you, Sarah. You've got to handle this. But you damn well can't do it lying here feeling sorry for yourself in between hysterical phone calls from your mother. Forget what I said a minute ago, you go to England as planned."

"I want to, I'd hate to let you down." Sarah shook her head as if that would clarify her thoughts. "I just keep thinking that Jarib might call. . . ."

"Screw Jarib! If he calls, it won't kill him to find out you didn't fall apart and shift all your plans. And the change will be marvelous for you. Look, I'm not saying you'll have a great time and feel like a million bucks. But you'll be busy as hell, and Tim Durant will look after you. When you come home, you'll have a better sense of perspective."

"What if I'm so distracted I screw it up?"

"You won't," Ivy said firmly. "Besides, you're forgetting about Tim. For one thing he's got the hots for you; for another I've worked things so he makes more if I get stuff for less. A reverse sliding scale. He'll guard you like a prize lamb." She came back to the bed and sat on the edge, taking Sarah's hand. "What do you say, pet?"

It was difficult to resist Ivy's enthusiasm. Sarah sat up, staring at the backs of her hands. She thought they looked old and wrinkled. Just twenty-five three months ago and she had hands like an old woman. She stopped contemplating her skin and looked at Ivy.

"What do you say?" Ivy repeated.

"I'll do it," Sarah said. "Thanks for giving me the opportunity."

The words were out before she had a chance to think about them. Willpower can achieve anything. So Jarib had said.

In Paris Dov Levi was drinking his dinner in the dingy café he frequented. Suddenly a shudder went through his body. It was as if some pattern of the tapestry of his existence had been altered, some thread pulled out preparatory to being rewoven. He was frightened of the insight. Confused. But along with that was a sense of excitement, a crazy kind of happiness. After all this time, happiness.

The sensation lasted only a moment; when it was gone, Levi was sure he'd imagined it. In its wake the brief euphoria left only his usual low-key depression, the dull ache that was his life. Levi ordered another cognac and drank it quickly.

Rome was the smell of lemon verbena. And sunset glowing on dull yellow stone, as it did now on the brick-fronted houses along the Via Santarsi. Monsignor Larry Donovan always thought of the city thus, particularly when he was home in Brighton. In winter, say, when the wind whipped across the Fenway and all odors, good and bad, were frozen from the universe.

The priest found the house he wanted and turned in. The path to the front door bisected an overgrown garden, lush even in November. The lemon verbena that scented the dusk was present on both sides; an undistinguished shrub, leggy and overgrown, indulged only for its heavenly smell. Small birds tittered their evensong in the slim, nodding branches. Donovan paused, inhaled deeply, then rang the bell.

The maid remembered him from previous visits, they exchanged formal pleasantries, and he was shown into the study. His host rose to greet him. "*Buona sera,* Lorenzo. I've been waiting for you. Everything is ready."

The professor of Middle Eastern history was built like a bull, thick and powerful. He had a square, aggressive face that could be identified as Semitic or Mediterranean, because in fact it was both, and a jaw permanently blued by traces of beard. Each time Donovan saw him he wondered how often the man shaved. Donovan was five feet three inches and had trouble keeping his weight up to 110 pounds. If he didn't shave for a week, no one would notice. Deficient in testosterone, no doubt. Not such a bad affliction for a priest bound by celibacy; he didn't often let it make him feel insecure. But when he sat, he was grateful that his eyes were now level with the Italian's.

On the desk between them was a stack of papers some two inches high, the results of the Italian's years of research into the scant records of what was known as the apostolic period in Church history, the years between the Crucifixion and the death of the last of the band of twelve with whom Jesus had been intimate. Today scholars agreed that none of the Gospels had been written until the end of that time. From which assumption flowed a number of interesting questions. Not all the possible answers were desirable from the Vatican's point of view.

"Here it is," the professor said. "But I don't imagine anyone will pay attention except you. Your *capi* aren't likely to approve of my hypothesis."

Capo merely meant "boss." Donovan knew that. Still, the word had a sinister sound. "I don't think it matters much," he said. "If the evidence is as strong as you and I believe it to be, they'll have to pay attention."

The older man laughed. "Lorenzo, all these years in a collar and you still have ideals. It's refreshing, and a little sad. I won't embarrass you by reciting the numerous times your Church has refused to believe the evidence." He pushed the manuscript toward the priest. "Anyway, take it. I hope it proves useful. This is an uncorrected proof, you understand. The book won't be published for two months."

"I understand, and thank you. I appreciate your confidence in letting me have this. It's going to be extremely useful for my committee."

"You can't wait to make your report until the book is out? There will be more support then."

"Yes, I know. But we've decided to release our findings just before Christmas. December twentieth. Frankly, I'd have preferred Holy Week."

The Italian looked at him. "Ah, yes, when you pray for the perfidious Jews."

"That wording has been out since '65. Now we say, 'Let us pray for the Jewish people, first to hear the word of God, that they may continue to grow in love and faithfulness to the covenant.' It was a great breakthrough."

"Sorry, I tend to forget the edited version. The first draft was with us for some fifteen hundred years." The Italian smiled wryly. "Ancient history, and not my fault or yours. Let's have a drink." He produced a bottle of Strega.

The two men drank each other's health; the glasses were refilled. This time the priest only toyed with his. He was marking time, looking for an opening, for the right words. Finally he plunged. "There's something I want to ask you."

"*Bene,* ask."

"Ever met Malachy Fanti?"

The other man's laugh was something between a snort and a cackle. "Met him? No, Fanti doesn't fraternize with Jews. Especially not now that he's a prince of the Church. You know about him?"

Donovan nodded. "Yes. But he's a real scholar, despite his peculiarities."

"Peculiarity," the Italian corrected. "In the singular. I'm told that except that he hates Jews, Fanti's a saint."

"He's a Benedictine," Donovan explained. "Released from his monastery to oversee Scripture studies here. That was twenty-five years ago, but he still lives like a monk. Among most of Rome's churchmen that makes him appear very holy."

"Is that why they want to make him pope?"

Donovan felt the blood drain from his face. "Where did you hear that?"

"Never mind where I heard. But it's true. Cardinal Bellini is pushing his candidacy all over Rome. Bellini's the great kingmaker, has been for years. I'll tell you something else: Word is the pope knows he's dying, and that he himself put the idea in Bellini's head."

"But Bellini's not an anti-Semite."

The Italian poured more Strega. "No, his is a different sin. He wants power. Make a fanatic the leader and then control him. It's been tried before; sometimes it works."

Donovan began to see the logic of it. "Bellini himself could never be elected. His excesses are too well known. There have been some scandals. . . ."

"Exactly. And the rest of them could be convinced to ignore Fanti's little obsession about the Jews, given that he's such a holy man. A little anti-Semitism more or less, what does it matter after two thousand years?"

"It can't be allowed to happen." Donovan finished his drink in one gulp.

"Relax. Your Church is supposed to be guided by God, isn't it? Never allowed to make a mistake."

"The doctrine's a little more complex than that. It hasn't prevented damn fools from screwing up a number of times, in case you haven't noticed."

"I've noticed." The professor spread his big hands. "But you can only do what you can. Your report, that's a step in the right direction. Concentrate on that."

Donovan frowned. "Listen, I brought up Fanti's name for a reason; I didn't know about this crazy rumor."

"What reason?"

"I was leading up to my real question. Ever heard of something called the Alexandria Testament?"

"Of course. But as far as I know, it's never been proved to exist. Do you know differently?" The Italian leaned forward, nostrils splayed, a hound on the scent.

Donovan shook his head. "No. I heard about it from Fanti himself. Twenty years ago. He's spent all his life looking for it. I wondered if there was a chance he'd found it, if you knew. It could have a lot of bearing on my committee's report. I don't want any surprises."

"Sorry, I've never heard even a whisper about its surfacing. As I said, I'm not sure it exists. If it does, and if Cardinal Fanti should find it . . . God help us, the very thought makes me sick."

Donovan nodded agreement. And after that there was nothing more to say. He rose and tucked the manuscript under his arm. "Thanks again for this."

"Thank you," the Italian said. "For everything you're trying to do. For what I hope your report will accomplish. Though getting them to listen to you will probably take a miracle."

"Miracles are not unheard of in my business," Donovan said.

The other man nodded. He shook the hand of the priest with warmth and affection. Which Larry Donovan judged to be at least a minor miracle. Considering what he and his kind had suffered at the hands of Christian clerics, not to mention what they faced if Malachy Fanti became pope.

Outside Donovan snapped a twig off the lemon verbena, crushing the leaves in his fingers and sniffing greedily. *Lippia citriodora* was its proper name; he'd looked it up years ago in a botanical encyclopedia. He had a passion for knowing the real names of things, the true origins of ideas and concepts. Moral decisions had first to be informed by facts.

He gripped the precious manuscript tightly, listening to the echo of his footsteps in the night. The professor's book was frosting on the cake. The committee's report was damn strong without it. But as soon as he'd heard of the Italian's work, he'd gone to see him. This was the result of that meeting. Until now Donovan had seen his role on the special ad hoc committee on Jews and the Scriptures as largely administrative. But this particular coup belonged to him, not the biblical scholars. He was glad of that. Something important to be done, and the means to do it. That deeply satisfied the priest from Brighton. It would have to make up for the fact that he was helpless to influence the election of the next pope.

The international departure lounge of Logan Airport was a mob scene. Milly Katz had not expected it to be thus. In November, she'd reasoned, there won't be many people going to Europe. That had worried her. But the situation was reassuring; she was unlikely to be spotted in a crowd like this. The high dollar, she realized. When they could be had so cheaply, people were prepared to take vacations even in November.

Milly worked her way slowly across the lounge, finally wedging herself into a corner beside a phone booth. It provided cover of a sort; so did the preoccupation of the small group she was watching.

There were four of them, Rita and Frank Myles, Sarah, and a

tall, flamboyant redhead she guessed must be Ivy Bell, Sarah's boss. The only one that really interested her was Sarah.

She looked exhausted, none of her usual vitality. She was wearing a black wool jumpsuit with a short and swinging red coat. Ordinarily bright colors suited Sarah; tonight they accentuated her pallor. And she was such a small girl it was hard to keep her in sight. Not a girl anymore, Milly reminded herself. Sarah was twenty-five. Which meant nearly a quarter century that this surveillance had gone on. And she'd never known exactly why. But she didn't have to. Some things you knew were right to do, regardless of the risks or the way they seemed to contradict conventional morality. She kept Sarah in sight and herself carefully hidden. She need not have worried; the Myleses and Ivy Bell were oblivious of her presence.

The loudspeaker rasped. The only intelligible words were *British Airways* and *London*. "Did you understand that?" Rita Myles asked her daughter.

Sarah shook her head. "No, not a word. I think it was about my flight, though."

"Maybe it's canceled," Rita said. Her tone was hopeful.

Ivy grinned at Sarah. "I'd better go ask what's doing." She was gone in a moment, pushing her way through the crowd. Given her build and her air of command, Ivy had no difficulty fighting her way forward. Sarah looked after her for a second or two, then turned to her father. Frank Myles was seated on a tiny portion of bench space.

He looked older and more fragile than ever, Sarah realized with a sudden sense of shock. Seventy-five had never before seemed so close to the end. The age difference between him and her mother struck Sarah with new force. How would Rita react when Frank died and she faced a long, young widowhood? What does any woman do when deserted? Sarah shivered and looked at her father again.

He had her large carry-on tote bag in his lap, and he seemed dwarfed by it. But it was Sarah's health that preoccupied him. And his wife's discontent. "Are you sure you're well enough to make this trip, honey? Maybe your mother's right, huh? I don't like to say it, but you look awful."

She knew she did, she'd caught a glimpse of herself in a mirror.

BEVERLY BYRNE

Haggard wouldn't be too strong a word. Green eyes framed in sooty hollows, skin drawn tight across high cheekbones. And when she spoke, her voice was subdued, shaded with fatigue. "I'm fine, Dad, really. And I'll be gone only a week or ten days. Stop worrying, both of you."

The senior Myleses looked at each other to avoid looking at their daughter. Ivy returned and said the announcement had been about boarding. It was taking place now at Gate Seven. Sarah took the bag from her father's lap. "Let's say good-bye here, shall we? There's no point in your battling through this mob."

Rita kissed Sarah fiercely, and clung to her. Frank was less demonstrative, but there was as much concern in his eyes. Ivy pressed her cheek against Sarah's for a moment. "*Ciao,* pet. Do right by me." She linked her arms through those of Rita and Frank and began shepherding them from the terminal.

Sarah hastened toward the boarding area; once she turned to wave, but Ivy and her parents were already out of sight. She allowed herself one searching look through the lounge. Maybe he'd come at the last minute to tell her it was all a mistake, that he hadn't meant anything he'd said in that dreadful letter. But there was no sign of Jarib. Tears stung behind her eyelids. Sarah blinked them away and took her place in the line of people waiting to pass through security control.

The watching woman noted Sarah's hungry inspection of the mob. Poor kid, she thought, but her sympathy for Sarah did not affect her determination not to be seen. She held her breath and shrank further into her corner; for once grateful for being a short, dumpy, typical housewife from the suburbs. It wasn't bad camouflage.

She waited until Sarah had walked through the metal monitor, and out of sight; then she stepped inside the phone booth. Milly dialed slowly, referring often to a slip of paper. The number had changed frequently over many years, and she had never made an effort to memorize it. Too much like what spies did in books, the idea made her uncomfortable.

The ringing tone that was so different from the American version began. Two rhythmic pulses, then a pause. It went on for a while. She wondered what time it was in Paris.

"Yes?"

"Hi, it's me."

"Milly, how are you, my dear?"

The old man always began thus, and his tone was warm and friendly, though they'd met face-to-face only once a long time ago. At a Hadassah meeting. Which explained a lot, if there were explanations required. "I'm fine. You?"

"Not so bad. A touch of arthritis. The weather's lousy in Paris this time of year. What's new?"

"I'm at Logan Airport. Sarah Myles left as planned; she just went through security. British Airways Flight Eighty-five to London. Due to arrive in London at seven A.M. English time."

"She's traveling alone?"

"Yes. Like I told you, it's a business trip. But what maybe you should know, Sarah's all upset. Apparently the guy ditched her. Jarib Baraak, the professor. I told you about him."

"Yes, you did."

"Well, this morning Sarah got a 'dear John' letter. You probably don't know what that means," she added hastily. "A letter saying he was through with her. But Ivy Bell, Sarah's boss, said she should go anyway. Therapy. Rita told me she didn't want her to, because she's so miserable, but Sarah hasn't done what Rita wanted in years. I'm not sure she ever did."

The man in Paris interrupted what was destined to turn into a long chat. "That's fine, Milly, dear. You've done an excellent job. Thank you. Go home to your family. Good night."

The woman hung up, retrieved her credit card, and started for the car park. She'd be well behind Rita and Frank. There was no possibility of their discovering that their friendly next-door neighbor had followed them.

In Paris the man to whom Milly had spoken was smiling when he put down the receiver. He took off his thick glasses and polished them carefully, a gesture that meant he was thinking, then went into the kitchen of the old flat and lit the gas under the kettle. He'd make himself a cup of tea.

But the drink didn't soothe him. He was trembling. With excitement, he realized. Because earlier today there had been the report from Ariel. Dov Levi was acting funny, Ariel said. Nothing he could pin down, just funny. Nerved up.

Inconclusive by itself. Except that unlike all the others, Ariel was a trained professional. The old man trusted him. And now this.

A year ago, when Milly Katz informed him the girl was seeing a parapsychologist, he'd been almost positive he knew why. She too must be a carrier. He'd been tempted to intervene then, but on reflection he'd decided only to watch and wait. Now Sarah was coming to Europe. He wasn't quite sure why that changed anything, only that he was certain it did.

The pieces in the game, the pawns if you will, were moving. Something was going to happen. He was sixty-nine years old, and the kind of life he'd lived had taught him to respect his instincts. Often they were all he had.

The tea grew cold in his cup while the man pondered various courses of action. In half an hour he'd made his decisions. He would stir the pot. Patience had been the best weapon for a long time. Now the stars of the drama were moving in their course. He would move, too, but carefully. Cautiously. Somewhere years ago he'd learned what American poker players meant by an ace in the hole. That's what he had, an ace in the hole. Only he knew all the ramifications, all the players on the stage. So he could afford a few risks.

At this hour all over Rome there were elegant private dining rooms where both new and old money fawned on Church dignitaries; restaurants where clerics with discreet touches of red or purple below their white collars enjoyed the choicest foods and drank the rarest wines to spice their endless gossip. As a bishop Malachy Fanti had never been part of that quintessential Roman scene; it was no different now that he was a cardinal.

St. Benedict had decreed that his monks, like peasants everywhere, should go to bed at sunset and rise at dawn. The monastic horarium was somewhat different in these days of electricity, but by ten-thirty in the evening Malachy had said compline, the last office of the day, and retired.

When the telephone rang, it startled him. His habits were well known; it was unusual for anyone to disturb him so late. He stared at the instrument a moment before answering it. When he did, he didn't say *"pronto"* in the Roman fashion. *"Benidicamus Domino,* Dom Malachy Fanti speaking."

The man in Paris knew the customary response was *"Deo gratias"*; he preferred not to make it. "Hello, my friend."

"Ah, it's you. How are you?"

"Well, Malachy. And sorry to disturb you. Were you sleeping? It's not yet midnight."

"No, I know. I still keep my monkish habits. It doesn't matter."

"I have news. Things seem to be happening with the subject. I'm not sure yet, but the indications are strong. I wondered if you've unearthed anything new."

"Not since the reference I wrote you about, the one in the *Curriculae Hebraica* from Florence in the ninth century. And I'm afraid I haven't had time to finish translating it. The language is very old and obscure."

"Too bad. I particularly hoped . . ." He left his hope unnamed. "But you must keep working. Harder than ever. Something is definitely happening here."

Malachy found himself clutching the telephone. "You think so? Good, that's very good! We've waited a long time, my friend."

"Yes, and this may be a false alarm. But I wanted you to know."

"Thank you, I'm grateful. And perhaps I can finish that translation tomorrow."

"Try. Any little clue might help. I'll call your office in the afternoon. Is six P.M. convenient?"

"I'll make it convenient. Nothing is more important than this."

"No, nothing. Good night, Malachy."

Fanti broke the connection and smiled to himself. In the Vatican they had coined the expression that the walls had ears. So what would a listener make of the fact that he, reputed to be such an anti-Semite, had just spoken in terms of intimacy with an old Jew in Paris? They wouldn't understand, just as few had ever understood his true feelings, why he did the things he did. The Church was beset by fools. Like Larry Donovan. Once he'd had real hope for the American. Now he was the enemy, and Fanti would do everything in his power to undermine the report of Donovan's committee. Perhaps this telephone call would help.

He tried to think how that might be, but it wasn't clear to him. Then he tried to go back to sleep. He couldn't, the news was too momentous, it excited him too much. Fanti rose. He'd put on no lights; the apartment was lit only by the moon. A cool white glow limned the high-ceilinged suite, accentuated the ornate plaster-work.

The sitting room was ill named. It was furnished in nineteenth-century stiff-backed, velvet-covered monstrosities, and there was no place comfortable to sit. He hardly ever used this room. His office in the Vatican Seminary, his combination bedroom and study here in the Tribunal Palace, and the small Church of the Magdalen in the Vatican Gardens—those were the points of his existence. Meals were brought to him on a tray by a nameless nun. Usually he ate them standing at the tall chest of drawers in the bedroom.

Fanti looked around him at the comfortless parlor. He was not an unthinking man; his austerities were not engendered by indifference. They were deliberate, both penance and petition. And now? Now perhaps God was about to answer. For a moment he contemplated the enormity of that. Then he knew what he must do.

The yellow BMW ate up the road. That's how the man behind the wheel always thought of it, a rapacious devouring in which he was the victor. He loved the drive home on a night such as this when the black asphalt shimmered under moonlight and the car surged, all its power at the ready under his fingertips. It was ten to midnight, no traffic on 128 at this hour. He liked that, too. He let his foot press a little harder on the accelerator; the speedometer edged just over the hundred mark. Then he saw the woman.

She was about thirty yards ahead, standing by the metal highway barrier, not signaling for a ride, just standing there. The BMW's headlights caught her for a few seconds. She didn't move. The driver registered a quick series of impressions. Tall, slender, very blond, inadequately dressed for the cold night. Then he'd shot past her.

He drove on for about a quarter of a mile, then eased off the gas, slowed, and finally stopped. He couldn't see her behind him any longer, it was too dark. No headlights either. What the hell, he'd chance it. He backed up cautiously, unsure now exactly where he'd seen her. There were no roadside features to remember, just the woman in the headlights. Maybe he'd imagined the whole thing. Maybe it was a religious experience.

The taillights picked her up a few seconds later. Exactly as he'd seen her the first time. Alone, still, simply waiting. He stopped and leaned over to the passenger side and rolled down the window. "Hello, aren't you cold?"

"Hello. Yes, I'm cold."

She was very pretty, much more so than he'd realized in that first fleeting glimpse. "Where are you going?"

"North."

He grinned. "Covers a lot of territory. I'm headed for Hamilton. Any use to you?"

She didn't answer; instead she reached for the handle of the door. It didn't yield until he pressed a button on the elaborate dashboard. The lock was released, and she got in. He noticed how graceful her movements were.

He didn't start up right away, just kept looking at her in the dim light of the BMW's interior. She was shivering, but with control. Odd, but that was his impression. He shrugged out of his jacket and slid it 'round her shoulders. It was Irish tweed, imported, very warm. "Better?" he asked.

"Yes, better. Thank you."

"I'm Sal Petrovski. And before you ask, I'll tell you. Salvatore because my mother was Italian, Petrovski because my father was a Pole. What's your name?"

She shook her head. Her hair was long and straight and blond, her profile astonishingly perfect. Her clothes weren't just inadequate for the temperature, they were an insult: a brown skirt in some sleazy material and a white cotton blouse under a blue cardigan. Acrylic, Petrovski thought, junk. He knew about knit goods. She ought to be in cashmere. "C'mon," he said. "Tell me your name. Everybody's got a name."

She shook her head again, but this time she turned her face to him. And she smiled. Petrovski caught his breath. God, she wasn't just pretty, she was gorgeous. Special. Very, very special. "Okay, if you won't tell me any different, I'll give you a name. I'm going to call you Purity."

"That's fine," she said softly. "Purity's fine."

The rearview mirror picked up the gleam of approaching headlights. Petrovski shifted into first. "Just north?" he asked.

"For now, just north."

The woman adjusted his jacket over her shoulders and sat back. The car smelled good. The upholstery must be real leather. A rich man's car. Mama always said she must never take rides with strangers. The newly christened Purity thought of that and smiled. No danger. Not to her. She dropped her hand to her hip. It was still there, tucked into the top of her panty hose. She kept her fingers over it, secretly caressing the plastic handle of the carefully sharpened screwdriver.

Sarah sat back in the narrow seat. A hostess walked up the aisle, clearing the last of the plastic trays that had held plastic food and lowering the shades at the windows. The lights were dimmed and an image flickered on the screen at the front of the cabin.

It was a Woody Allen film. She reminded herself that she loved Woody Allen and plugged in the earphones and tried to concentrate and make sense of the scratchy sound track. A pulsating rock beat accompanied the credits. The towers of Manhattan danced across the screen. She couldn't see anything but the tops. The seatbacks obscured her vision. She removed the earphones and pushed her own seat back. Maybe she'd feel better if she could sleep. Memories poured in as soon as she closed her eyes.

For a few moments she struggled against them, telling herself not to think about bad things, employing the lessons of evasion she'd learned as a child. None of those practiced techniques worked. She and Jarib talking earnestly while the fire popped in the grate in his tiny living room, laughing in his kitchen, walking on the beach, loving each other among the dunes or in his bed. . . . The pain was so fresh . . . so new. Have to get control, to relax. Concentrate on breathing, block out the anguish, follow the breath.

The mob was with her suddenly, instantly. This time she wasn't an observer made to see by the music and the woman's voice; neither was she deliberately thrusting herself into the woman's world. In the space of a heartbeat Sarah was hurled into the midst of calamity.

Hundreds of voices, shouting, brandishing torches. She couldn't see what the firelight illumined or understand the words. She was aware only of mortal terror, of the stupefying crush of bodies, of screams of horror. Death and despair. Not just sadness now, utter desolation. Death. She had to get out or she would die! The still point, she must find it. The still point where she could achieve control. The music was her bridge. *Do-sol-la-fa.* Concentrate on the music.

And slowly the terrible scene faded. Like a deep-sea diver surfacing through dark water, she rose through layers of obscurity to her own present: the steady drone of the aircraft speeding east, the silent movie still flickering up front, a child crying somewhere behind her. Total exhaustion, then merciful sleep.

The voice of the stewardess brought Sarah awake with a start. "Ladies and gentlemen, in half an hour we'll be landing at London's Heathrow Airport. We will now distribute landing cards to all passengers who do not hold British passports. Please fill them out carefully."

Sarah was bathed in sweat, still shaken by what had happened before she slept. She rose and made her way back to the rest room, splashing her face with the tepid tap water before she refurbished her makeup, twisting her hair into a coil at the nape of her neck. She didn't enjoy looking in the mirror. She still looked terrible. Maybe even worse. Not just her own grief, the horror she'd . . . what? Seen? Experienced? She didn't know how to characterize what had happened.

Jarib would know. But Jarib didn't care anymore. He wanted to forget her, ignore everything that had happened between them. Face it, in Ivy's choice phrase, she'd been well and properly dumped. The thought made her gag, and she fought back the urge to vomit and returned to her seat.

"British passport?" a stewardess inquired.

"No, American."

"Please fill this out for the immigration authorities."

Sarah took the card and found a pen in her bag and answered the questions, annoyed because her hand still trembled. What was her passport number? How long would she be in the United Kingdom? What was the purpose of her visit? Where could she be reached during her stay? To answer the last one, she had to dig in her bag again and find Tim Durant's address. Then it was done, and she could sit and wait and try not to think. Not of Jarib, and certainly not of the horror into which she'd been plunged. Don't be afraid, he'd always told her. I'm right here. But he wasn't anymore.

The little time that Anwar hoped would be all Sarah must spend making music in the soldiers' inn stretched into a longer time. Anwar fashioned and sold what he could, but it was never enough and he never earned a sufficient amount to release them from the bondage of poverty. The weeks passed and the months, the seasons came and went and came again, and Sarah stopped speaking about a journey to Jerusalem. Not only because they could not afford such a trip, but because Jerusalem had become a city under siege.

No nation had ever sat more uneasily under the Roman yoke than Palestine. Rome could swallow and digest all who would accommodate themselves to her ways, but the Jews with their insistence that theirs was the only God and their endless laws and customs were a lump that could not be absorbed in the vast Roman maw. The most fervent opposition to the Romans came largely from Galilee, from a band of rebels calling themselves Zealots. In 65 the Zealots fomented an uprising that pricked the sometimes lazy Roman lion. It ended with terror in the streets, house-to-house searches, and numerous crucifixions. In the Diaspora, those far-flung lands where Jews lived with their eyes turned always to Jerusalem, the holy city, they heard and shook their heads. Would the rebellious never learn? No, it seemed, never.

A short time later Eleazar, son of the former high priest Ananias and captain of the Temple—second in the hierarchy after the high priest himself—published a decree that henceforth no sacrifices would be accepted from any foreigner. The Romans could no longer pay for the twice-daily offering on behalf of the emperor. But Roman law demanded just such an offering, in every place of worship in the empire. Of course, Eleazar knew that. His decree was deliberate, open rebellion. To crown it, he mounted an attack on the palace.

Swiftly the word spread, and Jews everywhere repeated the stories. "They say," Anwar told Sarah, "just when it seemed Eleazar would win, he was attacked by Menahem, the Jew from Galilee. Menahem accepted the surrender of Eleazar's troops, and then he murdered Ananias, Eleazar's father.''

Sarah's eyes grew big with shock and fear. "But this is war! Will it come here next?"

Anwar laughed at her naiveté. "Alexandria is a mighty city, my love. Not a provincial outpost like Jerusalem. We are quite safe in Alexandria.''

Rachel was approaching her seventh birthday. She too heard the story her father told her mother. "You're sure, Papa? The Jews won't come here and murder us?"

"Hush," Sarah said at once. "You and I, we are Jews, too. And what they're doing isn't murder. The Romans have been cruel masters in Palestine.''

"And Papa, is he also a Jew?"

"No," Anwar said. "But I am a follower of Jesus of Nazareth. And so are you.''

Rachel nodded her head, prepared as children were to accept whatever she was told. She was a Jew and a follower of Jesus. For the time it was enough.

Soon there was more news from Jerusalem. Menahem had been captured by Eleazar and tortured to death. Then Eleazar promised the Roman soldiers they could move out of the towers where they had taken refuge. But this promise of safe passage was violated, and Eleazar's troops slaughtered all but their commander, who agreed to undergo circumcision.

It was open warfare, and it could no longer be contained. That night there was a riot and Alexandrian Greeks massacred dozens of Alexandrian Jews. Sarah heard this news, and though she learned that her parents and family were unharmed, she began to be afraid.

In 67 the Romans recaptured Galilee, but some of the rebel leaders escaped and took refuge in Jerusalem, still in Jewish hands. The Zealots were sure to venture forth again, and mighty Vespasian, now emperor, was preparing his response.

So it came, that time no Jew would ever forget.

In the summer of 69 the siege led by Vespasian's popular son, Titus, began. In its wake there followed the event which changed everything for Reb Michael, and Leah, and Sarah, and Farak, and Anwar, and Rachel . . . and all the others. The Second Temple, Herod's magnificent restoration of the great edifice built by King David, went up in flames and Jerusalem fell.

This was not news, not politics, not merely part of the ebb and flow of the tides of men's affairs. This was cataclysm, the rewriting of history. This was—must be—the judgment of Almighty God.

In the turmoil of those days, while Jews everywhere rent their garments and wailed their mourning, the Gentile followers of Jesus began to speak openly of the fact that they were not Jews. They were what the Romans had dubbed them, Christians, followers of Jesus the Christ. The disgrace and the judgment visited upon the Jews were not meant for them. They were no part of this accursed, pigheaded race; especially were they separate from those who, even while they lauded Jesus, insisted on the immutability of Jewish ways and laws.

From every corner the Jews were attacked, even in Alexandria, where they had so long been, where so many privileges were theirs.

"Sarah! Rachel! Come, we must go!" Anwar ran to his house just ahead of the rampaging mob. This was not a Jewish section, but by now the rioting and looting had spread far beyond any single quarter. "Come!" he yelled again.

Sarah took Rachel's hand and ran to join her husband. "Wait," she murmured to her daughter. "My lyre, I can't go without my lyre." It took only a moment to get it, but that was all that was needed. The screaming, cursing mob had reached the door, brandishing knives and torches, their faces made ugly by hate.

Sarah stared in horror, frozen by fear. She recognized a man she knew. He was a neighbor of Farak's, a follower of Jesus, albeit not a Jew. She opened her mouth to call out to him, to say that this was the house of Farak's son, of his grandchild, but she was too late. Another man sprang forward and the rest surged after him.

Anwar had been standing by the door, attempting to guard Sarah and Rachel, who were still in the house. He was trampled under the feet of the mob.

Screaming aloud her horror, dragging Rachel after her, Sarah turned and ran. There was a small window in the kitchen. She pushed her daughter through it, then climbed out after her. And they ran again.

The attackers did not follow her. It was not a woman and a child they wanted. The mob was intent on ransacking the house where they hoped to find the precious metals and jewels of Anwar's trade. By the time Sarah realized this she and her daughter had run far from the narrow street, into the countryside. Gasping for breath, they collapsed beneath a tree. Sarah was sobbing, but Rachel did not weep. She stared into the darkness, her small face set in a grimace of hate, her chest heaving.

Ten minutes passed, twenty. Then a man came. He was walking alone, followed by two servants. He saw the woman and the child and approached, lifting the lantern he carried so he could see their faces. "Sarah bas Michael, isn't it? And her daughter."

"Yes." Sarah pulled the child closer to her.

"Don't be frightened. You know me. I'm Nahaam, the vintner."

Sarah looked more closely at him. Yes, it was he. She did not know him well, he was a Jew, but he never went to the Temple or

to the synagogues to argue and pray with the other men. And he
did not live in the Jewish section. Vaguely she remembered that he
had a big house on the outskirts of the city. "We are trespassing on
your property," she guessed.

He had a big head and a full beard, and he nodded and bent
closer. Nahaam had kind eyes. "Yes, these are my fields. But it
doesn't matter. I have come out to search for a stray lamb. I did
not expect to find a stray woman."

"I did not expect to be here," Sarah murmured. Then, gathering
her strength so that she could speak without screaming in hysteria,
she told him what had happened.

"These are terrible times for Jews," Nahaam said sadly. "But
then, there have been many such. And our curse touches all who
are near us. You're sure Anwar is dead?"

"I'm sure. I saw. My child and I, we both saw." Sarah stared
into the night and tightened her grip on Rachel's shoulders.

Nahaam turned to the waiting servants. "Quickly! Go back to
my house, tell them to prepare for two guests, a woman and her
daughter." Then he spoke again to Sarah. "You will spend this
night under my roof. And as many nights as it takes you to regain
your strength and the city to be rid of its lust to spill blood. After
that, well, we shall see."

$\mathcal{S}ix$

**TUESDAY,
NOVEMBER 20**

In Paris it was 8:00 A.M. and Dov Levi slept; he seldom woke before 10. Below his windows the Rue du Bac was alive with early-morning street sounds. The cafés and shops of this Left Bank street between St.-Sulpice and the Seine were preparing for the day's business. Levi heard nothing. Probably because it was dawn when he staggered into the cheap residential hotel which the developers had somehow overlooked when the district became fashionable.

No matter how drunk Levi was, he could stagger up the stairs and manage to fall on his own bed. Such were the small triumphs of these days in his fifty-fourth year. A gray, uneventful life. Until now, when he suddenly screamed aloud.

Levi jerked himself awake and sat up. He was drenched in icy sweat and shaking. Not a hangover. That had nothing to do with this.

Sarah, listen to the music. . . . The most beautiful music in the world, Sarah.

Jesus! Nothing for years and years, now an experience just like the one around a year ago. He wrapped himself in the worn blanket. His frame was still muscular, despite everything, but the muscles sagged with disuse. He was so cold. And drunk, hearing things. No, not drunk now. Not hearing imaginary things. He knew the difference. *Sarah, listen to the music.* The Israeli shivered and dragged himself out of bed. He needed a drink.

Levi found his usual place in his customary bar, at the rear, hidden in the dimness. It was an old place with a zinc counter and sawdust on the floor. And high barstools that had metal rings circling the legs about ten inches from the floor. Levi particularly liked the stools. He was five feet five, and without the metal ring his feet would dangle. Too much already dangled in his life.

He liked, too, that the place wasn't shiny and modern and plastic and clean; it was crusted with old, comfortable dirt. He had learned to appreciate things that neither threatened nor demanded notice.

Levi raised his eyes from *Le Figaro* and glanced at the wavy mirror facing him. There were no bottles to interrupt his vision— the owner had never heard of impulse buying; he expected his customers to ask for what they wanted and take what they got. Levi's thick white hair was made yellow by the mirror and the lack of light. It wasn't like that; it was really white. The color had gone almost overnight twenty-five years ago, but he no longer thought much about why. Until lately, when the whole thing seemed ready to surface again.

Do-sol-la-fa. Crazy. After so long. A nightmare, he'd better forget it. He looked away from the mirror, ignoring that his green eyes were perpetually red-rimmed, his dark skin deeply lined. White hair, like a distinguished gentleman. That was okay.

He signaled the man behind the bar. "*Un cognac.*"

The man shuffled over and refilled Levi's glass. He pointed a grimy finger at the newspaper. "*Dans les journeaux il n'y ont que les catastrophes, vous gaspillez votre temps.*"

In French that was perfect except for its accent, Levi said that his time wasn't worth saving and he liked catastrophes. The barman grunted and moved to the other end of the counter, wiping the zinc with a filthy cloth that served to distribute the dust more evenly.

The Israeli went back to his paper. He read about the latest results of Mitterrand's program to create a million new jobs. Galloping inflation and a plunging franc. Just what the Socialist president had promised to avoid. Fairy tales. The French liked them, despite their reputation for logic and clarity. It was the language that was clear and logical; the people deluded themselves as readily as any other nationality.

He glanced at his watch. In a little while he'd go to the magazine. *Moyen-Orient* was the plaything of a wealthy expatriate Syrian, full of anti-Israeli and anti-American ravings culled from the newspapers of various Arab states. The Syrian paid Levi eight hundred francs a week to translate the garbage into English and French. It amused him that Levi was a Jew. For Levi's part, the job suited him. He could pick up the copy and take it back to the hotel. Two days later he brought the translations into the office and collected his money in cash. Less than a hundred dollars U.S., but enough for him. Considering the way he lived. And the small supplementary income from a source he preferred not to think about.

He was still shaken from the experience of the morning. The song had rung in his ears. So damn clear. After twenty-five years. He swallowed the brandy in one gulp and ordered a third. Stalling, not wanting to leave the dim, womblike atmosphere of the bar.

He continued to thumb through the newspaper. The auction page caught his eye. Not that he was an auction buff. He couldn't afford to be. But the ad was headed "Judaica—Hebrew Artifacts from the First to Eighteenth Century." He read the announcement quickly, then read it again. A few moments later Levi fumbled the last twenty-franc note out of his wallet and left the bar without waiting for change.

He found some coins in his pocket. Enough for the metro. Twenty minutes later he was at the Hôtel Drouot, doyen of French auction rooms but a glaringly modern black granite building erected in 1980 to replace a fire ruined, two century old wreck. Levi spotted a guard. *"Serais-ce possible voir l'Exposition Judaica?"*

"Certainement, monsieur." The guard nodded toward the main viewing hall. Levi moved tentatively, walking like a wounded man, his heart pounding in his chest. What the hell was he doing here? He had to come, that's all there was to it. Had to. He began pacing the aisles, searching. Oblivious of antiquity or beauty or the

multinational throng around him. Searching. For what? He wouldn't know until he found it.

Ten minutes later he did. A bracelet in a glass case at the very rear. Its presence called out to him, charged his body with an extraordinary electricity. Something he hadn't felt in years. And the four notes were playing repeatedly in his head.

The bracelet was with the minor offerings, among things that might be old but were not of sufficient craftsmanship or beauty to be coveted by the big spenders, be they private collectors or museums. Levi stared at it, breathing hard, his mouth dry. He'd picked up a catalog at the door. Now he feverishly turned the pages until he came to the section describing jewelry. The entry he sought was the next to the last listing. The information given was meager. No certain provenance could be cited, but the experts thought the piece dated from circa A.D. 100. Crude perhaps, but interesting because of its age. The estimated value was eighteen thousand francs.

Shit. Cheap in relation to other things, but where would he get eighteen thousand francs? He stared into the glass case. The compulsion to acquire the bracelet was a taste in his mouth, a ringing in his ears. A certitude when he'd assumed life offered him no more of those. Levi considered his boss, the wealthy Syrian. No. Not possible. It would have to be Yakov.

"I had to come to you, Yakov. There's no one else."

Yakov Tench was eighty-eight. A delicate, fragile shell whose body had all but disintegrated while the spirit remained alive within. His trembling right hand hovered over an African violet, pinching off a dead blossom which he transferred carefully to a plastic bag. "My daughter wants to enlarge her restaurant in Alsace. I'm going to lend her the money. Go to your friends in Mossad."

"I have no such friends."

The old man laughed softly. "You are a liar, Dov Levi. Just as all Israelis have become liars. Betrayers of the dream."

Levi sighed. He would have to listen to the old man's diatribe. That was the price of asking him for help. In 1922 Yakov had been one of the earliest Zionists, the intractable few who made Israel happen with their blood and their sweat and the sheer force of their will. In 1971 he'd left with his wife and Zelah, the twenty-seven-year-old daughter of their old age. In the long interval between arrival and departure the family Tench had become disillusioned and bitter.

French-speaking Swiss by birth, the senior Tenchs came to Paris and opened a greenhouse specializing in houseplants, in the fashionable suburb of Neuilly-sur-Seine. Zelah went to California. A few years later Yakov's wife died. He retired. Zelah returned to Paris and took over the greenhouse. They prospered. But the plants weren't enough for Zelah; she'd been infected with American ideas of success. Besides, she hated Paris. Last year she and a partner opened an *auberge* in Kohlburg near the German border. Dov knew that when Yakov died, Zelah would sell the greenhouse and move to Alsace. That thought saddened him enormously; not because of the old man, because of Zelah.

But Yakov wasn't ready to die; his bitterness kept him alive. Israel had betrayed him by becoming a modern state forced to compromise. Now he spoke to Dov Levi in swift, guttural Hebrew, cataloging the long list of sins which were the foundation of his discontent.

"Enough, Yakov," Levi said at last. "I know. We've been over this before. I don't live there either. What do you want from me?"

"You don't live there because Mossad prefers that you live here. So you can watch old men like me, and translate that dreck the Arab prints. Better you than somebody who's not in their pocket. Besides, I want nothing from you. It's you who want from me, remember?"

"Yes. Eighteen thousand francs."

"A fortune."

"A pittance. About two thousand dollars."

"What do dollars have to do with it?"

"Only a convenient measure of worth, Yakov. When Mitterrand gets through, the franc will be garbage."

Levi looked around the tiny room. The only ornaments were the plants. Some half a hundred African violets glowed in the cool north light provided by a window and a skylight. Their velvety dark green leaves and purple and pink flowers were the only color. Apart from them there was a narrow cot, two chairs, and a table. No carpet. Yakov Tench lived like a monk. And Zelah, too, was perverse in her way. Why live on the expensive Rue Jacob on the Left Bank and spend an hour each day getting to work? But at least downstairs Zelah had a comfortable home. Up here her father indulged his puritan conscience and cursed the past.

Levi had a sudden inspiration. "Listen, Yakov, if I don't get the bracelet, some New York Jew is bound to. The American collectors eat up things like this."

The old man blamed the American Jews for everything that was wrong in Israel. They'd come with their practical values, their desire to "get things done," their money; they had desecrated the dream. Even the ones who didn't emigrate, the ones who stayed in New York and Philadelphia and Los Angeles, polluted Israel with their contributions and their demands. "You think so?" he asked softly. "How will they even know it's for sale? You said the auction is tomorrow."

"I didn't see the ad until today, but it must have run all week. American Jewish collectors have scouts everywhere to warn them of such things." He sounded as much a crank as the old man. But it could very well be true.

"Why would they want it?"

"Judaica. What Jew doesn't want such a thing?"

"And that's why you want it? Because it's Judaica? You've become a collector of artworks now?"

"No. I told you the truth, Yakov. When I saw the advertisement, I knew I must go to the Hôtel Drouot. Then I knew I must buy the bracelet. Not why, just that I must do it." He'd decided that no lie would suffice; he must trust the old man's instincts, trust him to be the kind of man he had been, just once more.

"Your father," Yakov said in a soft, dreamy voice. "When he left Palestine, he mourned that he was not a better pioneer. I told him he was a good pioneer, just a bad fanatic. So many years ago, Dov. But you, you are a good fanatic. You and Mossad."

"I'm not part of Mossad, Yakov." Wearily, beginning to believe he'd failed. He wouldn't get the money. Levi rose to go.

"Wait. Eighteen thousand francs, you're sure it will be enough?"

"No. I'm not sure. That's the estimated value in the catalog. I may be able to get it for less." He hesitated. "Or it could go higher."

Yakov walked slowly to the table and pulled out a drawer. His trembling hands fumbled for a moment, then emerged clutching a checkbook. Saying nothing, he opened it, found a pen, and with difficulty signed his name in a spidery scrawl. "Here. You fill in the rest. Whatever it takes to get the bracelet, you buy it. Better you than somebody from New York."

Levi left the house in an ecstasy of relief, his hand deep in his pocket clutching the blank check. He did not see the other Israeli across the street. Not just because of his preoccupation, Ariel was quite expert at not being seen.

Ariel watched Levi until he rounded the corner. His face furrowed with speculation; it made him look older than his thirty-some years. Finally he walked off in the opposite direction from Levi. He'd report at once. Yesterday he wasn't sure of his hunch, although he'd reported it, too. Now he was sure. Something had definitely reactivated Dov Levi; the boss would want to know.

It took Sarah nearly an hour to get through passport control, claim her luggage, and satisfy customs. The process was irritating and tiring, and to add to it, she was nervous about seeing Tim Durant again.

Ivy was right. Tim had the hots for her. He'd made that plain. They'd had lunch together a few days before he left Boston. She'd felt constrained to tell him the truth. "Look, I'm involved with someone. I'm sorry, Tim, that's how it is. I like you very much, just not that way."

"I take it that's why you're never available on Mondays when Ivy's place is closed?" he'd said ruefully.

"Yes, that's why."

They hadn't said more, but there was a strain between them after that. Still, when she emerged from the encounter with bureaucracy Sarah was relieved to find Tim waiting.

"Welcome home," he said. "All is forgiven."

Sarah looked startled and uncomprehending.

"You know, the Pilgrim Fathers, that spot of trouble your lot made."

She wanted to laugh, but it wouldn't come. There was still so much pain in her. It sat in her belly, and every once in a while it rose and seemed to choke her. She managed only a small smile.

His car was a beautifully kept vintage Jaguar. "Just what I expected," Sarah said.

"That's me, never disappoint a lady." He stowed her luggage in the rear and folded his long body into the driver's seat. "We're on our way south to the old homestead. First sale's tomorrow morning in Bristol; that's nearby, so it's convenient, and the place is worth seeing."

"Fine by me," Sarah said. "I'm in your hands."

"A delicious thought. One thing first, however, I have to see someone in the city. Are you too tired for that?"

"No. I should be, but I'm not." She'd lost five hours traveling east, and a whole night's sleep, but she was full of nervous energy.

"Your first trip abroad, isn't it?"

"The very first."

"And you're not particularly happy about it," he added.

"Why do you say that?" She wondered if Ivy had phoned and told him something. Be specially nice to Sarah perhaps. But it wasn't like Ivy to spring for a transatlantic phone call for such a reason.

Apparently she hadn't. "No reason," Tim said easily, "just the look of you."

Unconsciously Sarah pushed at her hair. "I'm tired, as you said." She did not want to begin this trip with Tim Durant's pity.

"Okay, just settle back and relax. I won't bore you with a running travelogue. There'll be time for that later." After that they drove in silence. It was cloudy, and they kept hitting patches of fog; so Sarah couldn't see anything much to exclaim over or ask about, and Tim had to concentrate on the road.

Her first impression of central London was mad traffic, all in red and black: red double-decker buses that looked as if they must tip over every time they cornered, and black high-roofed taxis which always seemed on a collision course with the buses. "Do they paint them red so the blood won't show?" she asked.

"Never thought of it. I expect they do." He grinned at her. "A foggy day in London town . . ." he crooned softly. Then: "I promised to spare you the scenic wonders, but this is Kensington. The royal borough of, to give it its full title. Down there is Kensington Palace, where Wales, his blond princess, and the kiddies are sometimes in residence. On our left is the Royal Albert Hall. Impressed?"

"Should I be?" A bit tarter than she meant to sound, and he hadn't deserved it.

"No," he said. "Of course not."

Sarah could tell that he felt the rebuff. She didn't know what to say.

He maneuvered the car into a narrow street. "The woman I have to see lives here."

They were parked in front of a semicircle of perfect Regency houses, a curved ribbon of them; classically formal brick fronts were painted creamy white, the doors were lacquered black with gleaming brass fittings. "It's lovely," Sarah said. She turned to him and smiled. "I'm impressed."

He cocked his head at her. "Real beauty succeeds when famous names fail. I'm impressed, too. This crescent was designed by John Nash. It's a perfect example of its type. Care to come up with me? I'm calling on Lady Harris. Don't boggle at the title. She got it a few years back via her late husband. He made cough syrup. A knighthood for soothing the nation's bad chests."

"Do you have a cough?"

"No, and if I did, I wouldn't swallow any of old man Harris's rotgut. It's Her Ladyship's dad I'm interested in. He was a collector. His penchant was for things being done in his lifetime. Backed his own judgment as to what was going to prove valuable."

"And was his judgment good?"

"Well, he bought a lot of early-twentieth-century junk, mostly Edwardian kickshaws and Art Deco uglies, but he also happened to acquire two Mondrians and a Léger. Now the coffers are nearly bare, and Lady Harris is going to sell the lot."

Sarah gasped. "Are you trying to buy the paintings?"

"Hell, no, I'm not rich enough to buy the frames. I'm trying to get the old dame to let us handle the auction. Come along and see how it's done, or mucked up, as the case may be."

"I'm such a mess, I shouldn't be seen in public." The black jumpsuit was wrinkled.

"Not to worry. Wait till you see Her Ladyship."

They climbed three flights of graceful marble stairs to a flat so crammed with what Lady Harris called "my lovelies," there wasn't space to move. The woman herself was hung with ropes of pearls, armloads of bangles, and a flowing silk caftan in shocking pink. Her hair was rinsed blue, and her eyelids and lashes matched. "I must say," she trilled, "I am glad your father sent two nice young people to see me. I didn't much care for that old man who came for Sotheby's."

"Whom did Christie's send, Your Ladyship?"

The clotted blue eyelashes fluttered. "Now, Timmy, I didn't say Christie's had been consulted."

Tim smiled. "My dear Lady Harris, I know you're far too clever not to have called in both giants for an appraisal."

"Well . . . as a matter of fact, I did. And Christie's man was almost as young as you are."

"Does that put them in the lead?"

Celia Harris laughed, but she didn't answer. "Come sit down and have some coffee. We can talk business after that."

They had to dislodge three Persian cats in order to sit. When that had been accomplished, their hostess produced a magnificent Victorian silver service from which she poured a horrible brew of instant coffee and boiled milk. Sarah hadn't said a word up till now. But Ivy Bell had sold a service not half so beautiful for seven thousand dollars. And she was supposed to be looking out for Ivy's interests. "What a lovely thing." Sarah touched the twined and braided handle of the coffeepot.

"It is rather, isn't it? Mind you, it's not going in the sale. My late husband, Sir William, bought it for me for our silver wedding. I'm only considering selling Daddy's things. He always said they were an investment."

"Quite right," Timothy said. "And you want to realize the greatest possible return. Which is why you should let Durant's handle the sale."

The woman was enjoying this part. She sat back in her chair, prepared to be wooed. "And why is that, Timmy, darling?"

"Because if either Sotheby's or Christie's do it, they'll hive off the Mondrians and the Léger into a sale of modern masters here or in New York. The rest of the items you're offering will go in other, less well-publicized sales. You'll get a fortune for the paintings whoever sells them, we all know that. But Durant's will give you your own sale, the entire collection, of a piece as it were. We'll get the big spenders in because of the paintings, and we'll parade all your other treasures under their noses."

He sat back and waited. There was silence in the crowded living room. Sarah glanced sideways at Tim and realized that he'd taken his best shot. Up front, on impulse. If Celia Harris wasn't convinced, he had nothing else to offer. She was trying so hard to judge the woman's reaction that it took her a few seconds to realize she was being addressed.

"It is Miss Myles, isn't it?"

"Excuse me. Yes, Sarah Myles."

"Good, sometimes I forget names. You're American, aren't you?"

"Yes. This is my first visit to England, I arrived this morning."

Lady Harris wasn't listening. She was rummaging in a basket at her feet. "Here it is!" she said, producing a magazine. The cover flaunted a picture of the Princess of Wales. Below Diana's smiling face was the announcement of a new cancer cure. "I was reading the horoscope just yesterday." She thumbed through the pages, her scarlet nails flashing, the bangles jangling. "Now listen to this, Pisces for November, that's me, I'm a Pisces. '. . . on the twentieth you can expect good news from abroad'!"

The woman smiled in triumph, but both Timothy and Sarah looked blank. "Don't you see? Today is November twentieth, and Miss Myles here is obviously the good news from abroad. I'm sure it couldn't be clearer. Durant's will do the sale, Timmy, darling. Tell your father I want it to be as soon as possible."

"Walk, don't run, to the nearest exit," Tim hissed when the door of the flat closed behind them.

"Why are you whispering?"

"Shut up, I'll tell you later. Don't talk; don't even smile."

He pulled away from the curb with a look of grim concentration, but when they turned the corner onto Kensington High Street, he threw back his head and whooped. "We did it, Sarah, my girl! Wait till the old man hears."

His elation was infectious. "Don't forget, Timmy, darling, I want full credit for bringing the good news from abroad."

"Call me Timmy again and I'm likely to slaughter you. It's only permitted if you own magnificent paintings I can sell at a profit. I don't mind the *darling,* though."

He cast a sideways glance at her, and Sarah felt a sinking sensation in the pit of her stomach. She ignored his comment and his questioning expression. "Why were you so worried when we left? Did you expect me to rub my hands in gleeful triumph and make loud remarks about 'that awful old woman'?"

He looked sheepish. "I was a bit worried about that."

"Listen, you bastard." She turned on the seat so she was facing him. "Don't you dare treat me as if I'm stupid, or some kind of congenital idiot because I don't have an English accent."

"You're kidding, aren't you, you're not really angry?"

Sarah frowned, then broke into a grin. "No, I'm not, but I mean what I say."

"Agreed. And I apologize. Now why don't you try to get some sleep? It's a three-hour drive."

"Wake up, Sarah, we're in Avon, almost home."

Sarah yawned and stretched. "How long have I been asleep?"

"About two and a half hours. We made good time."

The side window was misted over, and Sarah rubbed it and tried to see out. Fog and drizzle still obscured the view. "Does it rain here all the time? I thought it was just a Hollywood trick. You know, fog swirling around a mock-up of Big Ben so you know the scene is London."

"Only most of the time," Tim said. But they were climbing now, into the Mendip Hills, he explained, and soon the fog had melted away, and through a gentle rain Sarah perceived a glowing green countryside.

"Here's home." He turned into a rolling drive between two massive gateposts crowned with dolphins. "Before we get there, I'd better warn you about dear old dad. He's somewhat eccentric."

"How?"

"I'll leave you to discover that for yourself. Just resist snap judgments and remember that we'll only be here one day."

They came to the crest of the final rise; Sarah leaned forward, then breathed a loud sigh. In front of them was the kind of building she'd only seen in books. It was long and low, just two stories, formed of muted rose-red brick. There were tall, narrow windows with vertical tracery that rose to a pointed arch and carried the eye upward to a series of hipped roofs. "It looks like perfect Tudor. Tell me it's not a reproduction."

"Guaranteed genuine," Tim said. "Built in 1525." Before he could say anything else, the clouds broke and a rainbow appeared in the sky behind the house. It was too perfect to seem real. They both giggled. "Welcome to Tiverton Manor," Tim said.

That was more than she got from his father. Hamish Durant met them in the front hall. He was short and enormously fat with a moon face below sparse fair hair. He wore a shapeless gray flannel bathrobe and slippers and had a large black cigar clamped in yellowed teeth. He paid no attention when Tim introduced Sarah. "Well, tell me. Did we get it?" he demanded.

"If you mean the right to sell Lady Harris's bag of tricks, yes, we got it. And it's largely thanks to Sarah here."

Durant turned to her, acknowledging her presence for the first time. "What have you to do with it, lass?"

His accent was difficult and different from Tim's, less clear, and his manner wasn't friendly. "I think it was because I'm an American. Lady Harris's horoscope said she'd get good news from abroad today."

He stared at them both for a moment, then grunted with satisfaction and left the room.

"Born in Leeds, up north in Yorkshire. Family from even further north, Scots," Tim explained while he led her to her room. "Dirt-poor working class, a miner's kid. But the genetic bank came up trumps. He was born brilliant, and somehow all the little gray cells arranged themselves around art and antiques. Married my mum to get a stake. She had a small trust fund, and he started the business with that."

"Why did she marry him?"

"That's what I like about you, Sarah. You're so discreet and subtle."

She blushed. "I'm sorry, I didn't mean to—"

170

"Yes, you did. And it doesn't matter, I'm not offended. Anyway, I don't know the answer. She died when I was born. Just Dad and me since then. Here's your room."

He opened the door to a bedroom that looked exactly as Sarah imagined it must, complete with four-poster bed, velvet draperies, a huge fireplace, and a fabulous series of early Ingres drawings on one wall. But it was horribly cold.

Sarah moved closer to the drawings; Tim plugged in an electric heater. "Too bad art can't keep you warm. This place would be remarkably cozy. As it is, we don't use the fireplaces. The chimneys need a lot of very expensive work. Hamish doesn't approve of such outlays, much less central heating. And as you'll quickly deduce, we live only in this wing. The rest of the house is used to store goods waiting for sale." He sounded a little defensive.

"I've never had such an exquisite bedroom in my life; thank you for bringing me here."

Tim smiled. "Thank you for coming." There was a pause; Sarah refused to look at him. Timothy reached out one hand, as if to touch her, then dropped it. "Lunch will be at noon; the only servant in this museum is a cook. Having seen my father, you'll understand the importance of that. You can sleep this afternoon if you like, or we'll take a walk. It's clearing nicely now."

"Can I make my choice after lunch?" Sarah asked. "I don't know when or if my second wind will run out."

"Sure. And I expect you'd like a bath. The bathroom's across the hall. It's bound to be icy, but there's usually plenty of hot water."

After he left, Sarah stood and shivered and thought about Tim and stared at the beautiful room, the priceless drawings, and the inadequate heater. She didn't know whether to bless Ivy Bell or curse her.

Hamish Durant was quite different at lunch. He was effusive and outgoing and made an effort to charm Sarah while he gorged on roast beef and something she thought was a giant popover sopped in gravy, but was told to call Yorkshire pudding. He hadn't changed his outfit, he still wore the bathrobe and slippers, but he'd omitted the cigar. He kept urging Sarah to eat more and refilling her glass with delicious red wine he identified simply as claret. "Art history, eh?" he said at one point. "Well, Tim tells me you're on a buying trip for Ivy Bell. So you must be bright, despite a fancy education. Ivy's not likely to have sent some idiot to spend her money."

Sarah suppressed a smile; his rudeness was so open it was funny. "I try not to be an idiot, Mr. Durant."

"Sarah's been impressing me all day with what she knows about architecture," Tim interposed hastily.

"I don't imagine Ivy wants her to buy any houses." But Hamish seemed content to let rest the question of Sarah's competence. "You know anything about music, lass?"

She froze with the fork halfway to her mouth. *Sarah! Sarah! Do-sol-la-fa* . . . She pushed the woman away. A conscious act, an effort of will. And it worked. Suddenly she understood. I'm the one who made it quiescent. I didn't even know I was doing it; Jarib didn't see that I was doing it. But after I moved to Ivy's, I just didn't let the woman in anymore. Jarib kept talking about my gaining control and I did, in a way neither of us understood. Then, on the plane, I was so upset my control slipped. So she got back in and showed me all that horror.

"You all right?" Tim asked.

"What? Oh, yes, fine. Sorry." There was no time to examine the insight now. "You were asking about music, Mr. Durant. I don't know much about it."

"Then it's time you learned. Myself, I always think of architecture and music as related. This house, for instance, Tiverton Manor, it's a madrigal. Contrapuntal rhythms meant for the human voice without accompaniment. Nearby there's the town of Bath. Roman origins tarted up by the Georgians. Bath's pure Handel. T'other side's Bristol. Used to be a shipping town, did Bristol. Gone all trendy and high tech. Young people from the university. Rock music. Can't stand it, never go to Bristol."

Dessert was a thick and soggy bread pudding swimming in runny custard. Hamish ignored Sarah's demurral and gave her a huge portion. She was still toying with it when he rose and unceremoniously left the room.

"You've been exposed to two of my father's four passions," Tim said. "Food and music."

172

"I expect antiques are the third, what's the fourth?"

"A sort of hybrid between religion and politics, his own home-grown version. Based on a minority interpretation of Catholicism that Hamish deigns to share with a select handful of people. I think they meet occasionally; apart from that, he seldom goes to church. Maybe it's not as crazy as it sounds since he's a certified genius."

"What about you?"

"Religion, you mean? I don't have any. Dad's a convert who came late to the Romans. Besides, he's not a proselytizer. He thinks a few are called and the rest of us left to fend for ourselves. Ivy told me you're a Catholic, too."

"I was raised to be, yes."

"Sounds like you have doubts."

Sarah shrugged. "Not anything I want to talk about. It isn't very relevant to my life right now. Let's leave it at that, shall we?"

He leaned forward and covered her hand with his. Sarah wanted to pull away, but somehow it seemed impossible. "What is relevant?" he asked.

"I don't know. Look, I had a bad shock just before I left home. There's nothing to be gained by dissecting it."

"Okay. The Monday man, I suppose. I won't ask any questions, but if he's out of the running, I mean to have a go, Sarah, love, and I can be very persuasive."

Out of the running. Like a racehorse. Not the end of the world, just a slight mishap. If you back one loser, you can always try again. So why was she so sure it would never seem like that from her point of view?

Tim was still looking at her; Sarah turned her face away and rose. "I think I'll pass on the walk if you don't mind. All that food and wine have done me in. I'm going to nap for a while."

"Probably not a bad idea. Tomorrow's a heavy day. We're off to Paris right after the Bristol sale. Tea here's at five," Tim added. "Shall I wake you for that?"

"Yes, thank you."

She escaped to the now slightly less frigid bedroom and burrowed under the quilts. There were three of them, thank God. She was afraid to dwell on the revelation about the voice. If she did, maybe it would start again. But she couldn't sleep. Religion, one of Hamish Durant's passions, according to his son. Well, time was when she'd have felt quite sympathetic to that. Only not anymore. Another empty place inside her. She'd wanted Jarib to fill up all the empty spaces; now he'd gone away, too. Sarah turned her face to the wall.

In Boston it was early morning. Jarib Baraak watched the sun playing on the Charles and fingered the gun in his pocket. It was because of her murderous rages, he reminded himself, that's why he had the gun. That's not why he bought it; he did that a few years back, when there was a rash of break-ins near the campus. He got a license and bought the gun, though he'd always doubted he'd use it. And he was far less likely to use it against Lenore.

When he admitted that, Jarib found a deserted side street and parked the car. Looking around carefully to make sure he was unobserved, he bent over a sewer. As if he were studying its function. Covering his action with his body, he dropped the gun into the depths. He felt more like himself after that, a little better.

Not good, of course. Exhausted and emotionally wrung dry. Sarah and Lenore weighed him down with guilt. Both rode with him.

He'd been driving for thirty-six hours, ever since he dropped the letter to Sarah in Ivy's mailbox. The same ten square miles over and over again; every place in Cambridge he could think of, every place that Lenore might go. But there was no sign of her.

It had seemed more useful to search than to go and talk with Lenore's embarrassed keepers. They weren't going to tell him more than they had on the phone. Now he realized that he was acting like a mouse in a cage. Repeating the same action constantly because he knew no way out of the trap. Crazy. He had to break the pattern. And maybe Lenore had been found. Jarib headed west on the Massachusetts Turnpike, toward Framingham.

It took him three-quarters of an hour to reach the very private facility. No, they told him immediately, Mrs. Baraak hadn't been found. And yes, of course, the director would see him at once. They'd been expecting him before this, as a matter of fact.

"Hard to say what she'll do," the psychiatrist told him. "She has fixed much of her hatred on you, of course. But she hasn't forgotten about North Carolina."

"How could this happen?" Jarib demanded. "How in God's name did she get out of here?"

The psychiatrist shrugged and looked grim. He'd already made all the explanations: the young orderly who was new to the job; the door left accidentally unlocked. . . . What difference did any of it make now? "Does Lenore know where you live?"

"Yes. That is, I suppose so. When I bought the house in Rowley, I brought in pictures to show her and said I was taking a sabbatical." And tried to explain about the television residuals, all the money he was making because the series was still being shown all over the world. Enough to keep her here, to allow him some luxuries. "I never know whether she listens to what I say. I'm not even sure she hears me."

The doctor made a few notes on a pad. "What about your Cambridge residence?"

"I probably told her about that years ago. I don't remember."

"I'll suggest to the police they watch both addresses. Meanwhile I think you should stay someplace else."

Jarib clenched his unlit pipe, something real to hang on to, anything real. "She's so obviously ill. Surely she won't get far. Anyone seeing her would recognize the situation and call the police."

"Not necessarily," the other man said. "When she sees you, it all surfaces. Her anger, her despair, her shame. We've talked about this before. But sometimes she's quite lucid, even charming. And she's very beautiful still."

"Still," Jarib agreed. Lenore's beauty was her undoing. If she were ugly, maybe none of it would have happened. "What do the police say?"

"They're extremely cooperative. But they're undermanned, of course. I've alerted the authorities in North Carolina as well, and the state police. We'll just have to hope for the best."

Jarib wasn't content to do that. He couldn't be. Because it was all his fault. The deaths, the anguish, Lenore's insanity. All due to him. He returned to Rowley, checking carefully before he went inside, making sure she wasn't there, hiding in some corner, ready to spring on him. The house was empty and silent.

175

He packed a few things in a small suitcase. Once the phone rang, and he looked at it longingly. Perhaps Sarah was on the other end. He could talk to her, tell her he loved her, that they'd be together again when all this was over. But she was doubtless in England now, and it wasn't ever going to be over. Not for him. He'd faced that truth at last. A clean break, it was the only way.

He ignored the phone and locked the house. In the car he examined his supply of road maps. They were adequate for the journey. Jarib started for North Carolina.

"But what are you doing here, Malachy?" The short arms made an expansive gesture; they included not just the tomblike Abbey of St. Louis in Montparnasse, but Paris itself.

"I like simple things," the cardinal said. "This suits me better than a hotel. As to why I've come, I thought it best. Because Mr. Levi is active again. Perhaps I can help you with him."

"Help me." The other man repeated the words as if the idea hadn't occurred to him. He took off his glasses and began polishing them absentmindedly. "Help me do what? All these years, Malachy, I have done my job and you have done yours. Why should we change now?"

"Things are coming to a head, you said so yourself."

"Yes. And frankly, I don't need any unexpected trouble at this stage."

Malachy wasted no time being offended. "It's my right to be here. If the Alexandria Testament is to appear at last . . ."

The layman was much the smaller of the two, but he dominated the room. His scorn seemed to bounce from the walls and reverberate in the stiffly furnished room. "You think that's what will happen, it will appear? Like a magician's trick. Levi will suddenly walk in somewhere and turn it over to us. Tied with a blue ribbon." He looked around him. "Maybe here. It's appropriate. This must be the gloomiest room in France."

It was night, and the curtains were drawn. They were faded cretonne of no identifiable color. Only one lamp burned, and its light was feeble. The shadows seemed invested with ghosts. Somewhere a clock tolled the hour. Nine P.M. And cold. The man shivered.

"The monks don't have much money," Malachy apologized. "This monastery used to be prosperous, but today so much has changed."

"Okay, Malachy, okay. I'm not so worried about interior decoration, not even about freezing to death. Only what are you going to do now that you've come? That's the question I keep asking and you don't answer."

"I don't know. Whatever you tell me to do."

The ingratiating attitude was beginning to get on his nerves. The man sighed. He pursed his lips and cocked his head, studying the Benedictine. "Maybe . . ." he said softly.

"Maybe what?"

"I'm stretched a little thin right now. I have other things to do besides this, you know."

"I've guessed that. So?"

"So there really isn't anyone else suitable, but I can't send my regular man tomorrow. Levi knows him. I prefer he isn't aware of our interest."

"Send him where?" Then without waiting for an answer: "It doesn't matter. Send me." The cardinal's eagerness was palpable.

It wasn't such a bad idea. Amateurs were always dangerous, but he was accustomed to working with them. A priest might be different, of course. What did an old Jew like him know about priests? Besides, Malachy had an enormous emotional investment in the outcome. But they all had that. He weighed the risks quickly, and made up his mind.

"Listen, there's an auction tomorrow. At the Hôtel Drouot. Judaica. Levi went to the viewing today. Tomorrow I expect him to go to the sale. If he buys anything, I want to know exactly what it is."

Malachy had taken a notebook from a pocket beneath the scapular of his habit. He was already writing busily. "Where is the Hôtel Drouot?" He noted the address carefully and asked the time of the sale. Then the critical question: "Remember, I've never seen Mr. Levi. How will I recognize him?"

"Mid-fifties, short but well built. Pure white hair, green eyes. Good-looking, but what he is shows, a guilty drunk. Tomorrow he'll probably look very nervous as well. This auction, Malachy, it's important. I'm sure of that, only as yet I don't know why."

"Very well. I'll handle everything, my friend, don't worry."

Yes. Just the sheer novelty of being given some task besides searching through endless ancient documents perhaps. The man felt better about his decision. "Good, I'm sure you'll do fine. Stay until the sale ends or Levi leaves. Then call me immediately. You have the number?"

"Of course. Both the office and your flat."

The Jew nodded and rose. Malachy had given him a glass of wine when he came in. He hadn't touched it; now he tipped back his head and drank the whole thing. He replaced the glass on the ugly yellow oak table with oversize splayed claw feet. "Where do they find such furniture?"

"Often it's given, donations from the faithful."

He smiled. He too knew about donations from the faithful. They kept his operation functioning. And he knew how giving a small amount could obligate, cause the recipient to become dependent. He'd worked both ploys for many years. When he went to the door, he was content. Malachy Fanti's sudden appearance in Paris might prove to be a good omen after all. And the edge was still with him. The cardinal knew nothing about Sarah Myles. He'd never so much as heard her name.

"I'm sorry my arrival surprised you," Malachy said at the door. "But we have the same goal, and I only want to help. It will be good, you'll see. We'll support each other, as we've always done."

"As we've always done," the layman agreed. They shook hands warmly.

Fanti remained in the doorway until the other man was out of sight. As if watching him were going to answer the question that had always plagued him. Why had the Jew cooperated with him all these years? What did he hope to achieve? He'd never known, he didn't know now. He was sure of only one thing: The Holy Spirit had forged this odd alliance. His own role was simply to use his best judgment and follow the promptings of that Spirit. All would be made clear in the end.

Sighing, Fanti went inside and found his way through the silent, darkened monastery to the room they'd assigned him when he asked for hospitality. Not a regular cell, though he'd have preferred that. A large room obviously intended for distinguished guests, furnished with the best the abbey had to offer. Which was poor enough, and ugly too. Malachy ignored it. He'd been born to something entirely different, but life had shown him much worse than this. In 1940 it was much worse. Nineteen-forty: he closed his eyes and allowed himself to remember.

On a night in 1940, two men walked toward a waiting sleigh, some twenty yards ahead. The older one stopped before they reached it. "You understand everything, Brother Malachy? If anything is unclear, this is the time to ask."

"No, Father Abbot. Nothing is unclear."

"Good."

They resumed their progress toward the sleigh. The driver was an old man wearing a rusty black lay brother's habit beneath the heavy sheepskin jacket of a laborer. He did not look at the abbot or the novice monk when they approached. But when young Malachy dropped to his knees in the snow, the driver snatched off his knitted cap and bent his head in reverence.

The abbot lifted his hand and made the sign of the cross while he intoned the blessing for brethren going on a journey. "*Benidicamus Domino,*" he ended.

"*Deo gratias,*" Malachy and the old man sang in reply. Their voices echoed and reechoed in the crystalline mountain air, reverberated from the vaulted roofs and rounded arches of the exquisite Romanesque buildings of the Abbey of Santa Pietà sheltered in this hidden depression among the soaring peaks of Switzerland's Monte Zucchero.

But the valley did not dare to magnify the abbot's final whisper. "Don't fail us, Malachy. We're counting on you."

The train was passing through Switzerland on its way from Italy to Germany. A link between the two mainstays of the Axis, it was crowded with men in uniform. Guttural Schweizerdeutsch blended with the High German spoken by many of the passengers. It easily overcame the soft, musical Italian, particularly that dialect native to this Swiss canton called the Ticino. Malachy Fanti had been born, bred, and schooled in the Ticino. At age twenty he had joined himself to one of the canton's great treasures, the twelfth-century Monastery of Santa Pietà.

Three hours later the train entered the St. Gotthard Pass. When it emerged and began the descent to the plains, he had left his canton behind. They were still in neutral Switzerland, but Malachy had the distinct impression of having entered the war zone. He adjusted the jacket of his elegant worsted suit. Two years since he'd worn lay clothing; it felt odd. But it was his battle dress, and he was not ashamed of it.

By nightfall they were at Lucerne; by ten, at Basel and the border. The Swiss train crew disembarked here and were replaced by German workers. One of them, bedecked in hunter green with a bright red belt diagonally crossing his chest and black boots that reached to his knees, began inspecting the papers of the passengers. In ten minutes he came to Malachy. *"Ich bin der Zugführer, geben Sie mir bitte Ihren Pass."*

Malachy reached into his breast pocket; his fingers trembled. Insane. His passport identified him as Malachy Fanti, student. It had not been changed two years ago when he became a monk. Moreover, he was a Swiss and thus neutral. He was in no danger. There was no way this petty official could suspect his reason for going to Germany. He handed the document to the inspector and waited.

"Ja, all is in order," the man said finally. But he didn't hand the passport back. "What is your business in Germany, *mein Herr?"*

Malachy swallowed hard. "My grandmother is ill. Perhaps dying."

"She is a citizen of the Reich, your grandmother?"

"Yes."

The man's eyes narrowed. "You speak excellent German, not with a Swiss accent."

"My mother is from the Schwarzwald. But she is a Swiss citizen since she married my father. . . ." Too much; he should volunteer no information unless asked.

But it was a lucky indiscretion. The inspector beamed. "Ah, the Black Forest. The most beautiful part of Germany, I too was born there." He stamped the little red folder and smiled when he returned it. "I hope your grandmother recovers, *mein Herr.* Enjoy your time in the fatherland." His arm shot up in a stiff salute. *"Heil Hitler."*

"Heil Hitler," Malachy murmured without the salute. He'd al-

ready decided to do that. It seemed the polite way of behaving, and least likely to attract attention.

The border formalities had become lengthy and onerous with the advent of war. After the *Zugführer* left, there were yet endless delays. It was nearly midnight when the train crossed the final fifty kilometers and arrived at Freiburg, but his grandmother's chauffeur was waiting. He recognized the old man instantly, remembered him from all the summers he had come with his mother to see her family. Malachy's father, Professore Pietro Fanti, never accompanied his wife and son on these visits. To the chauffeur, Malachy was *il signore* Fanti. He used the Italian as some imagined extra courtesy. "Welcome, Signore Fanti. The car is waiting."

The Mercedes was ancient, but it still ran smoothly. They left the city in minutes; in half an hour they'd climbed into the Black Forest Mountains, to the village of Sankt Ulrich. Schloss Brück was dark; the turrets and gables that had so delighted his youth thrust themselves into the sky as etched black-on-black outlines, clear only in his imagination.

"Your grandmother said she would see you at breakfast, Signore Fanti. She sent her apologies for not waiting up, but she hasn't been well."

"I know. Thank you, Gerhardt. I'm sorry to have brought you out at such an hour."

The chauffeur shrugged. "It's the war. These days you have to take any train you can get." He placed Malachy's suitcase carefully at the foot of the bed, on a polished mahogany stand expressly for the purpose. "The maid will unpack this in the morning, sir. Unless you prefer that I do it now."

"No, no. Of course not. The morning is fine."

Gerhardt turned to go; then, as if remembering, he turned back and raised his right arm. *"Heil Hitler."*

Malachy forgot his planned response. It was too out of keeping in this place of enchanted childhood memory. "Good night," he murmured.

When the old man had gone, he opened his bag. His breviary was protected by fine linen undershirts and carefully folded socks. He removed it, took a large, twisted candle from the heavily carved chest in the corner, and went out into the dark corridors of the *Schloss*.

There was no need to think about direction; he allowed memory to guide his feet. Finally he was at a wide door that rose to a graceful peak some four feet above his head. The door was guarded by a fourteenth-century carved wooden Madonna. Malachy knew without looking that she had strange fat cheeks and a cloak of vibrant cerulean blue unfaded by time. As a boy he'd spent hours gazing at this particular vision of virginity; he did not pause to greet her now.

There was an intricate wrought-iron key in the lock, and he turned it and let himself into the chapel. Flickering next to the tabernacle was the sanctuary oil lamp; it shed a dull red glow over the lovely stonework, the carved ebony pews, it lit Jan Brueghel's achingly innocent triptych of the Annunciation. He felt welcomed.

Malachy genuflected, then used the candle he carried to light one of the angled tapers on the wall. There was enough light to read by now. In this private church where his forebears had prayed for countless generations, where they had resisted Luther and clung to the old faith, where they had been a beacon standing for that version of truth among the surrounding peasants, where his mother had been baptized and married, where he himself had been baptized, Malachy Fanti began softly to chant the office he had missed during the long day's journey.

Freiburg was both the same and remarkably different. The next morning Malachy parked the little Volkswagen in a narrow alley a few steps from the cathedral. He'd insisted on driving himself to town and commandeered the smallest car in his grandmother's well-equipped garage for the purpose. Even so, he felt the object of attention. There seemed to be few private cars about, only military vehicles and uniformed men. But when he approached the market square in front of the cathedral, he was on familiar ground. Rising like a symphony physically erupted from the earth was one of the glories of Christendom. A mounting crescendo of towers and steeples, carved from red-brown sandstone in delicate lacelike traceries. The stonework was magnificent beyond belief, the cathedral a harmony which caught at his breath.

Malachy craned his neck and strained to see the exquisite angel Gabriel with his horn, perched high above the west transept. Some medieval stonemason had demanded it be put there, "where no one will see it but God." Unwittingly he'd created a legend and assured that everyone who visited the cathedral would pay attention to his masterpiece.

Malachy found the figure, looked at it as long as he could hold the uncomfortable position, then dropped his eyes. Clustered in the skirts of this pure Gothic vision was a bevy of *Hausfrauen* buying and selling the stuff of daily life. He crossed the square, wending his way among stalls displaying carrots and cabbages and potatoes, ever conscious of the architectural triumph behind him.

It took him twenty minutes to reach the university precincts. Twice he was stopped by military police, who asked for his papers. An able-bodied young man in civilian clothes attracted their attention. Each time they handed him back his Swiss passport and let him go on, but he was fighting fear and nerves by the time he reached the history building and asked for Professor Wolff.

"I regret, *mein Herr,* since last week he is no longer teaching here. Is there someone else who can help you?"

"No . . . that is, I think not. I have been asked to see the *Herr Professor Doktor* by my father, Professore Pietro Fanti of Switzerland."

The woman's eyes widened momentarily; then her noncommittal expression returned. Her business was to be equally polite to all, but in the world of academe some were more equal than others. Pietro Fanti was the acknowledged world's expert in ancient Roman history. "I see. In that case perhaps you would care to try the *Professor Doktor*'s home. . . ."

A short while later he was seated in a small, cluttered study in an apartment on the third floor of a building two kilometers from the university. The man opposite him looked to be in his seventies; he was of medium height, stocky, with heavy brows that beetled over deep-set pale eyes. He insisted that they speak Italian. "You don't mind my calling you Malachy? I met you a few times when you were a small child, in your parents' home. You probably don't remember."

"I remember that I was usually trotted in to meet father's distinguished visitors. He always speaks of you with great respect, Herr Professor; he will be sorry to learn you've retired."

The old man grunted. "*Retired* is a euphemism. We indulge ourselves in many euphemisms in Germany these days." He rose and went to the window, his back to Malachy. "Look at them down there. All the little boys are having a marvelous time, they are allowed to dress up and play at soldiers, and no one says they must eat their supper and go to bed."

"It does not seem to me they are playing," Malachy said softly. "Herr Hitler seems incapable of anything but victory."

The professor grunted again. "Do you know why I am sitting here rather than in my office at the university, Malachy?" He didn't wait for a reply. "My paternal grandfather was a Jew. It's well known. So it was useless for me to demand my rights of tenure, and soon those buffoons calling themselves the Gestapo will come for me and insist I wear a little yellow star on my sleeve. Soon after that I will be 'relocated' to a camp to await my deportation from the fatherland."

"But surely, a man of your reputation . . . To be one-quarter Jewish, what difference can it possibly make?"

Wolff turned back to his visitor and did not attempt to hide the tears in his eyes. "All the difference in the world, my young friend. All the difference."

Malachy was both embarrassed and moved. He opened his mouth but couldn't find anything to say. Wolff became businesslike again. "Forget this, I'm being maudlin. I am an old man, and it doesn't matter very much where I finish my days. Only the work matters. That's why they've sent you, of course. Your father and your abbot, they've explained?"

"Only that I am to collect some documents from you. Something you are anxious to have in safekeeping until this war ends."

Wolff sat down heavily. "Some documents . . . Yes, I suppose that is not a bad description." He leaned forward, pinning the young man with his pale eyes. "But these documents are the most precious I have unearthed in a lifetime as a historian. And in the present climate for them to remain here is disaster. The truths to which they point will never be made public. You must get them out of Germany, Malachy! No matter what, this you must do."

"I will try, Herr Professor."

"No! That is not good enough. You must not fail, my young

friend. If you do, madnesses like the one infesting Germany now will continue. And scholarship will be set back a millennium."

"I will get them out. I promise."

"*Gott sei Dank,*" the old man murmured, slipping into his native German, acting as if the word were itself the deed. "Now I can be at peace, whatever happens." He walked to the sideboard and poured two small glasses of whiskey. "It is early for schnapps, but this is an occasion. Besides, very soon they will take away my whiskey and my study and my books and everything else. They are doing that, you know. Confiscating all the property of German Jews, rich and poor alike. It is said to be reparation for the evils visited by them on the fatherland."

"But you are not a Jew," Malachy protested.

"You still don't see the point, do you? Anyway, what does it matter?"

They toasted each other and drank. When their glasses were empty, the professor opened a drawer in his desk and withdrew a folder. "This was my attempt to be clever. These papers are totally unimportant, a translation of parts of Josephus's account of the Jewish wars against the Romans. The material has been worked over a hundred times. It's ancient history in the most pejorative sense of the phrase. But I put my treasure among them." He withdrew four handwritten sheets, but he did not immediately pass them to Malachy.

Wolff stared at the pages for a moment, then looked up. "If I tell you that what is in here could prove the existence of an entirely new account of the years immediately after the death of Jesus, what would you say, Malachy?"

Malachy's spine stiffened. "I would say that people have been trying to discredit our Lord from the moment He was born until now. There is nothing new in that."

"Ah, the monk speaks. No, you misunderstand me. It is not the life of Jesus that is involved. Not even His death and resurrection. We are still left to make our own judgments about the truth or falsehood of that remarkable claim."

He drew his fingers over the papers, slowly, lovingly. "This is far more subtle, my friend. And for the world as it is, more important. Six years ago, before any of us knew what was really happen-

185

ing here, what the election of Hitler portended, I was in Egypt, doing research at the University of Alexandria. My find was simply an accident. I'm told you too have the makings of a scholar; by now you must know that the best discoveries are usually like that."

He smiled, and Malachy smiled back. "There is a delightful word for it in English," the younger man said. "Serendipity."

"Yes. I admire the language. Even nonsense sounds wonderfully complex with such an immense vocabulary. But we digress, and there isn't much time. Tell me, what do you know of your compatriot Carl Jung?"

It seemed a non sequitur, but Malachy didn't allow his puzzlement to show. "Very little. He's a psychiatrist, is he not?"

"Of a sort. An extraordinary mind. You must tell your father that I suggest he discuss my findings with Herr Doktor Jung. Your abbot, too. They will understand."

His grandmother, the Countess Maria de Brück, was waiting lunch for him. She could not come down to the great dining hall of the castle any longer. Instead he joined her in a small room in her private quarters. It looked out on the rolling foothills of the Black Forest Mountains, still covered in snow. But it was late March and the doors to a small balcony were open and the sun was warm, the air seeming to smell of spring. The countess lifted her cheek for his kiss. Her skin was creased and dry, and she seemed to him incredibly fragile; still, her eyes were sharp and clear, her words direct.

"So now you will take the time to tell me what you're doing here, Malachy."

"Mother wished me to see you, *Grossmutter*. She's been worried about your health."

"And because an old lady is ill, they let you out of your monastery and sent you here? In the middle of a war? When Switzerland protects her neutrality like a virgin her honor? Malachy, I am sick, but I'm not crazy, and my brains haven't dried up along with my body. Besides, your father wrote me about this visit, not your mother. Your father cannot tolerate me. So why are you here?"

He laughed. "To see you, whatever you think. And I will go home and report that you are as tough as ever."

She snorted and motioned for him to pour her more wine. "This is a 1912 Château Lafite, there are three dozen bottles left in the cellar, and I intend to drink them all before I die. Enjoy it, my little monk; you are unlikely to taste anything so extraordinary for the rest of your life. All the great vineyards will be wrecked in this stupid war."

Malachy leaned forward, holding his heavy crystal goblet, but ignoring its contents. "Do you think the war is stupid, *Grossmutter?*"

She shrugged. "All war is stupid. Grown-up men playing at soldiers."

"That's what Professor Wolff said."

"Ah, Wolff. That is another matter entirely. He's a Jew, you know. Did your father send you here to see Wolff?"

"He's not a Jew. He had one Jewish grandfather, that's all."

"It's enough. That is one area in which I agree entirely with the Führer. They have fed on us too long, these Jews. Germany will be well rid of them."

"Fed on you how? And where are they going?"

"Fed on our art, our wealth, our culture, our resources. We have not enough land for our own people, Malachy. Not enough *Lebensraum,* as the Führer says. We cannot continue to harbor these uncouth foreigners who even bastardize our language. As to where they are to go, that is not my concern. The Führer is putting them in camps from which he'll relocate them. In Palestine, I suppose. Where they came from."

"The British cannot allow hundreds of thousands of Jews into Palestine. It will upset their Arab allies."

She shrugged delicately and readjusted the lace shawl over her shoulders. "Some solution will be found, I'm sure. All I care about is that they are out of Germany."

"All their property is being confiscated. Do you think that's right?"

"Malachy, I have just told you, they have stolen from us for generations. Now, let us close this unpleasant topic. Since you won't tell me why you are really here, tell me about your life in that peculiar mountain hideaway."

"There is nothing much to tell, *Grossmutter,* I am happy there. I believe I am doing God's will."

187

"Can you say Mass for me?"

He shook his head. "Not yet. I won't be ordained a priest for three more years. When I am, I'll ask permission to come and say my first private Mass here."

She smiled. "If it is to take three years, I will attend your first Mass from heaven. Never mind, I could never feel right receiving communion from my own grandson anyway. I'm told your Abbey of Santa Pietà is a hotbed of scholars as well."

"Yes. There is fine work going on there." He touched the breast pocket where Wolff's papers were lodged, but if she noted the gesture, she didn't comment. Instead her eyes narrowed as she examined her grandson.

"I wasn't all that surprised to hear that you'd become a monk. You are much too beautiful to be a man, and there's not enough fire in you to satisfy a woman. I always thought so. You're too highly bred, Malachy. Hilda should have gone to bed with a shepherd or a farmer before she married your elegant father. No one would have been the wiser, and her son would have some toughness in him."

He was accustomed to his grandmother's outrageous statements. He laughed, and they chatted about inconsequentials for the rest of the luncheon. But Malachy remained aware of the four carefully folded sheets of paper near his heart.

It was after three before he got a chance to read them. The professor had said nothing about it, so he presumed he was permitted to do so. Which only meant that he needn't battle with his conscience before locking the door and settling down by the window. He'd probably have done the same thing anyway. The combination of secrecy and danger and historical revision was too tantalizing to resist. First, Wolff's covering letter.

> The existence of the document known as the Alexandria Testament has been hinted at for centuries. Herein you will find proof that there is indeed such a document, and the key, obscure though it admittedly is, to discovering the whereabouts of the Testament itself.
>
> According to the references I have uncovered, the Testament deals with events occurring during the period from

the Crucifixion until the presumed death of the last person to have been a member of the band of intimates surrounding Jesus—i.e., the apostolic era. Since none of the Gospels was written until *after* the end of this era, the Testament's value is obvious. However, it is rumored to be unduly favorable to the Jewish point of view; thus there has been both controversy and secrecy. . . .

Two hours later, while he was reading Wolff's remarkable notes for the fourth time, a maid knocked and insisted on coming in to light the fire in his room. Malachy waited until she had gone, then folded the papers and took his breviary in his hands. He had said no office yet today, but it was not prayer he had in mind. Instead he tugged at the book's spine and it came loose, the way it had in Father Abbot's office last week. "Leave your own breviary here, Brother Malachy," the abbot had said. "This one is very old, but it may prove useful. Look . . ." And he'd demonstrated the way the binding could be removed and a small hiding place revealed.

Malachy rolled Wolff's papers into a tube and inserted them in the breviary. When he was finished, it was impossible to tell that there was anything unusual about the slightly battered old prayer-book. "Almost two thousand years and considerable intrigue," Father Abbot had said. "We've learned a trick or two in this holy Roman Catholic Church."

Malachy put the breviary on the table and went to stand by the now-blazing fire. He was cold and his head ached. He'd asked both the abbot and his father the same question. Why all the secrecy? Now he knew. Given the way things were, it was justified. If Wolff were right and this so-called Testament existed, the Nazis would never let the fact be known. But was Wolff right?

It wasn't the Testament itself he found incredible. Such very early apocrypha were scarce, but when they could be found, of great scholastic value. Wolff implied that these particular writings would cause a reevaluation of the relationship of the synagogue and the infant Church. So be it. But the other business. This uncanny knowledge of the document which was supposed to exist in some of the descendants of whoever composed it—that seemed to him either insane or diabolical.

For a while he pondered his culpability in taking part in the spreading of such an idea. Then he reminded himself that he was a monk acting under obedience. His conscience could be absolutely clear whatever happened. Malachy's headache disappeared, and he began to look forward to his dinner.

Two days later Gerhardt brought him to the train station in Freiburg. "I am sorry you cannot remain with us longer, Signore Fanti," the chauffeur said. "Having you in the *Schloss* made it almost like the old days."

"I'm sorry, too. But I have promised my grandmother I will return when I'm ordained. To say Mass for her."

Gerhardt smiled, knowing how unlikely it was that the old woman would last that long, never for a moment considering saying so. "Please give my respects to your mother."

"I will, yes. Good luck to you, Gerhardt. And thanks for everything."

Gerhardt lifted his peaked cap in a final farewell and turned to go. Malachy watched him leave, slightly amused because the chauffeur had forgotten the obligatory Nazi salute. When the old man was out of sight, he walked to the gate where his train was to be found. But the gate was closed and locked, and there was a neatly lettered sign saying departure would be an hour late. He sighed resignedly and headed for the benches in the far end of the station.

There were very few people about, a couple of soldiers and one mother with an infant in her arms. Two old women in shapeless gray dresses were sweeping. He paid them little attention until he noticed that both had yellow stars stitched to their sleeves. After that he couldn't take his eyes from them. They were painfully thin and haggard. A uniformed man with a rifle was standing nearby and watching them impassively.

One of the women finished sweeping and propped her broom against the wall. She disappeared into a closet and came back with a bucket and a mop. She had just finished washing the aisle between the benches when the armed guard approached. "It isn't clean enough," he said. "Do it again. On your knees with a scrub brush this time." He was grinning.

Malachy half rose, then sat down again. He must not attract

190

attention. He could change nothing that was going on here. He put his hand protectively on the suitcase containing the breviary.

The woman with the mop said something to the guard, but Malachy couldn't distinguish the words. The other one made a placating gesture and went to the closet and came back with scrub brushes. Both of them got to their knees with difficulty and began pushing the stiff-bristled implements over the cold marble floor. Malachy couldn't stop staring at them. They were about the same age as his grandmother. They wore no stockings, and their feet were clad only in felt slippers. In a few seconds he saw that one at least had no underwear under her thin cotton dress. When she bent over her task, her bony buttocks and sparse pubic hair were exposed. He felt her shame with a sudden intensity. Like a pain in his chest.

The guard continued to oversee them. When they reached the end of the aisle, moving slowly and stiffly, their hands red and raw as they gripped the brushes, the guard came closer. Deliberately, and without losing his smile, he spit in the middle of the area they had just cleaned. "Do it again."

Malachy jumped to his feet. "What kind of a man are you? Do you take pleasure in proving you're stronger than two helpless old women?"

Silence greeted his words. The few people waiting with him looked away. The cleaning women looked away, too. Only the guard noticed him. "They are Jews. Give me your papers."

The guard held out his hand, and terror swept through Malachy; all his outrage evaporated and was replaced by fear. He reached into his pocket. "I'm a Swiss national. On my way home." He was burbling. The guard knew he was afraid, and his grin widened. He studied the red passport for long seconds; finally he looked up, but didn't give it back.

"Your train is late," he said. "It may not come at all. It is probably being used to carry vital supplies for the war effort. You will need someplace to stay for the night, Herr Fanti. The police station perhaps."

At that moment the waiting room reverberated with the whistle of an incoming train, and the loudspeaker blared the news that this was the noon express for Lugano with stops at Basel and Lucerne.

Malachy had only seconds to decide what to do. Almost of its own volition his hand shot out and he snatched back the passport. The guard laughed, and Malachy turned on his heel and began to run to the gate. Then he realized that his suitcase with the precious breviary inside was still sitting on the bench.

He turned back. The guard stuck out his foot. Malachy hurtled toward the marble floor. In the fractional moment before he hit he saw one of the women swing at the guard with her brush and he was aware of shouting and cursing. Then he lost consciousness.

There was a haze of time that was not time, of pain and darkness and confusion, of not knowing where he was or who he was. When at last this miasma began to clear, his head throbbed and he ached all over. Someone was bathing his forehead. He tried to see and could make out only an old man with a beard. The face was bent very close to his and seemed distorted.

"Don't be afraid," the face said. The accent was Bavarian, which detail of minor importance came into Malachy's mind instantly. The old man pulled back a little and began to look more normal. "They brought you in a few hours ago. You fell or they hit you. You're concussed. Not seriously, I think. I'm a doctor, by the way."

"Where are we?"

"In Dachau."

"The town near Munich?"

"Not exactly. A camp of the same name. Near the town."

Malachy's mouth was painfully dry. He had trouble phrasing the question, but knowing seemed extraordinarily important. Especially now that he was remembering the station and the guard and the woman without underwear. "A relocation camp?"

The doctor smiled. "*Ja,* a relocation camp."

"But I'm not a Jew."

"I know. I examined you." The man pointed to Malachy's crotch. "You have a piece we don't have." And when Malachy looked blank: "You're not circumcised."

Malachy tried to nod, but his head ached fiercely when he moved. "I'm a Swiss," he whispered hoarsely. "A Benedictine monk from the Abbey of Santa Pietà. They can't send me to Palestine."

"Don't worry," the doctor said softly. "That's not where we're being relocated to."

One week only. Years later, when he looked back, and sometimes he couldn't prevent that, it didn't seem possible that it was only seven short days. But that's all the time Malachy spent in Dachau. It was long enough to understand. He remembered Professor Wolff's remark about euphemisms. *Relocation* was such a word. A code for forced labor, starvation, total dehumanization; for torture, for two small boys buggered in the exercise yard before his eyes, for rumors of a special house where prepubescent girls were relieved of their virginity by officers before being given to ordinary soldiers to provide less rarefied pleasure, for tales of another house where the cause of medical science was being advanced without benefit of anesthesia. And later he always needed to remind himself that he was there in 1940, before the gas and the ovens.

Nothing particularly evil happened to Malachy Fanti. They tattooed a number onto his forearm, 66357; a high number because Dachau had been opened in 1933, the year Adolf Hitler was elected chancellor of Germany. But they did so in a passionless, businesslike manner. He was not otherwise abused, not even sent out to work planting potatoes like the other men in his barracks. No one could tell him why that was; the guards refused any explanation, and his fellow inmates merely shrugged and said that nothing in Dachau made any sense. He must wait and see.

He considered demanding an interview with the officers of this place, insisting on knowing the charges against him, telling them of his distinguished lineage, reminding them that he was a citizen of a neutral power. But somehow he could not muster the energy to do any of that. For one thing he was still disoriented by his injury; for another he was immobilized by pity which had not yet had time to turn inward. So he waited and he saw, and he heard the stories, and he refused half his meager daily ration so those who worked might have more.

"Are you a priest?" one man asked him his second night in Dachau.

"No, not yet. I'm a novice monk. In three years I will be a priest. That is, I would have if . . ."

193

The other man nodded. He was only a few years older than Malachy, among the youngest of the barracks inmates. He was short, and painfully thin, of course, but he looked as if he would be even if he were not living on a starvation diet. He wore thick glasses. The earpieces were broken, so he tied them to his head with a precious bit of string. Malachy was not surprised when he said, "I am—was—studying for the rabbinate."

The young man extended his hand. "Isaac Bekstein of Deggendorf. Tell me, what do you think is the meaning of the second friend who comes to speak to Job? Bildad the Shuhite, who asks him, 'Can sentence undeserved come from the Almighty?'"

And all that night the rabbinical student and the monk discussed the meaning of Scripture in general and the Book of Job in particular, and the others sat and listened, offering opinions occasionally. When dawn broke, Malachy was appalled because they must go out and work and they'd had no sleep. But they moved with more than ordinary agility that particular morning, and he understood that somehow the discussion had given them comfort and strength.

On the first Sunday in April, Easter Sunday he later realized, it was over—for him. Two guards came, *Kapos,* Jews who were cooperating with the camp authorities and were loathed by the others because of it. They brought him to the commandant.

"Sit down, Brother Malachy. I would offer you a cigarette, but I don't imagine Benedictine monks indulge in tobacco. A drink perhaps? Yes, I thought so."

The man bore the flashed lightning of the SS on his collar. He handed a large snifter of brandy to Malachy, then clicked his heels together sharply and introduced himself. "I am Acting Commandant Felix Wolhauser, temporarily in charge of Dachau. Your case has come to my attention and that of my superiors. We regret the confusion, a fault of the sudden death of the man in charge here and an overzealous minor functionary. I am to convey to you the Führer's personal apology. And my own."

Wolhauser waited, but Malachy didn't know what to say. He drank the brandy in one swallow and set the glass on the desk.

"You are not a Jew, of course," Wolhauser continued. "And when your abbot contacted your grandmother, the countess, she made inquiries. So we discovered the error which had been made. You will be put on a train for Switzerland in an hour."

Again the German waited for some word, but Malachy was silent. Finally the commandant called a *Kapo,* and Malachy was escorted to another office, where his clothes, freshly cleaned and pressed, were waiting. He changed under the eye of the guard, and when he was dressed, the man produced his suitcase. "You'll find all your things there," the *Kapo* said. "They're very efficient, these Nazi supermen."

There was something terrible in his voice, and Malachy, who had swiftly learned to despise the *Kapos,* looked at the man with a share of his newly wakened pity. When the *Kapo* led him to the door, he hesitated. He wanted to go to the barracks and say good-bye to the men with whom he'd lived this past week. Especially the doctor and young Isaac Bekstein. But he knew without asking that it wouldn't be permitted. Still, he hung back.

The commandant had come to bid him farewell. "Is something wrong, Brother Malachy?"

"No . . . only . . ."

"Yes?"

He couldn't form the words. I wish to stay, he wanted to say. I can be of some help to the others. They need so much. I can talk to them about God. His mouth was dry with terror, and nothing came out.

"Have you examined your suitcase?" Wolhauser asked. "My understanding is that all your things are in order. Perhaps it is better if you check. We wouldn't want to disappoint the countess."

Dumbly Malachy hoisted the case to a table and opened it. He riffled through the clothing and saw with a shock that the breviary was there. He had not thought of it, or of what it contained, from the moment he wakened in this place. "Everything seems to be here." The sentence came out in a hoarse croak.

"Good. Now, my car is waiting. Please . . ." the German gestured to the gate and followed Malachy out. Wolhauser opened the door for him himself, and when Malachy was inside, he leaned forward. "We are assured by the countess and your abbot that you are a young man of discretion, Brother Malachy. We count upon it."

In his head he shouted, No! I cannot desert these people in their need. Take me back. But the only sound was the commandant's loud "*Heil Hitler*" and the revving of the engine.

195

The train brought him as far as Friedrichshafen; from there he took a ferry across Lake Constance. The water was bright blue and very calm. Incipient spring green clothed the branches of the willows by the shore. Winter is over, he thought, and tried to smile. But his face was stiff. He crossed into Switzerland at Romanshorn. Only then did he take the breviary from the suitcase.

He was told the train for Lugano would be along in twenty minutes. Malachy left the suitcase on the platform; he held the only baggage that mattered in his hands, and found the men's room. His fingers shook, but he managed to loosen the binding of the breviary. The tube of papers was in place. Sighing deeply, he leaned against the tiled wall.

It was for this reason that he'd come back. God wanted him to get these papers out of Germany. Yes. Nothing to feel guilty about.

The train came and he boarded. He'd been provided with a first-class ticket, and he was grateful because the other five places in the compartment were unoccupied. For the first time since leaving Dachau he put his head back and closed his eyes. It was not sleep that came.

Malachy, Malachy, could you not watch with me in my agony? I am going to be crucified again, Malachy. Will you not stand beneath my cross?

The wheels of the train whispered the words over and over. Malachy Fanti wept.

No one understood. "But what do you propose we do, Brother Malachy?"

The monk, who was excruciatingly thin because he had lost more weight in the past month in his monastery than he had in Dachau, ran trembling fingers through his hair. "I don't know, but something. People must know what is going on in those camps." He brightened. "Perhaps I could tell my story to the newspapers."

The abbot smiled. "A monk giving a press conference. An interesting idea. But would they believe you, Malachy? And if they did, what could we Swiss do?"

"But if it was told here, the British would learn of it, and the Americans."

"The British are already fighting the Nazis," the abbot said softly. "And doing everything they can to involve the Americans. Would they fight harder for a few Jews, do you think?"

"It's not a few, Father Abbot." Malachy leaned forward, his hands pressed on the older man's desk. "It's all the Jews in Germany, even men like Wolff, who only had one Jewish grandfather. And in my barracks there were Bavarian men whose families have been German since the Middle Ages. They say there are camps full of Poles and Slovaks. Every Jew in territory taken by Hitler is at risk; there must be millions of them." He suppressed a sob. "The thing is, most Germans just want to be rid of them. If the Allies would offer to take them, arrange some kind of relocation . . ." His voice trailed away. There was no sob this time. His anguish was beyond tears.

The abbot laid his hands over Malachy's. "My dear brother, you have been through a horrendous experience and you're upset. But think of what you're saying, millions of Jews. Where could they be relocated to? Who would want them? And aren't you forgetting the most important thing, the papers you brought out with you? Miraculously brought out, I might add."

"Papers," Malachy whispered. "People are being enslaved, tortured—I brought out only papers."

"Your father would weep to hear you say that. Scholarship, Malachy. It's what makes man a civilized creature; for men like us it is the only way to save our souls."

"Yes, Father Abbot."

The abbot recognized acquiescence, not agreement. "Malachy, it is my opinion that this document of which Herr Doktor Wolff speaks may be of vital importance to the Church. It may become imperative that we control what it reveals, not the enemies of Christ." He rose and drew the young monk to his feet. "Walk with me awhile. Outside in the sunshine."

And in the ancient cloistered arcades of Santa Pietà the abbot and his charge walked and talked. The older man spoke of the great crime of the Jews, of their rejection of the promised Messiah. He reiterated the long history of Israel's infidelities, of her condemnation out of the mouths of her own prophets. "It is very sad, but perhaps they have brought this thing upon themselves. But you, Malachy, you have been given a life's work, I'm sure of it. You are to locate this document, this Alexandria Testament. And to see that it is never allowed to poison minds against our Lord's Church."

Malachy stopped walking and bent his head. He did not know what to say. Unconsciously he was rubbing his fingers over his tattooed forearm.

The abbot put his hands on Malachy's shoulders. "You have been tested like gold before the fire, my son. And you have been found worthy. You will do heroic things, Malachy Fanti. You will protect Holy Mother Church; our Lord has chosen you to do so."

$\mathcal{S}even$

WEDNESDAY, NOVEMBER 21

Bristol was exactly what Hamish Durant had said it was, trendy and high tech. When the town on the Bristol Channel saw its economic base slithering down the same ways that had once launched the thousands of ships it built, it created a new image: office towers of concrete and steel and black glass, arty red-brick shopping arcades with planters in the middle and little shops selling handwoven tea cozies and the latest fashions. Despite the self-consciousness of it all, it might have been fun if Sarah weren't so nervous.

Tim picked up her mood; it was impossible not to. "You're the proverbial cat on a hot tin whatever," he said at what seemed like the crack of dawn, over coffee and sticky currant buns in one of the few cafés already open.

"I know. I can't help it. I keep thinking it's Ivy's money I'm going to spend. And a damned lot of it at that." She bent over the catalog yet again. "You're sure we should go as high as a thousand pounds for this chest of drawers? It's not even a signed piece."

"Dead sure. It was made in London, mid-nineteenth century, but it's absolutely Georgian in feeling, not Victorian. And the workmanship is marvelous. The drawers are all fronted with rosewood, and the molding's ebony. The problem is whether you can get it for a thousand. I don't think any dealer will go higher, but a private buyer might."

Sarah had to accept his judgment; for one thing he'd been to the viewing over the weekend, for another, he simply knew more than she did. She swallowed the last of her coffee. "Let's go then. Sitting here is driving me nuts."

The salerooms were on the outskirts of town, in a building that looked like nothing so much as an abandoned warehouse. Rows of folding chairs had been set up, pushed as close together as was physically possible. The sale was to start at nine and it was only eight-thirty; the place was empty, cold, and forbidding. Sarah surveyed it with a sinking heart. "Looks like they're expecting a crowd."

"They'll get it," Tim said. "There aren't all that many lots, but there's some marvelous stuff going on the block. That's why we're here." He grinned at her. "Cheer up. This is supposed to be fun; there are those who even find it addictive. And here's your first lesson. Sit in the back. Novices always want to be up front, close to the auctioneer. That's no good. When you're bidding, they never miss you. But if you're in the front, you can't see who's bidding against you, and that can be important."

They took seats in the rear. Within minutes the room started filling up. Tim nodded to various people; he even introduced Sarah to a few. "A friend from America," he said. "On a buying trip, she's furnishing a new house." He lied without batting an eye.

Promptly at nine a man and two women made their way to the dais in the front. The man was the auctioneer; the two women were clerks. "Good morning, milords, ladies and gentlemen," he said. He smiled as if that were a bit of a joke. Were there any lords among the crowd come to buy? There could be. To judge by their dress, there was everything present from bag ladies to people who wore only things with designer initials.

The auctioneer cleared his throat. "This sale is taking place according to the Auctions Act of 1927, and its rules will be strictly adhered to." He spoke quickly, reciting a formula by rote. No one seemed to be paying any attention. He unfurled a sheet of hard-backed paper and hung it from the front of his desk.

"That's a copy of the act," Tim murmured. "It makes it illegal for dealers to conspire to hold down a price. That's what's called a ring."

He seemed prepared to go on explaining the seamy side of the business, but Sarah hushed him. "Ssh . . . I want to hear."

"All lots are exactly as advertised in the catalog," the auctioneer was saying. "All statements made therein are true to the best of our knowledge and belief, and no further warranty is made for them. All sales are final on the fall of the hammer, and payment will be collected immediately after the last lot is sold. Any credit arrangements must have been made beforehand. Now, let us begin. May we have the first lot, please."

Two porters wearing faded blue cotton jackets over nondescript trousers appeared from behind a curtained area. They were carrying a wicker rocking chair and two fat wicker lamp bases without shades. "Lot number one," the auctioneer said loudly. "A twenties-style woven rocker and two table lamps, not tested. Will someone start me off at thirty pounds?"

He waited a moment, but nothing happened. "Come along, folks, they're over fifty years old. And not being made any longer. Ah, a lady who knows value. Thank you, madam. I have thirty, do I hear thirty-five? Thank you. Forty? Thank you. Against you, first bidder. Forty-five. I'm looking for fifty. I see you, sir. I have fifty and I'm looking for sixty. Sixty in the front here. Looking for seventy. . . ."

It was incredibly fast. And the crowd who'd first indicated that none among them would pay thirty pounds for the three items quickly bid them up to a hundred and ten. "Going once, going twice." The man brought down his wooden hammer with a smart rap. "Sold for one hundred and ten pounds to the lady in the blue coat. May we have your name, madam? Thank you." The clerks wrote busily. "Lot number two," the auctioneer said.

By the fifth lot Sarah was having a marvelous time. The sixth was something Ivy had indicated she'd buy if she didn't have to go over a couple of hundred dollars. It was made up of three items, a small, unsigned etching depicting an unidentified eighteenth-century street, a nicely turned wooden candlestick, and a rather lovely wooden tray with unusual snake's-head handles.

Sarah scratched a hasty note and passed it to Tim. "Not a penny more than a hundred and twenty-five," it said.

"Pounds or dollars?" he hissed.

"Pounds, naturally," she whispered back.

The auctioneer was asking for an opening bid of forty; eventually he got it. The movement was swift up to seventy-five; then it seemed to stop. "I have seventy-five and I'm looking for eighty," the auctioneer said.

Sarah raised the hand holding her rolled catalog. Not too high. Casually, the way she'd seen the others do it. "Ah," the man said. "New money. Eighty bid, looking for eighty-five. More new money. Eighty-five and against you, madam."

He was speaking to Sarah. She gestured restrainedly again. The bidding went on. Two minutes later lot number six was knocked down to Sarah Myles at 110 pounds. "This is fun!" she whispered to Tim.

He grinned at her yet again. "Don't waste too much energy. We have to drive all the way to Dover after we get out of here."

"Don't worry," Sarah assured him. "I'm raring to go." Then she turned her attention back to the dais and the drama about to ensue over a pair of superb Queen Anne side chairs that Ivy wanted.

Three hours later the sale was ended. As a first effort it couldn't have been more successful. Ivy had selected six lots, and Sarah had managed to buy five of them, three for less than the limit Ivy had determined. They waited in the queue to pay, Sarah wrote a check on the English bank account Ivy had established, and it was done. Tim would arrange the shipments to the U.S. later.

"C'mon, Miss High-powered Tycoon," he said to her as she put away her checkbook. "We don't even have time for a meal, just some sandwiches on the fly. We've to be at the Dover dock by two."

It was Sarah who'd insisted they must cross the Channel by ship. "It's awful," Tim warned her. "The ferries are crammed with screaming kids. The ones who aren't screaming have plugs in their ears and move their lips and jerk their shoulders."

"All the same," Sarah said. "It's my first time. I want to savor it. Not just get whisked from one airport to the next."

She'd envisioned a long, slow sailing, something old-fashioned and romantic. It was nothing like that. They'd compromised on the hydrofoil and boarded at Dover at two-thirty. Thirty minutes later they docked at Calais. "Set your watch to four," Tim told her. "France is an hour ahead of the U.K."

He had a rental car waiting, and the three-hour drive from Calais to Paris made up for the too-speedy crossing. It gave Sarah a chance to realize she was really in France, headed for Paris.

The highway wound through isolated bits of farmland hedged about with suburbs and urban sprawl; there was nothing extraordinary about it, except for the plantings. "The French are the world's best arborists," Tim said with enthusiasm. "I don't think any French garden is as good as the best in Britain, but we don't do anything as wonderful as that."

He was referring to the roadside display of tall cherry trees faced down with spreading ornamental almonds. Even leafless, they were elegant sentinels. He told Sarah their names; she wouldn't have known otherwise. "In the spring they bloom one after the other. When the almonds finish flowering, the cherries start."

"I didn't realize you were so interested in horticulture."

Tim smiled shyly. "My secret dream. I want to buy some fantastic country house and make a great garden. The only problem is that it will cost millions."

"It would be hard to find anything more beautiful than Tiverton Manor."

"That's my father's. And as far as he's concerned, the gardens are nothing but a space to park lorries delivering auction goods."

She understood a great deal after that.

Doubtless there were many auctions taking place that day 'round the globe. In Paris there was one that to the world at large was far more important than the furniture sale in Bristol. Starting at 10:00 A.M., Judaica was going on the block at the Hôtel Drouot. Fragments of the long, painful history of a hounded people were to be sold to the highest bidder.

To Dov Levi the process was nerve-racking and obscure. Most of the time he couldn't tell who in the crowded room paid forty thousand francs for an old silk tallith, a hundred thousand for an ornate silver menorah. The buyers signaled their bids in what seemed to Dov invisible ways, but the auctioneer saw them. He would nod and prod the others higher.

Through most of it Levi simply sat and waited. The hall was cold and drafty. He wanted a drink. The whole thing was crazy anyway. How would he dare try to outbid these free spenders? Eighteen thousand, he'd told Yakov. But nothing here had thus far gone for less than twice that. He wouldn't dare spend so much of old Yakov's money.

The auctioneer announced a break for lunch. The sale would resume at two. Levi found a bar and ordered first a cognac, then a bottle of Bordeaux. Young but not bad. Not all that cheap either, but he needed it. Yesterday he'd been flat broke. Today he had four crisp new fifty-franc notes in his pocket, as well as Yakov Tench's blank check. The cash had been waiting for him this morning in an unmarked envelope at the hotel desk. Every week for ten years it had been thus. Since he'd been told he must leave Israel and come to Paris. He seldom thought about the source of the money. Now he was simply grateful that he could pay for his drink.

The barman was friendly. "You wish to eat something, monsieur? The choucroute garnie is good. Madame is from Alsace."

Levi ordered a plate of the sauerkraut and sausage, but only managed a few mouthfuls. His stomach was churning. At one-thirty he headed back, terrified that they would begin before the stated time and he'd miss out.

The doors to the auction hall were still locked. A few early birds like himself stood around and waited. Some compared catalogs and notes and discussed the merits of the offerings and probable prices. "None of the jewelry's worth a centime," he heard a man say.

A woman nodded and laughed. "They always think they can get away with that business of uncertain provenance. Not with this crowd. It's mostly dealers."

"What can they say?" the man said. "Provenance Printemps?"

Levi felt a surge of hope. If nobody here was interested in anything without a sure pedigree, he just might get it. He paced the foyer, feeling the sausage he'd gagged down roil in his belly. Somewhere chimes sounded and an old man unlocked the doors to the hall known since 1980 as Le Nouveau. As he went through them, Levi became aware of another man watching him. In his sixties, tall and slim, gray-haired, dressed in black with a small white collar. A priest. Levi met his eyes and nodded tentatively. Did he know the fellow from somewhere? No, probably not. The nod was barely returned.

The bracelet was lot 263. It was called at a few minutes past four. An auction amateur with no knowledge of technique, Levi responded to the opening request for two thousand francs. He waved his catalog in the air. The auctioneer acknowledged him and asked for four thousand. Apparently he got it, though Levi didn't know from whom.

"Do I hear six thousand?"

Levi waved his catalog again, harder this time. And again when the demand was for ten thousand, then twelve, then fifteen. He began to sweat, but he knew his arm would shoot up whatever the call. When he signaled his willingness to pay twenty thousand, he put his other hand in his pocket and grasped Yakov's blank check. He waited.

"Twenty thousand once," the auctioneer said. "Twenty thousand twice." He searched the faces of the crowd. Finally the small wooden hammer fell. "Twenty thousand three times. Sold to the gentleman in the front."

Dov realized that the gentleman in the front was himself, and he slumped against the back of his chair in an ecstasy of relief.

Malachy watched the Israeli leave the Hôtel Drouot. He knew the bracelet was in his pocket. He considered following him, but decided against it. That would be taken care of by the professional. His brief extended only to the auction. He watched until the Jew disappeared down the stairs to the metro. Then, rubbing his forearm unconsciously, he walked to a telephone kiosk on the corner.

In England Hamish Durant was waiting. Malachy had alerted him earlier. Durant's hand lay over the telephone on the museum-quality Jacobean desk. He wore a ruby signet ring which had once belonged to Alfred Lord Tennyson. It winked in the gloom of the unlit room, an odd contrast with his shabby bathrobe and slippers. When the phone rang, its sound was muted, something Hamish had carefully arranged years before. He lifted the receiver instantly. "Yes?"

"He bought a bracelet."

"Describe it, please."

"A copper bangle with three turquoises. He paid twenty thousand francs."

"Why so expensive? Were the stones extraordinary, the workmanship?"

"All I know is what it says here." Malachy read aloud the catalog description of the piece. "That's as much as I can tell you. I presume it was expensive because of its age."

"They were only guessing at its age," Hamish said tartly. "That's what 'Provenance uncertain' means. A trap for the unwary. Do you know where he got the money?"

"He must have borrowed it. I'm told he's friendly with an old man, another Israeli expatriate. He saw him yesterday. Levi was very excited at the sale. Almost hysterical. Something's happening."

"After so long," the man in England said with satisfaction. "Your patience has been rewarded."

"Maybe, if it's God's will. We must wait and see."

"And pray."

"Yes. Meanwhile, you will try to learn something about this bracelet?"

"Of course."

The connection was broken. Malachy waited a moment, preparing himself to make his next call, the one to his . . . what? Colleague? No, that wasn't right. *Accomplice* was the word, distasteful though it might be. The priest sighed. Dealing with the man in England was easier, Malachy understood his motives: a zeal for God's holy Church; an understanding of the threat international Jewry could pose.

But the other one, what did he want? The glory of the discovery? Perhaps. It was the only answer that occurred, but it was weak, and Malachy knew it. Yet without their alliance no progress at all would have been made. Malachy knew that, too. And he had to be dealt with carefully. So he'd admit to having called England; it was safer. No details, of course. He'd just say he knew an antiques expert and called him to ask about the bracelet. It would be good for the other man to realize that Malachy too could take a little initiative.

"Look, Yakov. The catalog put it around the first century of the Common Era. But it may be older. The copper could have come from King Solomon's mines." Levi's voice shook. Gently he laid the bracelet on the table, and he and the old man stared at it.

"Beautiful." Yakov sighed. "A beautiful thing."

It was a bangle about two inches wide, worked in dull greenish brown copper, rich with the patina of age. The three turquoises were inset in the copper, a large one in the center and two smaller ones on either side. "Beautiful," Levi agreed.

Tench's daughter, Zelah, joined them. "And for this piece of beauty you paid twenty thousand francs? So Papa thinks he's broke and he can't lend me any money."

"I have to consider my old age," Yakov muttered.

Dov and the woman looked at each other and grinned. Zelah was tall like her father, but without his stoop. She carried herself proudly. She was forty years old and wore her dark gray-flecked hair in a close-cropped helmet that hugged her head. Zelah was an attractive woman—as long as one didn't object to her strength.

Zelah spoke not to Dov but to her father. "Why don't you give it to me, Papa? I can wear it sometimes, which is more than either of you can do."

Dov snatched the thing from the table and held it in his hand. "No. That's not possible."

Zelah laughed, not unkindly. "Only a suggestion."

"The bracelet belongs to Dov," Yakov said. "Eventually he'll pay us back the money. On the same day the *meshiach* comes."

"I'm holding my breath," Zelah said.

207

Dov grinned at her. They understood each other. At least he thought so most of the time. Once, a few years ago, they'd been lovers for two weeks. He'd been surprised at how much joy that gave him, but Zelah put an end to it. "I don't want to feel like this about you," she'd told him. "I don't want your pain inflicted on me."

"I'm not in pain," he'd insisted.

"Yes, you are; you've lived with it so long you don't even recognize it anymore. It's part of you, like your breathing. But it's there, my darling. I smell it when I'm near you, feel it when I touch you. I can't live with it, Dov."

And she hadn't. They'd drifted out of loving back to something between that and friendship; neither of them could have said exactly what. In any case, it was Zelah's choice. Dov wanted a lot more, but his attempts to change things were halfhearted and ineffectual. Because in large measure he'd given up trying to change anything. These days he simply accepted.

Until he ran out and bought this bracelet with Yakov's twenty thousand francs. Why had he done it? Even now he didn't know.

He looked at Zelah as if she might have the answer. She shook her head, almost as if she'd read his mind, and took a Gauloise from the pocket of her jeans. She lit it before Levi could, blowing the smoke out her nostrils, watching him through narrowed dark eyes. "Okay, now you've got this eighth wonder of the world, Mr. Levi the collector, what are you going to do with it?"

No, Zelah didn't have the answer. Why should she? "I don't know," he said sadly. "I think I must wait."

He spotted the other man as soon as he got back to the hotel. Ariel was sitting in a chair with sagging springs next to a lamp that hadn't worked for three months. He was pretending to read a newspaper in the dark. Levi sighed deeply and crossed the lobby.

"This is a hell of a dump you live in, Dov," Ariel said in Hebrew.

"Yes, so why don't you just go away?"

"I will, as soon as we've had our little talk." He rose and took Levi by the arm, leading him out the door. Dov went without protest.

They didn't speak until they'd entered a nearby bistro and found a table. "The cassoulet is wonderful here," Ariel said.

"I don't like beans. Anyway, I'm not hungry."

"Eat, Doveleh, you should keep up your strength." The use of the diminutive was inappropriate; Ariel was some twenty years younger than Levi.

Levi recognized the tactic for what it was. He did not bother to protest. And he was conscious of the bracelet in his pocket. He wondered if Ariel could see any bulge. "My strength is sufficient for my needs, Ariel. What do you want?"

The waiter came and Ariel didn't answer. He ordered the cassoulet and a beer. Levi said he'd have a bottle of Alsatian Riesling.

"For yourself, a whole bottle?" the younger man asked when the waiter left. "You're drinking too much, Doveleh."

"Your concern is touching. Tell me what you want."

"We want you to take a little trip."

"Where? To do what?"

"To New York. Don't look like that. It will be good for you, it's exciting in New York. Take your mind off your troubles. Anyway, English is really your mother tongue, right? Not Hebrew."

"Not exactly. And I don't want to go to America. Get somebody else."

The food came. Ariel tucked his napkin into his collar and began spooning beans into his mouth. He prodded the dish to find the slices of smoked pork and preserved goose. "You should have ordered some of this, it's wonderful. You don't keep kosher, do you?"

"You know I don't. You and your boss have spent years convincing me you know everything." Dov poured a glass of wine. "Get some other poor fool to go to New York."

"Not my decision, Doveleh. We both serve the same master. I do what he tells me, and so do you."

Dov looked sour, but he didn't deny the fact. "When?"

"You leave tonight at ten. Be at Orly by eight-thirty." Ariel extracted an envelope from his pocket and pushed it across the table. Levi didn't touch it. "Tickets and a thousand dollars U.S.," the younger man said.

"What am I to do once I get there?"

"You'll be contacted."

"I have commitments here; you know that, too. How long am I to be gone?"

Ariel shrugged. "Can't say, my job is only to get you on the road."

"Shit," Levi cursed softly.

"Ain't it the truth," Ariel said.

Levi took the envelope and left the bistro. Ariel kept smiling until he was gone; then he frowned and pushed away the half-eaten cassoulet. He'd suddenly lost his appetite.

"A puppet on a string," he told the old man later. "What do you get out of this? Why keep jerking him around? The poor bastard isn't even useful. He's practically an alcoholic, and he doesn't know fuck all about intelligence work."

Yitzhak Beklem leaned back in his chair. It was a big chair, and he was a small man. He looked lost in it. He was completely bald, but he often ran questing fingers through his nonexistent hair. He did so now. "I lost it all in 1943. One morning it started falling out, and in a week it was all gone. Have I told you that, Ariel?"

"Oh, shit. Yes, you've told me. I know all the stories, Yitzhak, yours and the rest of them. Why else am I part of your cockamamy private army? But what's it to do with Dov Levi? He's a Jew, for chrissake. He's not a Nazi."

"I never said he was."

"So?"

"So he knows something. He doesn't know he knows, but I do. And when he finds out what it is, then we have to be in charge." Yitzhak removed his thick glasses and rubbed his eyes. "Levi is a pawn, but in a good cause. Don't feel sorry for him. Okay, he doesn't understand, but he's doing a *mitzvah*. So am I, in a way."

Ariel shook his head. "It's too convoluted for me. Too talmudic. You should have been a rabbi, not a self-appointed guardian of the nation."

Beklem laughed. "A rabbi. I had such an idea once. My studies were interrupted by my Nazi well-wishers. They showed me the importance of other things."

"What's Levi going to do for us in New York?"

"I don't know. I'll think of something. I'm trying to jog his memory, that's all. A *mitzvah,* as I said." And what in the old Irgun days they would have called a rearguard action. Better to get Dov away from Paris. Malachy Fanti was unlikely to follow him all the way to America.

In Los Angeles the phone rang at 7:00 A.M. Rhonda Kane woke with a start, instantly sure something terrible had happened to one of her three children. "Yes, hello. Who is this?"

"Yitzhak Beklem, how are you, my dear?"

"Oh, Jesus, have you any idea what time it is?"

"In Paris it's four P.M. Time for tea."

"Well, it's the crack of dawn here. You scared me to death. What do you want?"

"I want you to go see Sam. Tomorrow. Take Myra."

"I saw Sam two months ago. And Myra's in school. She's sixteen. I can't drag her to New York on a few hours' notice."

"Sam loves Myra, we both know that. Tomorrow, Rhonda, better yet, late tonight. After midnight maybe. Something that with the time difference will get you to Sam's in time for lunch."

Jack Kane was awake by now. He knew his wife was talking to Yitzhak. It couldn't possibly be anyone else. He lit a cigarette and listened to her argue with the Israeli. Not that it would do her any good.

"You're unreasonable. You think you can just push us all around, control our lives. Well, you can't."

"Of course I can't. Control, what a crazy word to use. Rhonda, darling, I'm asking you to do me a favor. So maybe it's a little inconvenient. If you don't want to, it's okay. We can talk about the December bookings instead."

The Kanes owned a travel agency. They'd opened it in 1959. Babies they'd been then, twenty-four years old and married two years. But things happened, and soon afterward Yitzhak Beklem entered their lives. Today there wasn't a U.S. tour operator with better Israeli contacts, or one with a bigger share of the lucrative trade. Kane Travel did an enormous business during the holiday season. Only if Rhonda didn't go to New York, she'd suddenly discover hotel rooms reserved months ago held by somebody else, and blocks of previously arranged airline tickets disappeared.

"Okay, okay. I'll go."

"Myra, too."

"Myra, too. What do you want me to do with Sam?"

"Nothing unusual. Just visit. Say you and Myra came to shop. Hanukkah presents from Fifth Avenue."

"There's nothing on Fifth Avenue we can't get on Rodeo Drive."

Yitzhak sighed. "You'll think of something, Rhonda. I have complete confidence in you."

"Yeah, I know. Your confidence is killing me. How long do we have to stay?"

"Until you hear from me. A few days probably."

She hung up without saying good-bye.

"Yitzhak?" Jack asked.

"Who else? You heard. Myra and I have to go to New York. More tender loving care for Sam Stein." She took the cigarette from his fingers and puffed angrily.

"Okay, it's not so terrible. Yitzhak's been good to us, honey. What's the harm in doing him a favor?"

Rhonda turned to him. "I don't know, Jack, what's the harm? Couldn't be that you'll be screwing Elaine twice a day with me gone, could it?"

Elaine was his secretary. He did screw her occasionally, but not twice a day. Rhonda was forgetting his age. "Don't be silly, honey, I stopped that crap years ago." He reached over and pushed the strap of her nightgown off one plump shoulder. "Maybe if I ever find anybody gives better head than you do, I'll be tempted. So far it hasn't happened."

Rhonda knew he was lying, but she giggled anyway, and worked her way down in the bed.

Beklem had gone home to make the call to Los Angeles because he was a little tired today. Now he remembered telling Rhonda it was time for tea, only what he really needed was something stronger. He poured himself a very small cognac. The apartment was overly warm, but he liked it that way, liked to walk around in his shirtsleeves even when it was cold and gray and drizzly outside, like now.

The window of his living room looked out on a neutral street in a neutral neighborhood; safe, stolid, middle class. The interior of the flat was the same. It had been rented furnished ten years ago, when France became a better center of operations than Israel. It was easier to bring in foreign currency here; the exchange rates were more stable. And it was harder for officialdom to look over his shoulder. The worldwide band of secret contributors who, often unknowing, supported Yitzhak's network could do so with more security.

He felt no guilt about those many strangers whose money was the lifeblood of his work, not even about those who had no idea where their contributions were really going. When a European group of Arab sympathizers was discredited, Israel was strengthened. When a few more Jewish families who'd managed to get out of the USSR were persuaded to go to Israel and forget about America, Israel was strengthened. When some misguided intellectual was convinced that he shouldn't publish a book that made Zionism suspect, Israel was strengthened. Yitzhak protected that tiny strip of precious Middle Eastern real estate in ways that Mossad and Shin Bet did not dare, because ultimately they were arms of the government. Yitzhak was wholly independent, answerable to no one but himself. And he did what he did for Jews everywhere, because if Israel died, they'd all be as good as dead. God knows he didn't do it for self-aggrandizement.

The nondescript things that had come with the Paris flat filled it yet: a round oak table on spindly legs, a couch covered in faded damask. Beklem sipped his cognac and sighed. In Jerusalem it was late morning. Probably it was sunny. And warm. It was usually warm in Jerusalem in November.

Despite his elected exile, Beklem yet owned a little house on the edge of what had been the Jewish quarter of the Old City, looking southwest toward Bethlehem. When he bought the house, neither Jerusalem nor Bethlehem belonged to Israel. They did now. Jerusalem would be theirs forever; the last Jew in Israel would die to keep David's city. Bethlehem was in the occupied West Bank; theirs de facto if not de jure.

There was an orange tree in his backyard in Jerusalem. This time of year it was starting to fruit, small, perfect spheres that gleamed in the sun. But sour. He'd tasted them often, and they never changed. He fed the tree and pruned it and did everything he could think of. The oranges never became sweet. The only thing they were good for was being hacked into bits and turned into marmalade. Maybe if he'd married, his wife would have made marmalade from the sour oranges. No wife, no homemade marmalade for his breakfast toast.

Yitzhak took his drink into the kitchen. It was much pleasanter than the living room. It too was old and shabby—a faded oilcloth covered a table with metal legs, and a chipped enamel gas hot-water heater hung on the wall—but it was cozy. His favorite chair was in here, a lounger covered in imitation leather, with a footrest that extended at the touch of a button, and a back he could adjust to whatever position suited him. He'd bought it four years earlier, when he realized his expatriate status could no longer be considered temporary. Which was okay; he didn't mind it so much anymore. Especially not since he got the lounger. Originally he'd intended to put it in the living room. Then he decided he preferred the kitchen.

A small table piled with newspapers was beside the chair. They were a polyglot collection—French, British, German, and American. Someone, usually Ariel but not always, bought them for him every morning at the Gare du Nord and delivered them to the house by seven. Often it was later than this before he got to read them.

Yitzhak picked up *Le Monde*. The bottom half of the front page was given over to a story about the weekend bombing of a synagogue. Nobody had been hurt; the vandals had chosen a moment when they knew the synagogue would be empty. That's what the paper called them, vandals.

The word had strayed from its origins. In the fourth and fifth centuries Vandals were Germanic barbarians who pillaged and slaughtered; now the reference was to ignorant destruction of property. Annoying, but not very serious; that was the connotation. The editorial page was less sanguine. A disgrace, it thundered, a national scandal. The authorities must do something. Small comfort. How many people read editorials? And how many "authorities" were moved by them?

He looked for the story in the other papers. The British were appalled but cautioned prudent, calm reaction; the Americans were self-righteous; in the two German papers he checked, the story was relegated to a single paragraph on an inside page.

Yitzhak went into the living room for more brandy. The phone rang.

"I called your office, you weren't there."

"No, I'm here."

"Early for you to go home, isn't it?"

"I was tired, Malachy. I'm getting old. We both are."

The monk spoke gently. "You sound discouraged, my friend."

"A little. Did you read about the synagogue that was bombed?"

"In Paris, yes."

"The German papers barely covered the story."

"Yitzhak, that's over. Forget it."

The Israeli laughed. "Okay, on your word I'll do it. Nothing to worry about anymore, so I'll stop worrying. Anyway, you didn't call me about that."

"No, I want to know what's happening with Levi. Has he done anything with the bracelet?"

"As yet, nothing. But I'm arranging things. I've sent him to New York."

Malachy was startled. "New York! But why? What's happening, Yitzhak? Why have you suddenly sent him away?"

Beklem countered with another question. "What did you find out about the bracelet?"

"Nothing yet. My contact is still checking."

"You're sure this 'contact' doesn't suspect your reasons for asking?"

"I'm sure," Malachy lied. He didn't like to, but this time it was necessary. "The real question is, Why is Levi active again? I think you know more about that than you're telling me."

"Patience, Malachy. All in good time."

"All these years we've waited and watched together. Why the secrecy now?"

"Call it an occupational hazard. Good night, my friend, I'll be in touch."

Beklem hung up and went back to the kitchen. He'd make himself an omelete. No, fried onions and eggs. The hell with his doctor.

Onions delighted him, not just because they were delicious, it was the way they were made. Layer after layer of papery skin hiding a juicy heart. And they made you cry. In his experience there were things worth crying about. But not the fact that he and Malachy were lying to each other. After all, their friendship had been born as part of an enormous, unthinkable deceit.

Malachy put down the phone with a distinct sense of unease. The strange abbey weighed upon him; similarities created by the fact that it was Benedictine were overcome by other things. Physical things for a start—this was a modern building by Santa Pietà standards, less than a hundred years old. And doubtless Montparnasse was a country district when the monks located here, but it had been absorbed by the sprawling city long since. His hosts didn't have a farm, not so much as a vegetable garden. They ran a school. The presence of small boys seemed to Malachy detectable everywhere. Even where he sat in the small basement office of the *cellérier*, the abbey's buyer and dispenser of wines and groceries.

He'd refused the offer of the abbot's office. There was more privacy here. But when he raised his eyes from the big black phone, they met shelves lined with boxes of cornflakes. Malachy shuddered. He put his fingers to his temples and tried to think. What was Yitzhak doing? Why had he sent Levi away? To keep them apart? To prevent Malachy from discovering something? What? And why? It was Yitzhak who informed him that Levi was active again. If he had not done so, Malachy would still be in Rome. And through the years, the many years, Yitzhak had shared everything he discovered. Admittedly for reasons of his own, which Malachy had never truly fathomed, but what had changed, why should he become devious now?

There was a discreet tap on the door. "*Je m'excuse,* Dom Malachy." The *cellérier* came into his office, murmuring apologies. "So sorry to disturb you, I just need to get my receipt book. The fishmonger is here. Such an hour to deliver. Things are crazy these days."

"Yes." Malachy rose quickly. "They are. Altogether crazy. No, no, it's perfectly all right. I'm quite finished. Thank you for the use of the telephone."

The bell for compline sounded; the old *cellérier* looked harried.

Tim had chosen a hotel on the Left Bank, across from the Luxembourg Gardens. It was new, but small and whimsically decorated in a combination of Art Deco and modern. And he'd scrupulously arranged for them to have rooms on separate floors. He was delighted with Sarah's obvious pleasure in everything she saw. "The Left Bank's not cheap and arty anymore; it's trendy and expensive instead. But it's still the most romantic part of town."

"I'm longing to go out and see it all, but I must shower and change first."

Tim glanced at his watch. "Almost eight. Meet me here in the lobby in half an hour. We'll have time for a short walk before feeding you your first proper French meal."

She debated about what to wear and settled on a new suit, a bon voyage present she'd bought herself in Saks last week. When she was happy. Before the letter came. Sarah pushed the thought away. She was in Paris; it had been a marvelous day and promised to be a wonderful evening. She was damned if she'd let Jarib Baraak spoil it.

The suit was of sheer wool in a dark blued purple. The jacket had broad shoulders and a nipped waist held with one button, and the skirt was perfectly straight and discreetly slit on the side. She added a white silk blouse with a high neck, and put her hair up, but not sleekly so. Sarah let it wave slightly around her face.

"Will I do?" she asked Tim.

"You're lovely, you should have sable and priceless pearls."

"Furs make me sneeze, and I read somewhere that pearls are bad luck. C'mon, I'm dying to get outside."

It had to be the Seine first; nothing else was adequate. They strolled along the embankment, beneath the legendary chestnut trees, leafless now, but subtly and beautifully lit. There was a moon, and it cast a lovely glow on the river. After a few minutes they reached the Île de la Cité and that stone poem which is Notre-Dame. "I only want to look at the outside tonight," Sarah said. "Otherwise it's just too much."

They looked until a clock somewhere tolled nine. "Time to eat," Tim said. "How about a small bistro I know? It's not famous, just a place Parisians go because the food is excellent."

"Sounds perfect."

Orly was a madhouse. Zelah and Dov had to elbow their way to the departure lounge bar after he'd checked in. "What I don't understand," Zelah said, "is why it had to be so sudden."

"It's not," Dov lied. "I just forgot to mention it before. The Syrian wants me to check on a story."

"He's never before seemed worried about the accuracy of anything he prints."

She was studying him, with her head cocked and the intelligent dark eyes narrowed. Dov reached up one hand and flicked a dangling earring playfully. "Stop being so inquisitive. Let me just enjoy a little time with you."

Zelah held his glance for a moment, then busied herself with her Campari and soda. "How long will you be gone?"

"I'm not sure. About a week, I imagine. I'll call you as soon as I get back, all right?"

She shrugged. There was something studied in the gesture, as if it weren't one she wanted to make, as if she were forcing her casual attitude. "Whatever you like. I may be in Alsace, of course. If it's the weekend."

"If so, can I come and see you? I've never seen the *auberge*."

"No," she said too hastily. "Don't push it, Dov. Please. It's no good. We both know that."

"No, I don't know it. Only you do." But there was no fight in his words. He signaled the barman to replenish his cognac.

"I have to go," Zelah said. "I start early tomorrow."

"Wait," he said impulsively. "Tell me why you came."

"To see you off, because you asked me to."

Dov leaned over and gently kissed her cheek. "Okay. That will do. I'll phone as soon as I get back."

"Suit yourself." Her voice was harsh, and she hoped he didn't guess the cause was unshed tears.

The restaurant was called La Vraie Grandmère and was tucked at the end of an alley off the Rue Jacob. There were four tables in the front and six in the rear. It wasn't particularly crowded. Too late perhaps. Tim chose a table at the back and asked for two Pernods. When they came, the waiter poured a few drops of water in each and Sarah watched the drinks turn milky and opaque. She sipped and tasted the essence of licorice. "Wonderful," she said.

"I'm glad. I want everything to be wonderful for you tonight."

The waiter returned with a chalkboard menu advertising four specialties. "The chef has outdone himself with the *poussins* this evening," he said. "And to begin, we have the season's first young turnips."

"We'll both have the turnips and the chicken," Tim said without consulting her. "And a bottle of Moët et Chandon '72. It's Mademoiselle's first time in Paris."

The food was exquisite. She'd never imagined turnips could be special. But these were meltingly tender and served with a piquant, crunchy walnut sauce; the baby chickens were described as "in half mourning," they had fresh black truffles inserted between the skin and breast. They finished the champagne and Tim ordered another bottle.

"You'll never save enough for your stately home and glorious garden this way," Sarah teased.

He started to answer, stopped when he heard his name called by a woman making her way to their table. Tim rose and kissed her ceremoniously on both cheeks and insisted she join them and share the champagne. "Sarah, this is an old friend, Zelah Tench, who runs a splendid greenhouse here and a reputedly remarkable restaurant in Alsace. Zelah, Sarah Myles, from America."

Sarah admired the tall, slim look of the woman. And her black slacks and man-tailored white shirt with the collar turned up. Above it her hair was very short, but springy and alive. It suited her, as did her amusing long gold earrings. She struck Sarah as remarkably gay and bright. The impression was heightened by her English, clear and colloquial with only a trace of an accent.

"That's because I spent three years in California," Zelah explained. "And today seems to be designed to remind me of America. I just saw a friend off to New York. Now I meet you." She smiled at Sarah, then turned to Tim. "I suppose you're here to take gorgeous things out of France and sell them in England."

"If I can. There are rumors of a few fine collections going on the block."

"Not in Paris, if the owners can help it," Zelah said. "When are they going to change their stupid system?"

"Not as long as the auctioneers are enjoying a free ride." Tim turned to Sarah. "In France auctioneers are members of the judiciary, licensed by a professional organization that takes something off the top of every sale, and divides it among the members at the end of the year. Half the buggers don't do a thing, but they still earn a nice commission. I know auctioneers here who haven't held a sale in a decade. And a lot of those who do are sloppy. Poor catalogs and damned little advertising. So the pickings are ripe for aggressive blokes like me." He grinned at Zelah. "Sarah's new to all this, but she's learning fast. How's the flower business?"

"Not bad. But the restaurant's really exciting. We're jammed all the time. Especially on the weekends. We wanted to add on during the winter. So we'd be ready for the tourists in the spring. Papa was going to lend us the money, but he's decided he's courting poverty, because he gave twenty thousand francs to . . . a man we know. To buy a bracelet at auction no less, so we'll have to wait."

"What kind of bracelet?" Tim was more interested in that than in any restaurant. "Maybe the man wants to resell."

"Not a chance." Zelah laughed. "And it was overpriced. The stones aren't valuable. The catalog made all kinds of claims about the thing's age, but they had to admit the provenance was uncertain. Sorry you can't see it. The owner is the guy who's just gone to New York."

Tim shrugged. "Without a provenance it's not likely to be important. And probably not worth twenty thousand francs. I suspect your friend got taken."

Zelah sipped her champagne. "I'm not surprised. That's the story of his life, I think."

She'd ordered only a salad and a glass of wine. Soon they had all finished eating. "Let's show Sarah a bit of Paris by night," Zelah said.

Sarah had read about Régine's, but Zelah shook her head derisively. "Too old hat. I'll take you someplace better."

As far as Sarah could see, it was just another disco, with the usual flashing lights and insistent music. The dance floor was raised, it seemed to be suspended in air, and it and the rest of the room turned in opposite circles. "This is obviously designed for people with cast-iron stomachs," Sarah said.

"The only solution is liquor, so you don't notice." Tim ordered more champagne.

The beat infected Sarah's blood. She swayed with it. They danced. The lights were purple and orange and warm pink, and the air seemed full of bubbles. Her hair came loose and she shook it free. "You're exquisite," Tim whispered.

"Zelah looks like she's trying not to be sad," Sarah said.

Tim glanced across the floor, to where the other woman was dancing with a big black man with a beard and an earring. "Zelah's tough as they come."

"Maybe," Sarah agreed. "I still think she's unhappy underneath."

Tim took her hand and led her back to the table. "I don't want to talk about Zelah Tench. Tonight you're the only woman in the world."

Sarah giggled and drank more champagne.

They didn't get back to the hotel till nearly two. "Stay with me tonight," Tim murmured in the elevator. His face was in her hair, his arms around her.

"No," Sarah whispered. "I can't."

"Why not?"

The elevator stopped; the door opened with a soft swishing sound. "Please," she said. "Let me go." She disentangled herself from his embrace, stretching out one arm to keep the door from closing. "I'm sorry, Tim. It's been a perfect evening, but I'm not sure."

"Bloody hell, Sarah, I'm not suggesting an immediate lifetime commitment. I want us to give each other a chance."

"Please, let's not argue about it."

She escaped into the corridor, heard the elevator move upward, and glanced over her shoulder to see if Tim had followed her. No. She stood in front of her room a moment, feeling oddly guilty. Within seconds the elevator started down again. She suspected Tim was inside still, going back into the Paris night to find an outlet for frustration. Well, what of it? She could just hear what Pinkie would say. "Jesus, sugar, y'all don't owe the boy a quick lay just 'cause he bought champagne. . . ."

But that wasn't exactly fair. Tim hadn't meant it like that. All the same, Pinkie would be right. No need to feel guilty. She should be excited, happy. She was in Paris, she was pleasantly high, an attractive man was pursuing her. Instead she wanted to cry. She went to bed and dreamed of Jarib, as usual.

The Air France jumbo jet moved silently through the night sky. Dov picked at the meal they provided, said he wasn't interested in buying any duty-free perfume, and ordered four more of the small bottles of Burgundy. He'd drink them slowly, pace himself. He didn't want to arrive in New York drunk out of his skull. Maybe his English would fail him if he did that. No, not likely. It wasn't the first language he'd learned; Ariel was mistaken about that. But it was the second. And in a sense, his mother tongue.

In 1922, when both were students at College of Physicians and Surgeons, Freida Silberman met Leo Levy. Neither Freida nor Leo was likely to roar with the twenties. Freida was small and dark, opinionated, strong-willed, and brilliant. Her German Jewish family were not in the least surprised when she insisted on becoming one of the first women admitted to study medicine at Columbia. Since they could afford to indulge her, they did so.

Leo was Freida's opposite in every way, including appearance. Tall, thin, fair; a student who achieved decent grades by endless studying rather than by innate gifts. Levy had been born and raised on the Lower East Side, and his parents were working twenty hours a day to pay his tuition. Perhaps it was simply that they were the only two Jews in their class which drew Freida and Leo together, but the bond became something more real and lasting.

They planned to marry as soon as they were through their internships. The Silbermans, as usual, resigned themselves to Freida's choice. The Levys were delighted that Leo had snagged a nice Jewish girl, who also happened to be rich. There was no reason to imagine that the marriage would lead to anything unusual. Except that one wintry evening in 1924 some friends took Freida to a Zionist meeting. She went merely out of curiosity, but that swiftly changed.

"You must come with me tomorrow night, Leo," she told her fiancé. "This speaker is extraordinary; I want you to hear what he has to say."

When Freida looked at him like that, Leo knew he'd have to do what she wanted. He tried a mild protest anyway. "I have no interest in Zionism, Freida. My home is here in America, not some godforsaken desert thousands of miles away."

"Godforsaken it's not, darling. Just come, listen, then we'll talk about it." Freida was always reasonable.

Within a year they were both completely caught up in the Zionist cause. Founded by the Austrian Theodor Herzl, who convened the first World Zionist Congress in Vienna in 1897, the movement was given impetus in 1917 by the British foreign secretary, Arthur Balfour. The so-called Balfour Declaration stated that His Majesty's government was in favor of the notion that the Jews of the world should be given a permanent homeland in Palestine, the place of their biblical origins. No mention was made of such a homeland being exclusively Jewish, nor was the opinion of the resident Arabs solicited.

It was the dynamic Chaim Weizmann, a Pole who had emigrated to England in 1904, who set fire to Herzl's idea and Balfour's suggestion, and caused the flames to spread among Jews on both sides of the Atlantic. It was to hear him speak that Freida dragged Leo to a drafty hall on Delancey Street. It was Weizmann's vision that took root in Leo's heart, and in Freida's.

On May 17, 1926, Freida and Leo were married at Temple Emmanu-El on Fifth Avenue. They spent their wedding night at the Plaza, and the following morning, glowing with happiness and expectation, they boarded the United States Line's flagship, *Leviathan,* and set sail for Southampton, England, whence they would take ship to Palestine. The Levys were to join the swelling number

223

of Jews returning to the place they hoped would one day again be theirs. They would prepare the way for those who would come after.

The newlyweds traveled third-class. Once they checked out of the Plaza, the beneficence of Freida's family came to an end. "I have indulged you all your life," her father told her solemnly. "But if you persist in this absurdity, in breaking your mother's heart, I'm finished with you. Don't come running home to me when you discover what a fool you've been, what a fool you've made of that poor, decent young man. If you board that ship, Freida, I never want to see you again."

Thus the words Freida heard in that tender moment at the end of the reception when her parents came to say good-bye. The senior Levys were slightly less adamant. They were overwhelmed by their new daughter-in-law and her fancy family. Mrs. Levy managed to mutter, "I can never forgive you," between her sobs. Mr. Levy looked at Freida and Leo in pain and disapproval while trying to comfort his wife.

So money had suddenly become a thing of major concern. They had their skills, of course, and they didn't doubt that they'd be welcomed on the kibbutz where they were to live, but the $1,500 they'd amassed in wedding gifts was all else they had in the world. Their third-class tickets cost $125 each, they had budgeted another $50 to see them through the time in England while they waited for a ship to take them east, and $200 for that journey. Freida and Leo planned to arrive in their new land with $1,000.

They steamed into Southampton Water on the morning of May 28, a shining, glorious day, golden with sunlight. Leo hung over the deck rail, entranced with the green embankments between which the ship negotiated. Even in these docklands there were flowers and leaves and the many splendors of that incomparable thing, an English spring. "Look, Freida. My God, have you ever seen such a country?"

"Never," Freida agreed. But she did not share Leo's immediate passion for England. She didn't have his essentially poetic soul for one thing; for another she was so single-mindedly committed to Zionism that she ate, slept, and drank Palestine. Particularly now while it was still a dream.

They were told they must wait two weeks for a ship to Haifa, so Freida found them a small room on Portbury Road in Southampton. A pound a week each for bed, breakfast, and an evening meal. "That's only eight and a half dollars, Leo. Isn't it splendid! We won't have to spend anything like fifty dollars. Twenty, more likely. Maybe less if we skip lunch."

"Yes, it's wonderful. But can we spare two shillings more, do you think? That's about fifty cents."

"Of course, Leo, but what do you want to buy?"

"A sightseeing trip. I saw one advertised in the newsagent's next door."

"What's a newsagent?"

Leo grinned, pleased with himself for picking up the local parlance so quickly, pleased that Freida had noticed. "British for a store where they sell newspapers and magazines. And they have a notice board in the window. That's where I saw the ad."

"Is it two shillings for one?"

"No, a shilling each. We go in a private automobile with a gentleman who says he knows every byway in Hampshire; that's the county we're in, sort of like a state. And the ad says he provides a packed lunch. What do you think?"

"You go, darling. I'm tired after the journey. And I want to go over the Hebrew grammar book they sent us."

Leo arranged his tour of Hampshire for the next day. The guide was an elderly man whom Leo liked at once. "Sort of close your eyes for this first bit, guv. Ain't much to see until we get to Lymington. That's where the real tour begins."

Lymington was a village at the edge of the New Forest, created in the eleventh century by William I. "Liked his huntin', did our King Billy," the guide explained.

Leo also liked King Billy. Any man gifted enough to create this place of enchantment must be likable. Endless little lanes and roads winding through a sylvan paradise, tiny villages that looked as if they'd been lifted whole from a child's picture book, exciting glimpses of the wild New Forest ponies that roamed free, and extraordinary pigs that took their ease in front of thatched roof cottages. Leo gaped at Eden.

He tried to tell Freida of the wonders he'd discovered and convince her to come and see, but she insisted she had to work on her Hebrew. At least one of them must have a few words of the language when they arrived in Palestine.

In the next few days Leo went sightseeing twice more. All of Hampshire delighted him. Freida said she didn't object to his spending the shillings, but she got a tight look around the mouth when he took the money from the drawstring chamois bag which contained their fortune. He chose to pretend he didn't notice. Very soon it didn't matter. They boarded the Cunard ship *Queen of the East* and set sail for Haifa.

Kibbutz Etz Hadar had been founded two years earlier. When Freida and Leo arrived, it comprised one four-hundred-square-foot building built of concrete blocks not yet covered in stucco, three temporary sheds made of tar paper, a struggling vegetable garden of about a quarter of an acre, and a seemingly endless vista of scrub and swamp. In this unlikely repository of dreams were housed twenty-seven people ranging in age from two years to fifty-six and representing five nationalities. The only common denominators were that all were Jews and all were passionate Zionists; with the possible exception of the two-year-old boy, who was passionate only about suckling at his French mother's ample bosom.

"Doctors, yes, I know. Well, I suppose we can use your medical skills."

Freida translated rapidly for her husband. Leo looked puzzled at the nature of the greeting.

Avrum Hamir, president of the kibbutz as well as head of the admissions committee, smiled. "We will speak in English. It will be faster. What I meant was that much as we value your medical knowledge, we need other labor as well. Hard physical labor."

Hamir was a Frenchman who had Hebraicized his name when he emigrated. He was thirty-nine, father of Benjie, the two-year-old, and an ascetic-looking man who studied the Levys from behind thick glasses. "You are our first Americans. You look strong."

"We are," Leo said. "We did not take this step lightly, Mr. Hamir. You need not fear that we're dilettantes."

"We're completely dedicated to Zionism," Freida added.

"Yes, I'm sure. But Zionism is one thing; the kibbutz ideal is something else. At least the two are not always identical. Besides,

226

we're all pretty healthy. Of course, we hope for more births; that's the key to our survival here, numbers. Maybe you can assist on both sides of that problem." He smiled and looked pointedly at Freida.

Leo put a protective arm around his wife's slim waist. "We will try to do everything asked of us in terms of work. As for births, well, even on a kibbutz I presume that is left to God."

"Unfortunately, yes," Hamir said. "I haven't yet thought of a more efficient method. Come, meet the others. Everyone's been impatient for your arrival."

The kibbutzniks were indeed healthy. In the first two months neither Freida nor Leo did more than dress an occasional wound. That didn't mean they were idle. They worked in the vegetable garden, they cast the concrete building blocks which were vital if they were ever to replace the tar paper shacks, and they dug the seemingly endless trenches which would drain the swamp. "Citrus fruits," Freida whispered one night when they lay stiff with exhaustion in their curtained cubicle in the dormitory. "In this wilderness. It's crazy. An insane idea."

"Maybe not. I was talking with Yakov, the Swiss horticulturalist, he thinks it can work. He's going to try grafting eating oranges onto wild orange stock. As soon as we build some sort of greenhouse."

Freida turned over wearily. "I don't know what you're talking about. I still think it's crazy."

"Wait, don't go to sleep yet. Yakov and Avrum, they both asked if we're going to change our names to something Hebrew. What do you think?"

"Freida and Leo sound pretty Jewish to me."

She, the one who had started the whole thing, the one who learned Hebrew so rapidly while he was still struggling, she sounded unhappy about the notion of changing their names. "That's not exactly the same, but okay." Leo thought it best to placate her. She was working so hard, was so tired. "Maybe we'll just spell it Levi, with an *i* rather than a *y*. Do you mind?"

"Why should I mind? It's your name."

They went on working. God, how they worked. And results showed so slowly. Everything was done by hand, with minimal resources and maximum strain, with guns slung over their shoulders if they were more than fifty yards from the main building. The friction between Jew and Arab, present occupant and returnee, was already making trouble. The Arabs and the ruling British were their constant preoccupation. Most of the kibbutzniks hated both equally. "All the old battles, the ones mentioned in the Bible between this tribe and that, we must fight them again. It is written."

"Written where, Daniel?"

The questioner was Yosef Hamir, Avrum's older brother. Like Avrum, Yosef was a fervent Zionist, a doubly fervent socialist, and a totally nonobservant Jew.

Daniel Kahane leaned forward intently. "In the Talmud. It says in Gemara—"

"*Merde!* I say shit on your holy books. In the fifth century, Daniel, that's when your Gemara was written. It means nothing for now, for 1926 in Palestine."

Daniel turned very pale; when he stood up, he was trembling. "You are a blasphemer, and I declare you anathema. Avrum!" he roared. "You must change my work assignment. At once. I will not spend one more minute digging trenches beside your foul-mouthed, blasphemous pig of a brother!"

Thus one of the major problems at Etz Hadar. Most kibbutzniks were like the Hamirs, committed socialists first, fervent Zionists second, and practicing Jews not at all. For others, a very few others, the kibbutz experiment was *Kiddush Hashem,* a sanctification of God's name, a chosen martyrdom, a holy thing that would give glory to the Almighty. They refused to accept that for the majority of their fellows, Judaism as a theological structure meant nothing, that their theology was socialism.

Such men and their women had come to Palestine to build a state where the fact of their Jewishness would not bar them from the corridors of power, where they would not be subject to the virulent anti-Semitism that had infected Europe for centuries. Praying and studying sacred books had no part in their lives. But the roots of a problem which was to grow beyond any of their imaginings were already sinking themselves deep into the ancient homeland. Jew would struggle with Jew over the meaning of their legacy.

At Etz Hadar the Orthodox faction was led by Daniel Kahane.

He was a Belgian who, like all those whose name was Cohen or some variation thereof, claimed direct descent from Aaron, the brother of Moses, founder of the Jewish priesthood. The function of that priesthood ended with the destruction of the Temple C.E. 70, but for many Jews, the *Kohanim* remained a special group. Sacred, set apart. Daniel's orthodoxy was nonetheless suspect in some eyes. His presence in Palestine assured that it must be.

According to strict interpretation of the Holy Books, the Jews could not return to Zion until the Messiah came and led them there. Had anyone seen him lately? But despite this break with tradition, Kahane was the opposite of the Hamirs and others like them. He believed, and he kept every one of the myriad rules laid down for devout Jews. He even pointed out to Leo that Levi was also a name associated with the ancient priesthood. Perhaps . . .

Leo listened to such pleadings and smiled and shook his head. Daniel retreated, but only momentarily. He never gave up. Daniel was the thorn in their collective sides.

Since the coming of the Levis and the birth of one little girl, there were thirty members of Etz Hadar; only five aligned themselves with Kahane. But these five had succeeded in establishing that the kitchen would stringently follow the laws of *kashruth* laid down in Leviticus and Deuteronomy, and that absolutely no work would be done between sundown on Friday and sundown on Saturday.

No matter how lengthy their labors or how exhausted they were, Kahane and his followers conducted morning and evening services seven days a week. Their greatest sorrow was that they lacked the required ten men to form a *minyan,* the prescribed unit for what might be termed "official" prayer. The little band of believers numbered only three men and two women. Maybe that was why they engaged the rest in endless discussions designed to convert them to observant behavior. These usually turned into harangues.

Leo learned to stay clear of the religious war being waged on the kibbutz. Freida couldn't resist an intellectual joust. But the arguments didn't refresh or stimulate her, they made her angry. Lately, Leo noticed, many things made her angry. Such as Avrum Hamir's reaction to her latest project.

When they'd been five months in Palestine, Freida started treating the Arab women of the village of El Ali, five kilometers east. It began by accident. She was working with one of the men at the far end of the kibbutz, digging yet another trench, when three women leading a camel passed by. As Freida looked up and debated whether to wave, one of the women staggered and fell. Freida didn't hesitate. "I'm a doctor," she explained, using the Hebrew word, hoping it was close enough to their language so they'd understand. In any event they understood her actions.

The woman on the ground was in sudden, premature labor. Deftly Freida made her as comfortable as possible. One of the others spoke a bit of English, and she explained that they'd gone to buy grain in a town twelve kilometers from their village. The pregnant one had been complaining of pain since they started back, but she wasn't due to give birth for at least a month. "Well, she decided not to wait," Freida said crisply.

A cursory examination indicated that dilation was complete and the child was being born in the breech position. Freida sent the man with her to the main building for medicines and water and remained with her sudden patient, whom she'd decided could not be moved. Two hours later she delivered a son to Fatima, youngest wife of the chief elder of El Ali. Mother and child both lived and prospered, and Freida became a respected and treasured friend in the village.

"I don't care what Avrum thinks," she told her husband. "I'm a doctor, not a ditch digger, a galley slave, or a broodmare. All he wants to know is if I'm pregnant. Well, I'm not. And if that's a crime, you're as guilty as I am."

"Freida, my love, nobody is accusing you or me of any crime. Avrum is charged with protecting the kibbutz. He worries, it's natural."

"It's also natural for a doctor to practice medicine. I'm thinking of offering to visit other villages in the area as well. I can do it nights if Avrum won't allow me to take time off during the day."

"I won't have you wandering around at night, Freida. It's unthinkable."

"Then talk to Avrum. He likes you better than me. Explain to him. I must have some time away from here, Leo. I just must."

He refrained from saying that coming had been her idea in the first place.

"And what about you, Leo?" Avrum asked when they discussed the subject. "Are you, too, feeling that your special training is being wasted here at Etz Hadar?"

Leo smiled. "To tell you the truth, no. I don't have Freida's drive, never have had. I enjoy medicine, but I'm not married to it. Frankly, I find Yakov's experiments with the oranges every bit as fascinating as infections and illness."

"Yes, he tells me you are a great help to him. You have the hands of a surgeon, good for grafting. And the soul of a poet, which is apparently a requirement of horticulture. I don't know, my friend, Freida's activities disturb me. And her attitude."

"Please, Avrum. She needs time to adjust, that's all."

"Very well, the secretariat meets tomorrow. I'll put it to them."

It was largely the presence of Yakov Tench on the committee that caused them to allow Freida three days a week to practice medicine in the surrounding area. Yakov understood the depth of Freida's discontent. He suspected that if they denied her, she was likely to convince Leo to leave Etz Hadar. They could not afford to lose Leo.

The Swiss was a man of thirty, so tall he'd developed a self-conscious stoop as a teenager. And he was thin, with a scrawny chicken's neck and a prominent Adam's apple. But his smile redeemed his appearance. Yakov had a gentle smile that lit his face. Moreover, he was a brilliant horticulturalist and a wise man. He'd been one of the original three founders of the kibbutz, a Zionist since his youth. It was a mark of his balanced character that when he came to Palestine, he changed his first name from Jacob to Yakov but retained the family name of Tench.

"It's good politics to let her go," Yakov told the secretariat. "We're here to stay. We've got to make friends of the Arabs or fight them."

"Good politics maybe," someone said. "But it's bad socialism." When the vote was taken, that turned out to be the minority opinion.

For three years this situation prevailed, and both Leo and Freida seemed at peace in the life they had chosen. Then, in 1929, Freida conceived. "I'd given up hope," she confided to Leo, held tight in his arms, both of them trembling with joy. "I thought I'd never give you a son. But I will, Leo, I will."

"You've been around the Arabs too much. A son, a daughter, what do I care? Our child, my darling. The fruit of our love, that's the only important thing."

In the chill desert night of January 23, 1930, Dov Levi was born. "Not David, or even Dovid," Freida insisted. "We'll call him Dov."

It was a little odd, just a whim of Freida's, but her pregnancy and her labor had both been hard, and Leo was overjoyed that she and the child had survived. "Of course, darling, whatever you want." He often found himself saying that to Freida.

When Dov was three months old—a wonderful baby, small but strong, with Freida's dark, curly hair and Leo's green eyes—he went into the communal nursery, which had been one of the first institutions established at Etz Hadar. For Freida the move signaled the beginning of the end. "He's too young," she protested. But she was reminded that all children were put in the nursery when they were three months old. Why should Dov be any different?

"We'll have him all to ourselves evenings and on *Shabbat,* Freida. Besides, this way you can go on with your medicine. I thought you wanted that."

"I do. What I don't want is for my son to become a pawn in the battle between Avrum and his ideologues and Daniel and his fanatics. That nursery is where they play their war games, fighting for the minds of the young."

"Dov is three months old, darling. Surely no one can yet influence his mind."

"It's the future I'm thinking of."

Indeed. Freida thought of the future almost all the time now. Her thoughts didn't make her happy. At the end of the first summer of Dov's life she voiced them. "I want us to go away from here."

Leo was not surprised. He'd suspected she was building up to just such an announcement. But he was made very sad by it.

Etz Hadar had become his life. He was astonished at how much he enjoyed the work with the orange trees, and the closeness and sense of shared purpose which, whatever their differences, marked the lives of the kibbutzniks. "I thought you believed in Palestine," he told his wife. "In everything that Zionism stands for."

"It's not Palestine, it's the kibbutz. The regimentation."

232

Leo raised a despairing hand. They'd had this argument many times; there was little point in repeating it. "Where could we go?"

"To Haifa. We can start a practice, Leo. The two of us together. There's a sophisticated European community in Haifa. You'd enjoy that, I know you would."

"I didn't come to Palestine to play doctor to the British bourgeoisie."

"I don't understand you. You're the one who was so impressed by England."

"I was, I am. But that doesn't mean I approve of their attitudes here, or the way they're dragging their feet about implementing the Balfour Declaration."

"If we were in Haifa, dealing with them every day, you might have some influence. What can you accomplish here, arbitrating between Daniel and Avrum day and night?"

They dropped the subject for a time, but came back to it frequently. Leo found the sense of inevitability more wearing than the fights themselves, and in the end Freida prevailed.

They'd both always known she would.

When Dov was two years old, they left the kibbutz. Avrum insisted they take back the thousand dollars they'd donated on their arrival. "All the work you've done here, it's a sufficient donation. More. Take the money, you'll need it."

They moved to Haifa and opened a joint practice. To allow her to work, Freida hired an English nanny to look after their son. Now Freida was free to insist that Dov speak English as naturally as the Hebrew which had been his first language. He learned quickly, but his accent became a strange blend of the American intonations of his parents and the Oxford English of the nanny; it was to remain thus all his life.

Dov throve in Haifa, but Leo became quiet and withdrawn. The only time he came alive was when he went to spend a day or two working with Yakov on the kibbutz. These visits became more frequent as time went by. Within two years Freida was carrying the medical practice almost entirely alone. If Leo wasn't at the kibbutz, he was meeting friends in town. These friends were largely people involved in active opposition to British rule, members of David Ben-Gurion's underground army, the Haganah.

Leo took part in no overtly criminal activities—he confined himself to attending political meetings and talking—but Freida knew the situation to be dangerous. She began to fear a thing that had never before occurred to her; she was afraid of losing her husband. And whatever else could be said of her, Freida loved Leo. She also loved Dov. With a consuming passion.

They had rented a big old house near the sea on the road to Qiryat Yam. It had a garden in the rear which Leo had lovingly restored with Yakov's advice and guidance. The chief feature was an allée of palm trees leading to a sunken bed of fragrant Persian roses. It was there that Dov and Miss Shalton, the nanny, would wait for Freida in the evenings when she came home from the office.

"Dov, my darling . . ." she would call from the terrace at the rear of the house, "Dov, Mama is home!" And he would race up the allée to meet her; sturdy five-year-old legs pumping hard, the sun filtering through the trees to make changing patterns on his dark, curly hair.

For Freida these homecomings soon became bittersweet. Because often Dov would greet her with words she had come to fear. He'd first uttered them when he was not yet four. "I heard my song today, Mama. It sang in my head all day."

At first she'd questioned him. What did he mean? What song? His answers disturbed her. Dov insisted that he heard music in his head, not just the melody of some nursery rhyme Miss Shalton had sung to him. No, his song was different. Once Freida took him into the music room they hardly ever used because neither she nor Leo was musical. She asked him if he could pick out the notes on the piano. He did so without hesitation. *Do-sol-la-fa.* She called the nanny to see if she agreed with the names Freida had assigned the notes. Yes, she was correct, and no, Miss Shalton had no idea where he'd heard them.

"Don't you want to hear other notes, too, darling? Not just those same four all the time."

"No. Anyway, I don't make the song happen. It just comes."

And within a few months there were other phenomena to worry Freida. Dov saw pictures as well as heard music. "A book, Mama. But not a real book. Sort of a wound-up book. With funny letters. Not like any letters I've ever seen."

234

"A wound-up book," Freida repeated to Leo. "The only thing I can imagine is a scroll. Where would he get such an idea?"

"From the kibbutz, of course. Daniel's Torah scrolls."

"He was two when we left the kibbutz. And anyway, I never let him attend Daniel's indoctrinations. Besides, he'd recognize Hebrew writing. He insists these are letters he's never seen."

"Relax, Freida. You're worrying about nothing. You're a hen with one chick, it's to be expected. But all children have a fantasy life. Dov's perfectly normal."

Maybe. But Freida wasn't convinced. And in her anguish and her fear she began to believe that Palestine was the cause of all things wrong in her life. It was a threat to her husband's freedom and disturbing to her son's mind. It had already caused an irreparable break with her parents. She wrote to them faithfully once a month, but they had never answered a single letter. Not even the one announcing the birth of their grandson. Leo's mother wrote to him occasionally, but the letters were just one long lament at his faithlessness, and Leo had come to dread them.

Such was Freida's state of mind the day in December of 1935, a few weeks before Dov's sixth birthday, when she came home to find Miss Shalton wringing her hands in agitation. "Dov went to sleep an hour ago, ma'am; he simply dropped off in his little chair. Just now I tried to wake him and I can't."

Freida raced up the stairs to the nursery, her heart pounding in her chest, her medical knowledge causing an encyclopedia of disasters to run through her head.

"Dov, it's Mama, darling. Wake up. It's time for your supper. Wake up, Dov!" The child did not respond.

She was taking his pulse when Leo came into the room. He'd been in town, meeting with the various people who had become his friends but not Freida's.

"Thank God you're here." Freida dragged her husband to Dov's side, her words an almost incoherent jumble as she tried to explain. "His pulse is only fifty-six, and his breathing is very shallow and unbelievably slow. Do something, Leo! For God's sake, do something."

Freida was any mother in a panic; that she was a trained physician didn't enter into it. Leo moved to the child's side. He put his fingers on Dov's wrist. The pulse was indeed diabolically slow. And the breathing. Gently he lifted his son and placed him on the bed. He was considering a stimulant, debating what might be safe for one so young, when Dov opened his eyes and smiled at his parents.

"Hello. You're home, and so am I. I went away for a long time."

Freida moaned—half relief, half terror—as if she guessed what was coming. It was Leo who asked, "Where did you go, son?"

"To visit with Sarah. She lives a long way away. It isn't easy to go there."

"Sarah who?" Freida whispered. She tried to sound normal and reassuring, but it wasn't possible.

"My friend Sarah, I've told you, Mama. The rolled-up book belongs to Sarah." And with that Dov turned his face away and wouldn't talk to them.

"We have to take him away from Palestine," Freida insisted. "If we do, he'll be all right."

"That's crazy, Freida. That makes no sense at all. If something is wrong with Dov, and I'm not convinced of that, where we live is irrelevant. There are good doctors right here in Haifa."

She turned very pale. "An alienist, that's what you're thinking of. My son doesn't need an alienist, damn you! He needs to get away from this terrible country. Leo! Are you listening to me, Leo? We have to take him away!"

She was screaming. He'd never heard her scream before. "Freida, please, darling, you're upset—"

She flung herself at him, beating her fists on his chest. Freida was small, but she was strong. Leo had all he could do to restrain her. Finally he convinced her to take a sedative and rest, but only after she had extracted a solemn promise that he would not spirit her son away to an alienist while she slept.

So began another campaign which they both knew Freida would win—as always.

England she decreed, as if offering Leo a consolation prize. "You liked England, remember?"

He did remember. But he loved Palestine, was committed to it in a way that the promise of beautiful, green England could not alter. Leo Levi went all the same. He did so because he knew that if he did not, his wife would take his son and go without him. Not even for Palestine, for the Zionist dream, could he sacrifice the two people dearest to him in all the world. "I'm not the stuff pioneers are made of," he told his friend Yakov. "I can't give up everything for the cause."

"That doesn't make you an inadequate pioneer, Leo. Only a failure as a fanatic. Go in peace, my friend, *shalom alekhem.*"

They arrived in Southampton in July of 1936. Freida had it in mind to go to London, where it would be easier to find work, but for once Leo insisted on having his way. "I go no further, Freida. We are settling here in Hampshire. And we're not renting a house. We're going to buy whatever we can afford; we're going to put down roots and not tear them up again while we live."

They had three thousand dollars—their original thousand plus two more they'd saved during the years in Haifa. When they exchanged it, they found themselves with seven hundred pounds. If they were frugal, they could manage for a year on three hundred. By then they should be earning. Leo decreed that they would pay no more than three hundred for a house. "That will leave us enough for a year's living and a hundred pounds over for emergencies."

"What about furniture?"

Leo frowned. He hadn't thought of furniture. "We'll find a furnished house. But no matter what, we don't go over three hundred."

In fact, they spent 275 pounds for a small cottage at the edge of the tiny village of Duxbury-near-Christchurch. It had five rooms, a thatched roof, a big fireplace in the sitting room, and an assortment of ill-matched but comfortable old furniture. It was called Mulberry Cottage, and there was nearly an acre of derelict garden out back, dominated by an old dowager of a spreading mulberry tree. Leo adored it. Surprisingly so did Freida. Somehow the gentle English countryside to which she'd been immune ten years earlier now wooed her and brought out a side of her nature neither she nor Leo had known she possessed.

Leo decided to invade their capital further and spend 150 pounds to buy a partnership in a general practice run by a charming old doctor in his eighties. It was obvious that Leo would have it to himself quite soon, and the Levis decided that Freida would no longer work. She would stay home and look after Dov and the house. Freida was willing. She could keep a closer eye on her son if she didn't work. She never practiced medicine again.

Dov didn't seem in the least disturbed by yet another uprooting. He was enrolled in the village school, and plans were made to send him to a nearby private secondary school when he was old enough. For a while Freida watched him constantly, waiting for him to mention the song and Sarah and the rolled book. Dov said nothing about them. She was convinced that the new environment, the friends he made so readily, and removal from the malevolent influence of Palestine had done what she'd predicted. Her son was cured of his disturbing fantasies. It never occurred to her that he'd simply grown old enough and wise enough to stop mentioning them to her or anyone else.

The Levis survived the war. Leo was on ambulance duty and Freida was a volunteer plane spotter. They gritted their teeth and bore the bombing. They endured the rationing that went on almost forever after victory had been proclaimed. They observed with interest the dramatic change in English society produced by Churchill's postwar electoral defeat and the subsequent dissolution of the empire. And they coped with the normal strains of life.

Dov had measles and chicken pox. He fell off a bicycle and fractured his arm. Following local custom, he was sent to boarding school when he was eleven. He had a bad time his first term, but straightened out after it, made new friends, and began getting excellent grades.

Leo and Freida made friends in the village and in the nearby town of Christchurch. They invited people for dinner, were invited to their homes in return. At twelve Dov developed a passion for horses, and Leo paid extra for him to have riding lessons at school. Dov's short, tough frame was admirably suited for the sport, and he became quite good. In large measure, the family Levi enjoyed life.

During all this time their Judaism was known but unremarked by those around them, and their customary nonpractice continued. All the same, when Dov was thirteen, Leo and Freida arranged for him to be Bar Mitzvah at a synagogue in Southampton. "It just wouldn't feel right if we didn't," they told each other. The Orthodox rabbi was inured to such attitudes and he agreed to train Dov for the ceremony. He was rewarded for his tolerance when he discovered that the boy had retained fluent Hebrew.

Leo donned the yarmulke and tallith he hadn't worn since his wedding, and Freida bought a new hat. Alone they went to the small *shul* and watched with pride while their only son repeated a ritual that spoke to something primeval in them, something to do with tribe and survival as much as God. To mark the event, they bought Dov his own horse.

He specialized in the grueling challenge known as three-day eventing, a seventy-two-hour test of man and animal. Two years later Dov made the Hampshire county team and was short-listed for the national, maybe even the Olympics, but he suddenly decided horses were taking too much time from his studies. Leo and Freida were astounded and rather pleased. Dov talked to them about it only once. After that he sold his horse and stopped riding.

When he was eighteen, Dov was admitted to King's College, Cambridge, and went up the following October. He took a first in Middle Eastern languages and moved to London, where he got a job at the research department of the *Times,* translating and interpreting news from what was now Israel and her surrounding, belligerent neighbors.

Dov's social life revolved around Fleet Street and the newspaper fraternity. As a King's man his credentials were impeccable, and he was recognized as competent besides. He was sometimes teased about his slightly American accent, but in general the people with whom he worked accepted him and liked him. He dated a number of women and slept with a few, but no one, not even his bedmates, considered herself his intimate. There was something reserved in Dov. Some distancing that was unbreachable and had simply to be accepted. No one of his acquaintances thought about him enough to bother analyzing it.

Dov was at the newspaper on the autumn morning in 1958 when he received a telephone call from the Hampshire police. A few hours before, around 2:00 A.M., Leo and Freida had been driving home from an evening with friends in Christchurch. They'd met another car in one of the narrow lanes. The other driver was drunk and driving without lights, and there was a head-on collision. The senior Levis had both died instantly.

Dov received the news with sad calm, accepted the condolences

of his superior and co-workers, then left the office. He wandered
up Whitefriars Street to Carmelite Lane and over to the Embankment. There he sat staring at the turgid Thames and remembering
his parents.

His most vivid memory was of the day after the British withdrew from Palestine, May 14, 1948. He had taken his Cambridge
entrance exam the month before, but didn't yet know the results.
He was home with Leo and Freida at Mulberry Cottage. The three
of them sat beside the wireless, listening to the BBC Empire Service, waiting for the promised transmission from Tel Aviv. Finally
the voice of David Ben-Gurion was heard proclaiming the new
state of Israel.

Leo had simply stared straight ahead, his face an unreadable
mask. Freida had wept bitterly. Dov thought she was crying for
joy, but his father had known better. "Don't weep, Freida," he'd
said gently. "We did the best we could. They managed without us.
It doesn't matter now."

In that long, sad and solemn vigil by the river Dov Levi came to
realize that Israel had done without him long enough. Two events
had coincided. The voice in his head, that muse who had never
ceased to dictate all his actions, was telling him he was ready, and
his parents had died. Everything that might have stood in his way
was eliminated. It was time to go home.

Would he have gone had he known how terribly it would end?
Yitzhak Beklem asked him when it was over.

"Yes," Dov told him. "I had no choice, you see."

Beklem's disgust was palpable. "They're both dead, but you had
no choice. You mystics and religious fanatics sicken me. You could
destroy Israel, all of us. Given a chance, you'd be more thorough
than Hitler."

Dov could explain no more. If he'd guessed how tragically it
would finish, anticipated the terrible guilt, known that Beklem
would own him ever afterward, he'd still have gone. In those days
the voice and the song ruled his existence. Now Beklem did. Hurtling through the night toward New York, Levi wondered if he'd
profited by the exchange. No, but then, he'd had no say over
making it.

Eight

THURSDAY,
NOVEMBER 22

"Wait till you meet Jenny," Tim said. "She's remarkable."

They were scheduled to attend an auction viewing in the afternoon, and Tim had decreed that the morning would be spent on a bit of business for Durant's. Sarah was glad he'd asked her to accompany him, and that he was bright and gay again, apparently as determined as she to forget the sour note on which last night had ended. "Tell me about her," she said. "Jenny who, for starters?"

"Fogel, she's German, though she's been in Paris many years. Taken on protective coloration. Hang on!"

The taxi in which they were careening through the Paris traffic lurched around a corner on two wheels. Tim had declined to drive. "We'll waste hours looking for a place to park," he'd said. "Besides, everybody should experience a Paris cabdriver at least once in her life."

The turning maneuver had flung Sarah into his arms, Tim held on for a moment, grinned at her, then let her go. The cab screeched to a halt on the fabled and fashionable Rue du Faubourg St.-Honoré, in front of a graceful granite building with shallow stone balustraded balconies in front of high French windows. "No time to tell you more," Tim said. "Come see for yourself."

A concierge intercepted them in the front hall. She wore a faded green smock over a black dress, her hair was in an untidy bun, and her hands were full of knitting. "If you say her name's Madame Defarge, I'm leaving," Sarah whispered.

"Haven't the foggiest what her name is," Tim hissed. And to the woman: "Madame Fogel is expecting us."

The concierge nodded, and they walked to the rear of the lobby and manipulated a large brass knocker. A maid let them in. "Madame is waiting for you in the garden."

She led them down a long hall, too quickly for even Sarah's keen eye to evaluate the surroundings, into a small space enclosed by high stone walls, where the late autumn sun was filtered through another of the ubiquitous chestnut trees onto a patch of worn grass.

"Timothy!" a woman exclaimed, rising to meet them and stretching out both hands. "At last. I've been impatient since dawn."

Women flutter around him like butterflies, Sarah thought. Because he's so beautiful. Why not me? What do they feel that I don't? His Bellini look was pronounced in this setting. The golden hair and the finely chiseled features were exquisite. Beautiful, there was no other word for him.

Tim's head bobbed quickly. He kissed each of the woman's hands, she both his cheeks. Only when this ritual of affection was ended did he introduce Sarah.

"You must call me Jenny," the woman said. "I prefer it. And you are too young and pretty to be Madamoiselle. I shall call you Sarah. Now, sit down both of you. The coffee is waiting."

They drank café au lait from exquisite Meissen cups and watched sparrows cavort in a startlingly grotesque birdbath becarved with monsters and covered in verdigris. Jenny resembled the sparrows. She was dark and small. She wore a black dress and a double string of pearls. Her low-heeled pumps gleamed; they molded themselves to her tiny feet. So too her stockings. No snags, no hint of a wrinkle. Perfect, like the tailoring of the dress, the lay of the pearls, the hair combed into a sleek chignon. Jennie Fogel was ageless and impeccably groomed and formidable. Sarah found herself wondering if her blue jersey dress was wrinkled and if the hem was straight.

"Well," the perfect woman said at last. "I suppose we must get to business." She rose and led them into the house, to a square, high-ceilinged room where the floor was covered with a glowing Oriental rug, the walls paneled and painted cream, the furniture upholstered in dark green velvet.

"My study," Jenny said. There was no sign that any intellectual pursuit took place here. The few books were leather-bound and carefully arranged on three shelves. The desk was bare except for a spray of orchids. Jenny sat down at the desk and moved the orchids slightly to one side. She motioned her visitors to chairs already drawn up. "Only a few pieces this time," she told Tim.

A drawer was opened, a tied cylinder of red velvet produced. Jenny undid the bow that secured it and rolled it open. "This pearl, for instance."

Sarah gasped. The pearl was gunmetal gray, tear-shaped, as big as the first joint of her thumb. She couldn't help herself. "Is that real?"

Jenny laughed. "Oh, yes," she said. "You didn't prepare her, Timothy. I thought she was your assistant?"

"On artworks," Tim explained, embroidering the cover story. "Not jewelry." He turned to Sarah. "Jenny's collection is fantastic. Her mother was a Russian princess."

"And my father a German conductor who didn't specialize in Wagner. He never managed to please the Führer. He died during the war, and Maman and I were under house arrest. We were living together in Berlin then, because my husband and my son were both in the army. Maman and I survived. Our men did not."

"I'm sorry," Sarah said. "I keep saying gauche, silly things and embarrassing Tim. In America that"—she pointed to the pearl—"would be in a museum. It astounds me to find it in private ownership."

Jenny cocked her head. "I think you have touched on a profound difference between American wealth and European pretension, *ma petite,* but it's too deep for me. Anyway, I'm not rich. I managed to bring some jewels with me when I came to Paris in 1948. A few of my own, mostly Maman's, she was dead by then. Now I sell them little by little, to keep myself. But unfortunately nothing's quite museum quality."

"Fortunate for me," Tim said, smiling. "If Jenny's things were wanted by the Victoria and Albert or the Metropolitan, she'd sell with Christie's or Sotheby's. That's the sort of thing they do better than anyone in the world."

"But when something falls off that pedestal," Jenny added, "it falls very far. They would take my little treasures, but I know I get more attention from Durant's. Besides, this way I get to see Timothy twice a year." She smiled at him and prodded the pearl with one slim finger. "Well, *mon cher,* what do you think?"

Tim took a notebook from the pocket of his cashmere jacket. It was fawn color and suited him. And it was very expensive. Timothy Durant had an appetite for the good life, Sarah realized, and he was willing to work hard in order to indulge it. He was focused entirely on Jenny now. Sarah might as well have disappeared. "Tell me the story of the piece," he said.

"The pearl belonged originally to my grandmother. At least originally so far as our family is concerned. Gran'papa brought it home from Jaipur, where he'd gone elephant hunting. As near as I can guess, that would have been the early 1870s."

Sarah leaned forward. "So you have your provenance, Tim. A pearl from a maharaja's turban."

"To the best of our knowledge and belief," he added, writing quickly.

"A ten-thousand-pound reserve, Tim," Jenny said.

"Too high, my love. Eight at the most. It's not a true black pearl, the color's not deep enough."

She frowned, but didn't argue. "How much for this then?" Jenny produced an ornate gold ring set with two sapphires. "Papa gave it to me when I was married."

"It's not antique and the setting isn't fashionable." Tim screwed a jeweler's glass into his eye and examined the stones. "A reserve of two thousand," he said finally. "We may get as much as thirty-five hundred with luck. The stones are large, but they aren't perfect."

244

The bargaining continued for half an hour. While Sarah watched in silence, Tim agreed to sell a heavy gold Florentine pendant and a lorgnette encrusted in diamond chips, as well as the ring and the black pearl. The reserves on the four pieces would total fifteen thousand pounds. If Jenny was lucky, she'd do a little better, and clear something over fifteen thousand after Durant's commission. "Enough to keep me for six months," she said. "So nothing more this time."

She wrapped the selected items in the red velvet jewel case. Tim signed a receipt and put the jewelry in his pocket. They all rose. "It's disagreeable, this haggling," Jenny said. "You know something about art, Sarah. Come see what I've not yet been forced to sell."

There was a door in one wall of the study. Jenny opened it and led them through to the salon. "My husband's family had a business in Egypt before the war. These pots and bowls are all I have left of their collection. A few of them are said to be very old indeed. Sarah, what is it? You look ill."

The bowls were mostly hammered brass, but one pot was terracotta. Uneven, hand-thrown, stained with use. Sarah couldn't stop staring at it. There were letters or symbols carved into the rim. "I don't know," she whispered.

The bowl seemed to grow bigger. It filled her vision, encompassed her universe. *Do-sol-la-fa.* The music in her head was deafening. A new rhythm, a kind of pounding, repetitive, insistent. Urgency. *Sarah! Listen, Sarah! Hear me! See . . .*

She didn't want to hear and see. Not here, not now, not ever if Jarib was no part of it. Sarah concentrated on only the notes, thrusting from her the woman and her demands. It took an enormous effort, it drained her, left a throbbing, sick-making pain in her head. The room was spinning. Sarah tried to clutch at Tim, but he was out of reach. She fainted.

Tim got her back to the hotel. The concierge produced a doctor, an old man with an elaborately curled mustache and thinning hair. He poked and probed and listened. "Mademoiselle is a bit overtired," he pronounced. "You think no sleep is necessary when you are young. And you eat always the hamburgers, while running. Unless, of course, Mademoiselle is *enceinte*?"

245

"No," Sarah told him, there was no chance that she was pregnant.

"Worse luck," Tim murmured under his breath, and grinned at her, but she was too weak to grin back.

The doctor prescribed strong tea and aspirin and rest. He left, still muttering about hamburgers. McDonald's was ruining the digestion of the young. Sarah didn't bother to tell him she hadn't had a Big Mac in months.

Tim sat by her bed for hours. Holding her hand, sponging her forehead, not talking because he knew she didn't want him to. Even though she hadn't said. Her thoughts were turmoil and anguish. This time it had been almost a direct confrontation. Between her and the woman. And the cost of winning had been to faint away like some Victorian damsel. And be left with another of the terrible headaches.

Without Jarib's guidance the whole thing was getting frighteningly out of hand. But if he didn't love her, she didn't want him. Just his professional help would never be enough, even if he'd give it. Too much, the whole damn thing was just too much. A tear rolled down her cheek, and silently Tim wiped it away. Sarah touched his hand, grateful for his kindness. Finally she slept.

Nahaam was a kind man, a good man. His house was big and comfortable, and Sarah and Rachel were safe there. They stayed because they had no place else to go and because no one suggested they leave. Nahaam's wife was kind to them, too. Not just because her husband demanded it, but because that was her nature. Besides, she was barren, and until Sarah and Rachel came, the house had been lonely. Now she shared with Sarah the repetitive household tasks which by custom fell to her and not Nahaam's numerous servants: the spinning and weaving and the tedious, endless milling.

Thrice each week, working side by side, the two woman made flour for the household's needs. The wife of Nahaam would grind the wheat by hand, using two cleverly matched stones; then Sarah would winnow it and pound it finer and sift it into the large clay pots which were sent to the kitchen, where the bread was baked.

Sarah envied Nahaam's wife her clay pots. They were a traditional part of a woman's dowry, precious things handed down from mother to daughter. They carried symbols around the rims, protection against souring milk or spoiled grain. If she had not been cast out of her father's house in disgrace but left it as a bride, Sarah would have such pots of her own. As it was, she had none.

Then, after Sarah had been in Nahaam's house for a year, his wife sickened and died. Sarah wondered if Nahaam would now wish to share her bed, but he never suggested it. He only asked her to remain and to take over the running of his household since he had neither daughters nor daughters-in-law to look after his wants.

In the year 78, when her daughter was fifteen, Nahaam told Sarah he wished to marry Rachel. He was almost forty, but still vigorous, and the girl told her mother that the idea was acceptable to her. Only one thing concerned Sarah. "We are followers of Jesus," she told Nahaam. "You are not."

"Religion I leave to the priests," he told her. "But I am a Jew for all that. As you are, despite your fool of a father's rantings. In my house Rachel will keep the laws of our people, as you have always done. As for this Jesus, I know nothing of him. Only that now Jew argues with Jew about one more thing, as if we did not have enough trouble before."

Sarah had to agree that all he said was true. And had she not seen the man who believed in Jesus among the mob that murdered Anwar? Sarah was confused, but in the end she agreed to the marriage. Rachel herself was convinced it was the right thing. "As it is, I have no name and no place," she told her mother. "Now I will be a rich man's wife. Besides," she added, "I do not wish to be a Christian. They killed my father. And his father says he believes in Jesus, who you tell me spoke of love and forgiveness, but he wants nothing to do with you or me."

That was also the truth. At last Sarah's conscience was easy about the marriage. Particularly because she was worried about Rachel. A husband and, if God willed, children would steady her. The girl was full of strange silences, and odd musings. Sometimes she seemed to know things before they happened. Like the day soon after she was married, when she went to her mother and said, "My grandfather is coming to see you."

She could not mean Reb Michael, who had died the year before. "Farak!" Sarah exclaimed. "Coming here? How do you know? Did you see him?"

249

"I haven't seen him, but I know."

That was all Rachel would say, and when Farak did not appear that day, Sarah was relieved and dismissed the girl's words as nonsense. But the next morning he came.

"For some time I have wished to speak with you, Sarah bas Michael," Farak said. "But I did not have the courage."

"And why have you come now?" Her voice was hard, for try as she might, Sarah could not forgive him.

"Because I am going to die soon. I am an old man." His hair and his beard were white, he stooped, and his eyes watered continually. Obviously he spoke the truth. "I do not wish to go to my judgment without asking your forgiveness, Sarah. And my grandchild's."

Sarah was moved by the old man's pleas, but Rachel refused to speak with him. "Very well," he said. "I understand. Your forgiveness will have to be enough, Sarah. I have brought you a present."

He sent word to the servant waiting outside, and a large box was brought into the room where Sarah and Farak sat together. The box was made of teak, itself a beautiful thing, and when the lid was pried off, she saw that it contained two wonderful silver candlesticks. "They are exquisite, Farak. Thank you."

"One is more than that," the old man said. He motioned for the servant to leave, and when he was sure they were quite alone, he showed her how in one candlestick he had created a secret hiding place. "Your song is well known, Sarah. I used it in my design. *Rube' nota, telaterba' nota, rube' nota, nuss nota.* Watch me and see how it is done."

He laid the candlestick on a carved stone bench and stretched out his arms so that one hand held the base, the other the top, and he made certain turns and the twined silver parted to reveal a wonderful hiding place inside. "The notes are the key," Farak explained. "If you know them, you know how many full, half, and quarter turns. But no one will ever guess unless you tell him. The secret is yours to use as you choose, Sarah."

"It is truly marvelous. But what will I put in this hiding place? I have nothing of value, no jewels. Only this bracelet that Anwar made for me." She held out her wrist encircled with the bangle. "I wear it always. When I die, it will belong to Rachel."

"Someday the secret place will be important," Farak promised. "I do not know how or why. Only that it is so. Believe me. In this I have been guided by the spirit of the Lord."

"But why?"

"I don't know," he repeated. And after that he went away, and the next month he was dead.

Sarah put the pair of candlesticks in her private apartments, and

Rachel saw and admired them, but they didn't really interest her. She was pregnant with her first child and it turned out to be a son and she and Nahaam had time for little but their own happiness.

The years passed and Sarah grew older and sometimes she thought she should tell the secret of the candlestick to Rachel, but she never did. Why she could not say. Perhaps because she still had nothing to put inside it. Sarah was a woman rich only in the memory of the things that had happened to her. And most of those memories were unhappy.

In the year 90 she began to wonder about the significance of her life and about the written chronicles of the sayings of the Lord Jesus which were beginning to take the place of the spoken stories known to Sarah and her parents. They were needed because since the fall of Jerusalem the churches were without real leadership. And they were more and more composed of Gentiles who did not understand the old ways and who wished not to be associated with the defeated Jews.

The written accounts were widely circulated. They were in Greek, which the Gentiles understood, rather than Aramaic. And often they seemed to Sarah to be slightly different from the stories she had been told. Particularly where Paulos and his teachings were concerned. This bothered her, but she reminded herself that she was a woman and such affairs were the province of men. Besides, she wasn't really a follower of Jesus anymore, only in her heart. She had not, for instance, shared in the Lord's Supper since she left her father's house.

She did not worry overmuch about these things. Sarah had six grandsons now, and the eldest was a promising silversmith. The other boys would doubtless grow grapes and make wine like their father, but Sarah was delighted to see one of Anwar's heirs carrying on his craft. Such things occupied her mind and filled her days—until she read the account of the first years after the Lord's death written by Luke of Antioch, whom she knew had been with Paulos for a time.

"He doesn't tell the truth!" she exclaimed to Rachel. "He says that Peter and the elders in Jerusalem agreed that the Gentiles need not follow Jewish Law. They never did."

Rachel shrugged. "What difference does it make? Men just look for excuses to argue and make war and kill each other. Who knows that better than you and I?"

Sarah shook her head. "But it was not like this, not as Luke says. James was the first leader, not Peter. And if Peter had such a dream, no one else ever heard about it or said everything must change."

"What dream?" Rachel went on with her weaving; she was merely indulging her mother, who was now old and inclined to dwell on the past.

"A dream that it was right to eat animals with cloven feet, and things that creep on the earth." Sarah shuddered. "No Jew would eat such things."

"The Christians are not Jews anymore," Rachel said. "I don't think they ever really were."

"You are prejudiced because of what happened," Sarah said stiffly. And she got up and went to her own part of the house and thought and prayed for a long time. Then she found a stylus and some sheets of papyrus and began to write. And she blessed her father, despite what he'd done, because it was he who taught her this skill which women did not normally have. Now she was convinced that she was using it to serve the God Reb Michael had served, and his Messiah, Jesus.

When she had finished, Sarah knew her testament was a simple thing. It was only the story of how things had been when she was a girl, of the many families she had known who were good Jews even though they accepted that the crucified Nazarene had been the promised Messiah, and of how they kept the Law and were supported in this by James and the elders of the Church in Jerusalem. "After the Temple fell, everything changed," she wrote finally. "And now the Gentiles want to pretend that Jesus himself somehow made the Law unimportant. But in the beginning it was not like that."

Sarah signed her name to the account and rolled it tightly and opened the candlestick and put it inside. Now she knew why Farak had been inspired to make it for her, and she was glad she hadn't told Rachel its secret. After Sarah was dead, Rachel might tear up the sheets and throw them away. She wouldn't think it was important. But Sarah believed it was. Some time from now, she told herself, perhaps in my great-grandchildren's days, someone will guess the secret of the candlestick and find my story. Perhaps people will be willing to listen then.

Three years later, in her forty-third year, Sarah became ill. She knew she was dying. Her heart beat so hard in her chest she could hear it, and she had difficulty breathing. Rachel sat beside her, sponging her forehead with water sweet with herbs. "Thank you," Sarah murmured.

"Ssh," Rachel said. "Don't waste your strength talking. Nahaam has sent for a doctor. He will bring leeches and bleed you and you'll get better."

"Perhaps," Sarah murmured. "But, Rachel, listen . . ." Her voice faltered, and she had to struggle to continue. "I have very little to leave you. My lyre, of course, and this bracelet." She removed it from her wrist and gave it to her daughter. "You know the story of the bracelet. And the candlesticks. Keep them always, Rachel. When you are old, give them to a daughter-in-law. They are very important. And listen, I have written the truth. Remember my music, Rachel. The four notes . . ."

Sarah could not finish. Her heart stopped, and she died.

Rachel puzzled over the things her mother had said. She took the candlesticks to her part of the house and she looked often at them, but they told her nothing. When she cleaned the rooms that had been Sarah's, she searched for the story, but didn't find it. "Just ravings," she told her family. "She wasn't in her right mind."

Nahaam merely shrugged; his sons and their wives did not seem to be listening.

Some years later Rachel died, and Sarah's things were divided among the wives of her grandsons. The woman who was married to the silversmith got the bracelet and the candlesticks, because her husband had been Sarah's favorite. Someone else got the lyre. Eventually it broke and was discarded. And some bedeviled member of a later generation was forced to sell one of the candlesticks in order to eat. But as luck would have it, all unknowing, he kept the right one.

Time passed. The family told stories about their ancestors and a secret testament was sometimes mentioned, but no one really knew anything about it, and eventually it was relegated to the area of legend; a thing that older, simpler people had believed which was now discredited. Sometimes certain Alexandrian Jews claimed to have more than ordinary knowledge, a few even to hear some mysterious music, but this was only whispered about. These were ages when the Church ruled, and such admissions could lead to a charge of witchcraft and death at the stake.

By the time of the family who were now not simply silversmiths but jewelers, the Al Ghawahergys, even the memory was gone. Albeit one candlestick and the bracelet remained.

Nine

It took Jarib two days to get as far as Virginia. He followed Route 95 most of the way, but he drove slowly peering into every vehicle that passed him, especially the trucks. He'd fastened on the notion that Lenore would hitch a ride with a trucker, somebody who'd be more interested in her gorgeous body than her nuttiness. He couldn't genuinely believe the psychiatrist's assertion that Lenore could be quite normal when he wasn't around.

He stopped at every restaurant on the highway, asked questions, looked. Nothing. He saw no sign of her, and apparently neither had anyone else. But that didn't prove anything. There were other routes and a hundred ways he could miss her. But not when he got where he was going, where he was certain she was going. It was a small place. Not big enough to be on any map, not big enough for Lenore to hide in. A small country place still locked into the old ways; that had been the trouble from the beginning. That and his pigheadedness.

. . .

The purgatory of Jarib Baraak began in 1969, in a Cambridge bar two blocks from Harvard Square—on the wrong side of the invisible divide between town and gown. His friend Tom Lasky found the bar while writing a paper for a sociology course. "It's real," he told Jarib. "We need a change from the ivory tower."

So they often spent an hour or so drinking beer among the blue-shirted men who worked at the nearby abattoir, enjoying the contrast with Harvard, feeling sophisticated and worldly. They were sitting there one night in March, during the last semester of their junior year, when Tom said, "Listen, I've got to tell you something. I don't think you're going to understand."

"That's an intriguing introduction."

"Next year, after graduation," Tom continued, "I'm going to enter the seminary."

Jarib was sufficiently startled to state the obvious. "You mean you're going to be a priest?"

"Yeah."

"What the hell for?"

Tom grinned. "Hell isn't the right word. It's the other place I had in mind."

Jarib was silent for a few seconds. "You really believe all that stuff, is that it?" He shook his head and stared at his empty glass. "I thought you went to church because of your mother, and your sister maybe."

Lasky's father was dead, and he was very close to what remained of his family. Jarib had always admired that. The Baraaks were intellectual and reserved. The family wasn't very Jewish or very eastern, and they were both, but that's how it was. So Jarib spent a lot of time in the Lasky apartment near the campus. He knew they were observant Catholics, but he'd assumed that Tom went along to placate the two women. Not that Lenore could really be called a woman. She was just seventeen. He fastened on that now.

"What about your sister?"

"What about her?"

"How's she going to react? Lenore depends on you. You say it yourself, you're the only father she's ever known."

"Yes, but she's growing up. She'll be eighteen by the time I go to the seminary. And there's her dancing. Did she tell you, somebody's forming a Boston ballet company and she's going to be part of it?"

"She told me. I still don't think it will take your place." He didn't know why he was so insistent on this element of Tom's decision. Maybe Mrs. Lasky would miss her son more than Lenore would. But there was something about the kid that always touched him. Not just that she was tall and blond and beautiful, as she was. Something else. Some element of extraordinary vulnerability that was a contrast with her physical grace and poise.

Tom moved the discussion to another plane. "I wish you'd see that all the stuff you're so interested in, the power of the mind, parapsychology itself, it doesn't make sense without God."

"Maybe," Jarib admitted. "But to me God and religion are separate issues. All this Chosen People stuff, for instance, it hasn't been much of a choice, has it?"

"No, I guess not."

And they'd drunk up and walked back to the campus, and on that particular evening said nothing more about Tom's decision. But Jarib always knew that had been the start of it.

He couldn't get Lenore Lasky out of his mind once he learned that her brother was to become a priest. At first he thought he was being particularly friendly toward her because she needed support. And when he realized that she did indeed see Tom's plan as a desertion, it confirmed and intensified his behavior. He spent more time than ever in the Lasky flat. Eventually he began taking Lenore places. For a while he didn't think of these occasions as dates; eventually he realized that's what they were. Lenore had become not just Tom's kid sister, she was his girlfriend.

One evening he took her to meet his parents. Mina Baraak tried to be kind, but the tall blond girl her son brought home seemed to inhabit a world about which Mina knew nothing and into which she could find no entry. Jarib's mother taught chemistry in a high school in Newton. She had nothing to say to a dancer preoccupied with art and painfully shy in the bargain. Sami Baraak was also a chemist; he worked in the research department of a large drug company. He said a few words to Lenore, then retired to his room to read medical journals. Mina tried a little harder, but to no avail. In the end she made them small cups of thick, sweet Egyptian coffee and produced a pastry soaked in honey and stuffed with ground nuts.

"How delicious," Lenore said. "Did you make this?"

Jarib's mother looked startled. "No, of course not. I haven't any time to bake. Anyway, I wouldn't know how."

After that they finished the snack in silence.

"Your folks didn't like me," Lenore said later.

"That's not true. They're not very demonstrative, that's all."

"I thought all Jews were."

"Propaganda. Or maybe it's only European Jews."

"When did your family come to America?"

"In 1949, right after the founding of Israel. The Baraaks had been in Alexandria as long as anybody knows. But once the Jews had their own state and the whole thing with the Arabs blew up, we weren't permitted to stay. It probably would have been pretty unpleasant anyway."

"You were born in Egypt then?"

"Sure. But I was a year old when I came here. I'm a U.S. citizen. A real Yankee-Doodle boy. You know that."

"Yes. But I prefer to think of you as foreign and exotic."

She'd pressed his hand and they'd both laughed and later, when he kissed her good night, there was an eruption of intense physical passion between them for the first time. Jarib hadn't thought he felt that way about Lenore. But obviously he did. And that led to the next step.

It never occurred to him simply to take Lenore to bed. He'd had his first girl the night of his high school senior prom, and at least half a dozen since he'd been at Harvard, but Lenore was different. For one thing he was sure she was a virgin; for another she subscribed to the same moral code her mother, and apparently Tom, maintained. The sexual revolution may just as well not be happening as far as the Laskys were concerned. Jarib woke up one morning in January of 1970 and found that he fully intended to marry Lenore, and to wait to possess her until that time.

That June Jarib was graduated summa cum laude. In August the wedding took place at St. Columkill's Church. The Lasky family had been parishioners there for years, but Lenore wasn't the one who mentioned being married at St. Columkill's. Tom broached the subject of a Catholic ceremony soon after his sister and his best friend became engaged.

"I don't want you to do anything you feel hypocritical about. It isn't that."

"I really don't mind either way, Tom. If Lenore wants a church wedding, it's okay with me."

"It's not just the wedding. I know she wants all the pomp and circumstance, for my mother, I suppose, but it's more than that. Lenore's a Catholic, Jarib. If she doesn't marry you according to our rules, she'll be outside the pale, refused the sacraments."

He'd sounded worried and earnest and embarrassed, and Jarib was loath to be the cause of so much discomfort. "Listen, it's okay. Really. I don't have to convert or say I believe in your religion, do I?"

"No, nothing like that. And thank God you don't have to sign anything anymore. They used to make you swear you'd bring up any children as Catholics. Now the Catholic partner only has to agree to use his best efforts."

Jarib hadn't thought much about children. He couldn't imagine delicate, indrawn Lenore as a mother; besides, he was going after his master's and his doctorate simultaneously. It would be years before they could afford kids. He didn't want to involve Lenore in a decision that would put her in conflict with her Church, so he planned to use condoms, but not to discuss the matter with Lenore. He did hint at it once, and she only smiled and he wasn't sure she'd understood. He decided it didn't matter. And he didn't say anything about his intentions to Tom. Only "No sweat, buddy. Bring on the incense and bells and whatever else you folks produce. I'm game."

Mina and Sami looked puzzled when he announced that the wedding would take place in a church, but in their usual manner they kept any objections to themselves. The Baraaks had no family in America. Few of their friends were Jews. Certainly neither of them was religious. It hadn't even occurred to them to arrange for Jarib to be Bar Mitzvah. He was circumcised only because he was born before they left Egypt, and in the hospital the process was automatic for Muslims and Jews. They had asked Mina if she wanted a religious ceremony. "No," she'd told them, "just do it."

So if their son was going to marry this blond dancer, whom they both suspected wasn't overly bright, he might as well do it in St. Columkill's as anyplace else.

The fellowship at Duke came through a few weeks before the wedding. "Rhine's semiretired now," Jarib explained. "But it's still the best parapsychology department in the country."

"Then that's where you have to go, I guess." Lenore didn't quite meet his eyes.

"What about the ballet company?"

She shrugged. "I won't be able to go on with them, will I?"

"Do you mind very much?"

"No. Your career is more important, Jarib."

And he didn't protest. He worried about her adjusting to life on a university campus, however. Particularly among the science types with whom he associated. So when they found the house in Pine Creek, Jarib decided almost instantly that it was ideal.

They'd arrived in Durham a week before, the day after they were married, and checked into the nicest hotel in the city. It was their honeymoon, a wedding gift from Mina and Sami, and they were using the time to explore the countryside and find a place to live for the next few years. They had a new Volkswagen Beetle, a present from Lenore's mother, and they went for long drives every day. That was how they stumbled on Pine Creek. It was in the prettiest part of the area around Duke, in the foothills of the Blue Ridge Mountains, about fifty miles west of the Chapel Hill campus.

This was apple country, and now in late summer the trees bent under the weight of the fruit and the air was heavy with the perfume of their ripening. The white pines and the creek which gave the place its name hugged the perimeter of a tiny town that consisted of little more than some houses painted in faded pastels and a combination gas station and general store. "It looks like a movie I once saw," Lenore murmured.

"A lot of movies," Jarib said. "C'mon, let's park and walk around."

They left the car on the outskirts of the settlement and walked along the bank of the creek. It was hot and still, and the water didn't seem to flow at all, just to sit and bask in the play of shade and sunlight which dappled its surface. The house appeared when they turned a bend. It had been blue once, but time and weather had rubbed it gray. It was small and single-story, with a barn that had obviously become a garage in some latter-day occupancy. "It looks empty," Jarib said.

"But somebody must own it," Lenore said. "All the shutters are closed and it's locked."

"Let's go back to the gas station and ask."

"Jarib, are you thinking we could live here?" She sounded astonished by the notion.

"Sure, why not? It's beautiful."

"Yes, I guess it is." Lenore turned and surveyed the scene. Her exquisite grace was somehow enhanced by the setting. Jarib caught his breath and felt himself get hard. But when she looked back at him, there was no answering passion in her eyes. Only fear. "It's pretty lonely. And a long way from the university."

"Not so far. Just about an hour's drive. And a country place like this may look lonely, but it's safer than big cities nowadays. I bet there aren't any muggings in Pine Creek. We can ask about that, too," he added, grinning.

But they didn't. They got caught up in negotiating the rent. The man at the garage said his name was Nate Summers, and in fact, he owned the old place down by the creek. His grandpa had built it. And sure, it could be rented, why the hell not, if they could agree a price and Mr. and Mrs. Baraak would pay a couple of months in advance.

Finally they settled on $90 a month and Jarib took out his pristine new checkbook from the Durham County Bank in Chapel Hill and wrote a check for $180 and Nate Summers looked at it carefully, then disappeared into a back office and came back with the keys. "Here you go. Hope it's okay for you. But remember, we agreed on two months either way. If you don't like it and don't stay, you ain't gotta pay no more rent. But I get to keep the hundred and eighty anyways."

"That's our deal, Mr. Summers," Jarib said, sticking out his hand.

Summers shook it, and as they were leaving, he called after them, "Got me all the groceries you're likely to need in my shop out back. And there's good fish in the creek. Got me all kinds of fishing gear, too."

Jarib waved his arm in response, and they hurried back to the house, laughing and talking to each other in a bad imitation of Nate Summers's Appalachian twang.

The lock turned easily, and they found the house less dirty than they'd imagined it would be. It appeared that someone had used it recently, and cleaned it when he left. There was dust, but it was a thin layer, and as soon as they opened the windows, the musty smell disappeared. There were even a few pieces of furniture. Among them was a couch covered in a flowered cotton slipcover.

Lenore ran her slim and elegant fingers over it. "Somebody just washed and ironed this," she said.

Jarib covered her hand with his and pulled her into his arms, and they made love on that couch in the September dusk, with the sound of crickets just beginning outside.

Jarib mounted his wife with deliberation and no haste. He was aware of the country sounds and the country smells, and of Lenore's exquisitely long legs sprawled on either side of his hips and her arms wrapped tightly 'round his neck, like a child clinging for comfort. "Bring your knees up, the way I showed you last night," he murmured into her neck, and she did as he bade her and he cupped one of her small, pointed breasts in his hand and wanted to go slow and try to make it good for her. He was pretty sure she hadn't had an orgasm yet, and he hoped she would soon, after she learned to relax. "Don't be scared," he said.

"Not so long as you're here with me," she whispered.

That wasn't what he'd meant, but this wasn't the time to explain. He couldn't have anyway, his body was making its own urgent twenty-two-year-old claims, and he thrust himself into her a few times, then finished with a great shuddering explosion of pleasure.

"Nate Summers has a son called Ruben," Lenore told him after they'd lived in Pine Creek for two weeks. "He's been off in Nashville at some country music thing, and he just came home. I met him today when I went shopping."

Jarib's classes had begun the previous day and he was preoccupied. He grunted and kept his eyes on the book he was reading. Tomorrow he'd conduct his first sophomore seminar.

"I don't think Ruben's pleased that his father rented the house," Lenore continued. "He says he was living in it. Now he's got to move in with his pa. That's what he calls him, Pa."

Jarib grinned. "I'll bet. Well, Ruben's not our problem; we've got a deal with old man Summers. I don't think he'll welsh."

Lenore shook her head. "No, I'm sure he won't."

She wanted to say that she wished he would, because she'd been terribly lonely these past two days in Pine Creek while Jarib was away. But she didn't; she ladled out canned vegetable soup she'd tried to improve with a little sherry. The soup tasted alcoholic and unpleasant to her, but Jarib didn't comment and neither did she. Nor did she say anything more about Nate or Ruben, or the way the younger Summers had looked at her and made her feel half naked in her thin cotton T-shirt and cutoff jeans.

They'd brought Lenore's stereo with them and her collection of records. Every day after Jarib left for school she changed into a leotard and played music and practiced at the barre Jarib had improvised in the living room. Sometimes she danced for him in the evenings, too. Jarib said he loved to watch her, and afterward he always wanted to make love. After that he'd get out of bed and go into the kitchen with his books and Lenore would lie there and try to sleep. The crickets made her nervous, and she tried to pretend they were cars in a Cambridge street, but it didn't work.

One morning toward the end of the month she cut her dance practice short because she had the sensation of being watched. She told herself it was ridiculous, but still she grew tense and angry. This was the one time of the day she really enjoyed and now it was spoiled. She stripped off the leotard and showered and pulled on her shorts and shirt and went out to the yard to bring in the laundry hanging on the line. Ruben was sitting beneath a tree at the edge of the clearing that surrounded the house. He held a knife and a chunk of wood.

"What are you doing here?" she demanded.

"Nothin' much. Pretty soon it's gonna be too damn cold for you to wear them things." He gestured to her cutoff jeans, and his eyes traveled the length of her legs. "Gonna be too bad for me then."

Lenore flushed and didn't answer him. Instead she busied herself with the clothes. She had to wash them by hand, and she noted that Jarib's shirts weren't as white as they should be.

"My girlfriend's named Stella Sue," he said. "She's pretty, but not so pretty as you."

"Look, I don't want you hanging around here. You'd better go or I'll have to speak to my husband."

Ruben hooted with laughter. "You will, huh? And what's that smart-ass city boy gonna do? Maybe set his spooks on me? Oh, yeah, I know what he's getting up to over there in his big fancy college. Stella Sue works in the cafeteria and she told me. Folks 'round here know all about that crazy ol' man Rhine and his spooks. Ain't scared of 'em neither."

Lenore turned away and carried the laundry basket into the house and locked both the back and front doors. She sat in the house all day, afraid to go out in case Ruben was still around. When Jarib came home, she blurted out the story.

"He had a knife and some wood?" Jarib asked. "Is that what you said?"

"Yes."

He threw back his head and guffawed. "God! I don't believe it. Whittling. Any minute some director's going to yell, 'Cut!' and this whole place will disappear."

"Jarib, please. I can't stand Ruben. He scares me. He looks at me as if—"

He put his hands on her shoulders and interrupted. "As if you were a beautiful woman. Because you are. Honey, don't take Pine Creek and its characters so seriously. We've stumbled on some nineteenth-century throwback. Years from now we'll remind each other of what we saw here and have giggling fits."

"He thinks parapsychology is about ghosts. Spooks he calls them."

"Yes, well, it's not surprising. People like the Summers' aren't likely to understand, are they?"

"No, of course not. His girlfriend's name is Stella Sue. She works at the university. In the cafeteria, he said."

"I'll bet she's the one who kept this place so clean. They were probably shacked up here before Nate rented it to us."

267

"I think so too. Jarib, why don't we move out and let them have it back? If we took an apartment in Chapel Hill, or even Durham, you wouldn't have to travel so far."

"I don't mind the drive. But if you want to move, we will, after we've used up our two months here. We can't afford double rent, honey. And Nate won't give us our money back, you know that."

Lenore nodded and went to get the tuna casserole she'd made for dinner. Later he asked her to dance, but she said she didn't feel like it, so Jarib spread his books on the kitchen table and she went to bed alone.

After that Ruben was there every time she went out. He was skinny and no taller than she, but Lenore began to think of him as some enormous shadow looming over her life. He had red hair that he wore in a fifties-style duck cut, and his jeans were always skin-tight and tucked into cowboy boots. "He fantasizes he's Elvis," Jarib said. "Does he carry a guitar?"

"No, only the knife and the wood. Always. Jarib, I don't want to wait another month. I want to move out of here now."

"We can't afford that. You're being childish and irresponsible," he told her. And they had their first quarrel and made it up later in bed. But later still, when he was studying in the kitchen, Jarib heard her crying and decided he'd start asking around. Maybe somebody knew of an apartment in town they could rent cheap.

She stopped going out of the house. All day, while Jarib was gone, Lenore sat behind locked doors with the curtains drawn. She didn't tell Jarib that, and he didn't seem to notice how tense and nervous she'd become. Once he mentioned looking for another place for them to live and said he had a lead on an apartment a few miles from the campus, but it wouldn't be available until December 1.

"We'd have to stay here until then?" she asked.

"I don't see what else we can do. Please, honey, be reasonable."

Lenore bit her lip and turned away, and Jarib pretended not to see.

It was mid-October when she smelled the fire. She was in the kitchen, the doors and windows locked as usual, and at first she told herself it was her imagination. But soon the acrid smell got stronger, and she ran through the house, looking for the source, and couldn't find anything until she noticed wisps of smoke coming in through the living room windows. She fumbled open the locks of the front door, all the while picturing herself trapped inside a burning building, and finally flung herself onto the front porch.

Ruben was standing there, grinning. A few feet away, shoved into the soft earth, was a crude six-foot cross made of planks of green wood, burning slowly and smoking. Behind the obscenity Lenore perceived more faces. They were all male, and they looked like Ruben clones.

"Me and the boys figured you oughta know."

Lenore clung to the porch railing. She wanted to throw up, and she prayed she wouldn't. It seemed the ultimate shame. "You're evil and crazy," she shouted hoarsely. "All of you. Get that thing away from here."

"Oh, we will, but like I said. We want you to know."

"Know what?"

"That we found out he's a Jew boy, your fancy husband. We don't hold with no Christ killers comin' to live in Pine Creek."

"I'm going to get the police," Lenore said. She straightened up, feeling a surge of strength as she made the declaration. Ruben had gone too far, she had him now. She'd be rid of him. "I'm going to have you arrested. There are laws about this kind of thing."

Ruben laughed softly. "Sure there are. Now why don't you just walk yourself into town and call the sheriff? You can use the pay phone at Pa's. You know the way." He nodded to the path stretching along the creek. The approach to it was barred by the four men he'd brought with him. They all watched her.

"Whatsamatter, honey? Maybe you ain't got a dime? Well, here. I'll lend you one." He stretched out his hand with a coin in it. "Now you just walk down to Pa's place and do your callin'."

Lenore looked from his evil grin to the faces of the others. The wind shifted suddenly, and the smoke from the burning cross changed direction and blew straight at her. Shuddering and coughing, she ran back into the house.

For a while she just sat on the floor in the front hall, shivering and sobbing. Then she realized that there was no noise from out front and the burning smell was gone. She crawled into the living room and peeked through the curtains. There was no one around, but she could see the black place in the earth where the cross had been. Jarib would see it when he came home.

Of course! That was the answer. Jarib would see the evidence of this vicious, obscene assault and he'd put her in the car instantly and they'd drive away. They could spend the night in that nice hotel in Durham where they'd had their honeymoon. And tomorrow she'd go apartment hunting while he was at school. She could do it herself, she didn't need Jarib with her. He'd understand now that it hadn't just been her imagination. Pine Creek was evil and Ruben was a monster. But he'd done her a favor today. He'd given her evidence.

Lenore stood up and went to the bathroom and washed her face and combed her hair. She'd start packing. Yes, that would be another proof that she was adult and responsible. Jarib wouldn't want to waste time once he saw what they'd done. She'd make it possible for them to get away from here while it was still light.

She got their suitcases down from the shelf in the closet and made herself fold the clothes with care. An adult would do that. She even carried the stereo from the living room to the front hall. Jarib would understand that she didn't want to leave it behind. She'd gone back to put the records in a cardboard carton when she heard the noise.

It came from the lean-to pantry tacked onto the kitchen, and Lenore froze and listened and told herself she was imagining things. But she wasn't. The sound of breaking glass was accompanied by that of splintering wood.

Ruben came in first. The smell of whiskey entered with him. He had his knife in one hand and a bottle in the other, and he leaned down and set the bottle on the floor before he spoke. "Me and the boys got to thinkin'," he said. "Here's a pretty cunt like you married to a Jew boy with half his cock cut off. Don't seem right. So we figured to be neighborly and give you a little of what you've been missin'."

She saw the others then and she opened her mouth to scream, but Ruben raised the knife and brought it close to her throat. "You do any hollerin' and I'm gonna have to slit that pretty neck," he whispered. He reached out and grabbed her arm and turned his head to the men behind him. "I'm first, just like we agreed. Jed, you come here and hold the knife while I gets her clothes off."

• • •

Jarib tried to convince himself the scene was real. He was truly sitting in the office of the district attorney of Durham County, hearing the man tell him not to press charges.

"Of course, I understand how you feel, Mr. Baraak. And I know how my advice must sound. But you have to realize that I'm being honest. For your own good and, most important, with Mrs. Baraak in mind. Rape is an almost impossible charge to prove."

"Gang rape," Jarib said dully. "There were five of them."

The other man didn't meet his eyes. "So Mrs. Baraak says. But she can't identify anyone but Ruben Summers. She can't even describe the others. And folks in Pine Creek say your wife was . . . well, a little odd. She was a recluse according to them. Never made any friends."

"She's very shy. And it was strange for her, coming from Cambridge to a place like that."

"Yes. Maybe it wasn't the best place for you kids to pick to live."

Jarib felt his belly knot with pain. "Maybe. But that's beside the point now, isn't it? That doesn't prove that Lenore made the whole thing up. They did burn a cross in front of the house. The sheriff found the evidence of that."

"Yes, at least of something having recently been burned there. And I'm not suggesting your wife made up the story, not exactly. The doctor says when he examined her, he had no doubt of recent, repeated sexual intercourse."

Jarib clenched his fists and leaned over the desk. "What the hell *are* you saying then? God damn you, I want some justice! Don't you know the meaning of the word here in North Carolina?"

"Spare me your northern superiority, my young friend," the man said quietly. "I was born in New Jersey. Came here to go to Duke and stayed. This isn't the movies, Mr. Baraak, and I'm not protecting the locals. I'm trying to protect your wife from a sordid, extremely unpleasant trial, which in my best judgment will achieve nothing but notoriety. Have you ever seen a pack of reporters on the trail of a story like this?"

Jarib slumped in his chair. "No, but I can imagine it."

"Well, take my word, it's worse than you're imagining. And

271

whatever lawyer defends Summers and any others who finally get charged is going to insist on putting your wife on the stand. And the kinds of questions he will ask are beyond your ability to imagine. And I have to tell you that in the end I don't think you're going to get whatever you think of as justice. The defense will claim that Mrs. Baraak enticed Ruben and any others into whatever happened. And I don't see how I can prove rape beyond a reasonable doubt."

The two men sat in silence for a time. Eventually the DA opened a drawer in his desk and produced a bottle of Jack Daniel's. He poured two drinks and shoved one toward Jarib. When their glasses were empty, he refilled them. Finally he spoke. "She's still in the hospital, isn't she?"

"Yes. The doctors say she's all right physically. It's just the shock."

"Shit," the older man said softly, without discernible passion. "Sometimes life is shit and my job is shoveling it from one place to another. Tell me what you want me to do, Mr. Baraak, and I'll do it."

Jarib didn't answer him, just tossed back the last of his bourbon and got up and walked out.

He brought her home from the hospital to an apartment the head of the department found for them. It was bright and sunny and cheerfully furnished and five minutes from the campus. Jarib set up her stereo in the bedroom and installed a barre in the living room. For a few days she just lay in bed and didn't eat or speak, but on the weekend Tom and her mother came and Lenore seemed to perk up and be more like herself.

Tom and Jarib went out that Sunday afternoon and walked a long time in the crisp autumn air along streets lined with gracious old houses and trees shimmering russet and gold. A Sabbath calm pervaded all; it was the quintessential American scene. "It's not your fault, old buddy," Tom said softly. "Take off the hair shirt."

"I can't. It is my fault. She hated Pine Creek, and she was scared of Ruben Summers the first time she saw him. She wanted to move, but we'd paid two months' rent and I said we had to wait until that ran out."

"It wasn't an unreasonable decision, Jarib. Making yourself a martyr isn't going to help Lenore."

272

"Sweet forgiveness," Jarib said. "That's what they teach you in the seminary, huh?"

"Something like that. But in this case there's nothing to forgive. Not as far as you're concerned."

"Jesus, Tom, don't you see? She knew. From almost the first minute Lenore knew that place was death for her, and I wouldn't listen. I'm breaking my ass to learn how to investigate phenomena just like that, to understand it, and when it happened under my nose, I didn't do a damn thing until it was too late."

Lasky stopped walking and eyed his friend. "Is that what's eating you, Jarib? Not guilt about what happened to Lenore, a failure of your skills?"

"It isn't like that. Don't twist what I'm trying to say. You sound like some damned Jesuit."

"Guilty as charged," Lasky murmured. They walked on. When they'd turned and were headed back to the apartment, he said, "Look, whatever blame may or may not be involved, isn't the important thing now to pick up the pieces? For Lenore's sake?"

"Yes," Jarib agreed. "That's what I keep telling myself, and that's what I'm trying to do. But it isn't enough. Someday, somehow, I have to make it up to her."

He insisted on nursing her himself, and he didn't go back to classes or teaching until after the first of the year. Under the circumstances the university was prepared to be very flexible. By the middle of January 1971, he thought she was over the worst of it. She'd started dancing again for one thing. And he could kiss her now without her pulling away in horror. Right after it happened she couldn't bear for him to touch her.

"We're going to be okay, honey," he told her the night before he started school again. "We're going to put all this behind us and pick up our lives. That's the best revenge on all of them."

Lenore didn't answer, but she smiled.

When the sheriff called him the next day, he thought it must be a mistake. He made the man repeat the words three times, and still he didn't believe them.

"Ruben Summers is dead, Mr. Baraak. Your wife shot him in the head in front of old Nate and a couple of other witnesses. You better get yerself out here. If I was you, I'd bring me a lawyer."

"Tried to kill herself afterward," the sheriff said before taking him to the cell where she was being held. "Only by that time one of the others had wrestled the rifle out of her hands. Too late for Nate's boy, though."

"But where did she get a rifle?" He'd been thinking about that all the while they'd been driving out to Pine Creek, he and the professor of law who'd consented to come with him. "Where would Lenore get a gun?"

"Just went and bought it, I expect," the sheriff said. "Lots of places 'round here you can buy a hunting rifle. That's what she had. A twenty-two. Small, used for rabbits mostly, but big enough to kill a man at point-blank range."

She was sitting on the narrow cot in the jail's only cell, staring into space and smiling. Jarib reached for her, and at first she seemed compliant and docile. Then she looked at him. "You! Get away from me. Christ killer! It's all your fault. It's because you're a Jew. That's why they did it, because you're a Jew!"

They pleaded insanity. There was no difficulty. Three psychiatrists agreed that Lenore was patently, painfully mad, and unfit to stand trial. Instead they put her in an institution for the criminally insane in North Carolina. She remained there for six years. Until Jarib could afford better.

He fell into the television series by sheer luck. The brother-in-law of a friend was a producer with the local public channel and was introduced to Jarib and plied him with questions about his work and was fascinated with the responses. He conceived the idea of the broadcasts, and hesitantly Jarib agreed, because an assistant professorship at Duke didn't pay all that much and he was offered two thousand dollars for five shows.

Then he was lucky with the writer, who, like Jarib, had been a science fiction buff in his youth and saw the way to make the series informative and scholarly—Jarib wouldn't budge on that—and at the same time twang the nerve plucked by stories of worlds beyond ours. All the episodes were a combination of two elements: First Jarib ripped up the charlatans and the deluded, exposing their hoaxes or explaining their "mysteries." Then he discussed truly inexplicable phenomena, documented their existence, and explained current theories about possible cause and implication.

When the broadcast went out locally, the station was inundated with calls and mail and the program got rave reviews. PBS picked it up and showed it nationwide, a second series was commissioned along with an accompanying book, and there were appearances on all the talk shows. Dr. Jarib Baraak was a celebrity of sorts. And a little bit rich. And very soon a full professor at his alma mater. That's when he arranged for Lenore to be transferred to the private hospital in Framingham, where he could visit her every Sunday.

Each visit was the same. "Jew!" she'd snarl in what seemed to him so obviously a crazy woman's voice. "Jew. Jew. Jew . . ."

When Sarah woke, it was dark and the clock by the bed said eight. One little lamp was lit on the far side of the room. Tim sat beside it, reading. "I'm sorry," she said. "This is terribly boring for you. Please don't feel you have to stay, Tim. Really. I'm all right now."

He closed the book. "How's the headache?"

"Tolerable."

"But still there?"

"Yes. I'm sorry." What was she apologizing for? It wasn't her fault.

"Nothing to be sorry about," he said, echoing her thoughts. "It's not your fault." He sat down beside the bed and took her hand. "Has this kind of thing happened before?"

"Not the fainting. I used to have the headaches all the time."

"When was that?"

"About a year and a half ago. After I'd been in a bad automobile accident."

He took the bottle of aspirin from the night table and shook out two for her to swallow. "How did you get rid of them?"

Sarah took the pills and wondered how to answer. "I learned relaxation techniques," she said finally.

Apparently he'd heard of such things, he didn't require an explanation. "Why not try some of that now?"

"I just can't. Don't ask me about it, please." How could she explain that if she did, the voice and the music would take over her mind, and that she couldn't face that without Jarib?

"Okay. Any idea what brought on this attack?"

"No," she lied. But it wasn't entirely a lie. The voice had precipitated the fainting and the headache, but what had started the voice? Vaguely she remembered the Egyptian bowls. She shuddered.

He cocked his head and stared at her speculatively. "Okay, how about distraction instead of analysis? This came for you a couple of hours ago. It's from Jenny, I think." He rose and took a small parcel from the desk. It was addressed to her and unopened.

Sarah undid the wrappings. He'd been right, it was from Jenny. A gift because "I'm crushed that you should have taken ill in my home. You must come and see me again as soon as you're well. Meantime I send this to cheer you."

This was a miniature Sixteenth-century icon, the face of the Virgin Mary, schematic and stylized, with deep-set Russian eyes. The colors were vibrant azure and jade green. Doubtless a reproduction, but beautifully done. Even more interesting was the frame. It was of a totally different period. Victorian, Tim and Sarah both pronounced. Gingerbread gold filigree with inlaid bits of mother-of-pearl. Charming.

"Turn it over," Tim said. "There's something on the other side."

Instead of backing, there was a little piece of glass. And behind it, in exquisitely small hand lettering, a text headed with the words *The Memorare*. "Too small to read," Tim said.

"I know it anyway. It's an old prayer. Attributed to Bernard of Clairvaux, a twelfth-century saint. 'Remember, oh, most gracious Virgin Mary' . . ." she began. Unaccountably her voice choked and her eyes filled with tears.

Tim took the little treasure from her hands and stood it on the night table. "Nothing works right today, does it?"

"Apparently not." She blew her nose and reached for her robe, conscious of his eyes on her when she climbed out of bed and started for the bathroom. "I'm going to take a shower. Why don't you go get something to eat? You must be starved."

"Maybe I will once you're back in bed. I don't want to worry about you fainted dead away in the bath. Too much like a Hitchcock film."

The hot water streaming over her skin was a blessing. Impulsively she decided to wash her hair. Her shampoo was still packed in her suitcase, and she couldn't go into the bedroom wrapped in nothing but a towel. Not with Tim there. She used bar soap, rinsing and rinsing and enjoying the strict squeaking cleanliness. Years ago Rita used to wash her hair with bar soap.

When she emerged from the shower, she realized she hadn't brought a clean nightgown with her. Sarah put on only her robe instead and made a turban out of a towel.

Tim was reading again. He didn't say anything when she came back and plugged in her blow dryer and sat at the small dressing table drying her hair. After a few minutes he rose and stood behind her and took the brush and the dryer from her hands. "Let me."

It was incredibly sensuous and relaxing. Sarah closed her eyes. It took a long time because her hair was so thick and long, and when at last it was dry, he didn't move away. He began to massage her neck and her shoulders instead. The way Jarib used to do. Part of their "work" at first, then, of course, something entirely different. She couldn't help it. She was imagining that Tim was Jarib, that when she opened her eyes and looked in the mirror, he'd be behind her, smiling his wonderful smile, looking at her with love. No! She wouldn't live in the past. She wouldn't mourn forever a man who betrayed her with a few words.

Sarah reached up and covered Tim's hands with her own. He stopped rubbing and waited. She opened her eyes and found his in the reflection opposite. She knew he was stiff with tension and desire. "Do you want me to go?" he asked.

"No."

"Are you sure?"

"Yes."

She rose and untied the belt of her robe and slipped it off and waited for him. Tim took both her hands and drew her to the bed and gently laid her down. In a few seconds he was naked and lying beside her, stroking her skin and kissing her mouth and whispering her name. Then he was over her and in her, and it was good. But it wasn't Jarib.

In Los Angeles Jack Kane drove his wife and daughter to the airport in time to make United's 2:00 A.M. flight for New York.

"Did you let Sam know you're coming?" he asked while they stood in line waiting to check their luggage.

"Sure, I called him first thing. He's meeting the plane. Myra, don't be so obvious."

Myra Kane had been studying a young man further back in the line; obediently she turned her eyes back to her mother. She never bothered hassling over the little things; go with the flow, that was Myra's motto. "There's no need for me to stand here, too," she said. "I'll go get a Coke."

Snort some coke more likely, Jack thought. But he didn't say anything. So far they'd been lucky with the kids. The two boys were married and settled; Myra was the last one at home. She'd never been in any serious trouble. Kane watched her move through the half-empty terminal toward the coffee shop. His daughter had the best-looking ass in California. And that was saying a lot. "I'll be glad when we get her through the next couple of years," he said to his wife.

Rhonda agreed with a nod and studied her nails. The line inched forward slowly. Finally it was their turn. Four bags, even though Yitzhak said they'd only have to stay a few days. Two of them were practically empty. "You're gonna buy out the town," Jack said.

"We've got to do something to explain our trip," Rhonda said.

"Yeah, sure."

Rhonda changed the subject to last-minute instructions about the office. Jack listened patiently and nodded as if he understood. In reality he didn't have to worry; besides being a great lay, Elaine was superefficient. She could practically run the office without either him or Rhonda. He'd have to talk Rhonda into giving Elaine a raise soon. They'd lose her otherwise. He thought about the arguments that was bound to produce and sighed.

"What's the matter?" Rhonda demanded.

"Nothing, honey. Just thinking that I'm going to miss my two favorite broads."

Myra rejoined them, and they went to the departure lounge and waited. Finally the flight was called, and he watched them until they disappeared into the passengers-only section. A few days of freedom. Kane walked from the airport with a spring in his step.

In New York Sam Stein felt good, too. Not like a bored, tired, overweight man of seventy-four. He was whistling under his breath while he made up the beds in the extra bedroom and put fresh towels in its private bath.

When he was convinced that all the preparations were complete, he took a cab to Kennedy. He'd be early, but he didn't mind waiting. The heady sense of expectation visits such as this produced was one of the highlights of his lonely life.

Sam Stein was fated to outlive those he loved. His wife, Bess, died slowly and painfully from stomach cancer in 1980, when Sam was seventy. They'd been married forty-five years; twenty-five of them they'd mourned together the untimely death of their only child. Bess's death reminded Sam yet again that he was an adept at saying Kaddish.

For six months after his wife's funeral Sam remained in his palatial house in the Hollywood Hills. Each morning he went to a synagogue on North Wilshire to pray for his dead. It wasn't a *shul* like the one he'd attended as a kid on Delancey Street in New York. This one was lavishly built and beautifully fitted, and it was Conservative rather than Orthodox. Temple Beth Shalom had been founded thirty years before, by one of Sam's contemporaries, Saul Plotkin.

Like Stein, Plotkin had been lured from the ghettos of the East in the late thirties, after men like Goldwyn and Mayer had established their empires and created the legend of California's golden promise. Many of that second wave of driven opportunists made their fortunes as producers, Plotkin and Stein among them. For years the two men had been vicious competitors who apparently hated each other, but they shared a bond of understanding beneath the surface animosity. That bond deepened when the movie business they'd known changed.

In the early sixties the studios lost control of the stars; in the seventies, much of their power and influence. Independent producers achieved growing importance during those decades, but the men profiting most from this weren't like Plotkin or Stein. They were young and brash; kids from middle-class suburban homes who hadn't stolen apples from pushcarts because they were hungry. Some of them weren't even Jews. "Typical," Saul said to Sam one day in 1981.

They were having breakfast together after the morning service at Temple Beth Shalom. Plotkin took a large bite of a bagel heavy with cream cheese and lox. "My doctor tells me I shouldn't eat this," he confided. "Too much cholesterol. Only I can't resist. Cigarettes I gave up, but not lox and cream cheese."

"That's what you mean is typical? Your doctor's advice?"

Plotkin laughed. "Maybe it is. What I meant was these cocksuckers who think they dominate movies now. A few Jews bust their kishkes to develop something; then the goyim come and try to take it over."

"They haven't put us out of business yet."

"Over my dead body," Saul replied.

The following day he dropped dead of a heart attack.

Once more Sam wore a black armband. It wasn't required, Plotkin wasn't a relative, but Sam spent a lot of time in the *shivah* house during the week of ritual grief. It was not merely his long association with Saul which drew him.

In 1959, when Sam's daughter, Amy, died in Israel, he developed a close relationship with Rhonda Kane. She was Saul Plotkin's kid, but more important, she'd been the tour guide in charge of the group Amy was with in Israel. Bess had needed to blame someone, so she'd fastened on Rhonda; she hated the girl. But Sam knew that Amy's death wasn't Rhonda's fault, not even the fault of Jack Kane, Rhonda's no-goodnik husband. He knew his daughter had been wild and spoiled and selfish. Rhonda Kane seemed the opposite of all those things; he was comforted by Rhonda's affection. As the years passed, he spent more and more time with Rhonda and her family. Because of Bess's animosity, he always went to their house, never they to his. Sam got to know the kids and Rhonda's husband. By the time Saul died, Sam was like family.

"Rhonda," he said when her seven days of deep mourning for her father were past. "Listen, darling, I'm practically retired now. I'm going to make it final. And I'm thinking of selling my house."

Rhonda had expected Sam to come to that decision sooner or later after Bess died. The Stein house had twenty-two rooms and three swimming pools. It required a staff of seven to look after it. All that conspicuous opulence had been Bess's pleasure; Sam's came from providing it for her. "Okay, it's a good idea," she said. "You can get something smaller. A condominium on Wilshire maybe. It'll be easier for you."

"Yeah, an apartment. What do I need with a house? But not here, I'm going home."

Rhonda looked at him in puzzlement. "What home? Where?"

"I'm moving back to New York."

"Sam, that's meshugga. It's cold in the East; it snows."

"You think I'm senile? I know it snows. When the weather's bad, I'll come to California for a couple of months."

"But why? Who needs that schlepp, and what about me? What about Myra?" Myra was then thirteen. She adored Sam and he doted on her.

"Myra and you don't need me. I need you, that's why I'll come out here often. And you'll come visit me. I'll get a place with a guest room." He poured himself another cup of coffee from the pot on Rhonda's terrace table. The table was glass on a wrought-iron frame. It had a central pedestal filled with artificial flowers. You looked down through the top at eternally perfect daisies. "I'm old and I'm tired and I want to go home," he added softly.

Rhonda understood enough not to argue. In the next months she spent a lot of time flying back and forth to New York, helping Sam furnish the apartment he bought on East Sixtieth Street between Second and Third avenues—at least he wasn't pining to live on the Lower East Side. After Sam was installed, she visited him a minimum of three times a year, and as promised, he came to California often. Rhonda never let him stay in a hotel. When he was in Los Angeles, Sam stayed with the Kanes. "If Rhonda was my own kid and Myra my granddaughter," Sam told people, "I wouldn't be treated better. I'm lucky."

It never occurred to him that he owed his luck to Yitzhak Beklem.

Most of Sam's days in New York were of a piece. He got up at eight and dressed and went to a coffee shop on Second Avenue for his breakfast. On the way he bought a paper and read it slowly, front to back, in a tiny booth in the rear of the restaurant. By ten-thirty he was finished, and he took a taxi to Houston and Broadway.

This was the edge of what was now called SoHo, a burgeoning district of tenements and warehouses turned into boutiques and art galleries and glitzy restaurants. It in turn bordered TriBeCa, a similar neighborhood. In the old days this had been the Lower East

Side, the starting place for Jews and Italians and Chinese intent on clawing their way up and out. Stein's delight was to walk for miles, identifying the old streets and alleys and the faint remaining echoes of his childhood.

At midday he had a sandwich in a deli not unlike those he remembered, definitely not one of the new eating places of the area. Around four he took a cab home, made himself some tea, and watched television. Sometimes he heated something for supper; occasionally he went out for a solitary meal; most often he did neither. He simply went to bed and waited for the next day to begin.

When the loneliness of this odd existence became more than he could bear, Sam went to California, laden with expensive presents for the Kanes. When they came to see him, he altered the style of his life, taking them to glamorous restaurants, where lavish tips and the name Sam Stein still curried favor, and using old contacts to secure seats for the latest shows. His totally introverted life when alone was unsuspected by Rhonda.

A crazy way to live, he told himself often. Meshugga, as Rhonda said when he first mentioned it. But the pattern had become a kind of comfort, and he could think of no better way to organize his remaining years, so he didn't try.

This November morning was pleasurably different. The flight from Los Angeles was even on time. Myra and Rhonda both looked wonderful. Tanned and healthy. Loyally he said that he thought Rhonda had lost some weight. And how could Myra keep getting more gorgeous than she already was?

The baggage appeared without undue delay, and when they left the terminal, the sun was shining. Earlier it was cloudy and he'd feared it would snow. "Even the weather's better when you're here," he told them. Grinning broadly, Sam hailed a cab. But when they'd settled themselves into the back seat, him in the middle holding each of their hands, he said, "Now tell me the truth, what's the matter?"

"Nothing's the matter," Rhonda said. "Why should there be?"

"You aren't having trouble with Jack? Or Myra's got some problem?"

"No, nothing like that. We just decided to take a few days off and do some shopping in New York. Tell him it's true," Rhonda commanded her daughter.

"As far as I know, it is," Myra said. "All of a sudden yesterday Ma said we were going to New York. And I had an English test today."

"You can take a makeup next week." Rhonda interrupted. "I just wanted a little break before the big Christmas rush at the office. It's holiday time for everyone else, not for me. We've got more bookings than ever."

"You're sure?" Sam asked.

"Yes, of course I'm sure. Stop worrying. If you buy an apartment across the street from Bloomingdale's, you have to figure I'm going to be tempted often."

There was a Bloomingdale's on Rodeo Drive, but Sam didn't bother mentioning that. He was delighted to have the two women with him, and if Rhonda said there was no problem, he would relax and enjoy the visit. "Okay, where do we go for lunch?"

"The Four Seasons," Myra said instantly.

Sam grinned. "I thought maybe you'd say that. I already made a reservation."

"Fancy tastes my daughter has," Rhonda said with some pride. "I'm amazed you could get a table on such short notice."

"Who do you think you're talking to, honey? Some four-flusher from Queens? Of course I got a table."

The Air France jumbo jet had landed four hours earlier, but Levi had been detained. First in the immigration line, because the man ahead of him was from El Salvador. The official seemed to find this suspect. He spent a long time asking questions, the Central American finally suffered a failure of his limited English, an interpreter was sent for. It took another twenty minutes for her to obtain and translate answers that satisfied the man from immigration. When Levi's turn came, his Israeli passport was accepted and stamped with no fuss. It occurred to him that the man had vented his spleen for the day. He followed the signs to the baggage claim area.

There was another delay here. The door to the baggage bay of the aircraft was stuck. It took an army of mechanics over two hours to release it and produce the passengers' luggage. Dov slouched by the carousel, waiting uncomplainingly, getting his first look at Leo and Freida's native land. On the face of it everything he'd read about America was true: loud, hectic, enthusiastic, no-culture elevated to the status of culture. A polyglot, multiracial mix formed into a people on the basis of exploiting the main chance.

He'd read about pickpockets, too; he kept his hand in his pocket, not clinging to the money Ariel had given him, just the bracelet. Eventually his battered black case appeared; he hoisted it and took his place in the nothing-to-declare line. The customs inspector was a woman, black, with a steel gray Afro above world-weary eyes. She asked him a few rote questions, Levi responded in the negative, she chalked a mark on his bag and waved him on.

BUSES FOR MANHATTAN the sign read. There was an arrow beneath it. Levi set off in the direction the arrow indicated. Finally he was in a line boarding a bus headed for Forty-second Street and Park Avenue.

He wanted a drink and cursed himself for not stopping in one of the bars before leaving the airport. Too late now, he boarded the bus and paid his fare with a crisp ten-dollar bill plucked from Ariel's envelope. There was a piece of paper in there, too. Hotel International it read, 200 West Forty-fourth Street.

A fleabag, as it turned out. Levi surveyed the room for which he'd had to pay sixty dollars a night, three nights in advance. It was about eight feet square, painted an ugly pale brown, splotched with pink where the brown was peeling and earlier decorative attempts showed through. The bed wasn't bad, though. And there was a phone beside it, which was more than he had in Paris. There was even a TV. He opened a door he thought a closet and found himself in a tiny bathroom, barely big enough for a toilet, a sink, and a stall shower. No bidet, he noticed. Another assertion about America that had proved true. The base of the shower was yellow with age; the toilet had rust marks around the bowl. The only ventilation was a minute window high up, the kind that pulls forward. It was tightly closed; the bathroom stank of urine.

He climbed up on the toilet seat and yanked at the window. It had been painted shut, but previous tenants had apparently worked most of the paint loose. Eventually it gave. He expected a rush of cold air, but the window opened on some kind of central shaft; flakes of soot drifted in, and a persistent whirring noise that was unbearable. Cursing softly, he slammed it closed.

Ariel had said he'd be contacted. So there was nothing to do but wait. But he wouldn't start the waiting just yet; first he'd go out and find a drink and maybe something to eat. He decided the safest place for the bracelet and his money was on his person. Bearing his treasures, Dov Levi sortied forth into the Manhattan streets.

Ten

FRIDAY,
NOVEMBER 23

Sarah woke first; the clock said six-thirty. She was afraid to move, not wanting to rouse Tim. He slept heavily beside her, one leg thrown over hers. He was tumescent; she could feel his organ pressing against her thigh. If he woke up, he'd want to make love again. And she didn't. She felt soiled and dirty, and it was horribly unfair because Tim had done nothing to deserve such a reaction. He acted as if he genuinely cared for her; all his actions, his patience, proved it. But she was using him as an antidote for the man she wanted and couldn't have. He deserved better.

The small lamp was still burning, and in its faint glow she could see the Victorian framed icon. It occurred to Sarah that God was laughing at her. A crazy idea. Besides, she didn't believe in God. No, that wasn't exactly it. Maybe there was some uncaused cause, some world-class explosives expert in the sky who arranged the big bang. What she didn't believe in was the Church; one, holy, catholic, and apostolic. She rejected the rites and the rubrics and the rituals, the concept of a savior, true God and true man.

"What are you thinking about?"

She hadn't realized he was awake. "God," she said.

"I hoped it was me; that's pretty stiff competition."

Talk was beyond her. She regretted her one-word honesty. God and Jarib, both the betrayers of her dreams.

Wordlessly Sarah turned and thrust herself at him, rolling on top, taking him inside her without preamble, moving her hips and wrenching a quick, almost hysterical orgasm from the union, an unsatisfying thing born of desperation and remorse. She sensed his excitement, his heightened pleasure in her sudden aggressiveness. Sarah allowed him to reverse their positions and seek his own satisfaction. Her sudden passion spent, she felt somehow disassociated from the act. And she consciously forbade herself to think of Jarib.

They slept an hour or so longer, hunger finally waking them. "I'm starved," Sarah said.

"Me too. Not surprising, neither of us had any dinner." Tim raised his arm and rang for the maid. "The French are marvelously civilized; they serve breakfast in bed as a matter of course."

Sarah was embarrassed at the thought of the maid's finding a man in her room, more embarrassed to admit the concern. She got out of bed and located her robe, still lying on the floor where she'd dropped it last night. Reminding her that she seduced Tim, not the other way 'round. She was conscious of his eyes on her body.

"You're beautiful," he said.

She knotted the robe firmly. "So are you." He was, even more so without clothes. His body hair was the palest possible blond. He'd thrown back the sheets, and Sarah found herself looking at his crotch. He wasn't circumcised; which was like Hal Watkins, but not like Jarib. There was a knock on the door. She admitted the maid, who didn't even glance at the bed, though Tim had covered himself hastily.

The breakfast tray came a few minutes later, and they drank café au lait and wolfed croissants with strawberry jam. "You seem to be a lot better," Tim said.

"I am."

"Up to the auction this morning?"

"Of course!" She'd almost forgotten. That wasn't very fair to Ivy.

"It's going to be difficult," he said. "We were supposed to go to the viewing yesterday, after Jenny's."

Sarah shook her head ruefully. The foul-up was her fault. "Will we have a chance to look today?"

"An hour or so before the sale. We'll have to make decisions pretty quickly. Don't worry, it will be okay. Just follow my lead."

The phone rang. It was the desk, asking if Monsieur Durant would take a call. Sarah turned crimson. They were too damned efficient, and the little maid hadn't missed anything after all.

"Tim, it's Zelah. I wanted to reach you before you left for the day. You weren't asleep, I hope."

"No, just finishing breakfast."

"Good. Listen, I've had a wonderful idea. You and the charming little Sarah, you must come to Alsace for the weekend. To see my restaurant."

"An intriguing thought. Hold on, Sarah's right here, I'll see what she thinks." He covered the mouthpiece with his palm. "It's Zelah Tench. She's inviting us to Alsace for the weekend. To see her restaurant."

They'd been booked to return to England the following morning. "Could we change our ferry reservations?"

"I expect so. Shouldn't be any problem going back on a Monday. Let's do it."

Sarah nodded agreement and the plans were made.

Since coming to France, Malachy had worn neither his Benedictine habit nor his cardinal's robe; just a black suit and a white Roman collar without the small red ribbon that would have told the world he was a prince of the Church. But even his simple cleric's garb attracted attention; nowadays almost all priests wore civilian dress. To make it worse, it was pouring with rain and Malachy carried a big black umbrella. Most Parisians didn't, apparently. He was the only one on the street with such protection. The others simply huddled into their raincoats and moved as quickly as possible. Still, they found time to glance at him.

He was aware of the scrutiny. France, the eldest daughter of the Church, the jewel in our Lady's crown, was becoming uncomfortable with the trappings of religion. A terrible shame, like so much that had happened since Vatican II, all in the name of modernization and reform. And it would be worse when Donovan and his committee issued their report.

Malachy knew he couldn't stop them. Yesterday he learned the report was definitely scheduled for release on the twentieth of December. But Donovan didn't know that there might be hard evidence for some of his wilder claims. It was up to Malachy Fanti to prevent his ever knowing, much less getting his hands on the Testament itself. If it existed. All these years chasing the will-o'-the-wisp, and he still wasn't sure there was anything to be chased. But Yitzhak was sure.

He knew the address of Yitzhak's office, though he'd never been there. It turned out to be a small room on the fourth floor of an old building behind the Gare du Nord. There was nothing impressive about it, just a single room with the words *Transport Maritime* on the door. Not even a secretary, just Yitzhak, dwarfed behind a big desk.

"You didn't have to come out in such weather, Malachy. I promised to ring you as soon as there was anything to report." Beklem gestured to the two phones on his otherwise bare desk.

"It's all right, I wanted to see you."

"You're shivering. Here, let me give you a brandy."

Malachy sipped the spirit gratefully. He glanced over his shoulder at the lettering on the door. "Do you actually do any shipping?"

Yitzhak smiled. "A little, sometimes. Mostly I move people."

"Like Levi."

"Yes, like Levi."

Malachy took a deep breath. "I need to ask you a question." Yitzhak remained silent, looking at him. "Why did you tell me about him, about Levi? In the first place, I mean."

Yitzhak didn't hesitate. "That was our agreement. When you gave me the papers. If I discovered anything, I would let you know."

"Only implied, we never discussed it. Anyway, that's the only reason, because of what you thought of as our agreement?"

The Israeli folded his hands behind his bald head and studied his visitor. "Why are you asking me this now? Why not years ago?"

Malachy didn't meet his eyes. "I don't know. Only I got to thinking . . ."

"Thinking what?"

"That we are on the verge of a breakthrough. And that I don't know your motives for cooperation, so I don't know what to expect." It was an entirely honest answer because he couldn't think of any equivocations that would elicit what he needed to know.

Yitzhak countered with a question. "Why did you give me the papers?"

"I'm not sure. An inspiration, I think. That day . . . It seemed absolutely the right thing to do."

"The right thing to do," Yitzhak repeated. "That's our problem, isn't it, my friend? We have both been struggling a long time to do the right thing. The debate occurs when 'right' isn't clear."

Malachy rose. "You aren't going to tell me any more, are you?"

Yitzhak spread his hands in a gesture of helplessness. "At this moment there's nothing to tell. I will let you know as soon as anything happens in New York, I promise."

That wasn't what Malachy meant. He knew Yitzhak understood that. But there was nothing more to say. He turned to go. "Thank you for the brandy. You can reach me at the abbey."

"St. Louis, in Montparnasse? I thought you'd go back to Rome now."

"No. I shall stay a few more days," Malachy said firmly. "Having come all this way, I might as well."

"As you wish," Yitzhak said. Then, just before the door closed behind the monk: "Malachy, it's time you got over feeling guilty. It was a long time ago."

The Benedictine didn't answer. Yitzhak stared at the door that closed behind him. A faint smile played about his thin lips. A masterstroke those last words. Reminding Malachy of his guilt was important just now. It was the hold he'd always had over the other man; this was no time for the grip to loosen. Malachy was right about one thing. They *were* on the verge of a breakthrough. Malachy knew a great deal less than he did, nothing about the girl, for instance; still, he sensed it. And there was that Monsignor Donovan in Rome, he was going to play right into Yitzhak's hands.

Beklem wondered whether the Swiss knew about the American priest and his committee. Yes, in all likelihood he did. Rome was full of spies. The same people who reported to him probably informed His Eminence Cardinal Fanti. The thought of all the power in the Vatican was a sour taste in Beklem's mouth. It gave him heartburn. The Israeli reached for an antacid tablet and chewed it slowly. His mind was on past pain, not the present insignificant discomfort.

On April 29, 1945, the liberators came to Dachau, and Isaac Bekstein, the former rabbinical student who in 1940 had discussed the meaning of the Book of Job with the Benedictine novice, was still miraculously, stubbornly, incredibly alive. He was twenty-nine years old, he had no hair, he weighed sixty-two pounds, he had three teeth left in his head, and because his glasses had shattered beyond repair two years earlier, he viewed the world through a haze composed as much of confusion as of pain.

The young infantryman who found him hiding among a mound of corpses did not at first believe him alive. But Isaac moved, preparatory to burrowing deeper among the debris of the dead because he did not realize that the man was his savior, and the soldier reached down and scooped him into his arms. Isaac recognized something human and almost forgotten in that touch. Pity perhaps, maybe even love. With difficulty he raised one hand and touched the other man's face and found it wet with tears.

The soldier carried him out the barbed-wire gates. Isaac could make no sense of the confusion, the shouting, the moving convoys of trucks and men and weapons. Because he did not yet speak English, a skill he would acquire some years later when he needed it, he didn't understand the argument between the boy who held him and the noncommissioned officer who insisted that now that the prisoner had been liberated, he was no longer the responsibility of the U.S. Fifth Armored Division.

"But this man needs a doctor, sir."

"Shit, soldier, half the people in this fucking country need a doctor. The other half need a firing squad. Put him down."

The boy tightened his grip on Isaac Bekstein's emaciated frame. "He can't walk, sir. He's too weak, he was crawling when I found him. Into a pile of corpses."

"Jesus Christ."

"Exactly, sir."

"Are you wise-assing me, soldier?"

"No, sir. I only meant you were correct when you reminded me about Jesus, sir. You know, the good Samaritan."

The sergeant cocked his head. He studied the soldier and his incredible, ugly burden. "Where you from, son?"

"Wichita, sir."

The sergeant was from the Bronx. He owned a garage on Bruckner Boulevard, and he'd never been farther west than New Jersey. "Jesus," he repeated, "Wichita. Well, you're either one smart-mouthed son of a bitch or the only saint in this outfit. Get that poor bastard out of my sight. And get back here. We're moving out."

"Can I take him up front to the medics, sir?"

"I don't give a shit if you take him to Kansas. Only do it quick."

"Yes, sir. Thank you, sir."

In those first days of the Allied breakthrough into Germany, anarchy reigned; chaos had invaded, a more effective weapon than bombs and guns. People wandered in the streets, clogged the highways, stumbled across the fields. The vanquished and their former prisoners formed a mourning, frightened mass that the incoming troops ruthlessly shoved out of their path. But thanks to the young soldier whose name he never knew, Isaac Bekstein was put in a makeshift military hospital.

They kept him for a month while they treated the countless running sores on his skin and fed him until he weighed just over a hundred pounds and made him false teeth and fitted him with new glasses. A month later some semblance of order was beginning to emerge, and they moved him to another hastily established camp.

At first he was terrified; finally he made himself believe that this time he was a refugee; not a slave, not even a prisoner. Slowly and painfully, Isaac began to reassemble the pieces of a once-strong personality. "From here where?" he demanded of his fellow inmates.

"America," they told him. "You must ask for papers to go to America. It's wonderful. You have relatives in America?"

Bekstein shrugged. "I don't know."

"Think," they urged him. "Think hard. If you can remember anybody, any name, they will look for your family and get them to sponsor you and bring you to America. You maybe can go anyway, but it's easier with *mishpocheh*."

Isaac could conjure up no relative who had gone to America in the long-ago days before the Nazis, when his family were comfortable, respected, prosperous Germans. Neither could he find any other Beksteins among the survivors. "Maybe France then, or England," somebody said. "They're taking some refugees too."

But Isaac remembered certain things he had read years before. "What about Palestine?"

"Don't ask," a woman said. "If you say Palestine, they put you down as a troublemaker. The British don't want us there."

Isaac listened and didn't ask—officially. Privately he found a few like-minded people who were well informed. They told him about Ben-Gurion and the Haganah. They had fought beside the Allies all through the war and now expected to claim their homeland as reward. "If that doesn't work, there's the Irgun," a man said. "The Irgun is going to make it so miserable for the British they'll beg to leave Palestine."

"And then?" Isaac asked.

"Then we fight whoever says it isn't ours."

A plan began fermenting in Isaac's mind.

The final notes of vespers died slowly, with a lingering echo that floated upward on the multicolored shafts of July sun piercing the stained glass windows. *"Adjutorium Deus sit semper nobiscum,"* the abbot intoned. May the divine assistance remain always with us.

"Et cum fratribus nobis absentium," the monks responded. And with our absent brethren. As one body they descended from their carved wooden choir stalls and filed two by two down the broad aisle dividing the nave. When each pair came to the foot of the high

altar, they genuflected, then passed into the cloister. Dom Malachy Fanti was the fifth man to exit the church, because the community followed an order of precedence based on the gospel, and thus the last were first. Dom Malachy was young in the priesthood; he'd been ordained two years previously in 1943.

The lay brother in charge of the porter's gate was waiting for him. "Dom Malachy, there's someone asking for you. An old German man. I've put him in the west parlor."

"Thank you, Brother Dominic." Malachy strode off to meet his visitor.

He wasn't expecting anyone today, but he was not surprised by the summons. Among certain scholars Malachy Fanti had the beginnings of a reputation in biblical exegesis. His father's name helped, of course. And the fact that his abbot gave him so much latitude for study and correspondence with the outside world. Distinguished visitors came more and more frequently to confer with the brilliant young monk. Especially now in summer, when the mountains were green and inviting.

Malachy let himself into the small plain room where the man was waiting. "You wished to see me, sir? I am Dom Malachy Fanti."

"Yes. I know. Don't you recognize me, Malachy? It was only a few days, of course. But in such circumstances . . ."

Malachy looked closely at his visitor. He guessed him to be about sixty, maybe a little more. His German had a southern lilt. Someone from Freiburg perhaps? Someone he'd known as a boy? "I'm sorry, but no." He was embarrassed, and annoyed that his visitor was making him play guessing games.

"Tell me, Malachy, what do you think about Bildad the Shuhite. 'Can sentence undeserved come from the Almighty?' "

Malachy stared hard. It all welled up in him again, the pain and the terror and the suffering that were Dachau. And he recognized something in the other's eyes. That mark of personhood which distinguishes one human being from another. "Isaac Bekstein," he whispered. "But it's impossible."

"So you do remember me. What's impossible? That I'm alive?"

"I prayed for you every day." Malachy sat down and motioned Isaac to do likewise. "But I can't believe it's you." He actually rubbed his eyes.

"Ah, my appearance, yes, of course. I was thirty last week, my friend. I only look like an old man."

Malachy continued staring and said nothing. Isaac reached over and patted his hand. "It's okay. So I don't look so wonderful, it's still a miracle. It got worse after you left, much worse. You heard about the gas and the ovens?" Isaac spoke the words flatly, without emotion.

"Rumors, yes." Malachy said. He did not meet his visitor's eyes.

"Not rumors. The truth. Our whole barracks, ninety-two men. All dead. I'm the only one who survived. I volunteered to work with the corpses. Looking for gold in their teeth, things like that."

Malachy listened to the confession and wondered if he should raise his hand and make the sign of the cross. *Ego te absolvo* . . . No, it would mean nothing to the Jew.

The Benedictine groped for something to fill the silence and found only his order's legendary hospitality. "You must have something to eat and drink." He jumped up and rang the bell by the door. A young novice appeared and was instructed to bring food. Only then did Malachy turn back to his guest. "Isaac, I agree, that you're alive is a miracle, but what are you doing here? Another miracle?"

Isaac smiled, showing his beautiful new teeth. "The day you disappeared with the two *Kapos,* we thought you'd been killed, of course. Then little by little we heard the true story. I never forgot you. You could have told them who you were right away. In 1940 it still mattered. But you didn't. Ever since I've wanted to ask you why."

Malachy gazed at the bulge his clenched hands made beneath his black scapular. "I don't know," he said softly. "I probably would have sooner or later. I wouldn't have stood it for long without trying to get out."

"Who would?" Isaac demanded, dismissing the self-deprecation in the monk's tone. "That's the point. Why did you wait?"

"I felt . . ." Malachy paused. "Overwhelmed," he added finally.

"With pity. Overwhelmed by pity, is that what you mean?"

Malachy nodded.

Isaac sighed. "I thought so. I hoped so." He did not seem prepared to say more.

The novice returned with a tray of bread and butter and cheese and wine. Isaac ate quickly, stuffing his mouth as if afraid the food would be snatched away momentarily. Malachy wondered if he would eat thus for the rest of his life. "You didn't answer my question, Isaac," he said at last. "What are you doing here?"

Isaac finished the last of the cheese and smiled. "I was passing by."

Malachy laughed. "You don't expect me to believe that." He nodded toward the window which looked out on the towering mountains and the remote fastness surrounding them.

"Why not? It's a crazy time, an insane world. Believe it, Malachy, it's best if you do. I was just passing by and I dropped in to see an old comrade."

Malachy's eyes narrowed, and he studied the frail-looking little man. "You're on your way to Palestine, aren't you? Illegally."

"I didn't say that."

"No, I did. It's the only explanation. There is talk that one of the routes being used is through the Ticino. Don't worry, I won't betray you."

"I wouldn't have come here if I thought you would," Isaac said. "Not that I'm admitting anything."

"No, I understand. What do you want from me, Isaac?"

"Besides the answer to my question, you mean?"

"Yes."

"Money."

"I don't have any."

Isaac shook his head. "Malachy, you pitied us once when there was nothing you could do. Now you can do something. I asked around, people told me things. You are the only son of a fabulously wealthy family."

The monk looked pained. "You don't understand, I'm a priest now, a monk with a solemn vow of poverty. I relinquished any claim on my inheritance. There are treasures in the abbey, of course. But only the abbot has control of them. And he is . . . not sympathetic. I'm not lying, Isaac. I have nothing to give you. I'm sorry."

The Jew shrugged. "So am I. Well, so be it. Anyway, I'm glad I saw you."

He rose to go. Malachy saw him slip the last piece of bread into his pocket, and he looked away. Together they walked to the door. Suddenly Malachy stopped. "Isaac, wait here. I've just thought of something."

When he came back, he pushed an envelope into Bekstein's hand. "It isn't money. It's more valuable. Wait until you're well away from here to read it; then you'll understand."

It was hours later, in the back of a broken-down old truck, by flashlight, that Isaac read the documents he'd been given.

TRANSCRIPT OF A CONVERSATION BETWEEN PIETRO FANTI, PRO-FESSOR OF ROMAN HISTORY, AND LUCIA DREKLER, FORMER AS-SISTANT TO DR. CARL JUNG, WHICH TOOK PLACE ON MARCH 5, 1943, AT 3:00 P.M. IN THE CAFÉ DES RONDELLES ON RUE VI-FORT, IN GENEVA.

P.F.: Thank you for seeing me, Miss Drekler. As you know, I have been unable to arrange an interview with Dr. Jung.

L.D.: He is very selective about whom he sees.

P.F.: So I've discovered. For the record, will you tell me again of your association with the doctor?

L.D.: I transcribed his notes and typed his manuscripts for six years. From 1931 to 1937.

P.F.: And you left his employ in '37 and have not seen him since, is that correct?

L.D.: Yes.

(Note: I had been given to understand that while Miss Drekler expected to be paid for speaking to me, she had another motive in that she had conceived a great passion for Jung during her time with him and that he had either tired of her or never reciprocated. In either case, Miss Drekler was said to see herself in the role of the woman scorned. I cannot prove any of this, but it was told me by a reliable source, and my observations that day in Geneva incline me to believe it. P.F.)

P.F.: Let us get straight to the point, shall we? I am inter-ested in Dr. Jung's theories about something I think he is calling the collective unconscious.

L.D.: Sometimes that, sometimes "racial memory."

P.F.: And it is his contention that such a thing exists?

L.D.: Oh, yes. He says that all our religious aspirations arise out of our collective unconscious. In our dreams they are represented by a person of the opposite sex.

P.F.: Every time I dream of a woman it's an inclination to religion, my part of the collective unconscious speaking?

L.D.: Nothing so simple as that. But if a peasant dreams of a woman in the form of a mythical creature described by the ancients, one that the peasant has never heard of, well, he's calling up a memory from the collective unconscious.

P.F.: And has Dr. Jung run into many cases where peasants tell him their dreams of creatures from mythology?

L.D.: That is only an example, Herr Professor.

P.F.: Yes, of course. What other proofs of the existence of this phenomenon has Dr. Jung proposed?

L.D.: He has taught himself to plunge into his own deep unconscious, even while awake. He did it first in 1913, and many times since then. I myself have often gone into his office and found him awake, but in a trance.

P.F.: And what are the results of these "trances"?

L.D.: You sound very skeptical, Herr Professor. You can read Dr. Jung's theories yourself. In 1916 he published a paper called *The Transcendental Function*. Early work, of course, but essentially it's all in there.

P.F.: I have read the paper, Miss Drekler. I do not understand it. I hoped you might cast some further light on the matter.

L.D.: I was told you were interested in similar phenomenon, that you were working on proof of its existence and might soon publish.

P.F.: Yes, well, you know how these things are. One must be skeptical to be effective. Now, tell me, in your time with him, did Jung ever speak of an inherited facility to plumb this racial memory? Something that may skip some generations but show up at random, as it were?

L.D.: I never heard him discuss exactly that. But from what I know of the work he has in progress, a book about memories and dreams, I think he would find it wholly possible.

P.F.: Thank you for your time, Miss Drekler.

Isaac Bekstein read the transcript over twice, then the copy of Pietro Fanti's covering note to his son.

Dear Malachy,

I don't know what you'll make of this. It seems a pretty poor substitute for speaking with Jung himself, but I've tried that without success. The woman was obviously hoping that I had the same theory by the tail and would publish before Jung and thus embarrass/wound him—which I believe to be her intention. What a professor of Roman history would be doing working on such esoterica I can't imagine; only she apparently believed it. Neither can I imagine how Wolff could credit the whole business. But obviously he was very excited. Incidentally, I've heard nothing from him for three years, and my letters are returned marked "address unknown," so the entire matter is now in your hands.

—P.F.

Imagine a man who signs a letter to his son with his initials. As the truck labored over the tortuous mountain roads, Isaac tried and couldn't do so. Nor fathom that in 1943, while the ovens in Dachau and Auschwitz and Bergen-Belsen burned, scholars discussed arcane theories. And wondered what had happened to a German colleague with a Jewish name like Wolff. Neither could he understand why Malachy had given the documents to him. Then he found the last sheet in the envelope.

Isaac,

I write in haste while you wait downstairs. I have reason to believe a manuscript exists which throws much light on the early history of your people and my Church. The key to it seems to be in Alexandria. Close to where you hope to be. Professor Wolff believed that some people, descendants of the manuscript's author, have a kind of racial memory about it. I give you this in hopes that if you ever

299

hear of anything which might have bearing, you will get in touch with me here. God go with you, as do my prayers,

—Dom Malachy, OSB

Isaac Bekstein crawled into Palestine on his belly, across a rocky beach that ripped at his still-sparse flesh, while above his head the Irgun exchanged rifle fire with a British army patrol. He wasn't at all frightened. Good, he thought. I like this, I'm not a slave, I'm fighting in a war. The experience helped to expunge the degradation of Dachau. It was another step in his healing.

The following day Isaac joined the Irgun. He also changed his name. Yitzhak, the Hebrew for Isaac, was an easy and obvious choice. But what to do about Bekstein? He did not wish to deny his parents, his long lineage. Beklem was an arbitrary rendering, it was close to the original but sounded vaguely Hebraic. Isaac/Yitzhak still had much of the mind-set of the talmudic scholar. That stood him in good stead in the Irgun.

"It's not just 'bang, bang you're dead,' " the ranking officer of his unit told him. "The British have more soldiers and more guns. We have to outthink them if we're going to be effective. Every one of us they kill or capture is worth more than twenty we get rid of."

"So?" Yitzhak asked. "What's the answer?"

"Cleverness. We've got to be smart, strike quickly where they least expect it. In and out. Fast! Fast! Fast!" He punctuated the words by banging his fist on a table. "Inflict damage and run. Never let them know what to expect or when."

It was a seminal description of terrorism, but that didn't occur to Yitzhak. In those days neither the word nor the concept was in common use. "Outthink them," he said slowly. "Yes, that we should be good at. Five thousand years of living by our wits, it should be worth something."

Yitzhak Beklem was among the select cadre of Irgun men who developed the code the British never broke. It was based on cabala. Yitzhak never forgot the day the idea was born. "What's a code anyway?" someone said. "Just a system of numbers. All we have to do is come up with numbers they can't figure out."

"Not always." The original speaker was contradicted by a former chemist who had shown extraordinary aptitude for making explosives from ordinary ingredients. "A code can be letters, too."

"Listen," Yitzhak said. "You're ignoring the obvious. We *have* such a system. Cabala."

It was the catchall name for an ancient system of mysticism. The cabalist *Book of Formation* appeared in Italy in the eighth century, the *Book of Splendor* in Spain in the thirteenth, but the roots were older and deeper. Cabalists claimed their revelation to be included in Scripture itself. At its basest it was hocus-pocus and superstition, at its grandest an intuitive effort to plumb the mysteries of the God who can never be known by reason alone; but Yitzhak was not interested in either interpretation at the moment. Cabala incorporated an amazingly subtle numerology known as gematria.

"We are Jews," he told the others. "The way of thinking involved in gematria comes naturally to us, not to goyim."

"Yitzhak," somebody said. "Gematria you use to figure out the date the *meshiach* is to come. That's not our biggest worry right now."

But Yitzhak was fired with his idea. "Look, according to gematria, every letter of the alphabet has a number; *aleph* is one, *beth* is two, and so forth. Then, when you add up the numbers, you get a value for a word. And you find a counterpart in Scripture for the numerical value. The scriptural reference gives you a concept. That's what will make it work. Adding up the numbers, that's easy. But finding the scriptural connection and the idea behind it, that's only obvious to a yeshiva bucher."

The group leader was a sabra, a man born and raised in Palestine. "Yitzhak, forgive me, but this whole thing is just too European for me. And it will be for a lot of us. We're not talmudic scholars."

"I know," Yitzhak said. He'd already fathomed the profound difference between these young men nurtured in the Holy Land, with their sophisticated political ideologies and absolutely no idea of holiness, and the wounded ones like himself. Those who had been taught to believe in a just God and whose beliefs had undergone a trial by fire in the Nazi inferno. "All the same, there are enough of us to leaven the rest of you. But the British, they have no yeshiva buchers at all, they don't send English Jews on tours of duty here."

That was largely true, and the primary reason that the Irgun code proved unbreakable.

On May 15, 1948, the day after Ben-Gurion proclaimed Israeli independence, the Arabs declared war. Not only did the new state defeat them, it took as spoils a third again as much land as the UN resolution had granted. Moreover, the war molded the Irgun and the Haganah into a single, formidable army. And the army spawned two remarkable intelligence organizations, Shin Bet and Mossad. Yitzhak Beklem could have had a high post in either. He chose instead to operate independently.

Ostensibly Yitzhak became a private detective in the international city of Jerusalem. It was excellent cover for the network he created and ran; people determined to protect Israel, even from herself, if necessary, and to do so without the restraints of laws and parliamentary committees. The people in Beklem's orbit were of two classes: his operatives—divided between those who worked for him full-time and those he could call on for occasional tasks— and his supporters. These were people who knew what he was about and undertook to raise the money that allowed him to do it. Often they didn't explain what the money was for, just that it was needed by Israel, but they never failed to keep him supplied, and as the years passed and the threats to the new state continued, the contributions increased in size and number.

Eventually there was enough money so Beklem could devote himself full-time to the secret commitment in which he believed so passionately. But in the early days he really did also operate as an ordinary private detective. Thus it was that in 1958 he took on an American client, a fat, florid man named Sam Stein, who smelled of money and of grief.

Yitzhak listened to the man's story of a daughter disappeared during a trip to Israel with a temple youth group. He sympathized, but that didn't prevent him from putting an exorbitant price on his services. When it was agreed to, he promised to continue the investigation officialdom had declared closed. The American went back to California, and Yitzhak sent him reports that said nothing, because no matter how deep he probed, there was nothing to say.

Until October 1959, when he met Dov Levi and learned the story behind the American girl's disappearance and that she was dead. And other things. One of which reminded him of the papers he'd received from Malachy Fanti twelve years earlier, which he'd neither lost nor forgotten. Now the whole damned thing had somehow fallen into his lap.

Yitzhak sent Dov away, but on a leash. He informed the American that his daughter was dead, but nothing else. There was too much at stake to worry about one man's guilt or another's grief. After he dealt with Levi and Stein, Yitzhak wrote to the Benedictine scholar, who had by then been summoned to Rome by Pius XII and made a bishop and given the task of overseeing the teaching of Scripture in the city's numerous seminaries. It was a most carefully composed letter which mentioned Levi's mental aberration, but nothing of the circumstances that had brought him into Yitzhak's purview.

It was still raining when Malachy left Yitzhak's office. And he didn't feel like going back to the abbey. He crossed the street and found a little café and went inside and ordered coffee. There was a table by the window; it looked out on the door from which he'd just exited. He took the coffee to the table and sat down to watch.

It was insane. He could never beat Beklem at his own game; it was foolish to try. Spying on his supposed friend and associate was nonsense; worse, it was probably sinful. But he felt utterly at a loss. The Jew was hiding something; Malachy didn't know why he was so sure of that, but he was. And he had come to Paris to see that the interests of the holy faith were protected. That was Malachy's job, his sole purpose in life. Why else had he agreed to be exclaustrated from his beloved monastery and entombed in the fleshpots of Rome? Why else had he been spared the fate of the vast majority of the inmates of Dachau?

He glanced at his cup, it was empty. He'd drunk the coffee unaware. A glance at his watch showed that he'd been in the café nearly an hour. Malachy got up and took his empty cup to the bar. He ordered another coffee and took out his wallet. "No charge, mon père," the barman said. The monk nodded his thanks and returned to the window.

A few minutes later a young man entered the building, the first person to go in or out since he started watching. Not really young, Malachy decided. Just youngish. Nice-looking. Medium height, medium build, medium coloring. Nothing distinctive about him. And he probably had nothing whatever to do with Yitzhak Beklem. Except that he did. Five minutes later, just when Malachy was deciding to end this futile exercise, Yitzhak and the other man left the building together.

The monk half rose, intending to follow them, then thought better of it. He hadn't been spotted here, but he could never get away with more. If he followed them, they'd see him. Bound to. They were experts at such things; he was a rank amateur. His vigil had gained him one tiny advantage: He knew what at least one of Yitzhak's associates looked like. Better to be content with that. And with his one other advantage. The one thing he'd never shared with Beklem, the extent of his ties to the auctioneer in England.

Hamish Durant had come into Malachy's orbit three years earlier. The Englishman wrote him a letter in response to a piece in a journal of biblical research. Malachy had written about the importance of the Zealots in Palestine in the time of Christ. He put forward the theory that it was their political unrest and warmongering that were behind the crowds who followed Jesus everywhere. In fact, he'd implied, though not said outright, it was doubtful that any Jews other than the apostles had been in the least interested in the messiahship of the Lord. They'd wanted a leader to overthrow Rome, nothing more.

Hamish Durant's praise for the article, and a few interesting historical asides of his own, had created a bond between the two men. They corresponded. In the summer of '82 Hamish made one of his rare trips out of England and visited Malachy in Rome. And Malachy had recognized a possibly useful ally.

At first he tried to be circumspect; the fewer people who suspected the existence of the Alexandria Testament, the better. But Durant was a genius. He had both a formidable array of facts in his head and an uncanny intuition which he trusted. His business was often a matter of detection, he'd explained. So it wasn't surprising that finally he'd fathomed the nature of the monk's quest. In the end Malachy told him as much as he knew. Not that it was a great deal. But Durant saw at once that if the document existed and were discovered, the Jews could exploit it to their own ends. He had become an ally indeed, capable of doing many things Malachy could not do. That had given him some sense of matching Yitzhak's enormous resources.

He examined that motive now. The fact was that even two years ago he'd been unsure of Yitzhak. So it wasn't just the pressures of being in a strange place. Something deep inside him told him to be wary. Not to trust the Jew too far. He must follow those instincts; they were quite possibly the promptings of the Holy Spirit.

He left the café, intending to return to St. Louis to make a phone call. The thought of the *cellérier's* tiny office deterred him. All those cornflakes. He fished in his pocket for change. Yes, enough. He ducked into a telephone kiosk.

"It's Malachy. I'm calling to see what you've learned about the bracelet."

"Interesting you should ring just now," Durant said. "I had word an hour ago. It was offered for sale by a Frenchman. Count François Lontesse de Montviron. Apparently a great deal of what was in the sale belonged to de Montviron. That's why he went to such pains to keep his name secret."

"I don't understand."

"The sale was composed of Judaica, was it not?"

"Yes. As the catalog I sent you showed."

"Indeed. And de Montviron is not a Jew. So the question would naturally arise, Where did he get all that?"

"And the answer?" Malachy held his breath. He had a sense that this conversation was to prove extremely important.

"The answer, and I'm guessing, but I'd wager a year's earnings on my guess, is that de Montviron pirated it. *Stole* might be a better word. He was in Egypt all during the war and for some years before. The family had a prominent exporting business there. He didn't return to France until 1950, two years after the Jews worked their will on those fools in the UN."

"You think this count got the things from the new state of Israel?"

Hamish was patient. "No, you're forgetting a bit of history, Father. There was a large community of Jews in Egypt. Had been since God knows when. But once the so-called state of Israel was

305

formed, they were persona non grata in the rest of the Middle East. The Egyptian settlement scattered all over the world. I suspect many of them sold their treasures to men like de Montviron for a pittance. To get foreign currency most likely. Egypt had severe currency restrictions; they weren't allowed to take much out."

"I see," Malachy said softly. But he didn't. What did Count François Lontesse de Montviron have to do with Dov Levi?

Hamish sensed his question. "I don't think Levi and this count have any connection. What I think is proved is simply that the lack of provenance in the catalog was a whitewash. Probably most of the attributed provenances were scarecrows, dummies erected to protect de Montviron. By the time they got to the bracelet they'd run out of ideas. But it really could be very old. Ancient, in fact. They were mining turquoises in Persia before the time of Christ."

Malachy drew a deep breath. "And that antiquity is what set Levi off. It triggered him, so to speak."

"Yes, that's my guess. But it's more your line of country than mine."

"So what do we actually know?" Malachy asked thoughtfully.

"Not a great deal," Hamish said. "Listen, my son is in Paris at the moment. Would you approve of my contacting him? I could ask him to see what he can learn about de Montviron."

"No," Malachy said instantly. Any investigating by amateurs was too likely to alert Yitzhak. He didn't want to explain that to Hamish Durant. He'd never told him anything specific about the Israeli, much less the connection between himself and the Jew. "My sources," that's how he always identified Beklem. It's what he said now. "I'll have my sources do any checking at this end. Thank you, Hamish, you've been most helpful."

The Paris auction Sarah had come to attend wasn't being held in the prestigious Hôtel Drouot but in a small, private gallery. There were few people compared with two days ago in Bristol, and the bidding was less frenzied. Sarah felt unsure and nervous all over again. Just as she had before Bristol. But Tim wasn't restrained by British law here, and he was able to be more actively helpful. In the end she decided it went better than could have been expected.

Particularly considering that they'd had less than an hour to examine the offerings.

Sarah bought three of the six lots Ivy had expressed interest in and two Ivy hadn't marked, but that she and Tim agreed were worthwhile. "I'm glad that's over," she said when the lots had been paid for and they'd exchanged the claustrophobic atmosphere of the gallery for the dusk gray streets of Paris.

"You didn't enjoy it as much as the other one, did you?"

"No. Still a little rocky from yesterday maybe," she admitted.

"What you need is just what you shall have, a weekend in the country. Which reminds me, I've got to call the old man. He's expecting us back tomorrow."

They decided to return to the hotel to make the phone call. Sarah noted that Tim followed her to her room almost as a matter of course. As if all that were settled between them now. It wasn't, not from her point of view, but she decided this wasn't the moment to say so. He seemed nervous when he dialed the international code for Britain, 44, then his father's number.

The elder Durant answered on the first ring.

Father and son exchanged pleasantries about each other's health; Hamish asked about Jenny Fogel's jewels and seemed satisfied with the response. "I think we should include them in the sale of Lady Harris's collection."

"Yes, my thought, too. I'll bring them straight to you on Monday."

"Monday? I thought you were due back tomorrow."

Sarah couldn't hear the other side of the conversation, but she saw Tim tense. He seemed a little like a small boy. "We've decided to spend the weekend here. In Alsace actually, at Zelah Tench's *auberge*. I've told you about Zelah."

"The Jewess from Israel, yes. But it would be best if the jewels were safe here at the manor right away."

"They're perfectly safe. They're in the hotel vault. Besides, Sarah's been ill. She shouldn't attempt the crossing for a few days."

"There are proper doctors in England, son." As if there were not in France. Which was what Hamish believed.

"She doesn't need a doctor. Just rest. She took a fainting spell.

At Jenny Fogel's, as a matter of fact. The sight of Jenny's Egyptian collection knocked her out." The attempt at levity sounded forced.

On the other end of the wire Hamish sighed. "Very well, Timothy. I suppose a lad your age is entitled to be frivolous. I'll see you on Monday then."

"Monday. Right." Tim hung up with a sigh of relief.

"Why do you get so tense when you talk to your father?" Sarah asked.

An impolitic question. Tim denied it. "Don't be silly, I don't. Now, forget about him. I've something much nicer in mind." He reached for her.

"Please," Sarah murmured. "I'm still not feeling very well."

"Not tonight, dear, I have a headache. The oldest dodge in the book." At least he was smiling when he said it.

"Sorry," Sarah said. "Maybe I'll feel better after dinner." But she knew she was still going to have a headache. Even after dinner. Only it would be a good idea to think up a more original excuse. Oh, Pinkie, where are you now that I need you?

After speaking to his son, Durant hung up with some sense of unease. It was a distinct contrast with his mood after he had spoken with Dom Malachy. It had pleased him that he could worm behind the facade of anonymity of the French auction system. Not that it was surprising, forty years in this business had established a great many contacts at home and abroad. But it was gratifying nonetheless. And nice to have been able to pass the information on to the priest so quickly. He knew the cardinal was in Paris, but not where. All their contacts were inaugurated by Dom Malachy.

In England it was five o'clock. He raised one pudgy hand and rang a bell beside his desk. It would signal the kitchen that he was ready for tea. The tray arrived quickly. Durant motioned for it to be left on the table on the other side of the room. Only after the cook had gone did he rise and seat himself next to it. Carefully, with loving gestures, he poured the brew into his cup, adding a dollop of milk and three teaspoons of sugar. He took a sip, then reached for the plate of crumpets which were also on the tray. They were warm, and they dripped with butter. Sighing with pleasure, Hamish ate.

When the crumpets were gone, and the teapot empty, he sat back. Burping softly, he reflected on the pleasures of his home and the dissatisfaction he always felt when he was forced to leave it. Imagine Timothy's choosing to stay two extra days in France. But then, Timothy was a disappointment in many ways. And he wasn't alone in liking "abroad"; many men did. Such as de Montviron probably. Unlikely he'd have remained so long in Egypt if he hadn't found it attractive.

Hamish thought about Egypt. Something was tugging at the back of his mind. Some connection. He relaxed and let it surface. He never lost any data once they were filed in his mind. Eventually he could recall anything he'd heard or once known. Just as now. He realized what was nagging him. Jenny Fogel's Egyptian collection. Tim had mentioned it. He said the girl Sarah fainted while looking at Jenny's Egyptian bowls. So there wasn't any real connection with de Montviron or the bracelet. Just a silly girl. He dismissed the consideration.

In North Carolina the midday sun shone brightly on Pine Creek. It had changed a lot, bigger for one thing. At least a dozen new houses that Jarib could see, little pastel-painted houses with carports and neatly fenced backyards. And there was a supermarket across from what had been Nate Summers's gas station. The gas station was still there, but it had been modernized—four pumping stations and a flashing sign that said TEXACO. He had to steel himself to drive in. A young attendant materialized quickly. "Fill her up, please."

Jarib got out of the car while the boy pumped gas. "How long has this been a Texaco station?"

The boy shrugged. "Don't rightly know. Long as I can remember."

Since he was probably no more than sixteen, that wasn't surprising. "Do much business?" Jarib inquired casually.

"Enough. Folk stop on their way up to the mountains." He nodded his head toward the looming Blue Ridge range on the horizon. He was a lean boy, blond, with a bad case of acne. "That'll be twelve dollars and sixty cents," he said. It occurred to Jarib that he both sounded and looked something like Ruben Summers. His hand shook a little when he reached for his wallet.

He paid with a twenty-dollar bill, and kept the change in evidence. "You the only attendant?"

"Naw, I'm Clarie Crock, the day boy. Guy named Will Tucker works nights. Why you wanna know?"

The boy was eyeing him warily. Jarib tried to look reassuring. He took out his wallet again, but he didn't put the money away. Instead he added another five dollars to the change from the twenty. The boy's eyes flicked from his face to the bills and back again. "I'm looking for a woman," Jarib said. "Tall, blond, early thirties, very beautiful. Not from around here, she's from Boston, has a Boston accent like mine. You haven't seen her by any chance?"

The boy grinned, displaying crooked teeth. "Sorry, mister, the state cops came and asked me the same thing. Never seen the dame. So I s'pose you better put your money away."

Jarib laughed softly. "Maybe, maybe not. I've got another question. Did you ever know the man who used to own this place? Nate Summers."

"The one whose son got shot by that crazy girl from up North—" He broke off. "Holy shit! She's the blonde everybody's lookin' for, ain't she? I heared she was in a nuthouse. She break out or somethin'?"

"Or something. What about old Nate?"

"Sure I know him. Everybody in these parts does. Lives down by the creek in the old cabin."

Jarib's gut wrenched. In the house he and Lenore had rented. "Thanks," he said. He proffered the money, and the boy took it.

He parked in the same spot they'd parked that first day and walked to the house. It looked different, better. The lean-to pantry was gone, the place had been painted, and in front of the porch a few marigolds and calendulas clung to the last of the long southern autumn. A dog barked ferociously, the front door opened, and Nate Summers stepped outside.

"Hello, Mr. Summers, I'm Jarib Baraak. Do you remember me?" The hardest words he'd ever spoken.

The old man squinted at him for a moment. "Sure I remember you. Been a long time, though."

"Fourteen years," Jarib agreed. "Can I talk to you for a moment?"

"Don't cost nothin'." Summers motioned for Baraak to join him on the porch. There were two wicker chairs, shabby but in good repair. They sat.

"I'm looking for Lenore," Jarib said. There was little point in being cagey. The state police must have questioned Summers, too.

"Yeah, the cops told me she got out. Ain't seen her."

"All the same, I think she's come here."

Summers was chewing tobacco; he spit expertly across the porch railing before he spoke. "You think she's gunnin' for the rest of 'em?"

It was the first time any resident of Pine Creek had admitted that the men with Ruben weren't a product of Lenore's imagination. Jarib registered that and passed it over; it made little difference now. "I don't know. She's sick, it's impossible to say what she'll do. I just have a hunch."

"Mebbe," Summers agreed. He studied Baraak openly. "If she comes, the coppers'll ketch her. They're real good at their jobs." He chuckled softly. "Ain't been a still 'round here in years." Abruptly he changed the subject, or seemed to. "Yore lookin' real good, boy. Still young. That Lenore, she still yore wife?"

Jarib nodded. "Yes. Legally."

"Yore a fool. Ain't no point in that. 'Tweren't yore fault. She wuz tetched in the head." He turned his face from Jarib and stared at the creek and the distant hills. "And Ruben was pure bad. I always knowed, just didn't like to face it. Anybody's to blame it gotta be him. Get yoreself a lawyer, boy. Get freed up and find another woman. Don't do for a man to sleep alone every night. And whores ain't the same."

Jarib swallowed hard. "Maybe," he said. Summers's laconic speech was affecting him. "I have to find her first. See she doesn't come to any harm." He stood up. "Thanks for talking to me."

Summers watched him walking down the path between the marigolds. "Take care of yoreself, boy. Get another woman."

Jarib turned back. "I'm sorry about everything," he said. It was the first time he'd been able to offer the man sympathy. Whatever Ruben had been, he was Nate's son.

"I know," the old man said.

He was staying in a motel on the outskirts of Durham. It was new, plastic, impersonal. It carried no memories of Lenore or his youthful, stupid stubbornness. There was something in the room called a minibar. A small refrigerator you opened with a key, supplied with miniature bottles of whiskey and cans of juice and mixers. He took two little bottles of Old Grand-dad bourbon and poured them neat into a glass. The first swallow went down hard past the lump in his throat. He opened the fridge again and added some ice. Better.

Jarib lay on the bed and stared at the ceiling and sipped his drink. He played back the conversation with Nate Summers. And he felt better. A predictable exorcism perhaps, but he'd never thought of it before. Never realized he needed or wanted it. Because he'd been flagellating himself so effectively for so long that he was out of touch with his own needs.

And he thought of Sarah.

Not Lenore, poor benighted creature that she was, Sarah. He loved her. She loved him. And he was allowing her to be swallowed by the vortex of tragedy that had engulfed Lenore and almost himself. After a few minutes he reached for the phone.

"She's in England, Jarib," Ivy said. "On a buying trip for me. She was scheduled to go the same day your charming little love note arrived. Remember?"

"Yes, I remember. I just thought perhaps . . . She took it badly, I suppose," Jarib said softly.

"What do you think?"

"I think I'm the world's prime candidate for horse's ass of the year. I've got to talk to her, Ivy. Please."

"You are a son of a bitch, Jarib Baraak. And you don't deserve Sarah."

His heart sank. "Please," he repeated.

Ivy's laugh jarred the wires. "Okay. I won't make you crawl

anymore. Hang on, I'll get the number." She was back in a few seconds. "She's based in a place called Tiverton. In Avon. With an associate of mine. Who, by the way, is young and gorgeous and mad about Sarah. Put that in your pipe and smoke it, you bum."

"Ivy, I'm miserable enough. The salt you're rubbing in the wound is superfluous. What's the number?"

She gave it to him. "They're going to auctions in England and France," she warned. "I can't say Sarah will be at the manor. But Hamish Durant, that's my associate's father, is bound to be. He should know where she is."

The international line was bad; Hamish pressed the telephone to his ear and shouted into the mouthpiece. "I'm sorry, Miss Myles is in France on business. No, I don't know where to reach her. I believe she's gone to Alsace for the weekend, but I couldn't say where. I expect her back late Monday afternoon."

"I'll call again on Monday," Jarib said, shouting in turn. "In the meantime, if you should hear from her, will you kindly tell her I called and it's urgent that I speak with her?"

"Yes, yes, of course. Please spell your name again, I'm afraid the line is so bad I didn't get it correctly."

Hamish wrote "Jarib Baraak" on the pad at his desk and broke the connection. It was 10:00 P.M., time for his hot chocolate. The cook had left it earlier in a thermos jug. He poured the thick dark liquid into a bisque ware stein and topped it with whipped cream from a little bowl that had been waiting on ice. Then he waddled over to the fireplace. Like the rest of the fireplaces in the house, it didn't work. But there was a gas heater in the opening. He turned it up and pulled his bathrobe tighter around his enormous bulk.

Jarib Baraak. An unusual name. Americans so often had peculiar names. The legacy of their miscegenation. Hamish frowned with distaste. A bunch of half and quarter breeds with more power than was good for them or the rest of society. No wonder the world was in such a mess.

Behind him shelves climbed to the ceiling bearing a reference library second to none in private hands. Hamish reached for *Thompson's Etymology of Family Names*. Published by Oxford University Press in 1922, it was long out of print. He considered his copy a treasure; it had served him well many times. *Jarib* was from the Hebrew, he found. God's strong arm. *Baraak* was Egyptian.

Hamish stopped midway through the motions of pouring himself another cup of chocolate. Egyptian. The third time today Egypt had played a part in his telephone contacts with the outside world. Too often to be a coincidence. He put down the stein and seated himself at his desk, pressing his fingers to his temples and closing his eyes.

Within seconds he had replayed in his head the entire conversation with the American. Every nuance and inflection was called back by his formidable recall. A northeastern accent, he decided. Most likely Boston. Young to middle aged, no more than forty probably. He thought a moment longer. Ten-thirty here, so it was five-thirty Eastern Standard Time. The office should still be open. He found the address book in his drawer and dialed. This time the telephone line was clearer. He could hear the man in Boston perfectly.

"Just the name, that's all you can give me?"

"That's all. Jarib Baraak. It's an unusual name, shouldn't be too difficult. I'll ring you tomorrow, ten A.M. your time."

"Tomorrow's Saturday," the man said. "The office is closed."

"Well, you shall have to open it, won't you, lad? I think my account substantial enough to warrant it."

He gave this particular research firm a good deal of business. Many treasures had found their way to Boston over the past two hundred years. Tracing their origins or present whereabouts was a frequent concern of Hamish's.

When he hung up, he was satisfied. If there was a connection, he would find it. But in the anxiety of a few moments ago he'd left the top off the thermos. His second cup of chocolate was stone cold. He felt deprived and angry as he lumbered from the room to his bed.

$\mathcal{E}$leven

SATURDAY,
NOVEMBER 24

Zelah's place was called Auberge California, but a less U.S. West Coast setting would be hard to imagine. It was located in a former mill, on the banks of a nineteenth-century engineering marvel, a concrete-lined canal that cut a precise furrow through the tiny village of Kohlburg. The village was a stone's throw from the mighty Rhine, and fifteen minutes by car from Strasbourg. "If you love old Alsace, as I do," Zelah told them when they arrived, "the place is a miracle. Still unchanged, despite being enormously convenient."

Sarah expected a restaurant, but this was something more, a classic *auberge,* ninety percent an eating place and ten percent an inn. Food and, for the lucky few, lodging, dispensed with hospitality and graciousness and oozing charm—the traditional European combination tourists always hoped to find and seldom did.

Built of old yellow sandstone, mellow with centuries, glamorized by Zelah's sense of color and her gift with flowers, the California was heaven. The dining room was enormous; it filled the main body of the onetime mill. But the space was divided by inspired grace notes: planters filled with herbs and lit by strategically placed skylights, folding screens of gray oak intricately carved in the local fashion, a pyramid of casks holding the wonderful Alsatian beer, and central to everything the watercourse and the wheel which had supplied the power to grind flour for nine generations. "It's perfect," Sarah said softly when Zelah proudly toured them 'round.

"How's the food?" Tim asked.

"Fantastic, of course," Zelah said.

And it was. They arrived in time for lunch. First came a light-as-air mousse of smoked goose, accompanied by carrots no bigger than Sarah's little finger and the tiniest, greenest string beans imaginable, then fresh trout au Riesling with sorrel sauce, and to finish, an estimable version of one of the glories of France, tarte Tatin— the apples tasting as good as apples smell, the caramel topping crisp enough to crackle beneath the fork and soft enough to melt on the tongue.

"You must drink a Wolxheim Riesling," Zelah had insisted. "It's from a vineyard just up the road; besides, that's what we poach the trout in."

Now Sarah took a last sip of the wine and pushed away the plate which had held her apple tart. "Paradise." She sighed. "Zelah, who cooks this ambrosia?"

"My friend and partner, Charles Corne. You'll meet him later, when the rush is over. But don't tell him I let you stay with the Reisling through dessert. He'll kill me. You should have switched to a gewürztraminer." She whisked the offending bottle from the table. No matter, it was empty.

Zelah said something about coffee and cognac. "I just can't," Sarah protested. "I'm too full, and too tired to lift the cup."

"What you need," Tim said, "is a brief tour of the district. Strasbourg at least. It's a wonderful city, and now that the rain's stopped you can see something."

Sarah agreed but insisted she had to change first.

Above the dining room were four guest bedrooms, each in reality a corner suite. "I didn't know for sure, *mes petites,*" Zelah said frankly, "so I reserved two. Do you share a bedroom?"

"Not today," Sarah said firmly. Tim looked chagrined. "I'm exhausted," she added.

Zelah read the situation at once. "In here." She opened a door and pushed Sarah through. "The key is on the inside, turn it. I'll put this ravening male animal next door. He can come through, but only when you unlock."

Ariel was on the stairs, just below where they turned. He could hear but not be seen. Too bad for the Englishman, the girl was a looker. Oh, well, he patted his full stomach, he, too, had dined on goose and trout; a man can't expect all of life's pleasures in one go. Still smiling, he went back to the dining room, paid his bill, and left.

Half a kilometer from the *auberge,* in front of the village chemist shop, was a telephone kiosk. He had no difficulty getting through to Paris.

"They're at Zelah Tench's place," he reported.

"I thought that might be where they were headed."

"Yes, well, you were right. Yitzhak, tell me something, who is the American dame? Why is she important?"

"No reason, she's just somebody I invented so you shouldn't lose your skills while Levi is in New York."

When he hung up, it occurred to Ariel that it might indeed be true.

"He's Dr. Jarib Baraak, a Ph.D., a professor at Harvard," the voice from Boston said.

Hamish jotted notes on the pad at his desk. "Age?"

"According to the *Harvard Register,* he was born in 1948, in Alexandria."

Hamish caught his breath. "In Egypt?"

"Yes, that's right. Came here with his family when he was a year old. They're Jews. Parents still alive, retired. The mother taught chemistry, father's also a chemist. I can get more on them if you want, but not until Monday."

"No, I don't think I want any data on the parents. What does Dr. Baraak teach?"

"That's off the wall," the researcher said with some glee.

"And what does that mean?"

"Off the wall, weird, you know." Hamish didn't, but he refrained from commenting. "He's something called a parapsychologist," the man in Boston was saying. "A ghost chaser near as I can figure out."

Hamish was too stunned to correct the American's narrow view of parapsychology. "I see, thank you. That's all for now."

He hung up without waiting for the other man's good-bye. For some seconds his hand remained on the receiver, fingers drumming nervously, eyes closed in thought. An Egyptian Jew, a parapsychologist, a connection of some sort with a young woman who fainted when shown a collection of ancient Egyptian pottery . . . Correction, of some intimate sort. "Tell her I called and that it's urgent." That's what this Baraak had said. One doesn't make urgent transatlantic telephone calls to idle acquaintances.

In the corridor outside the study there was an old Swiss cuckoo clock. It chimed every fifteen minutes and drove Hamish wild. He insisted that the clock remain silent. But someone must have disobeyed his instructions and pulled down the weights. At that moment the clock began chattering its silly message, coo-coo, coo-coo, coo-coo. Three in the afternoon if the mechanical bird spoke the truth. He glanced at the decently silent clock on the mantel. It did.

So it was four on the Continent. And Dom Malachy hadn't rung. Perhaps he wouldn't today. But that was not to be tolerated. Hamish picked up the telephone again. This time he called Fanti's office in Rome. He did not permit himself to wince at the thought of his bill.

"I regret disturbing you, Father," he told the cardinal's secretary. "My name is Hamish Durant. I am an associate of His Eminence."

"Yes, Mr. Durant. Dom Malachy has spoken of you."

"It's imperative that I speak with him. I know he's in Paris, but not how to reach him."

On the other end of the telephone there was a soft, sighing sound. The man was accustomed to intrigue and trained in discretion. "Of course, Mr. Durant. I will see to it that Dom Malachy hears of your desire to speak with him. Immediately."

Within half an hour Cardinal Fanti called. Clerics, Hamish noted, were well organized. He conveyed the information about Jarib Baraak and Sarah Myles succinctly, wasting no words but managing to include all his suspicions.

"It's too extraordinary to be a coincidence," Malachy agreed. "This young woman could be one of them, Hamish. One of the carriers I told you about. A descendant with a racial memory of the Testament. Like Levi."

"Yes. But she's not a Jew. Still, I suppose we must deal with the inconsistencies later, when perhaps we'll know more."

Malachy drew a deep breath. "You say she's in France now?"

"Yes, with my son, Timothy. They've gone to Alsace for the weekend. I don't have the exact address, but I can probably get it with a phone call or two."

The priest didn't answer immediately. He was thinking about Yitzhak. In the past he'd have passed on this information and left it to the Israeli to follow up. But not now. Now he suspected that Yitzhak already knew about this Sarah Myles. That he'd known about her for some time. That she, in fact, was what he'd been hiding. Now God had intervened, and the instrument He'd chosen was Malachy Fanti. "Hamish," he said slowly. "It probably sounds mad, but I think I should go to Alsace. To wherever this young woman and your son are."

"It doesn't sound mad to me." Hamish's voice was low. "It sounds absolutely imperative."

"But when I get there, what will I do? I feel so helpless. I have no experience in these matters."

"You underestimate yourself, Dom Malachy. I think we're dealing with matters of which you have every experience." He paused, weighing his next words. "For my part, I distinctly detect the stench of sulfur and burning brimstone."

"Yes," the monk said sadly. "So do I."

"Well then?"

"I'll go at once, if you can tell me where they are."

"If you'll give me your number, I'll have it for you before five."

"Of course. I'm at the Abbey of St. Louis." The precautions of a few days ago seemed absurd now. He'd wanted to keep Hamish somewhat removed, not let him too far into the inner circle composed of himself and Yitzhak; now he saw the Englishman as his only ally. Hamish Durant and God, that's all he could count on. "I'll wait here for your call," Malachy said before he hung up.

Getting the Alsatian address of the Jewess turned out to be easy. Hamish had thought he'd call her Paris flat or her greenhouse and make up some story that would achieve his end, but on impulse he checked first with directory inquiries in Strasbourg. Yes, there was a Zelah Tench listed, in the village of Kohlburg. Very simple.

"Kohlburg," he told Malachy. "According to my atlas, it's a village of under a thousand people. You should be able to locate the restaurant easily."

"There's a train leaving at seven, I'll be in Strasbourg before midnight."

Hamish Durant hung up and rose slowly from his desk, a man faced with an unpleasant task. He walked to the door of the study, the felt slippers making no sound on the thick carpets, the flannel bathrobe proof against the chill of the corridor. The cook was just bringing his tea tray. "I shan't have time for that," he told her. "And I won't be wanting dinner this evening. I'm going to Paris."

Rhonda had said it, Myra had fancy taste. Fortunately she looked like her father. She could wear the tiniest bikini, the clingiest cotton knit skirt. All her life Rhonda had coveted such things and known that though she could easily afford them, they made her look ridiculous. In Myra she had a surrogate.

Mother and daughter scoured Bergdorf's and Bendel's and every glittering marble and brass inch of Trump Tower. And as a last stop before going back in exhaustion to Sam's place, there was always crazy, wonderful Bloomie's. "It's true we have lots of the same stores in Los Angeles," Myra announced. "But somehow they're always more exciting in New York."

They brought their purchases back to Sam's apartment and gave him impromptu fashion shows. Myra adored being the center of attention, Sam loved the feeling of sharing a family, and Rhonda seemed content to watch them both. She'd bought things, too, of

course, a white silk caftan and a dark blue cape, but she had no
desire to model them. In the evenings Sam suggested taking them
out to dinner, but Rhonda always vetoed that plan.

The first afternoon she'd gone to Gristede's and stocked up with
first cut brisket and eye of the round, and she made Sam glorious
meals of pot roast with noodle dumplings and oven roast with
potato kugel. Tender loving care, just as she'd promised Yitzhak.
The hotel rooms and the airline seats would be safe because she was
keeping her part of the bargain. But so far she'd had no word from
the Israeli, and she worried and wondered how long this would go
on, and pictured Jack fucking the accommodating Elaine every
hour on the hour. So okay, in her saner moments she realized that
probably wasn't possible. Maybe only once a day. It was still too
damn much.

On Saturday morning Rhonda and Myra did Saks Fifth Avenue.
They were in designer dresses on the third floor. Myra spotted an
Yves Saint Laurent silk two-piece; the blouse was slit down to here,
the skirt up to there. "It's too old for you," Rhonda said. "You'll
look like a *kurveh*."

"What's that?"

"What you'll look like in that outfit."

"I'm just going to try it on, Ma, just to see."

Myra disappeared into the fitting room. And Rhonda spotted the
man for whom she'd been watching. He wasn't unfamiliar. It was
the same old guy Yitzhak usually sent when he'd promised to get
in touch with her about something. She knew him only as Morrie,
with no last name.

She did her best to appear casual as she moved to a rack filled
with the dresses of a Japanese designer. They were all shapeless
tents in black and gray. She waited and studied the price tags. Not
one of these *shmattes* cost under six hundred dollars. It wouldn't
occur to Rhonda to put her short, plump body in such an outfit,
but the display was at the far corner of the floor and no one else
was around.

Morrie approached. "Good morning, Mrs. Kane," he said without looking at her. He spoke English with only the trace of an
accent. It wasn't Hebrew. European, maybe German or Polish.
She'd never been sure, and she really didn't want to know. What

Rhonda wanted was to have this encounter over with before Myra came out of the fitting room.

"Well, what does he want me to do? I have to get home."

"Meet me today at three in the lobby of the Tudor Hotel. Come alone, please."

He was gone before Rhonda could say anything else.

Myra appeared in the Saint Laurent. "Look, Ma, it's gorgeous. I'll die if I can't have it."

"No, I promise you won't die," Rhonda said impatiently. "Take it off. I've got a rotten headache, and I want to go back to Sam's."

Sam had tickets for the matinee performance of *A Chorus Line*. "You and Myra go," Rhonda said. "I'm exhausted, and I have a headache."

"Okay, but tonight you don't cook," Sam said. "We go out for Chinese. What do you say?"

"Terrific," Rhonda said. "Only now get out of here and let me lie down."

She left the apartment half an hour after Sam and Myra did.

The Tudor was simply old. Neither elegant nor genteel, it spoke of no past glories, only a gradual, unremarkable aging. It was a solid red-brick edifice on East Fortieth Street, part of a large complex built in the twenties. Soon after the war, the UN Building went up and it got a new lease on life. The Tudor was clean and respectable and compared with newer, grander hotels, relatively inexpensive. It was also relatively empty, Rhonda had no difficulty spotting Morrie in the lobby. He was sitting on a shabby velvet banquette, and he rose and greeted her with a smile and a big kiss. Anyone watching would assume they were relatives or old friends.

"I thought you liked to practice your cloak-and-dagger stuff on me," Rhonda said. "Whispered messages out of the corner of your mouth." She always had difficulty taking Yitzhak's machinations seriously. And she never considered herself at risk because of them. Inconvenienced certainly, but she was rewarded handsomely for that. Nobody could accuse her of spying, for God's sake. Yitzhak and his cronies were Jews, Israelis. That was almost like being an American as far as Rhonda was concerned.

"Sometimes being obvious is the best protection," the man said pleasantly. "Let's go have a cup of coffee, shall we?"

There were few people in the coffee shop and no waitress, just a man behind the counter. Morrie collected two cups and carried them to a booth in the rear. Rhonda eyed a luscious-looking cheesecake, but he didn't ask her if she wanted anything else. "I expect you remember the first tour you took to Israel in 1958," he said.

Rhonda was startled. He was dredging up ancient history and the foundation of her relationship with Yitzhak. Was something wrong? Had she made some fatal error and angered her benefactor? "Of course I remember. What about it?"

"The boss wants you to meet somebody here. And get him to meet Mr. Stein. Somebody you met in Israel in '58."

"Who?"

"The fellow who took your group around Kibbutz Etz Hadar. Dov Levi."

She hadn't heard the name in more than two decades; now she inhaled sharply. "Jesus! He was the one the police suspected right away. Sam knows Amy was with him from the time she disappeared until she was killed. This Levi is here in New York? And you want me to—"

"Exactly," Morrie interrupted. "The boss says it's to jog Levi's memory. It will be fairly simple. Tomorrow morning you tell Mr. Stein you want to have brunch at a restaurant on West Fifty-ninth, across from Lincoln Center. It's called The Place. Mr. Levi will be there. All you have to do is recognize him and introduce him to Mr. Stein."

"You're crazy. Besides, I wouldn't know him if I fell over him."

"I thought of that." The man pulled a photograph out of his pocket. It was a Polaroid, probably taken when the subject was unaware. He was standing at a newsstand with his hand out, apparently paying or waiting for change.

Rhonda stared at the slightly blurred gray image. *Beaten* and *tired* were the words that came to her mind. But yes, she could just see the vestiges of vaguely remembered good looks. "You're crazy," she said again. "And cruel. Why does Yitzhak want to open all Sam's wounds? What's to be gained by it?"

"I don't really know, Mrs. Kane. Only what he said, to give Levi a nudge. But knowing isn't my job. I'm sure it's necessary.

Be there at eleven, no later. At three P.M. New York time you're to call this number in Paris."

He pushed a scrap of paper across the table. Rhonda stared at it. There wasn't any name, just the number. But she could guess who'd answer the phone. Yitzhak, wanting a progress report on the torture he'd devised.

Strasbourg, the cathedral town of Alsace, epitomized the history of the area. It was not quite French and not quite German; its personality was an amalgam of the two. There was a Germanic feeling to the small cobbled alleys of the old town, a definite French influence in the magnificence of the single-spired cathedral. Sarah loved it. She and Tim wandered around for a couple of hours; she bought a wonderful copper fruit bowl for Rita and earrings for herself. Tim was funny and knowledgeable, a delightful guide. She was unprepared for his change of mood as they drove back to Kohlburg.

"I must really be lousy in bed," he said suddenly.

"What are you talking about?"

"Last night you had a headache, and this afternoon you looked positively relieved when Zelah gave us separate rooms."

"Oh, that."

"Yes, that."

She played with the strap of her handbag, running it through her fingers, not looking at him. "I did have a headache last night." She'd insisted he go to his own room in the Paris hotel. And he hadn't been difficult about it. She'd hoped he wouldn't be tonight either. Because the truth was, she didn't want to sleep with Timothy Durant. The silence was growing ominous; Sarah had to say something. "I tried, Tim."

"You tried. Is that supposed to make me feel better? Am I such difficult medicine?"

"Oh, God, everything I say just makes it worse. Look, it isn't you. It's got nothing to do with you. That's the problem. I like you very much, and you're perfectly wonderful in bed, as I think you know. It's me, and—"

"And the Monday man," he supplied.

"Yes."

Tim sighed. "Okay, angel. No more advances. I know when I'm beaten. He must be quite a chap. Wish I could meet him and get a few lessons."

The British Airways 707 touched down at de Gaulle Airport at six-fifty, just ten minutes late. Formalities were brief for citizens of another member of the EEC. Hamish had no need to wait for luggage because he carried only an overnight case. By five past seven he was speaking with Jenny Fogel.

"My dear, this is outrageously short notice and I'm sure you're busy, but if by chance you're not, will you have dinner with me? I find myself in Paris, I've literally just arrived, and as soon as I got here, I thought of you."

"Hamish, for the pleasure of seeing you outside your manor fortress, I shall break my previous engagement. Where will you take me?"

"Wherever you suggest."

Jenny laughed. "That will prove expensive, but delicious. Give me the number and wait right there." Five minutes later she rang back and gave him an address and said she'd meet him at eight-thirty.

She'd chosen a Paris legend, Taillevant, on the Rue Lamennais in the eighth arrondissement, near the heart of the city, the Champs-Elysées. And it was Saturday evening. So it took Hamish's cab until well after eight to get there. By that time he was hungry and more disgruntled than he'd been at the airport. But he reminded himself of the importance of this unpleasant journey. And noted that from the outside Taillevant still looked like the private house it had once been: gray granite, three-storied, impressive. Hamish began to feel a bit better.

He made his way into the foyer, grateful for the immediate charm, the grace notes apparent everywhere. Sometimes "abroad" wasn't so terrible after all.

"*Bon soir,* monsieur."

"Good evening, you speak English, of course."

"Of course, monsieur."

"I'm meeting Madame Fogel. I believe she telephoned to book a table."

"Ah, of course!" The maître d' smiled. "A little over an hour ago, to see if perchance there had been a cancellation. *Et voilà!* there had been. On anyone else perhaps the gods do not always smile. But Madame Fogel is not anyone else. Would Monsieur prefer to wait in the bar or at the table?"

"The table, please." He did not want to lumber across the dining room in Jenny's presence.

The maître d' led him down a few steps. The tables were glorious, heavy with white napery, gleaming with silver, lightened with fresh flowers. The walls were paneled, the chandeliers of sparkling crystal. It was yet early; fewer than half the tables were occupied. But they all had little white cards marking them as reserved. "Will this be satisfactory, monsieur?"

It was. There was a deep and comfortable banquette, Hamish would not have to squeeze himself onto a chair inevitably too narrow. "Very good."

The Frenchman had known it would be. Madame Fogel had warned him when she rang. "My friend is rather large, Georges. You will be careful about the seating." Now Georges suggested an aperitif while Monsieur waited. They decided on a kir. The maître d' passed the order on. Hamish relaxed, suffused in a glow of comfort and having done exactly the right thing. By the time Jenny arrived he was beaming.

Not until after they'd eaten did Hamish pose the question he'd come all this way to ask. They were sipping armagnac. Jenny Fogel's cheeks glowed; her eyes sparkled. She must be past sixty, Hamish guessed, but she was still a lovely woman. She wore a black suit of heavy ribbed faille; the jacket was lined with red, and her blouse, a wisp of something Hamish had known in his youth as georgette, matched. Tonight her magnificent jewelry was represented by small ruby studs in her ears and one remarkable ruby ring. He leaned forward and covered the ringed hand with his own. "My dear, I have not been completely honest. I wished to see you not just for your charming self. I am in need of a favor."

Jenny smiled. She left her left hand beneath his, raised her snifter with her right. "I am not surprised, Hamish. But I'm curious.

Whatever this favor may be, did you come all the way to Paris just to see me and ask it? Despite your notorious hatred of leaving Tiverton?"

"Yes."

"I am enormously flattered. And curious." She waited.

"There is no one I know in Paris with more tact and better knowledge of . . . shall we say, the way things are. I wish to ask what you know of Count François Lontesse de Montviron."

"Why?"

"Recently he put some items up for sale, what's known as"— the thick lips made a sucking noise of distaste—"Judaica. And he took great pains to remain anonymous. Even at the expense of offering less than perfect provenance for some of the pieces. Among them was a bracelet that interests me. I can't tell you more than that."

He was conscious of her skin still touching his, and aware when she broke the physical contact, and of his own bulk. He had dined superbly, his mind was engaged, other pleasures he'd long since decided he could not have. "I hope you realize that I will find some way to repay your kindness."

"The next sale, perhaps," Jenny said.

"Perhaps. Or the one that follows it. I have an excellent memory, my dear."

"Yes, I'm sure of that, Hamish. Very well, I know your count. Everyone in Paris does. He's quite the man-about-town."

"What do you know of his time in Egypt?"

"Only that it was very profitable. His family had been there for generations. When the Egyptians gained their independence from your government, it was time for the de Montviron clan to pick up their toys and come home. François presided over the dismantling. He did not leave empty-handed."

"I wish to meet him."

She cocked her head and eyed him. "I see. How long will you be in Paris?"

"As short a time as possible. I wish to meet the count tomorrow. In the morning for preference, in the afternoon if necessary."

"You ask a great deal, Hamish."

"Yes."

She thought for a moment. "Very well, where are you staying?"

"The Georges Cinq. I haven't been yet, but I telephoned from the airport for a reservation."

Jenny picked up her elegant satin evening purse. "You must take me home now. I will phone you in the morning."

From behind the lace undercurtains of her drawing room Jenny watched the red taillight of the taxi disappear around the corner of the Rue du Faubourg St.-Honoré. When it was gone, she stepped back, letting the curtains fall into place, adjusting one fold of the taffeta drapes. Thoughtfully she removed the ruby earrings and the ruby ring. Things that had belonged to her mother and her grandmother. She'd told that story so often she almost believed it. Most of the time she managed to forget the high-ranking Gestapo officer whose patronage kept her safe after the house arrest that followed her father's last concert, his public denouncement of the regime. And she never thought about the source of the exquisite jewels the officer had lavished upon her. She went to the telephone.

"I'm sorry. It's very late, I know. But I must speak with you."

"Tonight?"

"Yes. I'm not sure. I can't be. But it could be extremely important."

"The usual place then. In an hour."

Jenny rang off and went to change her clothes.

In Kohlburg the last of the diners were just leaving the old mill. Zelah saw them to the door, then returned to the dining room. Tim and Sarah were there, sipping the last of their coffee and cognac, and Charles had just emerged from the kitchen and joined them. It was the first meeting between him and Zelah's guests.

She approached the table, grinning. "Now you know my surprise, would you have guessed?"

"That your partner and chef is—horrors!—an American," Tim said, laughing. "Never in a million years. Isn't there some French law against it?"

"Probably," Charles said. "So we just won't tell them, will we?"

"My lips are sealed," Tim promised.

"But your name sounds so French," Sarah said.

"Only after Zelah rearranged it. When we met in Los Angeles, I was Chuck Horn. Charles Corne is a translation."

"It's really not a secret." Zelah sat down, helping herself from the bottle of brandy on the table. "You couldn't keep any kind of secret in a restaurant kitchen, let alone a secret like that. And Charles has papers, he's not illegal. We just don't advertise it because the French are such snobs about food."

"Well, I'm not," Sarah said. "But I know marvelous when I taste it. The breast of duck with raspberries was heaven."

Chuck smiled his thanks and began eating his own late dinner. He was a big man, with tattoos on the backs of his big hands, a mermaid on the right and a sailor on the left. Self-taught, Zelah explained. And steeped in the witty, offhand elegance of California cuisine, which was just what she'd wanted. So she'd written and enticed him with an offer of a partnership, and he came. "My lucky day," Zelah said, smiling fondly at Charles.

Sarah was about to ask him about the tattoos when it happened. One minute she was laughing and enjoying herself; the next her head was exploding with the music, the woman's voice, and a kind of static unlike anything she'd previously experienced. It was as if the whole thing were garbled. As if a scrambler had been installed and, instead of either quiescence or communication, there was a new and terrible jamming. She grabbed her temples and moaned.

The others tried to help, demanded to know what was wrong. Sarah couldn't answer. She rose from the table and fled the room, reeling.

Outside the man in the black suit and white Roman collar saw her go. He could see everything in the well-lit dining room through the uncurtained glass doors that looked out onto the canal. He stood near it, sheltered from view by an old oak tree. He'd been standing there for almost two hours, unaware of the cold, the occasional spattering of rain. He'd simply stood and watched and tried to decide how to proceed.

He recognized Sarah Myles the moment he spotted her; she exactly fitted Hamish Durant's description. But having gotten that far, he was for a long time unsure of the rest. So he stood and looked and thought about the terrible and imminent danger posed

329

by Donovan's committee, of the Alexandria Testament, and of his long quest.

Then he saw it happen, saw her rise and leave the room in agony, and he knew. Everything Professor Wolff believed, what Jung said, what Yitzhak had told him about the Jew Levi, it was all true. And this American woman was another one. She, too, was a carrier. Malachy shuddered. But he understood what he could do. His line of country, just as Hamish Durant had said.

Larry Donovan was in Oxford, one more journey from Brighton made on behalf of the committee. The past eighteen months had confirmed his status as a veteran world traveler. This time he was in the sitting room of Blackfriars, the priory of the Dominicans. Not because they had anything to do with his reason for being in England, only because in the crowded university town hotels were expensive. The Dominicans had graciously offered a visiting monsignor hospitality.

A woman sat opposite him. She wore lay clothing, a tailored gray suit and flat-heeled black shoes, but she was Sister Miriam Frent of the Congregation of Our Lady of Sion. In addition to the letters OLS which traditionally followed her name, Sister Miriam had the right to add the letters of half a dozen degrees.

"Well, what do you think?" Donovan asked. It was a rhetorical question. They both knew what they thought about the inch-high stack of paper on the table between them.

"I'm too tired to think," Sister Miriam said. "It's nearly midnight."

"Yes, sorry to keep you so late." They'd been going over the final draft preparatory to Donovan's bringing it to America the next day. In America it would be printed and soon distributed. "But I did want someone to check the proofs with me," he added. "It's an enormous responsibility."

"Not one jot nor tittle of the law shall ye change . . ." Sister Miriam quoted, archaically and somewhat inappropriately.

"That's just it, isn't it? They changed the whole thing."

"In the Acts of the Apostles, yes," Sister Miriam said. "I think so. The entire committee thinks so."

The American leaned back and looked at her. "Do you think the world at large will agree?"

"Of course not." She smiled, and it magnified the tiredness apparent on her face. "But if it gets them talking and thinking, we've made a start."

Donovan rapped the pile of papers on the coffee table to line them up yet more precisely. Then he carefully inserted them in his briefcase. "Come along, Sister, I'm going to put you in a taxi and send you home. We've done everything we can. Now we'd better start praying."

He came back five minutes later and took his briefcase and put out the lights in the sitting room and climbed the broad stairs that led to his third-floor bedroom. It was small and utilitarian. Anyone accusing the Catholic clergy of living in unseemly luxury ought to visit Blackfriars.

The bathroom was down a long, cold hall, and he visited it hurriedly, brushed his teeth, and made his way back to the hard, narrow bed as quickly as he could. But tired as he was, the monsignor couldn't sleep. The first page of the report had burned itself into his brain. Deliberately dramatic to attract attention, it nonetheless was an accurate precis of the conclusions of the committee.

> To state our position briefly, we hold that the report in the Acts of the Apostles of an amicable solution between Paul and the leaders of the Church in Jerusalem on the question of whether Gentile converts were to be bound by Jewish Law is pure invention. Paul set out to Christianize the non-Jewish world, and he believed that his converts should not be bound to the Jewish dietary laws or the all-important circumcision of males—the sign of the covenant between Jews and God. But scriptural evidence, in the form of Paul's letters, which are accepted as predating the writing of the Acts, makes it apparent that this view, however correct and necessary for Christianity's future, was not accepted by the Church until much later, long after the death of Paul himself.
>
> Far from being an academic question, this, if we are correct, makes it apparent that Christianity was much more

331

Jewish in outlook and intent in its early days than has heretofore been admitted. And Paul, far from being a respected leader in that early Church, was an upstart and a radical who preached a minority view which proved to be prophetic and divinely inspired, but to have disastrous consequences for world Jewry.

For almost half a century after the Crucifixion, the Christians *were* Jews. They never intended to be anything else. The majority, including the apostles themselves, were not at all certain that the Messiah who had come, Jesus, had intended His message for anyone but Jews. This fact has been obscured not only by historical events but by *deliberate prevaricating on the part of those who first wrote the gospel story.* Moreover, they built into their tale the basis of a virulent anti-Semitism, the results of which have shaped the past two thousand years. In a sense, they laid the cornerstones of the ovens that later burned in Auschwitz and Bergen-Belsen and Dachau.

$\mathcal{T}welve$

For all its fabled gaiety, Paris, unlike New York or Berlin, was not a true all-night place. The ninth arrondissement was far enough from the Eiffel Tower and the Champs-Elysées to believe it had a right to sleep. Its streets were hushed and dim; the streetlamps, not augmented by flashing signs or well-lit windows, seemed barely adequate. On errands such as this Jenny Fogel avoided anything as traceable as a taxi; she had taken the metro from Madeleine to Poissonière. She emerged into the dark and walked north, her footsteps echoing on the wet pavements.

A west wind blew at her back, it was cold but dry, the rain clouds were blowing away. Jenny didn't look at the suddenly revealed full moon or the stars; she kept her eyes down, walked quickly. It took ten minutes to reach her destination. The Gare du Nord was well lit, a haven, not crowded at this hour, but as impersonal as railway stations always are. Full of tired-looking people with glazed eyes, for the moment strangers to themselves as well as each other. In one corner of the cavernous interior, tucked almost out of sight, was a small café. The man she'd come to meet was waiting for her there.

"Sit down, my dear. Will you have coffee? It's as awful as usual, but hot."

"Tea, I think. With lemon." She removed her gloves and the printed challis scarf tied 'round her head. The scarf had not disturbed her coiffure. Every dark hair was still sleekly in place.

She wore a light gray raincoat with a heavy lining in navy plaid. It was too warm for the steamy atmosphere. Jenny unbuttoned the coat and slipped it from her shoulders. Her companion offered to hang it up, but she refused. A waiter appeared and the tea was ordered.

"Now," Yitzhak Beklem said. "What's happened?"

Jenny laced her fingers beneath her chin and leaned forward on her elbows. "It may all be my imagination, but I have a feeling this concerns you."

"I rely on such feelings," Yitzhak said. "Particularly when they come from you. Go on, please."

Jenny started to speak, paused when the tea was set before her, then continued when the waiter had left. "Do you know an Englishman named Hamish Durant?"

Yitzhak smiled. "It concerns me," he said. "Right away I can assure you your instincts were sound. Until a week ago I'd never even heard of your Englishman. Now he has . . . entered my sphere, we might say."

"How?"

Yitzhak shook his head. "Later. First you tell me what this Durant has done to alarm you."

"He flew all the way to Paris to see me. Tonight. We had dinner, I left him barely two hours ago. And he practically never leaves his home. He's enormously fat, obese. Normally he sits in his manor in the south of England like a spider in the middle of his web. Waiting for the flies. Hamish is an auctioneer; he buys and sells. That's the basis of our association. My jewelry is my income, as you know."

Yitzhak nodded. She wore none now, he noted. Just an austerely plain navy sweater and skirt. Not Jenny Fogel-type clothes. But then, the woman with whom he'd been associated for twenty years wasn't the elegant society lady everyone else in Paris knew. "Did Durant come to talk to you about jewelry?"

"Yes, in a way. But nothing of mine. He was interested in a bracelet sold at Drouot last week. Part of a sale of Judaica."

"Better and better," Yitzhak said eagerly. "You confirm a number of suspicions, my dear." He leaned forward and studied her face. "Tell me the rest."

"Hamish wants to meet the original owner of the bracelet—that is, the man who put it up for sale, Count François Lontesse de Montviron."

"Him I've never heard of," Yitzhak said. "Is he a Jew?"

"No. And he's nothing extraordinary. Just another rich Frenchman with a title. The title is really quite old and distinguished; it dates back to medieval times. But for at least a hundred years the family has made their money in trade. They had a cotton business in Egypt. Actually François was a good friend of my husband's. He was one of the first people I got in touch with when I came to Paris."

"And this count is the one who put the bracelet in the Drouot sale of Judaica?"

"The bracelet and a good deal else. His name never appeared in any of the accreditations or descriptions of provenance, but Hamish has discovered that de Montviron was the owner of at least half the items in the sale. Information of that sort wouldn't be difficult for Hamish to acquire. He's a power in the auction world. There must be dozens of people who owe him favors. And they're all notorious gossips anyway."

"Yes, I see it," Yitzhak said thoughtfully. "And why does he want to meet de Montviron? How did he know you knew him?"

"The last he just guessed. He knows I'm not unwelcome in French society, and about my ties to Egypt, and François's background. As to the other question, Hamish says he wants to convince François to sell some more things, through him."

"This Gentile count has more Judaica?" He'd almost said "goy-ish," he always had to remind himself that Jenny was a sympathizer for reasons of her own, not a Jew.

"Possibly," she said. "Probably, in fact. He was in Egypt all during the war, until the early fifties. So he was there when the

Egyptian Jews were being turned out and their property confiscated. Many of them would gladly have sold their treasures to François for a pittance, as long as the price was paid in French francs and deposited in a bank here." She didn't meet Yitzhak's eyes.

"So what else is new?" he said softly.

Jenny took a sip of her tea. It had gone cold. She set down the cup in distaste. "I don't believe Hamish is telling me the truth. He could be, but I think if it were just a scouting mission, he'd send his son, Timothy. Tim has all the family charm, a remarkably handsome young man. And I happen to know he's in France at the moment."

"So do I happen to know," Yitzhak said, but he didn't explain further. "Let me get you some more tea." He rose and went to the counter before she could protest. Jenny watched him.

A small, ugly man with a head too big for his body. Made more obvious by his total baldness. Yet she loved him. Not sexually, of course. There was nothing remotely sexual about Yitzhak or her feeling for him. He was the savior of her conscience. All the guilt she might have, felt about the way she survived the charnel house that was Germany in '44 and '45, and afterward, remaining silent when the very stones cried to heaven for justice—all that Yitzhak Beklem and the small services she could do for him assuaged.

Yitzhak returned with another coffee for himself and hot tea for her; she smiled at him gratefully.

"Thank you. Listen, as I've said, it's normal for Timothy to do all the negotiating for Durant's, so why not this time? That's why I don't believe Hamish. I think he's up to something else. And all the while he spoke, during dinner, I kept thinking, This has something to do with Yitzhak. I don't know why. Perhaps just because I suspect Hamish to be a rabid anti-Semite."

"You are right again," Yitzhak said.

Absentmindedly he kept adding sugar to his coffee. Jenny counted at least six spoonfuls. "That's going to make you sick," she said.

Yitzhak shrugged and took a large swallow. "Like I told you, I never heard of this Englishman until last week. Then a young woman who interests me—never mind why—came to Europe from America for the first time. She went to stay with your Mr. Durant. I had some reason to check a bit into his background." He made a dismissive gesture with the half-empty cup. "I managed to find out a few things."

It was Jenny's turn to smile. "You're stuffed so full of secrets it's a wonder they don't make you as fat as Hamish Durant. If you ever decide to sell your memoirs, Yitzhak, half the governments in the world will fall."

"There's little chance of that," Yitzhak said.

Jenny sipped her tea, then set down the cup. "I know your American girl. At least I think I do. She's Sarah Myles, isn't she? I met her Thursday. She came to my house with Timothy. I had some things to give him to sell. As a matter of fact, they had to leave very quickly. Sarah became ill."

"I see. Did you like her?"

"Very much, a charming young woman."

Yitzhak drummed his fingers on the table. "Let's return to the auctioneer, he's meshugga, you know what that means?"

Jenny nodded.

"Dangerously meshugga."

"Dangerous to whom?" she asked. "Sarah?"

"Perhaps, I'm not sure. But in the late thirties Mr. Hamish Durant was part of the inner circle of Oswald Mosley, the British Fascist and Hitler supporter. Mosley was interned while Britain and Germany were at war. Soon after he got out, in 1948, he founded the British Union Movement. Just as meshugga and almost as dangerous. Only it went nowhere, thank God. Meanwhile, sometime in the fifties, Durant became a Catholic. Now he's unhappy about that; he doesn't agree with the decisions of the Second Vatican Council. He meets with a group that calls itself Catholic Loyalists. They make LeFebre and his friends look like liberals."

"So why does he want to get his hands on Jewish artifacts from Egypt?"

"I don't think he does. I think it's all about the bracelet he mentioned. He wants to know more about that. But how he knows it's important, and that it's connected with Sarah Myles, that I don't know." He smiled gently at the lovely woman opposite. "But I will find out, Jenny. I think I can promise that."

"I don't doubt it. What do you wish me to do? Shall I try to bring him together with François?"

"Yes. And if you can arrange to be there when they meet, it may prove very useful. You'll let me know what happens?"

"Of course."

The dawn came late this time of year. In Alsace it was after seven when the blackness faded to gray. The canal took on shape and form. Malachy could see the water move between the deep stone banks. He'd been staring into it all night, unaware of the cold, of his stiffening body, unheedful of what would be thought if he were discovered. He had simply emptied his mind of everything except the Alexandria Testament. He concentrated on it as if it were a mantra, a fixed point that would lead him to God. And he believed —no, he knew—that his thoughts were transmitting themselves to the woman called Sarah Myles. Somewhere in the *auberge* on the opposite bank she was being forced to concentrate, too. Later he would discover what she knew.

Malachy's overnight case was at his feet. He stooped and lifted it, ignoring pains in his arm and his back, and moved away from the tree. The walk to the village was short, less than a kilometer, but he was shivering with cold by the time he reached it. The single main street was just stirring to life. Predictably, the baker's shop was open. Malachy went inside, grateful for the warmth. Fresh *bâtards* were heaped on one side of the counter; next to them were mounds of croissants and brioches. He noticed an enamel pot on a small gas ring.

"Do you sell coffee?"

The baker took in the black suit and Roman collar. *"Certaine-ment, mon père."*

He ordered a cup of coffee and two croissants and ate and drank gratefully. His shaking had stopped, but he felt an increasing tightness across his chest and he sneezed a few times. The baker said something about colds and flu.

"Yes. I've been traveling. Missed my connection, I'm afraid. I shall have to spend a day or two here. Is there a room I could rent, do you know?"

The baker wondered what connection could be missed in Kohlburg. He dismissed the thought; priests were odd but not dangerous. "There's a new place just down the road, the Auberge California. It's mostly a restaurant, but they have some rooms, too."

"Ah, yes, I passed it. Too rich for me, I'm afraid. Perhaps some housewife in the village with a spare bedroom . . ."

The baker thought for a moment, then disappeared behind the shop. When he returned, he was accompanied by a woman twice his size. "My wife, *mon père*." The bell over the door jangled and a customer came in. The baker left his wife with the priest and went forward to sell the results of his night's labors.

The Frenchwoman inspected the priest. "Henri tells me you need a bed. For how many nights?"

"One, perhaps two. No more."

"There's my son's room. Last year he got married and moved to Lyons. It isn't very fancy, you understand."

"It will suit me perfectly, madame. God bless you."

"Fifty francs a night," the woman said, ignoring the benediction. "As much hot water as you like and your breakfast in the morning."

"Thank you, that will be perfect," Malachy repeated. He hefted his case once more and followed her to the rear of the shop and up the stairs.

The extra bedroom was on the third floor. It had a high, narrow bed covered with a spread in red and blue checks, a battered maple armoire, and in one corner a painted stand bearing a bowl and ewer. The only other furnishings were one small chair painted in chipped blue enamel and a large, realistic wooden crucifix on the wall behind the bed. The windows looked out on rolling fields, fallow now, that ended in a stand of beech trees. Malachy knew the canal was the other side of the trees. He couldn't see it, but he was looking toward the *auberge*. "Fine, madame, it's perfect. Thank you again."

"You're welcome," she said. But she didn't move beyond the open door. It took Malachy a few seconds to realize what she was waiting for.

"Oh, of course. The rent." He removed a worn black leather

purse from the pocket of his trousers and opened it. There was a healthy roll of franc notes inside. Malachy extracted ten ten-franc notes. "Two nights in advance, is that satisfactory?"

"*Oui, mon père.*" She pocketed the money and disappeared.

The bathroom was across the hall. There was an ancient tub on clawed feet with taps that looked as if they wouldn't turn without a wrench, a tiny sink, a toilet, and a bidet. He thought of a hot bath, but decided against it. There wasn't time for such indulgence. Instead he washed his face and brushed his teeth and shaved.

Back in the bedroom he pulled the chair to the window; then he took off his shoes and climbed on the bed. The crucifix was heavy, but it merely hung on a nail; taking it down wasn't difficult. Malachy stared at the image of his pierced and broken Lord. Tenderly he brushed his lips over the wounded feet; then he moved to the window and sat down, still cradling the crucifix in his arms.

Momentarily he looked across the fields to where he knew she was, and back to the wooden cross. "Unless the grain of wheat falls into the ground and dies, it remains alone," Malachy quoted softly. Even death was sometimes a good, a permissible thing.

He closed his eyes and imagined himself in his old stall at the Abbey of Santa Pietà where he'd learned to pray, in the presence of his abbot and his brother monks. In his mind he re-created the vibrant community of prayer and meditation of which he had been a part. He felt his entire body centering on the still point, blending into the universe's cry to its creator. Malachy fastened on the idea of the Alexandria Testament and excluded all else.

Sarah was too weak to weep. Exhaustion and pain had swallowed her tears. The woman's voice besieged her, but she couldn't hear it. Over the voice, between it and her, was the jamming, a high-pitched whining static she could not silence. She'd turned on all the lamps in the room, afraid of the darkness. She tried humming; she stared at the wallpaper and counted the mauve stripes. Nothing would replace the terrible cacophony in her head.

For a while she'd paced; now she lay on the bed, still dressed in the black cocktail dress she'd worn to dinner. Tim had come, and

Zelah. They'd tried to get her undressed and into bed, but she refused all their ministrations. "Leave me alone, please. It's just a migraine. I get them sometimes. Please, just go away. I'll be all right by morning."

So they'd gone. But it was morning now; she could see the dawn breaking slowly outside the window. And she wasn't all right. "Jarib," she whispered aloud. "Oh, Jarib. Please help me, you're the only one. Please . . ." Jarib was thousands of miles away. And he didn't want her anymore. Still the whispered plea, because it seemed to be her only hold on sanity and peace.

It was the middle of the night when Jarib turned his car into Willard Lane. Rowley slept silently. Frost rimed the path to his front door and crunched under his shoes. The house was cold. He'd left the heat turned low, just enough to prevent the pipes from freezing; now he turned it up and waited for the radiators to spread some warmth.

It occurred to him that he should go through the place carefully, see if there was any sign that Lenore had been there, might even be hiding and waiting for him. But he'd looked for her assiduously for six days without finding her; he couldn't believe he'd find her now.

He went to the living room and poured a brandy, which he downed in one swift gulp. It warmed him but also accentuated his tiredness. He'd driven for fourteen hours without stopping. As if it were important that he return at once. As if getting back to Rowley could reverse the clock, bring him together with Sarah once more.

"Jarib! Please . . ."

He heard her voice and spun 'round. The room was empty. Jarib dashed to the front door and threw it open. No one and nothing. Just his car parked by the curb, the sleeping town. He heard a noise in the kitchen and went in there, turning on every light he passed. The kitchen too was empty; the sound came from the radiators beginning to heat up.

He was trembling when he climbed the stairs to his bedroom. He must be even more exhausted than he realized. He was hallucinating. But he could swear it had been Sarah's voice he'd heard. Wishful thinking, no doubt. He was far too experienced in his field to attribute every oddity to paranormal phenomena.

It had been after three when Yitzhak got to bed; nonetheless he woke at seven. The habit of a lifetime. He opened the door and found the Sunday papers neatly propped outside. Ariel had delegated the responsibility.

Yitzhak carried the papers to the kitchen. He had an American percolator acquired some years earlier. He filled it with water and coffee and lit the gas stove. In a few minutes the rich smell of perking coffee filled the shabby kitchen. That's what he liked best, the smell. The taste was pallid; he used an American roast as well as the imported percolator. Because his doctor told him European coffee was much too strong.

He eyed the stack of papers ruefully. Too much for a morning when he'd had little sleep and his mind was refusing to concentrate. Later. Now he'd just drink his coffee. And sit and think. There was a lot to think about. He'd tried last night when he got back from meeting Jenny at the Gare du Nord, but sleep overtook him. Now he was distracted by the many things he hadn't done in this past week while Dov Levi and Sarah Myles monopolized his attention.

Beklem poured the coffee into a mug and settled into his favorite chair. He removed his glasses and closed his eyes. He was acting like an undisciplined amateur. He needed to get some order into his thought processes. But it wouldn't come.

Okay, he'd go to the office and take care of a few other things, forget about the Alexandria Testament for a couple of hours. When he'd tidied up the loose ends of half a dozen other matters, he'd come back to it afresh.

He had just the two hours he'd allotted himself. He got to the office at eight and Ariel's call came at ten.

"The girl's sick."

"Sarah Myles? What do you mean? How sick?"

"I don't know. I nosed around outside the place for a while this morning. They've got big glass doors right across from the canal.

342

It's easy to see inside. The Englishman, I call him gorgeous boy, had breakfast with Zelah Tench. Sarah was nowhere to be seen. Zelah and Durant took turns going upstairs. They looked worried. Ten minutes ago I saw an old guy with a little black bag going inside."

"A doctor?"

"Looked like one."

Yitzhak was silent for a moment. "Maybe it's got nothing to do with anything. People get sick. Even Americans."

"Yeah." Ariel's voice carried no conviction.

"You don't think so?"

"No. I don't like it. I can't say why. Only it stinks. Just a little bit, but it stinks."

"That's not good enough, Ariel. Something's bothering you. What?"

"I've got a crazy hunch."

"What?" Yitzhak repeated.

"Somebody could be poisoning her."

"Who somebody? Why? You're right, as hunches go, that one's crazy."

"It could happen," Ariel said doggedly. "I think maybe I should go in and get her out of there."

"You see too many movies, *tateleh*. She's sick, okay. A cold maybe. Or she's having her period. That's no reason for you to be John Wayne riding to the rescue."

"For a cold or her period she doesn't need a doctor."

"Please, Ariel, already this is complicated enough. Just keep watching and let me know what happens. Okay?"

"Okay."

"I don't mean you shouldn't stay close. The restaurant's open for lunch?"

"Yes. But I had lunch there yesterday."

"Big deal. One minute you're the cavalry and the next you're afraid to go for a meal. This is France, you liked the food, so you're coming back for more. A true believer, like a man who goes to *shul* morning and night. They'll think maybe you're a restaurant critic. You'll get treated good."

"Maybe. How come you're at the office?"

343

"A few things to do," Yitzhak said. "I'm leaving now. I'll be at the flat for the rest of the day. Stay in touch."

Jenny's cook had Sundays off; she'd have to do everything for her impromptu luncheon herself. The kitchen was small but cheerful, white tile walls and wooden countertops. The window looked out onto the street; if she craned her head, she could just see the gatehouse of the residence of the U.S. ambassador at 41 Rue du Faubourg St.-Honoré. The Americans owned the grandest *hôtel particulier* on the street. Jenny gazed at it and frowned. She didn't share the anti-Americanism that was so resurgent in Europe of late, but this morning the sight of the mansion bothered her.

Yitzhak said Hamish had something to do with Sarah Myles. She quite liked the little Sarah. And judging from Yitzhak's reactions, Hamish meant her no good. But Sarah wasn't Jewish; what could she have to do with whatever Hamish was mixed up in? Or with Yitzhak, for that matter. A clock chimed the hour, eleven. She'd better stop musing and see about giving her guests something to eat. She paused with her hand on the refrigerator; she wasn't in the mood to attempt cooking. She wasn't any good at it at the best of times, and this wasn't one of those. Jenny left the kitchen and went to the hall and got her coat.

Fortunately the Place de la Madeleine was just a short walk away; it was home to some of the most glamorous food shops in Paris or anywhere else, and most were open Sunday mornings. Jenny paused before Fauchon; its windows were a symphony of exotic fruits and exquisite charcuterie, but the sales floor was jammed. A large number of the waiting customers looked like foreigners. Instead she crossed the road and entered a shop called Caviar Kaspia. Ten minutes later she left. She was poorer by almost fifteen hundred francs, but her guests would dine well.

Hamish arrived first, at precisely noon. Jenny led him to the sitting room. "I have no help today," she told him. "So it's just a simple buffet lunch in here."

Hamish paused before the Egyptian bowls and pots displayed on a series of shelves that dominated the room. Behind him the heavy taffeta drapes were open and weak winter sun came in through the lace curtains. He turned back to the display. "Appropriate," he said softly.

"Yes, I thought so." The doorbell rang. "Excuse me," Jenny said.

She returned with an exceptionally tall, slim man. His thick hair was white, his skin pale. Startlingly blue eyes dominated a narrow, hollow-cheeked face. He wore a navy suit and a white silk shirt. The two top buttons of the shirt were open, and a long, crapulent neck rose above a printed ascot. "Hamish, may I present Monsieur le Comte François Lontesse de Montviron. Hamish Durant, an old friend from England."

The count extended his hand and accompanied it with a small bow of the head. His grip was weak, Hamish noted. And the print on the ascot was of becocked roosters. "Delighted, sir," he said. Only those who knew him well would recognize that his Yorkshire accent was broader than normal.

"Now, gentlemen, an aperitif. It's my cook's day off, and we're subsisting on blinis and caviar, so may I suggest vodka?"

Jenny poured small glasses of the spirit and served it neat. The two men drank and eyed each other. She watched them. Hamish was the one more in control. François had been reluctant to come on such short notice; she'd had to say it was in his interests to do so, and against them to ignore the invitation. Now he was wary. She knew him well enough to recognize the signs. And Hamish wasn't making him feel any better. He wore a black suit, the same he'd worn to dine with her the evening before. It was wrinkled now and pulled tight across his immense body. He looked like a great bird of prey. He sounded like it, too. "I have some questions for you," he said without preamble.

The count raised his eyebrows. "Indeed?"

"Aye. And let me begin by saying that I'm aware of the true provenance of most of the items in Drouot's sale of Judaica last week. So far I've told no one but Jenny here."

"Are you threatening me, Mr. Durant?"

"Indeed, no, what an idea." Hamish gestured expansively. "I'm simply assuming that we're two men of business who don't want to waste time. So I'm putting my cards on the table, as they say."

"And to what do your cards, as you call them, add up?"

345

"Well now, if our lovely hostess will permit us to fill our plates and sit down, I'll tell you." He eyed the blinis and caviar greedily. Jenny smiled and nodded.

"She's sleeping," Zelah said. "The injection the doctor gave her finally worked."

Zelah looked exhausted. Tim pulled out a chair and made her sit down. "You've been an angel. I'm so sorry we're causing so much bother."

"Don't be silly. Sarah's my guest. I'm only sorry the trip made her so ill."

"You think that's what's wrong with her?"

Zelah looked surprised. "Don't you?"

"I don't know. It's the second time she's been ill this week. It comes on so suddenly, and the attacks are so fierce."

"*La grippe*," Zelah pronounced. "She's probably had it for days, and she's fighting it. That makes it worse." She stood up.

"Where are you going? Can I help?"

"No, there's nothing you can do. I'm going to check on Charles. He went to Strasbourg to shop. If he's still not back, I can get into the kitchen for a little while. I'm not permitted if he's there."

"What's the attraction of the kitchen?"

Zelah grinned at him. "I want to make Sarah some chicken soup."

At 2:00 P.M. Jenny Fogel's guests were still sitting in her drawing room, speaking earnestly. The phone in the study rang, and she excused herself. Neither man seemed aware of her departure.

"It's me," Yitzhak said. "I'm sorry to bother you; are they still there?"

"Yes. Talking."

"What about?"

"About Durant's selling the rest of François's collection in England. And other things. I can't tell you now."

"No, of course not. Listen, my dear, I just want to ask one question. I've been thinking about something you mentioned last

346

night. The girl got sick in your house, you did say that, didn't you?"

"Yes. She fainted."

"Under what circumstances?"

"I'd just taken her in to see my Egyptian collection."

"And was the young man with you? Did he see what happened?"

"Timothy? Yes, of course."

Yitzhak sighed. "That's what I hoped you'd say. Thank you. Call me later when they've gone."

"So tell me why we gotta schlepp crosstown to have breakfast? Not that I mind," Sam added. "Only why?"

"I heard this restaurant was good. A friend told me it was terrific for brunch." Rhonda struggled to keep desperation and panic from her voice. Sam eyed her with cagey speculation.

"We were supposed to go to the Inn on the Park for brunch," Myra said. "I love that place."

"It's a cab ride, too," Rhonda insisted. "Now shut up, will you? Once in a while you don't need your own way. I promise, you won't die from it."

They got out at Lincoln Center and crossed the street. The Place was on the corner. Until recently autumn had been unseasonably warm; outside on Broadway there were yet tables and chairs and umbrellas, but this morning was cloudy and cold; there could be no thought of eating outside.

Sam pushed open the door and waited for the two women to precede him. A wave of acid rock hit them. There were no booths, only tables crowded hard on each other, sporting shiny plastic tablecloths in Day-Glo colors and hanging black metal overhead lights. The enormous room was jammed, the noise deafening.

"This is what your friend recommended?" Sam shouted in Rhonda's ear.

"Yeah. The food's probably worth it," she shouted back.

Myra was already swaying to the rhythm of the music. A blonde seated two inches from where they stood wore nothing beneath a blouse unbuttoned to the waist. The curve of her high, hard breasts showed, and her nipples strained the fabric.

347

"No food's worth I should get a headache and excited at my age," Sam said. "C'mon. We'll get a cab to the Inn on the Park."

"No," Rhonda begged. "Please, Sam, I want to eat here. So I can tell my friend."

A waiter appeared and motioned them to a table far in the back. Myra moved off quickly in the direction he indicated. Sam and Rhonda looked at each other for a moment; then Sam shrugged and they followed.

There was no ethnic loyalty displayed in the lengthy menu, pasta salad followed blintzes with sour cream, potato latkes were served with southern fried chicken. They ordered grilled kippers and scrambled eggs and croissants. Myra said she'd have hot chocolate with hers. "This better be worth it," Sam muttered. "But I don't see how it can be. Maybe the owner's got stock in Alka-Seltzer."

Rhonda had to strain to hear him. After a few minutes they gave up trying to talk above the noise. They studied the people around them instead. Young for the most part, often achingly beautiful, usually wonderfully slim. Rhonda shifted her size sixteen hips uncomfortably. She searched for the lined, tired-looking face in the photograph, but didn't find it. Thank God. Yitzhak couldn't blame her if this Dov Levi never showed up. She wouldn't have to do anything terrible to Sam after all.

She'd just started to relax when she saw him. Levi sat at a table some twenty yards to the right. He was alone, staring at his plate. There was a bottle of wine in front of him. Rhonda watched him for a few seconds. She clenched her hands into fists in her lap, remembered the agency and the bookings, summoned her courage. "I see somebody I know, I'll be right back."

Sam spotted a waiter moving toward them, holding a laden tray high above his head. "Our food's coming," he said. Rhonda was already squirming through the crush toward whomever she was determined to see. "I didn't know your mother had friends in New York," Sam said to Myra. Her eyes were closed; her head bobbed in time to the loud, cacophonous music. No more the little girl who'd told him he was her best friend, she'd moved beyond his orbit without either of them noticing. He sighed and looked at the kipper that had been set in front of him. The top was burned.

It seemed to Rhonda that it took her forever to get to the man's

348

table. When she reached it, he didn't look up. "Excuse me, you're Dov Levi, aren't you?"

"Yes." He looked at her without recognition, but didn't seem surprised. "Are you the woman I'm supposed to meet?"

"I don't know." She was yet more unnerved by his response, by the fact that he too was obviously being manipulated by Yitzhak Beklem or somebody like him. "I guess so. I'm Rhonda Kane. From Los Angeles."

Levi stared at her and waited.

"Come with me. There's someone I want you to meet."

"Okay." He said it without emotion, took another swallow of his wine and rose and followed her back through the chaos.

"Sam, Myra." She tried to sound bright and cheerful, as if she didn't realize what she was about to do. "Remember when Jack and I took our first tour to Israel? Before you were born, honey, in 1958. Well this is the man who was our guide at Kibbutz Etz Hadar."

Levi still acted like a zombie, without any reaction, but Sam half rose, then sat down again. He looked from Rhonda to the stranger, then back to Rhonda. "The tour my Amy was on?"

Levi answered for her, but not with words. He moaned, and the sound was loud enough to carry above the music and the shouted conversation. "You're Sam Stein, Amy's father, aren't you?" The question was a whisper, but like his moan, it carried.

Sam did rise then. His head was pounding, his stomach rolled, he had a burning sensation around the heart. It was this place, this crazy restaurant where no man his age should ever come. It must be curdling his brain. It couldn't be the same guy. How could Rhonda have recognized him after so many years?

But the stranger was staring at him with a look of such pain and grief he could be no one else. And Rhonda was white-faced and frightened. Something was happening here, something crazy. And somehow Sam Stein was supposed to be the victim. But victimhood wasn't his style. He'd scrambled too high, clawed his way over too many bodies for that.

He looked at Levi for a few seconds, and Levi looked at him. Then Sam turned to Rhonda. "Are you going to tell me what this is all about? Why'd you bring this bastard here?"

"I forgot," Rhonda said desperately. "I forgot his connection with Amy and everything—"

Levi interrupted her. "I'm sorry, Mr. Stein. It's too late, and God knows it's too little. But it's all I can say." He turned to go.

"Wait a minute." All the old authority was in Sam's voice. The legacy of the days when his word had the force of law and people jumped to do his bidding. He yanked an empty chair from the next table. A woman's handbag was on it; it tumbled to the floor. Sam didn't bend to pick it up; the woman muttered something about manners. Sam ignored her. He drew the chair close to his. "Sid-down," he said. Levi hesitated a moment, then sat. "Now tell me how it was with you and my Amy. Where did you go? Why?"

"Can I have a drink?" Levi asked weakly.

"You can talk," Sam said. "That's all, just talk."

Rhonda looked at the two men and tried not to cry. Myra nibbled a croissant and jerked her shoulders in time with the music.

Dov mumbled something Sam couldn't hear.

"Jesus. We gotta get out of this hellhole." Sam pulled a fifty-dollar bill from his wallet and threw it on the table. "That should cover both bills; let these schmucks figure it out."

Rhonda, Myra, and Sam rose. Dov remained seated. "C'mon," Sam said. "You and me are gonna go someplace we don't have to scream."

They found a big cab. Dov and Myra sat on the jump seats facing Rhonda and Sam. Only Sam spoke. "Rhonda, darling, I think it's time you went home. There's a plane to Los Angeles this after-noon?"

"Four o'clock from Kennedy," she said dully. Knowing flight schedules was her business.

"Good. You'll be on it. I'll call Jack and tell him to meet you."

"Sam, listen, I'm sorry. It's not what you think—"

"I don't think nothing, *mamaleh*. Whatever you're doing, I figure you got your reasons. Anyway, it's okay. Only me and this Mr. Levi, we got things to talk about. Better you and Myra should be out of the house."

"Now look, you mustn't do anything crazy. It was a long time ago. Amy's gone, Sam. Nothing will bring her back." She clutched his arm in desperation.

Sam patted her hand. "Rhonda, I'm not nuts. For dreck like him I don't make myself a lawsuit."

Levi acted as if he hadn't heard.

For most of the day Yitzhak sat in his chair and waited. He was anxious for another call from Ariel, but it didn't come. That only meant Ariel wasn't ready to tell him anything. Rhonda he wouldn't hear from until 9:00 P.M. Paris time, Jenny whenever she was free to make a comprehensive report. Patience was required now. And thought.

Somehow Hamish Durant had been thrust, or thrust himself, into the middle of the search for the Alexandria Testament. And Yitzhak was almost positive that Durant suspected Sarah Myles's connection with it. Part of her connection at least. If young Timothy happened to tell his father about Sarah's reaction to Jenny's Egyptian antiques, Durant would consider his suspicions confirmed. But how had he come by them originally? How could he know the Alexandria Testament existed?

In nearly thirty years neither Yitzhak nor Malachy had ever come across a reference to the document in any but the most obscure sources. But the man who originally told Malachy about it, Professor Wolff, had said some scholars had long suspected the existence of the thing, and Wolff found the proof of its existence when he was doing research in Alexandria. And his research had convinced him that descendants of the Testament's author had a racial memory of it. If Wolff could discover all that, so could Hamish Durant —independently.

Yitzhak played with that theory for a while. He didn't like it. According to everything he'd learned, Durant was almost a recluse. He sat in his grand house and nursed his grievances and fed his hatreds. Even the group he was part of, the Loyal Catholics, came to him. They met once a month at Tiverton Manor. Durant's only other interest was his work. He was an expert on antiques.

All at once he saw the connection he'd known all along, the thing that had been nagging at the back of his mind but wouldn't surface. Until now. After the sale Malachy said he knew an antiques expert who might be able to tell them something about the bracelet. Hamish Durant. It had to be. So maybe there was some kind of alliance between Hamish and Malachy; maybe the priest and the antiques dealer had more in common than just their religion? If that was so, Malachy could have been lying to him for years, not just the last few months, as he'd suspected.

Yitzhak went into the living room and poured himself a whiskey. A double. He kept the liquor in here so he wouldn't be tempted more often than was good for him. Not that he was a big drinker, he wasn't. But there were times when it was the only thing that helped. He didn't want those times to start coming too close together.

He didn't gulp, he sipped. It was good whiskey, Glenfiddich single malt. One of the few personal indulgences in his life. But this time it didn't warm and relax him as it usually did. He could taste the idea of Malachy's perfidy on his tongue. It was bitter. And that was stupid.

So one more goy had tried to double-cross one more Jew. What else was new? But he and Malachy. . . . Bah! That was meshuggaas. Because for a brief time they shared suffering, they were immune to lying? Was he? Yitzhak tipped back his head and downed the last of the whiskey. Then he went back to the kitchen and picked up the telephone.

Whoever was in charge of such things at the Abbey of St. Louis answered on the third ring. "No, I'm sorry, Dom Malachy isn't here."

"Will he be in later?" Yitzhak asked.

"I'm afraid I can't say. His Eminence is a visitor, you understand, not a member of our community. He left late yesterday and didn't say when he'd return. May I tell him you called?"

"No, thank you. That won't be necessary."

Yitzhak hung up and stared at the receiver for some seconds. He was starving. He hadn't eaten anything since breakfast. Besides, he always got hungry when things started coming to a head. His body seemed to know before his mind when something was going to happen.

There was a can of beet borscht in the kitchen, imported. The label was printed in Hebrew, French, and English. It promised that the soup was kosher for pesach. The only alternatives were one egg and some stale bread. Usually he shopped on Friday afternoon. This week he'd been too busy. He opened the soup and heated it. It was awful. He wondered what Jenny had fed the Englishman and the count. Not canned soup.

The phone rang, and he hurried into the living room.

It was Ariel. "Sorry I didn't call earlier. But there's not a damned thing to report. I ate lunch at the *auberge*. Sarah Myles never showed her face. Gorgeous boy was there, but not the dame."

"Ariel, did you see a priest by any chance? A tall, thin guy, late sixties, but still good-looking. A Swiss, but he speaks half a dozen languages, including French and English."

"A Catholic priest?"

"There's some other kind?"

"Sure, what about Greek Orthodox or Russian? Some Protestants even have priests."

"Wonderful. Thank you for the lesson, I'm delighted you're so learned. This one's a Catholic. I can't be sure, but I think he'd be wearing a black suit and a collar. I don't think he owns any other clothes."

"No, I've seen nobody like that."

"He's there, I'm almost certain of it. His name's Dom Malachy Fanti. Actually he's a Benedictine monk, and a cardinal. But he prefers that people think he's just an ordinary priest. Check any other hotels in the town."

"It isn't a town. That's why I slept in Strasbourg last night. Kohlburg's just a tiny village; there aren't any hotels. Only the *auberge*, and I'm sure he's not there."

"Good. That makes it easier. Ask in the village. Someone must have seen him. You know what to do."

"Yeah, sure. And if I find him, then what?"

"Nothing. Just call me and let me know."

Ariel left the phone booth and stared up and down Kohlburg's Rue des Magasins. The title was grandiose. The only shops were the pharmacy, a bakery, a hardware store, and a grocery. Not even a café. The baker served coffee at his counter, and the grocery had a tiny bar wedged in one corner next to the potatoes. He decided on the grocery.

Two farmers were bellied up to the homemade bar. They wore

353

expensive suede jackets with sheepskin linings, and their jeans were imported American. Times were good in Alsace. He only knew they were farmers because of their conversation. They were arguing about the best way to get the largest subsidies out of the EEC. *Vive la* common agricultural policy, and to hell with the butter mountain or the milk lake.

He stood next to them; the cramped space wouldn't have permitted him to do anything else anyway. The grocer lifted half the bar and inserted himself behind it. *"Que-ce-que vous voulez,* monsieur?"

He pointed to a small keg perched on its side. *"Un vin gris."* The local *ordinaire* wasn't really gray, more a cloudy yellowish white. He found it pleasant. The farmers took the opportunity to order refills. Ariel didn't waste time with subtleties. "They're all mad, these bureaucrats in Brussels, aren't they?"

"Of course," the older of the farmers agreed. "But it can be useful."

The grocer and the other farmer laughed. Ariel laughed too. "They think they're all-powerful. Like the Church. But ordinary people can always catch them with their pants down."

The three Alsatians agreed. "Of course, these days the Church isn't so powerful anymore," Ariel added.

"But still rich," the first farmer said. "Just today Henri told me about one who came into his shop with a wad of bills thick enough to plug up a cow's ass."

The second raised his eyebrows. "Henri talks too much. Half of what he says is stupid; the other half is lies."

The grocer produced a pack of cigarettes and offered them around. The cigarettes were American, too. Winstons. "This time Henri's telling the truth," he said. "His wife told mine the same story. The priest is staying with them. In André's old room. He paid Jeanne two hundred francs in advance for two nights, and so far all he's done is stay up there on the third floor."

"Jeanne always exaggerates," the younger farmer insisted. "If she says two hundred, it was one."

"Still, that's a lot of money for a priest to have." The grocer wasn't to be denied his role of true oracle.

"Maybe he's a bishop or a cardinal," Ariel said. "They're all rich."

"No, just a priest." In his guise as barman the grocer refilled all their glasses and poured one for himself. "Not French, though. Jeanne says he has some kind of foreign accent. Not that foreigners aren't welcome here," he added with a hasty glance at Ariel.

It was that simple. He drank his wine and paid, they asked if he was visiting someone in Kohlburg, and he said no, just touring the countryside around Strasbourg. But being a sightseer was thirsty work. They laughed and bade him good-bye with cordiality.

Outside Ariel paused on his way to the telephone kiosk. These locals might seem simple, but they weren't. A stranger who talked to them and went immediately to a call box was just a little too obvious.

His car was parked at the edge of town, and he began walking toward it. There was another public phone midway between the village and Strasbourg. He'd use that. The woman was on the other side of the street when he spotted her. She was coming toward him, carrying an unwrapped loaf of bread under her arm. Ariel knew he'd seen her recently. It took him only seconds to remember where.

He crossed the street with seeming unconcern, then made a great show of seeing her and smiling and saying good evening.

She was young and rather pretty and not unsure of herself. "Do I know you, monsieur?"

Ariel broadened his smile. "To tell the truth, not really. I've had two meals at the *auberge* and I noticed you." She was the chambermaid. He'd seen her coming down the stairs with piles of towels and bed linen yesterday. This afternoon during lunch she'd carried a full tray up and one almost as full down.

"Well, to tell the truth, I did not notice you. Good-bye, monsieur."

"Wait, don't go. I want to ask you something. I'm not dangerous, at least not to you." He remembered Yitzhak's joking suggestion. "I'm a restaurant critic."

The girl eyed him warily. "For what paper? I thought restaurant critics never admitted who they were."

"For a magazine," he improvised. "In Brussels. A travel magazine. We're doing a feature on Alsace. Usually I stay anonymous, but this is different, I'm worried about the Auberge California."

The girl's interest was piqued. She had a good, steady job at the

355

auberge, and a bad review could threaten that. "What is there to worry about? Didn't you like the food? Everyone says it's excellent."

"That's just it, it is. That's what I want to say in my critique. But I heard a rumor that one of the guests was poisoned. They say she took suddenly ill, and Mademoiselle Tench has been hiding her away in case anyone finds out it's food poisoning."

The chambermaid's eyes flashed. She had nice hazel eyes, and the anger made them all the more appealing. "That's a lie, monsieur. Whoever told you that is a vicious gossip. Probably someone who is jealous of Mademoiselle Tench. There is a guest at the *auberge* who is ill, but she doesn't have food poisoning. Only a very bad headache. Mademoiselle Tench called the doctor, and he says it's *la migraine.* You can ask him if you wish. He gave her something to make her sleep. Nothing for food poisoning."

Ariel sighed loudly. "Ah, I'm so glad you told me. I thought it must be a lie. Some people are jealous fools, aren't they?" He wished he had a hat to tip, but since he didn't, he bowed. "Thank you, mademoiselle. My magazine and I are in your debt. *Au revoir.*"

He called Yitzhak from the phone booth on the road. "You were right, he's here. At least there's a priest staying with the baker and his wife. Arrived early this morning, hasn't been out of his room all day. They don't know what nationality he is, but they're sure he isn't French. He never told them his name, but my guess is it's got to be the guy you're looking for."

"Yes, I'm sure it is. Fine, Ariel, that's fine. Thank you."

"Something else. I talked to the chambermaid from the *auberge.* Met her in town a little while ago. She says Sarah Myles's trouble is migraine. The doctor they called gave her a sedative."

Yitzhak sucked in his breath. "Not exactly migraine," he murmured. "But she's unlikely to tell them the truth."

"What do you mean?"

Yitzhak spoke slowly. "I owe you an apology, Ariel. You weren't exactly wrong. I think she's being poisoned, just like you said. But not physically, mentally."

"By the priest?"

"Maybe. I can't be sure, but I think so."

356

"Now you're the one who sounds crazy."

"Yes, I know. Just keep watching, let me know if anything else happens."

"What about the priest? Should I do something about him?"

"No, nothing unless he tries to see Sarah. That you don't permit. I don't care what you have to do, but don't let him near her."

The half-finished borscht was still on the kitchen table. It had sat there for over an hour, and it was stone cold by now. It was a noxious purple color that reminded Yitzhak of the stuff they made him soak his feet in in the refugee camp. Potassium permanganate, that's what it was called. Despite the memory, he picked up the bowl and drank down the rest of the soup. He hadn't thrown away a mouthful of food since 1945, no matter how awful.

His notebook was in here, on top of the mound of newspapers next to his chair. He'd been going over it when Ariel called, trying to see if there was anything he'd missed, any connection. Now he thumbed back through the pages and found the name he was seeking. Milly Katz's reports were always very thorough. She'd given him the man's address and telephone number as well as his name.

Jarib was trying to work, but it wasn't a very successful effort. He'd taken out his manuscript and even set up his typewriter, only the words wouldn't come. Talking about paranormal phenomena in the abstract seemed a useless exercise just now. Still, he needed to fill the hours until it would be Monday and he could call Sarah. That's when the man in England had said she was expected. Late Monday. He'd called Ivy and asked if she had a telephone number in Paris where Sarah could be reached, but she hadn't. At least that's what she said. Maybe she was still punishing him. In any case, the result was the same: He'd have to wait until tomorrow. He put a fresh sheet of paper in the typewriter.

He was startled by the sound of the telephone ringing in the empty house. The hospital perhaps, with news of Lenore.

"Dr. Baraak?"

"Yes, speaking."

"You don't know me, my name is Yitzhak Beklem. I'm calling from Paris, and I have a great deal to tell you. Is the line clear?"

Jarib pressed the receiver tighter to his ear, Paris meant Sarah, it couldn't be anything else. "Yes, I can hear you quite well."

"Good. Now listen carefully, I know that you're a parapsychologist, so nothing I say should come as any surprise. Sarah Myles is in a small village in Alsace. She's ill."

"I don't understand . . . ill in what way? Has she had a doctor? Give me the address and telephone number, please. It's very important that I speak with her."

"That's not likely to help right now. And she has had a doctor. The diagnosis is that she's suffering from migraine. But I believe that's not correct."

"Look, I don't understand, what has all this to do with you? What did you say your name was?"

"Yitzhak Beklem, and there's no time to explain how I'm involved. Sarah's mind is being . . ." Yitzhak hesitated. "Attacked," he said finally. "By someone well trained in mental prayer, what I think is called contemplation. Is that possible?"

Jarib hesitated. "I suppose so, yes. I can't say for sure without knowing a lot more. Nobody could. Now listen, about Sarah . . ."

"She's susceptible to such an attack as I describe, isn't she, Dr. Baraak? Originally she saw you about just such a phenomenon, isn't that so?"

Jarib hadn't time to deal with scruples about professional confidences. "In a way, yes. But that wasn't something being done by somebody else. Not the way you mean."

"I realize that. This time it is."

"But who? And why?"

"Who doesn't matter. Why is because the girl's part of something much bigger than you or she know about. You must trust me, Dr. Baraak. I think an effort is being made to make Sarah mad, or to make her tell things she doesn't want to tell. And I think you are the only one who can prevent it. Because of your skills and the relationship between you and Sarah."

Jarib clutched the phone. Crazy, the whole thing was crazy. But it made a strange kind of sense. And if there was even a remote chance of its all being true, he had to act. "You've got to give me a phone number where I can reach Sarah."

"Not good enough. I want you to come here. It's two-thirty

your time. You can get a flight to Paris this evening. I'll send someone to meet you at the airport and take you to Alsace. I realize this is very sudden, Dr. Baraak, but I can't put it too strongly. Sarah needs you desperately. I might say it's a matter of life and death."

Jarib didn't hesitate. "I'm on my way."

Yitzhak wasn't ready to ring off. "You have an up-to-date passport? And enough money for the trip?"

"My passport's in order. And I have credit cards."

"Good. I suggest you go directly to the airport. You won't have any trouble getting a seat. It's not too difficult this time of year. As soon as you have your ticket, call me here and tell me the airline and the flight number." He gave Baraak his phone number and made him repeat it.

"Okay," Jarib said. "I've got all that. But even with luck it's going to be many hours before I get to Sarah. If what you suspect is really happening, that could be too late." His voice broke on the words.

Yitzhak thought for a moment. "I don't have the number of the place she's staying just now, but I can get it. I'll give it to you when you call from the airport."

Only after he hung up did Jarib remember the experience of a couple of hours ago, the way he'd been so sure he'd heard Sarah calling him. An attack on her mind, the man said. That could precipitate a cry of need so intense it might even reach him, insensitive to such phenomena as he usually was. He took the stairs to his bedroom two at a time.

Rhonda called Paris at 3:00 P.M., as instructed, from Kennedy.

Yitzhak had been so involved with Sarah he'd almost forgotten about Dov. Rhonda's voice told him things had been happening on that front as well. "How did it go?" he asked.

"What do you think? Let me tell you, your Dov Levi is some kind of nutcase. He just sits and waits and does whatever Sam tells him. And Sam's all worked up. He made us leave them alone in his apartment. I don't know what's going to happen and I can't be responsible—"

359

"Rhonda, it's okay. I'm responsible."

"Oh, sure. Mr. Big Shot. Only you're thousands of miles away. What are you going to do if something terrible happens?"

"Nothing will. Everything's under control, I promise you. Would I hurt Sam? After all these years."

"Yes," she said. "You'd do whatever you liked to get what you want. Only this time I don't understand what it is."

"It's important, Rhonda. Believe me. And no one will be hurt. What did you think of the choice of restaurant?" Yitzhak chuckled softly. He'd briefed Morrie carefully, told him exactly the atmosphere he wanted. Morrie had assured him he'd found just the right place.

"Very funny," Rhonda said. "We had to scream at each other to be heard."

"A useful device, my dear. In this situation it's better if people are a little off-balance. You're on your way home I take it?"

The hair rose on the back of her neck. She hadn't told him she was calling from the airport. Yitzhak Beklem had eyes everywhere. "My money's running out," she said, and dropped the receiver.

No more, she promised herself as she made her way back to where Myra was waiting. I'm not doing anything else for him. The hell with the business.

Jarib wasted forty-five minutes getting gas. When he got into his car, the tank gauge read empty, not surprising considering how far he'd driven the day before. He turned right onto Main Street, but the local station was closed because of a death in the family. He had to wait until he was on Route 1, praying he wouldn't run out in the meantime.

The first station he came to was one of those serve-yourself places. You had to pay at a glassed-in booth before you could work the pumps. There was only one attendant on duty, and she was arguing with the man ahead of him. Neither the attendant nor the customer was prepared to hurry the process, and he didn't dare drive on. The only solution was to wait, cursing steadily under his breath.

Eventually the endless journey was over. It was four-thirty when he got to Logan. Baraak left the car in the long-term parking lot, retrieved his single bag from the trunk, and strode across the road to the terminal. The sun was down, and the wind biting. He hadn't taken the time to change; he still wore the jeans and sweater he'd been in when Beklem called. He'd grabbed a suede jacket from the hall closet as he left the house. His suitcase contained a suit, two shirts, some underwear and his shaving gear. If he needed anything else, he'd have to buy it.

A quick scan of the notices above the terminal doors pinpointed one marked INTERNATIONAL DEPARTURES. He headed for it. Inside there were signs listing every airline he'd ever heard of and a few he didn't know existed. There were lots of arrows. He hesitated. Directly in front of him was a British Airways desk. A bored-looking young man sat behind it. "Do you fly to Paris?"

"Certainly."

"When's the next flight?"

The clerk looked a little more interested. A bit glamorous this, not a tour group, a single guy in a hurry. The way it was in books. He hit some keys on the computer terminal in front of him. "Ten P.M. There are a few seats available."

"Not good enough," Jarib said. "Haven't you got anything earlier?"

"No, sorry. You're in a big hurry, huh?"

"Yes, as a matter of fact. Any suggestions?"

"Try Air France. Through that door on your left; it's in Terminal Three."

Jarib followed the directions. He'd been in Terminal One apparently. Two was home to TWA and something called Air Brasilia. He decided to go with the advice he'd been given and passed up TWA.

Terminal Three was busier than the first two had been. There were a number of people milling about and the tail end of a line at the ticket counter. There was a sign on a board that said "Flight 704 to Paris." Jarib hesitated; he could waste a lot of time in here finding out there was no room. Still, it seemed the best shot. He got in the rear of the queue. It took ten minutes for the three people in front of him to present their tickets, check their luggage, and receive boarding cards. When his turn came, a young woman held out her hand. She was a blonde, pretty. She looked Irish, not French. "Tickets, please. And your passport." Her English had a midwestern twang. Hurrah for the modern world.

"I have a passport, but no ticket. What time does this flight leave?"

"Five-thirty." She turned and glanced at a large clock behind her. It was quarter to five. "They'll start boarding in five minutes."

"Terrific. Room for one more?" He smiled as winningly as he knew how.

She grinned back. "I'll check." She did something with the keys of her computer terminal. After a few seconds she said, "Nothing in coach. First-class only."

"Fine, I'll take it."

"Don't you want to know the fare?"

"No." He pushed his passport and American Express card across the counter. "What time do we land? And where?"

"Orly Field. At six-forty A.M. local time. You're sure it's Paris you want to go to?" She looked hesitant.

"Quite sure. Doesn't anybody make travel arrangements at the last minute anymore?"

"Not with me at least. All I ever get are tour groups."

"Listen," Jarib said. "I really am in a hell of a hurry, and I've got to make a couple of phone calls. Will you keep my passport and credit card and make out the ticket and let me pick it up after I get off the phone?"

She craned her neck and looked behind him. There was no one else in line. "Okay, why not? Only you'd better be quick." The loudspeaker punctuated her words.

"This is the first call for Air France's Flight 704 to Paris. Will all passengers please go through security control to boarding Gate Number Six?"

There was no talking over the rasping PA system. Jarib gave the ticket agent a thumbs-up sign and hurried toward the phones. "What about your bag?" the girl called after him.

"I'll take it as carry-on."

The girl shrugged. It was oversize for that, but what the hell, he was traveling first-class.

He got through to Beklem as quickly as if he'd been calling Boston. And the line was perfectly clear. "Air France Flight 704, gets into Orly at six forty A.M. your time."

"A woman will meet you just outside customs. She'll find a way to identify you, don't worry. Just keep your eyes open."

"Okay. Do you have Sarah's phone number? Have you talked to her? Is she all right?"

"I can't answer those questions, Dr. Baraak. I've never met Sarah. Don't waste time now. She's in Alsace, as I told you, at a small inn." He gave Jarib the number.

"Wait a minute, don't hang up yet. I've been thinking about what you said before. If someone is really attacking Sarah in the way you describe, the important thing is to get her away from him. Physical distance may help. Get her out of Alsace. Back to Paris. I can be with her sooner that way, too."

Yitzhak had already considered that plan and rejected it. For reasons of his own, which he was not prepared to discuss with the American. "I'm sorry, I can't do that."

"Can't or won't?" Jarib asked. But the line had gone dead.

His luck was less good on the next call. The first time he dialed the international code for France he got a busy signal. Ten seconds later he tried again with more success. He got through. But no one seemed to be on the other end. The two rhythmic rings and a pause were repeated four, then five, then six times. Answer, for God's sake, please answer . . .

"Auberge California."

He hadn't studied French since high school, and he'd never spoken it. "Do you speak English?" A wave of static drowned out the answer. "I said, do you speak English? I'm sorry, the line is very poor. I'm calling from Boston, in America."

"Yes, monsieur. Can I help you?"

"I understand Miss Sarah Myles is there. It's urgent that I speak with her."

"Miss Myles is a guest, yes. But she isn't well. It's almost midnight here, I don't think I should disturb her. And she may not be able to come to the telephone."

"Please, she must. It really is very urgent. Will you tell her it's Jarib calling? Have you got that?" He spelled his name.

"Jarib, yes, I understand. Look, you'll have to wait. She's upstairs in her room."

"It doesn't matter. I'll hang on. But please hurry. And tell her I must speak with her."

He glanced at his watch. Five-ten. The blonde was heading toward him, waving the ticket and his passport, making urgent signals. He held up two fingers, and hoped she understood that he meant a couple of minutes more.

"Jarib, is it really you?"

Her voice was a faint whisper; he could barely hear her. "Yes, darling, it's me. Sarah, how are you? They told me you're ill."

"The voice, it won't go away. But I can't really hear it. It's like static, like a radio that's tuned to more than one station. Jarib, it's horrible, I can't stand it."

"Listen to me, you can fight back, Sarah. Do the breathing exercises. Keep doing them."

"I can't. The voice won't let me. Jarib, I need you so much. The letter . . ."

"Forget that stupid letter. It's the craziest thing I ever did. I love you, darling. I'm coming to France, to Alsace. I'll be with you tomorrow. Meantime you mustn't be alone. Don't just lie in bed and let the thing take over. Stay awake, Sarah. Play music. Make somebody stay with you and keep talking. You can do it, darling. You have to, for us."

"I'll try, Jarib. I promise I'll try. I love you so much . . ."

Her next words were muffled by static; then there was nothing but a hum on the line. They'd been cut off. Jarib cursed and jiggled the receiver. Nothing happened. The blonde was knocking on the glass of the phone booth. He slammed the receiver home and pushed open the door.

"C'mon, you've got to hurry. The last boarding call was four minutes ago. And you've got to sign this."

She handed him his receipt and a pen, then turned around so he could use her back as a leaning station. It was a very nice back. He scrawled his name, pushed the form into her hands, and grabbed his passport and ticket. "Thanks for everything; you've been great."

He started running toward security control.

.   .   .

Sarah put down the telephone slowly, keeping her hand on the receiver, as if that prolonged the contact with Jarib. The last of the evening's patrons were just passing through the foyer outside the little office where she'd come to take the call. Zelah was bidding them good night. Tim came to the office door. "You okay?"

She pressed her fingers to her temples. "It's still very bad. But I feel a little better."

"I take it that was good medicine." He gestured toward the phone.

She managed a smile. "Yes, the best." Then, realizing how he'd take it: "I'm sorry."

"Don't be. I'm pretty dense sometimes, but I've managed to get the message. Look, are you going to be well enough to go back to England tomorrow? I've already canceled the early reservation. But we could make a later boat if we left in the morning."

"I can't. Jarib's coming to meet me here."

Tim raised his eyebrows. "Anxious type, isn't he?"

She tried to shake her head, but it hurt too much. "It's complicated, I can't explain."

"Seems to me you've said that before. When's he due?"

"Tomorrow sometime. That's all he said. Tomorrow."

"Okay, I'll hang about until he gets here. Hey, what's the matter?" She'd suddenly stumbled and clutched the desk. Tim stepped forward and grabbed her arm. "I'd better get you back to bed."

"No, I mustn't. Jarib said I should stay with people, play music, talk . . ."

"Sounds like a queer prescription for migraine."

Sarah murmured something he didn't hear. Zelah came in. "My God, she looks awful. We have to get her back upstairs. Maybe I should call the doctor again."

"No," Sarah whispered. "Please, forgive me . . . but just till tomorrow . . . I need . . ." The strain was too much; her voice petered away.

"Her boyfriend's coming here," Tim explained. There was no emotion in his voice. "Apparently he knows what's the matter with her and how to deal with it. He says she's not to be alone. She's supposed to stay with people and talk and play music."

Zelah listened to this with an increasing look of wonderment. "Are all Americans really crazy?" she asked at last. "Just like they say."

Tim was still holding Sarah, but he managed to shrug. "I don't know. But I can't see anything else to try."

Zelah sat down hard in the chair beside the desk. She'd been on her feet since seven that morning. She was exhausted, and she looked it. Tomorrow she'd go back to Paris in the morning and work all afternoon in the greenhouse. "When is this miracle worker going to be here, did you say?"

"Tomorrow sometime, that's all I know."

Sarah tried to turn to face Zelah. "He's coming as fast as he can. I'm sorry . . . such a nuisance for you . . ."

"What nuisance," Zelah said with a burst of her customary energy. "I love music. And staying up all night is good for the complexion, whatever your mother told you. Come, we can go to my room. I have a stereo and a coffeemaker in there."

"You live in New York now?" Sam asked.

Dov shook his head. "No, I just got here Thursday. I was sent."

"What the hell does that mean? Who sent you?"

"A man named Yitzhak Beklem."

Sam stared at him. "Wait a minute, I know that name. Only I can't think . . . Yeah, I can. He was the detective I hired when Amy disappeared. Those schmucks that call themselves the Israeli police said there wasn't anything they could do. So I hired a detective. Only he didn't do nothing either."

"Yes, he did," Dov said. "He did a lot. Sit down, Mr. Stein. I'll tell you the story. You won't like it, but you're entitled to at least know what happened."

It was late when Dov stopped talking. Sam had said little; mostly he'd listened. First in anger, later in disbelief, finally in wonderment and pain. As for the Israeli, he'd poured it all out like a libation; a sacrificial offering. Once the gates of memory were opened, he'd resurrected every detail, every nuance. He sat motionless on Sam's expensive beige sofa with his feet planted on the thick chocolate brown carpet. All the while he spoke he stared at an oversize painting of orange and blue flames, as if the whole drama were being reenacted in their depths, unfolding before his eyes. Flames were an appropriate symbol. Finally he laid his head back—spent, talked out. "Can I have another drink?"

Sam passed him the half-empty bottle of scotch and watched in silence while Levi poured four inches into his glass and drank it in two gulps. Finally the older man stood up. "You gotta get something in your gut besides bug juice. C'mon, we'll make a sandwich."

Rhonda had stocked the refrigerator well. Sam took out a whole kosher salami and found a knife and cut it. Carefully he pulled the cellophane wrapping from the edge of each slice. There were braided rolls that had been fresh that morning. They were still acceptable. Dov watched while Sam opened them and made thick sandwiches. "I got some mustard in here." Sam fished around in a cupboard until he found the mustard.

He put the jar on the table and motioned for Levi to help himself. It was imported from France, shot through with small dark red grains. Dov put some on his roll.

"Siddown," Sam said, doing so himself. "You shouldn't eat standing up; it's bad for the digestion." They chewed in silence. Finally Sam looked up. "Tell me one thing more. Did you love my Amy?"

Dov put down the half-eaten sandwich and stared at it. He took a deep breath. "She was very important to me, Mr. Stein."

"Sam," the older man interrupted. "I'm like your father-in-law in a way. Call me Sam."

"While we were together, she was the most important thing in the world to me."

Stein winced. "Important. Okay, but did you love her?"

Levi thought a moment more. "Yes," he said. "Yes, I can honestly say I did."

"Thank you. The things she did, Amy was always looking for love. I loved her, but I didn't seem to be able to convince her of it. I hope you did."

"I think so."

•

Sam nodded and turned to the refrigerator. It was an arm's reach from the small breakfast bar, and he produced a cardboard tub of whipped sweet butter. "I'll let you in on a secret. Don't tell anyone, but one of the things I like best in the world is kosher salami with butter. Rhonda would die. As for my Bess, she'd roll over in her grave."

He made another sandwich, this one slathered with butter, and held it out. The other man refused. Sam took a large bite and smiled. "Delicious, you should try it." When the sandwich was gone, he looked at Levi. "Listen, according to you, this cocksucker Beklem has made us both schlemiels, right?" He didn't wait for an answer. "You know something, I don't mind. I'm grateful finally he brought us together. In the whole world you're the only other person alive who loved my Amy."

Thirteen

MONDAY, NOVEMBER 26

The pope's feet in the traditional white satin slippers were small; the steps they took, short and shuffling. His body, once merely thin, was now emaciated with illness. They had altered the white alb three times this month; still, he seemed lost in it.

"Let me help, Holiness." The monsignor put out a steadying hand.

Gently the pope pushed it away. "It's all right, Father," he said softly. "I can manage." The tiny feet continued their labored journey down the corridor. It was lit by dim bulbs; it was 6:00 A.M., before dawn in Rome.

The chapel had been prepared. The altar was covered in starched white linen; two candles in plain wooden candlesticks were lit; on a side table stood two glass cruets filled with water and wine; the simple silver paten and chalice which had belonged to a nineteenth-century French priest this pope had himself declared a saint were waiting. Everything was ready. In a few minutes the pontiff would offer holy Mass in a little-used corner of the Vatican, in a tiny room that had been the secret retreat of one of his predecessors. It was a whim, not his customary practice. The room was some distance from his apartments.

They'd wanted to take him in a wheelchair, but His Holiness refused. "I will walk; perhaps this is my last Mass. I wish to arrive at the altar of my God on my own two feet." But it was difficult.

The monsignor continued to keep pace with the old man, adjusting his stride to the short, labored paces. He was near enough to see the beads of sweat on the pope's brow. Two nuns who customarily served the pontiff walked behind them, and there would be a doctor and a nurse in the chapel. The monsignor prayed they would survive long enough for the professionals to be useful. They turned a corner; the door of the chapel was five yards ahead of them now. It was open; the altar was visible. A smile lit the pope's seamed, pain-racked face.

"We're almost there, Holiness," the monsignor murmured.

The pope nodded. "Almost there," he agreed. He paused for a moment, caught his breath, then gently took the hand of the monsignor. "I am coming to the end of a long journey," he whispered. He was still smiling.

The doctor had been kneeling in prayer; he rose when he saw his patient. He came to meet them, swiftly assessing the deterioration of the last few hours. "You are ill, Holiness. You must return to your bed at once. Perhaps tomorrow . . ."

The pope waved him away impatiently. The small procession moved on.

The vestments were waiting at a table by the door. The monsignor looked at them despairingly. The weight of the heavy embroidered chausible would surely be too much. The pope glanced at it, then at his master of ceremonies. "Not this morning, Father. Perhaps just a stole today."

The monsignor held the long scarf to the pope's lips for the ceremonial kiss; then he draped it over the bent shoulders. The stole was green, because it was still what was liturgically called "ordinary time," the period between the feast of Pentecost and the first Sunday of Advent. The trembling fingers of the pope stroked it lightly; then he moved forward. "I will go unto the altar of God," he whispered.

"To God who gives joy to my youth," the monsignor murmured in reply. It was an old prayer, an old response. No longer part of the official Mass rubric, but part of the history of both of them.

The pontiff moved behind the altar; the monsignor stood beside him as server; the others made up a tiny congregation. His Holiness looked at them, seemed to find a sudden reserve of strength. "I have wished to say this Mass here in this holy place because I believe it is my last," he said. "I offer it—" his voice faltered, then continued—"for the needs of Holy Church. May God protect her from her enemies, and from our sins."

He bent his head to kiss the stone beneath the white linen cloths. The frail hands clutched the altar to give the body support. Only the monsignor was close enough to see what happened next. The fingers splayed, the grip loosened. And the body of the old man sank gently to the floor.

"Holiness!" The monsignor dropped to his knees.

The doctor sprang up. He was beside his patient instantly, stethoscope in hand. The pope turned his head away from him. "Father . . ." His eyes were open; they found those of the monsignor. The younger man bent his head until his ear was almost touching the parched lips. "Fanti," the pontiff murmured. "We've had so many politicians; the Church needs a saint."

They were his last words. Ten minutes later the Catholic Church was without a pope. Within half an hour Vatican Radio made the announcement, and the world's press began booking airplane seats and hotel rooms. Plans for the funeral were being made, and for what would follow it, the conclave made up of the College of Cardinals. They would meet to elect one of their number as the Vicar of Christ. Rome settled into its favorite pasttime, mentioning names. The name most often heard was Malachy Fanti. Cardinal Bellini heard the rumors and smiled with satisfaction.

The flight was on time, six-forty on a cold dark morning. Orly was like most of the world's airports; tarmac and terminal were slick, characterless, and big. There was nothing to see, even had there been light enough to see it.

371

"You are a tourist, monsieur?" he was asked at immigration. Jarib said he was, and his passport was duly stamped. The customs area was empty of all but bored-looking inspectors. The other passengers were still waiting for their luggage.

Jarib put his single case on the counter. "Nothing to declare."

"*Très bien, bienvenu à France,* monsieur."

He'd never been here before; what time he had for travel he'd spent in the Caribbean and Latin America, except for one week in England years before. Another time he might be curious, not this morning. Hope and fear were riding a seesaw in his gut; the fear seemed more firmly seated.

It was barely seven when he was waved through the gate into the arrivals terminal. A line of people waited on the other side. In the harsh yellow lighting they looked bleary-eyed and not quite awake. About half of them wore some sort of uniform; the others had identifying badges pinned to their ordinary clothes. Each held a cardboard sign: ALL FRANCE TOURS, THOMAS COOK & SONS, AIR HOLIDAYS. . . . The tour guides were waiting for their first pigeons of the day.

He started past the queue, irrationally craning his neck and looking for Sarah. A woman at the end stepped almost into his path and held her sign a bit higher. It was crudely lettered, obviously a quick job. It contained only the words DR. JARIB BARAAK. Simple and extremely effective.

"I'm Jarib Baraak."

"Yes," she said. "I have the idea you are my man." Her English was heavily accented. "I know only a little your language. You speak French?"

"No, I'm sorry."

"Well, we will, how do you say, manage. Come with me. *Vite.*"

They did manage. She hustled him through the airport to a vast parking garage. Her car was conveniently placed in the nearest bay. It was a sleek gray late-model Peugeot. She took it expertly down the ramp and merely slowed at the toll booth. There was a rapid exchange of French, and she passed the exact number of francs through the window.

"We must be quick, so I drive and don't talk. *Vous comprenez?*"

"*Oui.*" His one bit of remembered French. He could also still

372

conjugate a verb or two. It was unlikely to help. She smiled at him. It was a nice smile; it made him feel a little better.

The woman was perhaps in her fifties. She wore dark trousers and a close-fitting blue nylon parka. Her hair was shot with gray and caught at the nape of her neck with a plastic clip. Only her skin was distinguished: very fine and fair, unwrinkled, close-pored. Jarib remembered reading somewhere that contrary to the legend about the English, Frenchwomen had the most beautiful skin in the world. Perhaps it was true. He thought of Sarah's skin. It was so soft. And her cheeks always glowed with color.

They moved out into the network of roads surrounding Orly. The sky was paling, and a rim of vibrant pink limned the horizon. "How long will it take to get where we're going?" Jarib asked.

She didn't answer immediately; she was negotiating the figure-eight entrance to a highway. The A4 according to the signs. Jarib repeated the question in case she hadn't understood.

"That is to depend on the traffic. If we have the luck, four hours and one half."

"How's Sarah? Have you spoken with her?"

For a brief second her eyes flicked from the road to his face. "I know nothing, monsieur le docteur, only to drive to Kohlburg. Is best that way, no? Now, we will be quiet." She reached beneath her seat and produced a thermos and passed it to him.

Jarib unscrewed the top. It separated into two small plastic cups. When he uncorked the thermos, the rich smell of coffee filled the car. He poured some and handed it to her, then took his share. It was half milk and very sweet. Nonetheless, he drank it gratefully.

In Kohlburg sunrise streaked the heavens with broad bands of dark yellow and orange, then disappeared in banks of cloud. A steady drizzle began shortly afterward. Malachy had not seen the transient glory; by the time he woke to his surroundings it was raining. He was not in bed; he still sat in the chair by the window. The crucifix was yet in his lap. He raised it to his mouth and kissed the wounded feet, then stood up.

He didn't manage to rise all the way. His legs buckled, and he grabbed the arm of the chair to keep from falling. The crucifix

373

tumbled to the floor. With difficulty he got to his knees and re-trieved it and half crawled to the bureau. Using one hand, he pulled himself up, put the crucifix down gently, and stood. The lower half of his body was completely numb.

Many times had he spent an entire night in prayer, but never almost twenty-four hours. And could he call what had transpired throughout all of yesterday and last night prayer? Yes, he decided. Deep contemplative meditation, the fruit of a lifetime's practice. Not thought, a plummeting into what an ancient mystic called "the cloud of unknowing." But focused. This time focused on the Al-exandria Testament and the woman.

He gazed out the window toward the *auberge*. He was somehow absolutely certain that she was still there, that his long vigil had excited whatever mysterious knowledge of the document she pos-sessed. It was time to reap the harvest of his labors.

He took a tentative step and found he could walk. Prickles of pain testified to returning circulation in his legs. He started for the door. It was more difficult than he'd expected because he was dizzy. No food, he decided. He'd eaten nothing since the previous morning. And before that there had been the long night spent in the open, outside the *auberge*. Naturally he was dizzy, and perhaps he'd caught a cold.

There was a brisk rap on the door. *"Entrez."* Malachy's voice sounded to him weak and faraway. There was an odd ringing in his ears.

"Bonjour, mon père. Here is your breakfast." The baker's wife pushed the door open with her hip; it was more than broad enough for the task. She set the tray on the small table. Malachy saw her eyes dart from the untouched bed to his face. "We worried about you, *mon père*. We did not see you since yesterday morning."

"I've been working." It was the only explanation he could think of, and it was true in a way.

"You don't look well. There is a doctor in the village, I can call him if you like."

"No, thank you, I'm fine. Only tired."

"Yes, and you must be very hungry. I brought a bit extra—"

"You are very kind, madame, thank you." Malachy pulled the door a bit wider, inviting her to leave. He knew she wanted to stay and talk, rather pry, but she took the hint.

There were two earthenware pitchers—one half full of syrupy black coffee smelling of chicory, the other brimming with hot milk already forming a skin across the top—two large rolls still warm from the oven, a small pot of honey, an egg, and a tumbler a quarter full of cognac. He ate it all, even drank the brandy. That made him feel hot.

Malachy put his hands to his cheeks; they were burning. And thick with stubble. He must wash and shave before he went to the *auberge*.

Twenty minutes later he descended the stairs and walked through the bakery. It was crowded with workmen and farmers having their breakfast. The smell of bread was a pungent presence in the air. Surprisingly it sickened him. Malachy moved hastily toward the door to the street. Two women eyed him with open curiosity. They held net bags, waiting for the next batch of loaves to come from the oven. He ignored them.

Outside, the rain had progressed from a drizzle to a downpour. He turned up the collar of his coat and wished he'd thought to bring his umbrella. There was nothing he could do about that now; the umbrella was back in Paris. Moving as quickly as he could on still-stiff legs, he started up the street. There were few passersby; the bakery was the only shop open at this hour. He came to the chemist's and paused. Perhaps some aspirin would help.

The door was shut and barred, but there was a light behind the curtained window. And the shadow of a man moved behind it. Malachy rapped sharply on the glass.

A few seconds passed. He knocked again. There was the rasping sound of turning keys. The man who opened the door wore a white coat and frameless glasses. "Yes, what is it? I don't do business until eight-thirty."

"I know, I'm sorry. But I'm feeling a bit ill. If you could just sell me some aspirin . . ."

The man adjusted the glasses and peered at his caller. "You're the priest, eh? The one staying with Jeanne and Henri?"

"With the baker and his wife, yes."

"Come in," the man in the glasses said. Inquisitiveness had overcome pique. "What's the matter, a headache? Are you sure aspirin is what you want?"

"I think so, I am a little dizzy and . . ." Malachy took a step

375

forward. He could manage no more. Suddenly everything was very dark and spinning frantically. The floor seemed to come up to meet him. His sore legs gave way, and he crumpled to the ground. His torso lay across the threshold, the rest of his body on the sidewalk in the rain. It wasn't possible to shut the door. The pharmacist cursed and knelt. He found the pulse in the stranger's carotid artery. Very fast, but steady. And he was breathing. Not dead, thank Christ. Just fainted.

The man's raincoat was still on the chair by the door; he flung it over the fallen priest's sprawled legs and went behind the counter to call the doctor.

On the radio a woman was reading the news in suave Oxford accents. Reports from the Vatican confirmed that the pope was dead. There was rioting last night in Ghana. The foreign ministers . were meeting this morning in Brussels to discuss the entry into the Common Market of Portugal and Spain. Italy and France were worried about the influx of cheap Spanish wine. Thus spake the BBC.

Zelah had a shortwave radio, and they'd tuned in the British World Service a couple of hours ago. After they'd played twice every record in Zelah's limited collection. Most of them were in Paris, she'd explained. Someday she hoped to sell the greenhouse and move here permanently, but she couldn't do that until her father died.

That was just one of the many things Sarah and Zelah talked about. At first it had been strained, almost manic three-way conversation, a desperate attempt to follow Jarib's instructions. Around three in the morning Tim had fallen asleep on Zelah's bed. That somehow relaxed the two women. They chatted more easily, exchanging confidences in the night that daylight would have delayed for a longer acquaintance.

Sarah lay on a chaise longue upholstered in mauve velvet. Behind her violet-sprigged curtains were drawn against the dark and the wet. Zelah sprawled on a mound of cushions on the gray rug. She looked up at the American woman. "Any better? Your color has improved."

376

Sarah lifted her hair from her temples with hands that had only recently stopped trembling. "Yes, as a matter of fact. I feel a lot better. Just in the last ten minutes or so. God, Zelah, I'm so sorry. What a night it's been for you."

"Not so bad. Kind of fun to tell the truth."

Sarah smiled; it turned into a grin.

The BBC announcer was saying something about Israel's invasion of Lebanon. Zelah got up and snapped off the radio. "If you're better, I don't have to listen to that anymore." They'd already been treated to three current affairs programs in which the British had made plain their disapproval of the Israeli actions. "The world only tolerates Jews when we're victims," Zelah said. "When we act like everybody else, the same feet of clay, the anti-Semitism all surfaces again."

"Do you think you'll ever go back to Israel?"

The older woman shook her head. "Never. It's claustrophobic. Any small country is. And I don't agree with Begin and the Likud party any more than the English do. I just hate it that they sound so self-righteous." She went to the dressing table and peered into the mirror. "My God, all the wrinkles are showing. I'm too old to stay up all night."

Zelah was forty, another confidence produced during the night. "You're a fantastic-looking woman," Sarah said frankly. "I've always wanted to look smooth and sophisticated. Instead I come across like a fragile child. Maybe I should cut my hair." She eyed Zelah's close-cropped head.

"Not this morning anyway. Your Jarib probably wouldn't like it."

Sarah pushed away the small taffeta-covered quilt that lay over her legs and sat up. "I can't believe it's real. That he's coming here."

Zelah crossed to her and put an arm around her shoulders. "It's real. I talked to him before you did, remember?"

Happiness was bubbling inside Sarah, despite everything. It had been thus since the phone call. There was the pain and the fear and the voice—and the joy every time she replayed Jarib's words. "I love you . . . forget that stupid letter . . . I'm coming." How did he know how desperately she needed him? Why was he coming

377

here rather than meeting her in Paris or waiting for her to come home? She didn't know the answers to either question, or half a dozen others, but it didn't matter. Nothing mattered except Jarib. "Yes, I remember," she said.

"Look, I've got to get back to Paris. My assistant opens the greenhouse on Mondays and the concierge looks after Papa until I come home, but they both expect me by late afternoon. It's a five-hour drive. I'll be terribly late if I don't go soon. Will you be all right? He's not much help." She nodded toward Tim, still snoring loudly.

"I'll be fine," Sarah said. She stood up. "The pain's gone entirely." The hours had unlocked many secrets, but she hadn't tried to explain about the voice and the music. Migraine, she'd insisted. The worst form. Something called cluster headaches. Jarib wasn't a medical doctor, she'd told them, but he was experienced in relaxation techniques, which sometimes helped. That's why she'd consulted him originally.

Zelah was thinking of Jarib, too. "If your friend was calling from the airport, he should arrive in Paris sometime this morning. There's a train to Strasbourg at noon. With luck he may make it. If so, he'll be here by three."

Maybe she could go to the train station and meet him. Sarah tasted the idea, and it was sweet, oh, so sweet. She stretched languidly. "It's crazy, I'm not even tired."

"It's called love, *chérie*. All the normal rules don't apply."

"No, they don't, do they? What about you, Zelah? Isn't there anybody special?"

"Just the man I told you about."

"The one who drinks?"

"Yes. And carries the troubles of the world on his shoulders. I don't need that kind of anguish, not even for love." Zelah unbuttoned her robe. Beneath it she wore bikini underpants and a half-cup wired bra. Her body was very good, long and lean with small breasts. A fashion model's figure.

"Too bad you can't reform him," Sarah said.

"There's nothing more stupid for a woman to try. No, I can't reform Dov. He is what he is. It's too bad, but nothing I can do will change it." The tone marked the subject closed.

"What I want most in the world's a hot bath," Sarah said.

"Me too," Zelah agreed. "That's the nice thing about living in an inn, lots of bathrooms and plenty of hot water. Meet you downstairs for breakfast afterward. The beautiful Timothy sounds as if he's good for another couple of hours." To confirm her judgment, Tim snored loudly.

The café in the Gare du Nord was busy at eight-thirty. Travelers and staff crowded in to have breakfast. Many of them fortified their coffee and rolls with cognac. Already the place reeked of alcohol.

Yitzhak looked around; there didn't seem to be a space not already occupied, and Jenny wasn't here yet. He spotted a man moving toward the door and pushed his way to the place that had been vacated. It was a tiny table. He saw an unused chair and dragged it closer and put his coat on it. Now it was a tiny table for two. The man had left a used coffee cup and brandy glass. Yitzhak pushed them away.

Five minutes later Jenny appeared in the door. She wore the gray raincoat again, although it was sunny in Paris today, and a different scarf tied 'round her head. Yitzhak held up his hand. She saw him and pushed through the crowd to his side. "I'm sorry I'm late, and that I couldn't see you last night. They didn't go until after five. And I had a dinner engagement."

"It doesn't matter. Thank you for coming. I apologize for bringing you out so early."

She removed her scarf and unbuttoned the coat and sat down. "It's not early for me. The older I get, the less I sleep. I rise with the birds."

She looked like a bird herself this morning. The delicate features were a little hard-edged, sharpened by fatigue. He smiled at her. "Now you're here to hold the table, I'll get us something to eat. There's only one waitress, and she hasn't even looked in this direction."

He took the dirty dishes and elbowed through the crowd to the counter. A few minutes later he came back, balancing a tray bearing café au lait and croissants wrapped in plastic film. These days

379

almost every public place served croissants thus. One of the glories of France had entered the modern era. There were Parisians for whom the search for a croissant that tasted as they remembered had taken on the aspect of a quest for the Holy Grail.

"Coffee," he told her. "You can't drink tea for breakfast; it's not civilized."

"Never tell that to the English, *mon cher*. But thank you, I like coffee in the morning."

They sipped. Yitzhak unwrapped both rolls and passed one to her. His own he broke in half and dipped in his cup. The first bite confirmed his suspicions. No one had so much as whispered the word *butter* over it.

"I think they make them with axle grease now," Jenny said. She pushed hers away.

Yitzhak ate every crumb of both of them in quick, nervous bites. "I can't ever forget how it was," he said quietly. "So I eat everything, even when it's terrible."

Jenny didn't look at him; she stared at her folded hands instead. She wore a ring this morning. A large garnet in an ornate silver setting. It winked up at her. Finally she raised her eyes and looked around. The crowd was noisy and self-absorbed. No one was paying them any attention. "They talked a long time," she said. "Hamish was incredibly clever."

"How so?"

"What he wanted was just what you guessed, the story behind a bracelet. But he led François on until he was salivating like a hungry dog. The man's a greedy fool. He was quite willing to be manipulated, and Hamish complied. He promised François a big sale in England. Something much better publicized than anything they do here."

"So your count does have more Judaica?"

"Oh, yes, a lot more, I think. Hamish is to see the collection this afternoon."

"He's still in Paris then?"

Jenny nodded. "At the Georges Cinq."

Yitzhak drew his narrow mouth back in a grin. "He takes good care of himself."

"The best care," Jenny said. "I gave them a luncheon of blinis and caviar. Hamish ate enough to gain another ten pounds. And he found out what he wanted to know."

Yitzhak leaned forward eagerly. The harsh light of the café played on his hairless skull.

"He started questioning François about the provenance of his collection. Said he couldn't produce a foolproof false provenance, and that was one of François's conditions, unless he knew the true story. By then, of course, François had mentally spent the profits a dozen times. He was prepared to tell Hamish anything just to get him to do the sale. Our suspicions were correct, by the way: He acquired his things in Egypt in '48 and '49. The Jews were being hounded out of the country in the clothes they stood up in. It was simple to milk them of whatever they had at outrageously low prices."

Yitzhak drummed his fingers on the table. They were long and tapered, his only elegant feature. "To me it seems odd that a man like de Montviron would have considered such things to have any value, to be worth collecting."

Jenny drank the last of her coffee and set down the cup. "Have you ever been to Rome?"

"No."

"Well, in the very heart of the city is a triumphal arch erected for Titus after he sacked Jerusalem. It's decorated with all the booty he brought back."

"Ah, yes, I've seen pictures," Yitzhak said. "Menorahs and candlesticks and Torah scrolls from the Second Temple. So maybe the count has been to Rome."

"You can be sure of it. And he comes of a long line of pirates. Take what you can get when you can get it. Someday, somewhere, someone is sure to be willing to pay a good price for it."

"So he bought the bracelet."

"Among many other things, yes. Hamish got him to talk about it because, unlike much else in François's collection, it isn't obvious Judaica. Harder to sell, he said. So how come it was included in the sale?"

"Clever."

"Yes, masterful, as I told you. Anyway, François said he never really thought about that. He knew the bracelet was an integral part of the collection because he got it from a woman named, just a minute . . ." She took a piece of paper from her black leather bag. The bag was emblazoned with the initials L. V. Vuitton, wildly expensive. Jenny's remorse for the past didn't make her reluctant to enjoy its fruits.

She perched elegant half glasses on her nose and stared at the bit of paper. "It's an unusual name. I had to run to the bathroom and write it down when I heard it." She looked up at Yitzhak. "So they wouldn't get suspicious, I mean."

"I know what you mean. What's the name?"

"Lily Al Ghawahergy. She was from Germany originally, married to an Egyptian Jew whose family had been in Alexandria for centuries. She told François the bracelet was a family heirloom. Very, very old."

Yitzhak took a notepad from his breast pocket. He wrote down the name. "It's Arabic for jeweler," he told her. Neither of them mentioned the obvious connection with the bracelet. "Any idea where this Al Ghawahergy woman is now?"

"Dead, according to François. Apparently she died just before she was to leave Egypt. Of a broken heart probably."

Yitzhak nodded. Then, without preamble: "Jenny, do you ever miss Germany?"

"The truth? Yes. I left because after the war it sickened me, and I'll never go back. Never," she repeated softly. "But I miss it sometimes."

"Me too," Yitzhak said. His voice was flat. "It's crazy, but I do. Sometimes." He cleared his throat. "What about the woman's family? Where did they go?"

"To America. New York, François thinks. But that's not certain. He had no reason to keep track of them."

"It's a place to start," Yitzhak said. For Hamish and Malachy as well as himself. He looked grim.

"I've brought you bad news," Jenny said.

"No, not really. Anyway, it's not your fault." No, it was his. Because he told Malachy something was happening with Levi, the monk came to Paris. Then he was crazy enough to send him to the auction, so Malachy knew about the bracelet. Because Yitzhak didn't suspect that Malachy was shrewd enough to have such a connection, his relationship with the Englishman had progressed to an alliance. Because by happenstance Sarah Myles crossed Hamish Durant's path, both the Englishman and Malachy had come to know about her. So all Yitzhak's best advantages had evaporated. But it wasn't Jenny's fault. Without her he wouldn't know they knew. It made him even with the other two men, better than being behind. "Thank you," he said.

Jenny left first. Yitzhak followed her a few moments later. In the terminal a newsboy was hawking a special edition. *"Le pape est mort!"* he shouted. So the pope was dead. Yitzhak grunted with satisfaction; a dead pope should give Malachy Fanti something new to think about. And get him back to Rome.

In Ipswich it was 3:00 A.M. Rita woke suddenly, summoned to consciousness by the perception that something was wrong. The room was brightened by moonlight streaming through the tied-back curtains at the window. They were unbleached muslin; authentic, but not heavy enough to shut out the light. Frank had suggested blinds, but she'd rejected the idea. They didn't have blinds in colonial times.

She looked over to her husband's bed. He was sitting upright. Doubtless that's what disturbed her sleep. "What's the matter, honey?"

"Nothing, a little gas, that's all. Sorry I woke you."

"It doesn't matter. Are you sure it's gas? Maybe you should take a heart pill."

"No, just gas. I ate too many of your baked beans."

"I'll get you something." She snapped on the light and padded barefoot into the bathroom. A moment later she returned, carrying a glass of fizzing liquid. "Drink it down, you'll feel better. And no more baked beans. I won't make them again."

"Okay," he said, handing her the empty glass. "Not until next weekend."

It was supposed to be a joke, but she didn't laugh. "Honey, you have to take care of yourself. I'll turn off the alarm; you sleep late in the morning."

Ostensibly Frank was retired; semiretired, he always said. Two years earlier he'd taken his sister's son, Ben Pollock, into the business. Ben owned twenty percent of it now. And he was in charge of the night shift, the most critical time at the bakery. Between 10:00 P.M. and dawn everything must work perfectly, both men and machines. If it didn't, they wouldn't be able to make their deliveries the following day. All his working life Frank Myles had been at his plant six nights a week. The only days they didn't deliver were Sundays and Christmas.

When the younger man took over the night shift, Frank claimed to be delighted. Too old for that stuff, he told everyone. But it was only pretense, both he and Rita knew that. Without the business he felt aimless, a man without a center in his life. So each morning he rose at six and walked to the factory and stood by the loading bays and watched the blue trucks take on their cargo of brightly wrapped sliced bread.

The trucks were small Chevy vans. They had yellow lettering on both sides. MYLES'S BREAD IS MILES AHEAD, it said. Ben had suggested they sell the fleet and subcontract the delivery operation. He produced a raft of figures to prove it would be cheaper. Frank wouldn't even look at them. Myles's bread is miles ahead. He'd thought that up himself. Hired trucks wouldn't display the motto.

"Leave him alone," the doctor had told Rita. "Don't nag. If he wants to go down there at the crack of dawn, let him. Just see he takes a nap in the afternoon."

She remembered that advice now and bit her lip. Still, for once he could be sensible, couldn't he? "Honey, please. Just one late morning. Ben has everything in control, you know that."

"Yeah, sure, maybe you're right."

But he didn't turn off the alarm; she did. And she lay awake a long time, listening to his breathing. Eventually it told her he was asleep, and she relaxed. Someday he wouldn't be there in the bed next to her. Someday soon probably.

Rita felt one hot tear escape and trickle down her cheek; she brushed it away impatiently. Death was waiting for everybody, her as well as Frank. How else could you get to heaven and be with God forever, the way the Church said? Frank was a good Catholic; he'd go straight to heaven when he died. There was only that one bad thing either of them had ever done, and that wasn't his idea, it was hers.

Rita felt again the weight of that memory; sometimes it seemed as if it would choke her. She pushed it away. They'd made their choice; it was too late to change anything now. It was just the idea of Frank's dying and leaving her alone that was making her so sad. She'd be the only person in the world who knew the truth then. Unless the man was still alive. No, he couldn't be. He'd been ancient twenty-five years ago.

Restlessly Rita turned over and tried to sleep.

Ariel phoned Yitzhak at ten. "Something's happened, now your Swiss priest is sick."

"How sick? An accident?"

"No. Seems he passed out in the village pharmacy. The doctor was called, and they took him to Strasbourg, to the hospital. I don't know anymore yet, but I thought I'd better bring you up-to-date right away."

"Yes. Good. Try to find out what's wrong with him, and how long he'll be in the hospital. I expect he'll be in a hurry to get back to Rome now. The pope is dead. And, Ariel, listen, there's someone coming to see the Myles woman. Another American, his name's Jarib Baraak."

"Got it. How's he getting here, train?"

"No. I arranged for Vita to drive him. With luck they'll be there by noon."

"I thought Vita was in Lisbon, following up on that Mengele rumor."

"I brought her back last night. I only agreed she should go because she insisted. And you backed her up. But this is more important."

"More important than Mengele?" Ariel's tone said he didn't believe it.

Yitzhak sighed. "*Tateleh,* listen, you want to chase Nazis already so old they're going to die any minute, go work for Simon what's his name in Vienna. I'll write you a nice reference. Me, I'm more interested in the future."

The line was silent for a few seconds. Yitzhak only knew they were still connected because he could hear Ariel's breathing. "Okay," the younger man said at last. "I guess you're right. You're right too damned often for comfort, Yitzhak."

"Whose comfort, mine or yours? Or maybe all the *mamzarim* out there just waiting to get us. Them I don't want to make comfortable."

The old man was doing his talmudic thing again. The argument was too complex for Ariel to follow, and he didn't try. "You want me to link up with Vita?"

"Maybe. I didn't plan on it, but probably she'd better make contact." He paused and thought a moment. Vita would call him as soon as she'd delivered Baraak to the *auberge*. He could tell her where to find Ariel. "I'll take care of it," he said. "Meanwhile, see what you can find out about Malachy. It may be that the Myles woman and Baraak will leave before he does. If so, two of you on the spot will be helpful."

Despite his anxiety, Jarib slept for much of the drive. He hadn't been able to do so on the plane, and it was the middle of the night for him. Besides, the woman was a superb driver. So he allowed the soft hum of the Peugeot to relax him, and he slept.

When he woke, they'd left the sun behind. It was gray and overcast. The dashboard clock said ten-twenty. His watch insisted it was four twenty-two. He hadn't changed it to French time. He did so now, giving the Gucci the benefit of the doubt as far as the extra two minutes were concerned, then opened the road map the woman had given him earlier.

The highway signs presented no difficulty; they weren't written in words but in clear, schematic drawings. They could be understood whatever language you spoke. The one that had just whizzed past indicated that ten kilometers ahead was a left turn for Verdun, a short way further on there was a right leading to Bar-le-duc. So they'd come two-thirds of the way.

"You are hungry?" the woman asked.

"No, not really. Are you?"

She shook her head, not taking her eyes from the road. They shared it mainly with trucks and buses and a few taxis, fewer private cars. The Peugeot dominated them all. "You must be tired," he said. "I can drive for a while."

"No," she said. It wasn't the kind of tone you argued with.

He felt constrained to say something more. "We've made good time."

"*Comment?*"

"We are getting to Strasbourg quickly. You are an excellent driver, where did you learn?"

She flashed him a quick grin before swinging her glance back straight ahead. "At Le Mans, monsieur, and Monaco."

A professional. He should have guessed.

A sign with a cup and saucer, a gas tank, and the letters WC appeared on the right. "We must stop for the petrol," she said.

Petrol, not gas; what English she knew she'd learned from a Britisher. He nodded and folded the map.

Six minutes later she took the exit ramp with customary skill and pulled into a service area. The line at the pumps was five cars long, and there was only one attendant. There was nothing either of them could do about that. She pointed to the rest rooms. "You go first, then me."

Orders, quietly given, but unmistakable. A good idea nonetheless. Jarib walked toward a green door with a man's head profiled above it. He remembered stories he'd heard about urinals that were simply filthy holes in the ground. It was nothing like that. Sparkling white tile and a wall to pee against, with water running down it perpetually.

When he returned, the Peugeot was parked on one side; the woman stood beside it. "Please, you will stay with the car?"

"Of course."

She returned quickly. No time wasted on hair or makeup apparently. Just a brief accession to the demands of nature. Moments later they were hurtling down the highway again. "I'd like to pay for the gas," Jarib said. "The petrol. Sorry I don't have any francs." He tried to pass her a twenty-dollar bill.

She shook her head impatiently. "No, no. It is all arranged."

Arranged by whom? Why? He put away the twenty and decided it was pointless to ask. She'd just pretend not to understand him. Maybe she really wouldn't.

Twenty minutes passed before either of them spoke again. It was the woman who broke the silence. "In the back there is food," she said.

Jarib turned and saw a red net bag on the rear seat. It hadn't been there earlier. He wondered if she'd bought it while he was in the men's room, or maybe it had been in the trunk and she'd just retrieved it.

There were sandwiches, chicken on thin-sliced dark bread, some cheese, and a couple of apples. A glass bottle without a label contained wine; another one, water. At the bottom of the bag he found two carefully wrapped glasses. Nothing she'd bought, it was obviously a lunch she'd packed at home. He took half a sandwich and passed the other half to her. She refused wine and asked for water. He left the wine bottle stoppered and took water, too. His stomach was too queasy for anything else; besides, he wanted to stay sharp. They ate in silence, the woman never losing her concentration on the road. Neither of them had cheese, just an apple each.

"Thank you," Jarib said. "That was delicious." She didn't answer, just smiled. "Listen," he added. "I don't know your name."

"Vita."

"Just Vita?"

"It is enough, no?"

"If you say so." What kind of name was Vita? A Latin root—life. It could be anything. French, Italian, maybe Czechoslovakian for all he knew.

The countryside was changing. It had been fields and herds of cows, dairy country apparently; now they were climbing a bit, there were dense stands of trees on either side of the road. It was ten minutes to eleven, a sign indicated that Strasbourg was seventy-five kilometers ahead. "In there"—she gestured with one hand—"is the green book. Please."

He opened the Peugeot's spacious map compartment. There was a two-inch stack of long, narrow green books: *Michelin Green Guides,* detailed descriptions of a small area. "Which one?" he asked.

"Alsace, the number eighty-seven." He found it. "Look, please, for the map of '*Strasbourg et environs.*' We go to Kohlburg, a small village between Strasbourg and Colmar."

She wanted to know if they must go through Strasbourg itself.

"No," he told her. "We can pick up the N four a little way ahead. Head toward Saverne. From there we take N four twenty-two."

She nodded and retired once more into silence.

They ran into rain at Saverne; when they turned onto the winding single-lane road that was the N422, it became a downpour. A sign appeared on their right. AUBERGE CALIFORNIA, 20 KILOMETERS. It wasn't a road sign; it was advertising, decorated all around the border with bunches of green grapes set on a purple field. A medley of pots and pans filled the center. The man calling himself Yitzhak Beklem had said Sarah was in a small inn. "Does *auberge* mean restaurant or inn?" he asked.

"Today usually a restaurant," Vita said. "But many times with some bedrooms."

"The Auberge California, is that where Sarah is?"

She shrugged. "It is where I bring you, monsieur."

Jarib's gut tightened.

Sarah soaked for twenty minutes in a tubful of steaming water and bubbles. Zelah had given her the bubble bath; it smelled of jasmine and musk. "Sexy," the older woman had promised with a grin. "Appropriate for this morning." Crazily Sarah had blushed.

She trailed her hands through the foam on the top of the water. Thick, satiny. Delicious. Her skin was tingling. She cupped her hands under her breasts. Jarib would touch them soon. The thought sent a shiver up her spine. And made her remember Tim. Should she tell Jarib about that night in Paris? She was debating that when the pain struck her again, a white-hot flame searing her temples, lodging between her eyes, lifting, it seemed, the top of her head.

Do-sol-la-fa . . . listen to the music, Sarah. Then the jamming, the awful buzzing.

She moaned. The sudden onslaught brought a wave of nausea. She retched, but it was just dry heaves; after thirty-six hours of such attacks there was nothing in her stomach to vomit. Breathe, she told herself, concentrate on your breath. Follow it in, down, up, out . . . breathe. And then it was gone. All of it, voice, pain, nausea—simply gone.

Shaking a little with the aftermath, she climbed out of the tub and toweled herself dry on one of the *auberge*'s thick monogrammed towels. Her motions were slow, preoccupied. It had never been exactly like this before. The jamming, for one thing. And the voice itself. Sustained for almost two days, then gone, then returned for brief minutes. She must remember to tell Jarib that; he'd want to know every detail. Such thoughts pushed the one-night stand with Tim Durant out of her mind.

She wanted to look marvelous, but there weren't a lot of choices as far as her wardrobe was concerned. She had only brought enough from England to carry her the three days they originally planned to be in France. And she hadn't had time to do any shopping in Paris. Finally she settled on the purple suit. It was a bit dressy for the country, but it looked terrific on her.

Zelah was already eating when Sarah went down to the dining room. She was sitting by the glass doors fronting on the canal, staring out at the relentless rain. It made the water look flat and killed the reflections of the trees on the far bank. She motioned Sarah to the seat opposite and signaled to a young boy who was watering the plants. She'd left extra coffee in the kitchen; would he bring it, please? And to Sarah: "Almost the entire staff has Mondays off."

Sarah looked at the rain. It had settled into a steady deluge. Not a nice welcome for Jarib. And not very pleasant driving for Zelah. "Will it be like this all the way to Paris?"

"Probably not all the way. According to the weather report, the storm is working its way east. Have some juice." She filled a glass from a large pitcher. "Something I got used to in America, orange juice for breakfast."

Sarah drank it all down, enjoying the unusual sensation of bits of orange pulp on her tongue. "You've improved on the custom. At home it's mostly frozen; that's fresh-squeezed, isn't it?"

"Absolutely. How do you feel now? Still okay?"

"Yes." She didn't mention the attack in the bathtub. "Any sign of Tim's waking up?"

"None. I sat in my bedroom in nothing but my skin and put on my makeup, and the bastard didn't even turn over. Now I know I must be getting old."

Sarah grinned. The boy brought two silver pitchers, and Zelah poured, holding one in each hand and mixing the milk and the coffee in the cup. "One thing I didn't adopt in America, your fondness for coffee that tastes like dishwater. Hope this isn't too strong."

"It's delicious, thanks." Sarah took a brioche from the basket on the table. It was warm, and it smelled marvelous.

"Does Charles bake these?"

"No, we have a baker. Charles is the head chef, different jobs here in France."

"Is he off today, too?"

"Yes," Zelah said. "He's gone to Basel, in Switzerland. Just for a few hours; he'll be back this afternoon."

Sarah was surprised. "How far is it to Switzerland?"

"About an hour's drive. And as I said, the restaurant's closed today, so there's no problem." Zelah drained the last of her cup and stood up. "Look, I've left instructions with young Louis there. Help yourself to anything in the kitchen. Until Charles comes back. After that you can't make free with his kingdom. I'm sure he'll do something for you for dinner, but if your man arrives, you may prefer to go out. An empty restaurant isn't very festive. In any case, the room is yours for as long as you like."

Sarah said a lot of things about how much she appreciated everything and how sorry she was to be a nuisance.

Impulsively Zelah leaned down and kissed her. "You're not a nuisance, *chérie*. I believe the correct English word is *friend*."

"I don't know what's going to happen after Jarib comes, but I'll get in touch."

"Do," Zelah said. "I'm dying to meet him and hear all about the ecstatic reunion."

They walked together to the foyer, but Zelah insisted Sarah mustn't go out into the rain. So she remained in the doorway, waving until Zelah's bright orange Citroën Dyane had pulled out of the parking lot and disappeared down the narrow road. It was eleven o'clock.

. . .

In Rome the morning had been one of concentrated activity, but it all proceeded calmly, dictated by centuries of tradition. Even the intense political lobbying was traditional.

Like those of Cardinal Fanti, the apartments of Cardinal Bellini were behind the walls of the Vatican, in the Tribunal Palace. That was all they had in common. Bellini's quarters were luxurious, supremely comfortable. He sat now in a capacious armchair covered in pale silk. Across from him Bishop Longo was seated on a matching sofa. The bishop was speaking. "I've talked with Fanti's office. He's been in France on personal business. His secretary assures me he'll be back in Rome shortly. So everything is going as we planned."

"Almost everything," Bellini said. "Fanti's name is being spoken all over Rome. But not all the cardinals live in Rome. I'd hoped the Holy Father might live a little longer, enable me to get around to see some of the others." He shrugged. "As it is, when they come, it may be different. Malachy Fanti may not be such a universal favorite."

"I have no doubt you will convince them all of the wisdom of your choice, my friend." Longo lit one of his French cigarettes.

"Only if I make them think it's their choice. I wish to see Cardinal Fanti elected immediately. By acclamation. Before there is a formal ballot. There is precedent for such things."

The bishop leaned forward. "Yes, but not frequent precedent. Why make it so hard on yourself? Why not elect him in the usual way? Let the other contenders have their day, just make sure none of them has enough votes to win."

"That won't work," Bellini said. "There is a complication; have you heard of this ad hoc committee on the Scriptures? The one chaired by the American?"

"By Monsignor Larry Donovan; yes, I've heard of him and his committee."

"Good, then you'll understand my concern. Their report will be published in a few weeks. In the normal way of things it will be after the election, but word has already leaked. The report accuses the Church of virulent anti-Semitism. According to Donovan and his friends, the origins go back to the authors of the Gospels."

Longo shrugged. "There's nothing new in any of that."

"This is more focused, more specific. And from our point of

view it has already done damage. The fact that the report is known to be forthcoming, that it's known to deal with the Jewish question means the subject will be on the minds of the cardinals. It won't take very deep probing for them to discover Fanti's . . . preoccupation. Or his antipathies."

"You think Their Eminences are all weeping over anti-Semitism?"

"Enough of them to matter," Bellini said. "A great many of them are young men; quite a few have never spent any time working in the Vatican. They don't understand the needs of the whole Church, only their own small corners of the world."

"Then it's up to you to educate them."

Bellini waved an impatient hand. "I'm not a magician, just a reasonably competent politician. And my job is not to argue the merits of the Jewish claims. That way lies certain defeat." He leaned forward. "We can only win if I create a mood of euphoria, a ground swell that concentrates on Fanti's well-known holiness, his austerity. In those first moments when the conclave feels its power, its history, the weight of its sacred obligations, that's when they can be influenced to choose a saint and worry about the practical consequences later."

The bishop tapped one knee thoughtfully. "You do yourself a disservice, Eminence. Not just competent, you are a brilliant politician. You're right, of course. It might work."

"It's the only thing that will work. If they have time to think about it, we lose."

"You didn't ask me here merely to tell me this. What can I do to help? Once the doors are locked behind you and your brother cardinals, I'm on the outside."

Bellini smiled. "This time, yes. But not next time, eh?"

"I hope not." That Longo lusted after a red hat was not news; he felt no need to linger over the subject. "We're talking about this time, about something that will happen a few days from now."

"Yes. And there is a role for you to play. The cardinals who come from a distance bring their own staffs, but they also have a number of temporary aides assigned to them while they're here. If those men can be carefully picked . . . if we know that they will have the name of Malachy Fanti on their lips. . . . If that is well handled, we can hope the newcomers will share in the fever that is mounting here in Rome."

"Ah, yes, I see." The bishop rose to go. "It's a big job. I'll have to get started immediately."

Bellini accompanied him to the door. "One last thing, when this is all over, when I propose your name to the new pope as his first cardinal, I hope you will do one more thing for me."

Longo studied the older man. "Yes, what?"

"Give up those damned cigarettes," Bellini said. "At least when we play chess. The smell is killing me."

Across the Vatican Gardens in Malachy Fanti's office the air was also blue with cigarette smoke. The monsignor who was the cardinal's private secretary had gone through half a pack in the last hour. All the while he was hanging on to the telephone, trying to find his boss, or explaining to other callers that yes, of course, His Eminence would be back in Rome by nightfall, or tomorrow morning at the latest. The problem was he didn't have the faintest idea if that was true, or where the cardinal was, or why. He wasn't at the Abbey of St. Louis, and they didn't know when he'd be back. The Englishman Hamish Durant might know something, but when he called England, he was told Durant was in France, and his housekeeper didn't know where he was staying. So the priest stared at the phone and tried to think of another way to locate Dom Malachy.

He had to reach him; he had to be sure that the cardinal knew the pope had died, that he'd be buried on Friday, that on Sunday the conclave of cardinals would begin. And most important, that the name of Malachy Fanti was everywhere being whispered as the almost certain choice to be the next Vicar of Christ on Earth.

There was someone else in Paris; the monsignor knew his boss had a longtime friend he spoke to often, but not the man's name or his address or telephone number. Dom Malachy was always very secretive about the man in Paris. So he was still debating the wisdom of searching the cardinal's private papers to see if he could find it. No, too risky. Too likely to infuriate the Benedictine. He'd wait another twenty-four hours. The secretary stubbed out his cigarette and lit another.

· · ·

The elderly doctor charged with caring for Malachy Fanti was not a happy man. Damned nuisance these foreigners. What were they doing in Kohlburg of all places? Yesterday the American young woman with migraine; today a Swiss priest who turned out to be a cardinal and have pneumonia. How had such people come to be his responsibility? He walked along the corridor toward the wards, and the busy hospital hummed around him.

Time was when he'd found this atmosphere exciting, stimulating. Now it burdened him, made demands on skills he'd half forgotten. He should have taken his wife's advice and retired last year. But there was no one to take his place, and he really didn't mind stitching the occasional wound or immunizing the children or jabbing antibiotics into the buttocks of the fevered. Of course, he no longer did prenatal. These days everybody in Kohlburg had a car. The women went to Strasbourg when they were pregnant. The young up-and-comers here in the city were the ones to be called when some farmer's wife went into labor at 3:00 A.M. Only these two foreigners, they hadn't gone to Strasbourg. They'd come to him, damn them.

Rather, damn that fancy new *auberge*. That must be the attraction the town had suddenly developed. Why else would such people be in his bailiwick? Apparently the woman was better, she hadn't required him today, but the cardinal, ah, that was something else.

He'd reached the head nurse's desk in men's medical. "Your patient is sleeping, Doctor." The nurse passed him the man's chart. He had to change his glasses to read it, and still, it required his holding it at arm's length and squinting. He could feel the nurse watching him. It wasn't his fault, damn her; it was the way people wrote nowadays. "We administered Nembutal ten minutes ago, as you instructed," she said.

"Yes. I see that. I can read." He put the chart back on her desk, not gently, and strode off down the corridor, conscious of keeping his back straight, not leaning over and shuffling like some half-dead old geezer.

It wasn't just the man's illness that worried him. It was his passport. Rather, passports. They'd found two among his things at the baker's. Ah! Jeanne really enjoyed that chance to paw through the stranger's belongings. One passport identified the priest as a Swiss, a Benedictine monk. The other was issued by Vatican City, festooned with special diplomatic stamps granting special diplomatic privileges, and said that he was a cardinal. The pictures in both were identical; there was no doubt the man was legitimately entitled to each of them. You didn't want to make any mistakes treating somebody with such credentials.

Considering all that documentation, they'd put him in a private room. The doctor stood by the bed a moment. There was an intravenous setup strapped to the man's thin arm, dripping fluid and antibiotics into his vein. The blue plastic prongs of an oxygen regulator were inserted into his nostrils and taped to his elegantly modeled nose. Sixty-six, according to the passports, but still exceedingly handsome.

The doctor was ten years older. He studied the apparently sleeping man, and his shoulders sagged, as if he felt the weight of that extra decade. Anyway, he'd never looked like that. Even illness didn't blur the thin, patrician features.

The man in the bed moaned, and his body jerked slightly. The doctor leaned forward and felt for his pulse. Weak but steady. Stop pissing with nerves every time the patient moaned. Everything was correctly done; accepted procedure had been followed. So a bad dream probably. Did sedated patients dream? If he'd ever known the answer, he'd forgotten it.

He glanced at his watch. Eleven-forty. If he left now, and if the Strasbourg traffic wasn't too bad, he'd be home for lunch. There was nothing more he could do here anyway. He'd eat his wife's good food, it was sure to be the remains of Sunday's *poule au pot,* and take a nap. Around four he'd return and check on his patient. And he'd make a decision about whether to call someone in Switzerland or at the Vatican.

Malachy was unaware of the doctor's presence or of his going. Vaguely he sensed the equipment attached to his body, but he was conscious of only one imperative. Within him. Fighting sleep. Alexandria. Yes, the Alexandria Testament. He grasped the thought, tried to hold it. It floated away. The Nembutal penetrated deeper into his brain; eventually it stilled all else.

At eleven thirty-five Sarah found a paperback book in English in the small sitting room reserved for the *auberge*'s overnight guests.

It was an old Dick Francis she hadn't read. She'd take it to her room; there was nothing else to do since Zelah said the train from Paris didn't arrive until three. She started up the stairs, wondering if she should wake Tim or let him sleep. She was just at the top when the pain and the voice and the static attacked.

The force almost knocked her backward; she grabbed the hand-rail and steadied herself. For brief seconds it was unendurable, and she cried aloud; then, with a suddenness almost as disconcerting, it was gone.

Tim appeared at the door of Zelah's room. He had a towel wrapped 'round his slim hips and another slung over his shoulder. He was holding a razor, and his face was masked in soap. "Sarah! I heard you shout. You okay?"

"Now, yes. Good morning."

"Good afternoon more like. Sorry I passed out. You're better today, aren't you?"

"Yes. Much better. Except every once in a while when it comes back. Only for a minute or so. That's what happened just now."

"It must be one hell of a pain to cause that reaction in less than a minute."

"It is," she admitted.

He eyed her speculatively, apparently suspecting that she knew more about whatever ailed her than she'd admitted. But he didn't press the point. He'd accepted that Sarah Myles and her private life were not to be part of his. "You and Zelah got on very well, didn't you? Right before I fell asleep you were starting to play just us girls together."

"Yes. I like her a lot." She climbed the last step and started down the hall, past a small window that overlooked the front entrance and the parking area. "She had to go back to Paris. I didn't know whether to wake you or let you sleep. I'm sorry about all this, Tim."

"Not to worry. I'll call the old man when I'm dressed, tell him not to expect me until tomorrow. Then I'll head for home. I take it you aren't planning to accompany me?"

"No, I can't. I have to wait for Jarib. We'll take a train back to Paris, I imagine."

"What time is the ugly American arriving?"

He said it without rancor, and she couldn't get angry. "I don't know. But Zelah says the first train from Paris gets in at three. There's another one tonight. He's sure to be on one or the other. I'm praying it's the first one," she added without looking at him. Why the hell had she admitted that? Because she couldn't keep all the joy locked up inside herself. When she opened her mouth, it spilled out.

Something attracted Tim's attention to the window behind Sarah, and he glanced over her shoulder. "Forget the train, love. Unless I miss my guess, that elegant Peugeot down there is delivering His Lordship just now."

She turned. It couldn't be Jarib, she wasn't ready. Then, overcome by excitement: "Yes, oh, yes, that's Jarib!"

"Sarah . . ." Tim's voice halted her dash down the stairs. "Just thought of something. The bastard's consistent anyway. It's Monday."

The parking lot of the Auberge California was covered in a thick layer of pale, pea-size gravel. It was puddled with rain. Vita avoided the worst of the muddy lakes and brought the car to within inches of the bright green canopy that stretched along the walkway to an elaborately carved oak door. Jarib glanced at it. Closed tight. And no other cars in the section of the lot he could see. "Doesn't look like there's anyone here. You're sure this is the place?"

"I am sure."

She hadn't moved, and the motor was still running. "Are you coming in?" Jarib asked.

"No, only to bring you here are my instructions."

He turned and held out his hand; she shook it firmly. "Thank you for everything, especially the delicious lunch," he said.

"Good luck, monsieur."

His bag was on the floor in the back. Jarib swung it and himself out of the car. Almost instantly the Peugeot accelerated and pulled away. He stood for a moment, staring at the door, praying to some God in whom he professed to have no interest that Sarah was behind it, that she was unharmed. And then that same door opened, and she was flying down the walk into his arms.

They stood thus for long moments, oblivious of the driving rain from which the canopy scarcely protected them, to anyone who might be watching from inside the *auberge* or the road. "Jarib, Jarib

. . . It's been so awful. Even after you called, I couldn't make myself believe it. . . . How did you get here so soon? Zelah said the train didn't come until three, so I was waiting till later to go to the station. . . ."

"I got a ride from Paris," he said. Then there was no more talk. He tasted her, drank her in, moved his lips across her cheeks, her forehead, her hair. She was trembling in his arms. "It's all right, Sarah. It's all right. I'm here. We're together. It's going to be all right." And finally: "Come, can we go inside? You're getting soaked."

"Yes, inside." She led him up the path and through the door, their bodies still pressed together, hands clasped tight enough to hurt had it not felt so good. "The restaurant belongs to a friend, Zelah Tench. She's an Israeli, but she's lived in France for years and America before that. I can't introduce you to her or her partner. Neither of them is here at the moment. But there's Tim Durant; he's Ivy's partner. He's upstairs getting dressed. The *auberge* is closed today, so there isn't any real lunch, but I can get you something if you're hungry—"

"Ssh," he told her, smiling gently. "You can tell me all this later."

She took a deep breath; nerves were making her sound manic. Then, in a moment of sudden, total relaxation of tension, she put her arms around his neck and laid her cheek against his chest. He wore a thick knitted sweater, and the unique, pungent smell of wet wool overlaid the beloved familiar smell of him. "Oh, Jarib," she whispered. "Thank God."

He held her very tight; for a few seconds neither of them spoke or moved. Until a voice broke in. "Sorry to interrupt. You must be the famous Jarib, I'm Tim Durant."

Sarah pulled away, but only just, and she kept hold of one of Jarib's hands. Tim shook the other one. He was dressed in the fawn-colored camel's hair jacket and dark slacks. A raincoat was slung over his arm and he was carrying a suitcase.

"I'm on my way," he said. "Phoned through to Calais, there's a ferry at seven this evening. Plenty of time, no reason I shouldn't make it. *Mirabile dictu,* the old man's not home. So I didn't have to listen to a diatribe. Let me know what you want to do about your things at Tiverton, won't you, Sarah? Perhaps you and Jarib can come and stay a day or two." It was obvious, at least to her, that he found the prospect appalling.

"Thank you, Tim. We'll see. But listen, you shouldn't travel on an empty stomach. There's fresh bread in the kitchen. And I can make you a couple of eggs."

"Not to worry. I'll eat in Strasbourg. You're staying on here?"

"I'm not quite sure. Zelah said we could. It will be fully staffed again tomorrow."

"You're all set then," he said. "So ta, love. Happy landings, or whatever you Yanks say." And to Jarib: "Nice to have met you."

"Good-bye," Jarib murmured.

Sarah didn't say anything. At the door Tim turned 'round and grinned at her. "Thanks for letting me have a go," he said. Then, with a final wave, he was gone.

"I expected you to look terrible," Jarib said. "You don't; you're beautiful." He put his big hands on either side of her face, pushing her hair back so he could study her. "A little pale maybe, but beautiful."

Sarah covered his hands with hers. "I knew everything was going to be all right once you got here; I hung on to that."

"No pain now? No headache?"

"No, not since early this morning. Except for two very brief attacks."

He bent his head and kissed her mouth softly; they didn't cling, both were waiting, and suddenly a bit tentative. "How about the static?" he asked when the kiss ended.

"It's there whenever the woman tries to speak. But at the moment they've both shut up." They were still in the foyer. Around them everything was silent, deserted. "We don't have to stand here," Sarah said. "There's a little lounge in there." She gestured toward her left. "Or I can get you something to eat if you're hungry."

"Not for food," Jarib said.

She smiled at him, a grave, serious smile, and took his hand, leading him up the stairs. They went into her room, and Sarah closed and locked the door—and suddenly they were both embarrassed; they could hardly look at each other.

"Look," Jarib said. "There's no hurry. We've got a lot to talk about."

Sarah started to agree, but instead she laughed. "I don't want to talk; I've been talking all night." Her voice grew serious, and Jarib detected a hint of strain. "It's only been a week, but I want . . . to know you again."

He took a step forward and unbuttoned the jacket of the purple suit, slipping it from her shoulders and tossing it onto a chair. She wore a pale lilac blouse with tiny silk-covered buttons; his broad fingers fumbled when he tried to undo them. Sarah did it herself. She shrugged out of the blouse, letting it fall. She didn't look at him, her eyes were closed, but she reached behind and freed the hooks of her bra and took it off.

Jarib put his hands beneath her breasts, drawing them toward himself. Sarah took one long breath. His touch was as she'd imagined it a thousand times this long week, most recently in the bath this morning. "I love you so very much," he said. He bent his head and kissed the creamy mounds of flesh, slowly tonguing first one rosy aureole, then the other.

She ran her fingers through his hair, reminding herself of the way it curled slightly at the nape of his neck, pressing his face closer to her skin. Then she unzipped the skirt and let it fall. It was lined with heavy taffeta; she wore no slip, just panty hose. Jarib peeled them down her hips and thighs, his fingers tracing a line from her waist to her ankles.

"No fair," Sarah said softly. "You have the advantage of me, Dr. Baraak."

For a second he didn't know what she meant; then he stripped hurriedly, anxious now, needing her. He remembered how his hands could almost span her waist and discovered that they still did. He pulled her close, but Sarah stiffened slightly. Instantly Jarib let her go. "What's wrong?"

She shook her head, the dark, heavy hair moving almost like a screen across her face. "Nothing's wrong. Only I want to lie down beside you." That was the way she had dreamed it over and over; that was the way she wanted it now.

They moved to the bed, together turning back the spread to reveal sheets of the violet-sprigged cotton that was the trademark of the *auberge*. She'd made the bed herself this morning, no chambermaid on Mondays. Impulsively Sarah had sprayed the sheets with her favorite perfume, Anais Anais, feeling incredibly wanton and not at all like a girl from Sacred Heart High School in Ipswich.

Now the scent rose to meet them, and unthinkingly Sarah giggled. She looked up quickly, to see if he'd misunderstood, if somehow she'd offended him, turned him off. Jarib only asked what the joke was. When she told him he laughed too. And for both of them that shared humor evaporated all the sudden strangeness. They were themselves again; Jarib and Sarah, not just lovers, friends.

They lay down, kissing, hugging, touching, tasting. Finally, ever so gently, Jarib put his hand between her thighs.

Sarah moaned with delight. "Oh, God . . ." It was a prayer of thanksgiving.

He did things he knew she liked, did them slowly and with concentration. He could feel the heat of surging blood warming her moist flesh, and she was trembling. Still he waited.

Until: "Now, darling. Now."

A violent gust of wind drove a sheet of rain against the window. For a long time that sound was the last either of them knew of any world outside each other.

Rita woke at twenty to eight. Almost an hour past her usual time. And she felt heavy-headed and still tired. The legacy of the interrupted night. She glanced over at the other bed. It was empty. Damn! Frank must have gone down to the plant after all. He just wouldn't listen to reason.

She swung her legs over the side and stood up. She'd have to hurry if she were going to be at the shop by nine-thirty, and she wanted to make Frank a good hot breakfast before she left. He'd be back in half an hour if he followed his regular pattern.

Rita was brushing her teeth when the phone rang. She answered it with the toothbrush still clutched in her hand.

"Rita, listen, it's Ben. Now don't get excited, but something's happened."

"Oh, my God! It's Frank, isn't it? What's wrong?"

"His heart, they think," her nephew-in-law said. "The ambulance just left, and I'm on my way to the hospital. I'll come by and get you. Five minutes."

"Yes . . . oh, God . . ."

"Look, get a grip on yourself. It may not be too bad. The ambulance was here in five minutes. They've got all kinds of emergency equipment now. He's getting the best possible care. Just hang in, Rita. I'm on my way."

Ten minutes later they were in Ben's car heading south. "Why'd they take him to Beverly? Gloucester's closer," she said. Her words came out sharply through pinched lips. And she was very pale.

Ben reached over and patted her hand. "Beverly's better set up for coronary patients. That's why they put all that stuff in the ambulance. So they can drive the extra fifteen minutes without doing any damage. You remember, there was a big story about it in the papers last year."

She didn't remember. She hadn't read the story. Rita had spent many years avoiding any thought of heart attacks. Ever since Frank had that small stroke and his health started failing. "Gloucester is closer," she insisted stubbornly.

Ben changed the subject. "I called Dr. Matthews. He's meeting us at the hospital."

She nodded. "Where did it happen?"

"On the loading dock. He was watching the trucks leave, like always. There was some argument about a new route." He kept his eyes on the road and didn't look at her. "I told him not to worry about it, that I had everything under control, but you know how he is."

The new route involved half a dozen grocery stores in Lowell and Methuen. It was territory untapped until now; Myles's Bread had previously not been distributed west of Lawrence. Ben both secured the accounts and arranged for them to be serviced by a private delivery company. "You should've bought another truck, goddammit!" Frank had said when the brown van pulled up and loaded four pallets of sliced bread in blue wrappers. "Jesus, Ben, can't you count? We sure as hell can afford another truck."

There had been no opportunity for Ben to say again that a new truck was an unnecessary drain on profits. Frank made his statement, turned red in the face, and began clutching his chest. Then

403

he fell down. Ben had frozen for a moment, staring at his uncle in horror. It was somebody else who dialed 999 and asked for the ambulance.

"It's going to be okay," he said now, reassuring himself as much as Rita. "You'll see. They can do fantastic things these days. Uncle Frank'll be good as new. Probably sitting up in bed by the time we get there."

He wasn't, of course. He lay white and silent, half obscured by tubes and machinery, in a bed in the intensive care unit. They had to gaze at him through a window.

Rita stood and looked for five long minutes. Until Dr. Matthews came up to her. He put his arm around her shoulders. "I've just talked to the man in charge; they're doing everything they can. But he's very weak, Rita. He's not been well since the stroke. You have to face up to that."

"What man in charge?" she demanded. "I thought you were Frank's doctor."

"Of course I am. But I'm not a coronary specialist. We want him to have the best. As soon as Ben phoned me, I contacted a colleague. He agreed to take the case. You'll meet him in a moment." Rita shook her head, as if refusing to see the strange doctor, but Matthews ignored her. He was familiar with all the irrational responses called forth by serious illness. "Where's Sarah? Maybe you'd better let her know."

Funny, she hadn't thought of Sarah once since Ben's call came. Only she and Frank, that's all that was important. The two of them. Together. The way they had been for thirty-one years. "She's in Europe," Rita said dully.

"Any way to get in touch with her?" Matthews persisted.

"Yes, I suppose so. I'll call Ivy, her boss."

The doctor patted her shoulder reassuringly. "Good, you do that as soon as we're finished here."

Finished. What did that mean? How could they be finished until Frank was out of that bed, sleeping beside her in his own house? Or in a box in the ground. The thought came unbidden, and she couldn't control a single sob.

Matthews tightened his grip on her shoulders. A much younger man in a casually cut tweed suit and a striped pink shirt strode toward them. His only badge of office was a stethoscope poking out of one patch pocket. "Here's the man we're waiting for," Matthews said.

Despite her fear and the irrational anger, Rita rose to the occasion. She managed a small smile while they shook hands.

She called Ivy from the hospital, and an hour later Ivy called her back. "God, Mrs. Myles, I'm sorry, but I'm not having any luck."

"Rita," the older woman said automatically. She'd told Ivy plenty of times to call her Rita.

"I got through to the Durants' house okay, but there's no one there. Some woman answered the phone. The housekeeper. She says Hamish, that's Tim's father, is away. She doesn't know when he'll be back. Tim phoned a little earlier, but he's in France. On his way back to England."

"Tim is your partner, isn't he?"

"My colleague. Sarah's working with him on the trip."

"So she must be with this Tim now, right?"

"I'm sure she is." Ivy tried to speak slowly. Rita's voice made it apparent that she was under terrible strain. "That's just the point; they're traveling, in transit right now between France and England. I can't think of any way to reach them. Unless you want me to call the American Embassy in Paris. Maybe they have some way to find them."

"No, no. Don't do that. I don't want to alarm Sarah."

"How's your husband?"

"He's holding his own," Rita said. That's what they kept telling her. Mr. Myles is holding his own. What did it mean? What was his own? What was her own, for that matter? Frank. He was hers, and now death was trying to take him away.

"That sounds encouraging," Ivy said. "I'm so glad. Look, I've left a message for Tim or Sarah or Hamish to call me immediately. Whoever the housekeeper hears from first. I'm sure it won't be long."

"Fine, that's fine, Ivy. Thank you."

"Will you be at home?"

"No," Rita said firmly. "Here at the hospital. They have rooms for relatives." They wouldn't have gotten her to leave even if they didn't. Doubtless the hospital knew that, which was why the support system for families got funded. "You can call me at this same number," she told Ivy. "The phone's right beside my bed."

When she hung up, Rita stared at the room they'd assigned her. God, it was awful. You'd think they'd do something to cheer it up, make people feel better when they were as miserable and worried as she was now. Maybe the garden club should donate some plants. A little green would help. She'd thought everyone knew that nowadays.

That's what made her think of her plants at home. She wasn't going to leave here until Frank was better. The plants would need watering. Milly Katz, of course. Milly would see to it. In Ipswich people knew what being a good neighbor meant. Even Milly. Years ago, when the Katzes moved in, Rita had expected them to be different because they were Jewish, but Milly was a wonderful neighbor. She'd call and tell her about Frank, and Milly would get the spare key from under the mat and take care of everything. It would be one less thing to worry about.

In New York on East Sixtieth Street at half past nine in the morning the cold made a mockery of a golden sun in a bright blue sky. Ten days ago it still felt like summer; today winter had arrived, and it was freezing. The man sitting and reading a newspaper in a parked car wanted to turn on the heater, but he couldn't. It would attract attention if he waited a long time with the motor running. Morrie shivered and wrapped his woolen scarf tighter around his neck. Was this the kind of day they sang about? "Autumn in New York . . ."

In Sam Stein's apartment it wasn't cold; it was too damn hot. The central heating was blasting away and ignoring whatever adjustments he made to the thermostat. He'd have to speak to the maintenance man. But not today. Today he had other things in mind. "Your people are from here originally?" he asked Dov.

"Yes, my mother and father were both born in New York. Their parents were immigrants. I think the Silbermans came from Germany; I don't know about my dad's people."

"There were plenty of Levys on the Lower East Side when I was a kid, but they spelled it with a *y*."

They were drinking coffee in Sam's tiny kitchen. He'd prevailed on Dov to spend the night; so far neither of them had spoken of their plans for the day.

"Spelling it my way is Hebrew," Dov explained. "Probably they changed it after they went to Palestine."

"You think it's possible any of your relatives are still alive? Your grandparents would be pretty old, but what about aunts and uncles, cousins maybe?"

Dov shook his head. "I don't know, and I wouldn't have any idea how to find out. To tell you the truth, I looked in the phone book the first day I got here. Just out of curiosity. But they're both common names. There are hundreds of them. My folks broke all their ties with the family. As I told you."

"Yeah. Too bad. People do crazy things. They have a fight and they nurse the grudge. They forget how alone they're going to be someday."

Dov knew the older man was speaking of himself. Stein had already said there was no one except Rhonda, and she wasn't a blood relative. "What do you do all day now that you're retired?" he asked gently.

Sam made a noise somewhere between a grunt and a laugh. "I shouldn't tell you. You'll think I'm crazy. I walk. Around the old neighborhood. It's all different now, nothing like when I was a kid. Still . . ."

Dov drank the last of his coffee—Americans made it so weak it almost wasn't worth the effort—and set down his cup. "You have something planned for today?"

"Nah, nothing. You?"

Dov laughed. "I'm not exactly my own man, as I explained. Whether Beklem has something planned for me I couldn't say."

"Screw him. You know what I think? I think the old cocksucker just sent you over here to put us in touch. Somehow or other he must've put the screws on Rhonda and got her to be the patsy. But this guy Beklem's gotta be behind it; otherwise how would she have known you after so many years?"

"I don't know. But if you're right, why? What was it supposed to accomplish?"

"That I don't know. But I'm working on it. Anyway, tell you

what, let's you and me go downtown. I'll show you where your folks came from. All different, like I said. But you're a man of imagination, you'll get the flavor."

"I'd like that," Dov said.

Morrie spotted them as soon as they left the building and turned east toward Second Avenue. He made note of the exact time, ten forty-five. They hailed a cab, and he followed to where it dropped them off, the corner of Houston and Broadway. Stein and Levi set out on foot and he trailed them for about fifteen minutes, but after that there was no need for further surveillance. "They're making a sentimental journey," he told Beklem.

The line was full of static; Yitzhak had to ask him to repeat the words.

"Sentimental. The way they're acting it's obvious, Stein's being nostalgic and taking Levi along."

"Ah, yes. I see. Listen, there's something I want you to do." He gave the instructions slowly and carefully and made the man in New York repeat them to be sure the bad connection hadn't obliterated anything. Finally he was satisfied. "Yes, that's exactly what I want. Thank you."

In Paris Yitzhak hung up and trudged back to the kitchen. A dozen times he'd promised himself he'd get the telephone company to put an extension in here next to his chair. But he never did it. Perverse. Maybe he secretly liked walking back and forth, wearing a path in the already shabby carpet. So much of his work was done by phone. It was ephemeral, impermanent; what was there to show for endless conversations with people you couldn't see? At least the marks on the rug were hard evidence of his labors.

He sat down in the black reclining chair and closed his eyes. It wasn't yet five o'clock, and already there had been over a dozen calls. Important calls, two of them from America. There was the man in New York and, before that, Milly Katz. Her call had been unexpected.

"I wasn't sure," she'd told him. "About calling you, I mean. Maybe it's not important."

"Everything's important, Milly dear. I appreciate your conscientiousness. What's happened?"

And she'd explained that Frank Myles had had a heart attack. "Rita said he was doing okay, but I called the hospital myself afterwards. I said I was a sister-in-law, and they told me he's on the critical list. That doesn't sound so okay to me."

"Not to me either," Yitzhak agreed.

"And Rita says she's trying to get in touch with Sarah, let her know what's happened. Only she hasn't been able to reach her."

There was a pause. Yitzhak didn't say anything. He'd become accustomed to these pauses of Milly's. They always preceded a question.

"Yitzhak, listen, if you know where Sarah is, maybe you could see that she calls her mother? I mean, it's serious after all. I know there's a lot I don't understand about Sarah and why you're interested in her and why she's important for us. But Frank maybe is dying, and he's her father, so after all . . ."

They kept him human, these few Americans that over the years he'd inveigled into working for him as well as giving him money. They could be as ruthless as Attila the Hun, but then they'd come up with some utterly ingenuous idea, suggesting that whatever it was was as important as the work, might perhaps take precedence over it.

He'd made ambiguous but reassuring remarks to Milly. She responded by saying that Harry had collected five thousand dollars from various people and was sending it in the usual way.

When they hung up, Yitzhak hadn't decided what to do. Fortunately a half hour passed between Milly's call and the one from the man in New York. That gave him time to make up his mind.

It was an enormous gamble. The one thing he'd never before dared to do. In a way he'd always thought of it as his secret weapon. But he was reluctant to use it, because if he did and it didn't work, there wasn't anything else. Well, too late for that now. He was committed.

Yitzhak returned to the living room and engaged in yet another series of telephone calls. When he'd finished, it was after six. He went into the bedroom and began packing.

Jarib's arm encircled her, Sarah's head lay on his chest, their limbs twined like vines; it was the best of moments, the pellucid afterglow. "I've got to tell you about Lenore," Jarib said. "She's Tom Lasky's kid sister; we were married in 1970."

It didn't take long in the telling; Sarah's luminous travel clock said six-thirty when he finished speaking. She'd said nothing during the recital, and a few more moments passed before she spoke. When she did, the comment sounded banal in her own ears, but it was exactly what she felt: "How god-awful for both of you."

"Worse for her, obviously."

Sarah sat up. "No, I don't think so. That's not just prejudice, darling. Lenore escaped to never-never land, that's tragic, but not as awful, not in the way I meant. You're the one who's carried all the"—she hesitated, searching for the words—"all the burden in reality."

"Perhaps. I can't assess it any longer. Old Nate Summers put it in perspective for me. I can't do anything more for her, I've got to live—we're entitled to a life."

"Yes."

And since there was nothing more to say about it, not here and now, they were quiet for a while. They dozed, woke, and made love again. Then, sometime after eight, Jarib announced he was starving.

Charles had returned. Sarah found him in the kitchen, poring over a menu list. "How was Basel?"

"Very Swiss, which means sturdy and efficient."

"Listen," Sarah said, "A friend's come from America."

He grinned at her. "Zelah left me a note with all the gorgeous details. Happy?"

"Mmm, very. We want to go into Strasbourg to eat. Suggest someplace wonderful."

He glanced at the clock. "Well, you can probably get to town by nine, so most kitchens will still be open. And it's Monday night, always slow. Hang on a minute, the best place in Strasbourg is usually booked solid weeks ahead, but the owner's a friend. Wonderful old guy with marvelous stories to tell. I'll give him a call."

He went to the phone hanging on the wall. Three minutes later he returned. "You're all set. Here's the address." He wrote the information on a scrap of paper. "Shall I call you a cab?"

"Please."

"Will do. I only hope you aren't too lovesick to appreciate what you eat. Three Michelin stars. Put on your most reverential attitude."

410

The rain had ended; the night seemed fresh and washed. The cab driver dropped them on a corner by an alley leading to the cathedral square. Too many one-ways to bring them to the door, he explained. They couldn't miss it.

They did, of course. They wandered the narrow cobbled streets for five minutes before at last spotting the mansard-tiled roof of what had once been a guild hall. CHEZ BECKER, a discreet sign proclaimed. The kind of place that didn't need to scream about its existence.

Inside, there were old stuccoed walls with blackened half timbers and swayed roof beams from which hung a collection of antique copper pots. The only other decorations were the white linen cloths and brown pottery tableware. Every chair was occupied by someone in some stage of serious eating. An elderly man approached them. "The American friends of Charles, no?" he asked in passable English.

They admitted to the distinction, and he led them to a table that seemed to have been specially set up between the cash desk and a display of fresh local fish. "I hope this is satisfactory. There really was not a free place, but Charles said you would not object, that you came to eat."

And eat they did. The man, who said his name was Emile Becker and that he was the owner of the restaurant, didn't give them a menu. "Let me choose for you," he said smiling, and Jarib and Sarah were content to do just that. First there were bowls of Alsace's famous Matelote, a soup made with freshwater fish from the river Ill. The bowls were whisked away, and a broad, round dish appeared. Cabbage and carrots and leeks and turnips and potatoes. The homeliest of vegetables, made extraordinary by the fact that each was cooked and seasoned to perfection.

When they didn't think they could eat any more, Emile returned, followed by a fat old waitress. "I do not bring you choucroute garnie; that you can get anywhere in Alsace," he said. Smiling broadly, the waitress presented a platter of fresh foie gras simply sautéed in butter and sliced exquisitely thin with a pungent sauce of watercress on the side. "Only a little of the sauce you must use," he warned. "To cut the richness of the liver, not disguise it. And with this you must drink a gewürztraminer." He removed the bottle of Riesling, poured their new wine, and left.

"Jarib, isn't it time you told me how you knew where I was and that I needed you?"

"I've been trying to decide how to explain. Telling you about Lenore was easier."

"Just the facts, sir," she said softly.

"Okay. Last night, at least I think it was last night, I'm thoroughly confused about time at the moment. Anyway, Sunday evening I was sitting in Rowley, waiting for it to be Monday. I'd tried to reach you at the number Ivy gave me, the one in England. A man there told me he didn't know where you were, but that you'd return late Monday. I was at my desk, pretending to work. And all of a sudden I heard your voice. Calling me. You sounded desperate."

"A paranormal experience? You?"

"I don't know. And I wasn't prepared to say that it was. It was too easy to assume that because I wanted so desperately to talk to you, I imagined the whole thing." He took a long drink of the rich, fruity wine and refilled both their glasses.

"Go on," Sarah encouraged.

"About an hour later a man called me from Paris. He said his name was Yitzhak Beklem." He looked at her questioningly.

"Never heard of him," Sarah said.

"Well, he'd heard of you. He knew where you were and how to reach you. And he told me you were in deep trouble and I was the only one who could help."

She drew in her breath sharply. "But how did he know all that?"

"I don't know. And I didn't waste a lot of time asking questions." He was drawing rings on the cloth with his glass. Sarah put her hand over his. Jarib gripped it for a moment. "This Beklem was very persuasive. He pushed all the right buttons. Said he knew that you'd consulted me and why. And it was obvious he knew a lot more about us, our relationship, I mean."

"And that's why you came?"

"Not only that. I wouldn't have assumed you'd welcome me in the role of white knight after I'd been such an ass, except for the rest of what he said." He told her about the theory of an attack by another mind. "Sounds pretty farfetched, sitting here with you perfectly fine. But theoretically it's possible. And Beklem claimed that whoever was doing the attacking was trained in mental prayer and meditation techniques. It could be true, Sarah. You said it was static, like jamming. That would fit."

They still held hands. She withdrew hers and toyed with her knife and fork. The sublime foie gras had ceased to attract her. "It's horrible. And I can't believe it. Who would do such a thing? And why? I don't know a soul in Alsace except for Charles and Zelah. It can't be either of them."

"No reason it has to be. According to Beklem"—he closed his eyes, trying to quote exactly—"you're part of something much bigger than you realize."

"That sounds like the corniest bullshit going."

"Yeah, it does, doesn't it? But when he said it, I believed it."

"He must be something if he can fool a pro like you."

Jarib hesitated. "I'm not prepared to say he was fooling, darling. He had too many facts, knew too much. And somebody working for him met me at the airport and drove me here. Everything was laid on and organized down to the last detail."

"But if it's true, why am I better?"

"I don't know. Maybe because your mind bested his, the attacker, I mean. Or because he left the area—physical proximity does seem to matter in the documented case histories of this kind of thing."

"You mean it is something you know about? It's been studied?"

"Yes, not by me directly. At least not in this context. But three years ago I spent a lot of time in the Caribbean investigating some voodoo claims. Essentially that's the same. The dolls and the pins and the other fetishes mean nothing. It's mind on mind, and a lifetime's worth of fear and belief."

Sarah was glad when the waitress appeared and took away their plates. She needed time to assimilate the whole crazy idea. It seemed absurd. Emile appeared, bearing yet another platter. This one held a great round brioche, its plump topknot askew and something that smelled heavenly peeking from the interior.

"I can't possibly eat any more," Sarah protested.

"But you must, mademoiselle. It is our specialty." The brioche had been hollowed out and filled with an ethereal pale golden soufflé. Jarib had no compunctions, he accepted an enormous serving.

"Please, only a quarter of that for me," Sarah insisted. The waitress complied, Emile hovered, Sarah took an experimental mouth-

413

ful, then paused. "Manna for the gods," she pronounced at last. "What is it?"

"The brioche you know; the soufflé is made with our little yellow mirabelle plums," Emile explained. While he spoke, he poured small glasses of a darker gold liqueur. "This, too, we call mirabelle. *Eau de vie* made from the same plums. It is my weakness." He took a small snifter for himself and raised it, bowing his head. "*A votre santé, mes jeunes amis,* to your good health. Perhaps after the coffee you will allow me to show you something of interest."

Forty minutes later he led them through the now half-empty restaurant to a set of stairs leading to the cellar. It was lined with racks of wine, almost all in the tall pale green bottles called flutes which were the traditional containers of the wines of Alsace.

"This section was built only ten years ago. When the old wine cellar became too small," he explained. "It's the old one I want to show you." He opened a heavy door and turned on a light.

There was a brass plaque on the wall; it was inscribed in French and in English. "In this room an American pilot was hidden from the Nazis for four years during the occupation of Strasbourg, while the Gestapo dined nightly in the dining room above."

"It was our way of protesting, you see," Emile said softly. "The entire staff was in on it, the whole town practically. He wasn't just a pilot, he was a Jew. No one ever gave him away."

Sarah and Jarib were silent. There was nothing they could say that wouldn't sound bathetic. "An American woman wrote a book about it some years ago," the Frenchman said. "But I don't think it was what you call a best-seller. We receive many American tourists at Chez Becker, and no one has ever asked about the wine cellar. I thought, because you are friends of Charles . . ."

"Thank you," Jarib said. "Thank you very much." And to Sarah: "That's crazy, too, isn't it? But it happened."

Sarah nodded her head.

It was midnight when they returned to the *auberge*. Charles was waiting for them in the foyer. "This arrived twenty minutes ago. I phoned Chez Becker, but you'd already left." He handed Sarah a telegram.

She glanced at Jarib, then ripped open the pale blue envelope. "Come home at once," she read. "Father very ill." It was unsigned.

Fourteen

TUESDAY, NOVEMBER 27

Frank Myles died at eleven forty-eight Tuesday morning, twelve minutes before Sarah got to the hospital. She found her mother sitting by his bed, holding his lifeless hand. Rita didn't turn when a nurse opened the door.

"Your daughter's here, Mrs. Myles." The voice was hushed, but the reverential tone didn't come through as real. They saw too much of death, these people; it was just another of the day's less pleasant events.

"Oh, Mom . . ." Sarah went to Rita, ignoring the small, still figure in the bed. When she put her arms around her mother, it was like embracing a rag doll. "I came as soon as I could; it was after midnight when I got the cable. We took the first plane we could get, but it just wasn't quick enough. . . ." A stream of words to excuse the inexcusable. She had left her mother alone in the only hours when parent genuinely needed child, when the symbol of continuity offered both consolation and meaning.

Rita Myles didn't take her eyes from her dead husband's face.

Already it was waxen and masklike, a caricature. She disengaged her shoulders from Sarah's arm and leaned forward, kissing the stretched blue lips of the corpse. "Good-bye for now, honey," she whispered.

Sarah choked back a sob, but silent tears ran down her cheeks. "I'm so sorry I wasn't here earlier."

Rita acknowledged her daughter's presence at last. "It's okay. Really. Nothing you could have done anyway. A massive coronary, that's what they said." Her voice sounded more normal with every word. Rita in control, cheerful, looking on the bright side. Rita being herself. "He wouldn't have been happy living with a heart condition or anything like that anyway. I'm going to get the nurse now. You want to kiss him good-bye?"

Dutifully Sarah bent and kissed her father's forehead. Only it wasn't his. It was no part of him, this thing lying in the bed. Where had he gone then, the man she'd known and loved? "Did he have a priest?" Not because she wanted to know, but because she knew instinctively what the answer would be, and that the telling would comfort Rita.

"Of course. During the night. It's not the last rites anymore, they call it the Sacrament of the Sick now. It was beautiful. Daddy wasn't conscious, but I made all the responses. And this morning he came to for a few minutes. Just when the priest was coming 'round with Holy Communion. He was right out there in the hall, and here was Daddy with his eyes open and everything. So I ran out and got Father, and Daddy took a tiny little crumb of the blessed sacrament on his tongue. And you know what, he looked so happy and peaceful just then. Wasn't that a miracle?" Rita's face glowed.

"That's wonderful, Mom. A real miracle." Sarah meant every word. The look on her mother's face was miracle enough to satisfy any skeptic. But it didn't last. She crumpled a bit, seemed to withdraw.

"I'll get the nurse now. They said I could have half an hour with him. But there's no reason to wait anymore, is there?"

"No reason."

They rang, and a nurse came with two orderlies. The mourners were shepherded gently out the door. Jarib was waiting for them. He went to Rita first. "I'm so sorry, Mrs. Myles."

"Yes, thank you."

Sarah knew from her tone that she hadn't recognized him. Perhaps because he looked so tired. Two transatlantic flights in thirty-six hours had taken their toll. "Jarib was with me in France when the cable came," she explained. "You remember Jarib Baraak, don't you?"

"Yes, sure," Rita said. But there was no thought behind the words. Sarah and Jarib flanked the older woman as they left the hospital, but it was as if she were not there.

Milly Katz got word of Frank's death almost immediately. She'd been calling the hospital every hour since early morning. At a few minutes past noon they told her he'd passed away peacefully and his widow and daughter were with him. "Her daughter's there, too? Sarah Myles, you're sure?"

It was a small hospital, and news the least bit out of the ordinary traveled fast. "Oh, yes, I'm sure. She flew in from Paris. Got here just a little while ago."

Thank God, Yitzhak had come through. Milly hung up the kitchen phone, tied on an apron, and pushed up the sleeves of her sweater. You could call it a wake or sitting *shivah,* it made no difference. Death was death and mourning was mourning, and since time began, good neighbors had been responding in like manner to the event.

Two hours later she carried a large wicker hamper across the road, went 'round to the kitchen door, and let herself into the house with the spare key. Rita and Sarah were already there. She'd seen the taxi arrive half an hour ago. There was a man with them. She couldn't be sure, she'd only seen him that one time at the New Year's party, but she was fairly certain it was Jarib Baraak. The man was in the kitchen making coffee when she went in.

"Hi, I'm Milly from across the street. I brought a few things."

He held out his hand. "Jarib Baraak, Sarah's—" Sarah's what? "A friend," he finished up.

Milly smiled at him. "I know, we met last New Year's Day." She put down her basket and nudged him away from the counter. "Here, let me do that. You look exhausted."

"Frankly, I am. Sarah and I flew in from Paris. Left this morning. At least I think it was this morning. I'm not quite sure. My internal clock's gone haywire."

"Yeah, just like when Harry and I went to Israel a couple of years ago. All that time-change business, somebody ought to do something about it."

Jarib turned away to hide his grin. When he turned back, he saw that she'd deftly reorganized the tray he'd been fixing and added some sliced cake. "Did you bring that? How kind of you."

"No, not the cake." She laughed lightly. "Rita Myles is the best baker in New England. You don't bring cake into this house, even at a time like this. It was in the breadbox over there. I just brought a few casseroles. Where are they?"

He was startled for a moment; the food she'd brought was on the counter. Then: "Oh, you mean Sarah and her mother; they went up to shower and change. I thought I'd take the coffee upstairs."

"Good idea. You do that. And if you don't mind my saying so, you should take a little nap, you look awful."

He put his hand to his cheek and felt the stubble of beard. "I'm sure I do. Sorry. It will help if I can shave."

"A nap first," Milly said firmly. "Go on now. Tell them I'm here and not to worry. I'll take care of everything. People will start coming any minute, but they shouldn't come down until they feel up to it."

They both heard a car pull up out front, confirming her judgment. Jarib took the tray and disappeared from the kitchen, and Milly went to the front door.

It was Ben Pollock and his wife and her mother. Ben looked like hell. "They're just getting washed and changed," Milly explained. "Go get yourself a drink, Ben. And check to be sure there's enough liquor and things, will you?" She kissed Ben's wife and his mother, the dead man's sister. "What can I say, you two? I'm sorry." And without missing a beat: "Can you give me a hand getting things ready?"

The two women accompanied her to the kitchen, gratefully allowing the stiff condolence thank-yous they'd feel so awkward uttering to die on their lips. People needed to be given jobs to do, orders to follow. That had been the same since time began, too. Milly understood.

By three the house was full of people, swirling in eddying waves around Sarah and Rita, rippling out to encompass in their embarrassed expressions of sympathy the sister and in-laws and cousins and nephew. What the hell did you say? What difference did words make anyway?

Milly surveyed the throng from the door between the living and dining rooms. From this vantage point she could keep an eye on both the ashtrays and the food. Ben was handling the bar; she didn't have to worry about that. The dishwasher was going in the kitchen. Rita's cleaning woman had come an hour earlier. The dishwasher would run repeatedly for many hours now, but the cleaning woman was competent. Milly didn't have to worry about that either.

Her glance settled on Ben, pouring a beer for the baker who'd been the first employee Frank Myles ever hired. Ben looked terrible. She was surprised at how hard he was taking his uncle's death. She'd not have thought there was that much affection between them. Oh, well, you never knew about people, did you? But usually they did the right thing. Like coming here this afternoon. It didn't matter that there was nothing they could say. It was not being alone; that's what helped Sarah and Rita. Having to respond to the greetings and the talk. You're alive, he's dead, but you're not. That's what it was all about. And it always worked. Always had, always would.

Sarah got up from her place on the couch next to Rita. "Excuse me," she murmured. The seat she'd vacated was instantly filled by an old friend, who took Rita's hand. Sarah made her way to where Milly stood. "I don't think I've had a chance to thank you."

"Don't be silly, darling. If it was the other way around, your mother would be at my house."

"Yes. All the same . . ." There were no adequate words; she hugged Milly instead.

"Have you eaten anything?" Milly demanded.

"Not yet. I will a little later. I'm just going to step outside for a bit of air."

"Okay, don't be too long. It's cold out, and it's not good for you to be alone. Where's Dr. Baraak?"

Sarah was surprised that she remembered both his name and his title. "Upstairs, sleeping, I hope. He hasn't slept in three days. He'd just arrived in France when Mom sent for me."

Milly nodded. Sarah went through the kitchen and out the back door.

The sun had disappeared, obscured by dark clouds. But it wasn't cold, despite Milly's assertion. It was surprisingly warm and humid. The smell of the ocean was drifting across the marshes. Soon it would probably rain. Sarah inhaled deeply. She'd always loved weather like this. It made some people nervous and tense, this humid, palpable warning of a storm, but not her. Because this was her turf, her home place. Twenty-five years had made it so, regardless of origins.

Behind her the white clapboard house loomed solid and stable and reassuring. The road was lined with cars. Comfort, something the small town knew how to offer. Envy, lust, malice; these people were as capable of sin as any others, and they victimized each other with normal frequency. But there was generosity, too. And a kind of knowing that spared them all the pain of anonymity. Sarah was grateful, not just for Rita, for herself.

Yet another car, a rather battered Volvo, turned the corner and parked some distance away. There weren't any spaces closer to the front door.

She recognized the man who emerged from the Volvo—Father Martin, pastor of Sacred Heart Church. He approached her with long, vigorous strides that belied his sixty-plus years. "Hello, Sarah." The priest took both her hands in his. "How's it going?"

"Okay, Father. Thanks for coming. Mom's inside—along with half the town. I just stepped out for some air."

"Had enough? Good, come along with me then. You can run interference."

She led the priest into the house, across the spacious foyer into the crowded living room. He greeted everyone with one all-inclusive nod and went straight to Rita. The people sitting next to her automatically made room. Sarah stood back a bit, feeling that somehow the quiet, almost whispered exchange between the priest and her mother was too private even for her ears. Then the priest raised his voice. "Okay, folks, Rita would like to say a few prayers. And I'm the professional prayer sayer, so I get to lead."

There were quiet chuckles, and those in the room who happened to be Catholics—almost everyone, Sarah realized—moved a little closer to the sofa where Rita and Father Martin sat. Closing ranks. The priest held his hand out to her. "Come sit with us, Sarah."

She had no choice but to do as she was bidden. She took her place beside her mother and made the sign of the cross automatically as Father Martin's voice shifted into official gear. "In the name of the Father and of the Son and of the Holy Spirit, amen."

Milly slipped into the dining room and quietly closed the doors between it and the living room. Mary White, the cleaning woman, was replenishing the stack of plates. Mary was a Catholic, too. "Here, I'll do that. You go on in and pray with them."

She was putting yet another load of glasses and cups and saucers in the dishwasher when the doorbell rang. Milly hurried into the hall. Most people around here didn't ring in these circumstances; they just let themselves in. It was more appropriate. A delivery maybe. Ben had called the liquor store awhile ago; they were running low on beer. But it wasn't a delivery boy at the front door. It was an old man she didn't recognize. "Yes, can I help you?"

He recognized her. Well, not her exactly. He hadn't seen her since 1960. Her voice. "Hello, Milly, dear. How are you?"

Milly's mouth opened, but she didn't say anything. Because it couldn't be him. But it had to be. She'd know the voice anywhere. "What are you doing here?"

"That's too long a story for standing in the door. Besides, it's starting to rain. Can I come in?"

"What . . . yes, of course." She stood aside. He preceded her into the hall, setting down the small case he carried. When he removed his old-fashioned soft hat, the naked skull confirmed her judgment. She'd never forgotten how utterly bald he was. So the man standing here in the Myleses' front hall in Ipswich was Yitzhak Beklem.

"Frank died this morning," Milly said. Making her report as always, as he'd trained her to do. "Sarah arrived a few minutes afterward. Too bad, she just missed him." It sounded crazy when she put it like that. As if it were a matter of seeing Frank off at the airport or something. She hastened to cover up with more words.

"The man's with her, Jarib Baraak. But he's upstairs sleeping. He's got, what do you call it . . . jet lag?"

"Yes, that's what you call it." Yitzhak removed his raincoat and looked for somewhere to put it. Milly took it from him and laid it on a chair because the coat closet was full to overflowing.

"The priest's in there now." She jerked her head toward the living room. "They're praying."

"I know." The sound of repeated Hail Marys burred softly from behind the closed door. Yitzhak smiled at her. "Don't sound so nervous. I'm not going to bust in and do anything terrible. I want to talk to them, Sarah and her mother, but not till later. Meanwhile, could I maybe have a little something to eat, Milly? That dreck they give you on planes isn't edible."

He'd eaten everything on the airline tray, of course, but asking Milly for food was putting her back in control, on safe and familiar ground. She responded as he knew she would.

"Of course. I didn't think . . . You must be starved. Come in here, there's plenty." She led him to the laden table in the dining room. "Try my eggplant casserole. You'll like it. I got the recipe when we were in Israel."

Yitzhak took a large helping and a large first bite. "Delicious. Just like in Jerusalem. Listen, I don't want to see them until this crowd's gone. Is there someplace I can wait?"

Milly had adjusted to his presence. She didn't understand it, but then she'd never understood his interest in the Myleses. "Come across the street with me. You can stay at our place. There'll be people here all evening," she warned him. "Probably you won't find them alone until around ten."

Yitzhak shrugged. "That's okay. You've got a sofa? I can maybe take a nap."

"What sofa? This is America, Yitzhak. We have a guest room."

"You're a day late, lad." Hamish didn't look at his son; he kept his eyes on the papers on his desk.

"I rang yesterday to explain, you weren't here."

"No, not till after midnight." He grimaced. "I had to make a journey."

422

Timothy took off his coat. There was a crystal decanter on a small table near the sofa. He helped himself to a glass of sherry. "I'm curious, since you do it so seldom. Something for us to sell? So important the negotiations couldn't be left to me?"

Hamish preferred to ignore the hurt and anger in the tone. "Yes. Where is the girl?"

"Sarah? I didn't think you gave a tinker's damn about the beautiful Sarah. In France, I expect, I don't really know."

The old man's head snapped up. "Don't know! I thought she was with you. I counted on—"

"She was 'with' me, as you put it, until yesterday around noon. That's when her boyfriend arrived in Alsace. I was rather a fifth wheel after that." He made his tone light, as if it didn't matter.

"My God, you're incompetent." Hamish spoke softly, his accent broad. "'T' think I sired such a fool. She's vital. You might at least have had the brains t' let me know what was happening. I thought—"

"Stop!" Timothy interrupted. "Stop right there. I don't give a bloody damn what you thought. And I'm sick to death of your moods and your insults and all the rest."

Hamish leaned back in his chair and made a tent of the fingers of both pudgy hands. He studied his son over the tops of them. "Insubordinate as well as stupid. Let's just salvage as much as we can, shall we? This boyfriend, I take it you mean Jarib Baraak?"

"Yes. And how the hell do you know his name? What's going on?"

"You wouldn't understand if I chose to explain, and I do not. You must go back to France immediately. You must find them. I wish to know where they are, and exactly what is happening with the girl."

Tim stared at him for a moment. He'd forgotten to drink the sherry. He did so now, one fast swallow that did no justice to its quality. Then he picked up his coat and started from the room.

"Ring me as soon as you arrive," Hamish called after him. "I shall want reports every few hours."

Timothy turned back. "Oh, you will, will you? Well you can bloody well wait for them till hell freezes over."

. . .

At ten forty-five the doorbell in Ipswich rang. Jarib put down the towel with which he'd been wiping silverware. Rita and Sarah were washing by hand the last of the coffee cups. "I'll get it," he said.

The final guests had left fifteen minutes earlier; this call was no longer a comfort but an imposition. "Tell whoever it is we'll be at the funeral home from ten tomorrow morning," Rita said wearily.

"And that the funeral's Thursday at eleven," Sarah added.

Jarib switched on the porch light before he opened the door. The man illumined in the yellow glow of the reproduction wrought-iron lamp was no one he recognized, but then, he knew very few of the Myleses' family or friends.

Yitzhak had the advantage; he knew instantly whom he faced. Milly had described Baraak very well. He noted the man's dark suit and tie. A little wrinkled, the clothes too must have made the journey to France and back, but he looked like one of the mourners. A member of the family now, de facto, if not de jure. "Good evening, Dr. Baraak, I'm Yitzhak Beklem."

"What the hell are you doing here?"

Yitzhak smiled. "A less-than-welcoming greeting, Professor. I must speak with Sarah and Mrs. Myles."

"Not tonight, for God's sake. They're both exhausted; Mrs. Myles's husband died this morning." Jarib cocked his head and looked down on the much shorter man. "But I suspect you know all about that."

"Yes." Beklem pushed past him into the hall. "I'm sorry. This can't wait. Will you tell Mrs. Myles I'm here? Just tell her my name, she'll see me."

Before Jarib could answer, Rita's voice came from the direction of the kitchen. "Who is it, Jarib?"

Jarib hesitated. "Tell her," Yitzhak said. He turned and went toward the living room. "I'll wait in here."

Rita came to the kitchen door, but Yitzhak had already disappeared from view. When Jarib didn't move, Rita went to him. "Who was it?"

Deliberately he pitched his voice low. Why? He couldn't say

424

exactly. Just instinct. "A man named Yitzhak Beklem. He's in there."

Rita didn't say anything for some seconds, but Jarib couldn't tell if she was shocked. There had been too much emotion this day. Rita simply seemed a bereaved and sad woman, her still silence and her downward gaze normal in the circumstances. "Yitzhak Beklem," she repeated finally. It was as if she were testing the words.

Sarah joined them. Her presence seemed to galvanize her mother, jerk her back into the present. "Yitzhak Beklem!" Rita said again, with an excellent imitation of enthusiasm this time. "Fancy that. Daddy and I met him years ago in the Holy Land. Imagine his turning up tonight to pay his respects. I'll just go and talk with him for a minute. No need for you to come, honey. Finish up in the kitchen, will you?"

She went into the living room and closed the door behind her. Sarah was surprised; that was an odd thing for her mother to do. They'd never been a family who lived behind closed doors. She took a hesitant step forward, but Jarib grabbed her arm and tugged her back to the kitchen.

Sarah allowed herself to be led, but she didn't return to the dishwashing. She was trying to remember where she'd recently heard the name, and in a few seconds she did. "He's the man that told you about me, isn't he? The one that called and said I needed you. What's he doing here?"

"I don't know."

Sarah started back to the hall. "I'm going in there. What's he want with Mom anyway?"

"Darling, wait. I don't know what the connection is, but she knew who he was." Beklem was at the center of a puzzle Jarib hadn't yet fathomed, but clearly at least one of the lines of inquiry led to Rita. "She wanted to see him alone, that's obvious. Shouldn't you give her a little time before breaking in?"

Sarah pushed her hair back impatiently. "She's in no condition to make decisions. And I don't like it. I don't like him knowing about you and about me and suddenly turning up here of all places."

"Five minutes," Jarib said. "I think you owe her that. Then we'll both go in."

Reluctantly Sarah agreed.

In the living room the man and the woman faced each other.

"Why now?" Rita demanded in a whisper that managed to be shrill. "After all these years, why now?"

"I told you." Yitzhak's voice was gentle, but not his words. "It's time."

"Time for what?"

"You've got to tell her the truth, Rita. You always knew you'd have to someday. I said that years ago."

Rita's shoulders sagged, and her face seemed to crease; it became a wrinkled map depicting pain and age. "I lost Frank this morning; now you're going to take Sarah away from me. What a terrible and cruel man you are."

"No. I don't think you'll lose Sarah," Yitzhak said. "But that's not in my control. You have to tell her, Rita."

"What if I refuse?"

"Then I'll tell her. But it would be a lot easier coming from you."

She went to the window. The rain had ended; she was staring out into a street lit by clever imitation gas lamps. The neighbors had gotten together four years earlier and put up the money to replace the ordinary town lights. The gas lamps were more appropriate for their lovely old houses, they'd agreed.

"There's no moon tonight," Rita said. "You can't see the marsh."

Yitzhak didn't reply.

And finally: "All right." A surrender spoken through stiff lips, almost too soft to be heard. "All right," she repeated. When she went to the door to summon her daughter, she found Jarib and Sarah waiting in the hall.

"Mom, what is it? You look terrible. What's he done? What does he want with us anyway?"

"Come in and sit down, honey," Rita said. "I have to tell you something."

Sarah followed her and sat. So did Jarib. But Rita didn't say anything more for what seemed a long time. Sarah looked not at her mother but at the stranger. "I don't think I like you, Mr. Beklem. And I want to know what you've come here for. Then I want you to get out."

426

Jarib put a hand on her shoulder. Restraint or comfort? Sarah wasn't quite sure, but she ignored either offer. "Mom, you don't have to tell me anything unless you want to."

"Yes," Rita said at last. "I do."

Wanted to or had to? It wasn't clear. Sarah waited. Her mother was silent.

"Go on, Rita," Yitzhak urged. "Just begin. It will be easier than you think. I'll fill in the parts you don't know."

Rita took a deep breath. "It wasn't Georgia, honey. Not exactly. I mean it was, but not at first. First Daddy and I went to the Holy Land."

Sarah shuddered once, then leaned back against the chair. *Do-sol-la-fa . . .* The song and the voice were trying to surface, but she forced them away. Rita's words were coming quickly now. Leading Sarah down a long, long path she'd always feared to travel, leading her back to 1958.

"The Lord said to Abram, Look about thee, turn thy eyes from where thou art to north and south, to east and west. All the land thou seest I make over to thee, and to thy posterity forever."

Rhonda Plotkin Kane repeated the words from Genesis in Hebrew. No surprise that she spoke the language and knew the quotation by heart, all her life she'd gone to religion classes and to *shul*. When she was thirteen and the rabbi refused her a Bas Mitzvah because he didn't approve of the ceremony for girls, her father built his own synagogue and hired a more cooperative rabbi. In Los Angeles neither was that a surprise, just a typical Saul Plotkin solution.

Now Rhonda's chubby face was flushed with intensity; her brown, close-set eyes skimmed the thirty-two occupants of the bus and came to rest on her husband. Her so handsome husband of one brief year. Jack Kane had red hair, gray eyes, and an incredibly boyish, open grin. He was looking at her attentively, waiting for her next words. She knew she should say more, inspire the younger kids with the true meaning of Israel, their reasons for making this trip.

Rhonda's glance darted to Amy Stein, then back to Jack. They weren't even sitting near each other. She was being crazy. Still, her throat was tight with tension. She turned to the driver, "That's it for now, let's go, Yosef."

She couldn't keep her eyes off Amy. The girl was staring out the window. Masses of curly dark chestnut hair hung almost to her shoulders. With her face turned away the big brown eyes didn't show, only the long lashes. Rhonda didn't need to see the eyes. She could picture Amy Stein's delicate features, her porcelain skin, her too pretty prettiness. She felt sick.

The bus jostled through the snarl of traffic that surrounded Tel Aviv's Lod Airport and headed toward the town. The bus had large signs in its front and rear windows. TEMPLE BETH SHALOM YOUTH GROUP, LOS ANGELES, they proclaimed in English and Hebrew. Instant magic. Everybody in Israel knew that Los Angeles was just a code name for Hollywood. People honked and waved. The kids in the bus waved back. Except Amy Stein, who ignored them. And was careful not to look at Jack.

"Jesus, Bess, did you see this bill from Magnin's? One month, eight hundred bucks. One lousy month! The kid's got no sense of money. None at all."

Bess Stein leaned closer to the gilt-framed mirror hanging over her vanity table and plucked a stray hair from a well-arched eyebrow. "So what do you want, Sam? What have you been killing yourself for if it's not so Amy can have things? There was a sale on cashmeres."

"Cashmeres. Eight hundred bucks for sweaters. That's more than my father made in a year."

"Your father's dead, Sam. You want to go back to the Lower East Side? Back to living over the store? That's what you want for your only child?"

"Do I need you to tell me my father's dead?" Stein sat down heavily; the bed sagged under his bulk. He folded his hands over his belly, staring at the pinkie ring he always wore. A big diamond in a circle of rubies. Bess was right. They'd come a long way from the Lower East Side. "Yesterday was Pa's Yahrzeit, you didn't say anything."

"Oh, God . . . I'm sorry, honey. I'll plug in the memorial light right away. A day late doesn't matter."

"Forget it. I lit a Yahrzeit candle at the office. That electric tsatske never seems right to me."

Tel Aviv was neither an old city nor a beautiful one. Founded in the early part of the century on the site of a tiny village, it grew frantically after it became the second-choice capital of the state of Israel. Jerusalem was unavailable according to the terms of the UN resolution, though every Israeli knew that was the nation's heart and soul. So the Israelis settled for Tel Aviv, but nobody bothered to make it more than functional.

The outskirts of the city were a sprawl of towering apartment blocks crafted in the ubiquitous white stucco of so many Mediterranean towns. Every flat had a balcony, and on each one people hung over the rails, watching the snarled traffic as if it were a phenomenon. It was a commonplace. The phenomenon was the way Yosef maneuvered his bus through the jam. In twenty minutes they were at the hotel on Yarkon Street near the beach. Also near the red-light district, but the tour organizers didn't mention that. Small and charming, they said, a place of character.

It was called the Savoy, and it was certainly small, the kind of place that could only survive on budget tours. The lobby was minute. The Los Angeles teenagers and their overweight suitcases filled it to overflowing.

"Beth Shalomers, stay in one group, please." Rhonda's voice. The high-pitched, nervous whine that had become habitual after the first three days of the trip, while they were still in New York, waiting to board their El Al plane. "Form a line to the right of the desk. Please, Beth Shalomers . . ."

Like the rest, Amy Stein pushed and shoved in an attempt to obey Rhonda's commands. She felt a hand on her buttocks. It wasn't snatched away in embarrassment; it stayed there. She turned her head slightly, saw Jack's broad grin, smiled back, then frowned a warning. He gave her ass a final pinch and took his hand away. A harried desk clerk began assigning rooms. The crush thinned as the group fought their way by twos into an ancient elevator.

"Everybody back in the bus in an hour," Rhonda shouted. "First tour of Tel Aviv . . . Jack, will you help with the baggage, please? Amy, you'll bunk with Sue, like in New York, okay?"

"Sure, Rhonda. Whatever you say."

"Okay with you, Sue?"

The other girl nodded enthusiastically. Amy Stein was the richest kid on this tour. Except for Rhonda, and she was the guide, so she didn't count. Amy lived in a fabulous house in Beverly Hills.

With two swimming pools. Rooming with her was a bonus. Sue got to borrow some of her clothes. Probably it would be the same as in New York; the price was to keep her mouth shut about Amy's slipping out during the night and not coming back for hours. What difference did it make?. Everybody had caught on right away. Jack Kane was balling Amy Stein. They all knew it. Probably even Rhonda. What could she say? When you looked like Rhonda and you had a husband who was a gorgeous hunk like Jack—a husband Daddy bought and paid for—well, it was inevitable, wasn't it?

"Listen, Bess, the other day, my father's Yahrzeit, remember?"

"Yeah, I know I forgot it. I already apologized, Sam."

"I'm not talking about that. I said it didn't matter. But it made me think of things. About Amy. I'm worried about her."

"Worried? She's a doll. She ever given us any trouble, Sam? Of course not. So she's a little extravagant. At her age it's natural."

No trouble, maybe Bess believed that. Maybe she didn't know their little girl had the roundest heels in California. Sometimes, when Sam looked at Amy's pretty, innocent face, remembered the kind of baby she'd been . . . so sweet, so damn sweet . . . he couldn't believe it either. But he knew it was true; he'd recognized the signs a couple of years ago, when she was sixteen. Muffled laughter out behind the cabana during a party, men his own age who looked at him half in pity, half in scorn. Guys old enough to be Amy's father. No trouble. Jesus! Bess was saying something more about his being cheap. "Will you shut up and listen to me? I don't give a fuck what the kid spends. What have we got it for? It's something else, Bess. She's got no values. No sense of roots. I'm not saying it's your fault. . . ."

"Roots, values. I don't know what you're talking about. Amy has a lovely home, she's just graduated from high school, she has two parents who love her. What more do you want, Sam, from her or from us?"

He sighed loudly. "I don't know. I didn't tell you everything the other day. It was Shevuoth. I went to shul to say Yizkor for my father."

"To shul? My God, Sam, it must be the first time since we're married. What shul?"

"Temple Beth Shalom. The new place Saul Plotnick built on North Wilshire. And it ain't the first time. I been going some Friday nights. Once or twice a month maybe. They got a youth group. I see the notices on the bulletin board sometimes."

"And you want Amy to join, right? So she'll have what you mean by roots and values?" Bess crossed to her husband and laid her hand on his shoulder. It was a pudgy hand with too many rings and bright red nails, but there was tenderness in her voice. "You're tired, honey. You work too damn hard. Especially now. Ever since you took the option on that book about the Italian gangster. I told you, Sam, what big star wants to play a wop crook?"

"You're changing the subject. We were talking about Amy."

"I know. But she's not religious, Sam. We didn't bring her up that way."

"Okay. That's our fault, mine. But I saw this announcement about a trip to Israel. Amy is always saying she wants to travel and why don't we send her to Europe. Let's send her to Israel. It'd be all right, Bess. Plotkin's kid, Rhonda, and her husband are the chaperons."

"Some chaperons. Rhonda's what, twenty-two, twenty-three? The boy can't be much older."

"I know, but it's a group from the shul, all nice kids. Amy would make some new friends. See a different side of life. Talk to her, Bess. See if she's interested."

"Okay."

"Promise?"

"Of course, I promise." She leaned over and kissed the top of his head.

Jack shoved the girls' suitcases into the elevator with his knee and handed Amy her carryall. She felt the note he was pressing into her palm and smiled. She didn't have to read it to know it would specify a time and a meeting place. Amy had known him less than a week, but when it came to screwing, Jack had shown a lot of initiative.

More of the ubiquitous white buildings; these far-flung and sprawling, surrounded by the orange groves which gave Kibbutz Etz Hadar its name. A symmetrical, carefully nurtured green presence in the scrub-infested, swampy landscape. A model of its kind.

The youth group had been force-fed facts in preparation for the visit. Etz Hadar was located north of Tel Aviv, not far from the Lebanese border; it was founded in the early twenties in what was then Palestine, before the existence of the state of Israel. It had survived war and terrorists and the more dangerous attacks mounted from within as diverse philosophies waxed and waned. Today the kibbutz produced a prodigious number of oranges for export, and served as inspiration for visiting Americans.

The bus with the Beth Shalom signs turned in past the barbed-wire checkpoint. Two men stood on the roofed porch of the main building and watched it approach. The older of the two was in his fifties, and spoke Hebrew with a Germanic accent. "Los Angeles. Doubtless full of nubile females, willing and eager to do their bit for Israel. Speaking English has advantages. The tourists I get are always Europeans with high moral standards and hairy legs."

The younger man was short, dark, and muscular. He looked like an athlete. One whose sport would be something tough and arcane, chosen because it didn't need height; kayak racing or mountaineering maybe. He didn't reply to the other man's banter, merely pushed himself away from the wall and went forward to meet the bus. His companion expected nothing else. Dov Levi was like that. He'd been on the kibbutz two weeks before anyone realized he spoke fluent, colloquial Hebrew, not the halting variety common to immigrants. It was a bit of a mystery, considering that he'd come to Israel from England six months earlier. But nobody got close enough to him to ask questions. And whatever the membership committee knew it was keeping to itself.

Levi stood by the door of the bus as the passengers got off, shaking each one's hand and saying, "*Shalom.*" That was prescribed. He had learned the drill some time ago and followed it precisely. The way he did every assigned task.

Amy was in the middle of the line. At first she couldn't see the welcoming committee of one. When she got close enough to the front to make him out, she was unimpressed. Short. She liked tall men. And he was dark. Amy was partial to blonds, or redheads like Jack Kane. She turned to smile at Jack. Rhonda obviously intended to say nothing about their relationship, and they'd become less cautious. Amy didn't look forward again until she was at the door. Her quick assessment put the Israeli at about thirty.

"*Shalom,*" he said. She gave him her hand. A few seconds passed; he didn't let it go. Amy looked up. He was staring at her. "*Shalom,*" he repeated.

"*Shalom.*" That one word was the total of her Hebrew. His eyes were studying her face. Nice eyes. Green. But too intense. She tried again to pull away.

"What's your name?"

He spoke good English, that was a bonus. "Amy Stein," she said. "What's yours?" It wasn't that she cared, only that flirting was second nature.

"Dov Levi." He was silent for a long moment, but still he didn't release her hand.

"Are you our guide for the day?"

He didn't answer her question. "I've been waiting for you." His voice was low and urgent, his accent something she couldn't place.

"Bet you say that to all the girls." Behind her the others were growing restless. This time she pulled her hand away, he'd have had to struggle visibly to keep it, and moved on.

She was conscious of his eyes on her all the while they toured the buildings and the orange groves.

Two days later she saw him again. The group had moved on to the ancient city of Ashdod. In the time of King Saul it had belonged to the Philistines. In those days it was coveted because of its location on the sea. The tour went there for the same reason. History would combine with relaxation. They were given a break, twenty-four hours of relative freedom. Most of the kids spent all day on the beach, but Amy's skin was so fair she had to be careful of the sun. In the afternoon she went shopping alone. She was just coming out of a boutique that specialized in hand-embroidered caftans when Dov Levi appeared.

"What are you doing here? I thought kibbutzniks were too dedicated to take a day off."

"I'm not a kibbutznik. Not the way you mean. Anyway, I told you, I've been waiting for you. No, don't look like that, it's not a line. I'm completely serious."

More crazy talk. He was a spooky guy. "Where are you from? Your English is terrific, but you have a funny accent."

"I'm from Israel. At least I was born here, back when it was Palestine. My accent is a combination of British and American." He stopped speaking, as if that much personal revelation were all he could manage, took the bundles from her hand, and started to walk away. If she wanted her things, she had to follow him.

433

"Hey! Wait a minute, where are you going? I'm supposed to be back at the guesthouse in fifteen minutes."

"And you're a good little girl who always obeys the rules, right?"

Amy grinned. "Wrong. Is this your car?"

"Yes, get in."

It was a much battered jeep. The passenger door didn't open. Dov lifted her over the side. She was surprised at his strength. She'd thought him weak because he was short; now she recognized her error. He threw the bundles in the rear and walked around to the driver's seat.

They drove for about ten minutes in silence. When he stopped the car, they were high above the town at the precipitous edge of some cliffs. There wasn't anyone else in sight. Amy began to feel slightly afraid. Dov climbed down from the jeep and went to the rear. She followed him, watching his movements with a mixture of trepidation and curiosity. A strangely exciting mixture.

The sun westered behind blue-gray hills; the air was still and warm. Dov took a blanket from the car and spread it on the ground. Then he turned to her. "Take off your clothes. I'm going to make love to you."

Amy stared at him. She was trembling, and the insides of her thighs were wet. It was always like this at first, when she realized that a man was crazy to have her. The disappointment came later. "Where I come from, it's polite to ask," she said. Her voice wasn't flip and gay, the way she wanted it to be. It quivered, like the rest of her.

"Stop it," he said. "I don't want to be reminded how frequently you've done this before. It doesn't matter anyway. This is different. You'll see." He reached out and trailed one finger down her cheek. Her skin burned where he'd touched it. "Take off your clothes," he repeated. More softly this time. "I've been waiting so long."

She wore a white off-the-shoulder blouse trimmed in eyelet embroidery and bright pink toreador pants that ended below her knees. Such clothes came off easily. She dropped them in a heap on the ground and stood facing him in a strapless bra and pink nylon briefs with "Tuesday" written above the leg. She had a pair for each day of the week.

Dov smiled for the first time. "Tuesday's child is full of grace, according to the nursery rhyme. A *mitzvah* for the day."

Amy barely heard him. Her ears were ringing, and she felt dizzy. The heat, what else could it be? She waited for him to kiss her, but he didn't. Instead he began to remove his own clothes. Slowly, deliberately. Watching her all the while. At last he took a step closer and reached behind her to unhook the bra. It fell away. Her breasts were on the small side. Amy always wished they were bigger. She saw no dissatisfaction in his face. His hands dropped to her waist, and he slid the pants down over her hips, staring fixedly at the triangle of dark hair between her legs. Still, he didn't kiss her.

"I've never been religious," he said softly. "But this is the day the Lord has made, like King David said. I should make *Shehecheyanu*. Blessed art Thou, O Lord our God, King of the Universe, who has kept us alive to this time."

He was crazy. Maybe even dangerous. The thought flashed through her mind for a moment. Then it didn't matter.

He lifted her up, and she recognized the extent of his strength, knew it in the iron grip of his arms, the hardness of his chest against her breasts. His mouth was pressed against hers, open, sucking her breath. She moaned and wrapped her legs around his hips. He dropped her slightly, and she was impaled on his penis. She moaned again. He knelt, lowering them both to the blanket, still staying deep inside her. His first real thrust brought him deeper still. Amy thought she would split apart, that she could feel him in her belly.

He moved in and out of her, slowly, over and over again. No one had ever done that before. She was accustomed to men who raced toward their climax, half afraid of discovery before it was attained. And he was looking at her. His eyes locked with hers, compelling her to maintain the contact. But she couldn't.

Suddenly her body was racked with a series of shuddering spasms that forced her to shut her eyes and writhe her head against the blanket. She dug her fingernails into his shoulders, feeling the flesh yield and break. "Aaagh . . ." For the first time in four highly promiscuous years Amy Stein had an orgasm.

Half an hour later he dropped her off in front of the guesthouse where she was staying. He'd said nothing all during the ride back.

435

Neither had she. She didn't know what to say, was too startled by the knowledge that somehow she had become the pursuer and not the pursued. When he stopped the car, she couldn't bear the silence any longer. "When will I see you again?" The question men always asked her. Only they meant, When can I get into your pants again? She didn't. She wanted to be near him. Screwing was just part of it.

"I'm not sure. I have things to arrange."

She pulled back as if he'd hit her. The brushoff words struck her with whiplike intensity. "Okay," she managed. "Bye." He thrust her packages into her arms, and she turned and ran.

The tour moved south, through Qiryat Gat toward Be'er Sheva. They were scheduled to see the Dead Sea and the excavations at Masada before finishing with five days in Jerusalem. Amy became more depressed with every mile, perceiving it as distance imposed between her and Dov. Who didn't want to see her anyway, wherever she was.

She avoided Jack Kane as if he carried plague, and he sulked for two days, then took up with Susan Cohen, Amy's roommate. Rhonda had retreated into a haze of misery and hurt, sometimes staring at Amy with intensified anger, as if her sudden uninterest in Rhonda's husband were some new and worse abuse. For the others it was all just something more to gossip about.

She lay awake nights thinking of other men, trying to tell herself that Dov Levi was just like them, worthless. She remembered the grip on the set of one of her father's films, who took her virginity in a hasty coupling behind Debbie Reynolds's trailer in 1956, when she was fourteen. He had blond hair and a scrawny beard, and she'd felt great for ten minutes afterward, like a real grown-up woman at last.

Then she'd discovered that he didn't want to repeat the experience because he hadn't known she was so young, let alone a virgin. And he didn't love her. And after a short while she realized she didn't love him. Nor the senior at Mojave Country Day School who had her next. He took her behind the super new gym donated by his father, pulling aside the elasticized leg of her bright blue gymsuit to gain access to her vagina, because removing the garment would take too much time. Neither did Amy love the delivery boy from Linda's Boutique, nor the aging director who was angry at her father for firing him from a picture and who was just screwing her to get even, nor the pretty-boy aspirant for stardom who hoped that by engaging Amy's affection he'd gain a friend at court. Not that Amy had that kind of influence with Sam, not now and certainly not at sixteen.

Sam treated her like a doll, a pretty little toy. She was sure he forgot she existed when she was out of sight. Probably some head doctor would say that's why she spread her legs for every male who came along. Maybe. What difference did it make? The fact was she was no good. Nobody knew that better than she. Some genetic flaw perhaps, some throwback to a lusty village whore back in Russia.

God! She had difficulty remembering them all. Dov Levi would be erased the same way after a while. But if that was true, the time was not now. Amy relived the minutes she'd spent with him over and over. From the moment she stepped off the bus at the kibbutz, to his abrupt dismissal of her in front of the guesthouse in Ashdod. She lingered as long as she could on the interval on the cliffs above the sea, but inevitably her mind insisted on recalling the last scene, and the pain of loss and rejection came back with appalling vividness.

"It is impossible to overemphasize the meaning of Masada in Jewish history. Not only because it proves that two thousand years ago Jews would choose death over surrender." Rhonda broke off and peered intently at the faces of her listeners. "It represents a truth that we in this generation have painfully relearned. It is better to fight and die than to be slaughtered like animals." She paused. "Never again." Her voice was heavy with emotion. "Never again."

The kids were silent, understanding her meaning, for once too overcome by feeling to wisecrack. Yosef braked at the bottom of the towering hill. They craned their necks to stare up at the geometrical gray-brown stone fortress above them. The quiet lasted a full minute longer; then Jack read aloud the brief history Rhonda had written out for him. She'd convinced herself things would be

437

better if she gave Jack more responsibility. But he was a terrible anticlimax. His voice droned on, sometimes he stumbled over the words, the mood of awe was destroyed.

Amy squirmed in her seat. It was hot, despite the air conditioning. Her yellow, dirndl-skirted peasant dress stuck to her legs. Beyond the window the ferocious heat was a shimmering haze. She knew the smell of the Dead Sea would be a pall in the atmosphere.

"All right," Rhonda said at last. "We'll walk up the ramp path and meet our official guide. The tour will last approximately an hour. After that we'll come down the snake path and have our picnic lunch here in the parking lot. Then you'll have an hour free to wander around." She rose from her seat; the air lock hissed as Yosef opened the doors. "Stay together, please, Beth Shalomers."

Amy endured the tour and the lunch, longed for the promised free time so she could be alone. When it came, she separated herself from the group, nobody invited her to join them anyway, and began to climb up into the east parapet. She'd noticed it when they were led through the fortress by the guide. It looked cool up there high on the restored walls, inviting. She was wringing wet by the time she reached the massive outcrop that overlooked the sea and the Jordanian border, but she was right: There was a breeze. She stood still, letting it move her hair off her neck, plaster the sheer cotton fabric of her dress to her body.

"Like Queen Esther," a voice said. "Or Sarah. One of the founding mothers anyway."

Amy turned to find Dov Levi leaning against the parapet, gazing at her with a big smile.

"How did you get here?" She was frightened again, that emotion warring with the intense pleasure of seeing him. "How did you know where to find me—that is, if you meant to find me?"

"Of course, I meant to find you. And it wasn't difficult. The Israeli tourist office keeps a record of the itinerary of all our visitors. I wanted to meet you here. It's an appropriate place for us to begin."

Amy stared at him. He wore faded jeans and a sweatshirt that said something she couldn't read because the letters were in Hebrew. A breeze ruffled his dark hair. "Begin what?" she asked. "I thought you didn't want to see me again."

438

He frowned. "What made you think that? I told you I'd been waiting." He crossed the distance between them and placed his hands lightly on her shoulders. He was only a few inches taller than she, and their eyes locked, the way they had when he'd made love to her.

"When you dropped me off the other day, I thought you were trying to get rid of me."

Dov shook his head. "I had things to arrange. For us. I expected you to understand that."

"I don't understand anything." She pulled away from his touch and turned to look down; the buses seemed like Tinkertoys. "I think you're some kind of nut."

"Oh, no," he said softly. "Don't make that very common mistake, Amy. Because something is extraordinary doesn't make it crazy. Now, there's no time left for this conversation. How long do you have before you're expected down there?" He jerked his head toward the parking lot.

"About half an hour now. Why?"

He didn't answer her question. "That's enough if we hurry. Come." He took her hand and began pulling her toward the steep stairs leading below. "I parked away from the buses. We won't be seen."

"Dov, stop! Where are we going?"

They were on the ancient narrow stairway, the massive walls of hand-hewn stone pressing in on either side. He turned and faced her. "We are beginning our journey of discovery, my sweet Amy, my *mitzvah*. All the waiting is over. Soon we'll know."

They drove for half an hour before she asked him again where they were going. "I could tell you," he answered, "but it wouldn't mean anything. Just relax. Trust me."

She watched his profile. He had a thin nose and a jutting chin, but full lips that softened his features. He didn't notice her scrutiny; he was intent on the narrow road, driving with all his senses alert, although they had seen only one other car. She hoped he was looking for a place to stop so they could make love. But he was letting it go a long time. "Dov, listen. I can play hooky for a few hours. But I'll have to be back at the hotel before midnight. Rhonda will call out the mounties if I'm not. She'll make it into a big deal."

439

He took his eyes from the road and looked at her for a long moment, then threw back his head and laughed. "Midnight. You really don't understand, do you?"

"No, I told you that. Maybe you'd better explain."

"We have been chosen, Amy. We're going on a quest. Into the desert. We may be gone a long time, even years, but when we return, we will know things that men have never dreamed."

She thought he was kidding, or talking more crazy talk, and she didn't say anything. Later she watched him unload things from the back of the jeep. He had everything neatly stowed: bedrolls, a tent, lamps, a small stove that worked off gas canisters, food . . . God! Why hadn't she looked in the back before she got in. Then maybe she'd have suspected something. But she wouldn't have; she'd just have thought he was going camping after they went somewhere and screwed for an hour or so. Men always had other plans once they were finished with her.

She swallowed hard, wished her mouth wasn't so dry. "Listen, Dov, I'm not sure this is such a good idea. I mean, there's Rhonda and Jack, the tour. They're bound to make a hell of a fuss when I don't come back. It will be a nuisance for you—"

"Don't worry, they'll never find us. I've taken precautions. Besides, we're on the Jordan side now. The Israeli police don't come over here, and in case you haven't noticed, there's not much co-operation between Israel and her neighbors."

Amy stared at him, fear crawling up her spine to the base of her neck. "The Jordan side, but how did we cross the border? I thought there were guards. Besides, isn't it dangerous? What about the terrorists?"

"The population of Jordan is composed of Arabs," he said quietly. "Get over the notion that the word *Arab* is synonymous with *terrorist*. It's a debilitating assumption." He pointed to a small carton. "Have a look in there; it's fresh food. Enough for a couple of days. Then we'll have to rely on tins, of course. See what you can put together for our supper."

Amy made no move to touch the box. "You didn't answer my question about the border."

"How did we avoid the guards, you mean?" Dov laughed softly. "My dear Amy, you see too many Hollywood films. The border

440

is long and mostly desert. There are very few official checkpoints and fewer guards."

He waved his arm at the bleak, forbidding landscape. "Unless you are very well prepared, this is protection enough. We, however, are superbly prepared." His voice gentled. "Don't be frightened. It's going to be fine, you'll see. Come on, be a good girl and do something about the food. They do teach you a little about cooking in Los Angeles, don't they?"

Woodenly she extracted a carton of eggs, some butter, and some bread. Dov lit the camp stove and produced a mess kit that included a frying pan. "There's coffee, too," he said. "Not instant, the real thing. And we have a percolator." He seemed delighted with his forethought, a child enjoying a picnic.

They ate in silence, Dov acting as if her quiet, like his, were simple companionship. The cool desert evening descended, turning the world a dusky blue. Soon it would be night; not cool, but cold. "Dov, I have no clothes, just this thin dress. Shouldn't we go back to Be'er Sheva? I could get some things; we can come out here again if you want." Never, she was thinking. If I can only get back to civilization, I'll never have to see him again.

He glanced up. His face told her he was reading her thoughts. "You're not just afraid of being out here, are you? You're afraid of me. Why?"

Humor him, that's what you were supposed to do with nuts. "No, no, it's not that. I told you, I don't have anything warm to wear."

Silently he rose and went to the rear of the jeep. Amy remained where she was, watching him, trying to gauge his mood. He returned and tossed a bundle at her feet. "Here, I told you I was prepared. Put this on."

It was the long robe of an Arab woman; there was even the funny head covering and veil. Amy stared at the black, coarse linen clothes, then looked up at Dov.

"The headdress is called a yashmak; the robe is an abba. Islam decrees it for modesty; out here it makes sense because of the blowing sand. And because it will help us blend with the locals. Go ahead, put it on." His voice was bitter, and strangely hurt.

She dragged the flowing abba on over her dress. At least it was warm. Dov moved closer to help her adjust the heavy garment on her small frame. His hands lingered on her shoulders. "Amy, tell me what I've done to frighten you."

She intended to go on humoring him, to say she wasn't scared, but there was too much churning inside her to be repressed. "What else can I feel? You appear at Masada like some ghost, you drag me out here without explaining anything, you talk about some quest. . . . It's insane, Dov, all of it. I'm not just scared, I'm terrified."

She regretted the words instantly, but all he did was drop his hands by his sides. "I don't believe you don't know, that in your whole life you've had no hint. Haven't you seen me, known I'd appear, the way I knew you?"

"Never! Nothing! Don't you understand? Everything you say sounds nuts to me. Crazy. I don't know what to think."

He bit his lip; she'd noticed he did that when he was concentrating. After a few seconds he went again to the rear of the jeep. This time he returned with a small musical instrument. Amy didn't recognize it.

"It's a lyre," he explained. "A very unusual ten-string lyre. I made it myself. Sit down, listen."

They sat on the ground. It was still warm from the day's sun. Dov folded his legs under him and settled the U-shaped curved wooden frame of the lyre on his knee. He plucked the strings with his fingers. Four notes. Amy listened. He looked at her. Nothing.

"Close your eyes," he said urgently. "Try to make your mind a blank. Just concentrate on the music." The same four notes. And a third time. "Nothing?" he asked finally.

"Nothing," she said. He looked so disappointed she almost felt sorry for him.

Dov replaced the lyre in the jeep. Amy waited. "Come," he said, "we're both tired, it's been a difficult day. We'll sleep, talk more in the morning."

Amy crawled after him into the tent; she couldn't think of anything else to do. They lay side by side. Not touching. Just before she fell asleep, she realized that at no time during the day had he tried to make love to her.

In the morning it was she who turned to him; just before dawn,

442

waking in a hazy, unreal dream, aware only of her aloneness, her need.

Amy remembered fear, the desert outside; she remembered Dov. Dov had made love to her in a way different from any man she had known. And he had prayed first, *prayed*. She wasn't just another screw to him, another piece of ass; Dov had made her feel important. Feel pleasure. And he'd come for her, all the way to Masada. It was an important place. Something to do with freedom. How wonderful to be really free.

She could hear Dov's gentle breathing beside her. She stretched out her hand, touched his face, let her palm stay against his cheek. She could feel the stubble of his beard. He was dark; naturally he had a heavy beard.

"Amy? What is it? You all right?"

"Yes. I mean, no, I'm frightened, Dov." Her voice a whisper in the desert dark.

He laid his hand over hers, pressing it against his skin. "Of me? Still?"

"No. I don't think so. Just being out here, being alone, everything."

"You're not alone." He turned to her, unzipping the bedrolls between them, moving closer until the lengths of their two bodies touched. "We're together, Amy. It's supposed to be that way. I wasn't lying, not last night or before. The first time I saw you, when you got off that bus with all those silly kids, I knew you were the one I'd been waiting for."

A sob caught in her throat, came out as a choked, wretched sound. "I don't know anything. Just that I'm alone."

"You're not, stop saying that." He put his arms around her, pulled her close. She was still wearing the abba and her dress underneath; in the closeness of the small tent she was sweating. Gently he helped her take off the clothes. Slowly, with infinite patience, like a father with a small, beloved child. She pushed up his sweatshirt, tangling her fingers in his matted chest hair.

When they were both naked, Dov pulled the sleeping bag around them, pressed her close. He stroked her skin, kissed her hair and her eyes and her cheeks; there was no urgency, no rush. They lay thus a long time, fondling each other like exploring children. The

443

passion built slowly and was blended with the sweetness that had gone before. When he entered her, they still lay on their sides, holding each other tight. Sex was a bridge between them, not a weapon.

Amy shuddered. "Dov, it's crazy, I think I love you."

"Not crazy. Planned, ordained."

He moved to insert himself deeper. They both moaned, together, sharing delight. She tugged at his shoulders, and he rolled on top of her. The ancient rhythm swept them up and carried them on its assertive wave.

"Jesus, Rhonda, it's twenty-four hours! We have to call the police."

Rhonda shook her head. Her eyes were red with weeping; her mouse-colored hair hung in dull strands around her face. "It will be so awful, my father—"

"Your father! What the hell does Saul have to do with this? Amy Stein is a little whore, but we can't just let her disappear and pretend it hasn't happened. Be reasonable, Rhonda, see sense. You wanted to wait, and we've waited. Now we have to do something."

"It's still afternoon. Maybe she'll come back tonight."

Kane ran his fingers through his hair and walked to the window of the guesthouse. Their bus was parked outside, but neither Yosef nor any of the kids were in sight. They'd been given an unscheduled free day because of the emergency. He turned back to face his wife. "Honey, listen to me. This situation can only get worse, not better. If we don't act to salvage it right now, it will be a disaster. Whatever's happened to her, wherever she's gone, you're letting her drag the rest of us down the same bottomless pit."

Rhonda stared at him. His face was lined with fatigue; he didn't look so handsome suddenly, just vulnerable. "That's just it," she whispered. "All the dirt will come out."

"I know. I understand what you're afraid of. I balled the kid a couple of times. It didn't mean a thing, Rhonda, you know that. But the police are bound to find out, make an issue of it. So what?" He crossed the room, took her cold, lifeless hands in his. "Our marriage isn't very old, honey; we're not going to let it collapse at the first sign of trouble, are we?"

"I don't want it to," she whispered. "That's just the point."

He shook his head. "I don't get it. As long as you and I are together in this, what difference can a little talk make? Rhonda, I had nothing to do with Amy's taking off. Nothing. You understand that, don't you?"

"Yes. I told you, it's my father. This is our big chance, Jack. He set us up to lead this tour; if everything goes okay, he promised me the money to open a travel agency in Los Angeles. You'd be good in a travel agency, Jack."

He was silent for a few seconds. "And not at much else. I get it. Okay, let me think."

Kane went back to the window, staring out at nothing, seeing only the future. He had two choices, Jack Kane, ne'er-do-well drifter, or Jack Kane, son-in-law of rich, respected Saul Plotkin. "Listen," he said finally. "I'm going to place a call to your father right now. You let me do it. I'll talk to him, make him understand. Okay?"

It was the first time since she'd known him that he'd offered to take any positive step. Until now all the moves had been hers. Jack just drifted with the main chance. "Okay," she said softly. "If you're sure it's the right thing to do."

"I'm sure."

There was a twelve-hour time difference; it was the middle of the night in California. That worked to their advantage. The international lines weren't busy, and the call went through in fifteen minutes. Jack gripped the receiver like the lifeline it was.

"Saul, that you? . . . No, of course, I'm not in California. I'm in Israel . . . No, no, everything's okay. That is, Rhonda and me, we're fine. But we've got a problem."

Once Saul Plotkin's initial panic calmed, he was quick to absorb the facts. Problem solving was his chief skill. That's how he got to the big house in Beverly Hills from a tenement on Houston Street. He listened to his son-in-law in silence, jotting notes on the yellow pad by the phone, waiting until Jack was finished to say, "Okay, I got it. And you ain't called the cops yet. Why?"

"We didn't want to go off half-cocked, Saul. Amy's no angel;

445

frankly her taking off didn't seem like a big deal. The kid's got hot pants." The grown-up sitting in judgment on reckless youth. The married man with responsibilities. "Besides, I figured this could be a problem for you. Sam Stein's a big *macher*, right? If we could handle it internally, no scandal, that would be better."

"True." Plotkin was impressed. The nebbish his Rhonda had picked hadn't seemed a good prospect to him; maybe he'd been wrong. "Okay, but it seems to me you gotta call the cops now. If they're anything like the LAPD, already they're not gonna be too happy."

"I know, but I'll handle them from this end. What I figure is you should call Stein. Better he hears first from you, not somebody thousands of miles away."

"Right. Soon as I hang up. I'll tell him you'll get in touch directly, say, ten A.M. our time. Keep him posted. Okay?" Plotkin listened to the boy's assent, said a few things about keeping Rhonda from being too upset. "And Jack," he added, "I'm proud of you. Good thinking, boy."

The police were predictably angry at having to follow a trail gone so cold, but there was little they could do about it. American tour groups were a vital source of foreign exchange; besides, Saul Plotkin's name carried clout, even over here. They swallowed their ire and got on with the job. Sam Stein was also a heavy contributor to Israel.

It took them little time to find out everything there was to know about the personal relationships of the tourists, including the fact that Jack Kane had a brief fling with the missing girl. But there was no evidence that Kane was implicated in her disappearance, none at all. Nor any other members of the Los Angeles group. They did trace the movement of the tour from its landing in Tel Aviv; they even visited Kibbutz Etz Hadar. When they found that the kibbutz-nik assigned to guide the visitors from Temple Beth Shalom had left a few days after their tour, they were intrigued. But that trail, too, was cold. In fact, it was icy. A few of the kids had seen Amy get out of a jeep in front of the hotel in Ashdod, and one of them was sure the driver had been the guy who took them around the kibbutz, but that was all. Nobody had seen him in or around Be'er Sheva.

The Steins were frantic. They filled the transatlantic telephone wires with urgent pleas, threats, and offers of any amount of U.S. dollars for anyone who could help. Three days later, after the Temple Beth Shalom tour had been allowed to continue with its now-abbreviated itinerary, Sam flew to Tel Aviv. The head of the Israeli police and the personal secretary of Prime Minister Ben-Gurion both told Stein he could do nothing to aid the investigation, but they understood his need to come and they received him with sympathetic cordiality. None of it made any difference.

At the end of three weeks the detective lieutenant in charge of the case said they could do nothing more. They were convinced that Amy was not in Israel.

"Nothing more! That's crazy, insane! A little girl disappears and you look for a few days; then you say that's it? What kind of a country is this?"

"A democracy, Mr. Stein. No, wait, I'm not giving you smart-mouth answers. I got kids of my own, I know how you feel. Please, I'm sick for you . . . But Amy is eighteen; she's not a little girl. We've done everything good police work demands, more. We care about the kids who come here; they're our hope for the future. But, Mr. Stein, there's no evidence of any kind of foul play. We're forced to assume that Amy went wherever she did because she wanted to. There's been no crime."

Stein leaned forward, gripping the edge of the man's desk, searching for something to change the decision. "She's got no passport. Rhonda Plotkin, that's Mrs. Kane, she carried all the kids' passports."

"I know. But that only matters if Amy officially tries to cross a border. We've alerted all the customs and immigration people. If she's wandering around Israel without proper documentation, that's a misdemeanor. Be reasonable, Mr. Stein, we can't maintain a full-scale manhunt for a misdemeanor."

"You said you don't think she's in Israel."

"No, personally I don't. None of us do. It's a small country. And we're well organized. If she was here, I think we'd have found her."

Stein was gray; his breathing came hard. He was listening to a death sentence. "But you also said she couldn't get across the border without a passport."

The Israeli didn't meet the American's eyes. "Officially. I said

447

officially she couldn't do it. The border is long and much of it's desert . . . nobody around for miles."

The two men sat silent for a few seconds. Finally Stein spoke. "What do you think?" he asked in a hoarse whisper. "You personally. If it was your kid, what would you do?"

The policeman stared at his desk blotter and made fleeting impressions on it with his thumbnail. "I think she took off with this Levi character. I think they're somewhere together. When they get tired of whatever game they're playing, she'll come back. As for what I'd do, I'm not a religious man, Mr. Stein, but I'd spend a lot of time in *shul*."

Sam Stein returned to Los Angeles and his shattered wife, and the two of them attempted to piece together the fragments of their lives. "Terrorists," they said. It was the explanation they offered to each other in the small of the night, when bravado no longer sufficed. "Everybody knows Israel is plagued with those fucking Arab terrorists." But if some Arabs kidnapped Amy, why was there yet no ransom note? What did terrorists want with a pretty, rich American girl if not money? The Steins tried desperately to avoid thinking about that question.

Sam also hired a private detective based in Jerusalem. The policeman, the one who had kids of his own, recommended him. Yitzhak Beklem was the detective's name. He sent reports first weekly, then twice a month. None of them said anything much.

For Amy the first six months were a time of insane, illogical euphoria. Six months when her only thoughts not centered in the present moment were fleeting sensations of guilt about her parents. Amy managed to suppress them because it was truly impossible to believe in any reality other than her and Dov and the desert—and the child growing in her body. Even that was a source of wild, improbable joy.

For years she'd agonized over the possibility she might get pregnant. If her period was even one day late, it was a disaster. Now she was ecstatic. And best of all, so was he.

"Dov," she said one night. "Do you remember the first time?"

"The first time I saw you?"

"No. The first time we made love."

"Of course. Do you?"

"Every second of it. The thing I remember best is that you said a prayer first. I think about that all the time."

He pulled her closer, settled her head on his shoulder, stroked her hair. "When our child is born, I'll pray then, too. The same prayer. A thanksgiving."

They were quiet for a long time. The moon shone through the open flap of the tent and filled it with light. "Dov, one more question. When you say it's important, what we're looking for, you sound so solemn. Is it just for us?"

"No, I don't believe that. I think it's for all Jews, maybe the whole damn world, I don't know. I hate to sound so grandiose, but it's what I believe."

Amy sighed. "Me too. It must be." That was the reassurance she sought. The balm for her one guilt, the thought of her parents grieving in California. They must think she was dead. But it would be okay. After Dov found whatever was so important, they'd go back to civilization. They'd get married, and her parents would be thrilled about everything, even their grandchild.

In the early days she had worried about practical things. How long would their canned food last? What would they do if they met any Arabs? That was before she realized how extraordinarily competent Dov was, how he had everything worked out.

He carried a huge supply of maps and a compass, and he always knew exactly where they were. More important, he knew how to make sure that when they needed something, they were close to someplace where he could get it. When they ran low on food or were down to their last spare tank of gasoline, he would leave her with the jeep and stride off alone. She didn't like that part, the waiting, but Dov insisted.

"There may have been some sort of alarm circulated for you, even here. And nobody would take you for an Arab woman, not if they looked twice."

If he wanted to, Dov could look just like a native. As soon as he put on a jellaba and wrapped his head in the crazy kerchief arrangement Amy found so funny, he seemed a different person. And when he returned to her, he had whatever he'd gone to get. Simple.

"How do you manage? Where do you find things like this?" Amy held up a can of Libby's corned beef.

He grinned. "A typical American. You think if there isn't a supermarket 'round the corner, you're bound to starve. This"—he gestured to the canned meat—"has become one of the most ubiquitous foodstuffs of the undeveloped world. They don't know it tastes like dog food. It's easy to find. I always pick a settled village, however small. Never a temporary camp. Then I go from house to house until I come across something we need. After that it only takes money."

Amy realized something else. "You can speak with them, can't you? In their language."

"Sure. That's what I went to Cambridge for. At least twelve dialects of Arabic fluently, and I can get by in a few others. I'd have been mad to come out here if I couldn't do that."

"Then you always knew you were going to do this?"

He never lost patience with her. "Yes, I told you that. When I was a kid, I got interested in riding. I was pretty good, but that was the problem. It started taking a lot of time. I knew I needed good grades to get into Cambridge. So I gave up riding."

"You said you pay the village people, for the food and stuff. What with?"

"A supply of local currency. I bought it in Israel on the black market. Don't worry, we have enough."

After that she stopped worrying about anything. Dov had everything under control, Dov was in charge of her and the future, Dov would take care of her, she loved Dov. Later she'd make it up to her parents. It was all beautifully simple. Best of all, she was convinced for the first time in her life that she too was loved. Perhaps not in the ordinary way, but she was all-important to this man. She was a fundamental part of his so vital, so carefully thought-out plan. For a girl who had never believed in her own worth, that was the headiest elixir of all.

Amy dated everything according to her pregnancy, kept a running calendar in her head. She was in her sixth month when Dov began to get moody. Not unkind to her, never that, just withdrawn and quiet. That was when they were camped in the rolling foothills near Jebel El Dabab. By the time she was eight months

450

along, her body heavy, her back sore, they'd moved south toward the Gulf of Aqaba. That's when Dov's headaches began.

Blinding pain. Terrible. He'd sit for hours holding his head in his hands, rocking back and forth in a steady, monotonous rhythm. She tried everything to help, massaged his neck and shoulders, rubbed his scalp; nothing relieved him. "Just leave me be, please, Amy, just leave me alone."

Finally, when she thought she could no longer bear to watch his suffering, he'd stand up and stretch, and she'd know it was over for a while. Always then Dov would get his lyre and sit next to her, playing over and over the four notes that meant so much and so little.

"You'll find it," she told him. "Don't give up, Dov, darling, whatever you're looking for, you'll find it."

Usually he simply smiled; one day close to her time he said softly, "No, I begin to think that's not meant to be."

Amy stared at him. Their mission, his long quest—was he abandoning it now, after everything that had happened, after the way he'd changed her life?

"Don't look like that," he said. "It's all right, we've done what we're supposed to do. Don't worry, Amy. Everything is going to be fine."

A few days later he went into a nearby village and came back with an old Arab woman. "She's a midwife, at least the local variety. I've brought her to examine you."

Amy shrank back. The woman's yashmak covered everything but her eyes; the skin around them was a network of veins and wrinkles. Her hands were brown and square, old hands with liver spots on the backs. "I don't want her to touch me."

"Don't be frightened. She looks strange to you, but she's delivered hundreds of babies, she knows what she's doing. And she's kind. Please, we need help now. Neither of us has ever done this before, right?" He grinned at her and mocked a punch to her chin. "C'mon, be a good girl. Otherwise she'll expect me to beat you. Good Muslim wives do as they're told."

Amy grinned back at him and let the woman examine her. Afterward the midwife and Dov spoke in words incomprehensible to Amy. "She says you're fine," Dov explained. "A strong female

451

who will bear me dozens of sons. She thinks the baby will be born in about two weeks. As soon as your labor starts, I'm to get her."

And so it was. At four in the morning on August 20, 1959, Amy gave birth to a daughter. The labor was neither particularly long nor difficult, and the Arab midwife came as she promised, bringing another woman from the village with her. They were kind to Amy and stayed with her throughout her ordeal. In the final minutes they showed her how to squat, and the second woman supported Amy's back and her shoulders while she pushed her child into the midwife's hands.

They tried to tell her it was a fine, healthy girl, but she didn't understand until they thrust the baby at her, letting her see its sex and that it had the requisite number of arms and legs. They murmured consolation that she had not borne a son, but Amy didn't understand that either. After they cleaned her up, Dov came into the tent. Amy and the child lay in the corner on the bedroll. She could see from his face that he was in the throes of one of the terrible headaches, but he tried to smile.

"Thank you," he whispered, kissing her gently. "Thank you for my daughter. Her name is Sarah." With that he left, and only after she'd slept and wakened did Amy realize that he hadn't said the prayer, the *Shehecheyanu*. He'd promised to do it, and he hadn't.

They stayed where they were, in peace, for seven weeks. Then Dov announced that he was leaving her.

The baby was at her breast when they drove into Jerusalem. Once more Dov had crossed the Israeli border without her being aware of it and with no need of officialdom. "I'll leave you off one block from the American Consulate," he said. "Just walk straight ahead. You won't have any trouble."

Amy didn't look at him. "Don't do this. Please, Dov, I'm begging you, don't do this to us." Her voice was a harsh whisper; tears streamed down her cheeks. Sarah suckled happily, oblivious of everything.

"I have no choice, Amy. We have no choice. I've told you how it is. We've been all over it."

"Your visions and your voices. Just like always. Take Amy into the desert, have a child, and then leave her, go off just like that. Amy isn't important anyway. Just a little whore you picked up.

And her daughter will probably be the same." She was sobbing now, anger and despair choking her.

"It's not like that. It's that everything I was so sure of has changed somehow. I have nothing inside me anymore, nothing to give you. You and Sarah, you'll both be much better off with your own people—" He broke off, his hands white-knuckled on the wheel. "What's the use? You won't understand because you don't want to. You have the money I gave you?" She didn't answer, but he knew she had. "Just tell the consul who you are. Say you want to call your father. Your folks will be overjoyed. You and Sarah will be fine. I know you will, Amy. I wouldn't leave you otherwise." He drew up to the curb.

She looked at him for the first time in an hour. "I hope you rot in hell, Dov Levi." Not shouting now. Just cursing in soft-spoken fury more vicious than any hysteria. "I hope you live for a long time first, though. A long time to remember what you've done, to beat your head against the wall because you can't undo it. And you never will, remember that. I'm never going to forgive you, and you're never going to get us back. You're never going to see your daughter again." She didn't look after him when he drove away.

They came to Israel in their thousands. Countless temple youth groups, endless tours organized by chapters of B'nai B'rith or Hadassah, droves of descendants of those driven from this place nearly two thousand years before, forbidden to return, scattered to the four winds. No matter what their loyalty to the land of their birth, no matter how brief a time they would spend here, for each this was the mystical homeland. Promised to their forebears, bought by their six million slaughtered, paid for with two thousand years of suffering and blood and sweat and skill. Whether Israelis or members of the Diaspora, they were Jews, and this was their place.

But it belonged to others as well.

The Methodist Golden Agers, the Southern Baptist Convention, the Episcopal Bishops' World Peace Tour, Our Lady Queen of Heaven Parish Jubilee Trip, the North Dakota Lutheran League, the Greek Orthodox Kyrie Society, the Friends of York Minister, El Sociedad de Nuestra Señora de Carmen de Madrid, La Société

453

de la Sacré Coeur de Paris, and a hundred hundred more. Christians of every stripe and nationality, come to see Nazareth and Galilee and Golgotha, come to walk the Via Dolorosa, to descend into the tomb which had been so briefly occupied, to wail, to weep, to laugh for joy. This was their holy land, too.

One thing they had in common; Christians and Jews, Europeans, Americans, Africans, Indians, Asians—all were pilgrims. They were like no other tourists in the world. They came expecting their lives to be changed in some fundamental way.

Rita and Frank Myles were no exception.

"Will the Washington St. Jude group line up over here, please? On the right, please. We don't want to get separated. . . ." The young priest struggled to make his voice heard above the din. His face was red and glistened with sweat. It was so crowded he couldn't get his handkerchief out of his pocket.

"Hang on to me, Rita. C'mon, we can get through here." The Myleses struggled to stay with their three dozen fellow travelers. A woman in a sari tried to push between them. Frank resisted. "Hey! Don't do that . . . just a minute, lady." The Indian woman muttered an apology and searched for another route. Frank pulled his wife to a place of relative calm against the wall of the basilica.

Rita found the crush unbearable. It was hard to breathe; her pink linen dress would be a mess. She should have worn the blue print; it was nylon, didn't need ironing. But today was special, the main event of the whole pilgrimage. She wanted to look her best. "Do you think all these people are going to be at the Mass?"

"God, I don't know. Hope not. But it's a big feast after all."

Rita nodded. The twenty-eighth of October, feast of Sts. Simon and Jude, apostles. Rita didn't know much about Simon. St. Jude was the patron of hopeless cases, things everybody said you couldn't change. That's why she'd reacted so strongly when she saw the notice in the Boston archdiocesan newspaper, the *Pilot*. A pilgrimage in honor of St. Jude, organized by the National Cathedral in Washington, D.C. Ten days in the Holy Land, October 21 to November 1, highlight of the trip to be a Solemn Pontifical Mass in the Church of the Holy Sepulchre in Jerusalem on the saint's feast day. Three hundred dollars per person, double occupancy.

St. Jude would help her to become pregnant, even though she hadn't in five years of marriage. Even though the doctors said it was extremely unlikely. It wouldn't matter then that the Catholic Charities Adoption Bureau wouldn't consider them because Frank was twenty years older than she was.

Rita glanced up at her husband. Fifty wasn't old, not too old to be a father. Frank was going to be a wonderful daddy for the baby they would conceive on this pilgrimage. She had a lovely thought: Maybe she was already pregnant.

Frank was hanging on to her, protecting them against the danger of separation from each other and the group. Impulsively Rita pulled their joined hands to her stomach and pressed. "Maybe," she mouthed. He looked at her and tried to smile.

He'd been telling her for months not to get her hopes too high, ever since they booked the tour. But since they'd been here, Rita had been floating. It was like she was drunk. What was the word for it? Oh, yeah, manic. She was so sure, she had so much faith in St. Jude. But what if St. Jude said no? What would happen to Rita then? Frank felt a knot of fear in his stomach. Maybe she'd get sick, or collapse, or leave him. He shoved yet closer to his wife to ward off any such terrible possibility.

"Wasn't it wonderful, Frank? So beautiful and solemn, and the bishop smiled when he gave me Communion." Rita sighed at the memory, and at the relief when she kicked off her high heels and stretched out on the bed. "I wouldn't care if we were going home this afternoon. I feel like we've accomplished everything we came for."

"Rita, listen. You mustn't let yourself get into a state about this. It's not the end of the world, you know." He sat down beside her and put his palm against her cheek. "A baby would be wonderful, but the most important thing to me is that we've got each other."

"I agree, honey. You know I do. But I'm sure St. Jude heard me. I feel it. I bet I'm a few days along already. I'll have a rabbit test as soon as we're back in Ipswich. It'll be positive, you'll see."

He opened his mouth, but he didn't know what to say. When she looked the way she did now, all happy and glowing, he loved her so much it hurt. How could he say anything to spoil this for her? He leaned over and reached for the typed itinerary on the bedside table. "Let's see, 'Friday Afternoon: Meet after lunch in hotel lobby, followed by bus trip to Masada on the Dead Sea. Return at six-thirty.' Sounds like fun. And we have dinner tonight in an Arab place in the Old Quarter. Good times, huh?"

"Mmm, but I think I'll just stay here this afternoon. You go, honey. Take the bus trip with the others. I'll just rest and get ready for tonight." She was staring up at the ceiling with a dreamy smile on her face. Frank wanted to cry.

Two hours later Rita Myles sat at a sidewalk table, watching the Jerusalem street life and sipping a cup of tea. She liked Israeli tea; it was stronger than at home, more refreshing. She glanced at her watch, just four-thirty; she had time before Frank and the rest would be back from their trip to the Dead Sea. A waiter passed by, and she ordered another pot of tea.

He'd not yet brought it when she saw the girl. She was holding an infant in her arms and looking for a place to sit. All the tables were taken. "Here," Rita called. "Share my table, I'm alone." The girl hesitated. "Do you speak English?" Rita asked.

"Of course, and thank you. I've been walking for half an hour and I'm tired."

"Why, you're American, aren't you?"

The girl nodded. Rita was surprised. The kid was so bedraggled-looking. And her yellow dress was too thin for a chilly day like today. She didn't even have a sweater. The infant was well wrapped, though. "What a darling baby!" Rita peered into the blankets. "Is it a boy or a girl?"

"A girl, her name's Sarah. I'm Amy Stein." Strange to say those words after so long. But she needed to do it, needed to establish some identity after what suddenly seemed a dream in which she had not really existed.

Rita registered the name. So the girl must be Jewish. Oh, well, naturally there were a lot of Jews in the Holy Land. "I'm Rita Myles. From Ipswich, Mass. My husband has gone sightseeing with our tour, but I was a little tired, so I stayed behind."

It was on the tip of Rita's tongue to say she was tired because she was pregnant, only she'd decided not to tell anyone but Frank until the doctor at home confirmed the fact. It might be some kind of jinx. "How old is the baby?" she asked instead.

"Almost two months."

"Is your husband with you? Are you in Israel on vacation or do you live here?"

Amy looked at the woman. A nosy, faded blonde with too pink cheeks wearing a cheap nylon blouse with a big bow. The blouse was pink, too. The waiter approached before she could think of an answer to the questions. He put a pot of tea on the table.

"Here, you have this, I'll get another." Rita gave the order and poured Amy a cup of tea.

Amy felt instantly guilty about her thoughts. Her misery wasn't this woman's fault. And she was kind. The tea was hot and refreshing, Amy drank it thirstily. "Do you know where the American Consulate is?" she asked, setting down the cup. "I was on my way there, but I got lost. I've been walking 'round and 'round, and each time I tried to ask directions, I ran into somebody who just spoke Hebrew."

Rita looked at her, conscious of the fact that the girl had avoided answering the questions about her husband and her presence in Israel. She was in some kind of trouble. Rita was sure of it. "The consulate's around that corner, I think. We can ask the waiter; he speaks some English. But first, are you hungry? How about having a sandwich with me? They have some nice chicken sandwiches."

"Thank you, I'm not hungry. I'd love another cup of tea, though."

Rita poured it. "Here, let me have the baby while you drink that. Your arms must be getting tired."

Rita pressed the child to her breast with a trembling sense of expectation. Soon she'd be holding her own baby. This one was so sweet, sleeping so peacefully; her little head had a fuzz of dark hair, and her tiny hands were clasped into fists beneath her chin. "Does she always sleep with her hands like that?"

"Yes. I think she's going to grow up and be a fighter." They laughed together. Amy's laughter turned to tears.

"Don't cry," Rita said softly. "You're in some kind of trouble. I guessed that right away. Tell me what it is. If I can help, I will." She fished into her bag with one hand and passed Amy a handkerchief.

"I'm sorry to break down. It's going to be okay as soon as I get

457

to the consulate and call my folks in Los Angeles. It's just that so much has happened. I'm still confused."

Rita nodded and waited. After a few seconds she said, "Sometimes talking helps. I don't want to pry. Tell me to mind my own business if you want."

"I can't explain . . ." Amy paused. She didn't really have any reason to tell this woman anything. Only she was so miserable and angry. Both at the same time. And maybe if she practiced explaining now, it would be easier with her parents. And the woman really was kind. A good soul, as her mother would say. "It all started a year ago September. . . ."

Rita listened in silence until Amy stopped speaking. "And all the time you were pregnant, you just camped out. You and this guy Dov?"

"Yes, we just camped out." So simple in the telling. And why was she so careful not to mention Dov's last name? Not for his protection, for Sarah's and her own. While she was lost and looking for the consulate, she started imagining things. Maybe somebody would try to take her baby away from her because she was an unmarried mother. Rita was waiting for her to say more. "We camped out," Amy said again.

"And afterward he just left you on the street? Just like that?"

"Yes, just like that. Me and Sarah."

"He should be shot," Rita said at once. "You've got to forget him and get over it. And don't worry, when your folks find out you're okay and see this gorgeous little baby, they're going to be too happy to be mad. You mark my words."

Amy smiled. "You really think so?"

"Of course. Don't you?"

"Yes, as a matter of fact, I do. I'll go and call them now."

"That's the spirit. Tell you what, I'll stay right here with little Sarah until you come back. It may be easier for you at the consulate if you don't have to worry about her."

Amy hesitated. "Well, she should sleep for another half hour or so. I just fed her. You're sure you don't mind?"

"Of course not. And after you've made your call, we'll go to my hotel. It's right there across the street. We'll get you a room. My husband Frank and I, we'll look after you until everything's straightened out. You'll love Frank. He's a wonderful man."

They called the waiter, and he confirmed that the American Consulate was indeed around the corner. Amy leaned over and kissed her daughter before leaving.

It only took ten minutes to convince them that she was who she said she was. The whereabouts of Amy Stein was still a live issue at the American Consulate; Sam and his private detective had seen to that. They tried to question her, but she wouldn't tell them anything. They kept asking where she'd been and if Dov Levi had been with her.

"I'm not saying anything more until you let me call my father." Amy had made up her mind to that before coming here. Maybe she'd broken some kind of Israeli law. She wanted her father to be in charge before anything happened about that. And it occurred to her that meeting Rita Myles was a blessing. This way nobody would know about Sarah until she told them. And she wouldn't do that until she was damn sure nobody could take her baby away from her.

She'd gotten as far as the Vice-consul's office; now the woman was speaking. "We just want to help you, Miss Stein. You've caused a lot of trouble and a lot of worry to everyone, you know."

"I want to call my parents," Amy repeated.

The Vice-consul sighed. She was a woman of fifty-six who knew she'd never go any higher in the Foreign Service, and she didn't want any black marks on her record at this late date. Certainly none put there by this inconsiderate, stupid girl. "Very well, if you'll just tell me the number." She reached for the phone on her desk.

Amy made an instant decision. She wouldn't tell her parents about Sarah either. Not yet, not while this old hag was listening. She'd call them back tonight from the Myleses' hotel and explain the whole story then. Now she'd just say she was safe and they should send her money for a ticket to get home.

Rita sat holding the baby, crooning softly to her, although the child still slept and required no comfort. In her imagination Rita was in her own pretty kitchen in Ipswich and this was her baby and they were waiting for Frank to come home from the bakery. It was a lovely fantasy. And it was going to come true. She could tell it was; it felt so right and natural to have little Sarah in her arms. Thank you, St. Jude. Thank you for answering my petition.

459

She said three Hail Marys in honor of St. Jude, rocking the child gently to the rhythm of the prayer.

A blue van pulled up to the corner and double-parked. Jerusalem was so crowded; the streets were so narrow. This van would hold up traffic for blocks. She watched the driver climb down from the cab and make placating gestures at the cars behind him. He shouted something. Telling them he'd only be a second, no doubt. That's what everybody said when they did something like that. The same excuse everywhere in the world.

The van was about twenty yards away. There was something written on the side. Rita couldn't read the Hebrew letters but below the words was a crude drawing of loaves of bread. She was thinking about the crusty Israeli bread, comparing it to the soft sliced variety Frank produced, when she saw Amy coming around the corner. Rita stood up and smiled and waved. Amy was smiling, too. So her parents must have taken the news all right. Wonderful, the story would have a happy ending. She couldn't wait to tell Frank all about it.

The explosion happened just at that moment. Rita was looking at Amy Stein's joyful face one second and the next it wasn't there. Neither was the blue van. All she could see was a haze of red and black and then smoke blinded her to everything. Clutching the baby to her breast, Rita ran from the chaos.

There was a long silence. Sarah didn't look at her mother. When she finally spoke, it was to the Israeli. "That doesn't tell me how you became involved." There was a rising note of hysteria in her voice.

Jarib had sat on the arm of the sofa all the while the tale was told; near, but not touching her. Now he gripped her hand and spoke to the stranger. "Who the hell are you, Beklem? How do you know about all this, and why have you been dogging Sarah?"

Yitzhak crossed his short legs and flicked a piece of lint from his trousers. They were crumpled, the crease only a memory. Milly Katz had wanted to press them, but he'd refused. "The waiter in the café where Rita and Amy had tea," he said. "The waiter worked for me. He saw the whole thing."

"Worked for you!" Sarah leaned forward. "What in God's name does that mean? Are you some kind of spy?"

"Nothing so glamorous. I'm a detective. Not in private practice any longer. Now I just try to do my country the occasional service."

It was so unilluminating neither Jarib nor Sarah knew what to reply, what to ask next. Rita spoke instead. The same voice she'd used to tell her part of the tale, low and without emotion, drained of every ounce of feeling.

"That same night, right after Amy was killed, Yitzhak came to see Frank and me in the hotel. We were arguing. I wanted to keep the baby." She didn't say "you" or look at Sarah. It was as if the infant in Israel and the young woman seated across from her were two different people.

"Frank said I was being crazy. Amy's family would want the child. Probably the Israeli police were already looking for her. Then Yitzhak came." Her words faded, she seemed too exhausted to say more. Beklem took up the tale.

"I told them that I knew everything and that I'd made inquiries. The American consul didn't know there was a child, and neither did Amy Stein's family. Sarah might as well not exist as far as anybody official was concerned. So if they wanted to keep her, I would arrange it."

"He didn't even want any money," Rita said. "He said he'd work everything out if we'd just do what he said. Frank still wasn't sure, but I insisted. I told him it was St. Jude answering my prayers.

"The next day Yitzhak came and got the baby and Frank and I went home with the tour group. Two weeks later I got a phone call from somebody saying I was to go to Georgia. To Macon. Sarah was there with a nice lady in a little house. A real pretty little house. And she kept you so nice, honey."

The acknowledgment that she was discussing the real Sarah was a kind of plea for understanding. "I mean, you could see they'd looked after you real well. No diaper rash or anything like that. And all the papers were in order. There was a judge and everything. Frank came, and we went to see him at his home. The judge, I mean. He declared the adoption legal and gave us some papers.

461

That's all there was to it. We never heard from him again until this morning." She jerked her head at the intruder.

"Why?" Sarah demanded. And once more her question was directed to Yitzhak.

"Ah, that. That's a much more complicated story." He looked at Rita. "Could I maybe have a cup of tea? I'm very dry."

She rose automatically and went into the kitchen; they could hear the sound of water running and the soft plonk of the kettle being put on the stove.

"It's because of your father, you see," Yitzhak said. "Your natural father, I mean. He heard voices, and I had reason to believe those voices were connected with something called the Alexandria Testament." He turned to Jarib. "Have you ever heard of it, Professor?"

"No, never."

"Never mind, we'll leave that for later. What I'm trying to explain is that I knew there was a chance the daughter, Sarah here, would be a carrier, too. So I had to protect her. Rita and Frank Myles were obviously good people. And America is a safe place."

"What about the man you call my natural father?" Sarah stood up and began to pace. "What about my grandparents? Who are you, God? Do you decide who's going to live and who's going to die?"

"Sometimes," Yitzhak said softly. Sarah stopped pacing and stared at him. "I made the judgment that Rita and Frank Myles would be more"—he hesitated—"more controllable than a Hollywood producer with a lot of money. I could have better liaison with the Myleses."

Sarah repeated the words he'd used. "Controllable. Liaison. You've kept tabs on me, had me watched?"

"Since that first day. Don't look so shocked. I felt responsible for you. Besides," he added, "I have seen what happens when Jews leave themselves vulnerable. Whatever I have to do to make sure that doesn't happen again, I do it."

"You're . . . a maniac." Sarah's tone was shrill.

"No, a realist. Don't waste your emotions hating me, my dear. There are more important matters to be dealt with. Your father, for instance. His full name is Dov Levi. He's in New York. With your grandfather, as it happens. I want to take you to them. It will have to be tomorrow morning."

Jarib rose and went to Sarah, putting his arm around her, physically inserting himself between her and Beklem. "You've kept your secrets a long time," he said. "Why the sudden interest in bringing them together now?"

"The Alexandria Testament," Yitzhak said. "When you understand about that, you'll understand everything."

Rita returned carrying a tray set with four cups of tea. The china was antique, something called flow-blue. A century and a half earlier it had come to New England as ballast on the clipper ships that plied the China trade. She was very proud of the cups. They were her best, and she used them only on special occasions. Sarah, Jarib, and Yitzhak turned to her. "I thought maybe we could all use something nice and hot to drink," Rita said. "It soothes the nerves, doesn't it?"

"Let me, Mom," Sarah said quietly. She took the tray and distributed the tea, leaving her own on the table beside the couch. Rita was standing in the middle of the room, staring at the cup in her hands as if she'd never seen it before. Gently Sarah led her to the couch and sat beside her.

"He wants me to go to New York and meet my . . . this man Dov."

"Okay," Rita said tonelessly. "Whatever you want."

Sarah put her arm around the older woman, ignoring the presence of the Israeli and even Jarib. "I'm going to go because I want to get to the bottom of all this. But not until after the funeral." There was a sound from the chair where Beklem sat. Sarah turned her head. "You've waited this long, you can damn well wait two more days." And to Rita: "Listen, whatever happens, whoever these people are. It doesn't make any difference. You're my mother and Dad was my father. I love you both. You know that." She saw Jarib's broad grin out of the corner of one eye, but she kept her attention focused on her mother.

Rita was intent on seeking absolution for some guilt of her own. "I couldn't tell you. You've got to try to understand, Sarah. If it had been something else, well, that would have been different. But Frank and I, we loved you so much right from the first minute. We couldn't tell you you were really a Jew."

Fifteen

Bromfield Street was washed and clean-looking after yesterday's rain. Ivy unlocked the shop door and stood for a moment, inhaling the freshened smells of the city. Then she went back to her office and the pile of customs forms she was preparing for the items that would soon be on their way from Europe.

Tim had sent a long telex detailing what they'd bought. The abbreviated language pleased her. It documented every item as a genuine antique, more than a hundred years old. Charges would be minimal. Sarah had done well.

Ivy bit her lip at the thought of the younger woman. Should she go up to Ipswich for the funeral tomorrow? She'd been debating the question for hours and not yet made up her mind. She'd met Rita and Frank only twice, and known Sarah herself less than a year. But Sarah's relationship with Jarib and their problems had served to thrust Ivy into the other woman's life. She felt close to Sarah.

The question remained in the back of her mind while she finished the paper work. By ten Ivy realized the decision was made, of its own volition, as it were. She'd have to go. She hated funerals, but she really couldn't avoid this one. She began organizing her time. There were two appointments to be canceled if she was going to Ipswich on Thursday. And the damn shop would have to be closed all day. But it couldn't be helped, and Ivy was not one to vacillate once she made up her mind.

Jarib let himself into the Rowley house shortly after ten. He'd spent the night in Ipswich, albeit Sarah relegated him to the guest room and wouldn't even permit a visit, but it didn't seem right for him to go to the funeral home first thing with Sarah and her mother. He'd go over this afternoon for a couple of hours. He wasn't officially one of the family yet, but he was going to be. He was sure of that now. He wasn't going to wallow in guilt anymore. Still, worries about Lenore had plagued him for hours. Funny, there was so much new information to think about since last night, but he couldn't concentrate on it. He was still stuck with the old problems.

He'd been gone only three days, but the house was cold and smelled musty. Three days. Incredible, it felt like months. Illogically he turned up the thermostat and opened the windows. Logic didn't seem to be his long suit at the moment. He couldn't, for instance, set himself to figuring out all the implications of the tale Rita and Beklem had told. Or what it meant in terms of Sarah's paranormal experience. Perhaps because he knew he had to deal with the situation that had been most urgent before he went tearing off to Paris. Reluctantly Jarib picked up the telephone and dialed the hospital in Framingham.

"Oh, yes, Dr. Baraak. I expected to hear from you before now." The director's voice was slightly accusatory.

"Sorry, I had to go out of the country very unexpectedly."

"Where are you now?"

"In Rowley. At my house."

"I take it there's still no sign of your wife?"

Jarib's heart sank. That meant that Lenore still hadn't been found. "No, not here. And you haven't located her?"

"No, not yet. The police . . ." The man hesitated.

"Yes," Jarib encouraged.

"The police say we have to face the idea that she may have . . . come to some harm."

"But if there's no evidence, how can we jump to that conclusion?"

The other man sighed. "That's the problem, isn't it? We can't be certain. Worse, they say maybe we'll never know for sure."

"But it doesn't make sense."

"I'm afraid it does. I reacted the same way until they lectured me about rivers and oceans and open building sites and swamps, and God knows what kind of hazards. Mrs. Baraak could . . . well, you see what I mean."

"Yes." Jarib's voice was a dull monotone. "You mean Lenore could be dead, but we'll never be able to prove it." He pushed away the vision of her lovely body mired in a riverbed somewhere, or under a ton of concrete poured all unknowing over her corpse. A grave unmarked, unmourned. He thought of Frank Myles and the family and friends now gathered around his remains, of Rita's story of his last moments on earth, of the priest leading the mantralike string of Aves that were Frank's due and his dirge.

"Never isn't exactly right," the medical man was saying. "I mean, I'm not a lawyer, but I think the law says Mrs. Baraak could be declared legally dead after seven years." There was a long silence on the other end of the line. "Dr. Baraak, are you still there?"

"Yes, I'm here." Seven years. Sweet Christ, seven years.

At one Ivy decided to close the shop for an hour and go upstairs for lunch. As usual, there'd been only one person in all morning, a woman looking for a frame for a photograph of her grandmother. Ivy didn't have anything suitable in the woman's price range; she sent her to a gift shop on Boyleston Street.

She was walking toward the front door, key in hand, when it opened. The bell rang, unnecessarily; she was face-to-face with the couple who entered, a man and a woman. They both looked vaguely familiar, but she could put a name to neither. She put on her greeting customer's smile. "Hello, can I help you?"

It was the man who spoke. He was short and stocky, and he had a broad Boston accent. Not the cultured Kennedy type, just the garden variety. "You don't remember me, I imagine. Sal Petrovsky. You sold me a Florentine writing desk three years ago. And a pair of urns."

Ivy snapped her fingers. "English lead urns, for your garden. Welcome back to Bell, Book, and Candle, Mr. Petrovsky."

The man grinned at her and stuck out his hand. Ivy shook it. The grip was firm. She remembered that she'd thought him okay —a little crazy, disgustingly rich because Papa had left him a few dozen woolen mills, and okay. He didn't seem to have aged since she saw him last. His hair was still blue-black and curly. Maybe he dyed it. In any case he looked the Salvatore part, swarthy and tough, nothing like a Pole. The woman with him was something else.

She was at least six inches taller than Petrovsky, and a good ten years younger. Late twenties was Ivy's first guess. Silver blond hair that she'd swear owed nothing to Clairol, aquamarine eyes, pale and perfect features. Stunning. She remembered Petrovsky as a bachelor and wondered if he'd married. But it wasn't likely. People usually said something like "This is my wife." All Petrovsky said was: "This is Purity."

"How do you do. Ivy Bell." She put out her hand, but the blonde didn't take it. Ivy withdrew, but kept looking at her. She'd swear she'd seen her someplace before. Only how could you forget somebody whose name was Purity? "Anything special you're looking for today?" she asked.

It was the man who answered. "Yes, as a matter of fact. Something for Purity to relax in. A chair, one of those, what do you call them . . . chaise lounges."

"Chaise longue," Ivy corrected. She shook her head. "Sorry, I haven't one. They're quite popular, though. You can probably order one made up in any fabric you like from a furniture place."

Petrovsky made a disparaging gesture. "No, we want an antique. Don't we, doll?" He turned to Purity for confirmation.

"Something old and beautiful, yes," she said. She didn't look at either of them when she spoke. Her eyes were ranging over the shop.

467

Ivy waited. Customers often saw something altogether different from what they thought they wanted. That accounted for over fifty percent of her sales. She kept looking at the woman, trying to place her, getting distracted by her beauty and her gorgeous clothes. Purity wore a camel's hair coat tightly belted at the waist. The collar and cuffs were of cinnamon-colored chinchilla. Her legs were encased in brown suede boots Ivy was fairly certain were Gucci, and her hair tumbled enchantingly around the fur that framed her face. Maybe a little older than she'd first thought. Early thirties. But a knockout.

"What's that over there?" Purity went toward the rear of the shop. Even her movements were elegant.

"Ah, now that could be close," Ivy said. "It's a daybed. Empire. Nineteenth-century French." The piece was half hidden by an elaborate Spanish candlestand. Ivy moved it out of the way. The daybed had a matching head and footboard of inlaid rosewood. It was upholstered in damask of a color that used to be called ashes of roses.

"It's lovely," Purity said.

Sal looked doubtful. "Yeah, but is it comfortable? It'd be too short for you to stretch out on."

"Try it," Ivy said.

Purity sat down, leaning against the back, raising her legs and setting them carefully on the wonderful old silk. "It's perfect."

Sal shrugged. "Okay, you're the boss." He turned to Ivy. "How much? And will you guarantee it's authentic?"

"Yes, to the latter. But it's expensive, Mr. Petrovsky."

"Sal," he corrected. "How expensive?"

Ivy named a figure. They haggled. This was part of the game; it's what people expected when they came to a place like hers. The stuff was secondhand after all, as one of her less reverent customers once pointed out. She'd quoted a price three hundred dollars over what she really wanted, but when at last they agreed on a number, Petrovsky had brought her down four hundred. Because she was distracted. That damned woman. For some reason Purity unnerved her.

"Okay," Petrovsky said. "For seventeen hundred I'll take it."

Almost absentmindedly Ivy got her receipt book and began filling in the details of the purchase. She was still preoccupied by her attempts to place the woman. Finally she turned to her. "I have the oddest feeling that we've met before. What do you think?"

Instantly the aquamarine eyes went cold. A mask seemed to form over Purity's face. Like pulling down a shade. "No, I'm sure we haven't. Can't you do all this later, Sal? I'm hungry." She began walking toward the door.

Petrovsky was in the middle of writing a check. He looked from Ivy to his companion, then back again. "She hasn't been feeling too good," he said softly. It was by way of apology and excuse. Ivy nodded. Hastily he signed the check and pushed it toward her. "I'll phone you later to arrange delivery. Hamilton, you remember." He didn't wait to see if she did. Just hurried out after the blonde.

Ivy followed them. She still had the key in her hand, and she locked the door, looking through the glass, watching the pair walk away. The woman's carriage was as perfect as the rest of her. She walked like a dancer. Jesus! That was it. Purity, hell. The blonde was Lenore Lasky Baraak. At least she had been.

Upstairs Ivy fixed a tuna sandwich. She should feel good about selling the Empire daybed; she'd had it in stock nearly a year. But she didn't feel good; she was upset and didn't exactly know why. To console herself she slathered Hellmann's mayonnaise on the sandwich and opened a bottle of Löwenbräu. To hell with the calories, she wanted comfort food.

But after everything was ready, she didn't feel like eating. She wrapped the sandwich and shoved it into the fridge. Then she took her beer and went to the living room. It was ten of two. She ought to open up again in a few minutes. But she didn't feel like doing that either.

Something was wrong. It didn't add up. So Lenore dumped Jarib, or he dumped her, and they went their separate ways. It happened every day. Ho-hum stuff unless it was your marriage breaking up. So maybe Lenore took it badly, maybe she wanted a clean break with the past, so she changed her name and took up with somebody else. Maybe a string of somebodies else. It was a free country. And the whole thing was what, thirteen or fourteen years ago? Why all the goddamn mystery? What was Jarib hiding?

Something. She was dead certain of that. "Gone," that's what he'd told her. "Lenore's gone." And he refused to talk to Sarah about his first marriage. And Lenore calling herself Purity was scared shitless at the thought that she might be recognized. The whole thing was nuts.

Okay, what it came down to was, Whose side was she on? Sarah's, definitely, she decided. But that wasn't the issue. The choice was between Lenore and Jarib. All Ivy's instincts put her in the woman's camp. Men were bastards. Period. But Jarib was less a bastard than most. At least she'd always thought so. Admittedly he had treated Sarah badly last week. But apparently they'd made it up. She'd spoken with Sarah yesterday. Jarib had gone to France to find her, then turned around and came back with her when she heard about her father. So Jarib had some brownie points in his column.

Her beer had grown warm; she didn't drink it, just held it in her hand. The clock on the Hepplewhite table beside her chimed twice. Ivy rose and went to the telephone.

It rang a long time. Probably he wasn't in Rowley. He must be at the wake with Sarah and Rita. Oh, well, it wasn't any of her business anyway. She'd think about things some more, maybe call him later. Maybe not. She'd see him tomorrow at the funeral in any case.

The funeral home was a cross between Victorian England and Hollywood. Who designed such places? Sarah wondered. Her father's open coffin was surrounded by a red velvet rope suspended from polished brass stanchions. The type of thing they'd had in movie theaters in Boston when she was a kid. To hold back the crowd.

Her folks used to take her to Boston once or twice a month. Rita would go shopping, and Sarah and her father would go to a movie; then they'd meet afterward and go to Chinatown for supper. It was one of her happiest memories. Frank always picked the movie; sometimes his choices were a disaster. Like the time he thought *The Graduate* was about teenagers, so Sarah, ten at the time, was sure to love it. Afterward he'd spent hours trying to explain to his daughter that really the lady just wanted to be nice to the boy and there were some things grown-ups did that kids couldn't understand. Sarah, who'd understood perfectly, had simply nodded. For months afterward she'd kept a picture of Dustin Hoffman on the wall of her bedroom and promised herself that when she grew up, she'd wear her hair like Anne Bancroft.

"So very sorry," somebody murmured in her ear. Sarah put the memory away. She smiled and nodded. Her cheeks ached with smiling, but a couple of hours ago she'd realized she didn't have to say anything. Everyone expected her to be silent. She was sitting a few feet from the coffin. The room was hushed. There was a prie-dieu nearby. People came and went; many of them knelt for a moment to say a prayer for the deceased. A good custom, she decided. More real than all the endless words of condolence.

The funeral home was big. There were at least three wakes taking place today. There was a sign in the foyer where you came in, white movable letters on a black background. It gave the names of the dead and a series of room numbers. The wake of Francis John Myles occupied the entire second floor: This small room the funeral director called the sanctuary, and a bigger room adjoining. The second one was for less formal contact. Rita was out there now. Talking with the endless stream of visitors. The sound of their voices penetrated the hush of the space where Sarah sat.

A few minutes later Rita came in. She looked awful. Black didn't become her, but she'd insisted on wearing a heavy black woolen suit Sarah had never seen. She wondered if her mother had bought it some time ago and put it aside to await this inevitable day. The twenty-year age difference alone would account for that. All her married life Rita must have been anticipating widowhood.

"I'll take your place for a while," Rita whispered. "Jarib just came. He's outside." She spoke with girlish enthusiasm, a conspiratorial kind of glee. Somehow Jarib had metamorphosized in Rita's mind. No longer the undesirable caterpillar, he'd become a butterfly—a man in a family suddenly bereft of that commodity. Moreover, one who had a house in nearby Rowley and wouldn't take Sarah far away. And now the fact that he was a Jew could hardly be counted a detriment. Sarah understood.

"You look so tired," she said softly. Rita's face was unnaturally flushed. The suit wasn't just unbecoming, it was too warm for the overheated rooms.

Rita shook her head. "No, I'm all right. Really, honey." She pressed her daughter's hand. Since last night she'd been hungry for physical contact between them. That was something new. Many times Sarah had felt smothered by Rita's love and devotion, but until now it hadn't been a touching thing. Normally Rita wasn't the hugging and kissing type. But since the revelations of the night before it was as if Rita needed constant, tangible reassurance. Despite what she and Frank had done, Sarah was still there. She was still her daughter. Yitzhak Beklem hadn't managed to spirit her back into the strange world that spawned her after all. This, too, Sarah understood.

But if Rita's feelings were transparent, her own were not. She hadn't had time to come to terms with them; she didn't yet know exactly what they were. Time for that tomorrow, after the funeral. Now the woman who had loved her and succored her, bestowed years of devotion on the child she snatched from a maelstrom, had pressing needs of her own. Impulsively Sarah leaned forward and kissed Rita's cheek.

"I'll just go say hello to Jarib," she said. "Then I'll come back in here."

Jarib was standing in the corner nearest the door. He looked uncomfortable. In Rowley he was always the temporary resident, the man from the city. Here the small-town ethos dominated all. "Not exactly your scene, is it?" Sarah said.

"Is it that obvious? I'm sorry."

"Don't apologize. It's not my scene either." After she said it, she realized how it could be construed. "I don't mean genes. Just that I always knew it was claustrophobic."

"Ssh. If you're overheard, we'll both be tarred and feathered."

"Only in the South. Here in New England we press people to death under stones."

Silly, inconsequential chatter. Wholly inappropriate to the time, the place, and the occasion. But they both felt better for it. "How are you doing?" Jarib asked. "Any headache?"

"No. I'm fine."

"No messages?"

She knew what he meant. "Nope. All quiet on the ghost front. No honest work for you here, Professor."

She didn't hear his reply because the woman who'd been her fifth-grade teacher came up to her just then. Sarah turned to acknowledge her presence and her sympathy. Jarib stepped back a bit and watched her.

Extraordinary that after everything she'd been through, Sarah looked marvelous. She wore black, of course, a plain black jersey dress, nipped with a wide belt of crushable leather. The belt was a soft gray and she'd filled in the neck of the dress with a few gold chains. Mourning, yes, but the outfit didn't bespeak inconsolable grief. Sensitive and entirely appropriate, Jarib realized. And she'd put her hair up, which always made her look older and more sophisticated.

All in all, it was the careful grooming that most struck him. The best definition of courage he'd ever heard, grace under pressure, came to mind. And that this small, strong, independent woman loved him. Once he'd thought her still half child. Today he understood that it was not so. Jarib felt a surge of pride.

Sarah continued talking to her onetime teacher; he couldn't enter into that conversation. Jarib stood and waited. Then he felt a light tap on his arm. He turned, and found himself looking into the eyes of Tom Lasky.

Lasky displayed the opposite of all the qualities he'd just been admiring in Sarah. The face above the black suit and stiff white Roman collar was drawn and haggard; he seemed to have aged ten years since Jarib saw him less than two weeks earlier. "Hello, Tom. How are you?" Never mind that he could see how Tom was. One automatically asked the question anyway.

"Fine, thanks." A meaningless answer to a pro forma question. Lasky's eyes darted between Jarib and Sarah, as if attempting to evaluate the state of their relationship. Jarib remembered Tom's plea last spring. "Give her up, Jarib. You're married." And so he was. And likely to remain so for at least seven more years. He wondered what Tom would say when he heard that. Maybe he'd already heard it. Doubtless he was in touch with the hospital. But his next words didn't confirm that. "Any news?" Lasky asked.

"Not since this morning. I called, but they have nothing to report." He'd save the suggestions of the police for another time and place. Tom didn't look as if he could handle it.

"I've been on retreat," the priest said. "I needed some time to think."

Jarib didn't have a chance to reply. Sarah freed herself from the former schoolteacher and turned to him. "Darling, I . . . Oh, hello, Father." Her voice cooled.

"Hello, Sarah. I'm sorry it's a sad time for you." He nodded toward the next room. "Is your mother in there?"

"Yes."

"I'll just go and see her then." He moved off quickly.

"He acts like he thinks we'll contaminate him with our sin," Sarah said.

"Don't be too hard on him. He's worried about Lenore; besides, he's the kind of guy who feels everything personally. He was always like that, even back when we were students. Another thing," he added. "We wouldn't have found each other without him." Their eyes met for a moment; then they broke the contact. It was too intimate. Almost like making love in public.

"I'd better go in to my mother. You don't have to hang around here."

Jarib took both her hands. People were kissing and hugging all over the place. He hoped his looked like just another gesture of sympathy. "If you're sure you're okay, I will disappear for a few hours. There's something I want to do."

"I'm fine. Really." She cocked her head, studying him, knowing instinctively that what he wanted to do concerned her. "What are you planning?"

"Just a trip to the Yard." She knew he meant Harvard. "I want to spend some time in the library."

"Looking for?"

"Anything that might be there about whatever it is."

"By it, do you mean the Alexandria Testament?"

"Yes, the Alexandria Testament. See you back at your house this evening. Around nine."

· · ·

474

Ariel was delighted with the posting. All his life he'd wanted to see New York. Of course, he wasn't working alone, the way he preferred. Yitzhak had insisted that he liaise with the old guy who'd been tailing Levi since he arrived in the States. Because the other man knew the city while Ariel did not. All the same, there'd been some talk of sending Vita and leaving Ariel to keep Malachy Fanti under surveillance. But that wasn't sensible, as Ariel pointed out. He spoke passable colloquial English; Vita didn't. So he was here, and Vita was doubtless stuck outside the hospital in Strasbourg. Entirely satisfactory.

"What the hell are they doing here?" he asked his cohort now.

"Same thing they did yesterday," Morrie said. "Walking around. Talking about how it used to be when Stein was a kid."

Levi and Stein were across the street, craning their necks to look up at a ramshackle building of stone blackened by over a century of grime, pockmarked with broken windows. On the ground floor there was a gallery displaying pictures that looked to Ariel like meaningless blobs. The gallery had been given a hasty coat of paint and a new door; the upper floors, the ones that interested the two subjects, seemed deserted. Ariel lit a cigarette with the dashboard lighter. "If that's any example of the old days"—he jerked his head at the crumbling facade and the broken windows—"they can have them."

A nearby street sign identified this as Broome Street; behind them was Canal. "Tenements like this," Ariel's informant said. "They're called railroads and dumbbells. Built like you expect from the names. Terrible—no air, no privacy, no sanitation. New York condemned them in the 1890s. Until a few years ago they were all still being lived in."

"And they tell us Americans always obey the law."

The other man grunted. "The people in those places, old people, immigrants, where were they going to go? What could they afford? Look down there." He pointed at the block in front of them. Ariel saw a cluster of brick buildings five stories high. "Hillman Houses," the man said. "Co-ops. You know what a co-op is?"

Ariel nodded.

"Guy by the name of Abe Kazan, he built 'em in the forties. Low-income housing they call it, but not a dole, not a handout from the government with social workers always nosing around. A real house that a working stiff, a guy with nothing, could afford because they made special mortgage deals. Kazan started in the Bronx; then came Hillman, and after that more. If a Jew can be a saint, Kazan's one. The money was put up by the union that broke the sweatshops, the ILGWU, and a Yiddish paper called the *Jewish Daily Forward*. But if Kazan hadn't been there to tell them they had to do it, it never would have got done."

Ariel wasn't really interested. Social subtleties and do-gooders weren't his line. He listened with half an ear, keeping his eyes on the two men still standing across the street. His partner continued talking.

"I'll tell you a funny one. In Hillman they made a big garden in the middle. A courtyard like. You think the people living there would use it? Hell, no. Trees, grass, who cares? All they knew, they couldn't see what was happening. So every day they took their beach chairs out on the sidewalk. Like in the old days."

Like in the old days. Ariel continued staring across the road. Dov and the American big *macher*, the Hollywood producer, they were laughing at something. Five years he'd been futzing around with Levi, one way or another. This was the first time he ever remembered seeing him laugh. Only in America. Just like they said. "You worked with this Kazan?" he asked.

The man made a sound between a laugh and a groan. "Not me. On the other side. I was a Communist. Wormed my way onto the union organizing committee, but the thing I wanted to organize was trouble. According to me, only way you're going to make things better for people, you got to have a revolution. So I was young. What did I know?"

"How long you been here?" Ariel asked.

"In New York? Forty years. I came right after the war. From Hungary by way of Mauthausen." The name of the concentration camp was given no special emphasis.

It figured. "That's how you got to know Yitzhak?"

"Sure. In the displaced persons camp. Didn't hear from him for years. Then one day in '59 he turns up at my front door in Brooklyn. Do I want to help Israel? he asks."

"And?"

476

"And I said, sure. I was a Communist, at least I had been, but when I looked around, there wasn't any Communist country where Jews were treated good. In America we make out okay, as long as we're not poor. So we need a place of our own, where we can do things our way."

"Right after the war, you never thought of going to Palestine?"

"I'm only a hero with my mouth," the other man said softly. "Not if somebody's gonna shoot at me. Once I survived. I didn't want to push my luck. Change things, yes. But with ideas, not bullets. Sabras like you, you can't understand that."

"I understand," Ariel said. "Besides, you're not a Communist anymore. And you're plenty useful to Israel here, right?" He clapped the other man on the shoulder. They always made him want to cry, these people, these survivors. Even Yitzhak, however long he'd known him. Every goddamn time he wanted to cry.

There was movement on the other side of the street. Stein and Levi walked a few yards. The man with Ariel put his hand on the key in the ignition. But the subjects didn't go far. "They're going into that delicatessen on the corner," Ariel said. "They'll be awhile. We can get something to eat, too."

They couldn't go into the same delicatessen. The subjects were oblivious of being watched and few precautions were necessary, but enough was enough. The remaining choices were a little place advertising whole wheat quiche and a pushcart a short way down the block. "Hot dogs okay by you?" the older man asked. "We can eat in the car."

"Fine. I've got to leave soon anyway. The boss is coming to town. I'm to meet him at . . ." Ariel took a notebook from his pocket. "LaGuardia Airport. You'll tell me how to get there?"

"Sure. Only if I was you, I'd take a cab. The subways are dangerous."

"No titles, please," the cardinal had said last night as soon as he could speak. "Just Dom Malachy, I prefer it."

The doctor used that form of address now. "I didn't alert anyone in the Vatican, Dom Malachy. It did not seem that you were in mortal danger and—"

477

Malachy held up his hand. "You did exactly the right thing. I appreciate your discretion. And the excellent care you've all given me. Now, Doctor, please ask them to bring me my clothes. I must leave today."

The old man narrowed his eyes. "You have a strong will, Dom Malachy. I suspect that, not medicine, is behind your apparent quick recovery. But frankly, I do not think you are as well as you seem. You only regained consciousness twelve hours ago; the body simply doesn't heal that quickly. You can confer with one of the younger men here. In fact, I'd prefer that you did. For my part, I'm sure you need more rest. There's nothing specific, but a bout of pneumonia like this in a man your age, it can affect the heart."

"My heart is in God's hands," Malachy said. "And I must go today."

The doctor shrugged. "As you wish. Oh, there's something else, have they shown you the newspapers?"

Malachy had a sudden premonition that this was important, perhaps vital. "No, not yet." His voice was calm despite his fears, despite his terror that whatever was of interest in the newspapers had something to do with the Alexandria Testament. For years he'd lived with that nightmare, that somehow the Jews would find it and publish their distortions and lies. "Is there something of special interest in the papers?"

The doctor smiled. "To you perhaps. The pope died on Monday."

Malachy felt a flood of relief. Death was natural; in the case of a man like His Holiness it was a blessing. He made the sign of the cross. "*Requiescat in pace*. He went peacefully?"

"The best way, at least I imagine you would think so. He was saying Mass."

"A beautiful death."

The doctor shrugged. He was not a religious man; dead was dead, and never a cause for celebration as far as he was concerned. "Now I suppose I've given you another reason to be anxious to leave. I imagine they expect you in Rome to help choose the next pope."

Malachy started to say no, that he had unfinished business in France. Then he paused. He wasn't simply an obscure bishop any longer. He was a cardinal, a member of one of the world's smallest, most influential groups. And he had a duty to do whatever he could to see that some so-called liberal didn't manage to take the chair of Peter. "Yes," he said slowly, "you're right, I must return to Rome."

"Very well, I'll tell them to bring your clothes. But if you value your health, you'll see your own doctor as soon as you get home. I'll call him if you like, explain what's happened and how we've treated you."

Malachy shook his head. "No, no, that won't be necessary. But my office, they must be looking for me."

"I'll have the nurse bring you a telephone."

"Yes—no, wait. I'd prefer to send a telegram. You can arrange that?"

"Of course." The doctor took a pad and a pen from his pocket. "Just write the message."

"Good, thank you." Malachy scrawled a hasty note. It said only that he was in France and had just heard the news, and that he was returning to Rome immediately. He much preferred that to getting embroiled in a long telephone conversation with his secretary.

Vita had been watching outside the hospital since Monday night, when she took over from Ariel. She saw the man in the black suit and the Roman collar come out. He fitted perfectly the description she'd been given. It had to be Fanti. She waited until he got into a taxi, then turned the key in the ignition of the Peugeot.

Fifteen minutes later they were at the railroad station. And a few moments after that she was two places behind him in the line to buy tickets. Near enough to hear what he said.

"Rome, please. When is the next train?"

"You're lucky, Father," the man behind the window said. "There's an express in an hour and a half. First-class?"

"No, no. That's not necessary. Third-class will be fine."

"You're sure, Father? It's not very comfortable."

Malachy smiled. "The third-class coach gets to Rome just as quickly, doesn't it?"

The ticket seller had to agree that it did. He took the money and issued the ticket. "Track Sixteen. At three-thirty."

It was only two, but Vita was in no hurry. Yitzhak had taught her to be thorough. At twenty past three she saw Fanti board the train; at exactly three-thirty she watched it pull out of the station. Only then did she go out and get back in her car and head for Paris. She'd check the office before wiring Yitzhak, just to make sure there was nothing of significance that had come in while he was away.

"I couldn't find anything conclusive in the library," Jarib said. "But it wasn't a wasted trip. I talked with a guy in the history department. He had a vague memory of hearing something sometime. He put me on to somebody else."

Sarah cut the ham and cheese sandwich in two and passed it across the kitchen table. "Are you sure you don't want something hot? There's piles of food left from yesterday. And Milly tells me she's cooking more for tomorrow."

"No, thanks, this is fine." He bit into the sandwich; it had a thick coating of mustard. He loved mustard; Sarah didn't. They knew many such things about each other. Small, inconsequential things that bespoke intimacy. He smiled at her.

They were alone, Rita had taken a sleeping pill and gone to bed. Alone sitting in the kitchen, eating a snack at ten in the evening. Something only a couple did. Jarib smiled at her. "I love you. That's apropos of nothing, I just feel like saying it."

"I love you. Who did he say you should see, and why?"

Jarib picked up the thread of the previous conversation. "A woman by the name of Susan Trilling, professor of Church history. The fellow I spoke with, the only person I knew who happened to be in his office, his field is the classical era."

"The Greeks and the Romans?" Sarah asked. "I'd have thought we needed a—what do you call it?—an Egyptologist."

Jarib shook his head. "I don't think so. This is something to do with religion, darling, with Jews. It has to be. The candles and the horn you saw for a start. Besides, otherwise what's Beklem's interest? And Alexandria is an ancient community. It's been under the rule of everybody who happened to pass by the Nile. From the Philistines a few thousand years ago to the British yesterday."

"I thought of something else," Sarah said. "Alexandria can be the name of a person as well as a place."

"Yes. If that's so, my line of inquiry is a dead end. But I don't think it is. Everything we know points to the city. And I've got to start somewhere."

"We," she corrected. "We've got to start somewhere."

"Agreed." He covered her hand with his. "But you've got the whole emotional load to carry tomorrow. The funeral and then the trip to New York, with whatever is waiting for you there. I'll be with you, of course, but I can't do much to help. So let me pursue the facts as far as I can."

"Okay. Did you get in touch with this Professor Trilling?"

"Not yet. I left a message." Jarib glanced at his watch. "I'd better get back to Rowley. Trilling's husband said she was expected home around eleven. I asked him to have her call me then if she could."

She walked with him to the front door. They clung together for a while; then she gently pushed him away. "Go on, get out of here."

"Sarah, when it's all over, will you live with me?" Insane. What made him ask that now? How could he explain in a few minutes standing by the front door of her mother's house?

"You called the hospital, didn't you?" she asked.

He didn't have to explain, she'd guessed. "Yes."

"And?"

"And they haven't found her and the police think she's probably had some kind of fatal accident, but there's no way to prove it." He took a deep breath. "I haven't checked it out yet, but it looks as if that would mean waiting seven years for her to be declared legally dead. I'll have to wait to be made a widower, probably no chance of a divorce earlier." He looked devastated.

Sarah put her palms on either side of his face. "Don't look so stricken. The legalisms aren't very important. Where have you been, Professor? Locked in your ivory tower? We'll be possums."

Jarib frowned. "What's a possum?"

"A cuddly, furry animal. Also, persons of opposite sex sharing a uni mattress." She laughed at his expression of relief. Then reached up and kissed him lightly. "Good night, darling Jarib. See you in the morning."

He got to Rowley at ten to eleven, and the phone rang twenty minutes later. Jarib answered eagerly, sure it would be Professor Trilling. It wasn't; it was Ivy.

"Listen, I've been vacillating all day, but I decided I'd better tell you."

"Tell me what, Ivy?" He tensed a little. Something in her voice made him wary.

But she didn't get to the point right away. Still vacillating perhaps. "Jarib, do you remember years ago, after you and Lenore split up or whatever, I asked you where she was?"

"I remember." His gut was churning now. But he knew better than to hurry her.

"Gone, that's what you said. I always thought it was a crazy answer. Gone where? But it wasn't any of my business. Still isn't, but—"

"Yes?"

"Do you know a woman named Purity?"

"No, Ivy. I've never met anybody named Purity. Does she know me?"

"Yeah, I think so. Purity's what Lenore is calling herself these days. She doesn't want to admit it, but I recognized her. It probably doesn't mean anything. Why the hell shouldn't she change her name if she wants to? Only the whole thing stinks. Something's not right. I figured I'd better tell you. Just in case."

Without realizing it, he'd been holding his breath. Now he let it out in a long, painful exhalation. "Yes, you'd better tell me. Your hunch was right, Ivy. It's very important and pretty ugly. Can you begin at the beginning and tell me exactly what happened? After that I'll explain." Jarib drew a pad of paper closer and took the top off his pen.

The train pulled into Rome station at midnight. Malachy was exhausted and in pain. His chest felt as if it were constricted with a rubber band, being squeezed tighter and tighter. He had not slept on the hard wooden benches of the third-class car. By now he looked like what he was, a man exhausted and ill.

"Dom Malachy!" The cardinal's private secretary was waiting. "I've met every train," he explained. "Since I got your wire. I had to get to you before the reporters."

"Reporters? What reporters? Why?" Malachy gratefully handed

over his small single suitcase. He wanted to explain that most of his things were still in Paris, but this new information distracted him. "Why should reporters want me?"

The younger man hurried his charge along the platform. "We'll go out this way; it's a side street. Safer. The reporters have been dogging me since yesterday. You're *papabile,* sir. They say you'll be the next pope. All Rome says it."

"Me? They're all mad! No one even knows me; I've only been a cardinal for a few months."

"I know, sir. But that's what they're saying. The last thing the dying pope said was your name. Cardinal Bellini has been try- ing to reach you for two days. And I didn't know where you were, so—"

Malachy held up his hand to end the flow of words. He stopped where he was on the platform and stared into the distance. "Pope," he whispered. "Can it be for this our Lord has been preparing me? To lead the Church, to counter the influence of the lovers of Jews and infidels, to find the Alexandria Testament. With the resources of the entire Church it could be done. . . ."

"Please, Dom Malachy. We must get you home. They mustn't see you like this." The younger man tugged on the arm of the wrinkled, soiled coat. "You have to meet with Cardinal Bellini."

Malachy straightened. "Yes, and when I do so, I must be in my habit. Bellini must know that whatever I am, I will remain a monk."

"Yes," the monsignor agreed, "that's why they want you. It won't hurt to remind Bellini."

The two men went out into the street and found a taxi.

Sixteen

THURSDAY, NOVEMBER 29

It was cloudy and very cold. Rotten weather for a funeral. But probably there wasn't any other kind. The cemetery was on a hill, exposed to the east wind. Sarah pulled the collar of the tweed coat closer around her neck. She wore a black knit suit underneath, but she didn't own a black coat. This one was old and she disliked it, but at least it wasn't bright.

"Go forth, Christian soul," Father Martin was saying. The wind whipped his white alb around his legs. He looked unnaturally plump, because he was wearing a ski jacket beneath the alb. Sarah could see its red polyester sleeve when he lifted his arm to sprinkle the coffin with holy water.

The pallbearers supplied by the funeral director did something to a system of pulleys and winches and lowered into the earth the elaborate mahogany casket on which Rita had insisted. Rita sobbed once, loudly. Sarah put her arm around her mother's shaking shoulders. The wind rose to a howl, almost but not quite drowning out the priest's voice. "Our Father who art in heaven . . ." The assembled company joined in.

Sarah spoke the words without thought, watching Jarib. He stood slightly apart from the family with the friends who'd accompanied the mourners from the church to the graveyard. Pinkie was there, too. She and Max had come back from Virginia yesterday and she'd called Ivy's, looking for Sarah, and heard the news.

Pinkie was reciting the Our Father along with the others. She looked very much at ease in this kind of setting; she'd once told Sarah that being raised to be a southern belle equipped you for all life's most dramatic moments. Jarib looked tense. And he wasn't saying the prayer. Perhaps Jews didn't. She'd thought it universal, maybe not. Only, was Jarib a Jew? By birth, yes. What did that mean? To the anti-Semite it was sufficient; you didn't get the job or the invitation to join the exclusive club. If you were unlucky in the political crapshoot, maybe you wound up being hounded from place to place, or in an oven. In that way Jarib was a Jew. Was she?

The prayer continued. Sarah's voice trailed off before the final amen. Not a conscious choice, just a mark of her confusion. She glanced down at the coffin. Good-bye, Dad. Thank you. Rest in peace.

Easy words, a formula she'd assimilated automatically, like so much else. But she knew what it was supposed to mean. ". . . I believe in the resurrection of the body and the life of the world to come." The Apostles' Creed, bedrock of Catholicism; the promise of personal immortality, unique to Christianity because it was incarnational, posited on a historical event that bonded the human and the divine. If Jesus was the Christ, true God and true man, everything else flowed logically. If not, pie in the sky, a myth to comfort children and fools.

The priest led them from the graveside. Sarah's tight black boots made crackling noises on the frozen earth. To her they sounded loud and clear above the wind. A requiem of a sort. Hollywood version, a lap fade of the feet of the living leaving the place of the dead.

Francis John Myles was buried and gone. Where? She didn't know. But if the voice in her head existed, if in Kohlburg someone had been able to enter her mind and come between her and the woman who spoke to her, if everything Jarib had been telling her for over a year was fact—then why not a heaven, maybe even a hell? Except that it wasn't about logic, not finally, it was about

485

faith. And that was not something you could argue yourself into or out of. It either existed or it didn't. And for her, right now, it didn't. Only this gray, cold day and the pain of her loss and her mother's grief.

Mother and daughter rode alone in the limousine provided for them. A wise custom perhaps. Rita didn't feel the need to keep bearing up. She held Sarah's hand and cried quietly. A line of cars followed the limousine, among them Jarib's. When they drew up to the house, Rita wiped her eyes with a wad of tissues, then shoved them in her pocket. She went up the front walk with her shoulders squared. Tough. A gutsy lady, despite her sometime silliness and lack of sophistication. Sarah walked behind her feeling proud.

Milly had gone to the Mass but not the interment. Instead she'd come home ahead of the others and made everything ready. Yet another buffet was laid out on the dining room table. "I think everything's done," Milly said. "How's your mother holding up?"

"Not too badly. The food looks wonderful, Milly, thank you yet again."

"The least I can do. I didn't know if you'd want the hard-boiled eggs. Only we always have them. I don't know why. Some kind of a symbol maybe. I did them anyway, just in case. You can take them off the table if you want."

Sarah shook her head. The bowl of austerely plain shelled eggs looked a trifle incongruous amid the casseroles and sliced meats. But she liked it. She'd always thought hard-boiled eggs beautiful, white and ovoid and perfect. Artistic considerations seemed a comfort at the moment. A reminder of who she was, at least who she'd been until the night before last. But she couldn't explain any of that to Milly Katz. "We—that is, Christians have them at Easter to symbolize new life. I expect that's why Jews have them at funerals."

Milly smiled. "It's nice to be smart. You're probably right."

She started to tell Milly that she had to catch a four o'clock plane for New York and that Rita would be staying with her sister in Newbury for a few nights. But she didn't. Suddenly, as she looked at the neighbor she'd known all her life, it occurred to her how Yitzhak Beklem had done it. Milly Katz was his liaison, his spy. She'd watched and reported to the ugly little man with the light of fanaticism behind his pale eyes. Because she was a Jew first and foremost, and certain convictions she would inevitably share with the Israeli. Sarah felt sick to her stomach.

"What's the matter?"

Milly's eagle eye missing nothing, as it had doubtless missed nothing for a quarter century. "Just everything," Sarah said flatly. "Go say hello to Mom; you always cheer her up." And she would continue to do so. Sarah wouldn't tell Rita about Milly. What was the point?

Milly left, and Jarib came into the dining room. Everyone else was still parking his car or getting a drink in the living room; they were alone for the first time that day. He hugged her quickly and kissed her lightly. "Okay?"

"I think the answer is, as well as can be expected." She wouldn't tell Jarib either. Not yet. Later maybe, when there was more time.

"Good girl," he said. "Listen, darling, I hate to do this at this minute, but I need to talk to you. Something's come up."

She studied his face. There were lines of tiredness around his eyes. She traced them with her finger. "Lenore?"

"Yes, Lenore."

"I'll go upstairs and wait in my room. You follow me in a couple of minutes."

Three minutes later she shut the door behind him. They didn't embrace; Jarib didn't even wisecrack about getting into her chaste girlhood bedroom at last. "I know where she is," he said. His voice was strained. "At least I think so. She's not dead."

Should she say "thank God"? She couldn't be that hypocritical. Lenore dead and proved to be so would simplify their lives enormously. "Who did you call, the hospital or the police?"

Jarib didn't say anything for a few seconds; then he shook his head. "Neither."

"Jarib! Why not?"

"I don't really know. Don't get upset, just listen for a minute, will you?" He told her about Purity and Sal Petrovsky. It didn't take long to relate everything Ivy had said.

"The guy's very rich, has an estate in Hamilton. Ivy found his address in her records. I . . . ." He hesitated. "I want to go and see her."

"Why?"

Jarib ran his fingers through his hair and turned from her to stare out the window. "I'm to blame for Lenore's being in a mental hospital in the first place."

"You're not. We discussed all that the other night in France." Sarah had a sudden vision of the two of them in the violet-sprigged room of Zelah's *auberge*. Three days ago; it hardly seemed possible. She pushed the vision away. The problem of the moment had to be dealt with. "It's not your fault, Jarib. Nobody thinks it is but you."

"Okay. But what I think is what matters just now. And what I know is that she's had a life of pure hell since the day she married me. Ivy says the woman calling herself Purity was dressed like a fashion model, that this Petrovsky guy obviously doted on her. Ivy says that until she said she knew her from someplace, Purity looked happy."

"And?"

"And if there's been some spontaneous cure, some remission of her illness because she's entered a fantasy land with a man who's willing to play along with her, the authorities won't recognize it. The only shot she has is that they don't know where she is. What right on earth do I have to take it away? Me, of all people."

Sarah went to her dressing table and began compulsively rearranging the silver-backed brushes and porcelain toiletry bottles. They weren't things she used. She'd taken all her own bits and pieces to Ivy's when she moved there. These were decorative items Rita had put in place to cover the void. She stalled as long as she could; then she said what had to be said. "Lenore's dangerous, she killed a man. You can't leave this Petrovsky to face that. If anything happens, you'll really have something to feel guilty about."

"Yes, I've thought of that. That's why I want to see him. The choice has to be his."

"You obviously have a plan; maybe you'd better tell me what it is."

"Nothing very elaborate. I want to go to Hamilton and look around. First of all, just to see if it really is Lenore. There's always the chance Ivy made a mistake."

"And if she didn't?" Sarah turned to face him.

"If it's she, I won't let her see me. That always sets her off. I'll find some way to get Petrovsky alone and talk to him. Then he can do what he wants."

He looked terrible; she hated to burden him further. But one thing more had to be said. "Listen, darling, could it be that you want this other man to make a decision so you won't have to?"

"I thought of that. It's partly true. But I don't know what the hell else to do."

She went to him and put her arms around his neck. "Okay, do it your way. There certainly aren't any clear-cut rights and wrongs. But, Jarib"—she leaned back and looked up at him—"be careful. You're mine now. Lenore doesn't have any more claim. I want you free of this one way or another. I want the life we're entitled to. Who else is going to make me a cuddly, furry possum?"

He kissed her, but it didn't last a long time. Downstairs the noise was increasing. Sarah belonged at Rita's side. "I'll leave now," he said. "It's not far. My suitcase is already in the car. Can you get to Logan without me?"

"Of course." Her own car was in the driveway. Better, Pinkie was downstairs, doubtless oozing charm and wowing everyone in sight. She could drive back with Pinkie.

"Okay," he said. "Meet you at the shuttle at three forty-five."

Pinkie sensed that Sarah didn't want to talk about the death or the funeral. "I'm thinking of going back to work a couple of mornings a week," she said.

"At the publishers'?"

"Nope. A school for brain-injured kids."

"But why? I thought you hated that."

Pinkie shrugged. "Seems like I ought to do something useful, besides recline gracefully and sip lemonade, I mean."

"Okay. I guess it's a good idea if you really want to do it." She wondered if maybe Pinkie and Max were having money troubles.

"What I want, sugar, is to have a baby." Pinkie's voice was just loud enough to carry over the sound of the car. She kept her eyes on the road and didn't look at Sarah. "Only seems like Maxie and I can screw till our back teeth ache and no little seed swims along and finds itself a little egg to love."

No, not money troubles. "I see. Any idea what the problem is? If there's a problem."

"There is sure a problem." The window was cracked, and a breeze ruffled Pinkie's short, thick blond hair. In profile her lashes looked a yard long. "Me. According to the best medical advice money can buy, I am an erratic ovulator. All those years I faithfully took my little pill in the morning were just a waste of precious time. Highly unlikely to conceive is the verdict."

"Oh, Pinkie . . . I'm sorry, darling."

"So am I, sugar. And so is Maxie and all the Schwartz clan. The Widow Arbuckle isn't so sure. She figures maybe the world doesn't need anybody half Jewish and half FFV."

"Have you guys thought of adopting?"

Pinkie shot her a quick glance and a grin. "Ask the man who owns one, huh? We've thought of it. With enthusiasm. Only there are very few babies around to adopt—that is, of the sort the Widow and the Schwartz clan could learn to love. White as snow. The doctor wants me to take baby-making pills."

"And Max?"

"Max says he can't face the possibility of sextuplets or more. And the only one who should be fucking around with my insides is him. He doesn't trust doctors, would you believe?"

Sarah stretched out her hand and touched Pinkie's arm. She would have grabbed it if the other woman were not driving. "Just don't get desperate about it. For God's sake, don't get desperate!"

"Easy, sugar. It's not high drama. A shame maybe, but not the end of the world. Max and I aren't foolish enough to think that." Then, after a pause: "You want to tell me what's been going on? Ivy implied that all hell broke loose soon as my back was turned."

"You might say so. But Ivy doesn't know the half of it. And there's no time to tell you now. Put it on your calendar for some-day soon. When I get back from New York, we'll start at breakfast and maybe by dinner I can tell you the whole story."

"Okay. I'll continue to resist asking why you're going to the wicked big city in the first place. Only I've got to drop you and run. Have to meet Maxie at a dentists' brawl. Wives to dutifully appear on cue."

.   .   .

490

At five to four Jarib still hadn't appeared. The knot of apprehension in Sarah's belly tightened. Everyone else had gone through the gate; the girl behind the counter was tidying her papers and getting ready to close the flight.

"Excuse me," Sarah said. "If I decide not to get on this flight, can I make the next one?"

The girl shrugged. "Sure. There's one every hour until eight. Then another at ten."

"No need to wait for me," a man's voice said heartily.

Sarah half turned. It wasn't Jarib; this man was short and kind of slick-looking, and he spoke with an accent. But he had plucked the boarding card from her hand and passed it across the desk with another one, presumably his own. In one fast movement he scooped up Sarah's overnight case, put his arm around her waist, and pulled her through the barrier. "Don't worry, Miss Myles," he hissed. "Everything's under control."

She was too startled to pull away. "Who are you? Did Jarib send you? Where is he?"

"Yes, Jarib sent me. Wait till we get on the plane," Ariel said. "I'll explain everything. But we must not be late." He hustled her up the steps into the aircraft.

Sarah was confused, but the man seemed totally in charge. And she clung to his words. Everything's under control. Jarib sent me.

"Sorry," the man said five minutes later in answer to her question. "I don't know anything about your Jarib Baraak. My job was to make sure you took the four P.M. flight as arranged." The plane lifted from the edge of the runway. Ariel didn't look at her; he stared out the window at Boston Harbor unfolding beneath them.

"You rotten bastard! This is his doing, isn't it? Yitzhak Beklem sent you."

"Yes. I work for him."

Sarah half rose, but her seat belt was still fastened. She fumbled with it.

"There really isn't anyplace to go until we land," Ariel said mildly. "And this man coming up the aisle wants you to pay for your ticket."

He was right. Until they got to New York, she couldn't do anything. There was no point in making a scene. Sarah gritted her teeth and fished in her wallet for a credit card.

She maneuvered herself to the front of the aircraft just before arrival and was the first person down the steps and through the gate at LaGuardia. The departure desk for Boston was on her right. Sarah turned. Yitzhak Beklem stepped into her path.

"Not that way, please. Come with me, we'll take a taxi."

"I'm not going anywhere with you. I'm going back right now."

Yitzhak remained where he was, blocking her way forward, but he looked inquiringly at Ariel. The younger man spoke in rapid Hebrew. "Her boyfriend didn't show up. I had to improvise."

"Dr. Baraak isn't with you?" Yitzhak looked surprised.

"No," Sarah said tersely. "Now let me pass or I'll yell and that guard over there won't like it. You two are foreigners here." There was no need to enlarge on the threat, and Sarah didn't bother.

"Wait a moment, please," Yitzhak said. "Hear me out. You're worried about Dr. Baraak, why?"

Sarah hesitated. There was no reason to explain anything to the Israeli, but on the other hand, there was no reason not to. And he might be useful. "He had something to do, so we arranged to meet at the airport. He didn't arrive in time, and your hired thug here" —she looked at Ariel with loathing—"hustled me on the plane. I could easily have waited for Jarib and taken the next one. But he had to flex his muscles."

"Then you expect Dr. Baraak on the six o'clock flight?"

Sarah didn't meet his eyes. "I'm not sure."

"You're worried, Sarah," Beklem repeated. "Tell me why. Perhaps I can help."

She didn't answer immediately, but the same arguments applied. This man wanted something from her; she might be able to extract an alliance in exchange. "Jarib was going into a potentially dangerous situation. If it didn't go as he planned . . ." Her voice trailed off. She either had to stop there or tell him the whole story. They still stood in the center of the terminal. People were milling around them; but it wasn't particularly crowded, and no one paid special attention. Just the Israeli. He had evaluated the situation as clearly as she had. Perhaps more so.

"Tell me the rest of it. If you want help, I have to know the details."

"Jarib's first wife was in a hospital for the criminally insane. She escaped about ten days ago. Jarib thinks he knows where she is; he went to see."

"Where was that?" No reaction. Like that old line from "Dragnet." Just the facts, ma'am.

"Hamilton. A town near Ipswich. A private estate belonging to somebody named Petrovsky. That's all I know."

Yitzhak nodded. "And you will go back, and if Dr. Baraak isn't at the airport, you will find this estate in Hamilton and go there. Correct?"

"Yes," Sarah said.

"And what will you do if in fact there is trouble? Are you trained to deal with such situations, Sarah?" He didn't wait for the obvious answer. "Ariel here is so trained. You don't admire him, but he knows his business."

"What are you suggesting?" Her voice was less certain.

"I will send Ariel back on the flight that is going in"—Yitzhak looked at his watch—"twenty minutes. At half past five. Meanwhile you and I will wait here. Ariel will call us when he lands. By then we'll know whether in fact Dr. Baraak took the next plane. If he didn't, Ariel will go to this town wherever it is and find out what is happening."

Sarah still hesitated. It sounded sensible, but she didn't trust Yitzhak Beklem.

"Ariel knows where we will be. He'll be able to bring Dr. Baraak to us as soon as he finds him. I am as anxious as you are for his presence, my dear; the business we're about is his specialty." He shrugged expressively. "I have no reason to wish any harm to Dr. Baraak."

"All right," she said at last. "Do it. But for God's sake, hurry."

The English had been too fast for Ariel to follow. Yitzhak told him the plan again in Hebrew. The whole business took less than three minutes. The two men went together to the nearest public phone, and Ariel copied down the number. Then he headed for the departure gate.

"Now we wait," Yitzhak said. "This will delay us an hour or so, but that's not so terrible. Come, there's a café. We can have something."

"I'm not hungry," Sarah said. But she followed him. Like most

493

people who had been giving orders for a long time, Yitzhak wove a spell. Charisma perhaps, maybe just leadership.

"I don't believe you," Petrovsky said. "Purity's a little strange, I know, but she's not nuts."

Jarib shrugged. "That's your word, not mine. I'm only telling you what happened and where she's been for the last fourteen years."

Jarib looked at the clock behind the other man's shoulder. They were in a drugstore in the small aggregation of shops that passed for downtown Hamilton. The drugstore was very trendy, designed to look like an old-fashioned apothecary. With a soda fountain. Perhaps that was an anachronism, but the theme had been carried forward with a vengeance. The clock was the old schoolhouse variety. It had large black hands on a white face. No mistaking the time, it was twenty past three. He'd have to leave immediately and burn up the highway if he was going to meet Sarah before four.

A lot of time had been wasted. First he got lost finding the winding road through the woods that led to Petrovsky's place. Then he spotted the two of them, the man and Lenore, through the French doors between a wide stone terrace and the living room, but they didn't budge from there for over an hour. They seemed to be listening to music. Lenore had a magazine on her lap and was thumbing through it. He'd studied her a long time. Beautiful still, in fact, as lovely as she'd been as a young girl. The distorting lines of tension that had marked her face each time he visited her in the hospital were gone. She was serene and relaxed. Purity indeed.

As he stood there studying her, his eyes had filled with tears. This was the Lenore that should have been, the woman she'd have grown to be if she'd married someone else and the whole terrible thing hadn't happened. But she'd married him, and Pine Creek wasn't a nightmare but a reality. Nothing was changed. Only the sadness and the waste were made yet more apparent.

He kept waiting because he was sure she'd get up and leave the room soon. Lenore was always terribly restless. But not this day.

494

Finally it was a little after two, and he realized he had to try another
tack. He'd drive back into town and telephone, tell Petrovsky that
if he wanted to hear something important about the woman he
called Purity, he should come and meet him. Alone.

That part of the plan worked, and Jarib cursed himself for not
doing it earlier. But once he and Salvatore Petrovsky were seated
at the marble table, drinking coffee, the whole thing fell apart.

"You want money, right?" Petrovsky said. He'd said the same
thing at least three times.

"No, I don't want any money. And I'm not on some kind of
vendetta aimed at you or her. I've told you the simple truth, Mr.
Petrovsky, all of it. The next move is up to you."

"Simple it ain't," the other man said. "Jesus."

Jarib sipped his drink. It was already too late to make the four
o'clock shuttle. And he couldn't phone Logan and have Sarah
paged. It would take forever, and he was afraid to break the tenuous hold he had on Petrovsky's understanding. He could only
hope she would hold tight for the next flight. And not worry too
much. "Your move," Jarib repeated. "What do you want to
do?"

"You aren't going to report her if I don't want you to, right?"

Jarib gripped the cup with both hands. It was warm, and he was
very chilled. "I'd like not to," he said softly. "Frankly, I'm unsure
what's the right thing to do. I told you that, too."

"Yeah. Okay, say I believe you, and I'm not willing to go the
whole way on that yet. But say I do, just for the sake of argument.
She got raped by four or five of those crackers? That's what you
said?"

"That's what happened."

"And she went back and shot the head off the ringleader?"

Jarib nodded.

"Hell, I don't call that nuts. Sounds like a damned good idea to
me."

"Maybe," Jarib said. "But there were other things. Then and
now."

"Like what?"

"It's hard to explain. Her illness is something you have to see
over a long time. The killing didn't take place until four months

495

after the rape. I lived with her all that time. I never suspected her mind had tipped, that she'd lost touch with reality. She hides it very well when she wants to. But she lives in a world of her own, a whole set of values relating to what she wants and feels and perceives. Those values aren't like yours or mine."

"So what?"

"That's just it," Jarib said quietly. "I don't know so what. Maybe with the right handling it doesn't matter. You're obviously a very rich man. Maybe your money can insulate her from the kinds of things that set her off. She's violently anti-Semitic, you understand that?"

"I guessed. Just a couple of things she said. But that's not so unusual. Frankly, I don't like Jews much myself. Too damned pushy and know-it-all." He didn't apologize, though Jarib had identified himself as a Jew in telling the story of what happened in Pine Creek.

"Okay. I don't really give a damn about your opinion of me or my kind, Mr. Petrovsky. I'm trying to do whatever is best for"— he hesitated—"for my former wife."

Petrovsky didn't let him get away with it. "I thought you said you weren't divorced."

"No, technically we're not."

The other man's eyes narrowed. "You want to get married again?"

"Maybe," Jarib admitted. "But that's not the issue now."

Petrovsky stirred the coffee dregs in his empty cup. "Ah, shit," he said softly. Then: "I've got to give her a chance. Don't call them."

Jarib exhaled. "Okay. I have to go to New York this afternoon. I'll be gone two or three days. I'll call you again as soon as I get back, and we'll talk some more. You'll have had a chance to watch her, knowing the facts. That suit you?"

The Pole rose and threw a couple of bills on the table. "It doesn't suit me, but it's the best thing I can think of. Let's get out of here. After everything you've said, I'm nervous about leaving Purity alone."

That was probably all he'd accomplished, Jarib thought. Making Petrovsky nervous. Which might put paid to any chance the couple had. As the man had said, ah, shit. "Call you by Sunday," he said as they parted. "One more thing, Mr. Petrovsky. Be careful."

"Yeah. And meanwhile there's something you ought to remember."

Jarib waited.

"I really love her. Maybe you never did. That might have been the start of all the trouble."

Everything looked normal when he returned to the house. "Purity! Hey, honey, where are you? Papa's home." Petrovsky's voice echoed in the silence.

He explored every sumptuous inch of this palace his father's money had bought and his mother's Italian sense of style had embellished. But the castle was empty; the princess, gone. He went back to the room he'd given her, the one adjoining his, and looked more carefully. All the beautiful clothes he'd bought her were there. The lovely white lace underthings, the dresses of soft silk and pure wool—the only things missing were what she'd had on. So the next thing to do was see if her coat was still in the closet downstairs.

Petrovsky stopped and stared at the picture he'd hung over her bed. An oil in a heavy gilt frame. St. Thérèse of Lisieux, the "little flower," holding a sheaf of roses and smiling her serene smile. He'd once read a biography of Thérèse that said the legend was distorted, that she got to be a saint through sheer guts and determination. He didn't like that version.

Innocence, a kind of untouched quality, that's what appealed to him about the blonde the first minute he saw her. Only according to this guy Baraak, it wasn't that. She was the way she was because there was nobody home upstairs. Shit.

Her coat wasn't in the closet.

Petrovsky returned to the living room; the magazine she'd been reading was still there, open to a picture of a villa in France. They'd been talking about going to France. Now she had gone somewhere without him. Nobody's business but his and hers.

At least that's how it would have seemed a couple of hours ago. Now he had an uncomfortable feeling that it was important. And that he ought to call this professor and tell him. But the guy said he was going to New York, and Sal had no idea of where to reach

497

him. All he had was the number of the hospital and the name of her psychiatrist. The Jew boy professor gave them to him before he left.

He crumpled the piece of paper in his hand and started to cry.

Yitzhak didn't watch the arriving passengers; he watched Sarah's face. He knew as soon as she saw him. Then he waited while they hugged each other and spoke a few hurried words he couldn't hear. Finally they turned to him.

"This is your party, Beklem," Jarib said. "What do we do next?"

"Did anything special hold you up, Professor?" The professional instinct to check every loose end. Yitzhak wasn't likely to ignore it.

"No, nothing special," Jarib said easily. "I missed the four o'clock flight and figured Sarah had gone ahead, so I took the next one."

"Very well. I have to wait for a phone call from my associate. Then we'll proceed."

"Tell me again," Sam demanded. "What did he say?"

"That he was coming to see us. This evening. That he's bringing something, or someone. That part wasn't clear."

"And you're sure it was Beklem you were talking to?"

Dov smiled, but without humor. "I'm sure."

Sam sat back in his chair and lit a cigar. He smoked very few of them these days. They aggravated his hiatus hernia. But so damn much had happened since Sunday. First Dov and his incredible story, then the inexplicable but real bond he felt with the younger man, a bond that Dov seemed to share. Now a telephone call from a man he hadn't heard from since Amy was killed. Not for him, mind you. The voice on the other end of the phone had asked for Levi. "How do you suppose he knew you were here?"

This time there was no mistaking Levi's snort for laughter. "Yitzhak Beklem has made a career out of knowing everything he wants to know. I imagine we've both been watched."

"Jesus. Just like a movie I probably should've made and didn't."

Sam drew deep on the cigar. It tasted wonderful. "What's he get out of it?"

"Yitzhak? He's a not uncommon breed. A fanatic. Could be anything—money, art, crime. With him it happens to be Israel. But the symptoms are the same in any case. Nothing and nobody are allowed to stand in the way of what he thinks is right and necessary."

Sam flicked an ash and stared reflectively at the glowing tip of the cigar. "After Amy, well, I found it hard to be a big Israel supporter. But still, I always bought the bonds. Every year. In '67, as soon as the trouble started, I pledged ten thousand dollars and got it up in five days. It's not hard to understand."

"No," Dov agreed. "And I don't know for certain, but I think Beklem was in one of the camps."

"Jesus," Sam said again. He stubbed out the cigar; it didn't taste so good anymore. And true to form, he had the beginnings of a wicked heartburn. "I gotta take some Maalox." On his way to the kitchen he asked, "You want something? A drink maybe?"

"No, thanks."

In three days Dov had taken only half a dozen drinks. Not a conscious reformation, he'd simply been enjoying himself too much to feel the need. Going around the Lower East Side with the old man had been a pleasure. Not least because he realized how much joy it gave Sam to show him the neighborhood. Now reality was intruding again. Yitzhak Beklem, the puppet master, was in New York getting ready to pull some more strings. Probably he really should want a drink now, but somehow he didn't. Maybe because for once he wasn't alone. He was sharing the burden of his guilt and Beklem's demands.

Your father and your grandfather. That's how Yitzhak had identified them. But Sarah didn't think of them like that. Until this moment, going up in the elevator of the apartment building on East Sixtieth Street, she hadn't really thought of them at all. Not as two separate individuals. She was too concerned with her own reactions to the truth about her birth and origins to wonder about the others whom the drama had affected. Even now they were simply people she'd promised to see.

The doors hissed open. The flashing counter overhead said they were on the seventh floor. "This is it." Yitzhak waited for her to precede him.

She started down a corridor carpeted in dark green, then stopped. "Listen, you said you didn't tell them about me, who I am. But the older man, Amy's father, he must be in his seventies. Maybe he has a weak heart."

"Sam Stein's as tough as they make them. Don't worry."

That's what he always said. Don't worry. But she couldn't help it. She looked at Jarib. He smiled encouragingly.

"Come, they're waiting for us." Yitzhak took her arm and prodded her forward.

The man who opened the door didn't say anything at first. He simply looked at the Israeli. Sarah had time to note that he was very fat and almost bald. Elderly. So he must be Sam. She felt no sense of kinship, but then, she hadn't expected to.

"Yeah," the man said at last. "You're Beklem. Even after all this time, I recognize you. You're a prize *putz,* you know that?"

Beklem didn't bother to respond to the insult. "May we come in? Dov's here?"

"Yeah, he's here." He glanced at Sarah and Jarib for the first time. "Who are they?"

"Later." Beklem pushed past him.

She had a quick impression of the apartment—expensive, glitzy, very decorated, a terrible painting over the couch—then of the man sitting on the couch. Dov Levi, it had to be. He looked surprised when he saw her. Some kind of recognition or just that a woman was present? She couldn't tell. He rose. Short, a few inches taller than she, beautiful white hair. She wondered what color it had been before, and if Amy had been dark. She was too far away to tell anything about the man's eyes.

"Hello, Dov." Yitzhak moved to the center of the room, took command effortlessly. "I think we should all sit down. Sam, you've got something to drink? A little brandy maybe?"

"I don't give liquor to cocksuckers like you." He glanced at Sarah, but not to apologize for his language. "The lady wants a drink, she's welcome."

"Please, don't go to any trouble."

Yitzhak smiled. "Get the brandy, Sam. It's not for me, but for you and Dov. You're going to need it."

Stein looked at him for a moment, then busied himself with a bottle and glasses.

Yitzhak motioned Sarah to a chair. Jarib found one on the other side of the room. Not a player, an audience of one. Sarah unbuttoned her coat and slipped it from her shoulders. She was still wearing the black jersey dress she'd worn to the funeral. There hadn't been time to change. She must be looking awful. Cold despite the warmth of the room, and pale no doubt. Dov Levi was staring at her.

Nobody said anything for a few seconds. Sam handed snifters of brandy around, and she took one gratefully, murmuring her thanks and noting that he had poured a drink for Beklem, despite what he'd said.

"Okay," the Israeli said finally. "I think I should tell you who this young lady is. Her name is Sarah Myles. At least Myles is the name she's used since she was three months old. That's when she was adopted."

He paused for a moment and watched the two men. Sarah, too, looked at Sam and Dov. Sam showed no reaction, just hostility, but Dov was staring yet more intently at her. He started to say something, then took a long swallow of his brandy instead.

None of that byplay was lost on Yitzhak. "You've guessed?" He directed the question at the younger man.

"I . . .my God . . .Is it true?"

"Yes."

Levi slumped back in his chair. He was visibly trembling. He didn't take his eyes from Sarah, but all he said was "my God" a second time.

"Will somebody tell me what the hell's going on?" Sam's voice was harsh with anger and frustration, but when Sarah looked at him, she saw other things. His jaw was clenched, and there was something in the back of his eyes. Some glimmer of a suspicion he perhaps didn't want to acknowledge. Because he was afraid, she realized. Afraid it might not be true. And he desperately wanted it to be true. She understood the whole thing instantly.

She turned to Yitzhak. "Shut up for once, will you?" No matter how tough he said the old man was, she was frightened by the play of emotion she saw on his face. Sarah rose and crossed the room. "Look at me, please, Mr. Stein," she said gently. She reached out a hand and touched his shoulder. "Please don't be upset. There was nothing any of us could do. He"—she jerked her head toward Yitzhak—"arranged everything. Everyone else was simply a pawn."

"I don't understand." It was the faintest whisper, incongruous coming from Stein, but as much as he could manage.

"I'm Amy's daughter," Sarah said quietly.

Sam stared at her a moment, then passed his hand over his eyes as if to wipe away a vision—or a tear. "I know there was a child. Dov told me a couple of days ago. But she died when my Amy did. The terrorist bomb got them both."

"No, it didn't. I was the child. I survived."

"Who says? Him? Why should we believe anything that *putz* says?"

"Not just him." She shook her head. "My mother—that is, Rita Myles, my adopted mother—told me the whole story the night before last. She met Amy when she was on her way to the American Consulate to telephone you. Amy left me with Rita. I wasn't with her when she was killed, everyone just assumed . . ." Her voice trailed off. How could she explain about Rita's desperate need, her decision not to look for the Steins and tell them that they had a granddaughter.

But Sam wasn't thinking of that. He raised his hands and put them on either side of Sarah's face, tipping it to the light. "It could be true," he whispered finally. "Dov, what do you think?"

Levi rose, still shaking, and took a step closer. He didn't say anything; he seemed incapable of it. Sarah turned to him. His eyes were green, the same as hers. "We have the same color eyes," she said.

"And something else in common." Yitzhak's voice, coming from the other side of the room as if to remind them of his presence, his role in orchestrating this scene. "Tell him about your experience, Sarah. Tell him what you hear."

She didn't say anything immediately, still captured by the mounting emotion of the two men on either side of her. It was

Dov who broke the silence. He began to hum. Before he reached the end of the four notes, Sarah chimed in. "Yes, that's the music," she said. "Over and over again, those same four notes. You've heard them, too?"

"All my life," Dov said softly. "In a way that's how you came to be born."

His acknowledgment that she was indeed his daughter passed without comment, but not unrecognized. Sam Stein began to sob.

Twenty minutes later some of the initial shock, and the emotion, were spent. "Mind my asking about this other guy here?" Sam had been introduced to Jarib, but he didn't seem to remember.

"Professor Jarib Baraak," Sarah said. Gently; she felt a need to be very gentle with the old man. "He's my . . . we're engaged."

"Hey, that's great! We can make a big wedding. What do you say, Dov? A big affair. I'll pay for the whole thing," he added quickly. "It'll be a pleasure."

Sarah looked a little desperate.

"Thanks, Mr. Stein," Jarib said. "We haven't set a date yet, but we'll keep the offer in mind."

Dov was looking at Jarib and at Beklem. "Professor of what, if I might ask?"

Yitzhak smiled.

"Parapsychology," Jarib said. "That's how Sarah and I met. She came to me because of her paranormal experience."

Sarah turned to the man she couldn't yet think of as her father. "When I was a kid, there was just the music. Then, a year or so ago, I was in an automobile accident. After that I heard a woman's voice calling my name, and I seemed to"—she fumbled for the right words—"to sense a great sadness. Not mine, I wasn't sad, but I could feel that she was. Terrible anguish. It was awful."

Dov nodded knowingly. "And did you 'see' things?"

"Yes. Candles, a kind of horn. And once there was a mob scene. A riot. Flames, people dying." She shuddered, and Jarib took her hand.

"The first thing I ever saw was a scroll," Dov said. "Eventually I realized it was a Torah, but not until years later. When I was very little, before my family left Palestine, a woman . . . I can only say she 'visited' me. Her name was Sarah. It seemed to me that I went away with her. I can't say where or why. Then—" He broke off, as if the rest were painful.

"Go on," Yitzhak said eagerly. He'd been quietly listening; now he leaned forward. "Go on, Dov. You and Sarah. If the two of you try, you can find out a lot more."

"Just hold on a minute." Jarib's words were edged with anger. "This isn't a parlor game, Beklem. What you're suggesting might work. But it will be an enormous strain on both of them. And Sarah has had a hell of a day. There's no way I'm going to let her go on now."

"We've waited a long time, Professor," Yitzhak said.

"I want to get it over with," Sarah added. "I told my mother I'd be away as short a time as possible."

"The professor is right," Dov said. "I'm pretty tired, too. Tomorrow. First thing in the morning. Sam, can we do it here?"

"What the hell 'it' is I don't know. But sure, you can do it here."

"That's settled then," Jarib said. "We'll meet you here at ten tomorrow morning. Now I'm taking Sarah to a hotel."

"You don't want to spend the night here?" Sam looked at Sarah hopefully. "There's still a lot we could talk about."

"Let her go, Sam," Dov said softly. "We'll both have plenty of chances to be with Sarah." He turned to her. "We will, won't we?"

"Yes. I hope so." She smiled at them both, excluding only Yitzhak. "But Jarib's right, I am exhausted. My father's funeral was this morning." She looked at Dov. "I mean . . ."

"I know what you mean. Your father. The man who loved you and raised you and gave you his name. I'm a very late entry, Sarah. I don't expect to take his place. Just call me Dov, okay? I hope we can be friends."

"You got a grandfather, too?" Sam asked wistfully.

Sarah grinned at him. "Nope. All my would-be grandparents were dead before Rita and Frank adopted me. You're the one and only." She crossed the room and kissed his cheek. Sam beamed.

"Can anybody suggest a hotel nearby?" Jarib asked.

"What suggest?" Sam started for the telephone in the bedroom. "I'm putting you kids up at the Helmsley. My guests. Don't argue, I won't listen." He paused at the door. "And I may be old, but I ain't senile. I'll make it a double room."

504

. . .

The Helmsley was ten blocks away on Fiftieth and Madison. It was after nine by the time they checked in. Once the Villard Mansion and later the residence of the archbishops of New York, today it was perhaps the most luxurious hotel in the city. For a moment Sarah was put off by the opulence: marble and gilt and crystal, a curved double staircase, the thickest rugs, the most exquisite fabrics. She'd wanted someplace quiet and cozy, a place to hide with Jarib. But they made it easy to love the Helmsley.

"Of course, sir," the desk clerk said in answer to Jarib's question. "The Trianon is still serving dinner. Or there's the Madison Room if you prefer a lighter meal."

They settled on the Madison Room. Designed in 1886, it was perfectly preserved—marble columns, a gilt and mosaic ceiling, elegant period furniture. But also lovely soft lighting, attentive service, a piano tinkling ever so softly in the background. Sarah felt the tension begin to ease from her neck and her shoulders.

"Nice," Jarib said.

"Very," she agreed.

And they grinned at each other and ate scampi loaded with garlic and said it didn't matter since they were both having the same thing. And they drank a bottle of fine French Riesling in memory of Alsace and toasted the generosity of Sam Stein. Then they went upstairs and made love, and later, while they lay side by side, Sarah cried a little; for Frank and for Rita and for Dov Levi and Sam Stein, and for herself.

Jarib held her and soothed her and, when she was calm, told her about Lenore and Sal Petrovsky and how things had been left. Soon they slept, and for a little while neither of them had to think about the Alexandria Testament.

Purity had known something was wrong as soon as Sal got off the telephone. She was sensitive to things like that, much more than he could ever realize. "Who was it?" she'd asked.

"Just a guy. Business. I have to meet him downtown. Back as soon as I can."

But Sal didn't have business meetings. He was just rich without doing anything. And there had been something in his eyes, something in the way he looked at her. So Purity had known the phone call concerned her somehow, and she'd waited until she heard the BMW drive away, then went up to her room and got the special thing she'd hidden and came down and put on her coat.

Taking the money was a last-minute idea. There was always lots of money around Sal's house. Tens and twenties and even fifty-dollar bills were poked into drawers and lying on shelves and stuffed into an unused ashtray in the kitchen. She went from room to room and gathered up what she could find, then set out to walk the mile and a half into the center of Hamilton.

The BMW was easy to spot outside the drugstore, and Purity got there in time to look in the window and see that she'd been right. Sal was talking to Jarib. Jarib had found her; now he'd tell Sal terrible lies. Jews all told lies. Maybe Sal was really a Jew too.

When the two men came out, she hid in a doorway so they didn't see her. But she heard them. And she kept her hand in her pocket, closed tightly around the sharpened screwdriver.

Never, since the time of the Ceasars, has Rome been anything other than crammed with people, noisy, dirty—and heart-stoppingly exciting. During moments of high drama in the Catholic Church all those things are intensified almost beyond possibility. Amazingly, the population can double and still everyone manage to find a place to sleep, there can be yet more traffic screaming its way through the streets, and the litter from all that teeming humanity can somehow be absorbed.

The three priests eating a late supper in a small trattoria in the district known as the Trastevere were ordinary clerics who found themselves in the city at this historic moment by sheer chance. Their only role would be to join the throng in front of St. Peter's and wait for white smoke. That and speculate. Speculating was the game of the moment and any number could play.

Monsignor Larry Donovan was the highest ranking among them and he was listening intently to the young man on his right. "Word is that the conclave will be ended by suppertime Sunday night.

They're going to make Fanti pope by acclamation, without even a ballot."

Donovan put down his fork. "Say that again."

"Haven't you heard? Malachy Fanti, the Benedictine. They're going to declare him pope. Everybody says so."

"Who's everybody?"

"Just everybody," the other priest repeated.

"Where did you hear this? C'mon, give me something specific. Somebody told you. Who?"

"Don't get so excited, Larry. I'm just telling you what's being said. I didn't start the story. As a matter of fact, I got it from a guy I know real well. He's an Italian, with the Secretariat for Religious."

"Can I talk with him?"

"Not now you can't. He's been assigned to the staff of some cardinal from Africa. Everybody with a specific assignment is busy as hell right now."

Donovan leaned his elbows on the table and put his head in his hands. "My God . . ."

A third man had been listening to the exchange. "What's the matter, Larry? Don't you like Fanti? I've heard he's a truly holy man. The story is he just got back to Rome last night, and he was shocked to hear that his name was being mentioned. He doesn't covet the job; apparently it was never his idea. That's got to be in his favor."

"In some ways he is a very holy man," Donovan agreed. "I used to work for him so I know that's true. He's saintly. He's also a rabid anti-Semite. The kind that believes in a world conspiracy of Jews out to take over everything and bring down the Church."

"That's crazy."

"Yes," Donovan said quietly. "That's crazy."

"If it's true, you've got to tell somebody."

"Who do I tell? I can't believe there's anybody in this town who doesn't know. Fanti's been like this for years."

The first man shrugged. "I saw some figures the other day, nearly half the cardinals aren't from Rome. And the percentage from the third world is higher than ever before. Guys like that don't know Vatican scuttlebut."

The second man leaned over and tapped Donovan's shoulder. "Bellini," he said. "I heard he was king making; I didn't know who. Now I'll bet it's Fanti."

Donovan frowned. "Bellini is power hungry, but I never heard he was an anti-Semite."

"Doesn't have to be," the other man said. "Probably he figures he can control Fanti if he's the one who puts him in office. It's happened before."

"You're right, I've got to talk to someone." Donovan toyed with his glass of wine. "My own cardinal, I don't know who else."

"Hey, you guys," the young one again, "where's your faith? What about the Holy Spirit? God's not going to let us have some nut as pope."

Donovan had already risen to go. "Read a little history, my young friend. Sometimes the Holy Spirit needs help."

Two hours later he said the same thing to the cardinal archbishop of Boston. "I'm not doubting the conclave will have divine guidance, Your Eminence; I just feel it's my duty to tell you what I know."

The cardinal nodded. He was familiar with Donovan's reputation, a sober levelheaded man. That's why he'd agreed to see him at this hour on such short notice. "Tell me again."

"Dom Malachy is as holy as they say he is, an ascetic and a man of prayer who never forgets he's a Benedictine monk. But he's convinced that some mysterious document called the Alexandria Testament exists. And that if the Jews ever find it, they can use it to discredit the Church, and that it's his job to see that doesn't happen."

"And does it exist?"

"Nobody knows for sure. Most other scholars reserve judgment. But it certainly may."

"And if it's found, will it discredit the faith?"

"I don't know. But if it's ever found, that's the time to deal with it. Eminence, the Church doesn't need a fanatic in the chair of Peter. We can't make all the noises we've been making about atonement for past sins and ecumenism, then elect a confirmed anti-Semite as pope."

The cardinal leaned back in his chair and sipped his whiskey. It was sour mash bourbon; he never traveled without an adequate supply. "Listen to me, Monsignor. I am just as concerned for the Church's reputation as you are. But I have no desire to be locked up in that medieval fortress one minute longer than necessary. And I have to believe that if all my brother cardinals are prepared to elect a man by acclamation, then that's the will of God."

"With respect, sir, not if they don't have all the facts when they make the judgment. Not if they're being manipulated by an old fox like Bellini."

"Ah, yes, Bellini. I don't doubt he's capable of playing hardball —and clever politics. But I don't think he's an anti-Semite."

"Dom Malachy can be disarmingly simple, Eminence. I wouldn't be surprised if Bellini had convinced himself that he can handle Fanti. Only I know better. He'll do irreparable damage. Just the fact of his election. Every important Jewish opinion maker in the world knows Fanti's reputation. What are we going to look like if we elect him pope?"

The prelate stood up and refilled his glass. "Okay, say I agree with you. There's not a lot I can do. The American cardinals aren't held in very high esteem at the moment. Our church is too radical for the old guard and too rich for the Young Turks."

"You can talk, sir. Just talk. Tell as many people as will listen about Fanti's beliefs."

The older man studied his visitor over the rim of his glass. "No chance of this report of yours coming out a few weeks early? Just so the Jewish issue is in the forefront of everyone's mind."

"No, sir. It's not ready. I couldn't rush the kind of scholars on my committee. Even if I wanted to."

"No, I suppose you couldn't. All right, Monsignor. I'll do what I can. But I warn you, it isn't going to be worth a great deal against a rising tide. Not unless you get me some kind of ammunition to use against Bellini."

Morrie had been instructed to wait outside Sam Stein's place until Yitzhak told him differently. He was there when the man and woman who'd arrived with the boss left, and still there ten minutes later, when Yitzhak himself came into the street.

"Go home, Morrie," Yitzhak said wearily. "Nothing more is going to happen tonight. I'll call you when I need you again."

"You want me to drive you someplace? A hotel maybe?"

"No, I think I'd like to walk for a while. Go on home. And thanks."

Morrie got to Flatbush a little before nine-thirty, just before the basketball game between the Celts and the Knicks started. He was a big Knickerbocker fan. His wife brought him a tray with a bowl of beef stew and a beer. There was something else on the tray as well.

"It's a telegram," she explained. "It came in the mail this afternoon. I guess maybe they tried to phone it earlier, but I wasn't here."

"What the hell do you mean you weren't here?" He ripped open the envelope.

"Don't use that tone with me, Morrie. I mean what I said. You told me you wouldn't be coming home last night. Business, you said. A little monkey business maybe? You and all your secrets, how the hell would I know? And I don't like to stay in the house alone, you know that. I went to Queens to stay with Rosie."

Rosie was her sister. "I'm sorry, honey," he said. "It's not your fault. And I wasn't away on any monkey business. I had stuff to do for Yitzhak."

She wasn't to be placated so easily. "Lately that's all I hear around here. Yitzhak, Yitzhak. For what he pays you, you shouldn't have to stay out all night. And you can tell him I said so."

"I'll tell him," Morrie promised. He left the stew and the television and went into the bedroom and found Sam Stein's number and telephoned. But Yitzhak hadn't returned there, and Stein didn't know where he was. He'd be back at ten the next morning.

"Tell him to call me first thing," Morrie said. "Morrie from Flatbush. Don't forget, it's important."

He wasn't sure whether or not it was. The telegram was in French, and he didn't know the language. It was signed Vita. He didn't know the name either, but it was bound to be another of Yitzhak's operatives. That gave him the idea of trying Ariel's hotel. But Ariel wasn't in. So important the message might be, but he had no choice but to sit on it until the morning.

By the time he returned to the television the Celtics had taken a seven-point lead and the beef stew was cold.

Seventeen

FRIDAY,
NOVEMBER 30

"All right," Jarib said. "Dov, you sit here, Sarah, right next to him." He turned to Yitzhak and Stein. "I'm not too happy about both of you being present. It would really be a lot better if you'd take a walk for an hour or so."

Both men shook their heads. They'd already had this argument. Yitzhak refused point-blank to leave; he didn't bother with an explanation. Stein insisted that if something weird was going to happen involving Dov and Sarah, in his house yet, he was staying.

Jarib waited a moment, to see if they'd changed their minds. Then he shrugged. Sarah and Dov had said it didn't matter. And as long as they weren't unnerved by the presence of the other two, it probably didn't.

"Let's examine what we know so far." Jarib's voice was low and matter-of-fact, calming. "Dov has had the experience of the woman's voice and the music for most of his life. Much less so during the last twenty-five years, but before that he heard it often."

"Always," Dov corrected. "Not necessarily in a specific way, but it was always there. And not just the limited communication

Sarah talked about. What I had for the first thirty years of my life was"—he paused—"a presence. I never made a decision without consulting it. Doing what it seemed the voice wanted was the focus of my existence."

Jarib nodded. Sarah's father, Jarib had known Frank Myles so little that he had no difficulty thinking of Levi as such, was an educated and intelligent man. That helped. Two thoughtful and perceptive subjects would make an experiment like this one at least feasible. He continued looking at Dov. "Thank you, that's clear. Let's see if I've got the rest of it. After Sarah was born, the thing you call the presence seemed to disappear?"

"Something like that. I'd been so sure I was doing what I was supposed to do, you see. I knew Amy was the woman I'd been waiting for the first moment I saw her. When we went into the desert, I was following instructions. I believed I was looking for something vital."

"The Alexandria Testament." Yitzhak's voice. Spoken low. Almost like a prayer.

Jarib glared. "If you want me to go on with this, Beklem, you'll keep your mouth shut. Otherwise I wash my hands of it."

"Excuse me," Yitzhak said mildly.

Jarib turned back to Dov. "But whatever you were looking for, you didn't find it?"

"No. What's more, I became convinced that I wouldn't, that I wasn't meant to. That I'd been . . . how to express it? Used. That the presence was laughing at me. Worse, I'd used Amy. I felt I had nothing to offer her, that I'd built our relationship on a lie. So I decided to send her back to her family in California." He'd been looking at Jarib; now he switched his attention to Sarah. "I wish I could make you understand. It wasn't that I didn't love you or your mother. It was a devastating realization that my whole life, as I saw it, had been built on a . . ."

"A lie?" Sarah offered. Her voice was gentle.

"No. Worse than that. On a joke."

He held her glance for a moment, then focused on Jarib again. "When I heard that Sarah and Amy had been blown up by a terrorist bomb, I blamed myself. They were only on that particular street because I put them there. I don't remember much about the days

512

immediately after the accident. I got drunk and stayed that way. Meanwhile, the police were looking for me. They had been since Amy was reported missing, but they didn't find me. He did." He gestured in the direction of Beklem. The old man didn't flinch.

Jarib understood Dov's need to explain, but also that it was his job to keep the encounter focused on the business at hand. "Very well, but what we want to know is if you've had any experience of the voice since that time."

"Not until a year ago last June."

Sarah caught her breath. "That's when I had the accident. And right after that I heard the voice for the first time."

"Yes, I think I actually heard the voice speak to you the first time," Dov said. "I remember it very well. I was in bed. Hung over, to tell the truth. All of a sudden I heard someone say, 'Listen to the music, Sarah.' "

"That's it! That's what the voice always tells me." She squirmed with excitement. Finally someone else had actually heard exactly what she heard. All Jarib's understanding and assurances that she was normal were helpful, but another human being who heard it too was far better.

"The thing is, I didn't realize the voice was speaking to you. As far as I knew, you were dead. But there's always been a Sarah in the presence for me," Dov said. "The imaginary playmate I mentioned. Except that I knew I wasn't imagining her. I thought of her as a woman who'd lived a long time ago. But one who visited me. In fact, that's why you're named Sarah." He reached out and touched her hand but didn't try to hold it.

"Tell us what happened after you heard the voice speaking to Sarah," Jarib said.

"For a few months nothing; then I heard it again, and I went out to a Judaica auction and bought a bracelet. I know that sounds insane and a non sequitur; but it was a compulsion, and I'm sure the two events were linked."

On the other side of the room Yitzhak moved in his seat. Dov put his hand in his pocket. "I have it here as a matter of fact."

"Wait!" Sarah put her hands to her temples and pushed back her hair. It was loose today. She and Jarib had slept late, then she'd spent ten minutes on the phone with Rita, she hadn't had time to put it up. "Don't show us. Let me tell you. A copper bangle with three turquoises."

"Yes." Levi was not surprised. None of the strangenesses seemed odd to him. He took the bracelet from his pocket and laid it on the table. The others stared. Sam half rose from his seat and leaned forward to study it. Then he sat back down with a shrug. It didn't look particularly impressive.

Jarib's briefcase was beside his chair. He lifted it onto his lap and took out a sheet of paper. "This is a sketch Sarah made for me about a year ago." He passed it to Levi.

"That's certainly the same bracelet. And the instrument's the lyre," the other man said. "That's part of it. The four notes, at least as I hear them, are made on a rare ten-string lyre. I've always known that. Years ago I made myself one."

"Where is it now?" Jarib asked.

"I buried it in the desert just before Amy and I returned to Jerusalem. I thought it was all over, you see. That I'd been tested in some way and found wanting. The voice wasn't going to use me anymore, so I didn't need the lyre."

"Pity," Jarib said. "It might help. But anyway, we have this." He lifted the bracelet and started to pass it to Sarah. Just then the phone in the bedroom rang.

Stein got up to answer it. "We'll wait," Jarib said. "Better not to have any interruptions."

Sam came back. "For you." He jerked his thumb at Beklem. "Same guy that called you last night, I forgot to mention it."

Yitzhak went to the phone. The others continued waiting.

"Here, let me see that thing." Sam took Sarah's sketch from Dov's hands. "You draw real good, darling. Just like your mother. Amy always got As in art."

"I majored in art history in college," Sarah told him. It seemed a small comfort to offer, one more of the tenuous links he so badly needed.

"You went to college? Good! Smart. That's terrific. I guess they did all right by you, these Myles."

"Wonderful," she said.

He nodded. In the bedroom they heard Yitzhak hang up, wait a moment, then begin to dial. "That schmuck thinks he can make free with my phone." Sam glared in Yitzhak's direction. But he didn't go into the other room to protest. Sarah began telling him about her job with the museum, idle chat to fill the moments until Jarib was ready to begin again.

Yitzhak dialed Ariel's hotel. He knew Ariel had returned to New York late the previous evening, after he'd spoken to him from LaGuardia and told him Jarib Baraak was safe and with them.

The switchboard let the phone ring for almost a minute before the operator said there was no answer.

"Keep ringing," Yitzhak said. "He's there." Finally there was a half-dazed voice on the other end of the wire.

"It's me." Yitzhak lowered his voice and switched to Hebrew. "I've had a cable from Vita. Malachy Fanti returned to Rome Thursday afternoon. And, Ariel"—he paused—"our people in Rome say he's going to be the next pope. It's practically a sure thing."

"Hey, that should be good, huh? You're wired into him. It can't hurt."

"You don't know what you're saying. He's the worst kind of Jew hater. As pope he'd be a disaster. It would be the Middle Ages all over again."

"Boss, that doesn't make sense—"

"Believe me," Yitzhak interrupted. "It makes sense. I want you to do something."

"Now?"

"Of course now. Haven't I just been telling you how urgent this is?"

"You want me to go to Rome and talk them out of it? Or maybe take out this Fanti?"

"Don't make jokes, *tateleh*. I'm not in the mood. It's too late for any action on the other side. I didn't get Vita's cable in time. It went to Morrie's and he wasn't there and his wife was away."

"That's your big problem, Yitzhak. Except for me you've got nothing but amateurs in this crazy army."

"So I want you to do something professional. I'm going to give you an address. Go there and watch the woman whose house it is. Don't do anything, just make sure we know where she is every minute. And check in with me every half hour. When I'm ready, I want to be able to find her."

In the living room they'd stopped chatting. There seemed little to say. Yitzhak's voice reached them as a low, unintelligible murmur. "What language is he speaking?" Sarah asked.

"Hebrew." Dov cocked his head. "I can't really hear what he's saying."

Sarah looked shocked. "I didn't mean to eavesdrop."

Dov smiled at her. A young woman from a world where listening to someone else's conversation was bad form. Refreshing. He knew only one other such woman, Zelah Tench. The thought of Zelah made him smile again. He wondered if she and Sarah would like each other. Yes, he thought they would. When this was over, he'd invite Sarah to Paris and introduce them.

"If that mamzer's putting transatlantic calls on my bill, he pays," Sam said.

Yitzhak returned to the living room. "Sorry. You can go on, Professor." And to Stein: "Not transatlantic, local. Stop worrying."

"Let's see," Jarib said, "where were we?"

"Just a minute," Dov said. "I have a rather fundamental question." The others looked at him expectantly. "Exactly what are we trying to accomplish?"

Jarib leaned forward. "What I hope will happen is that you and Sarah will interreact. The fact that you share the basic elements of the phenomena is extremely suggestive. And unusual. Hopefully, acting in concert, you can open the thing up. Go deeper and further. Find out what the voice is trying to say. If there's a message, if in fact, you are being told something specific and tangible, we may be able to find out."

"Rather like putting together two halves of a coin," Dov said.

"Exactly."

Sarah had been silent; now she spoke. "Jarib, do you really think a lyre would help?"

"It might. But we haven't got one."

"I can get one."

Jarib grinned at her. "I don't think they're on sale at Macy's."

"One of the curators of a museum here is a woman I know. We're part of the same network."

Yitzhak started and turned to stare at her. If Sarah was aware of his scrutiny, she ignored it. "Museum executives are largely males," she said. "Women with responsible positions in that world have formed some links. I've kept mine up. I can make a call and possibly borrow a lyre. May I use the phone?"

Sam beamed at her. "What a question to ask your grandfather. Go ahead. Call Hong Kong if you want."

She returned in less than five minutes. "She's sending it over by messenger. They have a ten-string lyre circa A.D. 50. She can't let that out, of course. But they also have a nineteenth century reproduction. She says the design is identical to those used in the Middle East. And it never changed much from one century to the next."

An hour later Dov cradled the instrument in one arm, resting it on his knee. He had long fingers, Sarah noted. The way he plucked the strings made it seem as if he'd done so all his life.

Four notes.

"Oh, yes," she whispered. "That's it exactly." This time it was truly what she'd heard. Not the approximation on a piano or any other modern instrument, *do-sol-la-fa*. Sarah sighed with satisfaction, leaned her head back against the sofa, and closed her eyes. Silently Jarib reached over and clasped the bracelet onto her wrist.

Again the same four notes.

Dov didn't need to watch the strings to pluck them; his eyes were closed, too. Jarib had thought to use relaxation techniques to start them off. It wasn't necessary; the lyre had done it effortlessly. It might be only a reproduction, but it was a beautiful instrument; carved ebony inlaid with ivory. And a tone that was both sweet and sad.

Four notes.

"*Fidha,*" Sarah said. She repeated the word. *"Fidha."*

"What does it mean, darling?" Jarib spoke very softly, not wanting to break her mood. He had his tape recorder out and running. "What does *fidha* mean? Is it a name?"

"*Fidha,*" Sarah said again.

It was Dov who replied, his voice low, measured, seeming somehow to reach them from far away. "It's Arabic. It means silver. I see it, too. Sheets of unworked silver." He stopped plucking the lyre.

Sarah opened her eyes. "I don't speak Arabic."

"But you knew the word." Jarib took her hand.

"I heard the word," she said.

"And did you see the silver?" Dov asked.

"I'm not sure."

"I saw it. But I don't know what it has to do with anything."
He thought for a moment. "My mother's maiden name was Silberman. But her family came from Germany."

They spent another hour at it. But there were no further results.
Only the single word, *fidha*.

"I have something to add," Yitzhak said finally. He'd been
glancing nervously at his watch for the last twenty minutes. Jarib
had seen him do it. For Beklem they seemed to be up against some
kind of time limit. But what or why only he knew.

"I have the name of a woman whose family once owned that
bracelet," Yitzhak said. "She's here in New York. Her name is
Claudia Al Ghawahergy. She's also a musician, a pianist."

Dov stared at him. "Al Ghawahergy's also Arabic," he told the
others. "Egyptian, to be precise. It means the jeweler."

Yitzhak removed his glasses, polishing them carefully. "There is
another connection. The woman's been in this country since 1949.
When you yourself came, Professor. She, too, is from Alexandria."

Jarib was past asking the Israeli how he happened to know so
damn much. "Don't tell me the rest, let me guess. She's a Jew. Her
family was forced to leave after the founding of Israel. Also like
mine."

"Correct. And that bracelet belonged to her family. Don't ask
me how I know, there isn't time. Professor, I have a suggestion."

Jarib was the logical person to do it, Yitzhak insisted. "Tell her
where you're from. She'll see you."

"I've been 'from' there since I was a year old."

"Try, Professor. For Sarah's sake." The old Israeli always knew
which buttons to push. "You've a better chance of getting willing
cooperation than any of us. If you fail, I'll do something else."

Jarib wasn't sure he admired Yitzhak's "something else." So he
was the one holding the receiver, listening to it ring in an apartment
over on the West Side.

"Hello."

"Mrs. Porter?"

"Yes, this is she." A nice, well-modulated voice, with just the
trace of an accent. Very like his mother's.

"You don't know me, and I apologize for disturbing you, but my name is Jarib Baraak. My family came from Alexandria. I believe you did as well."

"Yes, that's correct." A little hesitant now, wondering; that old con about relatives in the old country who needed money obviously on her mind. But his name was a bait she apparently couldn't resist. "I did know people named Baraak."

"My mother's maiden name was Ambar. Mina Ambar. My father's Sami. They live in Boston."

"Yes, yes. I do know your family. Not for years you understand, Mina and Sami were older than I. You're Jarib, that's what you said?"

"That's right."

She laughed softly, completely friendly now. "The Baraaks always have a Jarib. In every generation. I remember your grandfather, or maybe it was your great-grandfather. A very old man, at least he seemed so to me. I was just a little girl. He used to carry wonderful *ma 'amoul* in his pockets and dole them out to the children on the street. *Ma 'amoul.* They're a kind of little cookie stuffed with dates. Wonderful."

Jarib let the string of reminiscences go on for a while. Then he brought the conversation to the point. "I'm a professor of parapsychology, Mrs. Porter. At Harvard. I'm in New York at the moment working on . . . a case I'm studying. There's a bracelet which has come into it. A copper bangle with three turquoises." He heard her catch her breath. "I have reason to believe the bracelet once belonged to your mother. Would you be willing to come and identify it?"

"Copper, you said? A wide copper bangle? Is that it?"

"Yes. Set with three turquoises. One large and two small."

She didn't hesitate. "Yes, I'll come. Where?"

He gave her the address and hung up. The door between the living room and the bedroom was open. The others had heard everything. "Good," Yitzhak said. "Very good, Professor."

"She says she'll be here by one." Jarib glanced at his watch. "That's about forty-five minutes. I don't know about anyone else, but I'm starving."

Sarah and Sam went to the kitchen. There was toast bread in the freezer and some cans of tuna in one of the cupboards. They made sandwiches. Stein produced some beer. It was a subdued and quiet lunch. Mostly it was waiting.

Promptly at one the doorman buzzed. A Mrs. Porter was downstairs. Sam said to send her up. Jarib went to the elevator. The woman who got off was somewhere in her late forties, medium height, heavy. She had on a green loden cloth cape and black boots. Her hair, worn in a sleek chignon, was dark with no sign of gray. The eyes were dark, too, very large and beautiful in an otherwise undistinguished face. And her smile was warm. "Professor Baraak?"

"Yes, thank you for coming, Mrs. Porter."

Jarib put out his hand. Her grip was firm. He led her into the apartment, made the introductions, took her cape. Beneath it she wore a simple wool dress, plum-colored, and pearls. Elegant and poised, not put off by the unusual summons and all the strangers, as her first words showed. "Are you all here because of my family's bracelet?"

"More or less," Jarib admitted. "Dov, will you show it to her?"

Dov had put the copper bangle back in his pocket; now he brought it forth. Claudia Porter stretched out her hand. Dov hesitated for a brief moment, then passed it to her. She studied it for long seconds; when she glanced up, her eyes were moist.

"This was in my father's family as long as any of us know. It was always said that some ancestor, also probably a jeweler, had made it. When we had to leave Egypt, in '49, we had no money. They'd taken everything. My father was dead by then. There was just my mother, her sister, and me. My mother had managed to save two treasures. This bracelet was one of them. In the end she had to sell it. That's how we got the money to come to America."

"Who bought it, Mrs. Porter?" Jarib asked.

"I'm not exactly sure. I was only ten at the time. But I remember a man came to the house and Mama spent a long time with him. They were haggling. He was a foreigner, French, I think. Very aristocratic. And cruel. He gave Mama much less than the bracelet was worth, but at that time anything at all looked like a fortune."

"Please," Sarah interrupted. "Won't you sit down?" They were all standing; now they sat gratefully. Claudia Porter's emotions charged the atmosphere; her distress at the memory was palpable.

"Sam"—Sarah turned to her grandfather—"can we give Mrs. Porter some brandy?"

"Sure, of course. Why the hell didn't I think of that?" He got up, glad to have something to do, and poured a generous snifter.

The woman sipped it, still holding the bracelet, staring at it. "Where did you get this?" she asked finally.

She'd addressed the question to Jarib, but Dov answered. "I bought it at auction in Paris about a year and a half ago."

She nodded. "Then it's yours, isn't it?" She handed it back to him.

Yitzhak cleared his throat. They looked at him. "Mrs. Porter, I represent what I'll call Jewish interests in something that may involve this bracelet. At least something it may lead to. Can I ask you a question?"

"Of course." The dark eyes surveyed him calmly.

"Do you ever remember hearing mention of something called the Alexandria Testament?"

Her sharply indrawn breath was audible. "It's been mentioned to me, yes." The eyes had grown wary.

Yitzhak leaned forward. "In what context?"

"Like the bracelet, it was a family legend. Some story that an ancestor wrote, something that would vindicate the Jews."

"Vindicate them?" Sarah asked. "How? Of what?"

Yitzhak spoke. "It isn't vindication, it's proof that their Gospel, their anti-Semitic garbage about Jews murdering their Messiah are drivel. Lies. Two thousand years of lies and we've paid for them. Over and over and over." His voice shook. For the first time the measure of his commitment was apparent. Yitzhak the professional, the manipulator, was revealed to all of them as Yitzhak the survivor of unspeakable horror, Yitzhak the man.

"How do you know this?" Sarah demanded.

Yitzhak's pale eyes narrowed. She alone of the assembled company was in a way suspect. Sarah alone had been tainted by Christianity. It was his doing, and he knew well what risk he'd taken. "You're a Jew," he told her. "Don't forget that. I let them have you for a while because that kept you safe. But you're one of us. You know it now."

Sarah didn't rise to his baiting. "That's not what I asked you.

How do you know that this Testament, if it exists, says what you say it does?"

"I found out. In Dachau."

There it was. The irrefutable word, the ultimate weapon. None of them had been in a concentration camp; none of them could argue with the moral authority of a Holocaust survivor. Yitzhak let the idea sink in for a moment. Then he continued. "Malachy Fanti, the cardinal they're going to make the next pope, he was there, too. Only for a little while. A mistake. Even the Nazi bureaucracy made mistakes. He got out because he's not a Jew. He got out and left the rest of us behind. He said nothing, did nothing. Ever since he's been crazy with guilt. He told me about the Testament, because he's guilty. He's looked for it ever since, because he's guilty."

"And if he finds it?" Jarib this time.

"He'll suppress it. The truth will never come out. That's what Malachy wants. I know him, I've known him since 1940. He needs to see himself as savior of his Church; otherwise he has to face his own moral poverty. He'd seen it all, and he walked away and never said a word. Not a word."

"Where is he now?" Jarib again.

Yitzhak laughed, a soft sound without mirth. "In Rome. They're probably going to make him pope. Think of it, a virulent Jew hater as pope. Just like old times." He swept his eyes over all of them. "Don't you understand? This voice Dov and Sarah hear, it doesn't belong to them. It's not theirs to ignore if they wish. None of this little drama of the snatched baby and the dead mother and the drunken father is important compared with the Alexandria Testament."

Claudia Porter had listened to the diatribe in silence, knowing far less than the rest of them. Now she spoke. "What did you say about a voice?"

"As I told you on the phone," Jarib said, "I'm a parapsychologist. That's how I got involved. Sarah here and Dov, who is her father, have experienced what we call paranormal phenomena. A voice speaking to them and four notes of music."

The woman stood up and walked to the window. Outside, the traffic from the Queensboro Bridge was crawling west. She stared down at it for some moments; then she turned to face the others, backlit by the weak winter sun. "Ever since I was a child, I've been told that there were people in my family with the gift of second sight. My aunt had it. The one who brought me to New York after my mother died."

"Where is your aunt now?" Yitzhak asked.

"Dead. She died ten years ago."

Jarib took a step toward her. "What form did her 'second sight' take?"

Claudia shrugged. "Nothing very dramatic. Just that she could sometimes guess things before they happened. She had hunches. I never paid much attention. Old wives' tales."

"Nothing to do with music?" Dov asked.

"No. But lots of my family were musical. I'm a pianist. Nothing very grand, not a soloist, I accompany singers, play for rehearsals, things like that."

Dov rose and went to the bedroom. He'd put the lyre in there before the woman came; now he returned, carrying it. He plucked the strings. "Do these four notes mean anything to you?"

She cocked her head and listened. "Try again."

He did as he was bid.

"C, G, A, F. No, I'm sorry. Nothing."

Sarah was curled up in one of Sam's overstuffed chairs. Exhausted, buffeted by all the emotions, the claims and counterclaims. She had her head in her hands; now she looked up. "Mrs. Porter, earlier you said there were two treasures. The bracelet was one, and your mother was forced to sell it. What was the other?"

"A candlestick. Just one. Supposedly there'd been a pair once, but the other disappeared. God knows where or when. We had only the one. My mother always said it was as old as the bracelet."

"What was it like?" Jarib asked.

"Tall, almost two feet. A twisted rope, rather like a braid. Made by hand. Not perfect as it would be if it were done on a machine."

"*Fidha*," Dov said softly.

She faced him. "Why, yes, it is silver. How did you know?"

"Just a hunch," he said, smiling.

Yitzhak rose and took a step toward the Egyptian woman. "Mrs. Porter, please, it may be vital. Where is the candlestick now?"

She seemed surprised at the question. "Didn't I say? At home, in my apartment, on my dining room table. It was the one thing of value my aunt and I managed to take out of Alexandria."

The first cabby refused to take more than four of them. "Sarah and I will follow," Jarib said, taking her arm and drawing her back to the curb.

Claudia repeated the address. Jarib nodded and began searching the street for another empty cab.

Sarah carried the lyre, in the box in which it had been delivered from the museum. It had been signed out to her, and she refused to let it out of her sight. "Don't worry, I'm insured," Sam had said. But she insisted that she wouldn't rest easy unless it was with her.

Jarib spotted a taxi with a light on, hailed it, opened the door, and handed Sarah and the precious box inside. "I have to talk to you," she said as soon as he'd told the driver where to take them.

"That's the understatement of the century. Where in hell do we start?"

She shook her head, the dark curls framed her face, and he touched them gently. For a moment she pressed his hand with hers, then moved it away. "Listen, one thing bothers me more than anything else. Yitzhak's assumptions. He hates all Christians. I understand why, but I can't agree."

"You think he's right, that if this Testament exists, it will blow Christianity out of the water?"

"I doubt that. And if it did, if it could, that would be what Christianity deserved. If it really is all a lie, it's past time it was exposed."

"But you don't think it is?"

She didn't meet his eyes. "I don't know. Jarib, darling, I love you. And I don't have any clear feelings about this business of whether or not I'm a Jew. I don't even know what it means. But for twenty-five years the Catholic Church has been my—my place. My world. I can't just stand by and see it slandered by somebody as fanatical as Yitzhak Beklem. Whatever the Testament says, he and people like him will twist it to mean what they want it to mean."

Jarib didn't answer right away. The cab emerged from Central Park on West Sixtieth Street and continued toward the river. "I hear what you're saying," he said finally. "And I think I understand. I find it hard to be sympathetic, though. Seems to me we've been on the wrong end of the slander stick for a damn long time."

"Yes, I know. That doesn't change it, however."

"Two wrongs and all that. I suppose so."

The cabby slid open the glass and leaned toward them. "Seventeen hundred Riverside Drive, right?"

"Yes."

"Okay, must be this block." They were heading uptown between Seventieth and Seventy-first streets. One side of the street was lined with large old nineteenth-century buildings; the other was a shallow park fronting the Hudson. The cab eased toward the curb about midway. "Here it is."

Yitzhak, Sam, Dov, and Claudia were in the lobby, waiting for them. It was spacious and dim, a mosaic floor and walls lined with yellowed mirrors in worn gilt frames. "What a wonderful old building," Sarah said.

"We like it," Claudia said. "It went co-op about ten years ago, and we managed to buy our flat and the one next door." She led them into a self-service elevator with an old-fashioned folding metal gate and pressed number four. A few seconds later they were in a broad corridor. Claudia fumbled with her keys, got the door open, stepped aside to let the others enter.

A man moved out of the shadows further down the hall.

Sam noticed him first and stiffened. A New Yorker's reaction.

"It's all right," Yitzhak said. "He works for me." He went toward Ariel, and they spoke quietly for a few moments. "It's all right. Nothing out of the ordinary has happened," he said when he returned.

His tone carried menace, as if they were being pursued. Sarah shuddered, and Jarib slipped his hand into hers.

The Porters' apartment was large and sunny with a wonderful view of the river from the living room. The furniture was old and mismatched and charming. "Most of this belonged to my husband's family," Claudia said when Sarah commented. "I'd hate to live someplace with everything new and sterile." She glanced guiltily at Sam Stein, but he didn't seem to understand. She and Sarah smiled at each other.

"Can I get you something? Coffee perhaps?"

"Please," Yitzhak said. "Can we see the candlestick first?"

"Of course, it's in here."

She led them into the next room. There was an enormous table covered in a worn velvet cloth. On the table were a bowl of fruit and, dominating everything, a massive silver candlestick. Sarah paused in the doorway.

Music. Four notes, then six, then eight, then four again. Not a fragment, a theme. Repeated and repeated again, and yet again. Sarah reeled with the force of it; Jarib put out an arm to steady her. Dov simply stood.

Sarah turned to the almost stranger who was her father. "Do you hear it?"

Dov's face was animated by joy, an emotion newly returned to his life. First Sarah herself, now this. "Yes, I hear it." He moved closer to this child of his flesh, sired in the desert, abandoned, believed dead, and now miraculously resurrected. "I hear it." The voice hadn't used him, laughed at him—after all, there was a purpose. "*Shehecheyanu*," he whispered.

Yitzhak stared at the candlestick. He heard nothing, saw nothing. But they did. Dov and Sarah, the two whom he'd kept apart and brought together, who had reason to hate him for the role he'd played in their lives. They heard something vital, the sound of fulfillment. And the thing they were all looking at was the key, however obscure it seemed. "*Shehecheyanu*," Yitzhak echoed. "Blessed art thou, O Lord our God, King of the Universe, who has kept us alive to this time."

"Can you tell us what you hear?" Jarib asked softly.

"Where's the lyre?" Dov asked.

They'd left it in the living room. Claudia disappeared for a moment, returned with it, and handed it to Levi. He paused, listening; then he began to play. The four notes were dominant, but they were but the leitmotif of a larger melody. It was essentially simple, limited by the instrument; yet plaintive, haunting, both sad and joyful.

He played it through twice, then turned to Sarah for confirmation. "Exactly." She nodded her head.

"It's a good tune," Sam said. "Make a great theme for a picture."

"What else?" Yitzhak demanded. There was an edge of anger and frustration in his voice.

"Quiet." Jarib didn't shout, but the command lost none of its force for that. "Leave them alone, Beklem. When they're ready, they'll tell us."

Except that there was nothing to tell. Sarah went closer to the candlestick and touched it. It stood some two feet tall as Claudia had said, with a round, uneven base from which a twisted coil of silver ropes rose to end in a smaller flat circle mounted with a pin that held a candle. She ran her fingers lightly over the piece. Claudia stepped forward and removed the candle. Sarah lifted the thing in her hands. It was too heavy to hold for long. She closed her eyes and cocked her head, listening.

And there was nothing, only the lovely music.

Dov set the lyre on the polished mahogany table in Claudia Porter's dining room. He took the candlestick from Sarah and waited. Then he shook his head.

"There has to be something," Yitzhak insisted.

Jarib turned on him. "Once more and I put you out of here, bodily. And don't threaten me with your bully outside the door. I can take him, too."

"I'll help," Sam volunteered. "It'll be a pleasure."

Yitzhak made an impatient gesture. "I know, I know, the thing's very delicate. You're concerned for their mental health, Professor. But we haven't waited all this time and come all this way to hear a pretty song."

"Let's be practical." Dov looked at Claudia. "Have you ever discovered any moving parts in this thing?"

"Never. The story is that it was molded from one piece of pure silver. It's very soft, you can see all the dents." They showed as black deposits of tarnish, though the candlestick was obviously lovingly polished. "It's always been in my family. That's all I know."

527

Levi twisted the base; it didn't give. Neither did the top. When he turned it over, a hole running right up the center was revealed. "Do you have a torch?" Claudia looked at him questioningly. "A flashlight," he explained.

She brought one. They shone it up the center of the candlestick and studied the opening in turn. Claudia produced a wire coat hanger, and they untwisted it and poked it into the central shaft. Nothing.

Jarib was watching Sarah. Lines of fatigue and tension were showing in her face. "She's had enough for now," he said, moving to her side. "I'm going to take Sarah back to the hotel for a rest."

Claudia glanced at her watch. "Yes, it's nearly three. I'm due at a rehearsal at four."

"What time will you be finished?" Yitzhak asked her.

"Seven."

"Okay, we'll come back here at seven-thirty."

She was nonplussed. "My husband will be home then. I think he may be planning for us to go out to dinner. . . ."

"He's a Jew?" Yitzhak demanded. She nodded. "Then tell him you can't go out tonight. For the sake of Israel." He turned away as if the matter were settled. "Meanwhile, Ariel will stay outside. To protect that." He jerked his head toward the candlestick.

"Protect it from what? From whom?" Claudia asked. "It's been standing right there for years."

"I don't know," Yitzhak admitted. "I'm only sure that when we're this close, when Malachy Fanti is about to become the pope, I can take no chances."

Sarah wanted to walk for a while. They crossed the street and strolled downtown along the river. But before they'd gone very far, she stopped, leaning over the railing and staring into the water. "Do you think it's possible that the Church would make a man like this Malachy Fanti pope?"

"You'd know a lot more than I would about that," Jarib said.

"I don't. I don't even know if he's really what Yitzhak says he is."

"Does it matter?"

"Yes, to me. I want to know, Jarib. I think it may be important."

"Okay, but I don't know how we find out. Unless . . . how about calling Tom Lasky? He's the only priest I know; maybe he knows something."

They made the call from a drugstore one block east on Broadway. Jarib did the talking. "Never heard of the guy until a few days ago," Lasky told him. "That's when his name started coming up as *papabile,* somebody being considered for pope. But maybe everybody else has seen him as likely for years. I'm not much on Vatican politics."

"Know anybody who is?" Jarib asked.

"No . . . wait a minute, there is someone. My old ethics professor from the seminary. Larry Donovan. He's in Rome right now, I think."

"Tom, can you call him?"

"Well, yeah. I guess so. Somebody at the sem will know where he's staying. But what do I ask?"

"If he has any reason to believe that this guy Fanti is an anti-Semite. I'm not sure why, just that it may be important."

"Okay, I'll try. Got a number where I can reach you?" Jarib gave him the numbers of the Helmsley Hotel and Sam Stein's apartment. Tom repeated them to be sure he had them right, then: "Jarib, you haven't said anything about Lenore. Does that mean nothing's new?"

Jarib swallowed hard. "I can't say a lot just now, old buddy. But I think at this moment she's okay. In fact, I'm sure of it."

"Listen, that sounds like you know something. If so, I think—"

"Tom, trust me. Please. Just for a couple of days, just until this is over."

"Okay," the priest said at last. "And if I can get hold of Donovan and he knows anything, I'll get back to you."

Purity remembered what she had set out to do; before Sal picked her up on the highway and tried to lull her into forgetting. Now she understood that he'd just been waiting until he could tell Jarib, then they meant to take her back to that place.

But Sal didn't know everything, he didn't know about the weapon. Because she was smarter than he was. Smarter than Jarib, too. He didn't know she remembered the things he told her. Sitting there in the little room in that place and telling her things as if she were a child. About his new house, for instance. And that he was going to take a year off and stay in that house and write a book.

She waited until it was night, hiding in the woods around Hamilton. Then she walked to the highway, and this time she didn't just stand there; she stuck out her thumb. Pretty soon a truck driver picked her up and took her to the exit marked Rowley. She only had to walk for half an hour before she came to the town. And Purity remembered the address Jarib had mentioned. Seven Willard Lane. In the dark she walked around the sleeping little village until she found Willard Lane.

It was obvious at once that no one was there. But Purity knew Jarib would return. This was his house. This was where he lived. Probably he brought women here and did things to them. Awful things like those he used to do to her . . . It wasn't hard to break a pane of glass in the cellar window in the back and reach in and undo the lock. It wasn't even hard to climb inside.

The reproduction lyre had been signed out to Sarah until five. After they called Tom, she and Jarib took it back to the museum. An hour early. Sarah's curator friend was sent for and met them in the lobby. She was a woman in her fifties, small and thin with short black hair and intelligent brown eyes behind rimless glasses. She took the instrument back with a look of relief and passed it to a security guard.

"Thank you, more than I can say," Sarah said. "And may I introduce Jarib Baraak. Jarib, Wella Thompson."

They shook hands and exchanged pleasantries. Wella insisted they join her for coffee in the museum's restaurant. It was close to five when they got back to the hotel.

"Do you want a drink?" Jarib asked.

"No, just to lie down for an hour or so. I'm sorry, I seem to be fresh out of energy."

"That's hardly surprising."

They went upstairs. The room was charming, there was a fireplace and a balcony, but more important, it was supremely comfortable. Sarah lay down on one of a pair of king-size beds, too exhausted even to undress. "Jarib, is this going to end it?"

"Your voice, do you mean?"

"Yes, and Yitzhak Beklem, and all the rest."

"I don't know."

She sighed and turned over. "Come lie down beside me." She stretched out her hand.

Jarib took it, sitting on the side of the bed, stroking her forehead, leaning forward to kiss her. Sarah put her arms around his neck. "I think I want to make love."

"I thought you were tired."

"I am. That's got nothing to do with it."

He kissed her again. Then the phone rang.

It was Claudia Porter. "I'm so glad I found you. I thought I remembered your saying you were at the Helmsley. Listen, I've had an idea. It's too complicated to explain on the phone, but it may be worth having another try with the candlestick."

"Tonight, you mean?" Jarib asked.

She hesitated for a moment. "I'm not sure. I had the impression . . . well, perhaps you and Miss Myles would prefer to try on your own. It may not work anyway."

"Hang on a moment." He covered the mouthpiece with his palm and told Sarah what she'd said.

"Yes," Sarah said eagerly. "Yes, without that damned Beklem breathing down our necks. But how can we get past his guard dog?"

Jarib spoke into the telephone again. "We think it's a good idea, but don't forget Beklem's left someone guarding your apartment."

"Yes, I know. I'm calling from the rehearsal hall now. I can leave here early. I'll go home, tell that man I forgot something. I'll bring the candlestick to you. Forty-five minutes. Less if I can manage it."

"I should call Dov," Sarah said after he hung up. "He has a right to be here, too."

"You're sure? He's been in Beklem's pocket all along, don't forget. And he may not share your concerns about Church interests."

"All the same, he has a right."

Levi was in Sam Stein's apartment. He answered the phone. "Can you come to the Helmsley Palace Hotel?" Sarah asked. "Without Beklem's knowing anything about it?"

"I don't see why not. He's not here now. What's happening?"

"Claudia Porter is bringing the candlestick. She has an idea. I don't know if it will come to anything but I don't want Yitzhak Beklem here if it does."

Levi hesitated a moment. "He's not so terrible, you know. He's a fanatic where Israel is concerned, but he's probably got a point."

"Maybe," Sarah said. "Only it's not the only point. There are other considerations. Look, this may be a futile discussion. Nothing may happen. And the Alexandria Testament may not exist."

"And it may be unimportant if it does. You're right," Dov said. "I'll be there as soon as I can."

Ariel debated. He knew where to reach Yitzhak, in a cheap hotel off Times Square, a duplicate of the one where he was staying, but to phone, he'd have to leave his post. The nearest public telephone was in a drugstore around the corner on Broadway. Anything might happen while he was gone. On the other hand, he knew what was supposed to happen. Everybody was supposed to meet at the Porter woman's apartment at seven-thirty. Instead she'd returned at ten to six and gone out again immediately. There was too much he didn't know. Yitzhak hadn't had time to brief him properly. So whether this deviation was important, only Yitzhak could judge. He made up his mind.

Beklem had been sleeping, the ability to fall asleep instantly for even very brief periods of time was part of his armory; so, too, the fact that he was instantly awake and alert.

"Sorry to spoil your rest," Ariel said. "But something's happened. Maybe it's not important, but the Porter dame came in and went right out again. And she was carrying something. From the way she handled it, something heavy."

"The candlestick," Yitzhak said tonelessly. "It has to be."

"What candlestick?"

"Never mind, there isn't time now. Go back to the apartment.

I'll see you there or back here when I can. I've phoned Maurie, he'll relieve you at eight. He couldn't make it before."

"Why the hell not?" Ariel had been on almost continuous duty for two and a half days.

"His wife was making something special for supper," Yitzhak hung up before Ariel had a chance to comment.

Despite the import of the message, there was no urgency in Yitzhak's movements. He was quite sure he knew where Claudia Porter had taken the candlestick. If he was wrong, she might have taken it anywhere in this enormous city and he'd never find it. So either way, he had no reason to hurry. He'd have a shower and a shave and change his shirt. Then he'd go to the Helmsley Palace Hotel. If his suppositions were correct, the mystery was solved. It was a great day, the most important in his life. What mattered was that he arrive at the proper moment. Neither too early nor too late. Timing was everything. But then, his sense of timing had been proved infallible when he stayed alive until the last possible second in 1945.

Dov got to the hotel before Claudia Porter arrived.

"I'll phone down for some drinks," Jarib said. "I don't know about anyone else, but I can use one. Scotch okay?"

Dov smiled. "Fine. With me it always used to be wine. Cheaper and it goes further. Lately I haven't needed it as much." He turned to his daughter. "Someday, when we have time, I want to try to tell you what this last week has meant to my life. Not only discovering you but Sam Stein as well. For all his crudeness, he's a wonderful old man. And all of a sudden I have a family."

"There's no one in Paris then?" Sarah asked. He'd told her he lived there. "No wife, not even a girlfriend?"

"Not exactly. There is someone, but she wasn't too happy with me before. Too much alcohol and too many memories. I think that will change now; at least I hope so." He smiled.

He had a wonderful smile, Sarah noted; it made him look young and appealingly boyish. "I hope so, too."

The drinks came, and some sandwiches Jarib had ordered. "Will you come to Paris to see me?" Dov asked.

"Of course, I'd love to," Sarah promised. She was going to ask him more about the woman in Paris, but the phone rang. It was the desk announcing Mrs. Porter's arrival. Jarib told them to send her up.

Claudia carried a plaid satchel with a black plastic zippered top. Unlovely, cheap, battered, insecure—nobody would carry anything valuable in such a thing. The silver candlestick was utterly incongruous, emerging from its impromptu case. She set it on the dressing table. The four of them studied it in silence for some seconds.

"It's the four notes," Claudia said. "I've been thinking about them. I suppose it's natural I'd fasten on the musical part of the whole business. At first I didn't realize what it was that was nagging at the back of my mind. All my real training is in Western music, you see. As I told you, I was only ten when I came to New York."

"The scale is different," Dov said thoughtfully. "I'm not a musician, but it is, isn't it?"

"Yes. Egyptians today use tonic *sol-fa,* the *do, re, mi* scale, for convenience. But traditional Eastern music is based on mathematically denominated notes."

"I'm sorry," Sarah said. "I don't follow."

"When you tried to describe the notes you heard, before they were played on the lyre, you told me you picked them out on the piano, is that right?"

"Yes. *Do-sol-la-fa.* That was as close as I could come."

"Exactly. But it was an approximation because what you were hearing in your head were the notes as played on a lyre." She took a pad and a pencil from her bag. "I've worked them out. Expressed in traditional Egyptian terms, they are *rube' nota, talaterba nota, rube' nota, nuss nota.*"

"Quarter note, three-quarter note, quarter note, half note," Dov translated. "Yes, yes . . . I'm beginning to see."

Claudia Porter's dark eyes danced with excitement. "What if the notes were a code, some way to separate the ropes of the candlestick?"

Sarah gasped. "My God! How did you ever think of such a thing?"

The older woman looked suddenly embarrassed. "I'm a mystery story fan. I devour them."

"Have you tried it?" Jarib asked.

She shook her head. "I didn't dare. For one thing that man is still outside my apartment, and truthfully, I was frightened. Besides, whatever is involved here, I don't seem to have any part in it. I only own the candlestick. I've never heard a voice or had premonitions of the future in my life. Maybe it wouldn't work for me."

They all hesitated. The idea was so tantalizing, the disappointment would be so great if it failed. "Lately I've been thinking a lot about this question of family," Dov said. "I think I mentioned that my mother's maiden name was Silberman. Or Silverman if you spelled it differently. Considering names given for craft, the jeweler and the silversmith are pretty close. So maybe we're related. Maybe some Jews from Alexandria emigrated to Germany God knows how long ago."

"With Jews it's entirely possible," Claudia said.

There didn't seem any excuse to stall longer. Sarah touched the candlestick. "How should we do it?"

"Together," Jarib said. "You and Dov. Try the base first. If that doesn't work, you can try the top."

They lifted it a few inches from the table and began the sequence clockwise. A quarter turn, a three-quarter turn, a quarter turn, a half turn. But it was simply their hands that turned. At first there seemed a minute amount of play in the base; then it budged no further.

"Nothing?" Jarib asked.

"Nothing," Sarah confirmed.

"Try beginning counterclockwise," Claudia suggested. They did. Still nothing, not even that hint of movement they'd felt before.

Jarib took his pipe from his pocket but didn't light it; it was simply something to do with his hands, a break in the palpable tension in the room. "You two getting any messages?" Both Sarah and Dov shook their heads. "How about trying the top, the candleholder part."

Once more there was a barely perceptible amount of give; then the heavy silver remained inert. "There's only one thing left," Dov said. "Both together. You turn the top, Sarah. I'll work the bottom."

They made the motions simultaneously. A little more movement perhaps, but that could simply be the result of their efforts weakening the metal. "Let's try alternately," Sarah said. "I'll start the quarter turn clockwise at the top, next you do the three-quarter turn counterclockwise at the bottom, and so on."

"One more thing," Dov said. "Try to keep one finger on that pin thing. So the pressure is equal on it and the circle."

Jarib watched them. Unconsciously Claudia hummed the four notes under her breath.

Sarah made the first motion. "It definitely turned," she whispered. "Holding the pin is important."

Dov closed his eyes, concentrated, and eased the base three-quarters of the way 'round. There was a faintly audible click. "Did you hear it?" His voice was tinged with awe.

"Yes." Sarah wasted no more energy on words. She repeated the clockwise quarter turn with the top of the candlestick. Another click.

Dov made the final motion. And the ropes of silver disentwined themselves and parted in their hands.

In Rome it was very late. The funeral of the pope was over. Malachy Fanti was exhausted, but he did not sleep. He knelt on the bare floor of his austere bedroom, praying, begging God to allow him to serve the Church, begging that Yitzhak should not find the Alexandria Testament now, while Malachy was a prisoner of his own destiny here in the Vatican. Tomorrow was free, but that wasn't time enough to get to New York. And he had to be here on Sunday morning; that was when the conclave would begin. The cardinals would be locked up together, and they would choose a pope. And everyone said they were going to choose him. "Lord," Malachy whispered, "I wish only to serve you. Let your will be done."

Outside the Vatican walls, in a small *pensione* run by nuns, Larry Donovan had just gotten into his pajamas. He, too, was exhausted; even for those not officially involved in the ceremonies, it had been a long day. He crawled into bed and shut his eyes. He was almost asleep when there was a discreet tap on the door. Donovan opened it and found one of the nuns outside.

"Monsignor, I'm sorry to disturb you. But there's a telephone call. It's from America, so I thought . . ."

He had to pull on a bathrobe and pad downstairs to the front desk to take the call. "Tom Lasky?" They were friends, but not intimates. And he couldn't imagine why Lasky should be calling him here. "What can I do for you?"

"I'm not sure. Look, I know it's pretty late over there, but I'm calling for a friend, my brother-in-law, in fact. And he's not a guy who would ask me to if it weren't important. I'm supposed to find out if this guy Fanti is really going to be elected pope." Lasky hesitated. "And if it's true that he's a rabid anti-Semite."

Donovan snorted. "What's your brother-in-law do for a living? I bet I can guess. He's a reporter, right?"

"No, nothing like that. He's a Harvard professor, and his field is pretty esoteric. He's a parapsychologist."

Donovan gripped the receiver and spoke urgently down the wire. "Tom, let me get this straight, your brother-in-law's a parapsychologist? And he's asking questions about Fanti's attitude toward Jews?"

"Yes. I know it all sounds pretty weird."

"Not to me it doesn't. Listen, I have to speak to him, it's urgent. Have you got a number?"

"Two." Lasky repeated them. "Larry, what's this all about?"

"I can't explain, there isn't time. But go say your prayers, boy. You may just have been the prophet of the Lord, sent to save the people from doom."

When he hung up, Donovan was trembling. It was what Dom Malachy had told him all those years ago. The descendants of the author of the Alexandria Testament have some vestigial memory of it, a racial memory of the sort that Jung speculated about. And *that* might just interest a parapsychologist. Okay, get a grip on this thing. It's a long shot, a thousand to one. Or it's the hand of God, sending his Spirit to guide and protect the Church, just as He promised. He picked up the telephone and began to dial with shaking fingers.

. . .

There were twelve of the incredibly thin parchment sheets. They had been inserted into one silver rope of the candlestick, and for just short of two millennia they'd remained there. Airtight, waterproof, dustproof; they were as fresh as if they'd been placed in their hiding place yesterday.

"I can't do more than guess at ninety percent of it," Dov said. "Middle Eastern languages have changed dramatically, like all the others. This is a mix of what I think is Aramaic, liturgical Hebrew, and Greek. I don't recognize many of the characters. But some of it's clear. Mostly names. Yeshu, that's Jesus, and James, and Saul and Simon."

"Simon who is called Peter," Sarah said quietly. "And Saul who is called Paul. And James, the brother of the Lord." She'd been raised on those names, those gospel words. They came to her lips with ease.

"Perhaps," Dov agreed. "Certainly the thing seems to be about biblical events. There's another name." He looked at her. "I think the writer is called Sarah. It's confusing, she seems to be a Jew, but she calls Yeshu the 'master,' sometimes even the 'Lord.' "

Jarib poured drinks. "I think we all need this, I know I do." His hands were shaking as he distributed the glasses, and he kept glancing at the papyri. "I'm seeing it, but I can't entirely believe it's true."

Claudia Porter wept softly into a lace-edged handkerchief. "I'm sorry, I don't know why I'm being such an idiot. It's just that my mother was so upset when she sold the bracelet. She felt as if she'd betrayed something sacred. A trust. She died right afterward. Actually she'd been ill for a long time, but losing everything, having to leave Egypt, it certainly shortened her life. Only she didn't have to feel guilty, did she? She saved the most important thing." Her voice broke, and she took the scotch Jarib handed her and tossed it back in one gulp.

"Even selling the bracelet was part of it," Sarah said. "Part of a plan to bring us all here together now. So we could find the Testament."

"A divine plan?" Dov asked. He looked at his daughter.

"I think so, yes," she said.

He nodded. "Perhaps. Whatever divine may mean. Perhaps."

"The question is, What do we do next?" Jarib moved closer to Sarah. There was a loud, impersonal knock on the door. All four heads turned in its direction. "Who is it?" Jarib called.

"Room service."

Jarib got up. Dov stationed himself between the door and the table holding the Testament and the parted candlestick.

"We're all right for the moment," Jarib said. He only opened the door a crack. But that was enough for Yitzhak.

Beklem had surprise in his favor; it acted as an antidote to the other man's youth and strength and weight. He was in the room before any of them realized what had happened. "You've found it," he said. It wasn't a question but a declaration.

There was little point in lying to him. The evidence was too apparent. "Yes, we've found it." Dov spoke quietly, but all the defeat and abjection that had marked his previous conversations with Yitzhak were gone.

"That seems not to be the only thing you've found, Doveleh," the old man said. He smiled. "So now you're a man again."

"No thanks to you."

"Ah, but that's not exactly true, is it? First I kept you away from the police; then I brought you here. I made sure you met Sam Stein and were reunited with your daughter. So you owe me, Doveleh. And I've come to collect. That will do." He nodded toward the papers on the dressing table.

"No, Yitzhak, it isn't going to be that way. Twenty-five years and if you said go, I went, if you said come, I came. Why? For the pittance you paid me? Fear of the law? I don't know anymore. What were the police going to do to me that you didn't do? No, it wasn't that. Guilt. You were my hair shirt, Yitzhak. I wore you with a kind of crazy pleasure and told myself I was making atonement. But that's all over. This doesn't belong to you. It's ours. Mine and Sarah's and Claudia's. We're the heirs to whatever legacy this turns out to be. We'll decide what to do with it."

The only sign of Beklem's fury was that his face darkened. His voice was cool and controlled. "You're the heirs, eh? You've assigned yourselves the role. Well, let me tell you something: You're

539

mad, all of you. You don't own the Alexandria Testament. It belongs to the Jewish people everywhere. It's our payment for suffering I can never explain to you. It's our vindication. If there is a God, this at last is His justice."

Sarah moved toward the old man; she stretched out her hand as if to touch him, then pulled it back as she sensed his recoil. "Listen, what you say is probably true, but only partly so. We—that is, Dov—can't really translate it. But we've seen enough to know it concerns Christians and the time of Jesus Christ. The Church has a stake in this, too. I haven't had a chance to ask Claudia and Dov yet, but I think it should be shared."

"Shared." Yitzhak spit out the word. "Shared. You stupid child. What do you know of what's gone on? Besides, what do you care? You're tainted by them. I did it to you and I'm not sorry, it was necessary. But you're tainted."

"That's quite enough of that." Jarib saw the look in the old man's eyes. Momentarily he wondered if Beklem might have a weapon. "This whole conversation is insane. Scholars everywhere will rejoice to see what we've found. It's not a sectarian thing." It was, of course; he knew better than most the kind of petty intrigues of which scholars were capable, but right now the situation demanded to be defused. "All Sarah is suggesting is a compromise."

"Compromise?" Beklem's eyes had become black holes; behind them was an inferno of memory. "We compromised ourselves right into the ovens. No more." He moved toward the table and put out his hand. "Give it to me. It will go to the right place, I promise. Sarah is different, but the rest of you are truly Jews. Surely I don't have to convince you."

There it was, the ultimate argument. The one that carried maximum suasion. In the end we stand together, for our own kind. It had enabled them to survive for five thousand years; it activated Yitzhak's minions; it had brought them to this room; in a way it had preserved the Alexandria Testament. "Give it to me," Yitzhak repeated.

"No." Sarah almost whispered the word. "No, you're blind to any concern but your own, any pain or fear but your own. Everything that's happened to you, all those terrible things, they've warped you. It's tragic, but we can't give in to it. We mustn't." She turned to Dov and Claudia. "Even if this man Fanti is elected pope, even if he's as bad as Yitzhak says he is, not all Christians are like that. We can find somebody decent. Somebody who'll be fair—" Her voice broke; her eyes begged them to understand.

"You're a fool," Yitzhak said. "If they listen to you they're fools, too. Malachy Fanti has spent a lifetime trying to find the Alexandria Testament so he could suppress it. Now, when he's about to become the most powerful man in the Christian world, you're going to put it in his hands."

"Not his," Sarah insisted. "That's not necessary. Jarib and I have a friend who's a priest, someone we know and trust. We called him about this man Fanti; he's checking. We can also tell him about the Testament. Father Lasky will help us find the right person to talk to."

"Wonderful," Yitzhak said. "And as soon as he knows, the Vatican will, too. Malachy will know."

Sarah started to speak, then shook her head. There wasn't time to explain about Tom Lasky, no time to tie all the threads together for Yitzhak Beklem. Besides, he didn't want to understand, so he wouldn't.

"For God's sake, listen to me." Beklem's quiet voice was as urgent as a scream. "You have to understand. No priest can act independently of the pope in a matter like this. And Malachy Fanti is going to be pope."

"Perhaps not," Dov said. "You're not God, Yitzhak. You don't know everything." He picked up the parchment sheets and rolled them together carefully.

Yitzhak took a step forward. "It's time to end this farce. Give me the Testament."

Dov looked at the two women. "We'll take a vote. Sarah?"

"Not to him," Sarah said softly.

Dov nodded. "Claudia?"

She was staring at Yitzhak. "You're so sure you're right, Mr. Beklem. Your kind are always sure. But when you founded Israel, did you think about my mother? About what it was going to cost her to be hounded out of her home?"

The old man stared at the woman who was questioning the bedrock foundation of his reality. "Israel is the only salvation for us," he hissed through clenched teeth. "The only salvation."

"Maybe. But we have it now, a Jewish state. Only we have to

live in the world, with the rest of the human race. No vendetta, Mr. Beklem. I say we do it Sarah's way. I don't want to be a vigilante."

Dov looked grim. "Neither do I. Sarah's way, that's my vote, too. And that makes it unanimous. You don't get it, Yitzhak. This time you lose."

The Israeli looked from one to the other; then he sagged, as if the weight of his sadness were beyond bearing. "I thought I only had to fight them, Malachy and the goyim. But in my own breast I have nurtured vipers. *Shehecheyanu,*" he whispered; the word had become a curse in his mouth. "That I have lived to see this time."

He crossed the room slowly, each step seeming an enormous effort. When he reached the door, he turned and faced them. His eyes carried one final, mute appeal. It went unanswered. For some time the echo of the door closing was the only sound in the room.

When the telephone rang, Dov was closest; he picked up the receiver. "Professor Jarib Baraak, please. This is Monsignor Larry Donovan calling from Rome."

Eighteen

SATURDAY, DECEMBER 1

"You're sure that what they've found is authentic?" the cardinal archbishop of Boston asked.

"No," Donovan said. "I can't be sure. But it sounds as if it is. Near enough for you to be able to act on it in good conscience."

The cardinal took a large bite of bacon and egg. They were in his suite at the Excelsior Hotel. Where the kitchen understood about American-style breakfasts and didn't starve a man on just coffee and a roll. After tomorrow that was all he could expect, because he'd be sequestered in the Vatican until the conclave elected a pope. "Exactly what is it that you want me to do? In good conscience, of course."

"Threaten Bellini," Donovan said simply. "Tell him the document is dynamite as far as the Church is concerned, that it confirms everything my committee's report says about the writer of the Acts of the Apostles, that he distorted the truth in order to meet a political need of the time, that if Malachy Fanti is elected pope, the Alexandria Testament goes to only Jewish scholars. And that the persons who have control of it will make sure there's maximum publicity. The kind that's usually called sensationalism."

The older man leaned back in his chair. "Pour yourself some more coffee, Father. And tell me why you think Bellini will give in to this kind of blackmail."

"Because he really has no choice. You aren't just going to tell him, Eminence. You can tell a great many of your brother cardinals as well. Fanti's election depends on a euphoric ground swell. With this kind of controversy surrounding him there isn't a chance of that."

"The kind of controversy I'm going to make, right?"

"Yes, sir."

"Okay, and when I do, you know what will happen? We'll all have to start from square one. The Fanti bandwagon has been rolling so fast no one else has been seriously considered. So all the politicians will have to get into high gear. And we're going to be locked up in there for God knows how long."

"Yes, sir."

"Well, damn you, Monsignor, don't look so happy about it."

"I'm happy about the Church, sir. Because I think Divine Providence has stepped in and kept us from making a terrible mistake."

The cardinal burped softly. "So do I, son. So do I. Now, hand me that phone."

Across the city another telephone call was in progress. Dom Malachy's secretary was speaking with England. "His Eminence asked me to call, Mr. Durant. He's unusually busy at the moment, I'm sure you understand."

"That he's going to be pope," Hamish said with satisfaction. "Yes, I've heard."

"That seems possible," the secretary said. "But of course, it's in God's hands, and we won't know His will until after the conclave."

"Of course."

"And there are other matters to be dealt with," the man in Rome continued smoothly. "Even if Dom Malachy is . . . Well, there are some things it will be too late to change. The report of the committee on Jews and the Scriptures, for instance. That will be published in a few weeks, no matter what happens."

"And it will be the usual distortion?" Hamish asked. "The usual liberal pap?"

"Yes, so His Eminence believes. He thought perhaps . . ."

"Perhaps what, Monsignor?"

"The report will require much refutation. Perhaps you and your group in England will care to organize a response."

"We will. What would you suggest?"

"Oh, the usual thing, letters to all the influential journals, speeches, interviews. I'm sure you know better than I how such things are managed."

"I'll do my best, Monsignor."

"That reassures me," the man said. Then he rang off.

Hamish Durant sat for a moment, looking about him. A madrigal. He'd told the girl that when she first came. Tiverton Manor was an exquisite madrigal, contrapuntal rhythms meant for the unaccompanied human voice. But not necessarily a single voice. The house seemed so empty now. Perhaps he would hear from Timothy today. No, somehow he didn't think so. Probably not tomorrow either. Or the next day. He sighed, then realized it was after noon; he was late for lunch. Hamish rose and began to make his way to the dining room.

Ivy wasn't dressed yet; it was just seven-thirty in Boston. But somebody was leaning on the doorbell, and it was obvious whoever it was wouldn't go away until she appeared. Cursing, she started down the stairs. She was barefoot, her hair hung loose down her back, and she wore only a bathrobe. Timothy Durant looked a lot worse.

"What the hell are you doing here?"

He sagged against the door. "Looking for a cup of coffee and some sympathy. Can I come in?"

She didn't answer, just moved aside and waited for him to precede her up the stairs. His trousers were wrinkled, his coat had a rip in it, and when he was seated in her pretty kitchen, she could see he hadn't shaved in days. Still, he was an extraordinary-looking young man. Ivy pushed his curls off his forehead as she poured him a cup of coffee. "What happened? Care to tell Mama all about it?"

"I told the old tyrant to go to hell. Or words to that effect. I am unemployed, Ivy. And the bastard will probably blacklist me with every auctioneer in Britain."

"Is that why you came here? I mean, if it's Sarah you're looking for, I have to tell you—"

"That she's made it up with the love of her life," he interrupted. "I know. That may well be what started me on the road to ruinous rebellion, but it's not why I came here." He drank the coffee eagerly, then looked up. "Have you anything to eat?"

Ivy giggled. "Bacon, eggs, toast, and marmalade. That do?"

He nodded.

"Tim, are you stony-broke?"

"No. Not exactly. I have a bit put by. It's just that I got the notion of coming to see you yesterday. And I wasn't entirely sober at the time. No dollars and no traveler's checks and looking like this, I don't dare go into any restaurant that takes credit cards."

Ivy flipped a half pound of bacon into a frying pan, and in seconds it was sizzling and smelling wonderful. "Now that you're here, what do you want besides food?"

He eyed her with a theatrical leer. She wore nothing beneath the robe, and the curve of her breasts showed. "Part of the answer I'll reserve for later. When I've showered and shaved and rejoined the human race. The other part's easy. Work."

"A job with Bell, Book, and Candle?"

"Not quite. I want us to be partners. Since I'm not an auctioneer any longer, I can buy for you abroad. And we could consider opening a shop in London as well." He paused long enough to attack the plate of food she'd set in front of him. "But we'll have to renegotiate, love. A share of the profits, not just a commission."

Ivy studied him from behind the big glasses. "Maybe," she said. "But don't think you can scalp me, Timmy. Anything you skim off the top"—she leaned over, ignoring the fact that her robe opened further, and put her palm against his cheek—"I'll probably take it out in trade."

In Ipswich the Katzes were also at breakfast. Milly watched her husband devour a stack of pancakes swimming in syrup. "You shouldn't eat so fast, Harry. You'll get indigestion."

"It's late. I have to be at the store by eight-thirty."

"Why so early?"

"I'm meeting somebody. The young guy I told you about."

"The family that just joined the temple?"

"Yeah. I arranged to talk to him. About contributing."

There was no need to ask what he meant. "I tried Paris last night," she told him. "A woman answered. Somebody I never talked to before. She didn't speak much English, but I think she said Yitzhak was returning today."

"You'll call him later?"

"Yes, I suppose so. But I don't think I'm going to have to watch Sarah anymore. I think whatever that was all about, it's over."

Harry Katz got up from the table and put his hand on his wife's shoulder. "Good, if it is, you'll feel better. But you never did her any harm, honey. Don't worry about that. And Yitzhak's right, we have to look after ourselves however we can. Otherwise it could all happen again."

"Yes, I know."

She waited until he left the house, then began putting the breakfast dishes in the machine. She had nothing planned for this morning; maybe she'd do a little cooking. Chicken with green peppers and rice, and that wonderful meatball recipe she got last month. Rita was coming home from her sister's this afternoon. It would be nice to give her a couple of casseroles to see her through the weekend.

"You should come home with me," Morrie insisted. "No reason the two of you have to spend all day at the airport."

Yitzhak shook his head. "No, it's okay. We'll be all right here." He found a place to sit down. The International Terminal at Kennedy was half empty at this hour. He turned to Ariel. "You checked the bags?"

"Yeah, straight through to Orly. But our flight doesn't leave until this evening." He sat down beside the older man. Yitzhak looked terrible. "Maybe Morrie's right. We could go to his place for a few hours. You could get some sleep."

"I don't want to sleep," Yitzhak said. "I have to think. Whether or not Malachy is elected pope, they'll make it public. I'm sure they will. But with their own interpretation. We have to start figuring out how to react, how to discredit it. I know a man in Jerusalem. A biblical scholar. He'll cooperate."

Ariel wondered what hold Yitzhak could have on a biblical scholar. He dismissed it as foolish speculation. Scholars were as likely as anyone else to have things to hide. "Okay. If somebody has to go see him, send me. I haven't been home in three years."

"Maybe," Yitzhak said. "More important is to make sure you have a home to go to."

Morrie and Ariel nodded.

They met at eleven, in Sam Stein's apartment, Sarah and Jarib and Dov. Tom Lasky arrived half an hour later. He'd taken an early flight from Boston. He looked better than he had a few days ago at Frank's wake. The men with him looked positively jubilant.

Tom performed the introductions. "This is Rabbi Joel Wise."

"A Jewish rabbi?" Sam asked.

Wise grinned at him. "I don't think there's any other kind, Mr. Stein. Some of us talk to some of them these days."

Everyone laughed.

"I didn't mean—" Sam broke off and looked sheepish. "I just never had a priest in my house before."

"And a goy granddaughter," Sarah said.

"Goyishe, darling. And no, I never had that either."

Rabbi Wise shook his head. "Father Lasky has been trying to explain, and I talked with Monsignor Donovan in Rome, but I must admit I'm confused. Who are you people? How did you find this thing?"

"Never mind," Sarah said. "I don't think that part of it concerns you. Dov and I, and Claudia Porter, although she couldn't be here this morning, have a document which we believe is very old and very important. We want to be sure it's handled correctly."

"What exactly do you mean by correctly?" Wise asked.

"Fairly," Dov said. "My field is Middle Eastern languages, and I can promise you this isn't easy to translate, and we are absolutely certain of its age, though we recognize you'll want to apply your own tests. What matters is that when the document is made public, there mustn't be any distortions. No personal axes being ground at the expense of the facts. No suppressions to suit one side or the other."

"Scholarship is never simple," Rabbi Wise said. "It's always a matter of interpretation. And often argument."

"Fair enough," Dov said. "But we'd like to know the investigation is beginning from a neutral point." He turned and looked at his daughter. "Is that the correct way to express it?"

Sarah nodded.

Lasky leaned forward. "When Jarib called me, I told him Larry Donovan had been my ethics professor at the seminary, that I could vouch for his integrity. What I didn't know until Rabbi Wise phoned me was that Larry has been chairing a committee for the last year and a half. They've been studying Jews and the Scriptures. Rabbi Wise has been their liaison with the Jewish community. Larry called him from Rome, and that's what we're doing here. Also, the committee's report is to be published in a few weeks. Rabbi, would you mind telling them what you told me?"

"I've seen the preliminary draft. It's superior scholarship, and scrupulously fair. I think I can promise you that whatever you've found, it will receive the same treatment."

"Good enough, Sarah?" Tom Lasky asked.

"For me, yes. Dov?"

He nodded.

Tom turned to Jarib. "You haven't said, but I take it this is related to what you and Sarah have been working on. Do we want to discuss that?"

"No," Jarib said. "Maybe later, not now. Sarah and I haven't had time to discuss how much of it she wants to make public. And Mr. Levi is involved as well."

Wise cleared his throat. "May we see the document, please?"

Dov rose and went into Sam's extra bedroom and returned with it in his hands. Such a small, simple thing. Twelve sheets of rolled papyrus.

The priest and the rabbi stared. The latter reached out and touched it with one tentative finger, then pulled back. "The Alexandria Testament," he said softly.

"All we know is what Larry told us on the phone, but he thinks that's what it may be," Lasky said.

"There have been rumors of it for centuries," Wise said. "But no one has ever been sure if it really existed, let alone where it was."

"It exists," Sarah said. "This is it."

"But where did you find it?" Wise demanded. "How?"

Dov glanced quickly at Sarah. They'd arranged all this beforehand. "Hidden in a very old silver candlestick," he explained. "The candlestick belongs to Claudia Porter. It came here from Alexandria with her family. Mrs. Porter wanted to join us, but she's a pianist and she had an unbreakable engagement this morning; Sarah and I have her proxy as it were. Yesterday we discovered that the candlestick could be taken apart. We found this inside."

"But were you looking for it?" Wise sounded slightly suspicious.

"In a way. Let's just say we were looking for something."

"May I ask what is the relationship between all of you?"

"Sarah is my daughter," Dov explained. "As for Mrs. Porter, we're . . . distant cousins."

Wise nodded. Though nothing had been proved.

Sam had gone into his little kitchen; he returned with mugs of coffee. "Can I ask a question? What's supposed to be in that thing?" He jerked his head toward the papyri.

"If the rumors are accurate," the rabbi said, "a story that casts light on the period immediately after the death of Jesus."

Stein grimaced.

"Equally important for us, Mr. Stein," Wise explained. "It's the period when the groundwork was laid for a lot that came afterward. That's what Monsignor Donovan and his committee have been working on."

"Okay, if you say so. You take cream?"

The rabbi nodded. He took the coffee. "It will take time, you realize. There won't be any headlines tomorrow or the next day. We'll involve the best scholars all over the world. They will deliberate separately and together. The study may continue for years. I hope that doesn't disappoint you."

"On the contrary," Sarah said. "That's what we want."

Receipts were signed. Everyone shook hands again. Sarah went to the door with the two clerics. Wise had the Testament in his briefcase; he went out first; Lasky hung back. He looked questioningly at Jarib. "Tonight," the other man promised. "I'll call you tonight, and we'll talk about Lenore."

Lasky nodded, then turned to Sarah. "Is there anything else you want to talk about? I can stay in town a day or two if you like."

She smiled at him, then impulsively reached up and kissed his cheek. "That's for caring. But no, it's all right. I don't need priestly advice. Jarib and I are going to be together, and you mustn't worry. I'm on the way to getting it all straightened out in my head. Eventually I'm sure I will."

She told Jarib the same thing later. They were alone in the hotel room, getting ready to check out. "I feel—how can I put it?— peaceful about the whole thing. Finding out about everything has made it all a lot clearer."

"Finding out about your origins, you mean?"

"Yes. And that the 'other' exists. And that back in that earlier Sarah's time things weren't so simple either. I don't have to have all the answers, do I? Not everything spelled out and tied with a red ribbon."

"No." He kissed the end of her nose. "It seems to me that the only thing any of us has to do is continue looking and thinking and keep—"

"An open mind." She finished for him. "But if you don't mind, I think mine is going to be closed for a while. At least in one sense."

They said good-bye to Dov and Sam in the hotel lobby. "We'll stay in touch," Sarah promised. "As soon as Jarib and I are settled, I'll write. And you're to come to Boston and see us," she told Sam. "That's not a negotiable demand."

"I'll be there. But not for a few weeks. I gotta go to California first. To see Rhonda. I don't want she should eat her heart out about what's happened."

Jarib looked at his watch.

"Don't miss your flight," Dov said. He took Sarah's hand. "But don't forget I expect you to plan a trip to France very soon. Perhaps a honeymoon." His smile included Jarib. "If you don't wait too long, maybe you can come to my wedding."

"The woman in Paris?" Sarah asked.

"Yes. If I can convince her I've really changed. It's not easy to convince Zelah of anything."

Sarah's eyes widened. She remembered now, the night in Kohl-burg, the night they talked until dawn. Zelah said the name of the man she loved was Dov.

Dov cocked his head and studied her face. "Have I said something remarkable?"

"No, nothing." She grinned at him. "Only the lady may have a surprise for you."

He grinned back and kissed her cheek. "I see. Well, we'll leave it at that for the moment. Something to talk about next time we're together. The French have the best farewell, my dear, *au revoir.* Until we meet again."

"Au revoir." For a few seconds she clung to him; then Jarib was hurrying her out to a taxi.

It was later, when they were on the plane headed home, that Jarib said, "I wish we were planning that honeymoon Dov mentioned."

"We will be." Sarah squeezed his hand.

"Not if Petrovsky is going to stick with Lenore. If he is, I can't divorce her. I'll have to pretend she's still missing and wait the seven years or whatever it takes. Do you mind very much?"

"Not about the legalities." She laughed softly and kissed his cheek. "Don't think that gets you out of taking me on a honeymoon to France, Professor. Who says a wedding has to come first?"

She was lighthearted and gay because it was really over at last. And the other sad things—her father's death, Rita's adjustment to widowhood—those were just parts of life. They could be coped with; there was no reason to be afraid.

Jarib's car was parked at Logan Airport. "Mind if we stop in Rowley for a few minutes first? I'd like to call Petrovsky, and pick up a few things. Then we can go to Ipswich."

"Okay, as long as we're there before four. I don't want Mom to come home to an empty house." She glanced at her watch; it was two o'clock. There was plenty of time.

In Rome it was evening, 8:00 P.M. The window of Larry Dono-van's room in the little *pensione* looked up the Via della Conciliazione to Bernini's great piazza and the facade of St. Peter's. The American stood there for some moments, just looking. On the outside it was quiet now; a few strollers and some pigeons shared the enormous semicircle that was so often filled with cheering throngs. But behind the walls, in the Vatican itself, there must be a great deal of activity.

Since 1276 it had been thus; the election of a pope takes place while the cardinals are held incommunicado, locked up together and prevented from having any contact with the outside world. It was Pope Gregory X's inspiration, his attempt to insure there would be no delay in choosing a new pontiff. And it worked, and had therefore been continued.

It all worked. Because despite everything, despite the sins and the weaknesses and sometimes the evil of its members, the Church was unique; the only thing Donovan knew wherein the whole was greater than the sum of its parts. Thou art Peter and on this rock I will build my Church and the gates of hell shall not prevail against it. This time, too, the same forever and ever, or at least as long as time. He swallowed the lump in his throat and blew his nose.

"Monsignor, are you in there?" A light tap on the door accompanied the question.

"Yes, Sister. What is it?" He opened the door, and the little nun smiled at him.

"The telephone, Monsignor."

He followed her down the stairs to the front desk and picked up the receiver. And heard the rasping brogue-tinged voice of the cardinal archbishop of Boston. "Sorry to disturb you, Father. But I figured I'd better talk to you before I'm incarcerated."

"Yes, of course." Donovan glanced at the nun. She was already headed away from the desk, discreetly leaving him alone. Still, in Rome it always paid to be circumspect. "Did you speak with our friend?" he asked.

"Yeah, a few times. No dice."

"No dice? What does that mean, how the hell can he—" He remembered to whom he was speaking. "Sorry, sir. But I don't understand."

"It's okay, that's pretty much how I feel myself. But Bellini is one son of a bitch of a poker player. He's calling my bluff."

"Meaning?"

"Meaning he's never heard of this Alexandria Testament, not from anybody but Fanti. He doesn't believe it exists. And a lot of my brother cardinals share that view. Bound to. Nobody's ever seen the damn thing."

"So?"

"So as I said, I'm being called, and I have the feeling I don't have even a pair of deuces. Is there something you can do?"

"Between now and tomorrow morning? I don't know. I could call the man who has the Testament now. A good friend, Rabbi Joel Wise. But it's only a suspect old document at the moment, not translated, not age-tested. It will take months to verify the authenticity, maybe years."

"A rabbi," the cardinal said. "Somehow I don't think that's going to help much." There was a long sigh at the other end of the wire. "Okay, I just thought I'd fill you in, son; I'll keep trying. But don't be too disappointed if we lose. The Church will survive, you know, whatever happens."

Donovan hung up. There was a sour taste in his mouth, a knot of rage tightening in his belly. The gates of hell won't prevail. That was the promise. But if Bellini had his way, they were going to be brought to those very gates. He remained where he was for a moment. Then he made up his mind.

Half an hour later it had started to rain, a thin, misty rain from high clouds that blotted out the stars and the moon. The alley along which Donovan walked was dark, and his footsteps echoed. He thought he heard something, paused and listened. Yes, another set of footsteps. Good. The other man was on time.

Purity heard the car; then she heard the front door open. She was naked except for white lace panties, and it was cold in Jarib's house, but that didn't matter. She was free, unfettered, and strong. And at last he was here.

She crept up the cellar stairs, crouched low and clinging to the railings, moving on her hands and knees. Oh, she was clever. A clever, clever girl.

Jarib wasn't clever. He didn't know she was waiting for him. He didn't know about her weapon. The thought made her want to giggle, and she shoved her fingers in her mouth to hold back the sound. Then she pressed her ear to the door and listened.

"Jarib, I'm going to turn up the heat. Okay, darling?"

A woman's voice. Calling to Jarib from somewhere in the house. He did bring women here, just as she'd guessed. Slowly, oh, so slowly, Purity inched open the door.

One streetlamp lit the cobbled passage. It was about ten yards away, in the middle of the alley. Donovan went toward it. The other set of footsteps was approaching, too; they were walking in unison now, almost blended into one. The echo of their shoes on the wet stones bounced off the wall of the Vatican Gardens on the right. Simultaneously both men stepped into the yellow circle of light.

"Monsignor Donovan? Yes, it is you."

"Yes, Your Eminence. I apologize for bringing you out on such a night. But this seemed better than going to your rooms."

"Please, I still prefer just Dom Malachy."

"As you wish. Tell me, if you're elected pope, what will your name be then?"

Malachy smiled and shrugged. "I haven't bothered to think about it. Rome thrives on rumors. Few of them prove true. We both know that."

"I know a rumor that is true," Larry Donovan said quietly. "The Alexandria Testament has been found."

Only a hint of tightening around the jaw betrayed the older man's emotion; he'd had time to adjust to the first shock. "So you said on the telephone; that's why I'm here. But why should I believe you, Father?"

"Because I'm telling the truth." Donovan had already decided how to prove it. "Sarah Myles and Dov Levi gave it to . . . my representative. Because they had decided not to give it to an Israeli named Yitzhak Beklem."

"Those names," Malachy whispered hoarsely. "How do you know those names?" He staggered; the wet and the cold seemed to penetrate his bones. And the pain in his heart was more than physical. He gripped the lamppost for support.

"I didn't know them until yesterday. That's when I got a call from a friend in America. He told me what had happened. And asked me to help, to take charge of the Testament."

Malachy stared at the ground. "You. All these years I have prayed and done penance and waited. But you've been chosen. You of all people, you have it. . . ." Then he remembered. "But that doesn't matter now, does it? Because soon I will be . . . in a position to influence events. The Church is safe, Father Donovan, despite you."

"No, Dom Malachy. Not yet. Not unless you swear an oath to refuse the papacy." Donovan leaned forward. "Look at me. Come on, look at me! I'm not bluffing, I don't want you to kid yourself about that. I'll wait until we have white smoke, until the new pontiff steps out on the balcony to bless the crowd in the piazza. I'll be there, and I promise you, Dom Malachy, if you're the man who comes out when they announce, '*Habemus papam,*' I will turn the Alexandria Testament over to the Israeli. I'll tell this man Beklem to do whatever he wants with it."

"No! You wouldn't do such a thing. Why should you? Whatever your ideas, however poisoned your mind, you must love the Church." Malachy lurched forward and gripped the American's shoulders. He meant to shake him, but it was impossible. All the strength was flowing out of him. He was in such terrible pain. "You must love the Church," he repeated.

"I do," Donovan said. "That's why I won't let you be pope."

"I must save the faith, protect us from the Jews. . . ."

Donovan moved away; it was easy to escape the weak grip of the Benedictine. Dom Malachy's hands fell to his sides; he leaned against the wall. His face was wet with rain, and with tears.

"You will not be pope," Donovan repeated slowly. "If you are, the Israeli will have complete control of the Alexandria Testament."

"The Alexandria Testament," Malachy repeated. He said it again. "The Alexandria Testament. That's why I was saved from Dachau. That's why I had to leave my monastery and come to Rome. That's why I followed the young woman. . . ." He closed his eyes. He could see her, as he'd seen her that single brief time across the canal in Alsace. A small creature with long dark hair. And she was the carrier of the secret, she'd been brought to him by

God, it was his destiny to unlock the mystery in her mind. She filled the space behind his eyes, his whole body; she dominated the world. Her name was torn out of him. "Sarah Myles!" Malachy shouted into the Roman night. "Sarah!"

Sarah took down the coffeepot, humming to herself. Jarib was in the study, sorting through his mail. Stalling, but she understood that. What he really had to do was call that poor bastard Petrovsky and find out what was happening. She didn't blame him for putting it off a few more minutes. It wasn't going to be pleasant. She took the tin of coffee from the refrigerator and began spooning grounds into the paper filter.

Purity watched the woman. Small, dark. Probably a Jew. And right now she was between them. The little woman with the long dark hair was between her and Jarib. She was going to pay Jarib back for everything he'd done, so first she must get rid of this creature who stood in her way.

Suddenly Sarah heard her name. It was shouted aloud in the kitchen. "Sarah Myles! Sarah!" She spun 'round. And because she did, she saw.

The woman who could only be Lenore lunged for her. Sarah saw her breasts, high and wide-spaced, the nipples pink. She saw the strong dancer's body, naked except for white lace bikini pants. And she saw a weapon of some sort plunging toward her. "No, you mustn't!" She raised her arms to protect herself, but in a fraction of a second she knew she was no match for the insane strength of the blonde.

And in that same instant there was something between them. A man; slim, tall, clad in a long black habit. He was there, and his body deflected Lenore's; it gave Sarah a moment to twist away. Then she was behind the other woman, struggling to control her, to save the man as he'd saved her.

Neither woman screamed. Their battle was one of grunts and groans and gasping breath. Sarah locked her arms around Lenore's slim waist; she threw all her weight into bringing her down. They fell together. And all at once she was the victor. The body that lay beneath hers was absolutely still.

In the study Jarib did not hear the sounds of struggle. Neither did he smell coffee. "Hey, honey, where's that coffee you promised?" There was no answer. He rose and went toward the kitchen.

"Oh, Jesus, Jesus Christ . . ." They were lying on the floor, the two of them. Entwined like lovers. He could see Lenore's naked breasts and the back of Sarah's head. And he could see blood. There was a fraction of a second when he was frozen with anguish and shock; then he hurled himself at them, grabbing Sarah's shoulder and yanking her away, ready to use his weight to restrain Lenore.

"It's all right," Sarah whispered. "I'm all right. Here, take this." She held out the screwdriver. "She went for me with it, and this man saved—" She turned, and her eyes swept the kitchen, but there was no one other than she and Jarib, and Lenore's motionless body. "He was here. A man in black."

"Ssh," Jarib whispered. "We'll talk later." He took off his jacket and knelt to spread it over Lenore's nakedness. He must cover her face, because he was certain she was dead.

"Jarib, she's hurt, bleeding. We have to call an ambulance."

He stared at Sarah a moment, then looked back at Lenore. And saw her chest rise and fall in a slow, steady rhythm.

"Dom Malachy!" Donovan saw Fanti start to fall. He reached out, but was too late, the body of the Benedictine had already hit the ground. "Dom Malachy!"

Donovan knelt on the rain-soaked cobbles and bent his head and pressed his ear to the other man's chest. He thought he heard a heartbeat, but it was so faint he couldn't be sure. For a moment he hesitated, considered running for help; then he changed his mind. He pressed his mouth to Malachy's, forcing his own breath into the body of his enemy. After a few moments he had to stop and lift his head and suck in oxygen.

"No," came the faint whisper. "Please, give me . . ." Malachy was not strong enough to say the words. But Larry Donovan did not need to hear them.

He raised his hand in the timeless gesture of the priesthood. "May our Lord Jesus Christ forgive you your sins and I in His name absolve you of them, as far as I am able and as you need. . . ."

He spoke the wonderful, familiar words swiftly, and as he did, the life of the other man slipped away. Larry Donovan had seen death before; it was not difficult to recognize. "Rest in peace," he said softly. "In the name of the Father and of the Son and of the Holy Spirit." He made the sign of the cross, then gently closed the eyes of Malachy Fanti. And he saw that the monk had died smiling.

Jarib put down the telephone. "They say it's just a flesh wound. She must have hit her head when you pulled her down. But she's going to be okay. At least for her. The doctors say she may not remember a thing." He reached for Sarah, pressing her close, oblivious of the fact that they were in Ipswich, that Rita might come in and see them. "I still start shaking every time I think of it. That it was you she went for, not me. I could have lost you."

"Not a chance. Not big, mean Sarah Myles. And I was just the appetizer. I'm sure you were meant to be the main course." She buried her face in his chest, felt the comfort of his arms around her. "I'm toughing it out, darling," she whispered. "But I was scared out of my mind."

"I know." He kissed the top of her head. "It's all right, it's over."

"Jarib, who was the man?"

"I don't know. Are you sure there was one?"

"I'm sure. A man in a black habit. Tall, handsome, silver hair."

"At least you see good-looking ghosts."

"He wasn't a ghost. He was real."

He moved her back a little, so he could look into her beloved face. "Yes. Probably he was. It's just part of the whole thing, my love. Part of the mystery of who you are and what you are. Do you have to understand to be happy?"

She started to tell him no, she needed only him to be happy, but Rita arrived. She was carrying a tray.

"I've made some tea. Let's go into the living room and have it, shall we? I want to know more about this restaurant in France, Sarah. Do you really think I should go and see it?"

"Definitely," Sarah said. Arm and arm she and Jarib followed Rita. "As I said, the owners are friends of mine. I'm sure they'll be happy to arrange everything. You can have a tour of restaurants, see all kinds of marvelous French cooking first hand. And when you come home, I think you should start a baking class."

"You've got it all figured out," Rita said. "And you haven't even asked if I want to do it." But she was smiling.

"Sarah has taken charge of the future," Jarib said. "So what about me? May I ask if your intentions are honorable, Miss Myles?"

"Definitely. You're going to marry me and live happily ever after."

"You're sure?"

"Positive."

"Good," he said softly. "So am I."

It was dusk in Ipswich. Outside the windows a flock of gulls lifted off the marsh and whirled in the twilight before disappearing behind the house. "Because they're out of sight, they don't cease to exist," Sarah said.

Jarib nodded. "Exactly. It's our perception of reality that changes, not the reality itself."

"Yes, and we have to learn to live with the fact that we can't know everything, that some things are made apparent only by the passage of time."

Rita looked from her daughter to her almost son-in-law. "What was that prayer, the one Mr. Beklem told us about?"

"Dov's prayer," Sarah said. "Blessed are you, Lord, who has kept us and sustained us and brought us to this season."

Afterword

A novelist appropriating scholarly speculation ventures into cold country; the most adamently revisionist historian would not accept as proven any of the theses with which I've made free in this book. They are not, however, purely products of imagination.

Some years ago I read S. G. F. Brandon's *The Fall of Jerusalem and the Christian Church* (London: SPCK, 1978) and was fascinated. It was that book which gave me the idea for the historical story central to *A Matter of Time.* Further research led to many other books, the most important of which are listed below. It seems important to add that while these authors provided the nucleus of the story, in no way can I claim to have been true to their scholarship or vision. I've chosen to tread where doubtless they would not be dragged by a covey of angels, nor would they recognize their carefully worked-out hypotheses in these pages.

The question then remains, Is it true? Any of it? Was James the first pope? Did Peter and Paul never reconcile their differences while alive? Is the apparent anti-Semitism of the New Testament a deliberate ploy on the part of its authors, a response to a specific and almost forgotten political situation? And leaving history aside, do some people have a racial memory so strong it can erase the barriers of time and distance?

The short answer is, I don't know. But it *could be true* . . . and that is all the excuse necessary. If the book entertains, it serves its purpose. If perchance it provokes the reevaluation of some long-held ideas, the credit belongs to the erudite company of workers in the vineyard, whose grapes I unabashedly stole.

BEVERLY BYRNE
LANZAROTE, 1986

PARTIAL
BIBLIOGRAPHY

Brown, Raymond E., S.S. *The Churches the Apostles Left Behind.* London: Geoffrey Chapman, 1984.

Grant, Michael. *The History of Ancient Israel.* London: Weidenfeld & Nicholson, 1984.

Grayston, Kenneth. *The Johannine Epistles.* Grand Rapids, Mich.: Wm. B. Eerdmans Publishing Co., 1983.

Jung, C. G. *Memories, Dreams, Reflections.* London: Collins and Routledge, 1963.

Lapide, Pinchas. *The Resurrection of Jesus.* London: SPCK, 1984.

Payne, Phoebe. *Man's Latent Powers.* London: Faber & Faber, 1938.

Rhine, J. B. *Extra Sensory Perception.* Boston: Boston Society for Psychic Research, 1934.

———. *New Frontiers of the Mind.* London: Faber & Faber, 1938.

———. *New World of the Mind.* London: Faber & Faber, 1954.

Vermes, Geza. *Jesus the Jew*. London: William Collins Sons & Co., 1973.

Wilken, Robert L. *The Christians as the Romans Saw Them*. New Haven: Yale University Press, 1984.

Wilson, Colin. *Mysteries*. London: Hodder and Stoughton, 1978.

ABOUT
THE AUTHOR

Beverly Byrne was raised in Revere, Massachusetts. After some
time as a free-lance journalist in Boston and New York, she sold
her first book, a work of nonfiction, in 1967. Soon after leaving
the United States for the Isle of Wight in 1977, Ms. Byrne's first
novel was published. She has been writing fiction steadily ever
since. She lives with her family on Lanzarote, a Spanish island just
off the coast of Africa.

P9-ELG-831

Spymaster

takes you into the REAL world of cloak
and dagger——where truth is often
more fantastic than the wildest James
Bond adventure

Learn the TRUTH about:

- The 1942 mission of eight German
  saboteurs in the United States, with
  never-before-revealed information
  from the officer who was in personal
  charge of the operation

- Operation Cicero, the inside story
  from hitherto secret British files

- The amazing intelligence work behind the shooting down of Admiral
  Yamamoto in the Pacific

In his years with Naval Intelligence, Ladislas
Farago has known most of the great spies
of our time and has had access to information never before released to the public.

Also By Ladislas Farago

The Tenth Fleet

Spymaster

(Original Title: *War of Wits:*
The Anatomy of Espionage and Intelligence)

by **LADISLAS FARAGO**

WARNER

PAPERBACK LIBRARY
NEW YORK

WARNER PAPERBACK LIBRARY EDITION

First Printing: January, 1962

Second Printing: September, 1964

Third Printing: September, 1972

Copyright, 1954, by Funk & Wagnalls Company

All Rights Reserved

Library of Congress Catalog Card Number 54-6361

Warner Paperback Library is a division of Warner Books, Inc., 315 Park Avenue South, New York, N.Y. 10010.

Covers Printed in U.S.A.
Body Text Printed in Canada.

Preface

WHETHER IT WAS A SEQUENCE OF ACCIDENTS OR WHAT SIR Robert Howard called honest design, I have been running into the foremost "spies" of the century since the beginning of my career as a journalist exactly thirty years ago. I was fortunate enough to know Colonel Walther Nicolai and Admiral Wilhelm Canaris, Admiral Sir Reginald Hall and Sir Basil Thomson, General William J. Donovan and Admiral Ellis M. Zacharias, the six great modern directors of intelligence. I knew personally and well Captain Franz von Rintelen, Colonel George Sosnowski, Captain Sidney G. Reilly, Sir Paul Dukes, General Pavel Skoropadsky, General Walter Kriwitsky, and a host of lesser "spies." They frequently allowed me, as a writer, access to their memories and memoirs.

The purpose of this explanation is not mere name-dropping. It is, I believe, necessary to establish the credentials of anyone who writes such a book as this, and at the very outset. I have never done an hour of spying in my life, but I have watched and even directed other people in such activities and witnessed from several vantage points intelligence, espionage, and propaganda in both their technical and their adventurous forms.

My lifelong interest in the business, and my association with some of the greatest intelligence experts of our times eventually resulted in my working actively in the field. In 1942, I joined a branch of United States governmental intelligence work and spent almost four years inside this agency, working together with our opposite numbers in a similar British organization. Part of this work consisted of participation in a major intelligence and propaganda campaign against Nazi U-boats and blockade runners. Later I was connected with the operations which Captain—now Admiral—Zacharias conducted against the Japanese High Command.

After the war, I had a share in an adventure in propaganda known as Radio Free Europe; there I headed a clandestine "Desk X," combating Communism behind the Iron

Curtain. In line with the melodrama of this work, I went by different "cover" names, one of which, Colonel Bell, was to gain a modicum of prominence in the European underground. In the course of this work I had intimate contact with several intelligence organizations of various resistance movements. About these nothing more can be said, for obvious reasons.

During this decade in operational propaganda I invented at least two "characters" who managed to impress themselves vigorously on the imagination of their target audiences. One was a Commander Robert E. Norden of the U. S. Navy, whose broadcasts had, in the words of a captured German document, "a crushing effect on the morale of German naval personnel." The other was a certain Balint Boda, an omniscient and ubiquitous Hungarian forever moving surreptitiously behind the Iron Curtain, whose hypothetical body gained substance by the effectiveness of his patriotic appeals.

Thus, much that is related in this book is based on personal experience. Still more is based on material that came to me first-hand from the protagonists of some of the great espionage dramas. Secret agents have molded our destiny far more than is generally recognized. I feel that their historic role, frequently nefarious, should be brought forward from the limelight of pure melodrama into the less deceptive illumination of public discussion.

LADISLAS FARAGO

Contents

PART I

Intelligence

The War of Wits

Our very survival in the crisis of today is closely and inexorably tied to an exact, timely knowledge of what is going on in the world—everywhere in the world, and most especially behind the walls of the Kremlin. There is plenty of uninformed talk about the importance of such knowledge, and also every intelligent person is aware that efforts are being made on an unprecedented scale to acquire it by all means, some fair, some foul. The newspapers, in particular, treat their readers daily to a running spectacle in which men and women scramble for the secrets of nations, for the intimate details of their high policies, strategic plans, intentions, military capabilities, and economic potentials.

Behind the respectable façade of all great powers, their secret services work with blatant disregard for decorum and decency. Their agents seek secrets in the files of war ministries and in the vaults of foreign offices, but also in refuse cans and garbage pails. They break safes and codes, arrange kidnapings and assassinations, engineer conspiracies.

The melodrama of this conflict is widely featured. It is generally presented as a furtive war ranging on clandestine fronts, as if it were nothing but a series of plots for television scripts. And indeed, superficial facts are often close to equally superficial fiction. A stately blonde steps into a cab in Vienna and is never seen again. The briefcase of a stranger is snatched from his hands on a Hong Kong bus. From Indochina comes word that saboteurs have disabled a French destroyer. In Malaya, Her Britannic Majesty's governor general is killed on an inspection trip. In Frankfurt, the private diary of an American general is stolen from his hotel room. In Canberra, Tokyo, and Berlin, Soviet agents desert with documents to expose and incriminate the service to which they themselves owed allegiance up to the moment of their escape.

Members of Parliament complain in the House of Commons that "secret documents are even being stolen from Buckingham Palace." Phones are tapped, mail is rifled, people are trailed, homes are entered surreptitiously. Frontiers are crossed illegally and men are ambushed from Germany all the way to Australia.

Isolated though these incidents appear, they all have an intrinsic relation to each other. Combined, they form a single pattern. But the melodrama inherent in such incidents sometimes obscures their significance. For behind the plots and perfidies of individual operatives stand huge and rich organizations, the secret services of the great powers, which exist because there is a need—the need to know. Behind the melodrama and adventure there is today's grim business of survival. The total pattern is what can be called the war of wits—organized and waged because it is the function of prudent nations to watch their ramparts and bolster their defenses at the sources of danger. In this age of absolute weapons existence depends on the knowledge of the intentions, plans, and capabilities of the opponents.

Pearl Harbor taught Americans this lesson in 1941. But a sneak attack which at that time merely destroyed some elements of the United States Pacific fleet would today "take out," as the technical term goes, whole metropolitan areas. It could cripple a nation, perhaps beyond recovery, with a single stroke at the very outset of a new war.

Foreknowledge is needed to forestall such sneak attacks, to enable nations to make their policies and conduct their diplomacy in anticipation of strategic onslaughts or to provide warnings on the eve of disaster. Knowledge is needed to enable nations which are attacked to retaliate—knowledge of the enemy's hidden targets, his sensitive or weak points, the focal areas where his physical and moral resources are concentrated. In short, knowledge is needed to wage the cold war, to stage its maneuvers, to avoid its defeats and score its victories.

This is an important part of the war of wits in its organized form: this effort to acquire such knowledge. But that is merely a point of departure. In the past belligerents tried chiefly to out-gun each other; today they maneuver to out-think or outsmart each other. In this sense, the war of wits becomes a major operation by itself. The war of today, as it is waged relentlessly even in times of nominal peace, thus assumes new dimensions.

With the coming of the cold war, the ancient art of war—with its emphasis on the material and military aspects of conflict—has moved into the intellectual sphere. This is not to say that intellectual factors were absent in the conduct of past conventional wars. "In all ages," Henderson wrote in his brilliant essay on war, "the power of intellect has asserted itself in war. It was not courage and experience only that made Hannibal, Alexander, and Caesar the greatest names of antiquity. Napoleon, Wellington, and the Archduke Charles were certainly the best-educated soldiers of their time; while Lee, Jackson, and Sherman probably knew more of war, before they made it, than any one else in the United States."

But through the evolution of society itself, knowledge of war as an isolated technique has become insufficient. Wars include not only the armies which fight them in isolated theaters, but whole nations; not only the generals, but statesmen and the people; not only strategy but policy; not only military science, but diplomacy, economy, and the social sciences. The totality of war, the all-embracing, all-pervasive nature of modern conflict, tends to place greater stress on the non-military features of war and bring to the fore forces and means which stem from man's knowledge, his emotions, impulses, and urges. Up to now, stamina and courage have been recognized as the two main intangible forces of war; today we recognize that intellect and education play a more important part in it. What is more, intellect is no longer confined to aid in the conduct of conventional war, but is endowed with the power of conducting a kind of "war" of its own—what the Germans called *geistiger Krieg* or intellectual war—without resort to conventional arms, and waged with intangible weapons of its own which replace the implements of armed conflict.

This modern conflict of minds is the war of wits. In this new war, brainpower has come into its own to take its place alongside landpower, seapower, and airpower, the traditional powers of brute war. It may yet turn out that the coming of the cold war has brought an improvement in the art of war as a whole through a shift in emphasis from the material to the largely intellectual aspects of human conflict.

What Is Intelligence?

Some seventy years ago, George Aston, then a young officer of the Royal Marines, was ordered to London for duty in a mysterious branch of the British Navy, the "Foreign Intelligence Committee of the Military, Secret, and Political Branch of the Secretary of the Admiralty." His arrival caused a mild flurry of excitement in the old Admiralty Building and, on his way to his new post, the officer was buttonholed by a puzzled Old Salt:

"I say, Aston," said the Old Salt, "are you the new *intelligent* officer?"

Much of that old confusion still survives, even if today "intelligence" is a fashionable word. It is, in fact, one of those modern expressions, such as enzymes or existentialism or fission, that form the special vocabulary of an age of organized disorder.

The word keeps cropping up in official announcements and officious pronouncements. Recently *The New York Times* printed an article about the strength of the Red Army in Germany, and the correspondent stated that his facts and figures came from "Allied intelligence sources." He did not mean to say that they came from people who were just smart by nature. He meant that his sources were individuals whose business it is to gather such information and who have special means of finding out the exact nature of certain specified things. By slipping the word "intelligence" into his dispatch, the correspondent implied that his information was not mere hearsay, or gossip floating about in European coffee houses. He meant to say that it was factual, reliable, and confidential —that it was that inner-sanctum commodity—"intelligence."

Despite the aura of mystery that surrounds it, there is nothing occult about intelligence. In one sense, the word does, of course, mean the capacity to understand and manage ideas. But in the contest of wits, both in competitive human society and in the conduct of relations between nations, it means information that is handled as a commodity by people who specialize in it, much in the manner in which news is handled by newspapermen.

The dictionary definition of this kind of intelligence is "communicated information"—in other words, information that no longer merely stays in one person's mind, but that has been passed on to somebody else. In the agencies that specialize in the activity, intelligence is defined as "evaluated information," information the credibility, meaning, and importance of which has been duly established and appraised.

As a function or activity, intelligence is the organized effort to collect information, to appraise it bit by bit, and to piece it together until it forms larger and clearer patterns which in turn enable us to see the shape of things to come. It is a perpetual effort to pierce the fog of war and diplomacy so that we may draw with bold strokes the contours of tomorrow.

"In view of the present world situation," said General Matthew B. Ridgway, chief of staff of the U. S. Army, "it is more important than ever to have complete information upon which to determine the most economical deployment of Army forces commensurate with the military situation, to minimize the possibility or advantage of surprise aggression, and to assure the most effective employment of such forces should the need arise." He added: "Adequate intelligence constitutes the fundamental basis for the calculation of risks, the formulation of plans, the development of materiel, the allocation of resources, and the conduct of operations."

The acquisition of adequate intelligence is no haphazard activity or improvised function. It is a clearly defined effort in which a great many experts and specialists are engaged, for intelligence can be effective only if it is conducted along exact scientific lines in which causes and effects are meticulously linked.

The Maze of Information

The first weapons of men were the stone, the club—and intelligence. Surviving remnants of primitive races, like the American Indians, show that a crude form of intelligence figured prominently in their arsenals. It first took the form of minor scouting. Then it developed into reconnaissance. Then came the differentiation between scouting and reconnaissance on the one hand, and intelligence and espionage on the other.

When Noah sent forth the dove "to see if the waters were abated from off the face of the ground," he engaged in a strikingly modern form of intelligence activity—in aerial reconnaissance. The ancient Egyptians had organized intelligence services centuries before Christ, even if their deficient counterintelligence caused Sir Basil Thomson to remark: "If the Pharaoh Memptah had been given an efficient intelligence service, there would have been no exodus." Moses improvised a secret service under Oshea ben Nun on the way to the Promised Land in a somewhat sacrilegious quest to check up on the promise of the Lord.

The Crusaders went on their adventurous mission without an organized intelligence service and fared badly. Then they created one and fared better. Military classics like Sextus Julius Frontinus, Sun Tsu, and Maurice de Saxe stressed the importance of intelligence and wrote manuals for its practice. A few generals ignored their suggestions, but most of them scrupulously observed the manuals. Commenting on the mishaps of an adversary, Frederick the Great remarked: "Marshal de Soubise is always followed by a hundred cooks. I am always preceded by a hundred spies."

The crucial role of intelligence in victory or defeat was demonstrated most dramatically in a great historic event of the seventh century: in the establishment of Islam as the dominant secular and spiritual force in Arabia. In A.D. 622, Mohammed fled from his native Mecca where life had become unbearable for him. He moved to Medina with a few of his disciples and from there he led raids on Meccan caravans. In A.D. 624 he defeated a superior Meccan force in the battle of Badr whereupon the Meccans decided to get rid of Mohammed once and for all. They mobilized a force of 10,000 men against him.

The Prophet was not unduly worried. He had left efficient agents in Mecca who reported to him the plans of his enemies. But his adversaries had planted no agents with him. So when the Meccans reached Medina, they were stunned to find a trench and a wall that completely encircled the city and sheltered Mohammed from attack.

"This trench struck the Bedouin miscellany as one of the most unsportsmanlike things that had ever been known in the history of the world," H. G. Wells wrote. "They rode about the place. They shouted their opinion of the whole business to the besieged." The outraged attackers then encamped to discuss the unexpected developments. Then came the rains. "The tents of the allies got wet and the cooking difficult, views became divergent and tempers gave away, and at last this great host dwindled again into its constituent parts without ever having given battle."

The vast Meccan army was defeated without an arrow's discharge, by the failure of its commanders to gather information about the enemy. Mohammed, on the other hand, triumphed because he had exact information about the plans, disposition, intentions, and strength of the enemy. Had he not secured this vital intelligence, Mohammed certainly would have been defeated by such a superior host and whatever then existed of Islam would have been wiped off the face of the earth.

You do not have to penetrate the rarefied air of international politics to realize the importance of information and foreknowledge. We all need some sort of information at one time or another, in our business, in our private dealings, even in the most intimate phases of our personal lives. When we buy a house, we go to some length to find out everything there is to know about the neighborhood, termites, schools, stores, transportation facilities. In our daily lives, we continually seek information, if it is only to dial a number on the telephone to get a weather report. In normal times, the information contained in a weather report is freely available, but in times of war it becomes a piece of intelligence that the enemy needs for his plans.

The information that nations need for the conduct of their foreign relations is vast as to both type and subject. We live today in a highly complex world in which competition is acute and often ruthless. No nation today can any longer exist in an isolated position, sealed off hermetically from the rest of the world or protected automatically by natural barriers. Every nation must, of necessity, fit itself into the global pattern that technological progress has forced upon the world.

Communications and transportation have so shrunk the world that even a small and remote country may find itself in the direct path of military conquest or political or economic aggression. The unilateral proclamation of neutrality is no longer sufficient to guarantee the inviolability of a nation. In fact, neutrality is frowned upon by the great powers, which demand that all countries of the world choose sides.

As long as there remain nations that have expansionist aspirations and ideas of aggrandizement, or merely paranoiac grievances, other nations are in danger of being outwitted in diplomacy or infiltrated by economic and political influences, or even attacked by military force without warning.

Behind the shadow of the military threat lie, therefore, some very different aspects of intelligence which, though not so precisely definable, are equally important to a comprehensive interpretation and understanding of a nation's own position in the ever-shrinking world today. To illustrate this point, an outline of the major considerations of intelligence might appear in this form:

1. MILITARY: Offensive and defensive doctrines. War plans. Strategic concepts and tactical principles. Organization. Installations. Industrial base. Armed forces. Command structure. Command personnel. Materiel. Tactics. Morale.

2. GENERAL: Topographical and hydographic characteristics. Historical backgrounds.

3. DIPLOMATIC: Foreign policies. Alliances. Diplomatic establishment. Foreign-service personnel. Technique of conducting foreign relations.

4. POLITICAL: Ideology. Traditions. Institutions. Personalities. Areas of friction.

11

5. ECONOMIC:
   a. *Financial:* Monetary policies. Currency structure. Transactions. Institutions. Personalities.
   b. *Commercial:* Trade policies. Markets. Trading methods. Price policies. Personalities.
   c. *Industrial:* Structure and capacity. Manufacturing plants and processes. Raw materials. Energy resources. Labor relations. Personalities.
   d. *Mining:* Mineral resources. Production methods. Output.
   e. *Agriculture:* Policies. Crop structure. Cultivation methods. Mechanization. Financing. Specific characteristics of rural population.

6. COMMUNICATIONS AND TRANSPORTATION: Telephones. Telegraph. Wireless. Railways. Shipping. Automobiles and trucks. Highways. Aviation. Ownership. Policies. Organization. Personnel.

7. SOCIAL: Nationality structure. Classes and castes. Historical factors. Census. Personal aspects, characteristics, and mentality of peoples. Social legislation. Abnormal sociology of nations.

8. CULTURAL: Institutions. Intellectual accomplishments. Arts and sciences. Literature. Professions. Radio. Television. Press. Motion pictures.

9. INTELLIGENCE: Organization, methods, and personnel of competing intelligence systems.

Specifically, military information includes data about the military theories and prowess of individual countries, the doctrines of their armed forces, their war plans in general and their deployment and mobilization plans in particular, their strategic and tactical concepts in theory and practice. Also embodied are the tables of organization of the armed forces and their so-called Order of Battle, which, in turn, includes such general information as the location of military, naval, or air districts and such specific data as the names and ranks of offices and the insignia of units.

In addition, it includes data on weapon developments and the various arms, from the hydrogen bomb down to AA guns on PT boats and range-finders on fighter planes. It includes, too, detailed information about the strength and distribution of the armed forces in their components, the uniforms and the equipment of the troops, their health conditions, their morale, the *esprit de corps* of individual units, even such seemingly incidental information as the biographies of officers, the weak and strong points of their character, their preferences and prejudices, their circle of friends and off-duty hobbies.

12

Napoleon was keenly interested in the character traits of the commanders who opposed him. Karl Schulmeister, his chief of intelligence, had to procure for him all kinds of information about the personal lives and habits of the enemy generals. In his campaign plans Napoleon paid as much attention to the character and foibles of the generals who opposed him as to the disposition and equipment of enemy troops.

Military information on a monumental scale was procured by Sir Francis Walsingham in 1587, on the eve of the great running battle off Britain, about the plans, disposition, and strength of Spain's Invincible Armada. Since then, the war plans of nations have been the most closely guarded and the most sought-after military information. But even such seemingly general details as an army's tactics when fighting in wooded areas or a fleet's deployment of destroyers for night action are considered important.

Topographical or hydrographic information in the general category of intelligence has figured prominently throughout history. As a matter of fact, the first extant intelligence report was concerned with such information. It was prepared for Pharaoh Thothmes III in 1479 B.C., during his Armageddon campaign.

The army of Thothmes, moving on the city of Yemma, sixteen miles southwest of Megiddo, had the choice of three roads leading into the city. An approach march so close to the enemy was a delicate operation, and Thothmes was anxious to deploy his forces on the best of the three approaches. He sent out scouts, and they returned with information about the different roads. This information was then evaluated by the Pharaoh's chief of staff, who recommended that the middle road be used. Thothmes invoked the privilege of all commanders and disregarded the recommendation of his chief of staff. He moved against Megiddo by the northern road, which proved, in fact, ideal for his maneuver.

Modern military intelligence developed out of the gathering of topographical information which monopolized the interest of commanders in the nineteenth century. At that time, intelligence relating to terrain was considered more important than the knowledge of the nature and strength of foreign armies.

Today military surveys and the preparation and maintenance of maps and nautical charts still form a primary function of army and navy intelligence. Mapmaking is a continuous challenge to intelligence, an undertaking that never ceases, because the political boundaries and man-made changes of the earth never cease to take place. "Man comes along," Colonel A. W. Masters of G-2 said, "and he makes changes in the roads, in the rail systems, and in the cities, and all of those things affect the military use of the map, so there have to be revisions." Maps used by the military establishment must be "adequate"—complete, up-to-date, legible, and accurate—or else they are not only useless but dangerous since they might mislead commanders who base plans on the information contained in them. "Many historical examples could be given," Colonel Masters said, "as to the effect of lack of maps or the effect of map errors." In actual fact, from its early wars to the Korean campaign, the United States has never gone to war with adequate maps. "The resulting cost in men and materiel would be difficult to assess," Colonel Masters said, "but it could be assumed that it has been considerable."

During the Second World War, the Army spent a yearly average of $80,000,000 on military surveys, topographic maps, and geodetic data. The current annual average is around $40,000,000. At the present time, there are 8,123 persons in the U. S. Army permanently absorbed by this highly specialized intelligence activity.

The U. S. Navy keeps about 7,000 nautical charts up to date and produces more than 1,000 new charts every year. On this intelligence activity alone, the Navy spends almost $10,000,000 a year.

Maps are difficult to make, and especially difficult today with certain sensitive areas closed to our mapmakers. Maps of these areas must be prepared from data supplied by costly intelligence and espionage. And even under favorable circumstances mapmaking is expensive and time-consuming: an average 1/25,000-scale military map covering an area of fifty-six square miles costs about $150,000 and requires two years to make.

General intelligence also includes information about other physical characteristics of countries, such as the potability of the water from streams or the composition of the soil. Before the Allied invasion of North Africa in 1942, information concerning the latter was urgently sought; when obtained, it led to a wholesale resoling of GI boots to adapt them to the specific nature of the soft African soil on the outer fringes of the Sahara Desert.

In addition to geography, geology, and hydrology, general intelligence is also concerned with the history of nations, particularly their wars and political fortunes, since it has been demonstrated that history does repeat itself. An ambitious historical study along these lines was undertaken by the American Navy in 1944-45. It was conducted by a branch of the Office of Naval Intelligence in preparation for a psychological warfare campaign, conducted by Captain (later Rear Admiral) Ellis M. Zacharias, to persuade the Japanese high command to surrender. Considering the way the Japanese had been fighting the war up to then, the idea that they would ever lay down their arms en masse seemed almost preposterous at the time. Their troops were severely indoctrinated against surrender. They were drilled in the Samurai tradition —in the ancient code of Bushido—which regarded surrender as a mortal shame, far worse than death. The behavior of many Japanese units in battle had reflected this indoctrination.

Information was sought on the behavior of the Japanese in defeat, and Nipponese history supplied the clues. While ancient and medieval Japan had engaged in only two foreign wars up to the time of the Meiji Restoration in the nineteenth century, its history showed an unbroken chain of struggles between individual clans. It was then found by the American specialists who sought this information that the defeated clan never died in battle. On the contrary, it always surrendered. This background information, which also described the formalities of surrender, was then applied in the Zacharias operations plan, and used in its execution.

Diplomatic information today matches military information in significance and is particularly important in a cold war in which no armies actually meet. It comprises data about the diplomatic establishment of individual nations, the personalities of their foreign ministers and foreign-service personnel, the practices and techniques of their diplomacy, their foreign policies and alliances, the manner in which they conduct negotiations, their conference techniques, details of protocol.

Britain in particular has been interested in diplomatic information for the conduct of her foreign relations, sometimes to an almost ludicrous degree. Prior to sending a diplomatic delegation to a Moroccan potentate in 1879, the British obtained detailed information on the customs of the Sultan's court and also about the Sultan himself. When this information revealed that the Sultan was inordinately superstitious, the English delegation was enlarged by the addition of Douglas Beaufort, scion of the famous family of magicians. His assignment was to perform certain tricks before the Sultan, in order to impress the ruler with the supernatural powers of Queen Victoria, thus softening him up for the diplomatic pourparler that followed.

In preparation for the Berlin conference of the Big Four

15

Foreign Ministers in January-February, 1954, the American State Department studied all the information on file about the conference habits of Foreign Minister Vyacheslav M. Molotov of the Soviet Union. To prepare himself for the Moscow conference in 1945, Secretary of State James F. Byrnes even studied Lenin's writings, especially his treatise on compromise.

The Soviet Foreign Ministry puts a premium on such information and regards the gathering of intelligence as the primary function of Russian diplomatic missions abroad, especially intelligence relating to the frictions between countries opposed to the U.S.S.R.

Political information is derived partly from diplomatic information, but it also includes data about the leading personalities of states, especially the chief executives, prime ministers, leaders of the opposition, and politicians in general, their character traits, associations, influence, and particularly gossip about scandals in which they might have been involved. Beyond that, political information consists of data concerning the political institutions and systems of individual countries, their philosophies and ideologies, political parties, electoral systems, the influence of minorities, and the vast areas of friction present in all political systems. Information about foreign frictions monopolized the attention of Hitler up to 1939, as long as he thought he would be able to carry out his plans of expansion without going to war.

Information of decisive importance along these lines came into his hands in the summer of 1939, during the convention of an international organization called the Nordic Federation, held in Lübeck. One of the delegates to that conference was a certain Major Vidkun Quisling of Norway, leader of an extreme rightist party, the Nasjonal Samling.

During the convention, contact was established between Quisling and Alfred Rosenberg, a Nazi publicist who functioned primarily as Hitler's chief friction expert. Quisling supplied information on the Norwegian armed forces and on his country's international policies, and then organized a Nazi underground in Norway to provide additional information, including data on the defense installations of the strategic port of Narvik. This information encouraged Hitler to invade Norway in April, 1940, and to base his operations plan on the support he expected to get from Quisling's party, which was opposed to Norway's national government to the point of aligning itself with a foreign power. Hitler's Norwegian enterprise, which added the word "quisling" to the dictionary, is

16

the perfect example of manipulating political friction in foreign countries on the basis of pertinent information.

In the twentieth century, economic information gained equal importance with military and diplomatic information. Such information covers a vast area and ranges from data on the fiscal policies of individual countries to the blueprints of patents. Of particular interest is information pertaining to the monetary condition of a country, its foreign trade, and especially its industries, natural resources, and agriculture. Information about labor is of special importance, since labor-management relations frequently produce vast areas of friction, with violent strife and bloody strikes occasionally leading to revolution. There is a reciprocal relationship between industrial and military information, not merely in the field of production for the armed forces and in the special area of war economy, but specifically in technological fields, which are important sources of information.

The location of war-essential plants is the primary concern of what is called "target" intelligence, upon which stategic bombing is completely dependent. It is assumed, today more than ever, that the elimination of an army's industrial base is certain to paralyze the army in the field, and an enormous amount of information is needed about the nature and location of the industries of other countries to enable an air force to interfere strategically in an all-out conflict.

Industrial intelligence was much in demand even before industries existed in the modern sense. In A.D. 673, a Byzantine fleet wrought havoc on the fleet of the Saracens, chiefly through the use of an unheard-of implement of war which came to be known as "Greek fire." This was a deadly incendiary compound which the Byzantine ships hurled at the vessels of the Saracens, setting them on fire, disabling and sinking them all.

The Saracens set out at once to obtain information about the new weapon, which may properly be called the atomic bomb of that age. They discovered that it was the invention of a Syrian architect who had migrated to Constantinople, but they could not obtain the secret of the compound itself. For the next four hundred years, all the enemies of Byzantium sought information on this wonderful implement of war, but to no avail. Its secret is still not completely known today, when fire is again used with telling effect in the improved flamethrowers of armies and in "napalm" bombs.

With the emergence of the people at large as the major factor in a nation's life, sociological information has gained increased importance. Such information includes detailed

17

demographic data of the exactitude of a census bureau's inquiry, material on all strata of populations and their relations with one another. It penetrates to a nation's soul, as it includes knowledge about the people's ideas, desires, ambitions, hopes, preferences, prejudices, frustrations, morale, race consciousness, aptitudes, even family patterns.

Such information was highly regarded in Germany during the thirties, when special efforts were made to prepare composite pictures of the social structures of Great Britain, France, and the United States. Social scientists were sent to these countries by the Psychological Branch of the German High Command to collect data on the various manifestations of the nations' social existence. A psychologist named Walter Beck came to the United States disguised as a refugee scholar. He was received with open arms and given a job at an eastern university. Under this cloak, he gathered information about the American people for a study he was supposed to prepare for the Psychological Branch of the Wehrmacht.

In the course of his investigations, Dr. Beck visited all parts of the United States and studied the peoples in the East, Middle West, South, and Far West. When he tried to estimate what sort of soldiers Americans would make, he was unable to form any conclusions, until he watched a college football game. There he thought he had found what he was looking for. When he compiled his report, he represented all Americans as football players. He emphasized in the report that Americans have a highly developed team spirit, that they are aggressive in contests, that they have tenacity, and, above all, that they bring a scientific approach to everything they do, from football to war. He was convinced that the old frontier spirit was still very much alive in the people of America, and cautioned against the tendency in high German circles to regard Americans as materialistic and decadent. On the contrary, Dr. Beck reported, they were idealistic and virile. He ended his report with the urgent recommendation that Hitler refrain from provoking the United States to war, and predicted that America would certainly be victorious in war, not only because of its vast industrial superiority, but also because of superior social factors which would come to the fore in an open conflict.

It is interesting to note that the scientist who was sent to Britain to prepare a similar study returned with identical conclusions, reached on the basis of totally different information. This specialist also advised against becoming involved in war with Britain. However, the psychologist who was sent to France predicted flatly that Germany would win easily in a war against France, no matter how powerful the French army might be, solely because of dominant social factors in the life of the French nation.

Cultural information has an immediate connection with social information, chiefly because it provides the data needed for the manipulation of peoples and public opinion by intangible means. Such data includes information about the press, radio, and television, as well as other media of communication; the arts and professions; and the intellectual stature of nations. In a special category of rapidly increasing importance is scientific information, demonstrated most dramatically in the development of the atomic bomb in the United States, Britain, and Canada, and in the eagerness of the Soviet Union to acquire information about this.

Scientific information is always at a premium. In 1938, a notorious professional spy named Frederick Duquesne endeared himself to the Nazis by his self-declared ability to supply such information. This man made a good living by peddling information to highest bidders, beginning a shady career in the Boer War when he worked against England, continuing it in World War I when he again acted against the British, and then topping it on the eve of World War II when he proposed to work on a substantial scale against the United States. The information he promised to supply was almost exclusively scientific in nature and included the formula for certain textiles to be used in Army uniforms to neutralize mustard gas, certain devices developed by the scientists of the International Telephone and Telegraph Company, and information on bacterial agents in warfare.

While Duquesne was a dangerous operative, much of his information was useless. There were others, however, who did succeed in uncovering eagerly sought-after details of certain scientific achievements. During World War II, the United States employed teams of scientists for intelligence missions, including the famous *Alsos* operation, whose aim was to uncover information about Germany's atomic developments. The cover name Alsos was chosen because it was the Greek word for grove—and Leslie Groves was the name of the American general who headed the Manhattan Project. The information Alsos brought back was reassuring: it showed bungling, departmental jealousies, government interference, and relatively little scientific achievement.

Only once were the operatives of Alsos really afraid that the Germans might have made important progress in the development of an atomic bomb. They discovered that the Germans were hoarding thorium, an element that could be used in an A-bomb project in a well-advanced stage. From the moment of that discovery, the thorium mystery monopolized the attention of Alsos, since it might have held the key to some genuine and promising German effort. At last the thorium was traced to a certain German chemical firm, but nothing in this firm's set-up indicated that it was working on anything remotely resembling an atomic bomb. In actual fact, it was manufacturing toothpaste—thoriated toothpaste. In order to monopolize the market, this firm was hoarding all the thorium it could lay its hands on. This information about Operation Toothpaste was almost as important as if Alsos had found the thorium used in an A-bomb project, because it satisfied the Allies that the Germans were not using it for that threatening purpose.

It is quite obvious that information on the communication and transportation networks of foreign countries is of extreme importance in calculating the military potential of those countries. Comprehensive intelligence information is compiled on the rail nets, including such details as the number of tracks in railroad stations and marshaling yards and the location of switches and railroad crossings, in addition to major information about signal systems, junctions, key stations, and rolling stock. The importance of this information is demonstrated by the fact that in time of war a special corps of intelligence agents is assigned to its collection—people called "train watchers" in the lingo of intelligence. Their job is to observe the movement of troops and goods on rails, to record changes in the network, to keep track of schedules.

Like the weather report, the ordinary timetable is a casualty of war. It usually disappears on the day hostilities commence, since the movement of trains suddenly becomes military information to be carefully concealed from an enemy whose air force and sabotage troops are only too anxious to interfere with schedules.

The practical significance of such information was demonstrated in a most dramatic manner in June, 1944, during the Allied landings in France, when exact information about the French rail net enabled General Eisenhower to have the lines cut wherever it became necessary to retard the movement of German troops on their way to the Normandy battlefield. General Eisenhower later declared that the special operation based on this information was worth fifteen divisions in keeping the Germans away from the combat zone.

The state of chaos within the railway system became so serious that, by the beginning of July, 1944, it took the Germans eight days to go from the German-Swiss border to

Paris, a journey that normally requires seven hours. All told, nine German divisions were thus prevented from reaching the Normandy battlefields. When the 11th German Panzer Division was brought from the Russian front to reinforce the troops in France, it took them three times longer to cover the 450 kilometers in France than had been required to travel the 1,650 kilometers separating Russia from the French frontier. In order to effect this delaying action, the Allies needed information about the French rail network before they could organize the little band of rail cutters and bridge wreckers within the French resistance movement. Without adequate and accurate information, in which the exact location of a single switch often assumed key importance, the attempt to destroy German communications would have been doomed to failure, if it could have been made at all.

Last but not least, intelligence needs information about intelligence. Since the organized collection of information is among a nation's most competitive activities, those engaged professionally in intelligence work are never idle but must try forever to infiltrate competitive organizations. Such infiltration is difficult and risky and is virtually impossible without the most detailed and up-to-the-minute information about the opponent's organization. This information usually includes data about the opponent's method of collecting information, the items he is interested in (sometimes called the "shopping list" in the business), and, above all else, his personnel, both in the home office and in the field.

It is at this point that those who collect information may be most effectively destroyed. For knowledge of the opponent's intelligence enables one to manipulate information, to conceal certain items and dilute others, to put out bogus information, and so to destroy the value of information by destroying its accuracy. However, inaccurate information will occasionally avalanche and involve those who disseminate it as well as the intended victims.

The Need To Know

Obviously, a vast amount and enormous variety of information is needed to guard a nation against surprises—strategic attacks like that at Pearl Harbor, diplomatic coups like the conclusion of the pact between Stalin and Hitler in 1939, or economic moves like the devaluation of key currencies, as of the franc in 1930 and the pound sterling in 1949—and to supply the data on the basis of which a nation can form its policies, draw up its plans, and organize its moves.

Information is needed by the governments of all nations, and within these governments there are departments designed primarily for dealing with intelligence in all its forms.

Policy makers—the President of the United States, the Prime Minister of the United Kingdom, the premiers of France or Germany, and a few men in the Kremlin—require intelligence to carry out their work. Yet intelligence rarely goes directly to them. Intelligence services normally collect such vast amounts of information that no president, prime minister, chief of state, or secretary of state could possibly examine and evaluate it all and be able to distinguish between the essential and the trivial.

All this information, essential and trivial, factual and conjectural, has to pass through a large and intricate machine, which processes the raw material, filtering it and culling from it those individual items having a direct bearing on the policy under study by the policy makers at the time.

Let us see how this process works by looking at a specific example of some historical importance. In December, 1944, the policy makers of the Western Allies were deeply concerned with the seemingly stubborn determination of Japan to fight on to the bitter end, despite the gradual weakening of her war-making capacity in the face of our victories. The Joint Chiefs of Staff were extremely pessimistic and advised the White House that an invasion of the Japanese main islands would be necessary to subdue that country. They were convinced that Japan would never surrender. This gloomy advice was accompanied by the recommendation that the policies of the United States and Britain be based on the assumption that the war in Japan would continue until 1948 or 1949. This somber estimate of the situation was based not so much on hard military intelligence as on the innate cautiousness of General George C. Marshall, which dominated the Joint Chiefs of Staff and which had great influence with President Roosevelt and Secretary of War Henry L. Stimson. Both President Roosevelt and Mr. Stimson were deeply impressed with General Marshall's estimate and developed a policy for the fight against Japan which seemed to complicate the war and prolong it.

The results of this policy were the costly invasions of Iwo Jima and Okinawa. A large-scale invasion of Kyushu, one of the main islands of Japan, was scheduled to take place in the fall of 1945 with a force of millions and casualties estimated at one million men. The official Anglo-American attitude stiffened toward Japan and especially toward the Emperor.

These were tremendously important decisions in themselves, yet they were by no means all. Again upon the advice of the Joint Chiefs, a policy decision was reached to invite the Soviet Union into the Pacific war and to make considerable concessions in Europe for her participation in Manchuria. In its consequences, this policy had more serious results than any directly concerning Japan.

Whatever information lay at the bottom of these policy decisions, it was inadequate, one-sided, and highly biased. It was almost exclusively military information, consisting of such orthodox forms of intelligence as the order of battle and combat narratives, which are the chief sources of a *military* commander's information.

In December, 1944, however, a great quantity of political, diplomatic, and economic information arrived in Washington which should have placed the Joint Chiefs' estimates in an entirely different light. Included in this information was intelligence from two excellently informed diplomatic sources: the Vatican, and the envoy of a neutral country stationed in Tokyo. Both supplied the information that the Emperor himself had decided to explore the prospects of surrender, and that a peace party existing within Japan's highest echelons enjoyed the support of the Emperor and of top-ranking Naval officers.

The first definite information on this score reached Washington on Christmas Eve of 1944. From then on, additional evidence poured in. A special branch of the Army obtained reliable information indicating that Japan was being strangled by our blockade and was rapidly reaching the end of the road. Information was then obtained from a number of sources about Japanese peace-feelers, including direct appeals from Tokyo to Moscow asking the Kremlin to act as a mediator between Japan and the United States.

While the information on hand was considerable in volume and impressively persuasive, it was scattered among a great number of agencies. Some of it was in the Office of Naval Intelligence; some was in the Army's so-called Magic operation, which translated the codes of foreign governments; some was in the Office of Strategic Services; and still more was in a special intelligence branch of the Army attached to the assistant secretary's own office. Strangely enough, no information was forthcoming from the State Department, which is normally the chief clearing-house of diplomatic intelligence.

And there was no centralized agency that could have coordinated this scattered information.

Then, in February, 1945, an organ was created by Secretary of the Navy James Forrestal to concentrate this information, to evaluate it, and to prepare the necessary recommendations for the policy makers. To head this organization, Captain Zacharias was ordered to Washington. He was ideally suited for the assignment, since he had had three decades of intelligence experience and was the U.S. Navy's foremost expert on Japan. From then on, the scattered information became centralized. Captain Zacharias summarized the information in twelve major points, reducing it from reams of reports to a single closely typed page for the eyes of the President. When the information was processed for the policy maker, this is how it looked:

INFORMATION: (a) The Japanese main islands are now isolated *except from the continent* and are faced with threats from all directions.

(b) Our present and future position outside of the Japanese main islands will afford means of exerting all coercive pressure necessary.

(c) Certain members of the Japanese High Command realize that the war is irretrievably lost; the others of the High Command recognize the seriousness of the present situation, which is bound to deteriorate in the future.

(d) The plans for victory of the Japanese High Command are contingent upon continued unity of thought between the [Imperial] Army and Navy and upon an all-sacrificing prosecution of the war.

(e) Great conflict of opinion exists within the High Command as to the past, present and future conduct of the war.

(f) Field commanders in highest echelons are blaming the High Command for inept leadership in the war.

(g) Great difference of opinion and dissension exists among commanders in the field and at sea.

(h) For the first time since the Russo-Japanese war, the Premier has been instructed to participate in the deliberations of the High Command, thus establishing an immediate link between the political and military leadership of the empire, carefully separated since 1886.

(i) For the first time in 24 years, criticism of the government and the High Command is openly voiced.

(j) The Axis pact of September 27, 1940, was signed by Japan by the narrowest margin and only after extensive bribery in Tokyo and distribution of large sums of money.

(k) There are a great many highly placed individuals in Japan who realize that war with the United States meant "the finish of the Japanese empire and a great loss to the United States."

(l) It is known that foreign broadcasts are monitored in Japan and transcripts have a comparatively wide distribution.

24

Captain Zacharias then proceeded to make a policy recommendation on the basis of this information and also to draft an operations plan for the execution of that policy. This policy goal was worded as follows:

To make unnecessary an opposed landing in the Japanese main islands, by weakening the will of the High Command, by effecting cessation of hostilities, and by bringing about unconditional surrender with the least possible loss of life to us consistent with early termination of the war.

This summary of information, the policy recommendation, and the operations plan were then submitted to the Secretary of the Navy and through him to President Roosevelt in the White House. The document was on the President's desk at the time of his death. He had made a few penciled changes in it, a sign that he had read and considered it, but he never approved it. On May 8, 1945, however, it was studied by President Truman and, then, part of the Zacharias plan, based on hard information, became the policy of the United States government.

This, then, is an example of how information is coordinated, collated, orchestrated, evaluated, and summarized for presentation to the policy makers, and how such information then influences the major policy decisions of nations. Now let us see how an incidental piece of intelligence resulted in an isolated but major strategic move. In 1942, a prominent political scientist of the University of Pennsylvania, Dr. Robert Strausz-Hupe, was working in Washington on certain population studies in which President Roosevelt was personally interested. He and his staff surveyed all problems of peoples, including, of course, the question of food supplies.

The problem of food supplies in Japan was given special attention, since it was early recognized as one of the bottlenecks of the entire Japanese war effort. Dr. Strausz-Hupe surveyed all aspects of the problem and came to an important subsidiary problem: the question of agricultural fertilizer. He examined the sources of Japan's fertilizer supply and found that most of it came from the French possessions in North Africa.

Our invasion of French Morocco and Algeria and our control of the sea lanes cut off this source, but Strausz-Hupe found upon studying certain information emerging from inside Japan that there was no shortage of fertilizers in Japan, despite the loss of the North African sources. He then proceeded to ascertain all possible new sources of supply. He succeeded in pinpointing a Pacific island called Nauru, the surface of which abounded in leached guanos and phosphatized rocks. He assumed that supplies from Nauru were compensating for Japan's lost fertilizer imports from North Africa.

This information was then communicated to the military authorities, with the recommendation that Nauru be subjected to heavy aerial attack to knock it out as Japan's source of fertilizer supply and thereby to interfere with the food production of the country. The soundness of Strausz-Hupe's assumption was established when information was gained through aerial reconnaissance. Navy scouting planes took many pictures of the island and the usual examination of these aerial photographs revealed a number of interesting items. First, they showed a cluster of new installations. Second, they showed a number of cargo vessels loading at newly constructed piers. Third, they produced convincing evidence that Nauru had become the major source of Japan's fertilizer supply.

This information was then submitted to the Joint Chiefs, with a definite recommendation of action against Nauru. An operations plan was drafted and its execution assigned to the Navy. Energetic bombardment followed, and soon Nauru was knocked out. In time, information was obtained that showed a gradual deterioration of Japan's fertilizer stocks and a concurrent crisis in food supplies. The information that lay at the basis of this important operation was obtained by the orthodox means of library research and the unorthodox methods of aerial reconnaissance. The two combined to supply the intelligence needed for an important military operation. Of course, the details of the intelligence were never presented to the Joint Chiefs. They were merely given the results of the intelligence study and the findings of the reconnaissance, together with the recommendation based on both.

The far-reaching repercussions of the Zacharias and Strausz-Hupe operations, then, illustrate the need for knowledge of other countries in such areas as political, economic, diplomatic, social, and cultural matters. The Zacharias estimate was based on up-to-date information and also on a thorough knowledge of modern Japanese history. The summary combined political and military information, but, more important, it supplied data on the mood of the people, which is a social aspect, and on historic backgrounds, which is a general aspect of intelligence. The Strausz-Hupe estimate was based on information about certain basic needs of the population, on economic and geographical data, and on a great number of related factors across the entire spectrum of intelligence.

In the political area, knowledge of important personalities of the country under study is of crucial importance. This is called biographical intelligence. This type of information may be collected separately or within the various specialized intelligence systems. Thus, the diplomatic establishment has its own biographical file on foreign personalities, quite separate from the military establishment's, which maintains dossiers on the leading commanders of foreign armies, navies, and air forces. In lower echelons, biographical information is accumulated even on tactical personnel, such as crew members of U-boats and officers of companies in the combat zones. Information of this kind enabled us during World War II to address appeals to officers of all ranks opposing our forces and to make these appeals very personal indeed. A broadcast to a young lieutenant who commanded a machine-gun nest in Okinawa might mention his wife and children in Japan, and broadcasts to U-boat personnel could make use of similar intimate data, culled from the mass of biographical information accumulated in Britain's Division of Naval Intelligence and the U.S. Office of Naval Intelligence.

While such tactical exploitation of biographical data is useful, this information assumes decisive importance when used on the top level of national governments. With Stalin's death it became imperative to know as much as possible about the personality of the man who would succeed him. Intelligence in the past has supplied a picture of all personalities within the Kremlin. Certain information was available about all the probable successors to Stalin, including data on their character traits and personal lives. Consequently, intelligence did not have to start from scratch when the appraisal of Stalin's successor became necessary and urgent.

Previous intelligence operations had given a cursory picture of the men who were likely to take his place, among them Georgi Malenkov. Once Malenkov was designated as Stalin's successor, intelligence concentrated on him. Scattered data was pulled together and orchestrated until the picture of Malenkov appeared in sharp focus.

This information is needed because the personalities of political leaders play a major role in the formulation of policies. Before Roosevelt went to Teheran, he engaged in an elaborate effort to find out everything he could about the personality and character traits of Stalin. All intelligence agencies had to supply data for this study. In addition, Roosevelt interviewed persons who knew Stalin and tried to find

27

out from them certain specific aspects of his character. He then based his whole approach to Stalin on this data. He became supremely confident that he would be able to "handle" Stalin, because he knew not only his ideas, but also his whims, methods of negotiation, and various indelible personal traits.

And so, although information may not be of immediate importance, it must nevertheless be on file when needed, if only to round out a picture and thus aid in the formulation of policies and the direction of moves. Information may be available about certain mines in East Germany, but it need not be "live" information required for immediate action. Then, specific information may become available that will serve as tinder to start up the dormant fire. This information may reach us in a variety of forms and from a variety of sources, occasionally even from what would be normally regarded as a low tactical source.

Thus, an exile from East Germany who has worked in one of the mines may arrive in West Berlin with information that uranium has been discovered there. He knew it at first hand. He himself worked in that mine until his escape. Since uranium is essential in the Soviet Union's atomic developments, the mine found to contain this vital raw material acquires strategic importance. In such a case, all the available information is pulled together and additional information is obtained. This information may not be needed for immediate action against the mine. But it supplies crucial data for a greater pattern that shows, for example, the status and progress of atomic developments in the U.S.S.R.

We have seen before how important topographical information is, data on terrain and hydrographic information consisting of exact charts of seas and inland waters. The Sicilian charts lay neglected for decades in the hydrographic branches of the U.S. and Royal navies. But, when the decision was reached to invade Italy in 1943, these charts came to life and supplied much of the essential data needed in the drafting of the operations plan, actually influencing the operation itself. This type of information was considered so important that during the war special teams were sent surreptitiously into the Pacific area to acquire such data under the very noses of the enemy.

An isolated bit of scientific information may start a chain reaction in intelligence that explodes in a major operation which influences the course of history. On March 28, 1945, a go-between of the Soviet intelligence network in Canada had a luncheon meeting with one of his informants, a young scientist named Durnford Smith. The go-between tried to get information from Smith about the latest radar developments, but the scientist told him, "Radar is no longer important. What is really important today is the Anglo-American-Canadian effort to develop atomic energy for military purposes."

This was the first word Soviet intelligence in Canada had received on the momentous decision of the Western Allies to build an atomic bomb. The go-between reported Smith's remark to a Colonel Zabutin, resident director of Soviet intelligence in Canada, who in turn reported it to General Kuznetsov, director of the Center, as the U.S.S.R.'s central intelligence service is intimately called. The information was then called to the attention of Stalin himself and the enormous intelligence machinery of the Soviet Union was set in motion to acquire the details of this important development.

The Canadian branch of the network was instructed to obtain samples of the uranium used in the atomic bomb. The American branch was ordered to procure certain technical information: the scientific principles of the bomb, its trigger mechanism, its blueprints. Others were instructed to get information about the policy developments within the Allied governments in the wake of this historic discovery.

From scientists like Klaus Fuchs, Alan Nunn May, and Bruno Pontecorvo, from technicians like David Greenglass, from diplomatic informants whose identities are still unknown, Soviet intelligence received all the information Russia needed to determine the country's policies in the light of this development and to supply her own scientists with the necessary process for building their own A-bomb. All this was accomplished within three months. Since information is really useful only if available when needed, speed of acquisition is an essential aspect of intelligence. The success of Soviet intelligence was due to a perfect combination of the factors of accuracy, explicitness, and speed—the true criteria of good intelligence.

Scattered information is useful by itself. But to make it dynamic, it has to be pulled together piece by piece and developed to form distinct patterns for the enlightenment of higher echelons. This coordination of information is an important function of intelligence.

All intelligence is pulled together in concentrated form in a closely guarded and highly restricted area within the military establishments, foreign offices, and the executive departments of chiefs of states. This area is called the Map Room, not only because it contains a collection of maps, but because

29

much of the intelligence accumulating there is spelled out on maps and charts to visualize and relate it directly to the areas involved, and because huge maps dominate the interior decoration of these rooms. In international emergencies the Map Room is called War Room or Plot Room; that of the Joint Chiefs of Staff in Washington is called Situation Room.

It is a place of intelligence coordination where skilled officers form patterns of topical information on a minute-by-minute basis to the staccato rhythm of tickers. It has its own communication set-up and small army of dispatch riders who rush reports and estimates to this terminal nerve center of a nation's intelligence network. To the Map Room troop the policy makers and strategists to acquaint themselves with the situation as far as it concerns them. They review the scene presented on the maps and charts and listen to briefings by area specialists and experts who are called in to augment or explain the information supplied by the staff. The Map Room produces a vibrant thrill all its own. In it the humdrum world of intelligence acquires dynamism and drama with undertones reminiscent of Hollywood's concept of this romantic activity.

Another coordinating function of intelligence is the preparation of summaries and estimates, including those prepared for the highest policy makers and strategists. They are called "national estimates." This particular function is performed by carefully chosen specialists trained explicitly for this activity, or by committees in which several intelligence agencies are represented. In the summary or estimate intelligence reaches its most concentrated form and attains direct kinetic influence. The crucial importance of this function is clearly recognized by all countries. The Soviet Union maintains a special intelligence agency for this function, the so-called Confidential Bureau situated within the Kremlin and headed by one of the U.S.S.R.'s outstanding intelligence experts, at the time of this writing General Panyushkin, a former ambassador to the United States and China.

In Britain during the Second World War, the preparation of intelligence summaries for the War Cabinet was a job assigned to Professor Arnold Toynbee, the eminent historian. In the United States, summaries and estimates are prepared on various levels, most important being those handled by the Joint Intelligence Group of the Joint Chiefs, and by a special branch of CIA, headed by a Deputy Director for Estimates. The top-ranking official in CIA in charge of estimates is Dr. Sherman Kent, a former professor of history at Yale. The estimates prepared by CIA are presented to the

President and the National Security Council by the Director himself, who stands by to supply additional information or details if they are needed.

The Organization of Intelligence

Although the importance of information was recognized even in antiquity and organizations have existed throughout history which specialized in the management of information, intelligence remained a haphazard, improvised activity until the nineteenth century, when so many aspects of man's world changed.

Retreating from Moscow, Napoleon, traveling at top speed, covered the distance between Vilna and Paris—a distance of 1,400 miles—in 312 hours. This had been the speed of communication since time immemorial. This was the maximum rate of travel between Rome and Gaul in the first century A.D., and between Sardis and Susa in the fourth century before Christ. Then suddenly this classic rate was speeded up. Striking new inventions were added to facilitate human intercourse. The coming of the railway and the steamboat accelerated travel. In 1832, the electric telegraph came into being. In 1851, the first submarine cable was laid between England and France.

Man's interests were broadened and his powers enhanced; and the importance of intelligence in turn increased. The progress of technology improved its facilities. Gradually intelligence became an organized effort, promoted and stimulated by ambitious rulers to aid in not only the formulation but the execution of their plans. Napoleon III made political intelligence a permanent fixture in his government. In Britain, diplomatic and economic intelligence became fixed instruments of national policy. Then, during the Civil War in the United States, military intelligence, too, acquired organized form.

Although domestic in scope, the Civil War was really the first modern war in history. It applied for the first time many of the technological means developed since the turn of the century. Troops were moved by rail. The signal corps utilized the telegraph. A balloon was employed for aerial observation. Ironclad ships revolutionized naval tactics, and a practical step was made toward the development of the submarine. Major victories were scored simply because information

31

was available to the commanders and they could make their arrangements with exact knowledge of the enemy's plans, dispositions, and strength.

The first great triumph of modern intelligence was General Beauregard's victory over McDowell at Bull Run. The source of this intelligence was an aristocratic widow named Rose Greenhow, who maintained a fashionable salon on Washington's Eye Street. She was a descendant of Dolly Madison and a relative of Stephen A. Douglas. Politicians, diplomats, and generals flocked to her parties. She picked up whatever information she could and sent her reports to the generals of the Confederacy. The information about McDowell's plans came to her from one of her regular guests, a Union general. It was promptly forwarded to Beauregard, who used it in planning for his subsequent victory at Bull Run.

Recognition of the decisive value of intelligence persuaded both sides to establish active intelligence services. The American example was followed abroad. Britain established its Military Intelligence Service in the immediate wake of the American Civil War, then added a Naval Intelligence Service in 1887. In 1866, military intelligence was institutionalized in Prussia in preparation for the campaigns against Austria and France. France followed suit with the establishment of the Second Bureau of the General Staff, and Russia with the Seventh Bureau of the General Staff, both specializing in the collection of all forms of information for military and politico-diplomatic ends.

Today all countries have their intelligence services. They may be different in their organizations, efficiency, and methods, but they all have the same three basic functions.

As we have already seen, in the various examples listed above, these functions are:

1. the collection or procurement of information;
2. the evaluation of the information, which then becomes intelligence; and
3. the dissemination of intelligence to those who need it.

There is also a fourth function, called by the generic term counterintelligence. This activity is dedicated to the concealment and protection of one's own information from the intelligence operations of an adversary. Heretofore we have dealt with a single form of intelligence, the gathering of necessary information about other countries, called positive intelligence.

This fourth function, counterintelligence, is known as negative intelligence, and may be defined as the effort to protect

32

our own secrets and to apprehend those who try to gain unauthorized access to them. This is the defensive function of intelligence. In most countries of the world, these two activities are joined under one roof. Britain's Military Intelligence, the famous MI, has a branch called MI-5 which is the United Kingdom's major negative-intelligence agency. In France, the Second Bureau practices both positive and negative intelligence. In Germany, the now defunct *Abwehr*, as the High Command's central intelligence service was called, had three major departments: one for positive intelligence, another for such intelligence operations as sabotage and subversive activities, and a third for negative intelligence.

The United States and the Soviet Union are the only major countries in the world today which keep these two activities apart. The Intelligence Department of the Red Army, which is the Kremlin's *de facto* central intelligence agency, specializes exclusively in positive intelligence, while other agencies are maintained for negative intelligence.

In the United States, the top-ranking intelligence service is the Central Intelligence Agency, in which positive intelligence predominates. Negative intelligence is assigned to the CIC and the Federal Bureau of Investigation which, in turn, are not intended to conduct any positive intelligence.

At this point we are concerned with positive intelligence, and with the bureaucratic and less melodramatic aspects of intelligence proper. When information is procured solely by surreptitious means, by secret agents who disguise their true missions, the activity is called espionage. Reports of spies form an integral part of the intelligence summary, but spies only rarely represent an integral part of the inner intelligence organization. We will deal with espionage and negative intelligence in later chapters.

The purpose of a modern intelligence service was spelled out most lucidly by Allen W. Dulles, director of the American Central Intelligence Agency. This important service, which represents the most efficient centralization of intelligence functions ever attempted in modern times, came into existence after World War II, when the need for such an organization became evident. The CIA was established under the National Security Council by the National Security Act of 1947, and was approved on July 26, 1947. CIA itself was placed within the framework of the National Security Council. The duties of the Council are "to assess and appraise the objectives, commitments, and risks of the United States in relation to our actual and potential military power, in the interest of national security, for the purpose of making recommendations to the President; and to consider policies on matters of common interest to the departments and agencies of the Government concerned with the national security, and to make recommendations to the President."

The primary function of the Central Intelligence Agency, then, is to supply the data that the National Security Council needs for these recommendations to the President. According to Mr. Dulles, the Central Intelligence Agency performs five interrelated functions, described by him in what may be regarded as the classic definition of the purpose of a central intelligence service:

For the purpose of coordinating the intelligence activities of the several Government departments and agencies in the interest of national security, the Agency, under direction of the National Security Council:

1. Advises the National Security Council in matters concerning such intelligence activities of the Government departments and agencies as relate to national security.

2. Makes recommendations to the National Security Council for the coordination of such intelligence activities of the departments and agencies of the Government as relate to national security.

3. Correlates and evaluates intelligence relating to the national security, and provides for the appropriate dissemination of such intelligence within the Government using, where appropriate, existing agencies and facilities.

4. Performs, for the benefit of existing intelligence agencies, such additional services of common concern as the National Security Council determines can be more efficiently accomplished centrally.

5. Performs such other functions and duties related to intelligence affecting the national security as the National Security Council may from time to time direct.

The Central Intelligence Agency is not the only intelligence service of the United States Government. There are special intelligence services within the Army, Navy, and Air Force, and scattered among other government departments. But the Central Intelligence Agency is the top-ranking intelligence service of the United States, if only because it serves the highest organs of the state and has a dominant influence, through the information it supplies, on the recommendations to the President, from which the policies and actions of the United States then emerge.

As Mr. Dulles pointed out, collection, evaluation, and dissemination are the major functions of the Central Intelligence Agency, as they are of most modern intelligence services.

To perform these functions, intelligence services operate

with carefully drawn tables of organization. These are sometimes quite elaborate, as was the case with Germany's *Abwehr*, active during Hitler's reign, which had a labyrinth of departments, sections, divisions, and subdivisions, and employed 15,000 persons at its peak in 1938. The CIA is also organized along elaborate lines, with different divisions for the conduct of various forms of intelligence, for evaluation, for clandestine activities, and for distribution. Hanson W. Baldwin, military editor for *The New York Times*, estimated that it employs from 9,000 to 15,000 persons.

Intelligence organizations have a tendency to grow around their waists and to put on weight as they get older. However, experience shows that smaller and more tightly organized services are capable of functioning more efficiently, since they have less waste, duplication, and bureaucratic diffusion, none of which is conducive to effective intelligence work. My own experience convinces me that the smaller an intelligence organization is, the better it will function, provided, of course, that its personnel is first-class.

On many grounds, the PID, or Political Intelligence Division of Her Britannic Majesty's Foreign Office, is the most efficiently organized intelligence service of all. Supervised by the Permanent Under-Secretary of State for Foreign Affairs and headed by its own director, usually a man of exceptional qualifications, this branch of the Foreign Office is small and compact, serving as a clearing-house of information by making use of the various regional and functional divisions of the mother department.

Britain's Military Intelligence, the MI, is organized into about twelve branches (the number of branches varies with exigencies), in which the various intelligence functions are handled by specialists. As we have already seen, MI-5, quartered in the War Office in Whitehall, specializes in negative intelligence, under a civilian head. MI-8 specializes in so-called communication intelligence, i.e., the reading and translating of foreign codes and ciphers. MI-11 is in charge of clandestine or "black" propaganda. A semi-autonomous branch, called Special Intelligence, has supervision over strategic espionage and over the more secret phases of intelligence work. It is usually headed by an Army general, who is regarded as one of the top-ranking personalities within the British intelligence network.

In addition to PID and MI, Britain has at least thirteen additional intelligence agencies, including the Admiralty's Division of Naval Intelligence and the Air Ministry's intelligence department. Britain's counterpart of CIA is the Joint Intelligence Bureau of the Ministry of Defense, specializing in coordination, analysis, and evaluation, rather than in collection. It is headed by a Director under whom are a Deputy Director, three Assistant Directors, seven Principal Research Officers, twenty-one Senior Research Officers, and their staffs. The Joint Intelligence Bureau maintains a special branch for high-level political and military intelligence in the secret (or espionage) category. A majority of the department heads in JIB are senior officers of the armed forces. The primary function of JIB is to supply policy and strategic intelligence to the Cabinet together with national estimates.

In the Soviet Union, this function is performed by "RU" or Intelligence Department of the Red Army, situated in an old baroque palace at 19 Znamensky in Moscow. It is headed by a colonel general, who has the title of Director, and a major general with the title of Deputy Director. Under them are several major regional divisions, in charge of colonels, each with the title of Organizer. It also has a number of functional branches. This Department is called "the Center" in Soviet intelligence parlance.

The different regional divisions specialize in given areas, as the Western Hemisphere, the Far East and South Asia, Western Europe, and so on. Within each, individual countries are handled by subdivisions. Among functional branches are the Communications Branch, which handles the Bureau's own lines of communications, the Cryptographic Branch, which specializes in the translation of codes and ciphers of foreign governments, and the Authentication Branch, which supplies forged documents, manufactures bogus passports, and performs other functions similar to those of any other intelligence service.

There is also a semi-autonomous division called the Political Division, under the personal supervision of the Director, and charged with the evaluation of incoming intelligence.

In the United States, intelligence services are also organized along regional and functional lines, which means that they have separate branches for individual countries and others for the various technical functions of an intelligence service. The U.S. Office of Naval Intelligence, for example, has two major divisions, one specializing in positive intelligence, the other in negative intelligence or counterintelligence.

At the positive end, the ONI has a chief and a deputy chief. under whom there are major divisions for foreign intelligence, for technological intelligence, and for special activities, such as interpretation of documents, prisoner interrogation, psychological warfare, and similar functions. The foreign intelligence division is organized by desks, the major navies of the world each having its own desk, while the minor ones are lumped together under single officers. Communications intelligence is separated from ONI. It is handled by the Navy's Bureau of Communications, which has a special division for the reading and translation of foreign codes and ciphers. This is one of the most efficient intelligence organizations of its kind in the world.

The table of organization of central intelligence services is itself classified information, but we know from the Office of Strategic Services that the positive intelligence work of such central intelligence authorities is organized in three major divisions. One is concerned with research and analysis, or the exploitation of reference material in the public domain. The other is secret intelligence, which is engaged in the collection of information by surreptitious means. The third is morale operations, which is a branch designed to conduct propaganda in all its known shades, white, gray, and black.

The CIA itself is organized into five major divisions. Three of them collect or procure information by the various means of intelligence, both overt and covert; one conducts research and analysis and indexes evaluated information; and one division appraises all incoming information and prepares estimates on a daily, weekly, and monthly basis. These are complex functions, and the complexity of modern intelligence is reflected even in the physical set-up of CIA. It occupies more than twenty buildings and warehouses in Washington, some housing offices which in outward appearance resemble any Washington government office, others accommodating the various training establishments and the diversified apparatus without which no efficient intelligence organization can function.

Because the problems of positive intelligence are entirely different from those of negative intelligence, both functions operate best as separate organizations. Furthermore, the combination of both activities in the hands of one director might tempt him to use his organization, with its enormous power, to exploit the liberties of his fellow citizens.

The ideal central intelligence service should be headed by a director general, with three deputy directors to head the three major divisions of the organization: one to be in charge of information procurement, another in charge of evaluation and distribution, and the third in charge of administration.

The deputy director for procurement would thus direct a considerable organization of his own, in which basic separations are made between intelligence proper, secret intelligence, and intelligence operations. The first is concerned with research and analysis, i.e., the exploitation of published material and references accessible publicly, the monitoring of foreign broadcasts, the study of foreign newspapers and magazines, liaison with other governmental and private agencies collecting information, and the interrogation of citizens returning from travels abroad. This division should maintain a picture library, a very important tool of effective intelligence. Even amateur snapshots of such open and innocent scenes as bathing beaches often contribute essential topographic and hydrographic information.

Secret intelligence would logically handle undercover work or the acquisition of confidential material not easily accessible. It would direct outright espionage and would have as one of its tasks the job of infiltrating foreign intelligence organizations. It would also prepare, within its own organization, the technical facilities needed for undercover work and supply whatever documentation or authentication might be needed for secret agents working in the field.

Intelligence operations means exactly what the term denotes: the operational use of intelligence. It functions in five major branches. The business of one is liaison with friendly foreign organizations whose cooperation is essential for this kind of work. The second is in charge of sabotage operations. The third is devoted to the organization of guerrilla warfare, the supplying of tactical commanders, weapons instructors, radio operators, and other technical personnel essential for guerrilla action behind the enemy's lines. The fourth specializes in psychological warfare, while the fifth conducts conspiratorial warfare, or what may be called the dynamic subversion of an opponent's political organization.

An evaluation branch, headed by its own deputy director, would have important functions, including the publication of intelligence reports which might be of interest to wider circles within the government organization; for example, combat narratives, prisoner interrogation transcripts, analyses, and the like, and periodicals such as the brilliant *Weekly Intelligence Report* of the Admiralty's Division of Naval Intelligence, or the American *O.N.I. Weekly*. A special branch on a high level would be in charge of intelligence summaries, in which information is pulled together for the benefit of the policy makers.

A major section within this division should be responsible for the vital task of getting the evaluated information into the hands of those who could make the best use of it. This division would also have a liaison branch for the enlistment of experts and specialists needed for the best possible evaluation of individual items of intelligence. It would also serve as a link to the evaluators in other intelligence agencies, including those maintained within the military establishment.

The deputy director in charge of administration would handle the general management of the whole service (CIA actually has a General Manager), and supervise personnel, security, and finances, which assume special importance in an intelligence organization in which substantial funds are handled confidentially.

Two important activities of the intelligence service might also be placed under the deputy director for administration. One is training and indoctrination, which should be a subsection of personnel. The other is communications, which is not concerned with the translation of foreign codes and ciphers, but solely with the maintenance of the organization's own lines of communications. This branch is best placed centrally in administration where it is easily accessible to all those dependent upon its facilities.

Internal efficiency in an intelligence service is of exceptional importance for smooth and fast operation and is essential to effectiveness. Such efficiency might not be possible in an organization that overflows its banks, and consequently the diversification of the various activities must not be taken to mean that an intelligence service should have a great many employees in each function of the basic organization.

My experience in the Special Warfare Branch of ONI during World War II persuaded me that relatively few people are needed to make an intelligence organization efficient and effective, if the right people can be found for the right jobs. Thus Op-16-W, as the Special Warfare Branch was called within ONI, had an officer in charge, plus an executive officer who handled all administrative matters and supervised all activities. The branch had one officer in charge of liaison with operational agencies, and another to serve as a link to collection agencies. The latter doubled as a radio commentator, addressing German U-boat crews several times a week during the war.

Three regional sections, or "desks," were then maintained, one for Germany, another for Italy, and a third for Japan. The German desk consisted of three persons; the Italian desk, a single WAVE officer; the Japanese desk, two officers and three civilians.

The whole branch shared a single yeoman and two civilian stenographers. Its total annual budget amounted to less than the purchase price of two torpedoes.

Yet this branch was engaged in both the collection and the evaluation of intelligence, and also in various intelligence operations. It functioned efficiently and effectively, probably because it was small and closely coordinated.

In intelligence, quality is far more important than quantity, especially in organization.

In the field, an intelligence service may assume various forms. It may be organized within the offices of so-called service attachés, i.e., military, naval, and air attachés, or be set up as independent units, serving as foreign branches of the home office. Such organizations are usually headed by resident directors and maintain branches of their own, either to procure information about the country to which they are assigned or to stimulate the flow of information by developing and cultivating informants.

The Price of Intelligence

How much does intelligence cost or, to put it pragmatically, how much do nations spend on this important instrument of policy and security? It is quite difficult to answer this question in specific terms, because most countries prefer to keep their intelligence budgets under wraps. A distinction must also be made between the costs of orthodox intelligence, which may be fairly low, and the price of secret intelligence, which may be substantial. It is impossible to separate the budget of straight intelligence from expenditures on espionage, so the following account of the financial aspects of the trade will explain both.

In Elizabethan England, Sir Francis Walsingham had constant financial trouble maintaining his secret service and actually bankrupted himself in the end by investing his own money when he could squeeze no more funds from the thrifty queen. Cromwell, unlike the queen, expended large sums on his intelligence service as was attested by Samuel Pepys, who wrote in his diary on February 14, 1668, "Secretary Morrice did this day in the House, when they talked of intelligence, say that he was allowed but £700 a year for intelligence, whereas, in Cromwell's time, he [Cromwell] did allow £70,000 a year for it."

The financial affairs of today's British secret service emerge from obscurity just once a year, on Budget Day in the House of Commons. The Budget includes appropriations for "Her

Majesty's Foreign and Other Secret Services." In 1954 this was item No. 21 in Class I of the central government's appropriations under "Civil Estimates and Supplementary Estimates." It amounted to the sum of £3,000,000, highest in the whole history of the British secret service. Even this high figure is deceptive since it reveals only allotments from public funds. The bulk of Britain's intelligence revenue comes from private funds, such as dividends of the Anglo-Iranian Oil Company, some of whose shares are held by the Admiralty.

On the level of the individual, the glamour of intelligence is not reflected in the salaries paid to its practitioners. It was estimated that Britain employs 3,000 persons in secret service, most of them detailed from the armed forces. The secret agents of Britain draw an average salary of £1,500 a year (or about $4,400 at the current rate of exchange). Everything is paid in cash and such earnings are not reported to the tax authorities. Allowances are limited and agents are explicitly told to keep their expenses within bounds. While the British secret service in principle insists on paying for everything it gets, it is rarely willing to pay more than £1,000, even for data it is most anxious to have.

Before World War I, Germany appropriated only 450,000 marks (about $180,000) a year for all secret service activities within the Imperial Army, including counterespionage. At that time the Seventh Bureau of the Czarist Army was spending 12,000,000 rubles (about $5,000,000) a year. Russia was traditionally generous with money spent on intelligence, and the Soviet Union continues this expensive generosity. The total Soviet intelligence budget of today is impossible to calculate, but it may be safe to say that it amounts to several hundred million dollars—indeed *dollars,* since Soviet intelligence conducts all its financial transactions in American currency.

Probably the highest "fee" ever paid to a single agent—sums in excess of $100,000—was paid to Colonel Alfred Redl, chief of the Austro-Hungarian secret service who doubled as a spy for Russia. In more recent years, Soviet intelligence paid about $60,000 to an agent named Lucy (Rudolf Roessler) who operated in Switzerland from 1941 to 1943 and again from 1947 to 1953.

In the Soviet Union, professional intelligence specialists are paid only the regular salaries of their military ranks, while communists and fellow travelers receive but nominal compensation, their chief motivation being devotion to the cause.

41

In its summary on the motivation of Soviet agents, the Canadian Royal Commission stated, "Thus it is apparent that despite the relatively cheap method of inducing most new recruits to join the espionage network through non-monetary motivation courses provided by Communist study groups, nevertheless fairly substantial sums of money were in fact paid out by [Colonel] Zabutin [the Soviet military attaché in Canada], particularly to senior agents."

In the United States, there is only one such openly designated sum, the item called Activity 2100 in the U.S. Army's budget. It covers the total expenses of U.S. Army intelligence, including Activity 2131, its sole secret intelligence project. In the 1954-55 fiscal year, the U.S. Army asked for $54,454,000 to cover the expenses of intelligence. During the three fiscal years of 1952, 1953, and 1954, the U.S. Army spent a total of $176,400,000 on intelligence, or less than one half of one percent of the total Army budget.

The Army's budget reveals three additional intelligence items, totaling $88,363,000. This sum includes appropriations for the National Security Agency (not to be confused with the National Security Council), a top-secret intelligence organization about which nothing is spread on the record.

The budget of the Central Intelligence Agency is not known. General C. P. Cabell, Chief of Staff of CIA, wrote in a letter on September 4, 1953, "The budget of CIA is held very tightly; only four or five members in each House are shown the appropriation figures." CIA's appropriations are hidden in allotments to other agencies and the Bureau of the Budget does not report its personnel strength to Congress. "The amount is a classified figure," Senator Mike Mansfield of Montana said, "but published estimates of the annual appropriation run from $500 million to $800 million."

In the armed forces, intelligence officers draw the regular pay of their ranks. Civilian intelligence specialists are paid by Civil Service scales, from $5,000 to $12,000 according to their individual ratings.

The sum total the powers now spend on their secret services may amount to as much as two to three billion dollars a year. However, nothing may be gained by speculating on this score. It is safer to say that intelligence still represents but an infinitesimal part of the budgets. It should be remembered that the best intelligence is not always bought with money and that the amount of money expended does not necessarily reflect the quality of the intelligence effort or the results it may eventually produce.

The Collection of Intelligence

Collection represents the culling of information from overt sources, such as foreign newspapers, books, radio intercepts, and other material of a similar nature. On the other hand, "procurement" as used in intelligence parlance describes an aggressive effort to acquire certain specific information which may not be readily available. To this end a number of means may be used, including secret intelligence and espionage. In the vast majority of cases, however, even the procurement of intelligence is to a large extent a bureaucratic effort, a job that intelligence officers and specialists can do at their desks, without the adventure and melodrama that is popularly associated with the gathering of intelligence information. In fact, it was estimated that approximately ninety percent of all information accumulated within intelligence services comes from overt sources, even though some special knowledge and skill is often needed to produce the information. Today, the proportion of intelligence about Iron Curtain countries which comes from overt sources is, perhaps, half of the total.

Once an intelligence service is organized, it begins collecting the various kinds of information needed by its government: military, political, economic and industrial, scientific, social, and cultural information. The collection of diplomatic information, that pertaining to the conduct of international relations, is to a large extent the function of the State Department, whose own Foreign Service, the organization composed of career diplomats, is supposed to obtain such information through the conventional diplomatic channels.

Collection in an intelligence service is not performed haphazardly. It is the result of a thoroughly considered plan directed at the gathering of information of a specific nature. In this light, collection of specific information is undertaken by specialists who possess thorough knowledge of the subject to which they are assigned. Such knowledge may come from the specialist's educational background, from his familiarity with a foreign country, or from a professional knowledge of a particular subject.

For example, a specialist assigned to the collection of industrial information will logically have had some practical or scientific experience within the industrial field. As a result of this method of assignment to a familiar field, the specialist's

43

personal knowledge assures a familiarity with the subject under study, thereby eliminating the necessity for giving him time-consuming education within that phase of industry under study at the time. A specialist assigned to the gathering of information in any particular field moves with an ease engendered by knowledge of his surroundings.

For example, a person collecting information of a military nature should have a thorough knowledge of his own army and a similar knowledge of the army under scrutiny. Military knowledge is his specialty, and he will not be responsible for the collection of information outside of this immediate field. Any basic knowledge that the specialist already possesses is at the disposal of his own intelligence service, and it is the collection of additional knowledge within this field through largely overt means that is his primary function.

The collector, contrary to the popular conception, is not one who actually infiltrates by surreptitious means into the military or industrial organization about which he seeks information. He is, on the contrary, an official who is attached to a special desk where he scans such primary sources of information as newspapers and magazines, scientific and technical journals, radio transcriptions, books, official government publications, and financial and industrial bulletins issued by private firms. The collector, in scanning these media, looks for any information immediately or potentially relating to his individual specialty. When he finds an item corroborating information previously known to him or to his service, or containing information not previously known, he records it for future reference. Out of these very scattered items develops an enormous backlog of information, which ultimately forms that pattern from which policy is determined at the highest level of government.

Occasionally, items of great immediate importance are discovered, even if only by reading between the lines, which is one of the collector's special skills. Such information is then passed swiftly to the proper authorities on a higher level. Collection is a continuous function in which even the most trivial item, though usually not of such an immediate nature, goes into the weaving of a pattern that ultimately influences the policy of the government. This form of collection is known as research and analysis. It is supplemented by intelligence reports sent in by spies and agents, and by information supplied by other agencies, such as military attachés stationed abroad, consular agents and diplomatic personnel, and other informants. In wartime, collection is aided by censorship intercepts, such as letters and postcards, which are read and

44

copied by the censor, partly to prevent classified information from reaching unauthorized hands, and partly also to collect information.

There is also oral intelligence, in which persons possessing certain desired knowledge are interviewed. Such sources include specialists outside of the intelligence service, visitors to one's own country from abroad, and citizens returning from trips abroad.

An outstanding example of the effectiveness of research and analysis was supplied by a German journalist and military expert whose remarkable intelligence case became celebrated throughout the world. On March 20, 1935, this man, an author named Berthold Jacob, was kidnaped by agents of the German secret service from Switzerland. Jacob had written extensively about the German army that was then in its initial stages of rearmament. He had published a little book which spelled out virtually every detail of the organization of Hitler's new army. This book of 172 pages described the command structure, the personnel of the revived General Staff, the army group commands, the various military districts, even the rifle platoons attached to the most recently formed Panzer divisions. It listed the names of the 168 commanding generals of the army and supplied their biographical sketches.

When Hitler was shown the book, he flew into a rage. He summoned Colonel Walther Nicolai, then his adviser in intelligence matters, and asked, "How was it possible for one man to find out so much about the Wehrmacht?" Nicolai decided to find out the answer to this question from Jacob himself. An agent named Hans Wesemann was assigned to contact Jacob and lure him into a trap. Wesemann set up shop in Basel, in Switzerland near the German border, in the guise of a literary agent. He masqueraded as a refugee and struck up friendships with several exiles from Nazi Germany. Then he got in touch with Jacob in London and invited him to come to Switzerland to discuss a literary deal.

Jacob went to Basel with his wife and was received by Wesemann. They deposited Mrs. Jacob at a hotel, then went to a fashionable restaurant to lunch. At one point during this merry meeting, Jacob had to excuse himself to go to the men's room. His absence permitted Wesemann to slip a sedative into his drink. The unsuspecting writer returned in high mood and lifted his doctored glass for another toast.

Wesemann sat back in his chair and watched Jacob doze under the impact of the Mickey Finn. He then apologized to the waiter for his inebriated companion and asked him to help

45

carry Jacob to a waiting car. A moment later Jacob was on his way to Germany.

Berthold Jacob arrived in Berlin shortly before midnight, acutely aware of his predicament. He was driven straight to Gestapo headquarters in Prinz Albrecht Strasse and taken to a room on the second floor where a commission of officers and civilians awaited him. At their head was Colonel Walther Nicolai.

The moment Jacob was pushed into the room, Nicolai pounced upon him with the question: "Tell us, Herr Jacob! Where did you get the data for your confounded book?"

There followed an explanation that sounded like an exposition of brilliant intelligence work. "Everything in my book came from reports published in the German press, Herr Oberst," Jacob said. "When I stated that Major General Haase was commanding officer of the 17th Division and located in Nuremberg, I received my information from an obituary notice in a Nuremberg newspaper. The item in the paper stated that General Haase, who had just come to Nuremberg in command of the recently transferred 17th Division, had attended a funeral.

"In an Ulm newspaper," Jacob went on, "I found an item on the society page about a happier event, the wedding of a Colonel Vierow's daughter to a Major Stemmermann. Vierow was described in the item as the commanding officer of the 36th Regiment of the 25th Division. Major Stemmermann was identified as the Division's signal officer. Also present at the wedding was Major General Schaller, described in the story as commander of the division who had come, the paper said, from Stuttgart where his division had its headquarters."

This virtually ended the interrogation. Fortunately for Jacob, Nicolai respected good intelligence work. His admiration for the job Jacob had done secured for the writer humane treatment, in addition to which Jacob's wife left no stone unturned to secure her husband's release. The Jacob case became a diplomatic incident. Switzerland demanded that Germany release Jacob at once. The German Foreign Office was embarrassed and made a search for Jacob. He was discovered in the Gestapo jail. Some months later Jacob was returned to Switzerland where he related to me the details of his adventure.

Nicolai reported to Hitler on his findings. "This Jacob had no accomplice, my Fuehrer, except our own military journals and the daily press," he said. "He prepared his remarkable Order of Battle from scraps of information he discovered in obituary notices, wedding announcements, and so forth." He then added in a low voice in which there was suppressed a distant trace of admiration, "This Jacob is the greatest intelligence genius I have ever encountered in my thirty-five years in the service."

The case that at first looked as if it would explode into the greatest espionage scandal ever to rock the German Army was resolved. There was not a spy in it as far as the eye could see. It was a scoop scored by an outstanding civilian whose tools were a pair of scissors, a pot of glue, a file of index cards—and the mind of an intelligence officer.

I first witnessed the process of collection some twenty-odd years ago and, though it was a simple and relatively easy process, it impressed me even then as supremely efficient and effective. At that time, I was employed in the Berlin office of the New York *Times*, under whose auspices was a local agency called "Wide World Pictures," which sold news pictures to German clients. One of these clients was a tall, distinguished-looking, greying man called Herr Goetz. He arrived in our office every morning at 10 A.M. and went through all the pictures pouring in from Wide World's foreign branches and from its headquarters in New York. Hundreds of pictures went on sale every day, pictures of people, places, and events. Herr Goetz would spend a couple of hours every morning examining each fresh crop with great care. Then he would pick a few photographs and buy them "for his personal use," as he put it, at five marks each, their regular commercial price.

After Herr Goetz had come in this way for a number of years, familiarity inevitably developed. He relaxed gradually until we became friends. One day, for reasons known only to him, he revealed to us the true nature of his interest in our pictures. He was a major in *Abwehr*, the intelligence service of the German High Command, and he bought the pictures as a short cut in the collection of information.

"It would require no little effort," he once told me, "and perhaps a pretty penny, to get reliable information about, let's say, structural changes in the ships of the Royal Navy." He picked up a photograph that had just come in from New York and said, "But here is a picture of H.M.S. *Leander*, an excellent picture, don't you think, of that ship all decked out, during a courtesy visit to the Chilean port of Valparaiso. Now, we know a lot about *Leander*. She's the old lady of the new *Ajax* class of light cruisers. She was launched in 1931 in Devonport. We know all about her armor and her speed, her displacement and cruising range. As a matter of fact, we used to think she was pretty lightly armed for her size. I'm

47

going to buy this picture of the *Leander*, take it to my office, and compare it with older pictures we already have on file. I want to see if anything has been changed in her super-structure. We may find that nothing has changed. But then again, there might be some really important changes. It's quite possible that the caliber of her guns has been increased, her turrets moved or altered, or her silhouette modified. If any of this is true, let me ask you, where could you get such infor-mation for five marks?"

He went on, "This was how we found out that cruisers of the *Effingham* class had had the caliber of their main guns reduced, and that the armor on the battleships *Renown* and *Repulse* had been increased." He picked up another picture sent to us from Wide World's Paris office. "Here," Major Goetz said, "is a train wreck near Chateaureaux in France. Who cares? But there is a tunnel in the background and we might want to determine its dimensions." He turned to an-other picture, "How do you like this photograph? The usual stuff, you say? Maybe! Bank Holiday in Brighton. It is an unusually good shot of the whole beach, considering that it's only a news picture taken from a little commercial plane."

A few months after this amazingly candid explanation, Wide World sent me to Danzig on an assignment, and I re-turned with a scoop—pictures of a tiny island fortress called the Westerplatte, maintained by the Poles in the very heart of the Free City. Just at this time the Westerplatte figured prominently in the news. It was a bone of contention, since Danzigers protested vehemently that this Polish dagger was pointing threateningly at them. In Danzig, I requested per-mission from the high commissioner to take pictures in the Westerplatte and when permission was refused I took them anyway. It was a journalistic achievement for which I was given a bonus by Wide World. The pictures appeared in virtually every major paper in the world. Herr Goetz showed his personal appreciation by buying copies of every one of them.

Five years later in New York, on September 1, 1939, I stayed up the entire night to listen to the fantastic bulletins announcing the outbreak of the Second World War. Sud-denly I felt a chill when I heard the first official communiqué of the Wehrmacht, revealing that the war had begun with the old battleship *Schleswig-Holstein* bombarding the Wester-platte.

Photographs taken by professional cameramen, journalists, amateurs, or tourists are today eagerly sought by all intelli-gence organizations. They make the collection of information a simple and rewarding job. In intelligence parlance, these pictures are "Aunt Minnies," after the familiar relative who usually appears in such snapshots, with head half obscured and limbs magnified by bad focusing. But behind "Aunt Minnie" there may be a winding road, the particular bends of which are of interest to the topographer. Or high up above "Aunty's" head, on a protruding cliff, there may be a quaint little whitewashed church with a distinctive steeple, invaluable as a marker for target intelligence.

In intelligence work, snapshots and picture postcards are collector's items. Some of them, in demand when the lives of troops may depend on the intelligence they supply, may be worth more than a Rembrandt. Seven such pictures formed an important portion of the advance information the 1st Marine Division had when it went into Guadalcanal in August, 1942. They came from someone who had visited the Solomons in times of peace and then had given the prints to a friend in Washington when OSS's predecessor, the so-called Coordinator of Information, requested that citizens send in snapshots taken abroad. The collection of such "photographic ground intelligence," for example, is one of the few really centralized efforts in Britain's widely scattered intelligence network. It is localized in the Admiralty, which is the custodian of the photographic library of the entire British intelligence system.

Snapshots, news pictures, and picture postcards are but one group of the overt sources that supply the clues intelligence needs. Since the acquisition of information is the primary function of intelligence, it is also the most voluminous phase of the entire activity.

Among the most important basic intelligence sources, as said before, are foreign newspapers and periodicals, particularly specialty and trade journals, intercepts of radio broadcasts beamed to home audiences abroad, books of all kinds, especially yearbooks and reference books, and virtually any printed matter available on the counters of bookshops. Most valuable, however, are informants, or contacts, those individuals who supply information either voluntarily or involuntarily, sometimes even under duress. In the first category are patriotic citizens who might have obtained certain valuable information in the course of their routine activities, travelers returning from trips abroad with observations of immediate value to intelligence, and, especially in these days, refugees from countries behind the Iron Curtain.

Publicly available printed matter—from single issues of newspapers to encyclopedias—represents the chief source from

49

which information is usually culled. Some of the most rewarding missions have taken intelligence officers not into the vaults
of general staffs but into the reading rooms of public libraries.
In this respect, Soviet intelligence is in a much more advantageous position than any intelligence service in the West, if
only because so much of the sort of thing that is labeled top
secret in the U.S.S.R. is published freely in the United States,
Great Britain, and France. The Western press, in particular, is
an inexhaustible mine of information that continually feeds a
wealth of information to the alert intelligence specialist who
knows how to read between the lines. Recently one five-line
item printed by the Associated Press was actually revealed as
the sole source of a Soviet intelligence report when the dispatch of a Soviet agent was intercepted by the Sûreté in Paris.
This particular item reported the crash of two Lancaster
bombers of the RAF during maneuvers in the Mediterranean
near Malta, adding only that the seven members of one Lancaster's crew had been rescued. These five lines supplied welcome information to the agent. They told him that the Royal
Navy was holding exercises around Malta, and that it was
operating with land-based planes. Additional data was concealed between the lines, intelligible only to the trained
intelligence specialist.

Scientific and trade journals of the West supply specific
information, as do encyclopedias and handy reference books
like the *World Almanac* in the United States, *Whitaker's
Almanack* and *The Statesman's Year-Book* in the United
Kingdom, and the *Petit Larousse* in France. On pages 724 to
734 of the 1954 edition of the *World Almanac*, for example,
Soviet intelligence specialists can find, openly printed, vital
information about the armed forces of the United States.

Among other data, the *World Almanac* also prints the exact
number of nurses in the U.S. Air Force. This type of information was actually sought by the German intelligence service
in the United States in 1938-39 and was one of the assignments of German spies in this country. In addition, the *World
Almanac* describes in great detail the education and training
of American officers, the operation of the selective service
system in the United States, the pay scale of the Army, Navy,
Air Force, and the women's branches of the armed forces.
Although such information may not appear to be exceptionally valuable or conclusive by itself, it is useful to the intelligence specialist because it supplies the clues from which
major deductions may be made. As an intelligence manual of
the U.S. Army put it, "from the character, the measures, the
situation of an adversary, and the relations with which he is

50

surrounded, each side will draw conclusions by the law of probability as to designs of the other, and act accordingly."

Congressional hearings on American weapons developments, especially the use of the B-36 bomber as a strategic weapon, revealed to the Soviet Union virtually the entire American military doctrine. The hearings that followed General Douglas MacArthur's dismissal provided invaluable tactical clues, for both the North Koreans and Red Chinese, to the way the United Nations planned to prosecute the war in Korea.

In a similar manner, the debates in the House of Commons and in the French National Assembly furnish invaluable data to the Soviet intelligence service, for it has only to procure the records of those debates to obtain hard intelligence concerning those nations. Especially important information emerges from the so-called "question periods" in the House of Commons, during which members ask pointed questions about the state of Britain and members of Her Majesty's Government are required to answer just as unguardedly.

No such information ever emerges from behind the Iron Curtain, where even the legitimate functions of foreign press correspondents are regarded as espionage. Production figures of industries, even though they may not have any military significance, are labeled as state secrets, as are virtually all data concerning the state affairs of those nations.

By contrast with Western practice, the Soviet press prints little of direct intelligence value and great care is taken in general to withhold information from other overt sources as well. When I was in Moscow in 1937, I visited a foreign bookstore on Kuznetsky Most and tried to buy some thirty books printed in the English language, apparently intended for foreign readers. My selection completed, the clerk asked me whether I planned to take the books abroad. When I told him I did, he consulted a catalog and announced that only two of the books were approved for export—a slim volume about Stalin as a military genius, written by Marshal Voroshilov, and a report on a Russo-Japanese clash on the Amur River. The Soviet Union bans on principle the exportation of any book which may even remotely or inferentially contain intelligence data. It goes so far as to prohibit the exportation of the official journal of librarians on the theory that the reviews printed in it, or a mere listing of the books published in the U.S.S.R., might supply unintended information. Most of the Russian periodicals, and even some newspapers, are in this proscribed category, the ban representing an intense effort to withhold this important source of information from foreign intelligence specialists.

The Soviet effort to control these sources of possible information is unprecedented. It was unheard of in other totalitarian countries, even during the war. As a matter of fact, during World War II, a considerable part of our intelligence came directly from German, Italian, and Japanese periodicals. Recognizing the value of this source, the Allied intelligence services set up joint purchasing agencies in Europe and Asia which either bought the enemy's papers the moment they hit the newsstands or subscribed to his periodicals through neutral channels. They were then sent by plane to London, Washington, and New York. We thus received not only the daily papers of the enemy but also his scientific journals with gratifying promptness and regularity. At my desk in Washington, I was able to read Hitler's own *Völkischer Beobachter* within two days of its publication in Germany, and I culled an astonishing amount of hard intelligence from it, items no country can effectively conceal as long as newspapers are published on the open market.

Today, despite iron-clad censorship, ingenious intelligence specialists still can find valuable items in the strictly controlled Communist press. There is little the Communists can do about it. Since the press is an important instrument of their propaganda, they must continue to publish all kinds of printed matter. Often nothing is to be gained from an evaluation of items collected in this way, but the fact remains that even the thickest wall has its fissures.

One need not be a trained cryptanalyst in the breaking of codes and ciphers to obtain information from thin air. You need only tune in on the home beam of, let us say, Radio Moscow or Radio Prague to get a lot of valuable information. The exceptional value of such broadcasts was recognized by Britain shortly before the Second World War, and a special branch was established within the B.B.C. to monitor all foreign radio broadcasts directed at home audiences. Shortly afterwards, a similar agency was established in the United States, under the aegis of the Federal Communications Commission. Later called Foreign Broadcast Monitoring (Intelligence) Service, the special agency was transferred to the CIA where it now forms an important organ of collection. A daily digest of all such intercepts is printed, and the information is made available to a wide circle of officials. My own experience showed this to be an invaluable source of information.

Forming a third group of collection sources are the so-called informants. They may be "confidential informants," who supply information deliberately and voluntarily, out of sympathy with one's own cause, or they may be "incidental informants," who drop information carelessly and unwittingly. It is a primary task of good intelligence to seek out potential informants in both categories, then develop or cultivate them and keep them on tap. A seemingly innocent luncheon with an unsuspecting informant may yield more valuable information than an intelligence operation employing espionage agents.

If the battle of Verdun in 1916 ended in victory for the French, it was at least partly due to the indiscretion of an unwitting informant whose boastful remarks about the coming offensive were picked up by the various antennae of Allied intelligence. In January, 1916, an American merchant was traveling unhindered in Europe, since the United States was then still neutral. He visited Warsaw and accepted an invitation to a dinner during which a high-ranking German staff officer happened to be seated beside him at the table.

The German was interested in having an American as his dinner companion and proceeded to abuse the United States for her support of Britain and France. "But it won't do any good," he said, "because, you see, the war will be over very soon." He then proceeded to tell the American that there would be a decisive and all-out German offensive in the direction of Verdun that would certainly end the war. He went so far as to mention D-day of the offensive—February 20, 1916.

The American returned via London and while there related the Warsaw conversation to someone in the American Embassy. He was advised to report it to Admiral Sir Reginald Hall, director of the Division of Naval Intelligence, and regarded by Americans in London as the most outstanding intelligence officer in that field. The American went to the Admiralty but found that Hall was at home with a cold. He repeated the conversation to Hall's assistant, a young South African named Hoy, who, in turn, rushed to Hall with the information.

Hall invited Captain de Saint Seine, the French naval attaché, to his house and relayed to him the American's report. The captain left at once for France and, on the morning of January 11, reported to Marshal Joffre personally. As in the case of most unsolicited information collected from an unevaluated source, there were some doubts. Why should a high-ranking German staff officer, it was naturally asked, reveal such a secret to a stranger? However, there was intelligence already on hand that seemed to corroborate the American's story. French scouts had found that the Germans were building roads in the woods around Gremilly and Étain and in the scenic Bois de Caures. Then the sudden arrival of five German divisions from the Serbian front was reported by other informants.

Finally convinced of the authenticity of the American's information, Marshal Joffre issued orders to begin immediate preparations to meet the German onslaught. Hall and Hoy spent February 20 in their office, awaiting word from France that would confirm the American's story. The day passed, but all remained quiet on the Western Front. Hall grew restive and, since he did not cherish the prospect of appearing a gullible fool in French eyes, he went home deeply disturbed, even considering the possibility that the American had been a "plant" to mislead the French. Then at 6:30 next morning, Hoy called on the telephone. "A message from France, sir," he said. "At 0415, sir, the Germans opened up in front of Verdun, all the way from Brabant to Gussainville, with the greatest artillery barrage of the war." The battle of Verdun was on, exactly as reported by the American informant.

The recognition of the value of informants persuaded the intelligence services to deal with them systematically. Britain in particular has made the patriotic informant the backbone of her intelligence set-up. She maintains a relatively small nucleus of professional intelligence officers, and only a few specialists who may be called espionage agents, but depends on informants to supply the bulk of the information she needs. This works well in practice. "Britain's intelligence set-up," wrote E. H. Cookridge, "has never been seriously jeopardized. This is the best testimonial possible to her system of relying on the part-time agent to a great extent. A schoolmaster on a holiday, a businessman seeking markets, or a retired civil servant living abroad because of its attractions to a man dependent on a modest pension can all do useful work."

The other primary form of acquiring information, procurement, includes the gathering of data by both overt and covert means. To distinguish between the collection and the procurement of information, we may think of the latter as involving the gathering of data by going after it, in other words by contriving to acquire it rather than by culling it from various sources at the collector's desk. This may involve interviewing any person who can contribute specific information, during which interrogation he knows the purpose of the collector's visit and willingly supplies the information. It may also entail traveling to and within a certain area for the purpose of witnessing or studying it at first hand, or observing a subject open to survey without recourse to surreptitious methods.

Here the primary motive of the inspection may be concealed, but the object under scrutiny is open to observation by any and all. In this form of procurement, information of great importance is available to a specialist without his having to resort to clandestine means. In this category fall such events as the opening to public inspection of naval vessels, air derbies, military displays, and industrial expositions.

When Sir George Aston, one of Britain's great intelligence experts, was a young officer in Naval Intelligence, he regarded it as his duty to procure information through personal observation on every subject on which data could not be obtained by the simpler methods of collection. He frequently left his desk in the Admiralty and undertook special trips abroad, concealing neither his real name nor his rank, withholding only the fact that he was an intelligence officer on a procurement mission. When new fortifications were built in the French port of Dunkirk, it became imperative that his office observe the new lay-out, and also ascertain whether the fortifications had already been garrisoned. Since such information could not be obtained through routine overt sources, Aston decided to procure it personally.

In Dunkirk, posing as a British officer on a vacation trip, he climbed a lighthouse to get an "aerial" view of the fortress lay-out. Then he roamed around in the port, trying to see for himself where the troops, if any, were. Upon his return to his hotel in the town, Aston found a stranger waiting for him. "Monsieur," the man accosted him, "I know that you are a British spy. I also know the purpose of your visit." The man concluded with a Gallic flourish, "I am in a position to sell you the information you seek for a paltry 10,000 francs."

Aston answered with equal flourish, "Monsieur, first of all, I am not a British spy. Secondly, I am here on a vacation and I am not trying to find out anything. And, thirdly, monsieur, I already know what I came here to discover."

Aston had made his discovery by those simple methods of deduction that helped both Sherlock Holmes and the British secret service to some of their greatest triumphs. He knew that the soldiers of France had general-issue boots whose hobnails were arranged in a certain pattern. The ground around the new forts was muddy and revealed the prints of thousands of boot-nailed soles. Aston regarded this as sufficient evidence that the forts had already been garrisoned.

Personal observation does not always yield completely satisfactory results, as Aston was to learn occasionally on his inspection trips. From an announcement in a French newspaper he learned that there was to be an exhibition of new French weapons in Paris. Aston hurried to Paris to visit the exhibition. He inspected at leisure the various models on display, but whenever he attempted to sketch one or another a policeman would approach him and caution him to abandon his art.

As if permitting him special favor, the policeman then took him to a huge gun in the center of the exhibition and allowed him to make a sketch of it. Upon his return to England, Aston discovered that the gun had been a dummy, built of cardboard especially for the benefit of visiting intelligence officers.

Some time before the United States entered the Second World War, special agencies were created for the cultivation and exploitation of informants. One of them, called Oral Intelligence Group, was set up in New York to interview anyone with information that might be of use at one time or another. Members of the group buttonholed experts and returning travelers and plied them with questions with the utmost skill.

One of the specialists in Oral Intelligence was a middle-aged matron named Emmy Rado, a far cry, indeed, from the *femme fatale* of spy fiction. Swiss by birth and married to a prominent psychoanalyst, she qualified ideally for the job because she could speak German, French, Italian, Danish, and English, and knew how to coax information from people. Mrs. Rado studied the passenger lists of incoming ships, picked names and addresses from them, and wrote letters inviting strangers to call on her at her office. She was particularly interested in refugees.

One day such a refugee came to see her. He was a somewhat erratic and excitable man who knew only a few English words, but he repeated again and again, "Must see Roosevelt." When Mrs. Rado talked to him in French, he revealed that he was really a man with a mission. He had come to the United States as a special emissary of an anti-Fascist group in North Africa, bearing a message for President Roosevelt.

"Where are you from, monsieur?" Mrs. Rado asked.

"From Bône," the man said.

"What's your profession?"

"I'm a hydraulic engineer." It so happened that Mrs. Rado was at that moment intensely interested in Bône. A few weeks earlier, a directive from Washington had requested that Oral Intelligence collect information about Bône from its North

African informants. America was preparing for the landings in North Africa but had woefully little information about the port of Bône. And here was an informant who had helped to build the port and who knew many of the technical details of the installations.

Mrs. Rado persuaded the man to sit at a drafting board and reproduce maps and blueprints from memory. The man worked for three days, and, when he was finished, the harbor's defenses were down on paper. Mrs. Rado promptly dispatched them to the War Department, where the operations plans were being drafted.

When in November, 1942, British troops under Anderson took Bône, the stranger returned to Mrs. Rado in triumph. He was convinced that his information had reached President Roosevelt after all. He had a letter of thanks, beginning with "Greeting" and bearing the President's own signature, inviting him to join the armed forces of the United States.

When engaged in procurement, the intelligence specialist must sometimes leave his desk and go out into the field to secure information by personal observation. The classic example of this method was supplied by a German general named Zeitzler during World War II, not long before he was appointed chief of the Army General Staff. In the early winter of 1941, General Zeitzler donned civilian clothes and went personally to Greece to reconnoiter the terrain across which his tanks were soon to roll.

Today, such inspection trips are undertaken regularly by service attachés, and it might be remarked that they rarely visit out-of-the-way inns just because the food is reputed to be good. In fact, a service attaché or professional intelligence officer never makes a trip with his eyes closed or for his own private pleasure. Even his furloughs serve definite purposes. He usually spends his vacation in places that have some significance in his work.

One might naturally think that collection and procurement would be more easily performed during periods of peace than in times of war, but the exact opposite is true. Wars cannot be conducted behind closed doors. Ordinarily the real secrets of a country are not easily accessible, but during wartime the exigencies of the conflict make their exposure inevitable.

At the outset of the Pacific war, we had virtually no information on the Japanese navy beyond what was publicly available, and only inadequate or faulty hydrographic charts of many strategic Pacific islands. Either these islands had been altogether uncharted and unsurveyed, or there was only a narrowly restricted knowledge of their characteristics. An effort was made between the two world wars to get an American colonel onto one of the closed Japanese islands. Although his mission was not completely camouflaged and he traveled as a bona fide tourist, his trip ended in tragedy. His ashes were returned by bowing Japanese to the American authorities in Tokyo, with the explanation that the colonel had died during his voyage and his body had been cremated with all the solemn pomp of the Shinto ritual. A post-mortem was impossible.

The important work left undone in peace became pressing when war broke out. Guadalcanal, in particular, was a symbol of the careless indifference of peace and the urgent curiosity characteristic of war. It became the symbol of the ease with which intelligence can be conducted under wartime conditions when no holds are barred and nothing can be kept under wraps.

This famous island at the southern tip of the Solomon archipelago looked on the map like a bacillus under a microscope. The Guadalcanal operation was code-named Pestilence. It was to be the first offensive move of the American forces after more than eight months of humiliating retreat. Pestilence was scheduled for August 1, 1942, and the military planners at Pearl Harbor who had to draft the assault looked up Guadalcanal in the various intelligence files—and found precious little. They discovered only two good books about the Solomons; one in English had been published in 1893, the other in German had come out in 1903. They were not much help.

The American planners were fairly confident that British Intelligence would be able to supply some information, the Solomons having been in British hands since 1893. They had had plenty of time to survey the islands and chart the waters around them. But the charts were even older than the books. There was one based on Captain Edward Manning's journey in 1792. Even the newest was more than a hundred years old.

When the Japanese occupied Guadalcanal in May, 1942, they had excellent charts, so the idea occurred to Colonel Frank B. Goettge, G-2 (intelligence officer) of the 1st Marine Division, to get theirs instead of making our own. On July 1, Colonel Goettge flew to Australia and established contact with the intelligence authorities there. It soon developed that the situation was not as bleak as it seemed at Pearl Harbor. Although nothing had been done during the years of peace, considerable effort had been made to establish an intelligence network in the Solomons after the outbreak of hostilities in Europe in 1939. German raiders and blockade-runners were expected in the general area and a system of coast watchers had been established to report on them. The Australian Navy had a young lieutenant stationed on Tulagi and Guadalcanal, and there were four trained coast watchers or "Ferdinands," as they were called after the peace-loving bull.

Goettge sent two of his officers to "Ferdinand" headquarters and found that the officer, Macfarlan, and coast watchers had everything he needed. By then, in fact, Macfarlan had his own houseboy working in the Japanese camp and bringing back reports every week-end. "Ferdinand" had a string of agents all over the island, funneling information back from the jungle. While the Australians thus supplied information from under the enemy's nose, Goettge in Australia was interrogating refugees from Guadalcanal, missionaries, planters, and workers. What had been so woefully neglected during the carefree years of peace was nearly compensated for within a fortnight. Plans for Pestilence could be drawn up with knowledge of the enemy's disposition and strength on Guadalcanal, and the Marines could be supported with good intelligence when they stormed ashore.

If ever proof were needed that faulty intelligence or lack of intelligence results in confusion, delays, and high casualties, the invasion of Tarawa, in November, 1943, supplied this proof. In taking Tarawa, the Marines suffered the loss of about 1,000 men in dead and 2,000 in wounded. About twenty percent of all casualties were suffered during the first hours of the landing, as a direct result of a complete breakdown of intelligence. "The natural defenses of Betio were almost as formidable, and as little known, as those installed by the enemy," wrote Gilbert Cant in *The Great Pacific Victory.* "The atoll of Tarawa had not been the subject of an oceanographic survey since the visit of Lieutenant (later Commodore) John Wilkes, U.S.N., in 1841. His charts were still in use, 102 years later. In the meantime, the coral polyp had been busy, making Wilkes's charts inaccurate."

Since the landing craft could not traverse the reefs, whose existence had been unknown to our intelligence, the men had to wade ashore or be ferried to battle in little "alligators," cruelly exposed to enemy fire. American authorities were shocked. After Tarawa, collection of intelligence was vastly improved and new charts were made. In "Terrible Tarawa," three thousand American casualties served to point up the importance of intelligence.

Sources of Information

Indiscreet war which cannot keep its secrets supplies three categories of sources from which invaluable information can be obtained. In the first category are the prisoners captured in combat. In the second are the documents taken from the bodies of the dead after battle, from the raided headquarters of the enemy, and from his sunken ships. The third major source of information is reconnaissance. There is a fourth source, the constant monitoring of the enemy's radio traffic, but with that we will deal later when we discuss cryptography.

The use of prisoners of war as sources of information is as old as warfare itself. The first detailed account of a campaign in which prisoners were so used comes down to us from the thirteenth century before Christ, from the campaign of Pharaoh Rameses II against King Hattushilish III of the Hittites. In that campaign, prisoners were used in two ways. The Egyptians used them to obtain information about the Hittite forces. The Hittites used them in an elaborate ruse to plant misleading information with the Egyptians.

In 1271 B.C., the army of Rameses marched 400 miles in about a month and reached the upper Orontes, but with no sign of the enemy. Finally, two Hittite soldiers showed up in the Egyptian camp. They volunteered information that the army of Hattushilish was still some distance away and that it was full of mutinous soldiers who appeared anxious to desert to the enemy. Rameses thought that this intelligence sounded too good to be true, but he ordered patrols to reconnoiter the area and bring back prisoners to corroborate the desertion story. The patrol returned with two bona fide prisoners whose interrogation produced evidence quite different from the story of the alleged deserters. These prisoners reported that the Hittites were waiting with their infantry and chariots in the immediate vicinity of the Egyptian camp, that they were "more numerous than the sands of the sea," and that there was no dissatisfaction among the soldiers of Hattushilish. Rameses drew up his battle plan entirely on the information which he received from the new prisoners, in the exact manner in which such information was used thirty centuries later in World War II and in the Korean War.

Information that is obtained from prisoners of war ranges

60

all the way from the lowest tactical to the highest strategic level. A prisoner brought in by a patrol may disclose nothing more important than the identity of his regiment, but he may also be the source of information that ultimately influences the course of the war, or history.

By sheer numbers, prisoners represent a vast reservoir of information in modern war. During World War I, there was a total of 7,750,919 missing or prisoners of war captured by both sides, which meant that about twelve percent of the mobilized forces ended up in prison camps. The number of prisoners during the first two years of World War II totaled more than four million men; by the end of the war their number exceeded the fantastic total of fifteen million officers and men. In the Korean War, the enemy captured nearly 10,000 United Nations combatants, of whom almost 8,000 were Americans. Not only was information of inestimable value obtained from these prisoners, but they were also used in propaganda campaigns whose repercussions still plague us long after the war.

Prisoners of war supply an amazing amount of information involuntarily and not because they entertain any traitorous sentiments or thoughts. Capture and captivity undermine the soldier's power of moral resistance and create a psychological vacuum in which a man is hardly accountable for what he says or does. This state of mind is recognized by belligerents, and they maintain elaborate organizations to exploit it through various methods of ingenious interrogation. Under international law, a prisoner is not required to submit to questioning. He is obliged only to disclose his name, rank, and serial number, and nothing beyond that. The 1927 Geneva Convention specifically prohibits any organized interrogation of prisoners of war, but this provision of the law is violated right and left even by the ethical signatories of the convention.

The moment a man is captured, he is usually subjected at once to what is called "shock interrogation," when his power of resistance is at its lowest ebb. This is designed to establish whether the man knows anything at all. If he does, he is sent to a special interrogation cage where whole teams of interrogators go to work on him to obtain as much information as possible. If a man seems to have special knowledge, he is sent on to interrogation centers specifically organized for the purpose, and he is kept there until no information is left in him. Only then is he assigned to a camp where he will sit out the war.

During the Second World War prisoner interrogation was

developed by both sides to the point where it became an exact science. A number of gadgets were constructed to aid the interrogators. Stool-pigeons and decoys were used to get information from prisoners which they would not give in direct examination. Special interrogators underwent intense training, and teams were organized in which every interrogator was an expert on certain subjects.

The ordinary soldier usually cannot provide very valuable information. He is not privy to the secrets of the war, and he rarely has knowledge of more than the most routine functions of his own outfit. However, the interrogation of generals sometimes yields information of inestimable value about the plans and dispositions of the enemy. Field Marshall Sir Bernard (later Lord) Montgomery penetrated the most closely guarded secrets of his chief adversary, Marshal Erwin Rommel, when one of Rommel's top commanders, General Ritter von Thoma, fell into his hands. Thoma was not subjected to the usual interrogation. Instead, he was invited to Montgomery's for a series of friendly conversations which eventually provided all that the field marshal wanted to learn. In a somewhat more direct manner, the Russians learned virtually every secret of Hitler's Russian campaign from the generals of the VI Army captured at Stalingrad. In Britain, German generals were kept in a special camp where they not only submitted willingly to interrogation on a very high level but participated in exercises involving sandboxes and miniature military models, in the course of which they revealed intimate details of the Wehrmacht's tactics.

In the winter of 1942-43, during the battle of the Atlantic, Hitler's ferocious U-boat war against Anglo-American shipping was going badly for the Allies. On January 15, we suffered a most grievous defeat. Seven vessels of a convoy of nine tankers were sunk by wolf packs of U-boats, with the forfeit of millions of barrels of high octane gasoline that was needed urgently by the air forces in North Africa.

There were indications that the situation would grow worse. Allied agents reported that the Germans were experimenting with an acoustic torpedo that would be guided to the target simply by homing on the sound of the propellers. The Allies were groping in the dark. There is, of course, an eventual defense for all offensive weapons, but no such defense can be devised before the details of the enemy's new weapon are known. All efforts to obtain details of the mysterious new torpedo had ended in failure. There was uneasiness in the Allied naval high command as the admirals waited nervously for the first report establishing German perfecting of the deadly weapon.

Then, in February, 1943, a U-boat was sunk by an American destroyer somewhere in the Atlantic, and survivors were brought to an interrogation center near Washington. The prisoners had already been exposed to shock interrogation, and it was known that the group included a petty officer who had recently served at the German Navy's torpedo station in Kiel where the acoustic torpedo was being perfected. Immediately upon his arrival in the Washington cage, the man was taken in hand by a torpedo specialist of the ONI interrogation team, and before long this young reserve officer, whom war had made into a torpedo expert, was satisfied that the German petty officer knew all the secrets he was after.

A period of hide-and-seek ensued. The officer did not want to expose his own special interest in the new torpedo, and the German was reluctant to volunteer any information. But he was obviously impressed with the apparent knowledge his interrogator had of Germany's torpedo developments; and by using shrewd psychological methods to soften up his quarry, the officer soon had the man exactly in the state he wanted him. He taunted him by deprecating German torpedoes. This was too much for the proud German. To show how advanced his navy was in this field, he not only volunteered information on German torpedoes in general, but fell to boasting about the new secret weapon, the acoustic torpedo itself.

By then, a kind of intimacy had developed between the interrogator and the man. The officer pretended to be incredulous and scoffed at the man's story of a new torpedo. The German flew into a rage, finally offering to draw a blueprint of it. He was given the necessary equipment and within a few hours drew from memory an exact blueprint of the dreaded new weapon. The blueprint was rushed to Ordnance, and pilot torpedoes were constructed to its specifications. They worked. From then on it was simple to devise the defenses. When later the Germans fired their first acoustic torpedo, the Allied ships were well equipped to counteract them. The weapon the Germans thought would decide the battle of the Atlantic in their favor proved almost completely ineffectual.

This was a piece of intelligence that apparently no spy could obtain in the field and no amount of secret intelligence could turn up. If someone had come to an Allied agency in a neutral country with the design of the torpedo, he would have earned a fabulous sum for the secret. Yet it was obtained in exact blueprint form without the aid of a single spy. It was obtained by a young American sitting at a desk somewhere in Washington with another man whom the fortunes of war had made his prisoner. No unfair pressure had been applied. The Geneva Convention had not been violated. The German had actually volunteered the information.

I tried to do the impossible and compute the cost of this operation. Counting everything, including the expenses of the man's rescue from the sea, I came to a sum that was far below $1,000. Yet this piece of intelligence probably saved ships worth hundreds of millions of dollars.

Another major source supplies the hardest intelligence of all. This is the mass of documents that the gust of war inevitably scatters in all directions. Every high command is well aware of the dangers that the possession of its classified documents represents in unauthorized hands. Strict instructions are issued which prohibit the carrying of highly classified documents into a combat zone, prohibit the writing of diaries, and forbid the maintenance of files where they might fall into enemy hands. But human nature and the exigencies of war somehow combine to foil these excellent regulations. Certain documents obviously have to be carried into advanced areas, and some paper work is inevitable even at the front. No amount of warning will keep men from writing secret diaries. The Japanese, in particular, were avid diarists, and thousands of diaries fell into our hands during World War II, including some kept by top-ranking generals. Occasionally, however, the shoe is on the other foot. A few years ago, the diary of an American general fell into the hands of Soviet intelligence, causing grave embarrassment on this side of the fence and audible rejoicing on the other.

The Second World War was remarkable for the wholesale capture of vital documents. In 1940, the Germans captured the entire secret archives of the French general staff. Among the documents were protocols of conferences and arrangements the French had made with Britain's Imperial General Staff. France was then already knocked out of the war, so those documents concerned with French plans and dispositions were only of academic or historic interest. But Britain was still fighting, and the capture of the French archives caused inestimable damage to the British war effort.

Wherever Americans fought the Japanese on land, highly classified enemy documents came to the Allies by the ream. The Japanese gave far too wide distribution to very highly classified documents and even sent such precious papers regularly to commanders in the field. They probably acted on the vainglorious theory that we would never get near them. Furthermore, the Japanese had been indoctrinated in only the most superficial methods of destroying vital documents in emergencies. The result was that early in the Pacific war, when only low-level Japanese command posts were in the path of our advances, we succeeded in capturing documents of amazingly high-level strategic significance.

In August, 1942, we were testing Japan's newly formed outer defense perimeter with a probing invasion of Guadalcanal. While the main operation centered on the Solomons, two U.S. submarines, the *Argonaut* and the *Nautilus*, ferried combat teams of Colonel Evans F. Carlson's 2nd Marine Raider Battalion from Pearl Harbor to the island of Makin. The purpose of this operation was to harass the handful of Japanese on that outpost, to divert attention from Guadalcanal, and to give the troops some combat experience.

Alerted by intelligence reports compiled from loose talk overheard in the United States, the Japanese prepared defense positions against the anticipated "invasion." But when Carlson's Raiders landed, the enemy abandoned those prepared positions in unexpected haste and scattered inland. Some fighting developed, but such was the efficiency of the Marines that within forty-eight hours no living Japanese was left on the island. Going through the motions of a mop-up, the Marines blew up a radio station, burned substantial quantities of aviation gasoline, collected rations of canned meat and crackers—and paid a visit to the commandant's house. In Fletcher Pratt's lively description of the Makin raid, this phase rated exactly ten words. In actual fact, however, this incidental call on the absent commandant's house made the Makin raid one of the most rewarding enterprises of the whole war.

The Marines found the commandant's house deserted, although some warm dishes on a stove indicated that it had been only recently abandoned. The commandant himself had already joined his ancestors. But piled high in his office were stacks of highly classified documents, including operations plans, battle-order data, intelligence reports, combat narratives, virtually everything one would expect to find, not in the command post of such a remote outpost, but in a top-echelon headquarters.

Baskets of the papers were carried to the waiting submarines and, when they reached Washington, they revealed many closely guarded and otherwise inaccessible secrets of the Japanese high command. After that, documents in increasing number and importance fell into our hands wherever we went. By the time Saipan was reached, there was scarcely a Japanese document that did not have at least one copy in some file in Washington.

Like no other war in history, the Second World War opened up the files of the vanquished. At first, Germany was the beneficiary of such revelations, but, when the tide turned, she was on the losing side in this respect as well. When the end came, the complete files of the German General Staff, Foreign Ministry, and every other government department were captured by the Allies, including such invaluable historical documents as the original of the famous Schlieffen Plan itself, the blueprint drawn up before World War I for the military defeat of France. It was in this connection that an eminent German historian said after the war, "We not only lost the war, but we also lost all the secrets of our history and lost our national memory."

I recall how hard we used to work to establish the order of battle of the German Navy from telltale evidence that came to us through overt sources and prisoner interrogation and particularly through secret access to entries in the logs of individual U-boats. Then, in 1944, a U-boat surrendered, and everything that we had tried to piece together by painful and painstaking effort fell into our hands in a single day. The commander of the U-boat put into an Allied port that day with all the equipment that it normally carried absolutely intact. After that, it was no longer necessary to grope in the dark for information about the U-boat command. Everything that was needed floated in with the surrendering vessel, including code books and the German Navy's order of battle.

If ever a single document influenced history, it was a seemingly routine order signed by General Gerd von Rundstedt during the Battle of France in 1940 that fell into the hands of the helpless British and enabled England to evacuate her forces from Dunkirk on the eve of the French collapse. The story of this remarkable intelligence scoop may be told here for the first time.

Toward the end of May, 1940, the destruction of the Allied armies in Europe seemed merely a matter of days. The Belgian, French, and British armies were being pushed relentlessly to the English Channel. In the theater of operations there remained only the port of Dunkirk as a means of escape. The fate of the British Expeditionary Force appeared to lie, as Chester Wilmot expressed it, "in the hollow of Hitler's hand."

Evacuation seemed a possibility, but Prime Minister Churchill was advised that, at the most, only about thirty thousand men might be saved—less than one tenth of the forces involved. Churchill feared that it would soon be his "hard lot to announce the greatest military disaster in our long history." Confronted with what seemed imminent doom, and specifically and more immediately with the Panzer divisions of General Gerd von Rundstedt's Army Group B, the B.E.F. stood almost still, awaiting the *coup de grâce*. Rundstedt's tanks were barely fifteen miles away.

On the evening of May 24, Hitler suddenly intervened in the operation. He decided to change the center of gravity by pressing the advance on Paris, and to leave the British to their fate. He gave orders to halt Rundstedt's Panzers, a senseless and inexplicable order that no British commander or intelligence officer could have hoped for. Yet the order was issued, and, at dawn of May 25, it was carried to the Panzer commanders between Bethune and St. Omer by Colonel von Tresckow, one of Rundstedt's staff officers.

Colonel von Tresckow's command car skirted perilously close to the shattered British lines, and the unexpected happened. It was ambushed and fired on by a stray British patrol. The driver was killed and the car set on fire. Colonel von Tresckow jumped out of the car and escaped on foot, leaving his briefcase in the burning car. And in the briefcase was the momentous order that was to halt the advance of Rundstedt's Panzers.

The British patrol sneaked up to the car and snatched the briefcase from the flames. It was intact. A few hours later, its contents were examined by British intelligence officers. They were reluctant to believe what they saw. But the captured document was rushed to General Alexander and then to General Lord Gort, commander in chief of the B.E.F. Incredible as it must have seemed the British had but one alternative in their desperate situation—to accept it as a miraculous reprieve. Gort issued orders to strengthen his southern flank. Then he speeded up the march of the troops on Dunkirk.

Hitler's generals remonstrated with him, and with Rundstedt who had concurred wholeheartedly in the Fuehrer's order. But the order was not changed, and the British gained time to strengthen their defenses. The reembarkation proceeded virtually unmolested by German tanks. During those days, General Franz Halder, chief of staff of the German Army, wrote in his diary, "Bad weather has grounded the Luftwaffe and now we must stand by and watch countless thousands of the enemy getting away to England right under our noses."

By June 4, 338,000 Allied troops had been rescued from

the beaches—the nucleus around which, in Churchill's words, "Britain could build her armies of the future."

This was security at its worst where the Germans were concerned; but intelligence at its best on the British side. Colonel von Tresckow's conduct is difficult to explain, impossible to justify. He was not supposed to carry a document of such importance into the combat zone. He should not have carried it in a briefcase but should have carried it on his person, if he carried it at all. And he was grossly negligent in abandoning the briefcase when his car was set on fire. When he showed up at Bethune without the written order, he was called before a hastily summoned board of inquiry. He explained the incident and gave his word of honor that he had with his own eyes seen the order consumed by flames.

While prisoner interrogation and the capture of vital documents are primary sources of information for intelligence services, the real eye of the belligerent command is the airplane. General H. H. Arnold, the late great air chief of the U.S. Army, once said, "Introduce one lone airplane into the fifteen decisive battles of the world, and the course of history would have been changed." Aerial observation by balloon was first used in the American Civil War, and balloons were still used widely in World War I. By 1939 they all but disappeared from the skies over battlefields because they had become too vulnerable to the modern plane, which itself took over from the balloon the important task of observation, adding to it the more modern photo-reconnaissance and so-called "intelligence command missions."

The air force flies on observation missions for the ground command, to scout from the air the disposition of the enemy, his front lines, the location of his reserves, his maneuvers, his lines of supply and communications—in other words, the whole complex war-making machinery of the enemy in the active theater of operations. The entire enemy country is open to the observation planes. Planes have even been used to observe the habits and customs of the enemy population. They have been sent out to determine whether factories black out at night, whether business is being carried on as usual, whether the people still gather at racecourses or athletic fields, whether the schools in cities are still open or whether children have been evacuated to the country. This kind of observation produces so-called "morale intelligence" on the moods of the enemy's population, an important factor in calculating his total war potential.

There were times in the early days of aviation when commanders were dependent on returning pilots' reports of their personal observations. Later, the camera was placed in the plane, and today much of the aerial observation is recorded on film or photographic plates. While formerly troops in woods were hidden from the aerial observer, color photography has effectively countered such camouflage. Today, maneuvers and movements on the ground are almost impossible to conceal from the air observer and his camera. Frequently, commanding generals board observation planes and fly over the enemy, even while battles are in progress, to see for themselves. According to the most modern military theory, intelligence is bound to suffer some loss in the second-hand transfer of information. Commanders have come to favor personal observation from the air in order to compensate for this inevitable loss.

Aerial or photo reconnaissance, conducted for the benefit of the air force itself, is designed to establish the exact location of targets, to photograph them so that blown-up pictures may be available during the briefings of crews prior to bombardment missions. Bombardment units have their own intelligence kits, called "objective folders." These envelopes contain all available information about enemy targets and are kept in readiness in the event of the outbreak of hostilities.

One of the Second World War's outstanding intelligence scoops involving aviation observation was associated with a pretty, blue-eyed English girl named Constance Babington-Smith. She performed single-handed a major intelligence operation when she discovered one of the war's most valuable targets without leaving her underground office in a secret R.A.F. headquarters. The aerial target was Peenemünde, a German island in the Baltic, where Hitler was conducting experiments with the rocket bombs and guided missiles with which he hoped to decide the war in his favor.

These experiments had begun as early as 1933 and had been concentrated at Peenemünde since 1936. But British intelligence was unaware of this phase of Germany's war preparations and failed to evince interest even when information did leak out about the top-secret project. Between 1939 and 1943, a number of confidential informants tried to alert British intelligence. One report came in the form of an unsigned letter mailed in Norway. Another came from an old Dane in Nykøbing. Many others came in and were promptly lost in the fog with which blundering intelligence sometimes conceals its mistakes.

Somehow these reports were all filed and forgotten, without any action following them up. When the reports became more persistent, British intelligence simply dismissed the information as German "plants" or propaganda in line with Goebbels' efforts to advertise non-existent secret weapons. Whatever it was, Britain had to pay a heavy and bloody price for the complacency and indifference of its peacetime intelligence organs. It was only partly compensated by intelligence, which eventually and belatedly became concerned with the problem. Even then, the impact of this German "absolute weapon" would have been greater had not Miss Babington-Smith made her discovery.

She was one of a group of young officers whose job was the examination of reconnaissance photographs brought back by the R.A.F. from missions over Germany. One day in May, 1943, she scrutinized a picture taken the day before during a flight over Peenemünde. She used a stereoscope and a measuring magnifier, and, with these simple instruments, she discovered a small curving black shadow and a T-shaped white blot above it. It occurred to her that the curving black shadow was a kind of launching ramp, and that the T-shaped white blot was a small airplane placed on the ramp for launching.

Her superior accepted her hypothesis and ordered immense enlargements made of the photograph. In the enlargement, both the ramp and the little "plane" became clearly visible. Only then was British intelligence mobilized to procure additional and detailed information about Peenemünde. What followed was more or less routine intelligence work in which the old spy reports emerged as important clues, with new ones added to complete the picture. Peenemünde was then bombed by the R.A.F., and the production of flying bombs was retarded at least six months.

The Process of Evaluation

With the collection and procurement of information, the basic function of the intelligence service is essentially completed. Evaluation of this information is a superior intellectual task. It not only assesses the probability, credibility, and reliability of information, but it estimates its general importance and relates it to the general situation for the benefit of higher echelon policy makers.

Although it might seem imperative to leave the function of evaluation to the intelligence service, this is not always done.

Often only preliminary evaluation is made within the intelligence organization, leaving eventual evaluation to recipient agencies or to organizations specially created for this function.

Preliminary evaluation is usually done at the level of the lower echelons, mostly by the most immediate recipients of incoming data at the appropriate desks. They confine their evaluation to a rating of the information. Such ratings assess (a) the reliability or trustworthiness of the source, and (b) the probability of the information.

The reliability of sources or informants is usually rated with letters from "A" to "D." The letter "A" indicates that the source is highly reliable, and the letter "D" that it is an unreliable or untested source.

The probability of the information is rated with numerals from "1" to "4." No. "1" indicates that the information on hand is highly probable, accurate, and corroborated; number "4" that it is improbable or inaccurate.

I have rarely seen intelligence reports rated "A-1." The reluctance to bestow such a high rating on a report is usually due to a wholesome, but sometimes exaggerated, skepticism of individual evaluators. A "B-2" rating is considered pretty good. Even a rating of "C-3" is respected. Frequently, on the other hand, "D-4" reports turn out to be completely reliable and accurate. The whims of intelligence are inscrutable.

Evaluation continues on increasingly higher levels; the eventual attitude of the highest policy maker or supreme commander to a report or a piece of information represents only a more or less final form of evaluation.

While collection may not be particularly difficult, evaluation is. It requires broad knowledge, imagination, and intuition. It is often the banana peel on which hapless intelligence organizations slip up.

The decisive importance of evaluation has been demonstrated, both in its positive and negative consequences, virtually at every step of history. Stalin's negative attitude toward the reports of his secret service which indicated an imminent German attack in 1941 is not characteristic, because it was irrational and was motivated by Stalin's personal prejudices and innate suspiciousness.

The same information Stalin received was also accumulated by various British intelligence services. By the middle of March, 1941, there was ample information on hand in London to indicate that a German attack on the Soviet Union was definitely planned, and that it was due within three months. This was, in fact, the consensus of British intelligence of-

71

ficers on lower echelons. But then the information was relayed to the Joint Intelligence Committee, composed of representatives of the services, whose function was to sift the information and evaluate it for the Prime Minister and the War Cabinet.

The Joint Intelligence Committee surveyed the information and dismissed it on purely rational grounds, concluding that an attack on the Soviet Union would be a senseless enterprise on Hitler's part. They decided that, despite convincing data, a German invasion of U.S.S.R. was unlikely, chiefly because it did not seem reasonable. The Committee overlooked the fact that reason was not a Hitler characteristic.

Probably because the Committee disturbed the circles of his own thinking, Mr. Churchill decided to act as his own intelligence officer in this momentous case, and he gave orders that all raw reports concerning Barbarossa, the operation's code name, be sent directly to him without bothering him with further deductions and evaluations.

On March 30, 1941, a report reached his desk from a highly trusted agent in the Balkans, reporting the movement of five Panzer divisions into the deployment area of the projected operation, and involving about sixty trains. This report convinced Churchill that Germany was indeed preparing for the invasion of the U.S.S.R., and, although he still thought such a development too good to be true in view of Britain's plight, he concluded that the invasion was certain to come and that it was imminent.

Although relations between Britain and the Soviet Union, then Germany's "non-belligerent" partner, were strained, Churchill decided to share this information with Stalin. Churchill's message was delivered to Vishinsky on April 19 and given to Stalin on April 23. It is possible that it merely solidified Stalin's suspicion of similar reports presented to him by his own secret service and persuaded him that the whole flood of warnings was but a British plot.

In October, 1950, intelligence reports from Korea indicated, and actually predicted, that Red China would intervene at any moment in the war there. These reports received a high probability rating on lower echelons, but they were dismissed as improbable both by General MacArthur and by the intelligence committee in Washington to which they were referred for high-level evaluation. This evaluation prevailed, and it influenced policies, decisions, and moves made on the White House level, eventually causing embarrassment despite the explicit and timely nature of the warning.

The pitfalls of intelligence are many and varied. Discussing these dangers with jovial bluntness, Allen W. Dulles, one of America's greatest intelligence specialists, and at present director of the Central Intelligence Agency, once remarked: "It is often harder to use the product than to get it. The receivers of intelligence generally start out by discounting a particular report as false or a plant. Then, when they get over that hurdle, they discard what they don't like and refuse to believe it. Finally, when they do get a report they both believe and like, they don't know what to do about it."

The problem of evaluation represents a standing controversy among the students of intelligence. Some say, and I am inclined to side with them, that information should be evaluated somewhere within the intelligence organization that acts as the clearing-house of all information. There it may be evaluated by the chiefs of desks on their own level, if only because they have the broadest knowledge of their particular field, or by a branch whose function is general evaluation.

Others question the wisdom of leaving evaluation to those who collect the information. "Human enthusiasm is such," an observer remarked, "that it is difficult for me to believe that secret intelligence will be objectively evaluated by its collectors." Having separated its collection agencies from its analysis and evaluation section, the CIA has tried to prove in practice that effective evaluation work can be done within an agency that is also engaged in collection of information.

The Dissemination of Intelligence

Even the best intelligence is totally useless if it remains in the files of the intelligence service. This fact is fully recognized by the agencies themselves, who generally regard the distribution of evaluated information as one of their three basic functions. This part of their activity is called "dissemination of intelligence." It is usually handled by a separate branch of the service dedicated solely to this function and called the Dissemination Branch. The function of dissemination has many manual or technical aspects, such as the printing or mimeographing and the actual physical distribution of reports. Yet dissemination is essentially an intellectual activity involving great responsibilities, if only because it is the job of the men doing it to see that the proper information reaches the proper desks.

Intelligence material reaches the Dissemination Branch in

73

its classified form. Documents are given specific classifications to indicate their degree of secrecy. The scale of classifications begins with "Confidential." Next is "Secret." The highest classification is "Top Secret." Special documents involving highly confidential matters or operations are given individual classifications and often the term used in classifying such documents is itself in the classified category. During World War II, for example, the translations of the U.S. Army of foreign codes were classified "Magic." The operations plan of Overlord, the code name for the invasion of France in 1944, was classified "Bigot" and the men who were allowed access to such information were called "Bigoted."

The classification determines *ipso facto* how wide-spread the distribution of individual documents may be. An unclassified report, of course, may have unrestricted distribution, even though no official of any government is expected to hand over even unclassified papers to unauthorized persons. A report classified "Confidential" has a limited distribution but still may go to a great number of people who must be cognizant of its contents.

A document classified "Secret" has a far more limited distribution but it may still go to several hundred persons, but papers with the classification "Top Secret" are seen by only a few people, often no more than two or three. Even the physical transportation of such highly classified documents is severely restricted and prescribed. They are carried only by exceptionally trustworthy messengers specially cleared for the job, or in the armed forces by officer personnel who are required to carry side arms in transit. I recall the case of a "Top Secret" document of World War II that had a distribution of only seven specifically marked copies, and required that a brigadier general distribute them to their recipients, including the writer. Actually, the precautions taken with this particular document were out of all proportion to the value of the information it contained.

Even before such highly classified documents reach the Dissemination Branch, they are paraphrased or rewritten to prevent the identification of the codes used in their transmission and to safeguard the sources of their origin. Sources in general are indicated by established covers. "Top Secret" documents are numbered, and each copy is phrased differently. All these measures and many others are used to protect the sources of information even from the personnel of the Dissemination Branch.

Although it is widely recognized that dissemination is a crucial phase of effective intelligence work, it is very often the weakest link in the intelligence chain. Dissemination branches are frequently staffed by minor clerical personnel who carry out their responsibilities in a mechanical fashion. They give a perfunctory reading to the document at hand and then designate its recipients from a prearranged distribution list. As a result, certain vital intelligence material may never reach the person who could probably make the best use of it or, if it does, may reach him too late.

The sacroscant chain of command, observed religiously within bureaucratic organizations, also tends to interfere with efficient and effective distribution of intelligence. An intelligence report may originate on a rather low level of the hierarchy. The official who then handles it is supposed to pass it on through channels, which means that he gives it to his own immediate superior, who in turn relays it upward. Sometimes inefficient routing within the Dissemination Branch and the shackles of the chain of command combine to prevent vital items from reaching the final policy maker or commander in time for necessary action.

In December, 1944, an important piece of information was routed to a low-level official in one of the American intelligence agencies, simply because a distribution list showed him to be "cognizant" of the particular subject treated in the report. This report, however, contained intelligence of the utmost immediate importance to the highest policy maker, in this case President Roosevelt himself. It was a report from Tokyo, from a highly respected neutral source, advising us that Emperor Hirohito had established contact with the peace party in Japan and was actively working to create the preconditions for a possible cessation of hostilities. The official who received the report was quick to recognize its importance and possible influence on policy, but the chain of command separated him from the President by at least ten intermediate steps. Although the report was passed on at once, with a note urging that it be brought immediately to the attention of the President, it never actually reached Mr. Roosevelt's desk. It was sidetracked somewhere in the shuffle.

Although handled as separate functions, the close reciprocal relations between the three interlocking activities of an intelligence service—collection, evaluation, and distribution—are clearly evident. The efficient functioning of these three basic activities is essential if intelligence is to be effective and play its proper part in the great decisions that regulate international affairs.

The Influence of Intelligence

The highest form of positive intelligence is what may be called policy intelligence. The end purpose of all intelligence functions is to inform the policy makers at the highest level of impending moves of foreign governments, so that they may shape their own government's policies in the light of that knowledge.

On a somewhat lower level is strategic intelligence, which is designed to assist the higher military, naval, and air staffs in the development of their strategic plans and military policies. On an equal level is political intelligence, upon which diplomatic staffs depend for the formulation of their policies, negotiations, and treaties.

On a somewhat lower level is what may be called operational intelligence. The word "operational" is used here to identify the manifold interests and activities that fall somewhere between strategy and tactics. The term was originally coined in 1792 by an erratic Prussian military genius named Dietrich Heinrich von Bülow, who felt that a specific word was needed to express "lower strategy and higher tactics." He used the term "operation" to identify the coordination of several tactics for culmination within a single action, or the coordination of several minor actions toward the fulfillment of an intermediary step in the formulation of a definitive policy.

Accordingly, operational intelligence is designed to serve those who conduct the nation's diplomatic or military business on a high level in the field, but who have no policy-making power. Ambassadors and supreme military commanders fall into this category as the ultimate executors of a nation's policies abroad.

On the lowest level is tactical or combat intelligence, information of a localized or specific nature for use by all diplomatic and military echelons.

It may be said here that there is no critical division between the individual branches of intelligence, but that there is a very close reciprocal relation between them, since in the total intelligence activity each lower branch funnels its information upwards into policy intelligence.

Intelligence attains its greatest significance when it serves the purposes of the policy maker, and to the same extent national policy is dependent on intelligence. In this close relationship between national policy and intelligence, only a perfect equilibrium between the two can provide for the security of the nation.

In the middle thirties, high-level intelligence exerted its influence on Britain's national policy and grand strategy, and actually reshaped it. Some time in 1934, British intelligence received reports from its agents in Germany that Hitler was rearming in defiance of the Versailles Treaty and was secretly building an air force. To supplement the work of those agents already in Germany, the British Air General Staff developed a project to obtain absolutely reliable information from the Germans themselves. A number of young officers of the Air General Staff were instructed to feign friendship for the Third Reich and to worm themselves into the confidence of high Luftwaffe officials, for the purpose of getting whatever first-hand intelligence they could on the Luftwaffe's doctrine, strategy, tactics, personnel, and equipment.

The project succeeded beyond all expectations. A group commander even managed to get himself invited to Germany, where he was shown some of the Luftwaffe's most secret installations. He was eventually received by Hitler, who frankly disclosed to him confidential details of the Reich's aerial rearmament.

Influenced by reports about this surreptitious activity, His Majesty's Government decided to increase the Royal Air Force. However, this increase was only half-hearted. It was limited to seventy-five squadrons, of which forty-seven were bomber squadrons. At that time, the dominant R.A.F. doctrine still favored an offensive strategy. The British Cabinet had been persuaded by its air advisers that the four-engined heavy bombers of the R.A.F. would provide a war-winning weapon.

However, there was within the R.A.F. another school of thought, one that favored a defensive strategy concentrated in fighters and such electronic devices as radar, which was then in its earliest stages of development. This doctrine was represented most vigorously by Air Marshal Sir Hugh (later Lord) Dowding. Called "Stuffy" by his intimates and subordinates, he was a professional officer of the finest character, technical accomplishment, and imagination.

Dowding based his views on intelligence reports that indicated that Germany was increasing her Luftwaffe along offensive strategic lines, emphasis being heavy on bomber types.

Then, in March, 1935, Britain acquired, in a startlingly direct manner, a piece of policy intelligence of the greatest importance. Foreign Secretary Sir John Simon visited Hitler in Germany and was told by the Fuehrer personally that Germany had already achieved air parity with Britain. Hitler also told Sir John that he "intended to go on building until he had an air force equal to those of Britain and France combined."

This "gratuitous warning," as Chester Wilmot put it, jolted the Baldwin Cabinet. They decided to increase the Home Defense Air Force to 121 squadrons with 1,512 first-line aircraft by April, 1937, and to accelerate the development of defensive electronic devices. Thus, the intelligence Sir John brought back from Germany and the corroborative material supplied by British agents brought about the abandonment of a previous military policy and determined the drafting of a new one.

Subsequently, additional information was obtained by British agents confirming the offensive character of the new Luftwaffe and bearing out the assumption that it was designed as a threat to Britain, either as a deterrent in preventing her from interfering with Hitler's designs, or as the decisive weapon in the event of war. Additional information was obtained through the arrest of a Luftwaffe spy in Britain, a suave intellectual named Hermann Goertz. The mission of this agent was to gather information about the R.A.F.'s fighter fields ringing London. The planners of the Luftwaffe needed this intelligence for the strategic air war they were drafting against Britain.

When such details became known in Downing Street, Sir Hugh Dowding was appointed commander in chief of the Fighter Command. Britain's defense in the air was entrusted to him, and, in due course, the defensive strategy he had advocated superseded the original offensive strategy.

This thrilling chain of intelligence developments, and the evolution of policies and strategies based on that intelligence, yielded historic results in the Battle of Britain when it came in August and September of 1940. The combination of superior fighter aircraft and scientific and technical equipment that had been developed as a result of the alarming information from Germany saved Britain from defeat when Göring's offensive Luftwaffe did, as predicted by British intelligence, mount its all-out onslaught against the British Isles.

If ever intelligence had a decisive influence on the military strategy of a major power, and if ever it succeeded in staving off disaster, England's survival was the historic case. There was nothing haphazard about these developments, or about the close correlation between intelligence on the one side and

78

policy and strategy on the other. The intelligence maneuver that was designed to penetrate Hitler's plans was a superbly organized effort, in which all the branches of intelligence were employed. The information they produced was then carefully evaluated, and Britain's political leaders had the foresight to respect the information and the evaluation. The result was victory.

The United States was confronted with the necessity of making a similarly crucial policy decision in 1947 when the cold war began to take definite shape. The year before I had sat in on the deliberations of an intelligence group at which I heard the question raised for the first time, "Is the Soviet Union preparing for aggression?" Then subsidiary questions were posed, "Is the Soviet Union going to start peripheral conquests, in countries like Greece or Turkey or Germany?" and "Is she willing to risk a world war over her plans?"

It became the job of American and British intelligence to answer these questions on the basis of the hardest possible information, and then to prepare a long-range estimate of the situation on the basis of all the collected and collated information. This was a problem on the highest strategic level, since the policy of the United States would evolve from the answers intelligence gave to those questions. In a real sense, the future of the free world depended on the accuracy of the answers supplied by intelligence.

Nor did intelligence have to start entirely from scratch. It had a pretty good idea of Soviet intentions, and the idea had come straight from the horse's mouth.

During the last days of World War II in Europe, Allied troops captured intact the archives of the German Foreign Office. For years after that, American and British intelligence officers studied these papers and tried to educe from them information that had a meaning for the future.

Among the papers were the documents covering Germany's relations with the Soviet Union, including the period of intimacy between August, 1939, and June, 1941. And in this group of documents, American intelligence experts discovered the record of Soviet Foreign Minister Molotov's conversations with Hitler and Ribbentrop between November 12 and 18, 1940. They were exceptionally frank conversations of men who saw no reason to conceal their thoughts. You might call them most realistic conversations, if exclusive preoccupation with power politics or *Realpolitik* can be called truly realistic.

The intelligence experts discovered among the papers the drafts of a secret protocol, drawn up by the Soviet Foreign

79

Commissariat, for signature by Germany and the U.S.S.R. This draft, dated November 26, 1940, is probably the frankest revelation of a country's political aspirations ever to fall into the hands of another nation.

In the draft, the Soviet government stated in so many words that "the focal point of the aspirations of the Soviet Union south of Batum and Baku [is] in the general direction of the Persian Gulf." Turkey, Bulgaria, and the rest of the Balkans were described as other such "focal areas of Soviet aspirations," and the draft proposed that "in case Turkey refuses to join the Four Powers, Germany, Italy, and the Soviet Union agree *to work out and to carry through the required military and diplomatic measures.*"

While there had been cases in the past when the aspirations and intentions of foreign powers were disclosed through indiscretions or effective secret intelligence work, never before had the ruthlessly aggressive plans of a scheming world power been so thoroughly exposed on such a comprehensive scale. The capture of the archives and the subsequent discovery of these specific documents represented a rare intelligence scoop, which was further enhanced by the brilliant investigation and evaluation of Soviet policy by British and American intelligence officers.

At the very outset of its investigation Central Intelligence could expect, on the basis of the Kremlin's own secret plans, that Soviet aggrandizement would be in the direction of the Balkans, Turkey and the Straits, and Iran.

That this was by no means a theoretical project, and that it was not abandoned with the discovery of the documents, was evidenced by another intelligence scoop scored by the British secret service in Turkey and Greece. These two countries are traditional arenas of British intelligence activity. Some of Britain's most intrepid secret service maneuvers have taken place there, as far back as the eighteenth century. During the war, Prime Minister Churchill established a special secret service detail to watch the development of Communist influence in Greece. This group succeeded in infiltrating the various Communist organizations and intercepted directives received by those organizations from Moscow. The directives showed that the Soviet Union was prepared to translate into action the aspirations of its diplomatic draft of November, 1940, and to annex Greece and Turkey in the manner outlined during the Molotov-Hitler conversations.

These intelligence papers were also placed at the disposal of American Central Intelligence, where they supplied another set of indices for the formulation of answers to the crucial questions. The entire apparatus of Central Intelligence was then directed at the procurement of information on the issue under study. Before long, Central Intelligence had a mass of data, ready for sifting and evaluation.

The process was brought to a preliminary close in February, 1947, when a Soviet move on Greece and Turkey was reported imminent. Central Intelligence was asked to prepare an estimate of the situation, which was presented to the White House, on March 3, 1947, together with an evaluation of the situation prepared by the State Department. The result was the Truman Doctrine, the *direct* outgrowth of information gained through exceptional intelligence work.

After that, the White House requested that Central Intelligence make a comprehensive survey of the situation and present a definitive estimate, on which the future policy of the United States vis-à-vis the Soviet Union could be safely based. With this assignment, intelligence came of age in the United States.

In due course, the Central Intelligence Agency completed its estimate of the situation, based on the most painstaking preparatory work in the history of intelligence, and involving extensive scientific investigation of both open and covert intelligence material. The CIA regarded its analysis as foolproof and was determined to stand by this estimate for better or for worse. It answered the basic question in the negative, stating firmly that the Soviet Union would not within the foreseeable future, risk a global war, and that it would not interfere directly, by military means, with American action in the cold war.

President Harry S. Truman and Secretary of State Dean Acheson accepted the estimate of the CIA, although competitive estimates, especially those prepared by the Air Force, contained a more alarming picture. The Air Force predicted that the Soviet Union would automatically risk war to counter American moves in Europe and even described such a war as imminent.

The entire international policy of the United States since March, 1947, when in an address before a joint session of Congress Mr. Truman announced American aid to Turkey and Greece, has been predicated on (a) the original estimate of the CIA, and (b) its running intelligence summaries, which have presented a day-by-day implementation of the original estimate.

On the basis of the CIA's definitive estimate, the United States defied the U.S.S.R. with the Berlin airlift, confident that the Soviet Union would not seize upon this American move to counter the Soviet blockade of Berlin as an excuse for unleashing World War III. Also on the basis of the CIA estimate, the United States decided (a) that there was sufficient time to rearm, (b) to organize the defenses of Europe, (c) to expedite the development of the hydrogen bomb, (d) to prepare what Dean Acheson called a "position of strength," without which dealings with the Soviet Union appeared impossible.

The final decision of President Truman to intervene in the Korean War, convinced as he was that the U.S.S.R. would not expand it into a global war, was also based on the intelligence summary evolved by the Central Intelligence Agency. The CIA apparently was never shaken in its belief that its estimate of the situation was correct, even on a long-range basis.

I was myself involved in an operation which may be cited as an example of strategic political intelligence. I think it is important to present it in some detail, if only because it opens up several other views of the unspectacular desk work in intelligence and introduces still another important phase of the intelligence effort, the order of battle.

The enemy's order of battle is something every military, naval, and air intelligence service regards as its primary function to collect. It is a list of his forces, their dispositions, insignia, designations, organizational structure, and officers. It provides the basic raw material used by the commander in the field in the preparation of his plans.

British intelligence developed the compilation of the order of battle into an art. And, despite the enormous difficulties that the collection of information entailed in the Pacific war, the United States Army succeeded by some seeming magic in compiling the battle order of the Japanese army with some comprehensiveness.

I used the little red-bound volume of Military Intelligence as my sole source of information in answering a question of great operational importance, "How good was the much-vaunted Kwantung Army that the Japanese had in Manchuria?" In estimating Japanese military strength, it was assumed by the Joint Chiefs of Staff that the Kwantung Army was an extremely efficient, well-commanded, effective force. It was theoretically self-contained and autonomous. It was further assumed by Allied intelligence that the Kwantung Army was intact despite the war, and that it was kept in Manchuria as a strategic reserve which could continue the war, if necessary, from there, in the event that the main islands of Japan were lost.

For some strange reason, this phantom army in Manchuria held the same kind of fascination for G-2 (the intelligence branch of the U.S. Army's General Staff) that Hitler's new German army had for the American military attachés stationed in Berlin. Influenced by the respectful estimates that G-2 prepared on the military potential of the Kwantung Army, G-3 (Operations) drew up plans in which the distant and idle army loomed very large indeed.

The forces of the Western Allies were deemed insufficient to deal with both the Japanese armies in the active theaters *and* the Kwantung Army. So it became an obsession with the General Staff to draw the Soviet Union into the war and to assign to the Red Army the defeat of the Kwantung Army in Manchuria. In the summer of 1943, the War Department prepared "a very high level strategic estimate" to guide President Roosevelt's relations with the Soviet Union. It was called "Russia's Position," and stated, among other things: "Finally, the most important factor in relation to Russia is the prosecution of the war in the Pacific. With Russia as an ally in the war against Japan, the war can be terminated in less time and at less expense in life and resources than if we reverse the case."

When President Roosevelt went to the Yalta Conference in the early winter of 1944-45, he was handed what amounted to an ultimatum by his military advisers. "We desire Russian entry at the earliest possible date," the démarche read, "consistent with her ability to engage in offensive operations and are prepared to offer the maximum support possible without prejudice to our main effort against Japan."

The late Secretary of State Edward R. Stettinius, who was with Roosevelt at Yalta, spoke of "the *immense pressure* put on the President by our military leaders to bring Russia into the Far Eastern war." As usual, the strategy of the General Staff was based on intelligence and evaluation.

However, there were those who regarded this intelligence estimation as faulty and the evaluation erroneous. Among those who disagreed with the plan to bring Russia into the war were W. Averell Harriman, the American Ambassador to the Soviet Union, Major General John R. Deane, the American Military Attaché in Moscow, the high commanders of the Navy, and its Secretary, James Forrestal. But these men had no concrete information with which to back up their opposition. I knew that Mr. Forrestal and Vice Admiral Charles M. Cooke, Jr., Admiral King's chief of staff, were seeking for such information, and it became a determination with me to find it.

In the summer of 1944, after the capture of Saipan in the Pacific, I was astounded by a bit of incidental intelligence which stated that among the units we had destroyed on the island were the 50th Infantry and 135th Infantry. The Japanese battle order, according to G-2, listed it as part of the Kwantung force, stationed in Manchuria.

I checked, and there was no mistake on either score. The 135th Infantry was a part of the Kwantung Army and it was destroyed on Saipan, several thousand miles from its official garrison. This was the first indication I had that the Kwantung Army had been broken up, though it was only a straw in the wind. I immediately acquired a list of all the Japanese divisions we had encountered on the various Pacific islands, from Guadalcanal to Peleliu to Tinian, and from it I made a startling discovery. The Kwantung Army, as represented by our G-2, was nothing more than an imaginary force. None of the Imperial units which once formed that fine army were still in Manchuria to wage a dreaded separate war. Those crack divisions, "the cream of the Japanese army," as Colonel Carlson of the Marines called them, had all been transferred to the various theaters of active operations, to the Pacific islands, to China, and to the Philippines. A large percentage of the original force had been destroyed by us as we advanced from island to island. Others were pinned down thousands of miles from Manchuria.

I then began to collect intelligence on the new Kwantung Army. With the help of the British battle order of the Japanese army, I found that it consisted of third- and fourth-rate divisions, some of them maintained only at brigade strength and made up of inferior troops that Tokyo had scraped from the bottom of its manpower barrel.

Here was operational intelligence of the utmost importance, calculated to radiate its influence upward, to strategy and even to policy. It was obvious that if the Kwantung Army was only a phantom force, then the Allies did not need the Red Army to deal with it. And if the Red Army were not needed in the Far East, then Soviet intervention in the war against Japan was not required.

I was on a rather low echelon of intelligence, and the problem arose as to how this information could be channeled to the higher-ups. My immediate superior in the chain of command was a lieutenant commander, the executive officer of my branch. He reported to the officer in charge, a commander, who in turn reported to the Director of Naval Intelligence. Next in the chain of command was the subchief of Naval Operations. In turn came the Vice Chief of Naval

Operations and the Chief of Naval Operations, Admiral Ernest J. King, commander in chief of the United States Fleet. His superior was the Secretary of the Navy, and there the jurisdiction of the Navy ended. And this was clearly an Army matter.

At that time, the military leaders of the War Department believed implicitly in their intelligence. In the field, General Douglas MacArthur supported it to the hilt. On February 25, 1945, during a conference with Forrestal in Manila, MacArthur stated that "we should secure the commitment of the Russians to active and vigorous prosecution of a campaign against the Japanese in Manchukuo of such proportions as to pin down a very large part of the Japanese army."

On the other hand, Assistant Secretary of War John J. McCloy opposed this view. His opposition was based on information received from another intelligence unit of the War Department, under Colonel Alfred McCormack, which had reached conclusions similar to my own findings. But McCloy failed to make his influence felt, and the estimate of G-2 prevailed to the bitter end. Years later, in March, 1947, Mr. McCloy recalled this incident. "He said," Mr. Forrestal recorded in his diary, "this for him [McCloy] illustrated most vividly the necessity for the civilian voice in military decisions even in time of war."

Despite my own low position in the intelligence hierarchy, I prepared a memorandum of my findings and ventured to offer certain conclusions. I stated without equivocation that according to the most reliable information the Kwantung Army no longer existed as an efficient and powerful force. I stated as my second premise that its replacements consisted of inferior troops incapable of defending Manchuria. I concluded that Manchuria seemed unlikely to be slated as the battleground for a last-ditch stand of defeated Japan, and that these premises made Soviet intervention in the Far Eastern war appear unnecessary.

I had no means of ascertaining the fate of my memorandum. If it ever did get across to the Army, I do not know in what pigeonhole it wound up. However, I tried every possible way to publicize my findings and conclusions. I discussed them with higher-ups, and then I volunteered to survey them in a closed meeting of the American Military Institute, a scientific organization.

The meeting took place in a conference room in the National Archives in the fall of 1944. The chair was occupied by Colonel Joseph I. Greene, then editor of the influential *Infantry Journal*. After the meeting, I gave him a copy of my memorandum, and he volunteered to get it into the hands of General George Marshall. But still there came no signs that the War Department's high opinion of the Kwantung Army was dimmed.

In December, 1944, Captain Ellis M. Zacharias returned to Washington to serve in a confidential capacity directly under the Secretary of the Navy. I immediately acquainted him with my memorandum and, through him, the gist of it reached Secretary Forrestal. He used the report as one of the guns in the battery of his arguments against Soviet intervention in the Far East.

When it became known that President Roosevelt was planning to meet with Stalin at Yalta, and that position papers were being prepared for him to acquaint him with the backgrounds of the matters to be discussed, I managed to get copies of my memorandum to Harry L. Hopkins, and also into the office of Admiral William Leahy, the President's chief of staff. I have no means of knowing whether or not the memorandum ever reached his desk. But I do know from what happened at Yalta that it never made the slightest impression on the negotiations. General Marshall remained firm in his acceptance of G-2's estimate and urged the President to bring the Soviet Union into the Far Eastern war.

This attitude did not change even when the atomic bomb became a reality. According to Forrestal, "when President Truman came to Potsdam in the summer of 1945, he told [General Dwight D.] Eisenhower he had as one of his primary objectives that of getting Russia into the Japanese war." This determination was based on a canvass of his highest military advisers in Potsdam, but it was contrary to the advice of Secretary of State James F. Byrnes, "who was most anxious to get the Japanese affair over before the Russians got in." General Eisenhower also "begged" Mr. Truman "not to assume that he had to give anything away, . . . that the Russians were desperately anxious to get into the Eastern war and that in Eisenhower's opinion there was no question but that Japan was already thoroughly beaten." Ambassador Harriman also "begged" Mr. Truman to keep the Russians out of the war against Japan. But the opinion of General Marshall, seconded by Secretary of War Henry L. Stimson, prevailed. As events proved, it was based on erroneous intelligence.

The Russians did get into the war and the highly touted Kwantung Army crumbled away before them. When the Japanese divisions fighting in Manchuria were later identified it developed that the G-2 battle order was wrong and that the British battle order was right. It also developed that the conclusions I had drawn on the basis of the British battle order were correct.

Tactical Intelligence

Tactical intelligence is information of a local or specialized nature. It is generally of no immediate importance to the policy makers or to the commanders in war time. It is information that may subsequently be used to supplement and expedite a particular intelligence problem, and it deals essentially with facts and information of a minor nature which are only a limited aspect of the comprehensive intelligence operation.

In times of war, its military version is called combat intelligence, involving information about the enemy in a tactical sense. Comprehensively it is concerned with every military aspect of the enemy or potential enemy and with any form of information that has a direct bearing upon the prosecution of the war. It comprises such incidental knowledge as the location of gun emplacements, bridgeheads, invasion points, the caliber of enemy rifles, troop movements, the personal characteristics of enemy leaders, or the enemy's military tactics.

In time of peace, tactical information is continuously and vitally needed by the chiefs of political and diplomatic organizations, and in war it is essential information for all commanders—from the commander in chief down to the leader of a squad.

Since this is the most common form of intelligence, there are any number of cases—actually millions of them—that show tactical or combat intelligence in practice. My own favorite example is a quaint scoop from the Palestine campaign of World War I. It had nothing to do with carefully planned organized intelligence. It was entirely spontaneous, the product of that rare combination of erudition, ingenuity, intrepidity, and adaptation that in combat intelligence inevitably yields the best results.

On February 14, 1918, the British 60th Division was ordered by General Allenby to attack Jericho and drive the Turks across the Jordan. In preparation for the main attack they were to capture a small village named Michmash that was perched on a high rocky hill in the path of the drive. A brigade was detached to storm the hill and take Michmash by frontal attack from the substantial force of Turks holding it firmly.

When the name of Michmash was mentioned during the briefing, the brigade major felt somehow that it sounded familiar. Then he remembered. It was mentioned in the Bible. The major retired to his tent and by the light of a candle began to study the Bible, looking for the dimly remembered reference to Michmash. He found it in I Samuel, chapters 13 and 14.

The passage reads:

And Saul, and Jonathan his son, and the people that were present with them, abode in Gibeah of Benjamin: but the Philistines encamped in Michmash. . . .

Now it came to pass upon a day, that Jonathan the son of Saul said unto the young man that bare his armour, Come, and let us go over to the Philistines' garrison, that is on the other side. But he told not his father. . . . and the people knew not that Jonathan was gone.

And between the passages, by which Jonathan sought to go over unto the Philistines' garrison, there was a sharp rock on the one side, and a sharp rock on the other side: and the name of the one was Bozez, and the name of the other Seneh.

The forefront of the one was situate northward over against Michmash, and the other southward over against Gibeah.

And Jonathan said to the young man that bare his armour, come, and let us go over unto the garrison . . . it may be that the Lord will work for us: for there is no restraint to the Lord to save by many or by few.

Here was an important bit of combat intelligence about the approaches to Michmash. The major read on about how Jonathan climbed through the pass until he and his armor-bearer came to a place high up. The Philistines who were asleep awoke. They thought they were surrounded by the armies of Saul and fled in disorder. Saul then attacked with his whole army. It was, according to the Bible, his first victory against the Philistines.

The major roused his brigadier and showed him the passage in the Bible. "This pass," he said, "these rocky headlands and flat piece of ground are probably still there. Why don't we try to do what Jonathan did?" The brigadier agreed. Scouts were sent out to reconnoiter the ancient land. They found the pass exactly where the Bible described it, with the plateau above Michmash illuminated in the moonlight. "Very little has changed in Palestine," the brigadier said, "throughout the centuries."

The plan of the attack was promptly changed. Instead of

a whole brigade, the brigadier sent a single company against the sleeping Turks in Michmash. The few sentries the company encountered were silently eliminated and the biblical plateau was reached without incident shortly before dawn. The Turks awoke, as had the Philistines before them, and, thinking they were surrounded, "the multitude melted away."

The name of the young British major who was helped to this neat scoop by his knowledge of the Bible was Vivian Gilbert. "We killed or captured every Turk that night in Michmash," he said afterwards, "so that, after thousands of years, the tactics of Saul and Jonathan were repeated with success by a British force."

There can be, of course, no airtight separation between the various forms of intelligence, however they might be viewed. An item of seemingly general tactical significance may turn out to be of enormous strategic importance, and it may even have a direct bearing on final policy. Information about two strange new devices which arrived on Tinian in the summer of 1945, would have been a piece of combat intelligence had the Japanese been able to procure it. Yet the possession of this particular bit of information would have had enormous strategic implications to the Japanese High Command, since those two devices were in actual fact the atomic bombs destined for Hiroshima and Nagasaki.

Data about the arrival of certain Panzer divisions on the Western Front near Eupen-Malmédy in November, 1944, would have been regarded as *prima facie* combat intelligence, since the location and identification of enemy units in active combat areas is a tactical task of intelligence. In this particular case, however, such information would have had enormous operational significance, because those unidentified divisions formed part of the new German VI SS Panzer Army, organized and deployed specifically for what was soon to become the Battle of the Bulge.

We saw previously how an order by General von Rundstedt, which halted the Panzers converging on Dunkirk, had such a decisive influence when it was captured by a British patrol. Yet this coup was strictly within the framework of combat intelligence. Thus it is that intelligence in its practical application cuts boldly across categories and influences. A minute item may turn out to be of stupendous value, while what at first blush appears to be a major piece of information might prove to possess only minor tactical significance.

Pitfalls of Intelligence

Despite the size of the apparatus, the scientific scaffolding of the activity, the money expended on it—despite the conceit and arrogance of some organizations—intelligence is very far from being infallible. It is by no means a foolproof defense against unpleasant and damaging surprises in international relations, and the chances are that it never will be.

The modern history of intelligence is crowded with failures, blunders, and wrong estimates. Their respective secret services assured the Kaiser in 1914 and Hitler in 1939 that Britain would stay out of the war, and advised Prime Minister Neville Chamberlain on April 3, 1940, on the very eve of the conquests of Norway, Denmark, the Low Countries, and France, that Germany had "missed the bus." The Japanese secret service misled its government about the war potential of the United States. American intelligence failed to provide a definitive warning on the eve of Pearl Harbor. Stalin's secret service misinformed him about the power of the Finns in 1940. Marshall Göring's intelligence persuaded him the U.S. Air Force would never be able to develop a long-range fighter, and persisted in this estimate even when such planes had already been assembled on British flying fields.

Mussolini was constantly fooled by his secret service and went into all his wars, against Ethiopia, Greece, and the Allies, with inadequate or erroneous information. British intelligence only learned of the arrival of Field Marshal Rommel in North Africa fifteen days after a whole Panzer division of the Afrika Korps had landed. Allied intelligence never spotted the negotiations which led to the Russo-German pact of 1939. During the ensuing Polish campaign, Allied intelligence failed to ascertain that Germany had only 23 divisions in the West facing 110 French divisions, and that Hitler was ready to call it a day if the Allies started a real war in 1939.

Between the end of World War II and the outbreak of the war in Korea, American intelligence was guilty of five major blunders.

1. *It failed to predict the fall of Czechoslovakia.* Our intelligence assured the government that the crisis of 1948 was a routine change of government and not a seizure of absolute power by the Communists.

2. *It failed to predict and then to evaluate the meaning of Tito's defection.* We had no advance warning of impending events in Yugoslavia and no inside information on the circumstances of the break. The absence of hard facts prevented the U.S. government from acting promptly and exploiting the first serious emergency within the monolithic Communist orbit.

3. *It failed to anticipate the rapid disintegration of the Kuomintang in China.* "All our intelligence services save G-2," wrote Reid and Bird, "discounted the capabilities of the Communists to overrun China."

4. *It failed to provide accurate information on developments in Palestine in 1948.* The military abilities of the Arabs were embarrassingly overrated by the various intelligence groups. According to Secretary Forrestal, even such an astute observer as George F. Kennan was misled by State Department intelligence, exaggerating the strength of the Arabs and the weakness of the Jews.

5. *It failed to predict an uprising in Colombia in April, 1948.* This failure embarrassed the American Secretary of State who went to Bogotá to attend a conference of American states and found a revolution under way.

In 1950, the United States was caught *avec des pantalons bas,* as a French newspaper put it, when North Korea invaded South Korea. Remembering Pearl Harbor, Congress was understandably disturbed and invited Admiral Roscoe Hillenkoetter, Director of CIA, to explain this latest breakdown of American intelligence. Hillenkoetter produced a number of intelligence reports which his agency had received and circulated, all of them describing ominous moves and preparations north of the 38th parallel. Hillenkoetter persuaded Congress that insofar as Korea was concerned, CIA was "on the ball," even though other agencies of the government had failed to appreciate its warnings and were surprised when war came on June 25, 1950. In actual fact, however, Hillenkoetter had appeared in executive session before the Foreign Affairs Committee of the House two days before the outbreak of hostilities, on June 23, 1950, to report on the state of the world as CIA saw it. Congressman James G. Fulton of Pennsylvania then asked Hillenkoetter specifically about Korea and the likelihood of trouble there. The Admiral firmly assured members of the Committee that, insofar as his organization could tell, all was well in Korea and no trouble was expected then or in the foreseeable future. War came thirty hours later.

While the outsider is inclined to exaggerate the errors of

the secret service, there is a tendency on the part of intelligence services themselves to minimize their failures and cover up their blunders. Both attitudes are wrong, of course, and dangerous as well, if only because they tend to obscure the real potentialities of intelligence. In the words of Admiral Hillenkoetter, CIA's job involves "the systematic and critical examination of intelligence information, the synthesis of that intelligence information with all available related material and the determination of the probable significance of evaluated intelligence." But he added, "To *predict* the intentions of the enemy, real or potential, you would need a crystal ball."

The emphasis is on the word "predict." It implies deduction or rather an oracular venture even when it is based on masses of factual data. Yet prediction is an essential and inevitable function of intelligence. It is an integral part of its estimates and is necessary even though it involves risk. A prediction may be right and it may be wrong. Intelligence is on firm ground only when it makes its prognostication on the basis of exact knowledge of an opponent's proven intentions. There are at least four such cases on record, yet in three of those cases policy makers failed to accept the estimates of their intelligence services and act on the basis of corroborated information. In such cases, of course, it is the policy maker and not the intelligence service that must bear the responsibility for the consequences.

The pitfalls of intelligence are dramatized in its failures. It is, however, important to bear in mind that the errors of intelligence are not necessarily due to any basic deficiency of the service, but rather to the inevitable risks and difficulties inherent in this complex activity.

The failures of intelligence may be due to a number of causes. There may be too little or too much information on hand on which to base estimates. It may not be humanly possible to procure information about an opponent's intentions, or there may be too much information available, making selection difficult. On the eve of the Allied landings in North Africa in 1942, German intelligence had ample information about our intentions and so advised Hitler. The problem then became to acquire exact intelligence about the location of the prospective landings. Specific intelligence was obtained in substantial quantities, and selection left to the evaluators of the German High Command. In this particular case, the German High Command chose the wrong reports and expected the landings to take place near Bengasi and Dakar.

In December, 1941, we definitely expected Japan to start

a war, since convincing evidence had been produced in quantities by our intelligence organs. Yet when the reports were evaluated and estimates prepared, the wrong predictions emerged, and the striking area was fixed far from Pearl Harbor. In the hindsight of today this error is magnified and presented as a proof of the deficiencies of intelligence. In actual fact, such deficiencies cannot be remedied no matter how the facilities of intelligence may improve. The human tendency to err is an unavoidable pitfall in intelligence, and no technical competence is capable of eliminating it.

There are, however, other pitfalls which can be avoided: undue timidity, or undue recklessness, in collection and evaluation; or evaluation biased by deep-seated prejudices or preconceived notions. In March, 1948, for example, the Defense Department received information from General Lucius D. Clay in Germany indicating the imminence of a Soviet invasion of Germany. There was a tendency in Washington to accept the information at face value and to make the necessary arrangements to meet the onslaught. Secretary of Defense Forrestal, however, refused to act on the intelligence alone. He summoned the chiefs of the service intelligence agencies to his office and remained closeted with them for two days in an effort to determine the significance of what appeared in the surface-evaluated information.

It was then merely by the sheer force of Forrestal's personality and under the threat of serious danger that he succeeded in fusing their best thinking on the subject and producing an estimate that proved correct. Majority agreement was reached, with the Air Force dissenting, that the suspicious troop movements represented a build-up for the blockade of Berlin rather than preparations for a full-scale invasion.

Another pitfall is created in the inferior position of intelligence within the government organization. Colonel Nicolai pointed out that in the German Imperial Army, "in which the feeling of subordination was very strongly developed," the chief of the intelligence service was "by far the youngest departmental chief of the High Command"—a mere major. Anyone who is familiar with the sacrosanct institution of the chain of command knows how little influence even a colonel has in the greater order of things. "I must emphasize these personal considerations," Nicolai wrote, "because they help to make credible the difficulties which our Intelligence Service met with in its work."

In the United States, too, key intelligence officers have been hampered in their work and reduced in their influence

93

by their inferior ranks. Thus, for example, the fleet intelligence officer in Hawaii at the time of Pearl Harbor was a mere lieutenant commander. Throughout the military organization, old-line senior officers imposed strict subordination on their intelligence officers. The latter were prevented from influencing strategies and policies, despite the fact that by virtue of their preoccupation they knew first and best the trends and data on which such strategies and policies should be based. The echelon of intelligence is still far removed from the echelon of the policy makers and military planners. This distance alone reduces the effectiveness of even the best intelligence.

Worst of all is a condition common to all intelligence set-ups, in the United States as well as the U.S.S.R., in Britain as well as China. It is duplication within the intelligence effort. Tighter organization and a clearer demarcation of jurisdictional boundaries could ameliorate this situation, but we are still far from even a tolerable situation in this respect. In Britain, for example, intelligence activities are scattered among no fewer than fifteen intelligence agencies converging on the Joint Intelligence Bureau of the Ministry of Defence. While JIB is nominally the central intelligence agency of Her Majesty's Government, it shares its work with the Foreign Office, the Admiralty, the War Office, the Air Ministry, the Colonial Office, the Ministry of Commonwealth Relations, the Board of Trade, the Ministry of Supply, the Ministry of Civil Aviation, the Ministry of Transport, the Central Office of Information, the Medical Research Council, and the Department of Scientific and Industrial Research. Each has its own autonomous intelligence department.

The situation is not better in the Soviet Union where there are at least five major intelligence organizations, working parallel and even competing with one another. In the United States duplication is rampant with the work distributed among as many as twenty-five agencies. Aside from CIA, the State Department, the Army, Navy, and Air Force each has its own major and more or less autonomous intelligence department. In addition to these, there are a number of committees, conferences, and groups in operation. And the Joint Chiefs of Staff depend on their own Joint Intelligence Group.

This is a dangerous situation. It is not calculated to enhance the efficiency and effectiveness of intelligence. Contradictions, already existing by the very nature of the activity, inevitably develop from such decentralization. The situation is further complicated by the departmental jealousies which are rampant within intelligence services. The situation appears most detrimental when it comes to the appraisal of information. Corroborative evidence is as important in intelligence as it is in courts of law, but the scattering of intelligence interferes with effective corroboration. A piece of information may become available to but one major agency and then lack of corroboration may detract from its persuasiveness. Or a piece of misleading information may be fed to several intelligence agencies causing higher authorities to regard such information as "fully corroborated."

Centralization of intelligence is, however, only a partial remedy of this condition. There may be pitfalls even in this centralization, if only that assigning too much power and responsibility to a single agency leaves none at large to check up on it. When considering the potentialities of intelligence the pitfalls mentioned must always be borne in mind, and in thinking of intelligence as a first line of defense its limitations must be taken into account. Any absolute dependence on intelligence is itself a pitfall that must be avoided.

The Human Equation

The greatest, most intrepid operator in the business of intelligence is a mysterious American whom Radio Moscow calls "Colonel Lincoln." Not much is known about the man. He is said to be Robert T. Lincoln, the middle initial "T" standing for Throckmorton. He was born in Slippery Rock, Arkansas, on October 10, 1909. He used to be a rum-runner.

No superlative is strong enough to do justice to the skill of this man. He fought and won single-handed battles in the mountains of Iran against a whole army of Soviet operatives. He penetrated to Atomgrad, the mysterious Russian atomic city, and returned with a complete hydrogen bomb. He calmed unruly tribes in Afghanistan, and, on a Pacific island, disarmed a band of Japanese conspirators who plotted the assassination of General Douglas MacArthur. He also discovered Hitler alive in a cave in Patagonia some time after the world was satisfied that the dictator was no longer living.

Lincoln is known by a score of aliases and is frequently seen in a number of different places simultaneously. He is a champion marksman, a daredevil pilot, an expert mountaineer, a wizard in codes and ciphers, and a man of a hundred faces.

In every respect, Lincoln is the right man for the job. He

is modest and has a passion for anonymity. He is selfless and intensely patriotic. He is daring and resourceful.

There is just one thing wrong with Colonel Robert Throckmorton Lincoln. He does not exist.

He was conjured up over an after-dinner drink one night in Teheran by Ambassador John Wiley and his political officer, Gerald Dooher. It was 1948 and the two men were listening to the Moscow Radio. They were suddenly reduced to helpless laughter by a Soviet tale about a ubiquitous American agent. They decided to put their heads together and accommodate the Russians. The product of this whimsical conspiracy was Robert Throckmorton Lincoln, who emerged full-grown in all his classic and majestic proportions from the combined imaginations of the two inspired Americans.

Coming from nowhere, Lincoln was suddenly everywhere —to the bewilderment and dismay of the Moscow propagandists. His fame, given publicity by his creators, spread like wildfire. His name and exploits were on everyone's lips. It was soon quite common to meet people, especially in bars, who swore that they had actually seen Lincoln, or worked with him, or bunked with him.

When Supreme Court Justice William O. Douglas went mountain-climbing in Asia, Moscow charged that he, too, was an American secret agent and linked to Lincoln. When the associate justice of the Supreme Court came back to the States, reporters asked him to comment on the charge. "Oh, yes," Mr. Douglas said, "Lincoln was my constant companion on every one of my own secret missions."

Then the bubble burst in April, 1950. Cyrus L. Sulzberger of the New York *Times* was in Teheran and he picked up a lead about the fabulous Lincoln. The result was an article that announced Lincoln's death. It was not on the obituary page. Bob Lincoln was exposed as an amusing fraud! Some of us were very sorry to see him go and wished that men like him really existed. However, it seems that Sulzberger's scoop did not kill off Lincoln altogether. He continues to show up from time to time on Radio Moscow which claims that Sulzberger's story was printed to camouflage the fact that Lincoln is still as active as he ever was.

To be sure, the Lincoln myth is not all myth by any means. The colonel may be pure fiction (who knows?), but he is genuine, too, because he represents the epitome of the intelligence officer as he exists in the popular mind.

The people who thought up Lincoln made him active in all branches and categories of secret service. He was made what may be called the intelligence officer proper, a member of the "landed aristocracy" who donates his skills to his government without pay. He was made a secret intelligence agent, only slightly less important than the intelligence officer. He was a spy whose pedigree is perforce spurious. He was a saboteur, a conspirator, a guerrilla leader—a protean adventurer in the thrilling drama of intelligence.

This is not too unrealistic, since such zigzagging transfers and interlocking assignments do occur once in a while in actual practice. In Britain, for example, such jacks of all secret service trade were Baden-Powell, Dale Long, Lawrence, Paul Dukes, and, more recently, Keswick, Hutchison, and Picquet-Wicks, residents of the mysterious Norgeby House. In the United States, too, intelligence officers were frequently given assignments in the field, and may still be at large, walking boldly where even Lincoln never trod.

However, there are not many of them. With growth and specialization has come a stricter distribution of labor, and the casting of the right man in the right role has become the order of the day.

An intelligence specialist is like John Erskine's man—he has the moral obligation to be intelligent. But he need not be exceptionally brilliant or a creative thinker. The qualities sought in the rank and file are not so much inspiration, imagination, and bursting initiative as a professional knowledge of a particular activity, patience, application, persistence, and thoroughness. "The determination of facts relating to the enemy," Colonel Walter C. Sweeney wrote in his pioneering *Military Intelligence*, "the object of the labors of Intelligence Service personnel, is not arrived at by inspiration nor by any divine gift from a higher power. It is gained by the application of hard and patient work to the matter in hand, based upon knowledge, experience, and common sense. There is no mystery about it, only painstaking and systematic study of the recorded information. There is no royal road to success in the work of the Intelligence specialist."

Directors of Intelligence

The intelligence service need not be a phalanstery of geniuses —as long as there is a genius at its head. In the history of the secret service, great epochs have been linked directly and intimately not to any collective brilliance of the organization but to the individual brilliance of the chief. The history of the British Secret Service by no means shows uninterrupted efficiency, and there have been times when it was in rather bad shape, as well as others when it shone brightly. Those periods of greatness were marked by the appearance of exceptional personalities at the head of the Service.

Sir Francis Walsingham (1530-90) was such a genius during the reign of Queen Elizabeth, as was John Thurloe (1616-68) under Cromwell. After them, for about two hundred years, the luster of the Secret Service dimmed, not because England was unchallenged abroad, but simply because no great chiefs were developed at home.

In more modern times, the halcyon days of British intelligence were linked to such names as Sir H. M. Hozier (Winston Churchill's father-in-law), Sir Henry Brackenbury, Sir John Ardagh, and General Cockerrill, the genius who changed the art of intelligence into the exacting science it is today. Similarly the greatness of France's Deuxième Bureau is linked to General Dupont, who headed it during and after World War I and laid out a network of agents that reached from the Rhineland deep into the U.S.S.R.

The German Secret Service flourished under Bismarck's Wilhelm Stieber and Hitler's Wilhelm Canaris, and Soviet intelligence attained its greatest efficiency under such exceptional "spymasters" as Beldin, Davinov, Ulitsky, Fitin, Ossipov, and Kuznetsov.

These Russians were Marxist intellectuals raised in the Communist Party who had close personal ties with the party leaders. But otherwise they were hardly different from the great European chiefs. Common to all were exceptional organizing ability, the ability to inspire loyalty in subordinates, an innate flair for secret service work, a prodigious memory, a sense of history, an almost universal knowledge of complex technological matters, insatiable curiosity, and that aseptic intellectual ruthlessness and cold cynicism that Ambrose Bierce, bitingly satirical writer of horror stories, thought comes from a study of mankind.

The United States has found exceptional personalities as secret service chiefs whenever they were needed. The first man thus engaged was Major Benjamin Tallmadge, who headed George Washington's phenomenally efficient intelligence service. The latest is Allen W. Dulles, who today directs the Central Intelligence Agency. Two other able Americans in the field are J. Edgar Hoover, whose personality is reflected in the competence of the Federal Bureau of Investigation, an agency dedicated primarily to counterespionage but producing good results in positive intelligence as well, and

General William J. Donovan, wartime chief of the Office of Strategic Services and later American Ambassador to Thailand.

"Donovan was born in a lace-curtain Irish home in Buffalo," two of his wartime agents wrote. "He won the Congressional Medal of Honor while leading the famous Fighting 69th in World War I, and afterwards rose to such prominence as a lawyer that he was the Republican nominee for Governor in New York in 1933. Throughout his career he had a shrewd penchant for first names, for meeting the right people, and for expanding generously in every direction. OSS was a direct reflection of Donovan's character. He was its spark plug, the moving force behind it. In a sense it can be said that Donovan *was* OSS."

Britain's Division of Naval Intelligence, founded in 1887, was a stuffy and backward organization in which clerks, standing before high desks, recorded the characteristics of foreign warships with quill pens in huge ledgers chained to the desks. But this dusty office suddenly blossomed into a den of perpetual adventure when, in 1914, Captain Reginald Hall was appointed its chief.

There were some who thought that Captain (later Admiral Sir) Reginald Hall was the greatest intelligence chief who ever lived. In a letter to President Woodrow Wilson, Ambassador Walter H. Page wrote: "Hall is one genius that the war has developed. Neither in fiction nor in fact can you find any such man to match him. Of the wonderful things that I know he has done, there are several that it would take an exciting volume to tell. The man is a genius—a clear case of genius. All other secret service men are amateurs by comparison."

Colonel Edward M. House, Wilson's confidant, wrote directly to Hall, "I cannot think at the moment of any man who has done more useful service in this war than you, and I salute you."

William Reginald Hall was the personification of intelligence. He was brilliant, curious, eager, and industrious. In him intelligence reached a climax unprecedented until then, and it has remained unparalleled till now.

Hall had a relatively large staff in D.N.I. but he worked personally with every one of his men. He invigorated them and drew from them loyalties and sacrificial work. He was usually all over the place, supervising the breaking of German codes here, the surveillance of Irish spies there, and extending his interest to the land war in Europe where one of his scoops enabled the French to win the decisive battle of Verdun.

The overwhelming influence of chiefs like Hall on the intelligence service was pointed up by Colonel Walther Nicolai, one of Hall's opposite numbers as chief of German Military Intelligence during World War I. When I met him in 1934, he was an aging and broken man. Yet in his own days, Nicolai, too, had the makings of a great secret service chief. If he was to gain nothing but the disappointments of an indifferent career, it was only because the importance of his work and his own personal brilliance were not recognized by his superiors.

Frustrated in his own ambitions, Nicolai wrote in a melancholy mood of the role a good intelligence chief is supposed to play within the organization. He regarded the chief as the fulcrum of the organization, the sole person who really matters. "The intelligence service is a service for gentlemen. It breaks down when it is entrusted to others. The chief must, in every respect, stand head and shoulders above his agents. Or else, it is not he who rules but his subordinates, with all their inferior characteristics."

A few words might be added about the special responsibilities of the ideal intelligence chief. Enormous power is concentrated in his hands, and he can use it for good or evil, against foreign adversaries or against his own government's leadership. The Soviet leaders realize this danger and do not allow an intelligence chief to stay at the helm for too long. This explains, too, why the life of every chief of the secret service ends by execution in the Soviet Union.

In France, secret service chiefs tried repeatedly to gain dominant influence on domestic affairs and shook the nation to its foundations with their interference. The famous Dreyfus case is the classical example of such mischief. In Germany, too, Admiral Canaris turned on Hitler and joined a conspiracy against the man he was expected to serve without qualification.

Rebellions and ambitions of this type are unthinkable in a democracy, yet even it must be on the guard against such possibilities. This is why Hanson W. Baldwin, military editor of the New York *Times*, suggested that the director of intelligence should be a civilian who could be trusted implicitly to recognize this basic responsibility of his position. "Military personnel," he wrote, "are rarely suited by training for the collection or evaluation of strategic or national intelligence; some will be needed, but they must be men of particular talents; and they must rid themselves of departmental, or service, loyalties and acquire a higher loyalty to the national good. Above all, they ought to be strictly subordinate to the civilian director. The director should be a man of broad knowledge and intellectual attainments, thoroughly in accord with democracy."

The Rank and File

In the military branches, persons engaged in intelligence activity are usually called intelligence officers, and they are generally commissioned officers. Civilians of comparable position in the hierarchy are called intelligence specialists. Others constitute the rank and file of intelligence personnel: clerical staffs, security agents, and the various technicians needed in the trade for odd chores that range from safecracking to designing fountain-pen guns.

They are professionals who make a career of intelligence work, and amateurs who are used temporarily for *ad hoc* assignments. Whoever and whatever they are, they must possess certain personal characteristics to fit into the pattern. To excel in the war of wits, a man must combine in him such traits and qualifications as intellect and courage, percipience and enterprise, judgment and determination. He must love ideas as much as he loves adventure. He must be a man of erudition, with a good knowledge of history and geography. He must be thoughtful and articulate, with a philosophical turn of mind, a dash of cynicism. He must have technical competence and must be acutely conscious politically. He must be discreet.

He does not have to be physically powerful, and he need not have excelled in sports. Even a bookworm such as T. E. Lawrence, the fabulous Lawrence of Arabia, may surprise the professional in the field when he suddenly blossoms out as a buccaneer, leader of men, and guerrilla fighter. The rank-and-file intelligence officer or intelligence specialist is no adventurer. Above all, he is no spy. A majority of the personnel, even the officers, are chair-borne specialists who are never called upon to go on secret missions. Most of them acquire information simply by taking it from the "incoming" basket on their desks. Their most important assignments may send them no farther than the Library of Congress in Washington or the British Museum in London. Much of the information they are supposed to procure is accessible to anybody who has a library card.

Although the home office is usually their natural habitat, intelligence personnel may be sent into the field to serve as military, naval, and air attachés, or as "camouflaged" members of diplomatic missions. They may disguise their association with the secret service, but that is usually as far as disguise goes.

The function of the intelligence officer is the acquisition of information from legitimately accessible sources. Intelligence officers collate the reports that agents and informants send in and assign them to their appropriate dossiers. They write reports and so-called intelligence summaries, and they prepare position papers and estimates of situations under study, using files and libraries as the source of their information.

The intelligence specialist is essentially a bureaucrat who keeps office hours, attending to his duties during the working day and to his private affairs afterward. Once he is moved beyond this strictly circumscribed routine of activity and into the adventure of secret intelligence, he is no longer an intelligence officer or specialist but becomes a spy. This is an important distinction, but one that is not always recognized. In Britain, Reginald Hall was an intelligence officer, while Robert Baden-Powell, founder of the Boy Scout movement, was a professional spy. Both were among the greatest in their respective fields.

Women in Intelligence

Although intelligence is widely regarded as a man's world, there are many women engaged in its activities. They are employed as secretaries, occasionally as analysts, and more rarely as specialists, although there are fields in which a woman is superior to a man.

In Britain, two woman rose to the highest rank in intelligence—Gertrude Bell and Freya Stark. Miss Bell, a remarkable woman of considerable drive and enormous erudition, was responsible for the establishment of Iraq as an independent kingdom with the Hashemite prince Faisal as its head. Though she may not be as well known as T. E. Lawrence, she was equally as effective as Lawrence in the disintegration of Ottoman rule in Arabia. Miss Freya Stark also made Arabia her specialty and continued to work there after Gertrude Bell died.

We have already seen in the example of the brilliant Emmy Rado how effective women can be in American intelligence, and it may be said that, although women are numerically inferior to men in intelligence work, in every other respect they are their equals.

There is a tendency, however, to restrict women in intelligence activity and to confine them to the lower echelons. Hitler in particular had an extremely low opinion of women in intelligence and prevented their employment on higher echelons in his services. This was probably due to a painful experience he had with certain ladies, employed in the German High Comand, who were exposed one day as espionage agents for Poland. Because of the security risk, the German High Command made it a practice to employ as secretaries only the daughters of officers. However, in 1934, an intrepid and handsome Polish secret agent, Captain George Sosnovski, succeeded in enlisting two confidential secretaries working in the German High Command, both daughters of generals. He bribed them with his love in the old-fashioned romantic manner and got all the information he wanted from them.

In Washington, during the twenties, Japanese intelligence agents tried to obtain information by dating confidential secretaries of the U.S. Navy Department. However, experience shows that despite such incidents the great majority of women employed in intelligence work are as trustworthy and as security conscious as men. In fact, Colonel Nicolai expressed the view that they are, in the final analysis, even more discreet than men and pointed out that in the history of intelligence more men had been ensnarled by ladies than the other way round. Even fiction uses the beautiful woman to trap the male operator, but it ignores as unlikely the handsome male decoy.

Nicolai also held that the greatest German intelligence specialist of all time was a woman rather than a man. She was Elsbeth Schragmüller, a doctor of philosophy, a teacher in private life who attained fame in the lore of intelligence as the fabulous "Mademoiselle Docteur." Although she dealt with secret agents she was in fact an intelligence specialist who never worked in the field. Despite her achievements—and we shall see in due course that they were considerable—she was the exception to the rule that limits the employment of women in most of the intelligence services throughout the world.

The Intelligence Auxiliary

Aside from its professional practitioners, intelligence draws its personnel from the vast reservoir of the people at large. Among those who serve on an *ad hoc* basis journalists traditionally play an exceptional role, if only because they are themselves professional collectors of information. This is recognized by the Communists who suspect journalists as much if not more than they fear intelligence officers. In fact, Communist governments regard all Western newspapermen as *de facto* espionage agents.

Commenting on the arrest of Associated Press correspondent William N. Oatis in Prague in 1951, on charges of espionage, his colleague Dana Adams Schmidt of the New York *Times*, remarked: "Even though the prosecution disposed of every advantage and the defense of none, nothing was brought out at the trial that could, by Western standards, be called espionage. By those standards, Oatis was a perfectly legitimate, hard-working and enterprising reporter . . . But the Communists' conception of information and of the functions of newspapermen is different from ours. The idea that news might have value other than as propaganda is foreign to them. The only legitimately publishable information, so far as they are concerned, is that which comes from official sources. Anything else is espionage."

Frequently newsmen succeed better in procuring, evaluating, and transmitting information than professional intelligence people. A few days after Pearl Harbor, Raymond Clapper, the late columnist of the Scripps-Howard newspapers, commented with wry pride that a comparable debacle could not have happened in any self-respecting newspaper office in America. No newspaper, he said, could survive a similar blow to its prestige and certainly none could afford to be scooped on this scale by its competitors.

The occasional superiority of journalistic investigation over the largely bureaucratic methods of the intelligence services was demonstrated, for example, in 1912 when an enterprising Czech reporter named Egon Erwin Kisch discovered a major military secret which the intelligence services did not learn until it was too late. Kisch ascertained that the famous Skoda armament works in Pilsen had ordered hydraulic presses and tools of unusually large dimensions not justified by anything the plant appeared to be manufacturing at the time. Inquiry revealed that the Skoda target range was being enlarged. In the Hotel Waldek, Kisch encountered a group of artillery engineers. By talking to them and to a few workers, Kisch established that Skoda was making for Germany mobile howitzers of 30.5 mm. caliber. Kisch wrote up his discovery in a Prague newspaper, but his exposé failed to alert the interested intelligence services.

Then in the summer of 1914, these howitzers appeared suddenly in front of Belgium's "impregnable" system of fortifications and reduced them to rubble in no time. The Belgian High Command, as well as the Allied intelligence services, described these howitzers as Germany's new secret weapon "whose existence had been effectively concealed from the outside world."

The landing of the Anglo-French divisions in Salonika in October, 1915, came as a complete surprise to the Central powers. The move was described as "one of the best kept secrets of the [first] World War." Yet news of the impending landing was telegraphed by a Swiss newspaperman to his paper and the report was forwarded to Austrian intelligence headquarters in Vienna. What became of it when it reached the classified cemetery of intelligence nobody knows.

There is a great similarity between the work of intelligence services and newspaper offices, as was pointed out by General Donovan. There is, consequently, an inevitable relationship between bona fide working correspondents and diplomatic and intelligence personnel. The entries in Ambassador Dodd's diary show how close this relationship can be. It was a familiar sight during Hitler's occupation of the Rhineland, during the war in Ethiopia, and the Spanish civil war, as it is today, to see diplomats and intelligence officers frequenting the quarters of the press to "get the dope," although they have better facilities and the paraphernalia of "official espionage" for obtaining it themselves.

Even in the speed of transmission of information, newspapers frequently beat government agencies. The first report on Stalin's fatal illness, in March, 1953, did not go to the State Department. It went first to the Associated Press. It was from the AP's diplomatic correspondent in Washington that the responsible official in the State Department received the first news of this momentous event. The official asked, "How do you know it?"

"Our London monitor picked up the news from Radio Moscow," the correspondent answered.

"Then it must be the real McCoy," the diplomat said.

The news of the Communist invasion of South Korea, on June 25, 1950, reached the New York *Herald-Tribune* about an hour before it arrived at the State Department, and hours before it reached the Pentagon. This is remarkable, if only because the average editorial office operates with standard machinery that is inferior to the vast apparatus maintained by the intelligence services of the major powers. The ordinary foreign correspondent cannot, in his own interest, use some of the unusual gimmicks which should be normally available to good intelligence operatives.

Foreign correspondents have frequently served as unofficial intelligence agents, in the majority of cases for their own governments, but sometimes for alien regimes. Henri de Blowitz, fabulous correspondent of the London *Times*, provided much of the information Disraeli needed during the Congress of Berlin in 1878, and supplied the intelligence which enabled Britain to buy into the Suez Canal in 1875, a move that marked the beginning of British penetration of Egypt. But in 1935, a prominent British editor delivered classified information to the German Ambassador in London. It proved decisive in Hitler's efforts to forestall British opposition to the Nazis' occupation of the Rhineland. Documents which came to light after World War II revealed the existence of numerous such journalistic agents working for Germany, Italy, and Japan against their own countries, especially in Britain and France.

The extreme example of mixing journalism and intelligence is the Tass news agency of the Soviet Union, which is merely a branch of the Soviet intelligence service. If the value of a news agency is measured by the number of words printed from its correspondents' reports, then Tass is virtually useless. The total number of words which get into the Soviet press from dispatches cabled by a huge corps of Tass correspondents abroad is less in a whole month than the cables printed from a single special correspondent of the New York *Times* in one week. Yet if its value is measured in the number of words cabled to the home office, Tass is probably the most valuable news agency of them all.

In the United States, Tass maintains offices in New York and Washington. It has a number of editors and correspondents at both places, most of them Americans. While these men and women are recognized as functionaries of the greater Soviet intelligence apparatus, they have access nevertheless to the sessions of Congress, the press conferences of the White House, Congressional hearings, all the public functions of the American government. They are on the mailing lists of government agencies and private institutions, and receive releases on important developments which are actually confidential up to the release date. By cabling them to Moscow, Tass correspondents enable the Soviet government to find out about these events even before the American people learn of them.

When in 1945 the U.S. Government released the detailed Smyth Report on the development of the atomic bomb, every word of the lengthy report was cabled promptly by the Washington bureau of Tass to Moscow, but not a word of it appeared in the Soviet press. A Tass correspondent named Zheveynov was involved in the Canadian espionage ring, working under the cover name of "Martin." Tass correspondents in The Hague, Stockholm, and Canberra were found to be active operatives of the Soviet intelligence network.

It is important to distinguish between the bona fide newspaperman, who may perform occasional services to his country's intelligence organization as an *ad hoc* informant, and the intelligence agent who masquerades as a newspaperman. This distinction is acute in American minds, but it is somewhat hazy in the minds of Europeans and Asians. Americans, even those in the highest places, respect the basic integrity of the journalist and refrain from compromising or embarrassing him by drawing him into such extraneous functions. In Europe, however, newspapermen frequently double as full-time intelligence agents and sometimes operate as mercenary spies. British correspondents, for example, usually have a not too tenuous connection with the British secret service, or at least with the Political Intelligence Division of the Foreign Office. The journalistic front for intelligence work was used widely by Germany during the 1930's, by Italy and Japan, and by virtually every European country except the Scandinavian lands, which make the same distinction between journalism and intelligence work as do the Americans.

In addition to journalists, the auxiliary force of intelligence includes businessmen and industrialists, members of the academic professions, explorers and travelers, and engineers who may from time to time place information at the disposal of the intelligence services without actually belonging to any organization of this kind.

In times of emergency, such *ad hoc* informants are integrated into standing intelligence organizations whose wartime personnel is usually made up of "amateurs." An important secret branch of the U.S. Office of Naval Intelligence was thus headed by an officer who used to sell refrigerators abroad before the war. Most of his officers were newspapermen, college professors, and lawyers. The chief researcher of the branch was a stranger who used to make a living by selling stamps in a foreign country.

None of the British intelligence officers with whom I came into contact during World War II was a "professional." Some were former foreign correspondents, others were Oxford dons, still others were junior executives of various business enterprises. The exceptional effectiveness of American and British intelligence during World War II proves that rank amateurs can be as efficient in intelligence as the professional; it shows further that intelligence is by no means at its best when it is conducted by a cloistered caste—what General Smith called "a corps of professional intelligence officers"—but rather by a combination of highly trained professionals and enterprising and qualified amateurs.

The Education of Intelligence Operatives

The good intelligence officer, male or female, is not conjured up by any hocus pocus and is not molded by special calisthenics. He is the product of the educational system of his country. That Britain has produced some exceptional intelligence officers is probably a result of an educational system that stimulates the intellectual skills needed for this particular job. A young man who graduates from Cambridge or Oxford is almost ready to step immediately into an intelligence job, because of the emphasis those universities place on the humanities, on history, geography, and foreign languages.

This is why men like T. E. Lawrence or Peter Churchill or F. F. E. Yeo-Thomas were able to move directly from their peacetime specialties, in which they excelled, to wartime intelligence work in which they also excelled. There was a direct link between their education and the requirements of the secret service. Because of this, British intelligence has an atmosphere of culture and erudition, a civilized aura of intellectual accomplishment. I was frequently baffled by the style of British intelligence reports until I learned that they were composed by some of Britain's most gifted writers.

I recall in particular a magnificent report on Iran spiked with quotations from Homer, Sir H. M. Elliott, and Hamdallah Mustaufi, a noted Persian traveler who died in 1349.

Yet the report was as topical as that morning's newspaper and as informative as an intelligence report must be. It was written by a young man called Fitzroy Maclean, whose name I then heard for the first time, and who later became world-famous as the brigadier who represented Winston Churchill at Marshal Tito's headquarters in the mountains of Yugoslavia.

During the last war, in addition to writing such erudite reports, Maclean also organized the kidnaping of General Fazlallah Zahedi of Iran, who in 1953 became that country's premier, but who in 1943 had been conspiring to aid the Nazis. Before that Maclean had surveyed a good deal of the Soviet Union, covering a part of it on foot.

In the life of Fitzroy Maclean, as in the lives of Britain's most intrepid intelligence officers, there is that combination of Etonian erudition and the Cameron Highlander, of Cambridge and Oxford and the Coldstream Guard. Maclean was a graduate of Eton and Cambridge and had served in the Cameron Highlanders and in the Foreign Service. He learned the intelligence trade at first hand in Whitehall and Mayfair, Paris, and Moscow. Combining within himself elements of brain and brawn, he proved in the end to be good both as a writer of lucid intelligence reports and as a combatant on the secret front behind the enemy's lines.

By presenting these British examples, I do not mean to imply that only Britons excel in this field. The recent history of the French Secret Service shows that it had men who were the peers of Baden-Powell and Maclean, men like the late Jean Moulin, a provincial politician who commanded the French underground until his death at the Gestapo's hands in 1943, and the "Professor," Pierre Brossolette, and Colonel André Pierre Serot, a great intelligence officer who was killed by terrorists in Palestine at the side of Count Folke Bernadotte. I have known French intelligence officers of considerable stature, but I found that there was a wide gulf separating the "civilians" from the "military," and that the professionals were not particularly anxious to improve the efficiency of the brilliant amateurs.

Nor do I mean to say that Americans cannot graduate from their schools into intelligence work. However, in the United States it is often necessary to supplement formal education with some private extracurricular work. The American undergraduate must select a specialty that will come in handy later in an intelligence career, while such specialties are normally suggested by the special curricula of English institutions.

In intelligence work, on the level of the specialists, thorough familiarity with *specific* subjects is essential. It may be that a knowledge of a certain language is required. It may be archeology. It may be the geography of a foreign country, or some aspects of its culture. It may be the geology of remote regions. As we have noted, during the last war, an American intelligence agency was asked to supply information on the qualities of the soil of North Africa so that the boots of GI's could be adapted to that particular ground. This was one minute detail of the diverse information required of intelligence in the preparation for the North African landings in 1942.

Spectacular successes were scored by rank amateurs who served as intelligence officers during the Second World War. An American newspaper correspondent excelled in the interrogation of German U-boat men. A Wall Street banker charted the waters around the Pacific islands that were chosen as stepping stones in the slow conquest of Japan. They put to use skills and knowledge that they had acquired earlier in civilian pursuits. Intelligence often draws on the vast reservoir of a nation's civilian specialists, while it maintains only a relatively small corps of professional intelligence officers.

During World War II, the Office of Strategic Services included among the 12,000 people working for it a college president, presidents of large corporations, a gentleman jockey, a professional wrestler, an African big-game hunter, a missionary from Thailand, a Czarist general, and a Hollywood stunt man known as "the Human Fly."

The closest approach in the United States to a corps of professional intelligence officers was the small group of the Army General Staff assigned to military attaché duty abroad. A few of them achieved a modicum of fame, including Colonel Truman Smith, who became a highly respected, but by no means infallible, authority on Germany, and Colonel (later Brigadier General) Philip Faymonville, who came to be known widely as an equally controversial expert on the Soviet Union. There were a few such specialists in the U.S. Navy and the Marine Corps, including Ellis M. Zacharias, who began his distinguished career in intelligence as a language officer asigned to Japan.

According to General Walter Bedell Smith, a former director of the Central Intelligence Agency, the United States is now building its own corps of professional intelligence officers. I have known some of the officers and specialists who became the first members of the professional corps when it was decided that one be established at long last in the United

States. They are what the lingo of Sing Sing calls "lifers," in the service probably for the rest of their lives. They are without exception men of superior endowments. With them a new kind of "professional" was introduced into the field of intelligence—the specialist who combines all that is best in his British and French colleagues with the traits developed by the American brand of democracy, the enterprise, technological aptitude, adaptability, and ingenuity that is native to most Americans. There is still much of the old frontier spirit in these men. They combine a worldly informality with vast erudition and seem, indeed, to justify General Smith's opinion that Americans now make "the world's best professional intelligence officers."

"What enables the wise sovereign and the good general to strike and conquer, and achieve things beyond the reach of ordinary men, is foreknowledge." This dictum was expressed by Sun Tsŭ, a Chinese military scientist, in a textbook on tactics still highly regarded today. It was written five hundred years before Christ, and today, almost twenty-five hundred years later, the principle still can spell victory or defeat. In this atomic age it could mean the difference between survival and extinction.

Intelligence Service and the People at Large

Whenever power appears shrouded in secrecy we are inclined to view it with a certain amount of awe. The intelligence service is a mysterious power to the outsider, who is prepared to believe that its mystery conceals not so much national secrets and military strength as roguery, vice, and intrigue. A proper intelligence system, Hanson W. Baldwin wrote, is an institution with great potentialities for both good and evil. "It must utilize all men and all methods; it is amoral and cynical; it traffics with traitors and heroes; it bribes and corrupts; it kidnaps; sometimes, in war, it kills; it holds the power of life and death; it utilizes the grandest and the lowest passions; it harnesses in the same team the loftiest patriotism and the basest cupidity; it justifies the means by the ends."

He added: "Such an organization, of tremendous importance and terrible power, must obviously be blueprinted with care and maintained in a framework flexible enough to permit its efficient functioning, but not broad enough to develop as a danger to the democracy it must serve."

111

Those of us who have worked within an intelligence organization, and those who have participated in its clandestine work, can testify that this is the exact blueprint of the intelligence systems in countries like Britain and the United States. There is inevitably melodrama in the activity, because the very nature of secrecy breeds it; but the greater part of the activity is the uninspiring routine work that goes on behind the locked doors.

I recall my own first days in intelligence most vividly, since I approached my new profession with a great deal of romantic anticipation. I entered the inner sanctum with the melodramatic designation "Secret Agent." Even my hiring had elements of mystery. I had to use an alias during the negotiations, and my first meetings were arranged with circumspect secrecy.

My first day in intelligence served to develop in me a sense of mystery. I had no permanent pass as yet and was given a temporary slip that expired at 4:30 P.M. I had worked to a late hour, and when I was ready to leave my office building in Washington I was taken by a guard to the Provost Marshal to be checked out. A phone call was put through to my new chief to identify me, but, when my name was mentioned on the telephone, my chief said bluntly, "Never heard of the man!"

I was in a pickle. I was trying to explain my presence in the building in some excitement, when the door opened; my chief walked in and checked me out. "I'm sorry," he said. "Regulations! Your name is not supposed to be mentioned on the telephone."

Once I settled down to the routine, I still respected the importance of secrecy, but I no longer regarded my work as romantic or melodramatic. It was little different from work in a newspaper office where I had worked before, and where information is also collected for a purpose. There were the usual files and reference books, and there were the dispatches of the "correspondents" from their posts. My job was to collate them, to piece them together, to file them for future reference, and to prepare from them composite pictures which the policy makers, planners, and commanders could use when needed.

Once in a while a colleague from a neighboring office would come in to say good-by. He might be going on a secret mission—to the Philippines, then occupied by the Japanese; to Sicily, which was to be invaded; or to some European city, to contact a mysterious go-between. Such episodes never

112

failed to bring home to me some special melodrama about the activity. These men had a job to do and they did it in the most impersonal fashion.

The Citizen's Role

In view of the important role the civilian specialist—indeed, the informed citizen—plays in the work of intelligence, the activity opens up and becomes of direct interest to persons in all walks of life. It is, therefore, important to desecretize the secret service and introduce it to the citizenry, somewhat in the manner in which warships are thrown open for public inspection on Navy Day.

In a democracy where the secret service has its basic roots in the people of the country, damage ensues from attempts to isolate the service, cloak it in impenetrable mystery, and thus separate it from the people on whom it depends in emergencies. In a country such as the United States there is a dual responsibility that converges in intelligence. Those attached to it should familiarize the people with the purposes, importance, and need for the secret service, and conversely the people should interest themselves in the work of their intelligence service, to be available when needed.

In the United States, neither responsibility is properly understood. The authorities do little to acquaint the people with the secret service, unlike J. Edgar Hoover whose policy is to establish the Federal Bureau of Investigation firmly in the popular imagination. The close relationship between the people at large and the FBI has yielded enormous dividends for both. But no such collaboration exists between the intelligence services of the government and the intelligent people of the nation.

The extreme of this attitude was expressed by General George C. Marshall during his appearance before a Congressional committee which, among other things, discussed intelligence. General Marshall bemoaned a tendency to discuss intelligence too widely in the United States and praised the secrecy that surrounds the activity in Britain where, he said not even the name of the organization is known to the public.

In may be true that the exact designation of the British secret service is concealed, even though Britain rarely hesitates to label intelligence services as such. I was frequently baffled when, while abroad, I encountered British officials whose doorplates described them openly, in such sensitive areas as Egypt, Palestine, and the Sudan, as Intelligence Officers. And I was amazed by the frankness with which they discussed their jobs with me, a stranger and an outsider. "My dear fellow," an intelligence officer once told me in Khartoum, "if you don't know what I'm doing and don't know where to find me, how on earth can I expect you to come to me when you have a bit of information you think I ought to know about?" Obviously, however, no iceberg is wholly above water.

In Britain, MI, which is the Military Intelligence branch of the War Department, is as popular as the FBI in the United States, partly because the section called MI-5 is in charge of the romantic job of counterintelligence and counterespionage. But much is known about MI in general, and the director of MI-5, Sir Percy Sillitoe, even disclosed the exact location of his office in his biography in *Who's Who*. "War Office, Room 505," he wrote without undue security pangs, for "Room 505" is famous throughout Britain, a romantic synonym for excellent intelligence work.

Contrary to the impression that General Marshall tried to convey, it is the policy of the British government to publicize and popularize certain intelligence activities. This policy evolved from the realization that the government needs the close cooperation of the public to do a thorough and successful job of intelligence. A public kept in ignorance of the existence, methods, and needs of the intelligence service cannot be expected to provide the support it requires.

This deliberate effort to acquaint the people at large with the delicate work of intelligence extends to all of its branches, military as well as political, positive as well as negative. The British authorities not only encourage outstanding secret agents to publish their exploits for popular consumption, they not only collaborate with writers who prepare works on intelligence, they actually promote such books, including spy fiction. The outstanding example was that of the late Alfred Duff Cooper (Lord Norwich), who at one time served in high positions in the British secret service. He told about his career in a brilliant book of memoirs, later expanding the material into a novel.

Sir (later Lord) Robert Vansittart was often described as a former chief of Britain's top-echelon secret service, one of those glamorous and brilliant "chiefs" we have met before. He regarded it as a part of his job to educate the greatest possible number of people to the intricacies of intelligence work. He used a pseudonym in writing spy fiction and also

114

the scenario of a motion picture dealing with the adventures of certain spies. Motion-picture firms are encouraged by Britain's highest intelligence authorities to prepare such movies as will serve to help familiarize the public with one of their most essential government agencies.

If such a policy exists in the United States, or if anything is being done to educate the people on this score, I am not aware of it. On the contrary, I think there is a deliberate effort to mask the secret service and keep it cloaked from the public view. After the Second World War, two books appeared dealing with the theories of strategic intelligence and secret intelligence. They represented excellent beginnings of a high-level education program, but the practice was abandoned abruptly and completely. Mr. Allen W. Dulles, present head of CIA, permitted the publication of his remarkable exploits in Switzerland during the war, and since that time he has written a book on Germany's underground activities. He has also written a number of fascinating book reviews of other peoples' work, all revealing his exceptional skill in this field.

The efficiency of an intelligence service depends on a number of things: the government's attitude toward the activity and the service's place in the governmental table of organization, the so-called intelligence doctrine of the organization, the methods employed, and the tools used.

In the final analysis, however, its efficiency is dependent upon the men and women who make up the service. The secret service is a human organization; it represents a high form of intellectual activity. In the past society has been inclined to assign the solution of national problems to soldiers, a tendency prompting Georges Clemenceau to warn that war is too serious a matter to be entrusted to generals. And, probably, peace is far too precious to be entrusted to the diplomats and the politicians alone.

PART II

Espionage

The Art of Espionage

One spring day during the late war, a young officer came into my room in Tempo-L, the long temporary building that housed the secret branches of Naval Intelligence in Washington, to bid me good-by. He was a boisterous little Italian with enormous shoulders and bulging biceps, and a huge round head in which two laughing eyes flashed under bushy eyebrows. He often came over from his office a few doors away to discuss the war and tell stories whose punch lines, shouted in ribald Italian, brought forth the most appreciative guffaws.

Now he seemed solemn and, while his eyes still shone, they had a different luster. This office was hardly a place for histrionics. There was nothing romantic in our bare environment—the desks, the typewriters, the maps on the wall, and the huge safe with its combination locks. But as I stood up behind my desk to bid him good-by and bon voyage his solemnity impressed me deeply. He stretched out his hand, and I pressed it a bit more firmly and a little longer than usual.

For this man was about to go out into the field, to leave behind his desk job in intelligence, to become an espionage agent behind enemy lines. For a moment or two, I came to *feel* something of the great difference between intelligence work and espionage.

Intelligence on the whole, despite its elaborate secrecy and occasional drama, is transacted above ground. Espionage is carried out below ground, a clandestine operation. But behind the melodrama espionage has as exact a scientific and moral structure as intelligence. Moreover, it possesses its own dignity, often not apparent in the methods it is forced to employ, for espionage, like intelligence, is a legitimate and essential function of every government that is aware of its responsibilities. It is justified by the fact that all nations conceal important phases of their activities, and it is necessitated by their urgent need to acquire information about things concealed which may influence or threaten their peace and security.

Nations go to extreme lengths to conceal their affairs. They have made secrecy into a fetish and an institution and have set up elaborate machinery to protect their secrets. They have enacted severe laws to safeguard them. The United States has a complicated system of espionage laws and security regulations. Britain depends upon its Official Secrets Act of 1889, which punishes an official for communication of information concerning the military and naval affairs of Her Majesty to any unauthorized person. An article of the Soviet Constitution describes the keeping of secrets as "the fundamental duty" of every citizen, and calls the betrayal of secrets "one of the most heinous crimes." An American judge recently called the betrayal of our atomic secrets "worse than murder." Nations rate their secrets equivalent to human life and frequently punish the betrayers of highly classified information with death.

Different nations have different attitudes toward secrecy, the extreme viewpoint being that of the Soviet Union, where even production figures of industries manufacturing consumer goods are concealed. The Soviet Union regards concealment, as Andrei Y. Vishinsky stated in a speech before the United Nations, as her first line of defense.

Secrecy may conceal strength or weakness, the design of a new weapon or the location of the plant where it is manufactured. It may conceal the position of a single military unit in a tactical situation or the strategic plans of an entire army. Naturally, a potentially aggressive nation must obscure its intention of making war until it has marshaled its forces and is ready to strike.

There are today all kinds of secrets, little secrets and big secrets, state secrets and military secrets, official secrets and private secrets. Secrecy has always been recognized as one of the main conditions of success in war, as a highly effective form of diplomacy, as a necessary phase of private enterprise, and as an expedient even in simple, everyday human relations.

The very fact that concealment exists, and that it is maintained for the advantage of one side, makes it imperative that the opposition penetrate the secrets of other countries. This is the fundamental task of espionage.

Some years ago, in England, I discussed the moral aspect of espionage with Captain Franz von Rintelen, one of the most successful German spies of the First World War. Rintelen said: "Each country is entitled to its secrets and is at

117

the same time duty bound to protect them. By the same token, each country is entitled to find out the secrets of other countries. You have to approach espionage in the spirit in which Darwin regarded vivisection. It is justifiable for real investigation, but not for mere damnable and detestable curiosity." He then added, "There is really nothing base about espionage. It is as much part of human nature as is the keeping of secrets."

This element of secrecy is responsible for the distinction we must make between intelligence proper and espionage. A clear understanding of this distinction is important for a proper appreciation of the activity that we are about to outline in detail.

What Is Espionage?

Espionage is that part of the total intelligence effort that is designed for the surreptitious inspection of the activities of foreign countries, to ascertain their strength and movements, and to communicate such intelligence to the proper authorities. It is the effort to discover by concealed methods the guarded secrets of others. Because of the circumstances and the difficulties of espionage, it is an autonomous function but, in the final analysis, still an integral part of the over-all scheme of intelligence.

Espionage, like intelligence, moves on different levels. We distinguish between strategic espionage, in which the surreptitious search is for important stakes, and tactical espionage, in which the objective is some secret of limited or localized importance.

In addition, there are political espionage and military espionage, whose respective designations indicate the nature of the activity. There is, too, industrial espionage, a widespread and highly developed activity practiced both in peace and war, by governments as well as by private enterprises.

At the top, there is a distinction between positive espionage, which is conducted aggressively to acquire the secrets of foreign countries, and negative espionage, or counterespionage, which is designed to protect one's own secrets and to apprehend those who try to penetrate them for the benefit of a foreign power.

Among the practitioners of espionage, operatives are usually grouped together under the generic and somewhat derogatory designation of spies. But there are all kinds of spies. Persons who are engaged in direct espionage, who go out under false pretense and disguise their identities in order to procure secret information, are called secret agents or operatives. In this category are so-called resident agents, who reside permanently in certain locations and operate on a permanent or long-range basis. Resident agents may be assigned to general espionage work, picking up whatever incidental information they can, or carrying out specific tasks such as watching trains, roads, or coasts. There are also so-called transient agents who go on *ad hoc* missions, hit or miss, hit and run.

In addition, there are couriers, whose job is the maintenance of liaison with agents in the field. They do not engage in espionage directly but merely relay the information procured by the operatives. Also there are a number of technicians and specialists essential to the system, such as clandestine radio operators, cryptographers, and secret-ink chemists. Another group of specialists comprises the authenticators, who forge documents and prepare or manufacture the other paraphernalia a spy needs in action. And there are the so-called double-agents, who work for two masters simultaneously, sometimes with the knowledge of at least one of the two employers. There are the agents provocateurs, whose job is to infiltrate the adversary's espionage organization, to compromise it or force it into the open, to expose its methods and personnel.

There are spies engaged solely in recruiting, who work like Hollywood talent scouts, trying to round up likely prospects for use in the net. There are the "cut-outs," or go-betweens, who, like couriers, do not engage in espionage themselves but form a link between two spies, or between a spy and a higher-up whose identity is usually concealed from the operative. In addition, there are so-called "mail-drops," or "letterboxes," who serve merely as relaying points in the communications system of espionage, often innocent-appearing persons not even remotely suspected of any illicit activity. They are usually located in neutral countries to receive communications from the operatives and in turn forward it to the headquarters of the espionage organization.

There are free-lance spies who work for the highest bidder on a professional and mercenary basis, and also "patriot" spies who engage in this dangerous pastime as a service to their countries, frequently without recompense, moral or material.

In negative espionage, operatives are called special agents

119

(as in the FBI) or investigators (as, for example, in Naval Intelligence). Popularly they are called "gumshoes" or "shoeflies." Television and radio script-writers prefer to call them counterspies. Also in negative espionage there are the informers, whose job it is to supply information about their own fellow operatives, much in the manner in which stoolpigeons squeal on their fellow criminals.

Espionage has a more complex hierarchy than intelligence, chiefly because the activity is essentially more complex and its functions are more specialized. At the top is what may be called the spymaster, the head of the espionage organization or of that branch of an intelligence service that specializes in espionage. His proper title is usually director.

Under him are the resident directors, who conduct the business of the fixed, long-term, foreign branches of the espionage organization.

Then come the so-called collectors, who procure secret information from a great variety of sources.

Below them are the transmitters whose job is the forwarding of information acquired by the collectors.

Even lower in the hierarchy are the couriers who act as messengers. Then come the drops and cut-outs who relay information from collectors in the field to headquarters, maintain contact between the various echelons, and act as blinds for active agents.

And, by themselves in a separate category, are the specialists. They are the expert saboteurs, whose activities will be discussed in another section of this book.

What, then, is the difference between an intelligence specialist and an espionage agent?

The intelligence specialist is engaged comprehensively in the collection, evaluation, and dissemination of information—all kinds of information—most of which comes from overt and accessible sources. He performs a highly intellectual function in the integration of seemingly unrelated data. He is not required to masquerade, and although his activities are protected by considerable secrecy he is still able to retain his true identity.

The espionage agent is engaged exclusively in the procurement of secret information, performing a function that is but a part—often a small though extremely important part—of the total intelligence effort. Unlike the intelligence specialist, he is required to conceal his identity, the exact nature of his mission, and his lines of communications, by assuming a false identity and by applying airtight secrecy to his activities.

thus, training and indoctrination of personnel, and the ex-

The Espionage Organization

In Britain, the most secret phase of the intelligence service,
concerned with the procurement of secret information and
clandestine operations, is called special intelligence, the word
"special" being frequently employed to designate surreptitious
intelligence. During the war, Britain called its major espionage organization "Special Operations Executive," and even
this designation was further protected. It was housed in
Baker Street, not far from Sherlock Holmes's mythical abode,
in a building called Norgeby House. The plaque on the
building identified the agency as "Inter-Services Research
Bureau." Members of the organization referred to it as the
"Old Firm."

In the United States, the most elaborate espionage organization maintained prior to the establishment of the Central
Intelligence Agency was the Office of Strategic Services, the
word "strategic" being used to camouflage the true activity
of the agency. Its headquarters was openly designated, but it
maintained a number of hide-outs for the pursuit of its secret
business. Today, espionage activities are separated from the
headquarters of CIA, whose address is available to all in the
Washington telephone directory. But, while the location of
its central headquarters is common knowledge, only the initiated know the location of its special branches.

Only a relatively small part of the espionage business is
conducted at headquarters, most of it being transacted in the
field. Headquarters personnel, in charge of preparing missions, selecting targets, and directing the activities of agents,
represent a distinct minority, while the great majority of
personnel consists of secret agents working in the field. These
agents may never visit headquarters, may not even know
where it is located. The only direct contact between headquarters and the field is maintained by resident directors and
their aides, who in turn direct the network of agents in their
respective areas.

The headquarters organization of espionage is usually split
into a secret service section and an espionage subsection. The
secret service section is largely a bureaucratic agency charged
with the supervision of all offensive and defensive measures
and with the administrative functions of this activity.

The duties of the espionage subsection embrace the selection, training, and indoctrination of personnel, and the assignment of missions to secret agents in the field. While it examines, analyzes, and verifies incoming reports, it does not usually evaluate them. It is primarily concerned with the forwarding of agent reports to a superior division where they are subsequently evaluated.

How an espionage organization functions in practice may be shown in a historic example—the procurement and transmission of information concerning Germany's impending invasion of the Soviet Union. Hitler had decided to attack the Soviet Union some time in 1940, but the detailed invasion plans were not drawn up until December of that year. Preparations for the execution of the plan, which was given the code name Barbarossa, began at once and, in May, 1941, a definite D-day for the commencement of operations was designated, June 22, 1941. Anti-Nazi elements within the German High Command, whose identity is still unknown, secured this information and decided to communicate it to Soviet authorities.

On June 2, the information was transmitted to a confidant of the anti-Nazi group in Switzerland, who then established contact with a go-between named Schneider, then working for the Soviet espionage apparatus in "Sicily," as Switzerland was called by Soviet agents. The confidant of the anti-Nazi group communicated his information to Schneider, alias Taylor, who in turn submitted it to a professional Soviet spymaster named Rado. The resident director, Rado, then drafted a report and gave it to his transmitter, a clandestine radio operator named Alexander Foote, for immediate transmission to Moscow. The radioman coded the report and radioed it at once. The code consisted of five-figure groups and read in part: "85862 70113 48931 66167 34212 42883 76662 18984." In view of the extreme importance of the message, Rado instructed the radio operator to repeat the message for two full hours to alert the receivers in Moscow to the urgency of the report.

In Moscow the report was picked up and immediately forwarded to a Captain Ivanov who was in charge of the decoding section of the Soviet intelligence office. Ivanov recognized the urgency of the message and set out at once to decipher it. Within half an hour he had the first part of the message decoded. It read:

DORA TO DIRECTOR, VIA TAYLOR. HITLER DEFINITELY FIXED D-DAY OF ATTACK ON THE SOVIET UNION AS JUNE 22.

Ivanov called his superior at once and read to him the decoded part of the message. Then he deciphered the remainder of the report, which read:

HITLER REACHED DECISION TWO DAYS AGO. REPORT ARRIVED HERE VIA DIPLOMATIC COURIER OF SWISS GENERAL STAFF TODAY. WILL CONTINUE 0130. [*signed*] DORA

When the decoding of the message was concluded, Captain Ivanov's superior brought it at once to the attention of the "Director," General Golikov, who in June, 1941 was chief of the Soviet Intelligence Service. General Golikov was attending a meeting of the Red Army General Staff, but he left the conference room to receive the call from his subordinate. He gave instructions that a copy of the decoded signal be sent to the Kremlin and, when it arrived by special messenger, he immediately laid it before the chief of the General Staff.

Forty-eight hours later the same information was transmitted to Moscow by another agent, a high-ranking German official named Arvid Harnack, listed in the Soviet espionage network by the cover name of Coro. Despite this corroboration, and despite the Red Army General Staff's evaluation that the information was accurate, Stalin refused to accept it as bona fide. The machinery of Russia's espionage system had operated with perfection, justifying its existence by acting to preserve that nation in the face of military aggression through the penetration of the secret intentions of another nation. In this respect positive espionage constitutes a defensive action that vindicates its clandestine methods.

Prototype Organization

However specific information may finally be regarded in high quarters, the fact remains that in organization and efficiency the Soviet secret service towers over that of most other nations where espionage is concerned. There is a tendency to regard Soviet espionage as ruthless and sinister. To be sure, some of its activities may be so described. But it would be more profitable for the opponents of the Soviet Union to recognize its system as supremely efficient in organization, attainment, and amorality.

While Western countries like Great Britain, Germany,

123

France, and the United States place greater emphasis on the intelligence phase of the activity, Russia traditionally has emphasized espionage. In no other country's history has espionage played so dominant a role as in Russia's. No country's foreign policy has been as basically determined by its spy system as Russia's has. This was no accident. It was a deliberate design that began with Peter the Great in the seventeenth century and was continued without interruption by both czars and commissars.

During Czarist days, Russian spies succeeded in acquiring Napoleon's plans for the invasion of Russia, and, at the beginning of this century, they penetrated to the entire secret archives of the high Austro-Hungarian General Staff, including its campaign plans against Russia and against its own allies. This tradition was continued in 1941, when Russian spies managed to obtain Hitler's Russian invasion plans, complete to the exact date of his attack. As if to remind the world again of their efficiency, in 1945 Soviet spies procured the atomic secrets of the United States, Britain, and Canada.

There may be deep-seated psychological reasons for British preoccupation with intelligence and Russian preference for espionage. The Englishman's approach to the secret service has always been positive, influenced by his philosophy, character, and political tradition. There was sophistication, cynicism, and ruthlessness in the so-called empire builders, but there was also subtlety, elegance, and a sporting spirit. Frustrated critics of British imperialism from Bossuet to Goebbels, from Napoleon to Hitler, have called England perfidious for her devious ways in foreign affairs, but Tolstoy's characterization of the Englishman was far more accurate. "An Englishman," he made Baron Pfuel say in *War and Peace*, "is self-assured, as being a citizen of the best-organized state in the world, and therefore as an Englishman always knows what he should do and knows that all he does as an Englishman is undoubtedly correct."

Baron Pfuel regarded the Russians as nihilists at heart, but he found that they derived enormous self-assurance, drive, and an impetuous curiosity from this nihilism. Looking skeptically upon the world, Russians have always groped for knowledge, forever suspicious that part of it might escape them. They became insatiably curious and suspicious, and gravitated to espionage like ducks to water.

Virtually the first organization the Bolsheviks restored to the predominance it had attained under the czars was the espionage organization. At first it was tucked away in the military council, where it worked along conventional lines

124

inherited from the Czarist organization, to some extent with its old personnel. But it was soon established as the Fourth Bureau of the Red Army General Staff, where it was assigned new personnel of the generation that had grown up under the Soviet regime. Its methods were revamped and improved. It was lavishly endowed with funds and given a unique autonomy in a state where every function of government is strictly controlled and coordinated. Today, the Intelligence Bureau of the Red Army General Staff must be regarded as the perfect prototype of all agencies in the world dedicated to the conduct of espionage.

Formerly called Fourth Bureau, then renamed Main Intelligence Department, or RU for short, it is one of several agencies that the Soviet Union maintains to satisfy its insatiable curiosity. At the top is the Kremlin's own espionage bureau, called the Confidential Administration of the Communist Party's Central Committee. This is not a collection agency. It is rather the Soviet espionage network's highest organization for the evaluation of espionage reports pouring in from all quarters, the summarizing of their contents, and the delivery of the summaries to the few men in the Kremlin who control the Soviet Union. The agency is headed by a secretary general, who is aided by so-called "specs," or specialists, who possess specific knowledge or special qualifications for evaluation.

The direction of Communist espionage is in the hands of six separate agencies. As we have seen, one is the Fourth Bureau. Another is the Ministry of Foreign Affairs. Still another is the Foreign Department of the M.V.D., the Ministry of Internal Affairs. Fourth is the intelligence section of the Ministry of Foreign Trade. Fifth is the Tass News Agency. The sixth agency is the intelligence apparatus of the Communist Information Bureau, the Cominform, which continues the world-wide espionage activities of the defunct Comintern.

A German journalist named Richard Sorge, one of the foremost operatives of the Soviet network, who was hanged by the Japanese in 1944 for his espionage activities, had occasion to work with every one of these agencies. In his opinion, five of the six were not too efficient but were, as he put it, "somewhat one-sided, and therefore unable to meet the growing demand of the top leadership for comprehensive information."

Such comprehensive information is supplied by the General Staff's Intelligence Department. According to Sorge, it cannot be considered "a narrowly specialized organization whose activities are restricted to military espionage, nor can it be equated with the *Abwehr* of Germany. Pure military espionage is only one of its activities," Sorge wrote. "It engages in the collection of intelligence in the spheres of military affairs in general, military administration, and economics. Reports accumulate there from military attachés serving with embassies overseas, military committees, wartime economic committees, secret intelligence groups, and spy rings. It also handles and studies a great deal of legitimate and semilegitimate material on the military governments, purely military problems, and wartime economies of other nations. Finally, there is a political section within the bureau where incoming information is fashioned into highly competent reports or summarized for top army and party leaders."

Sorge thought that "from the standpoint of technical level and seriousness of purpose, this agency was probably without equal." For all practical purposes, the Red Army's RU is the central intelligence agency of the Soviet Union, not in name, but in actual practice.

The RU is organized into three great strategic regional sections which comprise the entire world geographically, and into several functional sections for the execution of such technical tasks as communications, authentication, cartography, codes, and cipher work. Evaluation, according to Sorge, is the responsibility of the Political Section, while dissemination is handled by another branch.

At the apex of this Intelligence hierarchy is the Director. He is an old and trusted Communist Party member who knows all the top party leaders personally and shares their confidence. He is in close daily contact with them and reports to them weekly when the Kremlin leadership meets for its comprehensive conferences. The Director holds the rank of colonel general in the Red Army. At the time when the atomic secrets of America were procured Colonel General Fyedor Fyedorovich Kuznetsov was Director of Military Intelligence.

Second in command is a Deputy Director, with the rank of major general. He is to a large extent responsible for handling administrative problems. The various sections or desks are headed by Organizers, who hold the rank of major general or colonel in the Red Army. Under them are other members of the hierarchy, whose military ranks range from captain to colonel. Technical personnel and younger aides generally are lieutenants.

In the field, resident directors are in charge of what are called individual "rings." They are assisted by persons who take care of organizational matters and communications respectively. Networks of agents work for them, and a hierarchy exists even among the operatives. Each agent has his own "net," within which he is charged with the supervision of subagents, informants, and communications specialists, the latter called "musicians," since a radio is called a "music box" in Soviet espionage parlance.

Supplying a connection between the Moscow headquarters, called the "Center," and the rings and nets in the field are highly placed cut-outs or go-betweens. Only technical specialists are actually trained at the Center in Moscow, since agents are selected for their preeminence in certain special fields and therefore require no specific training. They are prepared for their missions in informal meetings with the Director and Deputy Director, and receive their assignments from the Organizer in whose area they are to operate.

The recruiting of agents is done primarily by the Cominform, while the selection of personnel for the Center is the task of a special "educational commission," which observes young students during their formative years or their term of compulsory military service and then transfers such men to work in the Center.

Soviet Agents in Action

In the field, the agent's first job is to establish his cover, set up his communications, and then organize his sources. The Soviet espionage organization operates in complete secrecy, far greater than is usual in intelligence proper. Cover names are assigned to all members of the espionage organization, a practice common to all espionage agencies of the world, but carried out to an extraordinary degree by the Soviet agency. Great care is taken that individuals are known only within a very limited circle. In Richard Sorge's Japanese ring, only Sorge knew all the subagents, including such important aides as Hozumi Ozaki, who was his link to Prince Konoye, the Prime Minister of Japan, and Yotoko Miyagi, his contact with General Ugoye. Most of the subagents of the Sorge group met for the first time, and found out about each other, only when they were brought together by the Japanese secret police after their arrest.

It then developed that the Sorge spy ring was organized into two echelons. One was Sorge's own, composed of himself, Max Klausen, who served as his radio operator, Ozaki, Miyaki, and a Yugoslav journalist named Branko de Voukelich. On the second level were twelve subagents, who were also in contact with a great number of informants. Most of the informants did not know that the data they had given, usually during casual or friendly conversations with acquaintances whom they trusted implicitly, actually wound up in the archives of the Fourth Bureau.

Soviet agents in the field are required to establish plausible covers for themselves. When in Japan, Sorge functioned as a foreign correspondent, which is one of the most effective covers. Klausen set himself up in business, and Ozaki worked as a respected journalist.

In Canada, the resident director was Colonel Zabutin, who had the legitimate cover of a military attaché. His Canadian agents used their real occupations as covers while they engaged in espionage on the side. In Switzerland during World War II, the resident director was a partner in a respected firm of cartographers.

Information is acquired through individuals who have either personal knowledge of certain secrets or access to them. The agent in the field begins his operations by gathering around himself a number of subagents from among clandestine party members or trustworthy sympathizers, men and women who in turn have good contacts with persons in government, the armed forces, the press, business, and elsewhere. Either directly or through subagents, the resident director, or the chief agent of a net, then exploits his sources for whatever information can be acquired.

Such sources usually are drawn from eight major groups whose members are in a position to supply valuable information: 1. politicians; 2. diplomats; 3. military, naval, and air personnel; 4. journalists and foreign correspondents; 5. scientists; 6. businessmen; 7. engineers and chemists; and 8. professionals such as writers and artists.

The exploitation of these sources is rarely left to the scouts who discovered them. In 1936, for example, a Soviet agent named Hede Massing appeared in Washington, where she collected a number of informants among the younger government officials. She posed as a German refugee from Nazi persecution and frequented various Washington parties where many young but influential officials congregated. She began by striking up seemingly innocent friendships with some of them. She continued by slowly drawing certain ones of them into the net. Once a prospect was thus caught, Miss Massing handed him over to the agent whose job it was to develop him as a source.

The development of sources is a tedious process that follows a circuitous but carefully plotted route. How sources of vital information are developed was demonstrated in a dramatic fashion in the great Canadian atomic espionage case, which broke in 1945. The most important single source of Colonel Zabutin, the Soviet military attaché, was the informant who gave one of the first tips that the Anglo-American-Canadian combine was building an A-bomb.

When Colonel Zabutin arrived in Ottawa in 1943 to take up his post as the Soviet Union's fully accredited military attaché, he brought along a list of prospective contacts to assist him in the establishment of his spy ring. This list had been prepared for him by the *cadre apparat* of the Comintern espionage organization, that section which keeps, in a central section in Moscow, the roster of all Communists and sympathizers.

Among the suggested contacts was a man named Fred Rose, a member of the Canadian Parliament and of the Labor Progressive Party. Rose was among the first Canadians enlisted by Zabutin to serve as a scout, to develop and recommend individuals who could themselves supply information or who had access to other possible informants.

During a train trip, Rose met an old acquaintance named David Gordon Lunan, a Scotsman by birth, working in the Canada Wartime Information Board.

During the trip, Rose discovered that while Lunan himself had no information of any real value he did have a number of acquaintances who had access to enormously valuable scientific data.

Rose reported Lunan to Zabutin as a promising prospect, and Zabutin in turn assigned Colonel Rogov, one of his aides, to recruit Lunan for the ring.

Shortly after, in March, 1945, Lunan found an unsigned note on his desk in his office inviting him to meet someone at a certain time on a street corner in Ottawa. Lunan kept the appointment and was accosted by a man who introduced himself as "Jan," in fact Colonel Rogov. The colonel openly invited Lunan to join the ring and form a net consisting of himself, as go-between, and three of his acquaintances, Isidor Halperin, Ned Mazerall, and Durnford Smith, all scientists employed by the National Research Council and the research division of the Department of National Defense. They were known to be sympathetic to the U.S.S.R. and to possess much valuable information that the Fourth Bureau was most anxious to acquire.

When Lunan agreed, Rogov assigned to him the cover name "Black," and told him to proceed with the organization of his net and with the subsequent exploitation of his sources.

Lunan began by inviting Smith to lunch in order to sound him out. The two met in a downtown restaurant where, after some preliminary sparring, Lunan broached the question: Would Smith be willing to supply information for the Soviet Union? Smith asked for time to think it over, but at their next meeting agreed to the proposition. After their second meeting Lunan wrote to Rogov: "Badeau [Smith's cover name in the ring] warmed up slowly to my request and remained non-committal until he had checked independently on my *bona fides*. Once satisfied, he promised to cooperate." Durnford Smith, a scientist of impeccable reputation who had access to some of his country's most sensitive information, was in the Soviet net.

Durnford Smith proved to be a most valuable informant, and on March 28, 1945, Lunan reported to Rogov: "Discussing the work of the National Defense Council in general, Badeau informs me that the most secret work at present is on nuclear physics (bombardment of radioactive substances to produce energy). This is more hush-hush than radar and is being carried on at the University of Montreal and at McMaster University at Hamilton. Badeau thinks that government purchase of a radium-producing plant is connected with this research."

This was momentous information, the first the Soviet espionage organization had received about atomic developments in the Western sphere. The information reached Soviet intelligence three months before the first experimental A-bomb was exploded at Alamogordo. But from the time Lunan's report reached Zabutin the Canadian spy ring concentrated on the acquisition of additional information about the A-bomb.

Scattered data was then received from a number of other sources that Zabutin had succeeded in developing in Canada and the United States, and, in time, a major scoop was scored when samples of the uranium used in the A-bomb were acquired through another source.

A British scientist named Allan Nunn May was listed in the Comintern files as a clandestine sympathizer, willing to cooperate. Contacts in London reported to Zabutin that Dr. May was working in Canada on the same project Smith had mentioned to Lunan. May was already in the net, but he was not yet active. Zabutin then instructed another one of his aides, Lieutenant Angelov of the Fourth Bureau, to call on Dr. May at his apartment in Montreal and ask him to obtain samples of uranium 235. A few days later, May again met with Angelov and handed over samples of both uranium 235 and uranium 233, thus making what was probably the greatest single contribution to the Soviet Union's own atomic energy project, equal in importance to the contribution of Dr. Klaus Fuchs, another source, who had been developed in the United States.

This is the most common method of developing and exploiting informants (sources), and it is followed by espionage organizations everywhere. Yet while the methods may be the same everywhere, the results are not. Neither is the zeal, skill, and pitiless efficiency with which they are applied. Where both quantity and quality are concerned, Soviet espionage is far superior to any other in the world. Of the 1,902 espionage cases reported by the New York *Times* between 1917 (when the Bolsheviks came into power in Russia) and 1939 (when the Second World War broke out and espionage became a wide-spread activity practiced extensively by all belligerents), the Soviet apparatus was aggressively involved in more than 1,500 cases, while only about a dozen cases involving spies working against the Soviet Union were reported.

Although the number of Soviet spies caught by the counter-espionage agencies of the world is enormous, this does not mean that Soviet spy rings are inefficient or insecure, or that Soviet spies are easily trapped. The vast majority of Soviet agents were caught only *after* the completion of their missions, when they had already delivered the information they were sent out to acquire. The atom spies, for example, were not arrested in Britain and the United States until 1950, a full five years after the completion of their missions, and many of them were not caught at all. The British branch of the atomic espionage ring, for example, was never fully exposed.

The numbers cited above merely indicate the extent to which the Soviet Union engages in espionage throughout the world. It is generally figured that only about ten percent of all spy cases are exposed, and that not more than one out of ten operational spies is ever caught. If this calculation is correct, the Soviet intelligence service may have had approximately 15,000 espionage missions in operation in just twenty-two years. If only ten agents were engaged, on an average, in each operation, there were then some 150,000 persons working for Soviet intelligence service during those years. Actually, I am inclined to place the number of Soviet spies even higher—as many as 250,000 to 400,000 men and women working in all echelons and all capacities for the acquisition and transmission of information by surreptitious means.

The efficiency of Soviet espionage is reflected in its results. In the United States alone Soviet spies succeeded in procuring information on the following highly classified subjects:

Details of the hydrogen bomb; the theories and plans of the atomic bomb; the defense details of the Panama Canal; blueprints of the proximity fuse; data on the gaseous diffusion plant at Oak Ridge; American cosmic ray research; details on the Hanford atomic plant; samples of U-233 and U-235; the experimental layout of Los Alamos; the identity of America's atomic scientists; the designs for atomic aircraft; the dates of atomic tests; plans for the so-called Earth Satellite, a project involving the construction of a "space fortress"; the formula of RDX high explosive; data on American turbo-prop aircraft; jeep plans; blueprints of the research equipment of Edgewood Arsenal, test center of American chemical warfare; details of experimental bacterial warfare; radiation data; blueprints of the B-29; aircraft production data; techniques in breaking codes; the formula of the Dina explosive; sonar antisubmarine devices; the formula of the Torpex explosive; details of radar and scanning radar; progress in guided missile research; data about air-borne distance indicators; waterproof maps.

Between 1947 and 1953, a single Soviet spy stationed in Switzerland supplied the following information:

The location of RAF airports in Germany; a roster of all American officers stationed in Germany; the battle order of American troops in Germany; a critique of the various maneuvers and exercises staged by Allied troops in Europe; the organization of the U.S. Air Force in the United Kingdom; Allied military installations and constructions in Germany; the battle order of the French Army in France and in Indochina.

Between 1930 and 1945, the Soviet espionage organization reputedly had agents, some of them very highly placed, in the following key posts of foreign countries:

THE UNITED STATES. In the office of Naval Intelligence, the State Department, the Department of Justice, the Counter Intelligence Corps in Germany, the Manhattan Project, and thirty-nine other government departments.

FRANCE. In the Ministry of Foreign Affairs, the high command of the resistance movement during the war, the cipher department of the French Admiralty, the scientific department of the French War Ministry, the minister's cabinet in the Air Ministry, the Sûreté Nationale, and at least fifty other sensitive government departments.

THE UNITED KINGDOM. In the code rooms of the Foreign Office at London and the British Embassy at Moscow, the American division of the Foreign Office, the Admiralty; the Harwell center of atomic developments, and many more government agencies and departments.

CANADA. In the cipher department and passport division of the Ministry of External Affairs, all branches of atomic research and other scientific developments, the Bank of Canada, the Canadian Wartime Information Board, and numerous other key departments.

GERMANY. In the highest command of the Wehrmacht, the Reichs Ministry of Air, the Ministry of Construction and Supplies, the Propaganda Ministry, and at least sixteen other sensitive government departments where Soviet spies were identified but not necessarily caught.

JAPAN. In the private cabinet of Prime Minister Konoye, the confidential office of General Ugoye, the House of Representatives, the Foreign Ministry, the headquarters of the South Manchurian Railroad, various government research departments, Japan's so-called China Research Institute (itself an intelligence organization), various Manchurian administrations in Tokyo, and many other sensitive agencies.

The highest tribute to the efficiency of Soviet espionage was paid by Adolf Hitler, who attributed his own setbacks in Russia not to the superiority of Soviet arms but to the superiority of the Soviet intelligence system. On May 17, 1942, he hold his intimates, "If we don't know what to do with the armored divisions of the Russians, this is because the Soviets are so highly superior to us in just one field—espionage." In praising the supreme efficiency of Soviet espionage, he bemoaned the apparent inferiority of his own espionage system. He overlooked the fact, however, that in espionage technical efficiency is no more essential than the zeal and determination with which a country pursues it, or the mental and physical aptitude that the people of different nations bring to the task. In the highly civilized countries of Europe, where Christian ethics influence the thinking processes and instincts of the individual, espionage cannot be developed to the high level of efficiency that it attains in countries where no equally limiting influences affect this particular phase of intelligence.

133

The Scheme of Espionage

An espionage organization is by far the most delicate precision instrument operated by a government, and it is also the most unethical and lawless activity in which a nation may engage, apart from final unwarranted military aggression. Partly because of the amoral and immoral aspect of espionage agencies, governments painstakingly camouflage them or deny that they exist at all.

In general, spies are regarded as expendable, and they are aware that they must be regarded, even by their own governments, as criminals and outcasts. When the English writer W. Somerset Maugham was recruited in World War I to serve as a British agent in Switzerland, he was told by a superior: "There's just one thing I think you ought to know before you take on this job. And don't forget it. If you do well you'll get no thanks, and if you get into trouble you'll get no help."

When caught, spies are disavowed by the governments for which they have worked, and any association with them is emphatically denied. While governments publicly and brazenly disavow their espionage agents when they are exposed, they do everything possible behind the scenes to aid and protect them, to facilitate their work, and to make their survival possible. The basic protection of a secret agent is the over-all efficiency of his organization, its secrecy, and the efficacy and practicability of the entire espionage plan.

Espionage services are so organized as to provide for a maximum of efficiency while keeping the danger of compromise at an absolute minimum. Within the organization everything is arranged and planned with clocklike precision. The organization is kept tightly knit and as small as possible. It is maintained at a permanently high level of efficiency with every person assigned to a specific detail, the nature of which is meticulously defined.

The work of the organization in general, and of the agents in particular, is further protected and facilitated by a basic operations order, called the "espionage plan." It is patterned after the operations plans of armies in action. The "general espionage plan" involves the current needs of a government concerning information that can be procured only by surreptitious means. It includes the table of organization of the espionage service, the principles of recruitment, and personnel policies. The plan also outlines the methods of operations, the system of concealment, and the rules of internal security. Such a general espionage plan is outlined at the inception of the service, and changes are afterward made in it only when circumstances make them advisable or necessary.

For individual missions or special operations, directives or field orders are issued. In the British secret service such orders are called "Operations Instructions." They prepare each mission with meticulous care and outline every maneuver in advance, always trying to anticipate every possible exigency.

In view of the complexity of espionage, the difficulties involved in spying, the difficulty of securing reliable agents, and the complications of maintaining agents at large and keeping contact with them, even countries which engage in the activity on a substantial scale employ only a relatively small number of operational agents or full-time professional spies. The great majority of the people who procure information are not full-time or professional spies but *ad hoc*, part-time informants.

Espionage is an expensive and extremely difficult activity, often producing no return whatever for an enormous investment. Much of the information needed, even that of great strategic value and immediate importance, can be obtained from open sources by the simpler methods of intelligence proper. Experience shows that spies in general produce insignificant results and add little to the information obtained by conventional intelligence. An agent-at-large sent to a foreign country with instructions to obtain whatever he can, with no mission specified, is unlikely to produce data justifying the investment in time, money, and effort. Occasionally such an agent will pick up information of real value, but this is the exception rather than the rule.

Agents on special missions produce better results and are sent out to procure information about specific subjects. A great number of spies were sent from Britain to the Continent to obtain detailed information about the "V" weapons of the Germans after the existence of the Peenemünde project had been established through the examination of aerial photographs. Although most of these agents returned empty-handed, when they returned at all, one of them did bring back a blueprint of the V-1. She was a small, raven-haired Frenchwoman who is still known today only by her cover name, *La Souris*, The Mouse. She got the name from her secret recognition signal, a delicate scratching on a windowpane, like a mouse. She managed to obtain the blue-

135

print from a Vichy French engineer who had spent some time working in Germany and who helped reconstruct the design of the V-1 from memory. The assignment of *La Souris* was a specific mission. Recalling the days of these missions, Winston Churchill wrote: "Every known means of getting information was employed, and it was pieced together with great skill. To all sources, many of whom worked amid deadly danger, and some of whom will be forever unknown to us, I pay my tribute."

Instead of using secret agents sent out from headquarters on special missions, espionage services often utilize inhabitants of foreign countries to obtain whatever information is needed, whether general or specific. To this end, a clandestine network of local residents must be established within foreign countries, the members of the network acting as spies and agents on a free-lance, part-time basis, usually for monetary rewards. This network then feeds the information to full-time representatives of the espionage organization who pass through the target countries at irregular intervals or reside there for longer periods, and who confine their own activities to relaying the information instead of going out and acquiring it themselves.

In this way, an espionage organization needs to maintain only a limited number of full-time, professional spies, even while it has a very large number of part-time spies on its roster. This is the method now used by most espionage agencies, in particular by the Soviet intelligence service. The Soviet system has the advantage of drawing on local Communist parties in foreign countries to produce the spies and informants it needs. These agents are then used either directly by themselves in supplying the information to which they have immediate access, or indirectly by acquiring information from contacts who may not actually be in the net.

The establishment of a network of local spies is not as difficult as it may seem. When Colonel Zabutin arrived in Canada in June, 1943, for example, he found only a skeleton ring which had been functioning since October, 1942. It consisted of a total of sixteen persons, of whom five are still unknown. Of the remaining eleven individuals, three were Soviet nationals serving as organizers and eight were Canadians serving as spies.

Colonel Zabutin arrived in Canada with a substantial staff. It consisted of eleven members of the Fourth Bureau, all officers, and even such assistants as door guards and chauffeurs were actually lieutenants in the Red Army. In addition, he had three civilian aides who were on diplomatic assignments to camouflage their real activities. Zabutin's inner staff did not engage in direct espionage action but served merely to establish the network of Canadian spies, direct and supervise their activities, handle administrative matters and disbursements, and maintain the line of communications both within Canada and to the Center in Moscow.

Zabutin's ring of active spies consisted of one Englishman, two Americans, and twenty-four Canadian subjects. Among them were scientists with direct access to Canada's most carefully guarded secrets, a registrar in the office of the United Kingdom High Commissioner, an official of the Bank of Canada, officials of the Department of Munitions and Supply, a cipher clerk in the Department of External Affairs, and a member of the Canadian Parliament.

This phenomenal network was established within six months of Zabutin's arrival in Canada and functioned without interruption until September, 1945, a total of twenty-six months. It is significant that the ring was exposed, not by any of its Canadian members, but by Igor Gouzenko, a Soviet national, Zabutin's own cipher clerk, who deserted to the Canadian authorities with a great number of documents, thereby exposing the activities of the entire network. Gouzenko proved the only weak link in the Russian chain, while the local agents of the ring, those who owed their allegiance to Canada, proved to be loyal and reliable Soviet instruments. This Canadian example serves to show that a local network, composed of citizens who are willing to spy on their own country for a foreign power, is usually trustworthy and dependable when properly organized.

Another ring of comparable efficiency operated in Switzerland between 1937 and 1943. Unlike the Zabutin ring, it was not connected with the Soviet diplomatic mission but operated independently under a resident director whose "roof"—as a respectable or plausible cover is called in the Soviet espionage lingo—was established in advance. The ring consisted of the resident director, three cut-outs, three wireless operators, and one courier, altogether only eight persons serving as the ring's inner administrative and communications staff. These eight then tapped a local network of sixty sources who supplied the information. Among these sources were officials of the League of Nations and the International Labor Office, members of the French, Chinese, and Yugoslav military attaché staffs, officers of the Swiss general staff, an official of the Swiss Passport Office, and several clandestine members of the Swiss Communist Party under a man named Leon Nicole, who was the Swiss representative of the Comintern's espionage bureau. Not a single member of the Swiss ring was a Soviet national.

The main Japanese ring of Soviet espionage under Richard Sorge consisted of thirty-five members, but only two of them, Sorge himself and a radio operator, were full-time agents of the Fourth Bureau. All others were local residents and, with the exception of one Yugoslav, all of them were native Japanese. Two of them were women. The average age of these people was 40 years, the youngest member of the ring being 21, the oldest 61 years old. Among them were editors and journalists, researchers, manufacturers, businessmen, brokers, government officials, railroad officials, a member of the Japanese House of Representatives, and a physician. The thirty-three local members of the Sorge ring had access to a network of 160 informants, among them the Prime Minister of Japan and an influential general, neither of whom, of course, suspected that data supplied by them was going to the Fourth Bureau. None of the members of this entire ring was a Soviet national.

The Germans and Japanese operated similar rings in the United States before World War II. They sent to America only a few trained professional spies, Japan only a handful attached to the Japanese Embassy, and Germany only two or three agents to organize the networks of local residents. The active members of the ring were all Americans, both native-born and naturalized, including a former officer and a former petty officer of the U.S. Navy and a number of businessmen, all working as part-time spies through cut-outs.

Before the outbreak of World War II, Britain made an effort to establish such a network of local agents inside Germany, operating from headquarters in the Netherlands. This ring was infiltrated and exposed on November 9, 1939, when its two British directors were lured into a trap and kidnaped by counterintelligence agents of the Gestapo. After the ring was smashed, Britain apparently never succeeded in establishing a substitute network in Germany during the war. The main Soviet network within Germany was smashed by the Gestapo in 1942. The elimination of the British and Soviet networks left only one such network at large in Germany, the one established by the Office of Strategic Services from its headquarters in Switzerland.

The establishment of this network of agents working for the United States, none of whom was an American citizen, represented a new departure in the traditional attitude of the United States toward espionage. As late as 1924, Colonel Walter C. Sweeney, a former chief in the Military Intelligence Division of the U.S. Army's General Staff, described the method of procuring information through the establishment of a network of local resident agents in foreign countries as "a system whose use would not even be considered by the United States." The idea of using foreign nationals as spies was repugnant to the American government, even when the need of the information they could have supplied became increasingly pressing.

Several recommendations were submitted to the authorities in Washington urging that a network of resident agents be set up inside Japan to supply information concerning her plans of aggression and military organization. One plan of this kind, known as the M-plan, was prepared and submitted by Colonel Sidney Mashbir but it was rejected without ever being considered seriously. The result was that the United States had no network of agents inside Japan on the eve of Pearl Harbor and obtained no direct information from spies on impending events. The military and naval attachés, whose job it was to collect such information, were deceived both by an efficient camouflaging of Japan's actual war preparations and by their acceptance at face value of information deliberately planted by the Japanese High Command to mislead them. On the very eve of the attack on Pearl Harbor, the American naval attaché in Tokyo expressed the opinion that a surprise attack was unlikely, convinced that the fleet was still at its main base at Yokosuka simply because of the great number of sailors who could be seen crowding the streets of Tokyo. In acual fact, the fleet was at sea, on its way to its wartime destination. The sailors so much in evidence were soldiers dressed in naval uniforms and sent into the streets of Tokyo for the sole purpose of misleading people such as the American service attaché.

Had the United States maintained an espionage network in Japan as proposed by Colonel Mashbir, it would have been possible to anticipate Japanese intentions. This was proved by the fact that the Soviet network of Dr. Sorge did actually acquire the information that Japan would commence operations against Britain and the United States on December 7, 1941, and that it would not attack the Soviet Union as was expected. This information proved to be of extreme value to the U.S.S.R., since it enabled the Soviet leaders to demilitarize their Far Eastern provinces and transfer their garrisons to fronts in Europe where they were urgently needed. We may perceive on the basis of this strategic example how essential the maintenance of an espionage network in sensitive areas of the world can be, and how disadvantageous the absence of such a network can be to the intended victim of an aggressor. This is no longer solely a matter of international ethics or moral scruples. In our competitive human society it is a matter of survival.

During the war the United States made no serious effort to establish a network of spies within Japan, since the difficulties of such an effort were far too great in proportion to its possible value. It is virtually impossible to set up a local network in an enemy country under wartime conditions; it has to be established prior to the outbreak of hostilities. Even the Russians failed to reestablish one within Germany when their original network, known as the *Rote Kapelle* or Red Orchestra, was smashed. They managed to create such networks only in the countries of their wartime allies, Canada, the United Kingdom, and the United States, and in neutral Switzerland, traditional battleground of international espionage.

But where the Russians failed and the experienced British dared not tread, the United States succeeded, largely because of the exceptional skill, ingenuity, and tenacity of the American intelligence genius, Allen W. Dulles. Mr. Dulles arrived in Berne, capital of Switzerland, in the fall of 1942, a few months after the establishment of the Office of Strategic Services. He was to set up a Swiss branch of the OSS for the purpose of procuring information about neighboring Germany. In a brownstone house in Berne's quiet Herren Street, Dulles devised a new operation to which the whole underworld of espionage was soon beating a path. "My first and most important task," Mr. Dulles later recalled, "was to find out what was going on in Germany. Among other things, Washington wanted to know who in Germany were really opposed to the Hitler regime and whether they were actively at work to overthrow it. As far as the outside world could see, it often seemed as though Hitler had succeeded in winning over, hypnotizing, or terrorizing the entire German nation.

"From Switzerland I was able to establish contact with the German underground and for many months before the culmination of the plot on July 20 I had kept in touch with those who were conspiring to rid Germany of the Nazis and the Nazi state. Couriers, risking their lives, went back and forth between Switzerland and Germany with reports. . . ."

The network Mr. Dulles succeeded in establishing within Germany was large in numbers and exceptionally high in quality. In all the history of espionage there had been no precedent for this achievement. While this type of network usually is maintained only to procure tactical information of a specialized or localized nature, the high quality of the Dulles system produced at least one strategic result of the greatest significance. Through this network Mr. Dulles managed to start a conspiracy within the high command of the German armies in the south and to bring about the surrender of the very army on which Hitler was dependent for the prolonging of the war from behind the legendary "Alpine Redoubt."

The grand scheme of espionage is all-embracing. It is world-wide in scale, and so detailed as to be concerned with every phase and aspect of life in individual countries. The most important job of all is the infiltration of the opponent's armed forces. Yet here, just where spies are needed most, the difficulties of planting them appear to be greatest. All civilians are automatically suspect in combat zones. Passing from one front line to another presents great and often insurmountable difficulties. Espionage agents have to be dropped behind the lines of the enemy and then, disguised as soldiers, approach the front from the rear areas.

Contrary to common belief, spies are rarely used in this manner in the combat zone since conventional methods of intelligence, aided by the practical exigencies of war itself, are capable of supplying most of the information that commanders need. Whatever additional or specific information is required may be obtained from local residents or *ad hoc* agents recruited on the spot. Often such information may be procured from a few scattered espionage agents established at fixed positions before the commencement of hostilities and activated during the war when needed.

One of the outstanding cases of such wartime espionage involved an elderly couple in Germany, named Müller, and a British agent sent specially to assist them. The Müllers owned an inn on Brunsbüttelkoog, the southern terminus of the Kiel Canal that connects the Baltic with the North Sea. The Müllers were great favorites with the German submariners who passed through the canal on their way to operational cruises in the Atlantic. As a matter of fact, it became their custom to visit the Müllers' inn for a last glass of German beer in the Fatherland, donated as a patriotic gesture by the friendly innkeepers.

A little ritual developed around these calls. At the end of each farewell celebration, old man Müller would produce a guest register and invite his guests to sign their names as a memento of their visit. Then, as soon as the men had departed and the coast was clear, Müller would descend to his cellar and, through an underground passage, make his way to a neighboring house and hand the guest register to a friend awaiting him there. This friend was the British agent. He would copy off the names and radio them to England from a transmitter operated by the radioman of his team.

In this manner, Naval Intelligence in the Admiralty was promptly informed whenever a U-boat departed on an operational cruise. From the name of the U-boat's commanding officer, Naval Intelligence determined the number of the submarine and thus established her class and tonnage, her cruising range, and occasionally even the nature of her mission.

The case of the Müllers illustrates several points in the grand scheme of espionage. First of all, it demonstrates the complex nature of organization and the need for establishing such nests long in advance of war. The Müllers were recruited by a full-time itinerant professional agent of British intelligence when he became aware of their anti-Nazi sentiments during a trip to Brunsbüttelkoog before the war. He realized the strategic location of their inn and accordingly planned the whole scheme, including the parting glass of beer "on the house" and the guest register.

Another important point that the case of the Müllers demonstrates is the difficulty of keeping secret even such an isolated military move as the passage of a single submarine in home waters. Also, the case shows the personal danger inherent in this kind of operation and the high price spies must often pay for their part in it. The Müllers paid with their lives.

The Ideal Spy

Whatever contributions good organization, iron-clad secrecy, and meticulous planning might make, the success and survival of the individual spy will ultimately depend on factors within himself, whether innate or acquired. It is often assumed that men must possess certain specific character traits to qualify as effective spies, and that many of these traits are morbid or else a man would not select such an odd vocation. It is true that the secret agent must live by a special code, in which conventional morality is of necessity secondary to more immediate and less ethical motivations. Since elaborate deceit is the essence of espionage, it is often believed that if the spy is not an unprincipled scoundrel to begin with, his character inevitably disintegrates during his life as a spy.

Undoubtedly there have been psychopaths among the spies of history. Some of them were show-offs, egotists, what William Bolitho called truants from obligation. Others were sheer adventurers who sought and found satisfaction, not in the aims, but in the thrills of espionage. Still others were driven into espionage by jealousies, persecution and inferiority complexes, overweening ambitions, deep hatred, and violent prejudices—or simply by the love of money or the urgent need for it.

It has been gossiped that some of the famous spies of recent history were notorious homosexuals. Actually, in the entire history of espionage, there are only two renowned spies who were proven homosexuals, and only one whose homosexuality caused him to engage in espionage. The legend is that sexual deviates are vulnerable to blackmail and so forced into spying activity. In point of fact, very few homosexuals have been trapped by their sexual aberrations compared with the great number of normal men who have succumbed to the charms of the opposite sex acting as decoys.

Scientific studies of the psychology of espionage show that psychopaths and freaks do not make good spies. On the contrary, such studies prove that the effective spy is neither a freak nor a psychopath. He is rather the "citizen spy," who acts upon the incentive of enlightened patriotism and to whom deceit and intrigue are only temporary expedients that he knows how to keep under strict control.

The personality problem has long baffled all organizations engaged in espionage. They have tried by all kinds of methods to establish the pattern of what is called the "ideal spy," although this is admittedly a futile quest for unattainable perfection.

Different countries have different concepts of the perfect spy. The British, for example, visualize the ideal spy as a sporting young man of excellent birth and independent means, with a better than average education, inconspicuously handsome, rationally courageous, tenacious, and mildly philosophical. He feigns snobbishness, dullness, cynicism, disinterest, and a tendency to swagger, while in reality he is sensitive, alert, poised, erudite, and inquisitive. The personalities of British spies I have known were made up of all those traits, both natural and pretended.

The Russian approach to the personality problem of espionage is at once pragmatic and dogmatic. The Russians envisage their spies as eager and practical intellectuals with enormous book knowledge, serious, industrious, with an un-questioning respect for rules and regulations and an unshakable reserve, to whom all action is a conditioned response. The actual Russian agent, on the whole, is a kind of polished automaton who does everything exceedingly well as long as the sailing is smooth, but who is immediately lost in a crisis since he does not know how to deal with problems not treated in his textbooks.

In the United States the spy is popularly thought of as an easy-going rugged individualist, not necessarily brilliant in all fields, but a wizard at his own specialty, ingenious, instinctive, and intuitive, with little liking for pure reason, adventurous and brave, adaptable, friendly, dexterous, a quick improviser in tight situations, somewhat indiscreet, and a daredevil. In actual fact, successful spies possess all of these traits to some degree.

Several scientific efforts were made, especially in the United States where psychological prognostication is a fad, to establish the personality structure of the ideal spy. On the basis of these studies, there was drawn up a catalogue of ten major groups of traits which the good spy is supposed to possess in order to qualify.

First of all, his morale must be high and he must be genuinely interested in the job ahead.

Second, he must be energetic, zealous, and enterprising.

Third, he must be resourceful, a quick and practical thinker. He must have good judgment and know how to deal with things, people, and ideas. He must be proficient in some occupational skill.

Fourth, he must be emotionally stable, capable of great endurance under stress. He must be calm and quiet, tolerant and healthy.

Fifth, he must have the ability to get along with other people, to work as a member of a team, to understand the foibles of others while being reasonably free of the same foibles himself.

Sixth, he must know how to inspire collaboration, to organize, administer, and lead others. He must be willing to accept responsibility.

Seventh, he must be discreet, have a passion for anonymity, and know how to keep his mouth shut and preserve a secret.

Eighth, he must be able to bluff and mislead, but only when bluffing and misleading become necessary.

Ninth, he must be agile, rugged, and daring.

Tenth, he must have the ability to observe everything, to memorize details accurately. He must be able to report on his observations lucidly, to evaluate his observations and relate them to the greater complex of things.

Naturally, it is the rare individual who combines all of these traits in his personality. Men who were highly intelligent were found to be strong in leadership, excellent observers and reporters, and good salesmen. But their emotional stability was often low, their discretion left something to be desired, their sociability was deficient, and they generally lacked a physical skill.

Emotionally stable persons were found to be sociable and good leaders, adequately discreet and fairly skilled, but their intelligence was somewhat lower. They were also poor observers, inaccurate reporters, and not good salesmen.

It was found that the ideal spy was not so often the brilliant spy but the average spy. This averageness extended even to his personal appearance.

Spies in Action

Now that we have seen how espionage is organized and have examined the basic qualifications for an effective spy, let us see in some detail how espionage operates. For the individual drawn into this activity, service begins on the day of his recruitment and ends with the termination of his mission. A mission may terminate either with the man's arrest or with his return to his base. Naturally most of the best known espionage cases had unhappy endings, although once in a while a spy returns from his mission to tell his own story when circumstances or security no longer impose silence on him. Often the agents who return come back from the shadow of death. However melodramatic this may sound, it is a grim reality in the espionage business.

The narrative of the famous *White Rabbit*—F.F.E. Yeo-Thomas, one of the foremost British agents of World War II and Mr. Churchill's personal liaison with the underground in France—demonstrates most dramatically the odyssey of even the best spy. The story of his adventure, as told by Bruce Marshall, covers 256 pages. But his mission ends on page 99 with a breathtaking description of his arrest by the Gestapo in Paris, after he violated a cardinal rule of the trade and waited a few minutes for a tardy contact. The rest of the narrative describes his interrogation and torture, his anguished years in German concentration camps, his every minute awaiting the seemingly inevitable end.

Another great British agent, a woman named Odette Sansom, the only living female spy to wear the George Cross, was also caught, as were about ninety percent of her colleagues in the field. Life expectation is low in wartime espionage; the mortality rate is high. The balance sheet of espionage shows that despite the enormous investment of money and effort expended on this most complex and difficult of human activities, failure is far more frequent than success. Some of the world's best spies did not live to tell their own stories, even though most of them managed to send back invaluable information before their untimely death.

Agents in the field may operate as lone wolves, going out by themselves and carrying through their missions without outside aid. But missions of this kind are rare and very seldom successful. They are mounted when a man or woman is planted permanently in an opponent's organization.

More often spies are sent out in teams, usually in pairs, one man to procure information, another to transmit it. Even the smallest team needs a communications apparatus to back it up. It needs a contact in the home office, one who conceived and organized the mission and remains essentially in charge of it by remote control.

Spies in the field obviously cannot go to banks and withdraw the funds they need, for a bank account may eventually betray even the long-term resident agent. He cannot account for the source of his funds, or be expected to pay taxes on his espionage income in the normal manner of the wage-earner. Most of the monetary transactions in espionage are handled on a cash-and-carry basis, the cash ordinarily being supplied in the currency of the country in which the spy operates and brought in by special couriers.

Nor can the espionage agent buy his supplies in the country where he operates. If he buys the chemicals he needs to mix his secret ink, or the film on which he photographs his documents, his periodic purchases may trap him. Virtually all the supplies a spy needs in the field—the chemicals, the films, the tubes for his radio set, the bullets for his gun—have to be smuggled in from headquarters.

Even in the field the spy is rarely left to himself. Small though the operating circle may be, there are always a few people at the point of his assignment who work with him and on whom he depends. He has an *agent-de-liaison*, a kind of espionage apprentice who performs his errands, usually a native of the country in which he is working. He often has a host assigned to provide a roof over his head, a trusted but peripheral member of the organization. He is given the names of contacts and guides, and supplied with accommodation addresses where he may hide out in emergencies, operate his radio transmitter, or remain for a while to camouflage his movements. Despite this circle of aides, contacts, and associates, the spy is a lonely man, necessarily keeping to himself as much as possible, since any association may compromise his security.

Espionage organizations strive to anticipate every possibility and eventuality that will confront an agent in the field. Among other things, they try to warn him of the possible ways in which he may be trapped, and suggest alternate means of evasion and escape. They try to prepare him for every possible emergency, and to arrange everything in advance so as to reduce his chances of exposure or arrest. Espionage organizations are perforce eminently practical and ingenious. They conduct their operations in the field in ten different stages, each stage having exact rules painstakingly outlined in manuals and operations orders.

These ten stages are: 1. recruiting and selection; 2. training and indoctrination; 3. establishment of cover and authentication; 4. routing, or the agent's journey to his place of assignment; 5. the establishment of his cover on the spot; 6. development of local sources of information; 7. the surreptitious procurement of confidential information; 8. meetings with contacts, subagents, cut-outs, and couriers; 9. communications and transportation; and 10. safety and security, often the most difficult part of the operation. We may now examine these various stages one by one.

Recruiting and Selection

Because agents usually operate in alien lands whose language and customs are different from their own, persons who speak the language and know the customs of the countries to which they are assigned are preferred. This is a primary consideration in recruiting. Agents are sought who fit this basic condition by virtue of an exceptional linguistic ability or by long previous residence in the foreign country of assignment. In other instances, agents may establish a temporary nationality as a cover. A British agent, for example, may be sent to work in Rumania posing as a German, provided he speaks German fluently and without a detectable accent and is thoroughly familiar with at least certain parts of Germany. At any rate, fluency in some foreign language and familiarity

147

with a foreign country is an essential prerequisite in recruiting.

Recruiting poses no problem to the Soviet espionage organization, which draws its agents from the vast reservoir of international Communist parties. Nor is it too great a problem in the United States, which can draw its agents from its foreign-born population, or from among refugees, escapees, and political exiles.

It is not so simple in Britain or France. To overcome this obstacle, Britain selects prospective spies at an early and impressionable age. Very young men are encouraged to take up residence abroad and fade into their environment, become bilingual, and prepare themselves for whatever mission might at one time or another be assigned to them, either in the countries where they have grown up, or in countries to which they might be sent, pretending to be nationals of the country of their long residence. This may seem a tedious process in the breeding of spies, but it is actually followed.

The Japanese had an even greater problem to overcome in the selection of their agents, since their physical features automatically set them apart from much of the rest of the world. They solved the problem by using their own trained agents only as administrators, organizers, and supervisors, and hiring Caucasians to act as operational spies. The Germans prefer their own nationals, or recruit their agents among German residents abroad. The Italians do the same, often using agents who are absorbed into the large Italian populations of the countries where they operate.

Actual recruiting is usually done by specialists assigned to that sole function. They are the "talent scouts" who bring likely prospects to the attention of the special branch of the espionage organization which is in charge of undercover personnel. The candidate is gradually introduced into the organization, invited to become a spy in due course, and initiated only when he passes severe tests.

In the Soviet Union, a man's competence in certain special fields is the decisive factor in his selection. His aptitude for a job is assessed subjectively through personal observation and interview.

The United States is the only country in the world that selects its secret agents on the basis of scientific tests. These tests were developed during World War II by the assessment staff of the OSS, operating at a secluded estate in Virginia. Here candidates were required to spend three days, during which they underwent a number of ingeniously devised psychological and aptitude tests, under conditions simulating

148

those met in the field. They were given cover names and bogus identities. During their tests they were exposed to strange situations and required to participate in hazardous procedures.

One such procedure was, for example, the "Belonging Test," designed to test a candidate's ability to observe a situation and draw the correct conclusions from his observations. He was taken into a bedroom which, the candidate was told, had been occupied several days earlier by a transient. On his departure, the transient had left behind a number of his belongings, twenty-six items in all, including articles of clothing, written material, newspapers, clippings, and a timetable. The candidate was told to examine them carefully and, from the clues these objects offered, to make a try at sizing up the guest in exactly four minutes.

The three-day trial period ended with a test designed to measure the candidate's ability to endure stress and strain. An arrest was simulated and the candidate taken to a small room in the basement where he was placed in the glare of a blinding spotlight. The room was otherwise dark, but from the darkness came harsh, relentless voices which tried to confuse and unnerve the candidate, to make him betray his original cover story. The test was a good imitation of interrogation by the secret police of a totalitarian state.

Men who passed these tests were then assigned to that branch of the OSS which seemed best suited to the candidates' particular talents revealed by the examination. Similar methods are used today in the selection of agents for the CIA.

I think the United States is probably the only country in the world that goes to so much trouble and expense to select its secret agents. But the investment has paid off in the field. The record of the Medical Branch of the OSS showed that men and women passed by the Assessment Staff had fewer neuro-psychiatric symptoms and fewer breakdowns in the field than those who obtained assignments without this screening.

Training and Indoctrination

Indoctrination of prospective secret agents is an abstract educational process. It is designed to cultivate inner strength in an agent's personality, to impress him with the basic nobility of his effort, and to develop in him loyalty, responsibility, and reliability. It is undertaken in the form of lectures that possess a high degree of emotional appeal but have little bearing on the actual work for which the candidate is being prepared.

Training, on the other hand, is a concrete and functional exercise or practice to teach the agent all the practical aspects of his trade. It is designed to equip him with certain skills that he will need in the execution of his missions, and to prepare him for all eventualities and emergencies. An agent's training is less concerned with the teaching of specialties, since it is assumed that anyone slated for the job already possesses certain fundamental knowledge or experience in the field to which he will eventually be assigned.

Secret agents are trained in special espionage schools. During World War II, the Allies maintained sixty of these schools, since many agents were required in meeting the exigencies of war, and many more to work with the various underground organizations. The present-day number and location of existing schools is, of course, classified information, as are some of the details of the curricula. Even so, it is possible to describe the training of secret agents in general terms, or on the basis of past or foreign examples.

The primary training of all personnel follows certain uniform lines and later branches into the various specialized fields, somewhat in the manner of teaching at medical schools, which require the mastery of fundamentals before allowing the student to specialize. In intelligence and espionage there is a distinction between basic and advanced training. Basic training covers all the subjects every agent needs to know. Advanced training is designed for developing specialists with individual skills.

In the training of secret agents the so-called "applicatory system of instruction" is used. In this method, theory plays only a minor role, whereas the heaviest stress is placed on practical factors. Candidates are given problems in which all possible situations are assumed, and they are required to solve these problems under simulated field conditions.

Since the agent's primary purpose is the procurement of information, his training is primarily concerned with this phase of activity. First of all, the meaning, nature, and value of every type of information is explained generally, after which its collection is taught in detail. It is ordinarily emphasized that any information at all is important, although it may not seem at a given moment to be of immediate or actual value. Agents are thus conditioned to recognize information in general, then to recognize that of some specific value, and finally to recognize the value of specific information to individual branches of government.

150

The next step is the development through training of the candidate's ability to observe and to record his observations. Obviously, the candidate must bring to the job some natural aptitude and ability. His training is then designed to sharpen and channel this ability. Students are taught to read maps quickly and accurately, to interpret aerial and ground photographs, to examine and study documents, to identify military and civil installations, and to identify airplanes and naval vessels by silhouette, to recognize machines, devices, and the equipment, uniforms, and insignia of the various branches of armed forces.

They are taught methods of recognition, identification, and location. They are instructed in the proper and efficient use of compass, telescope, and field glasses. They are told how to make observations and what to look for during apparently routine train trips, hikes, and journeys in airplanes and on ships.

Instruction is given in the recording of observations, the making of notes, maps, and sketches, and the taking of photographs both openly and surreptitiously. Candidates are taught how to write reports in which information is properly coordinated and focused, and in which observations are described in a concise and graphic manner. During this phase of the training, in addition to the art of interrogation, languages are improved and candidates are acquainted with the national characteristics of the peoples they will later work among.

The Russian system makes a sharp distinction between the training of secret agents or spies, and of conspirators, who may be agitators, propagandists, or revolutionary agents. The training of secret agents is short and to the point, and stresses such technical matters as the arranging of meetings, microphotography, the use of radio, coding and decoding, and the various methods of establishing and maintaining covers. This training is conducted within the Fourth Bureau, which has a special division for the training of its own agents and technicians. Some are trained by the MVD, and others by the foremost college of conspiracy maintained anywhere in the Communist world, the Lenin Academy in Moscow.

In the Lenin Academy students from all countries are taught: how to handle light arms of their own and of other countries; how to use the weapons at the disposal of the police abroad, and how to defend themselves against such weapons; how to break codes; how to enter offices and plants surreptitiously; how to search files, pilfer documents, make photostats of microphotographs; how to assemble and operate

151

radio transmitters; how to wage what is called conspiratorial warfare—street fighting, action behind barricades, partisan operations, civil war; how to ascertain the location of food stores, armament dumps, warehouses, public utilities, communications nerve centers, railway stations, junctions and marshaling yards, telephone exchanges; how to wreck trains, sabotage ships, slow down or stop production, destroy installations in key factories, demolish centers of resistance such as hostile newspaper plants, police stations, etc; how to publish clandestine newspapers and operate secret radio stations; how to print leaflets; how to induce labor disputes and organize strikes; how to propagandize members of the armed forces; how to organize meetings and raise the "mob spirit"; how to infiltrate governmental apparatuses and sensitive private institutions, such as public utilities plants, newspaper offices, banks; how to conduct counterespionage and maintain the security of their own espionage organization and of individual agents.

The German system of training was originally developed by a great intelligence specialist who became famous in the literature of espionage under the pseudonym "Mademoiselle Docteur." She was Elsbeth Schragmüller, a graduate of Freiburg University and a teacher by profession. At the outbreak of the First World War, Dr. Schragmüller volunteered her services to Colonel Nicolai of the High Command's intelligence bureau. She impressed Nicolai with her ideas about the training of spies and was allowed to organize a spy school of her own. Her pioneering methods have since been adopted by most of the modern espionage schools, not only in Germany, but in Britain and the United States as well.

Dr. Schragmüller's school was in Antwerp, at 10, rue de la Pepinière. She chose the house because it was inconspicuous and because it had a rear entrance on rue de l'Harmonie. Her students were brought to the school in curtained cars which stopped at the Harmony Street entrance. As soon as a car arrived the back gate was opened from the inside, and the student was whisked into the house. Inside he was received by Dr. Schragmüller, who showed the newcomer to his quarters. This was always a large and well-furnished room. It was equipped with a small library, manuals and maps, a phonograph, and games that a person could play alone. From then on the student was kept to himself. His door was locked from the outside and opened only when his meals were brought to him.

On the door was the given name by which the student was known in the school, common and impersonal, such as Hans or Karl or Willy. For the first few days, the new man was observed closely although never given a chance to see his observers. Every room had a mirror on the wall that was actually a screen, authentic in appearance from within the room but transparent from the opposite side. In this way Dr. Schragmüller could observe certain personal characteristics of her pupils, especially their ability to endure solitude.

After a week instructors began coming to the room one by one. Language experts came to teach the dialects and idiomatic speech of the country to which the man was to be assigned. Cipher experts taught cryptography, and communications specialists the use of secret inks, radio, and telegraphy. In time, all of the many arts in which the accomplished spy is adept were introduced and mastered, and for his final examination the student was taken to demonstration rooms where he proved his aptitude for the manifold requirements of espionage work.

Dr. Schragmüller herself wrote the manuals used in her school as texts, which today still serve as standards in the most modern espionage organizations. There was a basic manual in the Schragmüller school that is regarded as the best document of its kind ever produced for the instruction of secret agents. Here are a few items from it, as valid today as they were four decades ago:

1. Conceal whatever linguistic gifts you may have, to encourage others to talk freely in your hearing.
2. Never write or speak a word of your native tongue while on duty in a foreign country.
3. When procuring information, make your informant travel as far as possible from his place of residence and away from your immediate field of operations. Make him go to the meeting by a devious route, preferably at night. A tired informant is less cautious or suspicious, more relaxed and expansive, less disposed to lie or to bargain shrewdly—all advantages in the transaction which you should reserve to yourself.
4. Collect every available bit of information without indicating undue interest in any of it. Never fasten upon some item of intelligence you think you can or *must* acquire. By pursuing a single item, by making inquiries conspicuously, you expose your determination to learn a particular thing.
5. Always disguise newly acquired data with some apparently innocent cover. Figures or dimensions that have to be recorded may best be put down as items of personal expenditure.
6. When burning a letter or other papers, do not forget that their charred or ashen remnants are readable. Microscopic examination can do a great deal with paper ash. Tearing up papers and throwing them away does not mean that they are destroyed effectively. Paper scraps are never disposed of with absolute security, even in lavatories.

7. Never talk or behave mysteriously, except when trying to make a talkative person talk to you about things he knows.

8. Avoid every temptation to show off, to be too smart or too original or inventive. Remember what Talleyrand told his young diplomats: "Above all, no zeal!" You will certainly get farther by moving slowly. The best genius in espionage is the one who is never conspicuous. Remember, too, what Henry Austin said: "Genius, that power which dazzles mortal eyes, is oft but perseverance in disguise."

9. When securing a lodging, try to obtain a room or apartment that has more than a single entrance and exit. Plan and rehearse your escape in advance.

10. Always make sure that you are not being trailed, and learn the technique of eluding your follower.

11. Do not drink to excess. Cultivate the company of only those women you know and can trust.

12. Never take anything for granted, neither proffered friendship nor apparent hostility, neither the reliability of a report nor the seeming uselessness of some bit of information.

The ideas and methods of Dr. Schragmüller were studied in the United States when the OSS established its espionage schools during World War II. These American schools incorporated many of the methods of foreign institutions in their own curricula and, as a result, turned out some excellently trained personnel. One such OSS training station was established at the Congressional Country Club in Washington, where students were taught an amazing variety of subjects. Among its courses were cryptography, clandestine meeting, tailing, interrogation, residence searching, mine laying, arson, the handling of explosives, the use and maintenance of firearms, judo and other forms of self-defense. Students learned to read maps and to draw them, to make a lethal weapon from a folded newspaper, to immobilize automobiles by pouring sugar into their gasoline tanks, and to duplicate the imprint of rubber stamps with half a potato.

The British secret service operated a great number of schools of this type. At one of them, located at the municipal airport in Manchester, agents were trained in the art of parachuting from planes into hostile areas. Probably the best Allied espionage school of World War II was in Canada, an institute for advanced studies where instructors went to be taught.

Establishment of Cover and Authentication

When the training and indoctrination of a candidate is concluded and he is initiated into the organization as a secret agent, he is required to give up his former identity and as-

154

sume an entirely new one called a cover, under which he then operates in the field. This metamorphosis is accomplished through a carefully plotted procedure in which nothing is left to chance. It begins with the preparation of a "legend," or "cover story," which is the bogus biography of the agent.

The construction of a cover story requires considerable effort. In the legend, the agent's knowledge of trades, peoples, and places is taken into consideration. It changes his birthplace, his educational background; it conceals his real work, his actual place of residence, all that is real about him. However, it must be plausible and easy to remember in the most specific detail, since a man is supposed to be able to maintain and defend his legend under exhaustive grilling and even torture.

I once saw a bogus biography that covered eighteen closely typed pages. Before it was finished, the agent not only had a new name, a new set of parents and grandparents, and a new birthplace, but also new hobbies and a new name for his pet dog.

In the Soviet Union every official of the Fourth Bureau is required to prepare a legend before going abroad. Igor Gouzenko, the Russian who exposed the atom spy ring, described the meticulous care with which his legend was prepared before his assignment to Canada. The compilation of his cover story took several days. "The idea behind these 'legends' is rather curious," Gouzenko wrote. "In case the authorities of a country, to which the subject of a 'legend' is assigned, wished to check on him, they would communicate with their embassy in Moscow. The embassy, however, would find itself incapable of attempting a private investigation, for the simple reason that practically all such 'legends' give phony home addresses outside Moscow, and even an embassy representative would hardly be permitted to conduct enquiries in towns and cities beyond Moscow." Gouzenko's legend, submitted to the Canadian authorities when the passport visa was issued, was accordingly completely false.

After the completion of the cover story, the agent is given an alias for administrative purposes within the organization. In internal communications and in his relations with other agents, he is referred to by this alias, which is really a code concealing the identity of the person in the event that the communications network is tapped or decoded. While generally any code name that comes to his superior's mind might be assigned to an agent, sometimes a system is employed in its selection. During World War II, for example, the French

155

secret service picked aliases for its agents to indicate their specific assignments. Military delegates used geometric nomenclature, officers in charge of aerial operations utilized titles such as Count or Archduke, while saboteurs were given cover names from maritime lingo.

The melodramatic designations of spies, such as "Q-43" or "Z-8," which occur in thrillers or motion pictures, are seldom used in practice. If used at all, they are bureaucratic designations, indicating the agent's number in the personnel index file.

The cover story of the secret agent usually determines the disguise he will use. Contrary to common belief, secret agents rarely use elaborate disguises on their missions but conduct their secret activities under the cover of a legitimate profession or blind. Once I heard it said of a not-too-popular individual that he went to a costume ball in the disguise of a gentleman. This quip tells a lot. The guise of gentleman is an excellent one in the espionage business.

"The spy requires not merely an appropriate disguise," Winfried Lüdecke wrote, "but the skill to play the part he undertakes. He must be a good actor, and especially a first-rate quick-change artist, capable of meeting with boldness and presence of mind even the most perilous situations." Generally, a secret agent will require only temporary disguises for brief tactical missions. He may have to pose as a waiter, barber, telephone repairman, or night watchman in order to enter a hotel room, office, or plant. In other instances, spies may pose as priests, monks, hospital attendants, tourists, workers, farmhands, businessmen, traveling salesmen, or writers. Secret agents are sometimes obliged to pose as members of the foreign armies against which they operate. Ordinarily, the illegal donning of a foreign uniform is resorted to in only the most stringent cases, although instances have been recorded in which an agent was thus disguised for many years.

British agents are past masters in the art of disguise and have worn the uniforms of many foreign countries. One of the best of their practitioners of the art of disguise was Baden-Powell, the officer-spy, who was blessed with an exceptional gift for altering his appearance. In these transformations he rarely changed his costume. He merely assumed the personality of someone else. Once, when he had been assigned to establish the caliber of the guns in the Dalmatian fortress of Cataro, Baden-Powell decided to go as an entomologist. In preparation for the mission, he not only studied entomology but also the personal habits of the professors who instructed him, copying their ways of carrying the butterfly net and of keeping notes in the field book.

He embarked on this particular mission carrying a box of paints and brushes and a sketch book that contained a number of completed drawings of butterflies done by him beforehand. His pursuit of lepidoptera brought him close to the fortress of Cattaro, and into his sketch book went the outlines of the fortification intricately woven into the details of a beautiful butterfly.

At another time, in an attempt to get close enough to a secret German military installation to study its armaments, Baden-Powell stuck a bottle of brandy in his coat pocket and approached his target. He had almost completed his mission when he was discovered by sentries who had been ordered to arrest any intruder, but, finding the stranger badly intoxicated and his clothes soaked with the liquor, they ordered him away from the fort, too certain of his condition to bother with a staggering drunk.

To be effective a disguise should be inconspicuous and commonplace. The less it entails in the way of costume and gimmicks the better it is. Disguise by costume should be the exception rather than the rule. Outside of such changes as can be accomplished with the hair and eyebrows, and a beard or mustache, there is little that can be done to disguise the facial characteristics without resorting to plastic surgery, which, incidentally, has often been done. The ability to change one's bearing and gait is invaluable. The spy is served well by a spare necktie, different in color and shape from the one previously worn. Experience has shown that, in a brief encounter, the color and shape of a tie leaves a greater impression than features of the face or the color of the eyes. A spare hat may also be kept handy, since a Homburg or a bowler will change a man's appearance more effectively, and with less danger of detection, than false eyebrows or a wig, whereas sunglasses make a man immediately conspicuous.

The making over of an agent is completed with his "documentation," the false papers he is given to provide his new identity. Among them may be his passport, identity card, registration of residence, trade-union card, and such papers as are carried by the people of the country where he is to operate, including ration cards, draft board registration, and driver's license. To make his new identity even more convincing, the agent may be issued season tickets for certain commuter lines, correspondence with friends, stubs of used theater tickets, and such scraps and papers as might be found in the pockets of a person anywhere.

157

His passport is the agent's most important document. Frequently the passport he carries may be genuine. The espionage organizations of all countries have on hand an assortment of foreign passports for use by their spies. The only change made in them is the substitution of the spy's photograph for that of the legitimate owner. A Russian agent assigned to the United States was provided with a Canadian passport made out to a certain Ignacy Witczak. This Witczak fought on the Republican side in the Spanish civil war, and his passport was taken from him by the political commissar of his battalion and never returned. The document later turned up in the possession of the Soviet agent, who was operating in California.

Routing

The agent is now ready to depart on his mission. All that is left to do is to prepare him for his specific assignment. He is required to rehearse his mission at headquarters, to participate in "dry runs," to exercise on mockups. In the United States, during the last war, agents who were to be sent out to obtain information about factories abroad were first sent into factories here to secure similar information, never knowing when the FBI or plant security forces might expose them. German saboteurs sent to the United States in 1942 were similarly prepared for their mission. Since their targets were the aluminum plants of the United States, they were planted in aluminum factories in the Reich and there went through all the motions of their mission, short of actually blowing up the factories.

Agents are given operations instructions in which every phase of their assignment is outlined in detail. A typical document states the nature of the mission, enumerates the specific information sought and what part of it is already available, states the cover name of the operation and the alias assigned to the agent, reiterates his cover story, and lists the code names of all those who participate in the mission. In addition, it outlines all the information and so-called assumptions on file about the target, lists the names and locations of contacts in the field, in particular the spy's *agent-de-liaison*, his route, alternate routes, and hide-outs, his accommodation addresses, means of evasion, his lines of communication, transportation and supply, and his code—everything to the smallest detail. Such operations instructions are memorized before the agent's departure on the mission, since he obviously cannot carry a document of this nature with him.

The agent is now completely prepared for his mission. Although he may have a base on which to fall back and at least some connection with his headquarters, he is by and large left to shift for himself.

The agent's trip to the place of his assignment is a delicate operation within itself. It is planned with painstaking attention to every detail by his home organization, where special traffic managers plot every stage of his journey from departure to arrival. Occasionally, his cover enables him to travel directly and more or less openly to his destination. In other cases, an agent may have to be smuggled into a country by being dropped from a plane, landed from a submarine, or put across a frontier at night by surreptitious means. Frequently, agents approach their places of assignment by circuitous routes, especially when they assume a false nationality as a part of the cover. In such cases, the agent will first go to the country whose citizen he later pretends to be and settle there for a few months before approaching his final destination.

Upon arrival, the agent will notify his organization, by radio signal, postal card, or possibly the insertion of a fictitious ad in a newspaper's classified section, that he is ready to begin his work. He then contacts any other persons slated to work with him. Frequently, his mission is well prepared in advance on the spot, where he is awaited by contacts, and his lodgings are provided for him so that he may begin the mission at once. Timing is important in espionage, for time lost may be a life lost, or it may result in the failure of a mission.

Establishment of Cover on the Spot: Local Contacts

Earlier in the chapter we have seen how a plausible cover is established upon arrival and, secondly, how the agent will go about developing his ring or net, his circle of informants, his sources. The next stage, of course, is the mission itself: the acquisition of information.

Surreptitious Acquisition of Information

Such information is obtained either directly or through informants and go-betweens, but espionage organizations are like courts of law. They are impressed only with hard facts supported by convincing documentation. Information based on hearsay is rarely accepted by the agent's organization, nor is data accepted if it is submitted without an exact description of its source. The need for exactness and documentation makes the work of an agent tedious and difficult, and it keeps him extremely busy. In addition to all of the effort of preserving his identity, and to the work of the mission itself, the agent must attend to the job assigned to him as a cover.

An agent always strives to obtain actual documents or blueprints from his sources, either in their original forms or as photographed copies. There are manifold problems involved in the acquisition, copying, and transmission of documents, and everything must be accomplished with the greatest possible speed, since most documents cannot remain long in the possession of the agent but must be returned to their legitimate sources.

In order to obtain such documents, the agent develops contacts within the agencies of the foreign government, people who will "borrow" them temporarily for his use. In the early thirties, Soviet intelligence was eager to obtain the blueprints of a new American tank developed by the inventor Walter Christie. Contact was established with a high-ranking American officer, who lifted the documents from the War Department files at the end of the office week on Friday and delivered them to a go-between, who in turn transmitted them to the agent. They were returned to the officer in time for him to replace them in the files early on Monday morning.

Photographed copies of original documents represent the best possible intelligence material any espionage organization can acquire. This type of information is ordinarily obtained only from persons who have immediate access to it, and, of course, surreptitiously. In handling the documents, the agent acts as a trustee or clearing-house. His chief problem is to develop sources who have access to such materials, and then to receive the documents without attracting attention. In order to camouflage this part of the activity, personal contacts are arranged with extreme circumspection and, therefore, meetings with contacts are regulated on the basis of the espionage plan of all such organizations.

Meetings with Informants and Couriers

There are three major groups of espionage personnel with whom an agent may engage while on a mission. In the first group are routine social contacts; in the second are contacts with informants and cut-outs who supply or relay the information; and in the third are meetings with couriers who carry the information back to headquarters.

General social contacts are made and pursued overtly. They

do not differ from those made by the average person within his own circle of friends and acquaintances.

Contacts with informants and cut-outs, and meetings with couriers, are in a different category and constitute some of the most melodramatic aspects of a secret agent's work. It is in these contacts that the often routine business of espionage approaches most closely the Hollywood version of the activity.

An agent may use a number of different ways and means to keep in touch with his informants. A very simple way was described by Whittaker Chambers. Mr. Chambers was not a spy, inasmuch as it was not his function to acquire information at the source. He was a cut-out or courier. His function was to pick up information from the source and relay it to the collector. Chambers would simply go to the house of an informant, pick up a number of documents, and take them to a drugstore in downtown Washington where he would meet the technician of the net whose job it was to photograph them. This technician then would take the material to his home in Baltimore, photograph the documents, return with them to Washington, meet Chambers again, and return the material to him.

While such straightforward traffic is simple enough, it is actually a perilous phase of espionage work. First of all, if a cut-out or courier makes numerous visits at regular intervals to the home of an informant, he will invariably attract attention in any country where counterespionage is alert. If the cut-out is under surveillance he is certain to lead the counterespionage agent to the informant, thereby destroying this vital source and compromising the whole operation. Secondly, documents should not be in transit for too long a time or over great distances. Their security might be easily compromised en route, they could be lost, or something could happen to the person who carries them. If Chambers actually used such a procedure to relay documents from their source to the collector, he not only employed the most primitive and precarious method, but he also violated a very important rule in the Soviet spy book. The Soviet espionage organization prescribes special procedures for the meeting of informants and the transmission of documents. These procedures specify that the Center in Moscow must make all arrangements for meetings, some of which might take place thousands of miles away.

In Soviet espionage, meetings are arranged by go-betweens. Informants rarely meet with collectors or even with couriers. They are contacted by cut-outs to whom they hand the information. The cut-out then relays the information to the collector by the shortest possible route in the least possible time. It is a strict rule in Soviet espionage, for example, that all meetings in the course of which documents are transferred from one person to another must take place on a street or in a public place. A Soviet instruction sheet prepared for the orientation of cut-outs stipulates:

"Any meetings [with informants] must take place outdoors, on the street and, moreover, separately with each, and only once a month . . . The material they supply must be received the same day on which you must meet me in the evening. The material must not be kept by you even for a single night . . . Wives of informants must not know that you work with and meet their husbands."

The lengths to which espionage organizations go in arranging meetings of cut-outs and informants was shown in the contact that a Soviet go-between was supposed to make with Dr. Allan Nunn May in London in the fall of 1945. This meeting was originally prepared by the Soviet military attaché in Canada. He had to submit his plan for approval to Moscow, where it was completely revised. When the final arrangements were made, they were spelled out in an operations order that is reproduced here as a typical sample of such arrangements. The order was signed by the "Director" personally and sent to the military attaché on August 22, 1945, almost two months before the meeting was to take place.

The document read as follows:

1. Place: In front of the British Museum in London, on Great Russell Street, at the opposite side of the street, about Museum Street, from the side of Tottenham Court Road repeat Tottenham Court Road, Alek [May's cover name] walks from Tottenham Court Road, the contact man from the opposite side—Southampton Row.

2. Time: As indicated by you, however, it would be more expedient to carry out the meeting at 20 o'clock, if it should be convenient to Alek, as at 23 o'clock it is too dark. As for the time, agree about it with Alek and communicate the decision to me. In case the meeting should not take place in October, the time and day will be repeated in the following months.

3. Identification signs: Alek will have under his left arm the newspaper *Times*, the contact man will have in his left hand the magazine *Picture Post*.

4. The Password: The contact man: 'What is the shortest way to the Strand?' Alek: 'Well, come along. I am going that way.' In the beginning of the business conversation Alek says: 'Best regards from Mikel.'

Meetings with couriers are invariably arranged by the

162

headquarters of the espionage organization. Before a courier is sent out, the place and time of the meeting and the signals of identification are communicated to the agent by the best available means, frequently by radio. Richard Sorge emphasized in his testimony the circumspect care with which the Soviet espionage organization arranges meetings with couriers. Similar procedure is practiced by all espionage organizations.

For example, Sorge once received instructions from Moscow to go to a certain restaurant in Hong Kong where he was to meet a courier. Sorge was to be seated at a table at a certain time, and the courier was to enter the restaurant a few minutes past 3 P.M., take from his pocket a long Manila cigar, and hold it in his hand without lighting it. As soon as Sorge saw the signal, he was to approach the counter of the restaurant, take a pipe from his pocket, and hold it in his hand without lighting it. When this signal was recognized by the courier, he was to light his cigar and Sorge his pipe.

The courier was then to leave the restaurant and Sorge was to follow him to a park. There the courier would approach Sorge with the words, "Greetings from Katcha." Sorge was to answer, "Greetings from Gustav." This was the exact procedure the two men followed. Sorge had to go all the way to Hong Kong from Tokyo for the meeting, an added precautionary measure to avoid detection by the Japanese secret police. It was assumed that two total strangers would not attract the attention of the authorities in Hong Kong.

The manner in which documents are actually handed over is very strictly outlined to avoid attention. The document is often concealed inside a folded newspaper, which the agent places on the bench beside him, and, at the end of what appears to be an innocent, and often chance conversation, the newspaper is picked up, not by the agent, but by the courier.

Such precautions are essential for the security of all personnel involved in espionage, their organizations proceeding from the assumption that their agents are known to the counterespionage authorities of the countries in which they operate, or at least that they are under surveillance. It is, therefore, essential to perform all functions connected with the mission only when it is absolutely certain that nobody observes the operation, or when it is painstakingly camouflaged. Even so, secret agents are in the greatest danger of being trapped when meeting with others, whoever they may be. Judith Coplon was arrested on the street during a meeting with her Soviet go-between, as was British agent Yeo-Thomas while awaiting the arrival of his *agent-de-liaison*. Such meetings are unavoidable, but they are kept at a minimum.

No matter how isolated a secret agent is, he must maintain a line of communications with his headquarters, to which he must forward whatever information he collects—unless his instructions are to bring back personally. The latter instance is extremely rare, since there is an important time element in espionage. The value of an item of information is computed on the basis of its significance and the speed with which it comes into the hands of the organization. Any item, even of the greatest intrinsic value, is obviously useless if it reaches the organization too late to be used. Therefore, espionage services do their utmost to expedite the transmission of information, at the same time maintaining iron-clad safety and security. In this phase of the activity, which often involves a great number of people, all moves involving collector and transmitter, sender and receiver, are coordinated and synchronized. Every member of the team must attend to his own duties on the split second and in the exact manner prescribed in the operations plan.

In addition to word of mouth, there are fifteen means of transmission used by espionage agents. In the order of frequency with which they are used, they are: the mail, couriers, radio, underground telephones, telephone, telegraph, carrier pigeons, airplanes, runners, dogs, hand flags, signal fires, heliograph, rockets, and flares. Also, freak methods may be used when circumstances compel them. Messages have been transmitted by lighting bonfires on hilltops, or by turning lights on and off in the windows of houses to spell out words in Morse code. Even smoke has been used, as in September, 1914, in Poland when, according to a communiqué of the Austro-Hungarian command, "the troops suffered great losses owing to the espionage and treachery of the natives who indicated the positions of artillery and infantry by employing columns of white and gray smoke by day, and light signals by night." In the Boer War, native spies working for the British would mark out a trail by cutting the bark of trees, and indicated a direction by inclining treetops or laying bundles of grass. Cases are on record in which the hands of clocks in church steeples were so set as to indicate the location of enemy troops, or in which the movement of the sails of windmills communicated a specific message in a complex and unsuspected code.

Of all the means of communication, the mail is still used most often, not only in times of peace, when censorship is relaxed or non-existent, but also in wartime when every single letter, postal card, telegram, or cable must pass the scrutiny of censors. Espionage agents use ingenious methods to outwit or evade the censor, often writing their letters in code or with secret ink. The progress of microphotography makes it possible to reduce even the longest espionage reports to the size of a dot over a typewritten "i." Even when no censorship is feared the agent must disguise his communications, partly to protect his own cover and security, and partly to conceal the contents of his message. Letters are never mailed directly to an espionage service, but instead to cover addresses, the so-called letterboxes or mail-drops. These drops then forward the mail to the home office of the secret agent, sometimes via several intermediary drops.

Frequently, agents are instructed to send in their messages in duplicate or triplicate through several drops located in two or three different countries. If all letters arrive safely at their destination, it is assumed that all is well. If, however, one or two of the letters fail to show up it is assumed that certain drops have been found out, and they are then promptly abandoned and new ones are set up.

Espionage reports may be sent in letters whose real contents are camouflaged by the use of a code. This method was used by a German agent operating in the United States in 1941 who sent his reports to Berlin via drops in Spain and Portugal. He would write an ordinary business letter in which every sentence had a dual meaning. This same agent used secret ink and chemicals which made writing invisible but which could be made visible at the receiving end. The message was written in secret ink and inserted between the lines of the ordinary letter. In this manner, in the spring of 1941, the German agent reported on the ships loading at New York piers ready to depart in convoys with war material consigned for Britain. It so happened that his letters were intercepted by British censorship in Bermuda, which also exposed the writing in secret ink.

Despite the elaborate organization and efficiency of modern censorship, the mail still continues to deliver innumerable communications sent by spies. One of the great secret agents of our times was a self-effacing, industrious little man named Jules Crawford Silber. He actually operated under the cover of British censorship in which he had a modest job on the German desk. There he made good use of the suspect list, composed of persons suspected of espionage and for whose correspondence the censors were constantly on the alert.

165

Silber culled information from the very mail he examined. He then wrote out his own reports, placed them in envelopes, stamped them "Examined by Censor," and posted them to addresses in neutral countries picked at random from the suspect list, which listed them as possible drops. Every one of his unsolicited but extremely valuable reports reached the German secret service in Berlin.

The preparation of an agent's report for mailing follows a set routine. Whenever information is received, the agent will write it up and encipher it. The message is divided into portions of about 500 cipher groups each. These portions are then individually microphotographed until they produce a negative about the size of the head of a pin. This tiny negative is pasted on a postcard in a predetermined position and sent to a drop, who either sends it to still another drop or to the diplomatic mission of the country for which the spy works.

A special corps of couriers is maintained by all espionage services, men and women who maintain personal contacts with agents in the field. They carry to the agent the funds and supplies he needs and pick up whatever information or documents he may have for transmission. This is an unexciting but extremely important phase of espionage work, and, although couriers never do actual spying themselves, they run as great a risk as any spy engaged in the collection of information.

There is a great variety of methods employed by couriers to disguise the messages they carry. Messages have been found in soles and heels of shoes, in buttons and linings of clothing, in sweatbands of hats, in false bottoms of suitcases and food cans, in toothpaste and cakes of soap, in cigarettes and cigars. They have been tattooed on the body of the courier, or written in secret ink on his skin. Once the label of an overcoat was found to contain a coded message. A pretty espionage courier plying between Hungary and Turkey during World War II carried microfilmed messages in the glass eye of her silver-fox scarf.

Although radio does not play so dominant a role in the transmission of information as is commonly believed, it is nevertheless widely used, especially in wartime when the mail is slowed down by censorship and when the traffic of couriers is complicated. The development of radio as a tool of spies has changed the complexion of the battle of espionage. It has broadened the field of secret war enormously. In the Second World War, in particular, constant liaison could be maintained between headquarters and spies in the field, and between groups of resistance fighters, by the use of clandestine radios. Every espionage service maintained extensive networks and hook-ups of clandestine transmitters, especially the Soviet Union, whose espionage service operated several hundred secret radio stations in German-occupied Europe.

The radio operator is responsible for the setting up of his technical installations, and, since he obviously cannot establish himself in a hotel or a boarding house where he might be surprised in the midst of transmission, he must find a suitable apartment from which he can operate. The top floor of an apartment house is desirable, if only to make detection by counterespionage agents somewhat more difficult. The apartment should be self-contained and situated so that the operator may hear anybody approaching and thereby gain time to conceal his transmitter before having to answer the doorbell.

Radio sets used in clandestine operations are small and handy instruments about the size of portable typewriters. They can be assembled easily and just as easily concealed. Radio operators usually set up their instruments in kitchens, bathrooms, or closets. Unexpected visitors are not likely to penetrate to such places immediately, and the operator often has time to conceal his set.

Naturally, all messages go out in cipher. Usually the operator of the radio will encipher messages handed him *en clair* by the agent, but once in a while the agent takes care of enciphering. The purpose of ciphers and codes is to prevent the enemy from reading the messages, while the constant changing of wavelengths, transmitting times, and call signals confuses the enemy's listening posts. To avoid detection, several transmitters are used to service the same ring or net.

Generally, radiotelegraphy is used, since it is more reliable than radiotelephone, and because Morse signals are more difficult to intercept. Telegraphy uses a very narrow band of only one kilocycle, while radiotelephony needs a band of six to seven kilocycles. A radiotelephone message can be easily overheard and the voice recognized, often leading to the identification of the transmitter. As a matter of fact, the radio operator of an espionage team is its most vulnerable member and yet, without him, the operational spy would lose his voice.

When putting his message on the air, or when he entrusts it to the mails, the spy gives up a bit of his cover. He not only reveals himself to a certain extent, but in fact runs the risk of exposing his mission.

We have already seen in general terms what security means and how it is maintained. Now we may examine the problem more specifically on the basis of actual examples.

By security, espionage services mean the sum total of all measures designed to preserve the secrecy of the central organization and its branches and agents operating in the field, the concealment of methods used in the collection, transmission, evaluation, and dissemination of information, the concealment of all individual items in which the service may either be interested or actually already possesses, the concealment of individual missions, codes, and ciphers, and the protection of personnel from exposure.

To insure the safety and security of agents operating in the field, a broad foundation is laid during the agent's indoctrination and training, when the importance of security is impressed on him and when he is acquainted with all the possible pitfalls of his profession. He is then taught in great detail how to avoid them. The counterespionage methods and institutions of foreign countries are studied, and precautionary measures based on these investigations are devised.

But, however efficient an agent's preliminary indoctrination may be, it may still prove insufficient to protect him in practice. The agent in the field is secure only as long as absolutely nothing is known to the opponent about his clandestine activities. Once even the slenderest lead points to him the counterespionage agents of the country where he operates will inevitably develop that lead and expose him. One arrested agent can unwittingly lead the authorities to others, and in due time the whole ring or net will be exposed.

If the security of agents seemed far greater during the 1930's, this was a result chiefly of the laxity of counterespionage measures which, in most countries of the West, were almost non-existent. In countries where counterespionage was pursued effectively, agents were insecure.

The precautionary measures used by the Sorge ring in Japan were unusually excellent. They were all described during the interrogation of Sorge, Klausen, and Miyagi, and became known when the transcripts of their interrogation fell into American hands at the end of World War II.

Sorge himself went to extreme lengths to camouflage his espionage activities. He was painstaking in establishing his legitimate cover as a foreign correspondent and sought continuously to maintain it. He did not engage in any espionage activities for several months after his arrival in Japan because he knew that in most countries foreigners were watched by the local police authorities. He examined carefully every sign that indicated such surveillance. In order to avoid suspicion, he made his movements widely known and advertised his legitimate activities to direct attention away from those of his mission. He employed only one housemaid, a dull old woman, and made her live away from his quarters so that she could not identify visitors who called on him late at night, after her departure.

Max Klausen listed the precautionary measures he considered essential for agents in the field, as follows:

All members of the ring must have rational, legitimate, occupational covers. The radio cipher must be altered by the use of different scramble numbers at each transmission. The transmitter must be dismantled, packed in a case, and moved after each operation. Messages must be sent from different locations, never from a single house over long periods. Liaison with couriers must be carried out in the utmost secrecy, never mentioning real names on either side. Each member must have a cover name. Real names must never be mentioned either in messages or in conversations. Place names must be disguised in code. Documents must be destroyed immediately after they have served their purpose.

How precarious the security of any espionage ring may be in the field was shown dramatically in the exposure of the Sorge organization, which was discovered despite the most scientific measures of protection and the high internal security of its top echelon. Sorge followed his instructions from Moscow never to have any contacts with the Communist Party in Japan, a standing rule prescribed for most Soviet spy rings. Their sole contact with the "corporations," as regional Communist parties are called in Soviet espionage parlance, is with those "corporants," or party members, who have already gone underground and are enlisted in the espionage apparatus of the Cominform.

This is usually resented by local Communists, who are left outside the rings. Just such a frustrated Communist was Ito Ritsu. He suspected that a Soviet espionage ring was working in Japan and became jealous when he was not allowed to have any connection with it. He suspected that one of his acquaintances, a woman named Tomo Kitabayashi, was a member of the Sorge ring and shared this suspicion with the Japanese authorities when he himself was picked up in a raid against Communists in general.

It so happened that Mrs. Kitabayashi was a minor member

of the Sorge ring. She was a dressmaker by profession and managed to secure some information from her customers. She then transmitted these items to her own contact within the Sorge ring, the artist Yotoko Miyagi.

Working on the tip they received from Ito Ritsu, the Japanese police arrested Mrs. Kitabayashi and forced her to confess her relationship with Miyagi. Then Miyagi was picked up and tortured. A frail consumptive man, he broke under torture and revealed his contacts, including Hozumi Ozaki, who then disclosed his association with Sorge and Klausen before succumbing to the brutal tortures of his Japanese interrogators.

Ito Ritsu was first picked up in June, 1941. He tipped off the Japanese police to Mrs. Kitabayashi in early September, and she was arrested on September 28, 1941. Following that it did not take long for the police to blow up the whole ring. Sorge himself was arrested on October 18, 1941, and within a few months no member of his ring was at large.

In those rare cases when an agent succeeds in preserving his security to the very end, he will leave his assignment and return to headquarters, often by simply purchasing a steamship ticket or a place on a plane and leaving the country. Occasionally, the termination of a mission requires as circumspect preparations as its establishment, especially when an agent is required to hand over his ring to a successor.

Once in a while, completion of a mission means the end of a man's connection with espionage. There are hundreds of former secret agents living among us to whom espionage is only the memory of past adventures. Others, however, are destined to stay in the business for good, not necessarily because they choose to, but because they are considered indispensable. Others are forced to remain active because their organizations feel that they know too much to risk letting them go.

Cryptography and Cryptanalysis

In conclusion, there remains to be reviewed just one other form of what may be called "applied espionage": cryptography in its various manifestations. In John Eglinton Bailey's classic definition, "Cryptography is the art of writing in such a way as to be incomprehensible except to those who possess the key to the system employed." Cryptanalysis is the organized effort to translate such writing into its original meaning and to make it again comprehensible.

Cryptography is properly placed under the heading of espionage, since it plays an important role as a major tool of concealment. Cryptanalysis is itself a form of espionage. Every major government utilizes it today in an elaborate and complex effort to penetrate the most closely guarded secrets of other nations by breaking their codes and solving their ciphers.

In cryptography we distinguish between codes and ciphers. A code is a system of words or groups of letters or symbols, selected arbitrarily to represent other words. Under this system a single word may have several meanings, it may represent several words combined, or it may be the equivalent of an entire predetermined sentence or paragraph.

An Austrian code of World War I, for example, used the word "Mama" to mean "three torpedo boats of the *Avanti* class"; the word "Easter" to mean "in the direction of Cattaro"; the word "doctor" to mean "depart" in its various tenses; the word "sun" for "heavy cruiser *Italia*"; the word "apartment" to mean "launching"; and "garden" for the month of August. A message an agent sent in this code read: "Three torpedo boats of the *Avanti* class departed in the direction of Cattaro; heavy cruiser *Italia* will be launched in August," actually read when it was encoded: "We expect Mama to move after Easter. She went to see the doctor yesterday, since the pain in her shoulder was getting worse. He suggested that she spend a lot of time in the sun and this will be no problem, since her new apartment has a lovely garden of its own."

A cipher may use any letter of the alphabet as a substitute for another, it may transpose them, spell words backward when enciphered, make arbitrary divisions between words, or substitute numerals or certain characters for letters. Ciphers are made increasingly complicated by the multiple use of transpositions or substitutions and the scrambling of numerals, and by the insertion of dummy letters.

The cipher is a very ancient form of concealment. The prophet Jeremiah, for example, wrote (xxv, 26) *Sheshach* for "Babel" (Babylon) to conceal the meaning of his prophecy. Jeremiah made up this cipher by transposing the letters of the Hebrew alphabet. Instead of using the second and twelfth letters from the beginning, Jeremiah wrote the second and twelfth from the end. Julius Caesar devised a special cipher for his own secret correspondence. He wrote *d* for *a*, *e* for *b*, *f* for *c*, and so on, using the third letter after the one standing in the original text. This particular system is still called "the Caesar." There are other more modern systems, including the "Beaufort," named after the famous British cryptographer Admiral Sir Francis Beaufort, the Sliding Alphabet Cipher, and various French systems called "St. Cyr," after the famous military academy. They represent considerable improvement over the primitive Caesar, but employ the same basic principle.

The fundamentals of cryptography are also ancient and unchanged. They were first enumerated by Bacon centuries ago when he stipulated that "a cipher must be simple to write and read; it must be impossible to decipher; and it must not arouse suspicion." These are perfectionist rules. If they appear to be unheeded it is not because cryptographers do not try to live up to them. But the art of cryptography is so complex and exacting that it is humanly impossible to devise the perfect cipher or code.

Individuals engaged in this activity are called cryptographers. They may be encoders or decoders, encipherers or decipherers, or cryptanalysts, according to the nature of their functions. Code and cipher experts specialize in encoding or decoding, enciphering and deciphering messages, that is, in translating a plain or *en clair* message into code or cipher and then retranslating incoming messages into clear. Cryptanalysts are the actual "spies" of this traffic. Their job is to break the codes and ciphers of others, to find a key to their solution, and then to expose the contents of the concealed message.

This is an exact science involving mathematics and statistics, as well as the ingenuity of the specialist. Cryptanalysts base their operations on the fact that in each language certain letters occur more frequently than others. In the English language, the letters e, t, a, o, i, and r occur most frequently, and v, k, x, j, q, and z most rarely. In French, the letters e, a, i, s, t, and n, and in German, the letters e, n, i, s, r, a, d, and t, are the most frequent. The first thing a cryptanalyst does is to look for such "frequencies" in the text. He will then prepare a "frequency table," in which all letters of the text are catalogued according to their frequency. After that, a number of complicated methods are used, and really skilled and imaginative cryptanalysts usually succeed in breaking even the most complicated cipher.

Ciphers are often as treacherous as any other type of security leak. While every country hopes and trusts that its systems are the best and safest, the history of cryptography shows that there have been very few ciphers in the world which survived the ingenious assaults of expert cryptanalysts.

The same is true of codes. Codes are specially prepared in the form of books, or "dictionaries," in which each word means a different word, sentence, or phrase. Although codes are more difficult to break than ciphers, they are still vulnerable, especially when code books fall into unauthorized hands. As a result, coded books are among the favorite targets of spies. Divers have actually been sent into the hulls of sunken ships to recover whatever code books they might find in them. And agents are used to entrap individuals engaged in the code rooms of government agencies and diplomatic missions, to acquire through them the secret code books entrusted to their care. The Soviet Union once gained access to the diplomatic code of the British Foreign Office by luring a code clerk into espionage. In an almost identical manner, the Germans and Italians acquired American diplomatic codes by persuading an American code clerk named Tyler Kent, working in the Embassy in London, to spy for them. The outstanding espionage case of our times, which resulted in the smashing of the Soviet spy ring in Canada, had a code clerk, Igor Gouzenko, as its pivot.

Every intelligence service has its own cryptographic department to handle the codes and ciphers used by its agents, and some of them maintain cryptanalytic branches to break the codes and translate the ciphers of others. However, some governments keep this function separate from the intelligence service and maintain it under the signal corps of their armies or the communication branches of their navies. These departments are usually shrouded in supersecrecy, and their methods are protected as carefully as the personnel working in them.

While every country in the world has practiced cryptography and cryptanalysis, England and the United States have made the greatest contributions to the science. Britain, in particular, pioneered the art in modern times. The great Reginald Hall, director of Britain's Division of Naval Intelligence, first recognized the overwhelming importance of cryptography as a source of information, and he made elaborate arrangements immediately after the outbreak of the First World War to monitor German radio communications and break the codes and translate the ciphers of the enemy. With the help of Sir Alfred Ewing, a professor whose hobby was the solving of intricate puzzles, he set up a cryptanalysis branch of Naval Intelligence in the famous 40 O.B. and broke virtually every code the Germans used during the war. Among his great achievements was the reading of telegrams which the German Foreign Office sent to its envoy in Mexico, urging him to bring Mexico into the war against the United States. His unusual ability to break operations orders sent to fleet units of the German Navy on the seven seas enabled the British Admiralty to make its own arrangements in the fullest knowledge of the enemy's plans, intentions, and strength. Thanks to the information Admiral Hall culled from coded German signals, the Royal Navy triumphed in the battle of Dogger Bank and in the battle of the Falkland Islands.

On September 16, 1945, Hanson W. Baldwin, military editor of the New York *Times*, wrote in a column: "It is not, has not been, and since the Battle of Midway never could be a secret that the [United States] Navy broke the Japanese code fairly early in the war and, by interception of Japanese radio messages and other means, learned in advance of many Japanese operations." John A. Beasley, Australian Minister of Defense, came out with the flat statement that "U.S. Naval Intelligence Officers had cracked Japanese naval codes even before the Battle of the Coral Sea" in 1942.

Admiral Chester W. Nimitz, commander in chief of the U.S. Pacific Fleet, was later asked in a press conference, "How were we able to shoot down Admiral Yamamoto, commander in chief of the Japanese fleet?" He answered with a frankness that is quite rare when discussing these matters, "We had broken the latest Japanese codes and ciphers and knew where Admiral Yamamoto would be at a certain fatal minute of a certain fatal day."

In April, 1943, the cryptanalysts of the U.S. Navy's Communication Intelligence intercepted a top secret signal sent from Japan's naval high command to its China stations and units in the South Pacific. When the signal was translated, it was found to contain a message of enormous immediate importance. It advised the various commanders of the Japanese fleet that Admiral Isoroku Yamamoto, their commander in chief, would make an inspection of their units. The intercept included an exact itinerary of the admiral's trip. It revealed that he would go to China, then to Truk, and then to Bougainville. Every stop-over was listed, as were the exact date and time of his arrivals and departures.

The information was relayed immediately to Frank Knox, then Secretary of the Navy, who rushed it to President Roosevelt. The American leaders were confronted with a grave dilemma. The question before them was: Shall we attempt to intercept Yamamoto's plane and destroy him, and thus deprive Japan of the guiding genius of its war effort, or shall we let him pass despite our knowledge of his itinerary?

During the more chivalrous days of warfare there used to

174

be an unwritten code that somehow protected the lives of leaders in war. Kings and generals were frequently killed in battle, and Napoleon III was captured by the Prussians, as was Leopold III of the Belgians in World War II. In World War II, however, several deliberate efforts were made to destroy the leaders of the enemy. A German U-boat tried to torpedo the ship on which President Roosevelt was sailing to one of his wartime conferences. During the Battle of the Bulge, the Germans devised a plan to assassinate General Eisenhower. An attempt was made to shoot down Prime Minister Winston Churchill as he was flying back to London from a vacation in the Mediterranean, but the Germans blundered and shot down the plane in which the famous actor Leslie Howard was traveling, mistaking it for Churchill's plane. The secret war book of the Germans did, in fact, advocate "the assassination of war leaders" as a legitimate and justifiable method "if it led to the prejudice of the enemy."

The United States normally deplored such practices. There were several opportunities to participate in attempts made to assassinate Hitler and Mussolini, but the United States refrained even from lending a helping hand. The case of Yamamoto was different. He had outlawed himself on "the day of infamy" and had forfeited the protection of the articles of war when he himself violated them with the sneak attack on Pearl Harbor. Moreover, he was traveling in a combat zone, where a top admiral is as fair a target as any sailor manning a gun.

The issue was decided by President Roosevelt. He ordered that an attempt be made to intercept Yamamoto's plane and shoot it down. An operations plan was drafted under the personal supervision of Secretary Knox and the decision reached to ambush Yamamoto's plane as it was approaching Bougainville.

The order and the plan were then sent to the operations officer of a Marine unit in the South Pacific, directing him to make a "maximum effort" to intercept Yamamoto's flight. "Destroy the target at any cost," the order read, "then break off and return to base, evading all further action." Utmost secrecy before and after the operation was enjoined.

At exactly 4 P.M. on April 17, 1943, two Army Air Force pilots were summoned secretly to a dank, musty room on Guadalcanal, the office of the Marine operations officer. They were Major John W. Mitchell and Major Thomas J. Lanphier, Jr. They were shown the Navy's signal and told that they had been chosen to carry out this supersecret mission. Various plans were discussed at length. The Marine officer suggested that Yamamoto be attacked in Kahilli harbor where he was expected to conduct his inspection aboard a sub-chaser. But the pilots said, "How do you expect us to pick out that particular craft with all those ships in the harbor?"

They suggested that Yamamoto's plane be intercepted in midair while flying from Truk to Kahilli. Yamamoto was known to Naval Intelligence for extreme punctuality in his schedules. The decoded itinerary said that he would reach Kahilli at exactly 9:45 A.M. on April 18, in a flight of two Mitsubishi bombers escorted by six Zeros. He was to be accompanied by his entire staff. "I'll bet my last silver dime," Major Lanphier said, "that he will be on time!"

A map was produced and the very spot chosen where Admiral Yamamoto was to be intercepted. It was fixed at a point thirty-five miles from Kahilli, just eleven minutes flying time from the airport where he was scheduled to land. Then the detailed arrangements for the interception were made. Two groups of Lightnings would fly out from Guadalcanal to ambush him. One group, commanded by Major Mitchell, would fly high as a decoy to draw off Yamamoto's escorts. The other group, commanded by Lanphier, would then attend to the destruction of the Mitsubishis.

The planes were chosen and their crews picked. On the morning of April 18, the men received their last briefing from two intelligence officers, Lieutenant Joe McGuigan of the Navy and Captain Bill Morrison of the Army. At exactly 7:35 A.M. the Lightnings took off. They flew in a 435-mile semicircle to avoid all known Japanese positions. They kept radio silence all the way. Using only compass and air-speed indicator to navigate, they reached the chosen spot at the prearranged time, only fifty seconds before the expected arrival of Yamamoto's flight. Then at 9:34 A.M., Lieutenant Doug Canning called out on the intercom, "Bogey! Ten o'clock high!"

Exactly as predicted by the original intercept was Yamamoto's unsuspecting convoy, the two bombers and six Zeros. Major Mitchell's group climbed to 20,000 feet to draw off the Zeros, whose pilots immediately left the bombers unprotected to attack the American fighters. Below, and unseen, Major Lanphier climbed straight into Yamamoto's course. He had his engines wide open as he tried to cross ahead of the Mitsubishi. He was followed closely by his wing man, Lieutenant Rex Barber, and by Lieutenant Joe Moore, leader of the second element, and his wing man, Lieutenant Jim McLanahan.

At last Lanphier and Barber were even with the two

Mitsubishis. Too late, the protecting Zeros noticed them for the first time and wheeled into power dives in an attempt to cover their admiral's unprotected bomber. Lanphier opened up with a long steady burst, and in a moment the right engine and then the right wing of Yamamoto's Mitsubishi burst into flames. As the bomber fell away towards Kahilli, Lanphier poured another burst into it. The wing of the bomber flew off and the big plane plummeted earthward. Its fuselage exploded among the trees of the jungle, only a few miles from its destination at Kahilli.

In spite of the desperate efforts of the returning Zeros diving to the rescue, Rex Barber shot down the second bomber, which carried members of Yamamoto's staff. The mission was accomplished.

An operation that had begun in the secret offices where the Navy housed its Communications Intelligence in Washington was completed in Bougainville as planned.

Although the importance of secrecy had been enjoined upon the personnel engaged in the operation, news somehow leaked out that Yamamoto had been shot down. Except for the alertness of the naval censor at Pearl Harbor, who was able to intercept the news reports, this unique incident in the history of espionage would have been broadcast right then to the world—and, more important, to the Japanese. Fortunately, the secret was preserved. Stunned by the disaster, the Japanese tried to find out what had happened, but their intelligence services could never supply a single clue. Unaware that their code had been broken, they believed that Yamamoto's death was a freak accident, and left it at that. Their ignorance of the actual facts prevented them from taking precautions against the repetition of such leaks.

Agents at Large

For every espionage exploit that becomes known, there must be dozens of cases which will remain secret forever. Among these, indeed, are the true epics of espionage, in which the identity of the agent is never exposed, not even deduced from the sometimes monumental clues he leaves behind in the frequently historic consequences of his successful mission. Before World War I, the French General Staff obtained an authentic copy of the famous Schlieffen Plan from a mysterious man who traveled to Paris disguised as a seriously injured patient in the care of a nurse, his whole face and part of his body covered with bandages. The document was concealed in the bandages. But although the case became known after the war, no one actually knows who the agent was.

Throughout both world wars, the British had a high-ranking officer of their secret service planted within the German General Staff. But only a handful of initiated persons knew the identity of the spy. During the Second World War, scores of Italian submarines were lured to their destruction by using the top-secret code of the submarine service. It was stolen by a British spy. But only the initiated knew the identity of this agent, and the counterespionage organs of Italy were never able to identify or catch him.

While Britain succeeded in unmasking most of the German agents of World War II, one truly effective German spy managed to evade the net. This man succeeded in outwitting Britain's entire counterespionage machinery for seven years, from 1937, when he entered Britain allegedly from Canada, to 1944, when his trail eventually vanished. During those seven years, this phantom spy supplied the German secret service with a remarkable collection of intelligence. Among his deliveries were:

1. A top-secret report prepared by Sir Alexander Cadogan, then British Permanent Under-Secretary of Foreign Affairs, representing the Foreign Office's estimate of Anglo-German relations. This document existed in only four copies, one each for the Cabinet, the War Office, the Admiralty, and President Roosevelt.

2. A dossier of maps showing the emergency system of food and fuel distribution in the United Kingdom.

3. Information about the deficient defenses of the great Scapa Flow naval base in the north and the delay in the arrival of submarine nets and booms. This enabled German Lieutenant Commander Gunther Prien in submarine *U-47* to penetrate to the heart of the "impenetrable" base and, on October 14, 1939, to sink the battleship *Royal Oak* with a loss of more than 800 lives.

4. Blueprints of the docks of London and Hull, as well as detailed maps of both key ports.

5. Maps of the system of airfields in Kent built to protect London from attack by the Lutwaffe. Later, this phantom spy was said to have directed the Lufwaffe raids on these airfields in preparation for the Battle of Britain.

6. A complete report on the dispersal of British industries and on the organization of so-called shadow industries concentrated around Birmingham and Coventry. The spy was

later credited with the guiding of the German bombers to these crucial targets.

This is only a partial list of the man's achievements. His activities still baffle British counterespionage and even such a taciturn spy-catcher as Colonel Hinchley Cook of MI-5 pays an unstinted tribute, if not to the efficiency of the German secret service, then to the competence of this one agent. Who was this formidable adversary? How could he remain undetected? How could he escape?

Even today, no one professes to know the answers to these questions. Some say that all these scoops were scored by a single operative, probably one of the greatest spies who ever lived. Others presume that there were, in fact, three different men behind those coups, none of whom was ever caught. Still others insist that they were the work of a brilliant network of Germany's ace operatives led by a single genius who not only understood how to direct his men but also how to protect them from the spy-catchers.

Whoever he was, this phantom was still going strong in the fifth year of the war, on the very eve of the Normandy invasion. When, in March, 1944, General Eisenhower moved his headquarters from London to Busy Park to evade German spies, the phantom reported the transfer to Berlin within 72 hours. Later, he reported the exact date of D-Day, but Hitler trusted his intuition more than a report from his master spy. He simply refused to believe that the Allies would have the audacity to invade his continent.

It may be that this elusive Scarlet Pimpernel was someone whom MI-5 and Scotland Yard did meet, but only as a corpse, in a deserted air-raid shelter in Cambridge, with a bullet in his head and a German revolver at his side, apparently a suicide. From the papers in his pocket he was identified as a native of Holland, Jan Willem Ter Braak, but it was obvious that this was an alias. Later the body was recognized by a landlady who reported one of her boarders missing. In Ter Braak's abandoned room, the spy-catchers found forged documents and a powerful German-made radio transmitter.

However, it is more likely that the phantom spy was a German-Canadian who called himself Karl Dickenhoff. He lived quietly in a villa in Edgbaston. His real name was Hans Caesar. His is a weird story, somewhat in the Conan Doyle tradition. Caesar is said to be still alive and in England, the demented, amnesia-stricken inmate of an insane asylum. Nobody will say whether he is really unbalanced or merely simulates insanity to escape the consequences of his wartime activities.

Sometimes not even the boldest spy is caught, even though his escape may be due more to luck than anything else. During the war, one of the most successful Allied spy rings operated in neutral Sweden. It was a ring of amateur spies composed of German anti-Nazi refugees, led by an intrepid agent named Kurt Englich. He discovered that the center of German espionage in Sweden—a kind of clearing house of all incoming secrets—was in a vaultlike room of the German air attaché's office in Stockholm. Englich found out, too, that the room was always abandoned at night, left in the custody of a single guard.

Englich got a lead to this guard and established that the man was not too well disposed toward the Nazis. The adroit refugee went to work on him, and the guard was soon convinced that Germany would lose the war. So he joined the anti-Nazis and permitted Englich to enter the air attaché's office every night to copy important documents that were left lying on the desks in the locked room.

Kurt Englich worked in the room night after night, and, only once, for a few tense moments, did he nearly get caught. That was the time an aide of the air attaché suddenly showed up in the office. At first, Englich was undecided as to how to meet the emergency, but then he decided to go on copying the document on which he was working as if he belonged to the place. The young Luftwaffe captain walked straight to one of the safes, opened it, and removed from it a bottle of Scotch whisky. Then he locked the safe again and left.

"There is no end to espionage," Alan Moorehead wrote in his account of the Klaus Fuchs case, "it flows on, in a private world of its own, through wars and centuries." As it flows on, it increases in cunning and violence, until it overflows the banks of espionage to leave physical destruction in its wake.

PART III

Sabotage

What Is Sabotage?

The term sabotage is derived from the French word *sabot*, a kind of wooden shoe worn by the lower classes in some European countries. The *sabot* came to be regarded as the symbol of rebellious farm laborers or revolutionary workers who trampled the properties of squires or threw their wooden shoes into machines in the factories during the periodic unrest of the eighteenth and nineteenth centuries. When later a word was needed to describe the act of wanton, deliberate destruction of property to further one's own ends, the act was called sabotage, and the perpetrators of such acts became known as "saboteurs."

In the official language of the secret service, sabotage is usually called "special operations." The saboteur is listed merely as a secret agent, or as a "specialist."

Sabotage is a form of subversive warfare. It is usually physical action designed to damage the enemy's military or economic machinery. It is action against an enemy's administration, industrial production, food and commodities production, armed forces, lines of communication—everything, in fact, that aids his war effort.

Sabotage takes different forms, not all of them necessarily physical or violent. There is direct action, or active sabotage, sudden violent actions against key targets. There is indirect action, or passive sabotage, directed at an opponent's morale or his material resources by non-violent means. There is an intangible form called psychological sabotage, whose purpose is the manipulation of crowd psychology to cause strikes, panic, or riots.

Direct action is carried out in a number of ways and on various scales. It may be aimed at major targets, such as factories or entire regions in which the enemy may have important installations. Such operations are usually performed by scores, sometimes hundreds, of men. They are called sabotage troops: in Britain, Commandos; in the United States, Rangers; in Germany, the Brandenburg Divisions; in the Soviet Union, partisans. Sabotage may also be directed at

181

smaller, pinpointed targets, such as boiler rooms in factories or single railroad switches. These operations are carried out by small sabotage crews of two or three men, and often by only one man.

Arson, explosions, and mechanical interference are the most common forms of sabotage by direct action. Fires may be started either by conventional methods or by such ingenious means as substituting incendiary solutions for non-volatile fuels, or deliberately overloading machines in essential industries. Explosives, including bombs and infernal machines, are used against the enemy's system of communications and his military and economic installations, such as command posts, government offices, ammunition dumps, telegraph lines, radar stations, and the like. Other forms of direct action are the damaging of machinery by placing emery dust in delicate bearings, tossing bolts into dynamos and turbines, jamming steel waste into machine works, or simply dropping keys into the mechanisms of conveyor belts. Direct action may also involve anti-personnel operations, in which sentries and guards are killed, key personnel kidnaped, or important personages assassinated.

Indirect action, or passive sabotage, aims to achieve similar ends without open violence. Encouragement of absenteeism or deliberate slowdowns in industry are common forms of passive sabotage. By feigning a cold and having to leave his job periodically, a worker may effectively interfere with production. Failure to lubricate machines will inevitably lead to breakdowns. Spare parts are often deliberately mislaid. A worker may pretend to need a wrench to tighten a loose bolt, using this excuse to effect sabotage. The cumulative effect of even scattered passive sabotage is enormous. In the spring of 1949, a quarter of a million workers used such methods in the metallurgical industries of Italy, causing a sixteen percent reduction in output. Periodic and systematic looting of enemy stores is another form of sabotage, designed to withhold from the enemy raw materials, fuel, and spare parts which he needs for uninterrupted production.

Psychological sabotage is designed to cause strikes, panic, or riots, and to harass an opponent in his own country or in those that his forces occupy. When small boys in China during the Second World War sprayed Japanese officers with evil-smelling liquids, they were conducting a form of psychological sabotage. At one point during the German occupation of Czechoslovakia the public was persuaded by the underground not to buy newspapers on certain days. In satellite countries of the Soviet Union audiences watching Russian movies sometimes laugh at the wrong time or break out into exaggerated applause at the performance of a collaborationist or a Russian actor.

Psychological sabotage may have serious physical consequences when, for example, a saboteur calls a factory to tell the switchboard operator that a bomb is about to go off in the plant. This method was used repeatedly by German saboteurs in the United States during the Second World War. When such a call is received production is usually stopped and the plant evacuated while guards and police search for the bomb, and without using violence or resorting to any direct physical harm, the saboteur causes the loss of innumerable man-hours and reduces the output of equipment that might be urgently needed.

Maritime sabotage is a very special branch of clandestine warfare, designed to interfere with ships, maritime installations, and navigable waterways. Aboard ships compasses are disturbed by tampering with the magnets. Fires are started in ships, especially in hot weather, by pouring gasoline on the coal. Cargoes of meat and other perishable goods are drenched with kerosene. Ships are occasionally sunk by opening the sea cocks and flooding the holds with water. A very common form of sabotage aboard vessels, both at sea and in port, involves the cutting of electrical cables where the repair of such damage is extremely costly and delays the ship's departure.

In port the saboteur will often interfere with the operations of cranes, thereby delaying loading and unloading, or he may alter the shipping marks on cases containing essential goods to delay their delivery, often by months. Saboteurs working as agitators may induce certain key personnel of ports to go on strike. Even if only the crane operators walk out, the whole port comes to a standstill.

Navigable inland waterways may be sabotaged by destroying locks, bridges, and reservoirs. In this manner saboteurs succeeded in delaying for three months the supply of Ruhr coal to the industrial regions of Lorraine during the Second World War.

Effectiveness of Sabotage

Sabotage, or the calculated destruction of an opponent's vital material resources and installations, is relatively recent as a means of warfare. It may be that American recognition of its value was the result of an unstaged disaster that befell the Germans in 1916. In a munitions dump near Spincourt in France the Germans had stored 450,000 fully fused heavy shells. It is not known how or why, but the dump blew up and all the shells were exploded. With their heavy shells gone, the Germans were unable to supply their artillery with adequate ammunition during the battle of Verdun. This "accident" helped save Verdun.

In the Allied camp, a French general named Palat was the first to recognize the value of such "accidents" and urged that the deliberate use of sabotage be considered. But the Allies felt uneasy about it, largely on the same ethical grounds that prevented the use of poison gas and that retards the employment of atomic weapons.

The Germans, on the other hand, had no such qualms. As early as 1915, their military attaché in Switzerland suggested that Russian communications be sabotaged by blowing up the bridges of the Yenisei River on the Trans-Siberian Railway. At about the same time, the German high command decided to conduct history's first organized campaign of sabotage and picked a neutral country, the United States, as its target.

On the night of July 29, 1916 the Germans blew up the freight terminal of the Lehigh Valley Railroad in lower New York Harbor, opposite the Statue of Liberty. Thirty-seven carloads of high explosives, several large warehouses filled with sugar and food, a dozen barges and ships, and a complete railway yard went up in the explosion. Then on January 11, 1917, the Kingsland Assembling Plant in Kingsland, New Jersey, was blown up by German saboteurs. The plant, "Black Tom," was extremely important since American supplies were finally crated there for shipment to Russia.

If sabotage was but a minor phase of World War I, it became a large-scale operation in World War II. The Germans regarded it as a definite weapon and prepared for it long in advance by training saboteurs in great numbers. Adolf Hitler actually initiated his aggression in the Second World War with a most cynical sabotage operation. It was a staged attack against a German radio station on German soil by six German saboteurs disguised as Polish irregulars. Behind this strange operation was Hitler's desire for "justification" for his unprovoked attack on Poland. With one eye on history, Hitler tried to preserve decorum by putting the onus of aggression on the attacked. Once before, on April 18, 1938, he had seriously considered the assassination of the German envoy in Prague by one of his own strong-arm men to "justify" a strategic attack on Czechoslovakia.

The Czech coup was abandoned, but an SS man named Alfred Helmut Naujocks, according to his own account, was ordered "to simulate an attack on the radio station near Gleiwitz near the Polish border and to make it appear that the attacking force consisted of Poles." The operation was given the code name Canned Goods. The idea was to seize the Gleiwitz radio station and hold it long enough to enable a Polish-speaking German to make an incendiary speech against Germany. The operation was to be carried out by five SD men, terrorists of the Secret State Police, headed by Naujocks. A prisoner taken from a German concentration camp and carrying forged Polish credentials was to be left dead on the ground to "prove" that the attack was mounted by Poles.

The sabotage operation was executed, exactly as planned, at 8 P.M. on August 31, 1939, about nine hours before German troops crossed into Poland. The Gestapo delivered their human prop directly to the radio station. He was unconscious and dying from a fatal injection administered by a Gestapo doctor. The six German saboteurs seized the station, held it for four minutes while the prearranged speech was broadcast in Polish, fired a few shots, and departed, leaving the dead "Pole" at the entrance of the station. Hitler had his justification for starting World War II with what he then called "counterattack with pursuit."

German sabotage never succeeded in interfering seriously with the Allies, partly because the Nazi leaders of the military intelligence service, which was responsible for sabotage operations, opposed such action on the grounds that it was ineffectual. When these opponents of sabotage were removed and the job was assigned to a fanatical Nazi, an Austrian soldier of fortune named Otto Skorzeny, there was insufficient time to cause serious damage before the war ended.

But where the Germans failed the Allies succeeded brilliantly. Sabotage became accepted as a legitimate means of war chiefly because its value and effectiveness were recognized in the type of war the Allies were compelled to wage in Europe and Asia between 1940 and 1944. Whatever qualms might have existed before were overcome. "This form of warfare," Bruce Marshall wrote in his account of the exploits of Yeo-Thomas, "was both more accurate and benign than aerial bombardment. An agent insinuated into a factory could sabotage effectively and without loss of human life a piece of essential machinery which a squadron of bombers would be lucky to hit by chance."

Sabotage expectations were fully borne out by achievement

in World War II. It required more than 175,000 incendiary bombs dropped from squadrons of Royal Air Force planes to create damage equal to that caused by German saboteurs in 1916 in New York harbor alone. In one instance, seven separate air raids failed to destroy a bridge in France which later fell after a single charge was laid surreptitiously by only two saboteurs. In twenty-six months of the Second World War, a single group of Soviet saboteurs destroyed 52 railway trains, 256 bridges, 96 munition dumps, 2 oil refineries, 150 miles of track, and 20 tanks, and killed over 1,000 German soldiers. Sabotage groups operated as far as 600 miles behind the German lines.

After the war, sabotage was the chief weapon of the Communist guerrilla forces in Greece. In August, 1948, for example, when sabotage operations were at their peak, they wrecked 91 trains, destroyed 153 railroad stations, and sabotaged 21 factories.

We may witness the truly decisive effectiveness of sabotage with an example from the Israeli-Arab war in which a combined operation actually saved the Israelis from defeat.

Israel was proclaimed an independent state in May, 1948. The young state was then promptly attacked by an alliance of Arab countries. An Egyptian army, led by a tank division, crossed into Palestine, overcame feeble military resistance, and rolled along the coastal road toward Tel-Aviv, the temporary capital of the new state.

The danger to Israel was extreme. The fall of Tel-Aviv would have ended the war and established Egypt as the virtual ruler of Palestine. At that stage, the Israelis drafted a plan in which they assigned a major role to a single and seemingly minor sabotage operation. The Israeli Air Force had a total of four planes, smuggled in from Czechoslovakia, antiquated German Messerschmitt fighters. Their purchase and arrival in Israel had been kept secret. Maintenance crews went to work behind the locked doors of the hangars at an airport that appeared deserted to Egyptian reconnaissance planes. The grass was allowed to grow high over the runways. Spare parts, left behind by the Royal Air Force, lay rusting in the sun.

While the Israeli mechanics worked frantically in the hangars to assemble the four planes, the Israeli intelligence service managed to obtain the operations plan of the Egyptian tank division. The division was to reach the outskirts of Tel-Aviv on June 10, 1948. The tanks were to halt there and then move on next day, the schedule calling for them to arrive in Tel-Aviv on the 12th.

186

Just outside of Tel-Aviv the Egyptian column had to cross a bridge, which immediately became the focal point of the Israeli counterplan. A team consisting of four saboteurs was chosen as a suicide squad. Their job was to wait under the bridge for the approach of the Egyptian tanks, and to blow it up just as the first tank reached it.

At dawn of June 12, the Egyptians rolled toward the bridge. There was no resistance and consequently no reason for them to disperse their tanks. They moved along the excellent highway, tank following tank, armored car after armored car, forming a column several miles long. The rear was brought up by huge army trucks carrying Egyptian infantrymen to serve as occupation troops in Tel-Aviv.

The first tank was sighted by the four saboteurs, waiting with their charges already laid. When the tank was within a few yards of them, the saboteurs blew up the bridge with tremendous force, throwing debris on the approaching tanks. The driver of the lead tank brought his vehicle to an abrupt stop. The second tank halted instantly, and so on, until the whole column was stalled on the open road, stretched out for five miles.

At that moment, the closed doors of the hangars on the airfield were pushed open and the Israeli "air force" rushed out for the take-off. The newly assembled planes were not even flight-tested. Although built to take off from hard runways, they now had to use the strips on the neglected field overgrown with high grass. As if by sheer will power of the pilots they were pulled into the air and headed for the immobilized Egyptian tanks. They swooped low over them, raked them with round after round from their machine guns, and dropped bombs on them.

As the planes appeared overhead, coming so unexpectedly from nowhere, the Egyptians were seized with panic. The orderly column of the Egyptians was thrown into confusion. At headquarters, Israeli military intelligence listened on monitoring sets to the excited chatter of the tank radios and shortly afterwards picked up a signal issued by the commanding general of the Egyptians ordering the tanks to disperse and await further instructions. Later that day came the decisive signal from the Egyptian general. It ordered the tanks to reform and retire. And so, at 9 A.M. on June 12, 1948, Israel was saved by the suicidal daring of four saboteurs.

Sabotage is a major weapon in a cold war. Today it is conducted by the various resistance forces in eastern Europe and Asia, and within the Soviet Union, especially in the Ukraine.

It is part of a greater operations plan, about which more will be said later.

Due to the physical aspects of sabotage, it becomes a complex operation even when only a single agent is involved. Sabotage, like intelligence, is an exact science, which demands exceptional military, economic, technical, and psychological preparation. It must have a general or strategic plan for campaigns, and tactical directives for individual operations. It requires large standing organizations both at headquarters and in the field, both at home and abroad. It must have its own lines of supplies and communications, and it uses personnel especially chosen and trained for the job.

The combination of these major elements represents the over-all scheme of sabotage. Now let us survey them one by one.

The Sabotage Plan

Even though in the final analysis everything will depend on the courage, inventiveness, and initiative of the individual saboteur in action, sabotage operations evolve from a general plan drawn up originally on the strategic level and then broken down into tactical directives for individual operations.

The sabotage plan is prepared at headquarters on the basis of general military requirements and detailed intelligence. It considers and evaluates the total potential of an opponent's resources accessible to sabotage. This potential includes raw materials, power sources, basic industries, military strength, food and water resources, auxiliary industries, and lines of transportation and communication. Information about all the resources is obtained by what is called general reconnaissance. It is designed to establish the military and economic importance of a country's industrial regions and to locate the various installations within them. After that, so-called special reconnaissance is used to supply data for the technical and tactical details of individual operations.

These are intelligence functions which must precede all sabotage operations and, indeed, must supply any information needed in the drafting of the basic sabotage plan. When such a plan is organized it follows logical lines which promise maximum effectiveness with a minimum of compromise. A logical plan, based on proper strategic considerations and exact information, will not ordinarily destroy assembly plants that produce finished products. Instead, it will attack the sources of raw materials needed by a great number of factories, or it will strike at auxiliary plants manufacturing special parts and accessories upon which final production is dependent.

The basic sabotage plan must determine in advance the extent to which a country is to be sabotaged. All such plans must be prepared on a long-range basis, the planners bearing in mind that indiscriminate destruction is bound to interfere seriously with postwar reconstruction and, during the war, with one's own operations in sabotaged areas. A wise military commander does not conduct wholesale sabotage operations against regions that he expects to occupy within a short time. He may find that indiscriminate sabotage, which often leaves bridges blown and rail lines cut in its wake, will hinder his own advance or retreat far more than it interferes with the enemy's operations.

In a blind fury of destruction, Hitler ordered large-scale attacks against Warsaw, capital of Poland, even though it was obvious that the city would fall to him within a few days. The destruction his own forces wrought eventually proved detrimental to the Germans, and Warsaw, instead of being an asset to Hitler, became a liability.

Within a sabotage plan, each target is treated separately, much in the manner in which an air force treats its aerial targets. Individual objectives are chosen in advance and all information concerning them is placed in separate "objective folders." These folders contain the operations instructions, evaluated intelligence reports and maps, information about protective measures, all worked out to the most minute detail. The objective folder also contains an estimate of the over-all situation, an evaluation of the target, and an assessment of its relative value to one's own plans, to the military organization of the enemy, and to his national economy.

The Sabotage Organization

Sabotage operations are generally conducted, first, by citizens against their own government or industries; second, against the occupation forces in a defeated country; third, by one country against another, either in the latter's own territory or in territories occupied by its forces; and fourth, in support of over-all military operations or as an independent effort to take the place of conventional military operations.

Despite the special nature of individual operations, sabotage is regarded as an intelligence function and is placed organizationally within the intelligence service, where it represents the brawn in a brainy function. This activity is included under intelligence chiefly for two reasons: because it requires the most detailed advance information to be effective, and because it has to be conducted in the deepest secrecy, which can only be achieved within intelligence services.

During the late war, sabotage operations represented one of the main functions of the OSS. There they were conducted by an autonomous branch called Special Operations. German sabotage was handled by a division of military intelligence, with saboteurs directed by what was called the Brandenburg Division for Special Operations. In Britain, sabotage was used as a major weapon between 1940 and 1944 to harass the Germans on the continent and prevent them from consolidating their victories.

The Italians and Japanese made very limited use of sabotage. The Russians, on the other hand, practiced sabotage on a truly gigantic scale. For domestic reasons, this activity was separated from the Fourth Bureau and established within the Ministry of Interior, and also in a special organization which served as headquarters for all partisan forces. This separation is explained by the fact that members of the Communist Party of the Soviet Union were traditionally experts in sabotage, having used it extensively in their struggle for power. Today it is further motivated by the Kremlin's fear of domestic saboteurs who might, if not closely controlled, use it as a weapon against their rulers. As long as all sabotage activities are controlled by the party, the men in the Kremlin feel secure against being sabotaged themselves.

Within underground movements, sabotage is usually one of three major "networks," the other two being intelligence and propaganda. Sabotage is sometimes called "action network," and is organized into regional, departmental, and local committees which conduct sabotage operations with crews, and guerrilla warfare with *francs-tireurs*, or partisans. Usually a separate network is maintained for the reception of material smuggled into the country. This network is also organized along regional lines, each sabotage region handling separately its own problems of supply from reception to distribution.

Sabotage organizations now generally maintain their own means of transportation and systems of communication. The former is often composed of speed-boats, submarines, and small planes for landing in hostile territory, and larger planes from which agents can be parachuted. Early in the war, sabotage organizations were dependent on regular navies and air forces to provide the means of transportation, but they since have developed their own means, since it was found that because of interdepartmental bureaucracy transportation from the other services could not be depended upon.

The communications net consists of couriers, wireless operators, and any of the other means of transmission used in intelligence operations. The communications center at head-quarters is the nerve center of a sabotage organization. In addition, field transmission centers act as a kind of switch-board to maintain liaison between various communications posts on a regional basis. In sabotage operations, radio is con-sidered the best medium of liaison. However, other media are also used to maintain personal contacts and to transmit mes-sages by less direct means.

Permanent sabotage organizations are rarely maintained in times of peace, outside the Soviet Union. Whatever sabotage operations are conducted in peacetime are handled by small special teams detached from the intelligence service for such special missions on an *ad hoc* basis.

When employed on a nation-wide scale, in an armed con-flict or in a cold war, sabotage organizations cannot subsist in the field as totally independent and self-contained units. Even though composed entirely of citizens of the country being thus attacked, organizations cannot survive when left to themselves. In order to be effective, they have to be organ-ized, directed, and supplied from abroad. Material aid is of prime importance, but political and diplomatic direction is also necessary. Consequently, liaison is a vital function of all sabotage organizations, not merely to sustain sabotage groups in the field and to supply them with whatever equipment and tools are needed, but also to provide them with policies, stra-tegic directives, and tactical guidance. This is necessary in order to integrate them into the greater strategic aim which sabotage, on whatever scale it may be conducted, must ulti-mately serve.

The Perfect Saboteur

Like an intelligence service, a sabotage organization stands or falls on its personnel. If possible, the question of personnel is even more important in sabotage than in espionage. In view of the complex nature of these operations, and the fact that far more persons have to be employed in them than in espionage, sabotage organizations usually involve the greatest personnel problems of intelligence services. The membership of such an organization is classified according to the specific functions they are supposed to perform. There are directors and planners, agents, couriers, guides, weapons instructors, and specialists. There are also the various technicians, including radio operators, pilots, naval personnel, signalmen, and many more. While each man is assigned to a highly specialized function, he must know something about the functions of others and be capable of coordinating his work with the whole. In the field, the distribution of labor so neatly drawn in tables of organization is seldom apparent. A man who starts out as a follower may suddenly find himself in the position of leader. Or a specialist may go on a mission to operate a clandestine radio and wind up mixing explosives or laying charges.

Like the "ideal spy," the "perfect saboteur" is actually only a figment of the imagination. Yet all sabotage organizations go to great lengths to select men best qualified for a perilous job, and to train them scrupulously for special missions of all types.

Let us see, then, who the men are who go out to create destruction. Are they unbalanced persons whose urge to destroy is morbidly overdeveloped? Are they depraved, incapable of recognizing the traditional limitations that humanity has imposed on the means of conflict? Are they low-class, low-intelligence brutes whose personal background predestines them to such deceit and violence? By no means. As a matter of fact, history's best known saboteurs have been men of superior background and standing in their own societies. The chief of German sabotage in the United States in 1916 was Captain Franz von Rintelen, a member of the old Reich's historic nobility. Italy's most effective sabotage expert, a naval officer who infiltrated British ports in tiny underwater craft and single-handed attacked battleships and carriers, was a prince, a descendant of the Borgias. The leader of the British Commandos was Lord Louis Mountbatten, a great-grandson of Queen Victoria, and his most efficient lieutenant was Simon Christopher Joseph Fraser, 15th Lord Lovat, whose barony was created in 1485. The "brain" behind most of Britain's wartime sabotage actions was Nathaniel Meyer Victor, 3rd Baron Rothschild, a member of the famous family of bankers and a brilliant scientist in his own right.

According to Colonel F. O. Miksche, who was chief of operations in General de Gaulle's secret service during World War II, "it is not altogether a question of military ability, for the technical knowledge required is of a relatively simple nature." It calls more for psychological instinct and political skill. "They are less chiefs in the military sense than they are chiefs of popular tribes," Miksche wrote. "They must be men who have risen from the people, and are accustomed to a simple life. By achieving distinction among their fellows, they gain the individual confidence of their followers. The best training for guerrilla chiefs (or, for that matter, for leaders of sabotage teams) is a hard life."

The sabotage leader must be a born conspirator. He must be able to deceive not only the enemy but his own comrades, since in sabotage operations one of the cardinal rules is that each man should know only what is essential to his own task. In addition, he must have quick judgment and appreciation, an alert and inventive mind. He must possess the moral courage to assume responsibilities and the will to accomplish what often may seem impossible. He must be physically vigorous, ascetic and austere, capable of adjusting to the strangest environment.

The sabotage chief must be deeply devoted to his cause and imbued with strong political convictions. Otherwise he is no better than the mere *sabot*, a man driven by impulses of senseless destruction too difficult to control. In practice, organizations strive to indoctrinate their personnel along ideological and political lines, and to impress upon them the nobler motives of their destructive occupations. Responsible nations approach sabotage with certain fundamental misgivings, and they try to impress at least a basic self-restraint upon their operatives. Sabotage, when engaged in over long periods of time on an active scale, tends to destroy the conscience of a man, to lull him into a false sense of justification of its methods. Men long accustomed to the violent struggle are inclined to believe too readily that any end justifies the means, and without a proper balance between the conscience and the evils of destruction may find it difficult to readjust to a normal positive life.

"Was it a wise policy on a long-term reckoning," Captain Liddell Hart, the British military writer, asked when assessing the implications of secret warfare, "taking account not only of winning the war but of securing the peace that should follow victory? Was its contribution to victory outweighed by its legacy of disorder?" He answered his own questions in a dubious mood. "The habit of violence," he wrote, "takes much deeper root in irregular than it does in regular warfare. In the latter it is connected by the habit of obedience to constituted authority, whereas the former makes a virtue of defying authority and violating rules."

Gunnerside: The Mission That Succeeded

One of the historic feats in the annals of sabotage is an operation identified by the code name Gunnerside. This was the fantastic mission of a small group of Norwegians during World War II who proved conclusively that, unlike crime, sabotage does pay. When the United States decided to develop the atomic bomb, plans were made simultaneously to prevent the Nazis from acquiring one first. Special intelligence groups were formed in Britain and the United States. Their mission was to find out where the Nazis had their own atomic plants and laboratories.

Such a plant was discovered in the Norsk Hydro factory in Vemork, in the Norwegian province of Telemark, known the world over for its fine skiing. Norsk Hydro was the world's largest producer of heavy water, a substance needed in the construction of the atomic pile. The possession of the plant, and the heavy water it produced and stored, gave the Germans an enormous potential advantage in the development of atomic weapons.

It was decided, therefore, in the highest councils of the Allies, to sabotage Norsk Hydro at any cost. On March 28, 1942, a Norwegian agent whom I will call Einar was parachuted into Telemark province to pave the way for a sabotage party to follow. He worked alone for months in this enemy-infested land, gathering invaluable data essential for the drafting of the eventual operations plan. From his observations on the spot, and the observations of others, the plan was evolved. Since this became the greatest single operation in the entire history of sabotage, and since this operations plan has become the classic type for all such directives, I will reprint here its salient features, to show the care and detail that go into the drafting of such directives.

INTELLIGENCE

Fifteen Germans in the hut-barracks between the machine room and the electrolysis plant. Change of guard at 1800, 2000 hours, etc. Normally two Germans on the bridge. During an alarm; three patrols inside the factory area and floodlighting on the road between Vemork and Vaaer. Normally only two Norwegian guards inside the factory area at night, plus one at the main gates and one at the penstocks. All doors into the electrolysis factory locked except one that opens into the yard.

From the advance position at the power-line cutting, the following will be brought up: arms, explosives, a little food. No camouflage suits to be worn over uniforms. Claus to lead the way down to the river and up to the railway track. Advance to the position of attack some 500 meters from the fence. The covering party, led by the second in command, to advance along the track, followed close behind by the demolition party, which the Gunnerside leader will lead himself. The position for attack will be occupied before midnight in order to be able to see when the relieved guards return to the barracks. According to information received from sketches and photographs, we have chosen the gate by the store-shed, some 10 meters lower than the railway gates, as being best suited for the withdrawal and as providing best cover for the advance. The attack will start at 0030 hours.

COVERING PARTY

Duty: To cut an opening in the fence. To get into position so that any interference by the German guards, in the event of an alarm, is totally suppressed. If all remains quiet, to stay in position until the explosion is heard or until other orders are received from the demolition-party leader. The commander of the covering party to use his own judgment if necessary. If the alarm is sounded during the advance into the factory grounds, the covering party to attack the guard immediately. When the explosion is heard, it may be assumed that the demolition party is already outside the factory grounds, and the order is to be given for withdrawal; the password is, "Piccadilly? Leicester Square!"

After that, the operational order reached its own climax, the detailed instructions for the sabotage action proper:

DEMOLITION PARTY

Duty: To destroy the high-concentration plant in the cellar of the electrolysis factory. At the exact moment when the covering party either take up their position or go into action, the demolition party will advance to the cellar door. One man, armed with a tommy-gun, takes up position covering the main entrance. Those carrying out the actual demolition are covered by one man with a tommy-gun and one man with a .45 pistol. An attempt will first be made to force the cellar door; failing that, the door to the ground floor. As a last resort, the cable tunnel is to be used. If fighting starts before the H.C. plant is reached, the covering party will, if necessary, take over the placing of the explosives. If anything should happen to the leader, or anything upsets the plans, all are to act on their own initiative in order to carry out the operation. Any workmen or guards found will be treated in such manner as the situation may demand. If possible, no reserve charges will be left behind in the factory.

It is forbidden for the members of either party to use torches or other lights during the advance or withdrawal. Arms are to be carried ready for use but are not to be loaded until necessary, so that no accidental shot raises the alarm.

The order concluded on a highly melodramatic note, spelled out in the matter-of-fact language of such an operations plan: *"If any man is about to be taken prisoner, he undertakes to end his own life."* These were the only lines underscored in the whole document.

Planning required eleven months. Then on February 27, 1943, two teams composed of gentlemen saboteurs stood ready to execute the plan. One group went by the code name Swallow. The other was called Gunnerside. Here, in the very words of their own log, is the story of this part of the operation.

FEBRUARY 27

. . . left our advance base, a hut in Fjosbudalen, about 8 P.M. We started on skis, but were later forced to continue on foot. . . . At Vaaer Bridge we had to take cover, as two buses were coming up the road with night shift from Rjukan. . . . We advanced to within about 500 meters of the factory's railway gate. Carried on a strong westerly wind came the faint humming note of the factory's machinery. We had a fine view of the road and the factory itself.

FEBRUARY 28

. . . once more I checked up to make sure that every man was certain about his part in the operation and understood his orders.

Cautiously we advanced to some store-sheds about 100 meters from the gates. Here one man was sent forward with a pair of armorer's shears to open the gates, with the rest of the covering party in support. The demolition party stood by to follow up immediately.

The factory gates, secured with padlock and chain, were easily opened. . . . At a given sign the covering party advanced toward the German guard-hut. At the same moment the demolition party moved toward the door of the factory cellar, through which it was hoped to gain entry. The cellar door was locked. We were unable to force it, nor did we have any success with the door of the floor above. Through a window of the high-concentration plant, where our target lay, a man could be seen.

During our search for the cable tunnel, which was our only remaining method of entry, we became separated from one another. Finally I found the opening and, followed by only one of my men, crept in over a maze of tangled pipes and leads. Through an opening under the tunnel's ceiling we could see our target.

Every minute was now valuable. As there was no sign of the

196

other two demolition party members, we two decided to carry out the demolition alone. We entered a room adjacent to the target, found the door into the high-concentration plant open, went in, and took the guard completely by surprise. We locked the double doors between the heavy-water storage tanks and the adjacent room, so that we could work in peace.

My colleague kept watch over the guard, who seemed frightened but was otherwise quiet and obedient.

I began to place the charges. This went quickly and easily. The models on which we had practiced in England were exact duplicates of the real plant. I had placed half the charges in position when there was a crash of broken glass behind me. I looked up. Someone had smashed the window opening on to the back yard. A man's head stood framed in the broken glass. It was one of my two colleagues who, having failed to find the cable tunnel, had decided to act on their own initiative. One climbed through the window, helped me place the remaining charges, and checked them twice while I coupled the fuses. We checked the entire charge once more, before ignition. There was still no sign of alarm from the yard.

We lit both fuses. I ordered the captive Norwegian guard to run for safety to the floor above. We left the room.

Twenty yards outside the cellar door, we heard the explosion. The sentry at the main entrance was recalled from his post. We passed through the gate and climbed up the railway track.

For a moment I looked back down the line and listened. Except for the faint hum of machinery that we had heard when we arrived, everything in the factory was quiet.

It was calculated that 3,000 pounds of heavy water were destroyed, together with key parts of the high-concentration plant. Five men of the Gunnerside team skied 250 miles to safety. They were flown out of Norway and back to England shortly afterwards. The sixth man, Knut, stayed behind for another mission, together with the entire Swallow team. Only one member of the two teams ever encountered the enemy, so well was the operation planned and staged.

He was Claus Helberg, a member of one of the advance parties who did most of the original intelligence work for the operation. On March 25, 1943, on the high, snow-covered Hardanger Vidda plateau, Helberg was ambushed by a German patrol of three soldiers. He turned around and skied away from the spot, but was pursued by one of the Germans, himself a master on skis.

Claus stopped and turned, then drew his pistol and fired one shot from his Colt .32. The German had a Luger. Helberg knew that the man who emptied his magazine first would be the loser, so he held his fire but exposed himself as a target at a range of fifty-five yards. The German fell into the trap and emptied his magazine at Claus. Then he turned and started back.

Helberg was unscarred. And now it was his turn. He fired a single shot at the retreating German and saw him stagger, then stop, hanging over his ski poles. Claus raced away, apprehensive that the two other Germans, attracted by the gunfire, might join the fracas after all. By then the countryside was enshrouded in darkness, but Helberg kept going for two more hours, groping his way as he went, until the inevitable happened. He stumbled on a protruding rock and fell over a cliff. He dropped forty-four yards, but escaped with a broken arm and a bruised shoulder. But he was safe—and a few days later he, too, was flown back to England.

By November, 1943, spies in Norway reported to London that, despite the initial success of the operation, Norsk Hydro was back in production. This was bad news, since no more teams were available then to repeat the coup of Swallow and Gunnerside. It was decided, therefore, to bomb the plant from the air. On November 16th, strong formations of the 8th United States Bomber Command attacked the Vemork power station and electrolysis plant. But where the handful of saboteurs had managed to blow up 3,000 pounds of heavy water, the costly air attack destroyed only 120 pounds. Even so, the Germans had had enough. They resolved to dismantle the plant and ship it to Germany.

Then on February 7, 1944, another agent report reached London from Norway. It announced that the transportation of the plant would take place on February 20, in the Lake Tinnsjøe ferry boat *Hydro*. Her orders showed that she would be going to Hamburg.

The new situation was discussed by the British War Cabinet, and orders went out to destroy the *Hydro* by sabotage. The operation was extremely hazardous, if only because it had to be carried out under the noses of an alerted enemy. Special SS detachments were assigned to the whole area. Each day, German planes patrolled the mountains in that vicinity, and security guards were stationed along the railway line from Vemork to the *Hydro's* pier. Yet not a single guard was posted on the *Hydro* herself.

February 20, 1944, was a Sunday. At one o'clock in the morning, four saboteurs led by Knut, the member of the Gunnerside team who had remained behind after the first operation against the factory, left by car specially requisitioned for the purpose. They drove up to the *Hydro's* pier and Knut went aboard with two of his men. His third aide stood by at the get-away car.

They saw the crew gathered below deck, engrossed in a rather noisy battle of poker. The engine room was occupied. Two of Knut's men pushed through a hole and crept along the keel to the bow. Knut laid his charges in the bilge, coupling them to two separate time-delay mechanisms which he tied to the stringers on each side. The charge was big enough to sink the *Hydro* in five minutes.

Knut then set the time-delay charge, home-made from an old alarm clock, for 10:45 A.M. This was the time the boat was expected to arrive at the best place for its destruction. It was now only four o'clock in the morning, but the saboteurs were finished with the job. Knut and his partners crawled back through the bilge and escaped undetected. They got back into their car and drove away, and by nightfall were safe in Oslo, lost in the hustle and bustle of the Norwegian capital.

The *Hydro* sank at 10:45 sharp that morning just as planned. It went down with priceless machinery from Norsk Hydro and 3,600 gallons of heavy water on board. "So it was," the official report of this operation concluded, "that the manufacture of heavy water ceased in Norway; and so it was that all stocks available to German scientists from that source were lost."

Sabotage and the Cold War

The global battle of sabotage continued up to the very last hour of the Second World War, after which a new type of conflict descended upon the world, what we call the cold war. With it came a new phase in the war of wits, in which we are confronted with a different type of secret agent, the Communist operative to whom all means are justified, in peace as well as war.

Although little is published about them, considerable damage is done by Communist saboteurs. They are especially active in France where they hamper anything aiding the war in Indochina, especially ships and cargoes. In Britain, they boldly attack the vessels of the Royal Navy. The list of sabotage perpetrated against Her Majesty's ships is frighteningly long, and growing daily. It is even more alarming that British security organs seem incapable of coping with the problem. Some of the damage to the warships has been serious, indicating careful and painstaking organization, and none of the saboteurs have been found despite the narrow confines of their operations.

199

Maritime sabotage is the strongest arm of the Communist secret service, partly because it is regarded as vitally important, and partly because the Communists have genius guiding this type of work. He is the dean of saboteurs, the German Communist leader Ernst Wollweber. At the time of this writing, Wollweber is no ordinary outlaw, no roughneck, no lowly saboteur. He is Minister of the Interior in Eastern Germany, the Russian zone's top policeman directing law and order. He was appointed to the post—the first in his life that carries with it the slightest appearance of dignity—in the wake of the great patriotic uprising of June 17, 1953, that shook the Communist regime of Eastern Germany to its foundations. Wollweber is expected to prevent the recurrence of such outbreaks and to deal with them in his customary fashion—ruthless intolerance.

I knew Wollweber in Germany in the early thirties, at which time he conducted his world-wide sabotage activities as if they were a respectable business enterprise. He had his headquarters in Hamburg, in an office that masqueraded as a labor union of merchant seamen. From his office he engineered the mutiny of the Royal Navy at Invergordon and the rebellion of the sailors of the Royal Netherlands Navy. I have seen him there, sitting at his desk beneath a huge maritime map of the world on which colored pins marked the positions of the ships in which he had a personal interest. He had bloodshot, narrow eyes, and was a squat, dark, truculent, vulgar-looking man. When he laughed, he displayed a row of bad teeth stained by the tobacco from the pipe that was never missing from his mouth.

Wollweber's whole life had been wasted on violence. He was one of the "Kaiser's coolies," a sailor of the High Seas Fleet of Imperial Germany. Theodor Plivier wrote a classic book about him and about the mutiny Wollweber stage-managed at Kiel in 1918.

After the collapse of the Kaiser's Germany, Wollweber set himself up as a specialist in maritime sabotage. He formed Communist cells on innumerable merchant vessels sailing under the flags of all nations, and also on warships. He established sabotage schools where hand-picked sailors from many countries were trained as strike-makers, mutiny inciters, spies, and saboteurs. He organized merchant ships all over the world into a network for smuggling spies, transporting couriers, ferrying his gunmen, and shipping his prisoners to Soviet jails.

At that time, in 1930-33, Wollweber had a number of Americans on his staff: a tall, heavy-set, lazy Negro agitator named James Ford who later became the Communist candidate for the vice-presidency of the United States; George Mink, Thomas Ray, and Mike Pell, "activists" all; and a notorious triggerman known as Horseface, whose real name was Roy Hudson.

After Hitler's seizure of power in 1933, Wollweber moved his headquarters to Copenhagen, Denmark, and continued his global sabotage with even greater vigor. Today, although he occupies a position of apparent respectability, he still works at his old trade from the former German port city Stettin, given to the Poles at Yalta.

Wollweber is a Soviet agent of the worst type. His activities are directed and financed by the Kremlin. The not inconsiderable funds that he requires for his operations come from the treasury of the Sovtorgflot, the maritime trust of the Soviet Union, through the Profintern, the Communist center of labor conspiracy.

In fighting against men like Wollweber, the free world has been forced to invoke the doctrine of Zeno: knavery is the best defense against a knave. The spy and saboteur of the free world, operating in the countries occupied by the Communists, are remarkable for their courage and selfless devotion to their cause. Their sabotage, on however large a scale, is hardly more than a symbolic act under the circumstances. It is designed to remind both friend and foe that men are still willing to live dangerously and die heroically so that liberty shall not perish from the earth.

An example of this symbolic fight was supplied by saboteurs of the Hungarian underground in April, 1952, on the anniversary of the day of their country's occupation by the Red Army. It was a big day for the Communists, and they tried to make the most of it. Delegates from the whole Communist world converged on Budapest to attend the festivities. From the Soviet Union came Marshal Klementi Voroshilov, a powerful member of the Politburo. Top-ranking Communist leaders came from the other countries, from Czechoslovakia to China.

There were many overt acts the anti-Communist underground could have undertaken on that day. They could have sabotaged the train that carried the Soviet marshal or placed a time bomb under his reviewing stand. They could have committed innumerable acts to spoil the Communist fun by killing the guest of honor, but the Communists would have taken savage reprisals, killing hostages and exiling the innocent to forced labor camps. There was no point in defying the police state with useless, senseless, pointless acts of murder and sabotage, and the underground acting behind the

Iron Curtain was made up of sensible and responsible men and women.

And yet, Marshal Voroshilov's presence in Hungary was too good an opportunity to miss without at least a symbolic act of defiance. The underground leader in charge of the arrangements was a simple workingman known to his fellows only as Pete. He prepared his plan in great secrecy. Nothing leaked out to the secret police, despite the fact that this was to be a major demonstration at a time when Communist vigilance was increased in preparation for the marshal's visit.

Voroshilov's train reached the Hungarian frontier at 8 A.M. on April 20. A reception committee was on hand, and a band played the Communist anthems. Suddenly flames sprang up from the freight yard of the huge frontier station. Within a few minutes several warehouses were on fire.

At the same moment, a train carrying the French delegation reached the city of Györ and was received with the firing of a boxcar factory near the station. A power plant was set on fire to greet delegations from Czechoslovakia and Eastern Germany, while the Rumanian and Bulgarian delegations were greeted with fires in Hungary's great tobacco plant in Szeged.

The moment Marshal Voroshilov's train pulled into Debreczen, Hungary's third largest city, fire broke out in its biggest industrial plant, a sheet-metal factory. And as the trains arrived in Budapest, the capital, the city scarcely knew which spectacle to watch, the arrival of Voroshilov at the head of the foreign delegations, or the fire raging over several city blocks, consuming the Wolfner plant, Europe's biggest tannery and leather factory.

The honored guests could not sleep their first night in Budapest, for the city was kept awake by the sirens and bells of the fire-engines racing to the various conflagrations.

At the height of the fires the underground struck for a second time. It sabotaged the water works, forcing the firemen to stand by idly and watch helplessly as everything the patriot arsonists had put on fire burned out.

Operation Torch, as the demonstration was called, ended as planned. Nothing went wrong. The Hungarians showed the assembled Communists that the spirit of resistance was literally aflame in their land. Of all the men who participated in the demonstration, only the leader, Pete, had to flee. He reached the free world by way of Czechoslovakia and Austria. His comrades remained at their posts—to carry the torch for freedom.

PART IV

Counterespionage

Negative Intelligence

Negative intelligence is a generic term meaning three different things: security intelligence, counterintelligence, and counterespionage. By security intelligence, we mean the sum total of all efforts to conceal national policies, diplomatic decisions, military data, and any other information of a secret nature affecting the security of the United States from unauthorized persons. It is the effort to deny information to unauthorized persons by restricting it to those who are explicitly authorized to possess it.

The basis of security intelligence is concealment in general: the classification of documents according to the degree of their secrecy; various screening operations, which include the spreading of deliberately falsified or bogus information to mislead an enemy; the enactment of legislation to deter people from even trying to gain unauthorized possession of classified information; the selection and indoctrination of trustworthy and security-conscious personnel; and a protective plan designed to secure natural resources and industrial production against the intelligence, espionage, and sabotage efforts of an enemy.

A finely drawn line separates security intelligence from counterintelligence, which is the organized effort to protect specific data that might be of value to an opponent's own intelligence organization. One of its chief instruments is censorship. By censorship of the printed word, of correspondence, broadcasts, telecasts, telephone conversations, telegrams and cables, and other forms of communication, counterintelligence aims to prevent the dissemination of any information that might aid an opponent. Other instruments of internal security are the maintenance of files on suspects, the surveillance of suspects by observing their movements, reading their mail, listening in or recording their telephone conversations, and the infiltration of the enemy's intelligence organization to procure information about its methods, personnel, specific operations, and interests.

Up to this point, negative intelligence is a protective and anticipatory function. It is designed to prevent certain information from becoming public or from falling into unauthorized hands, whether accidentally or through the positive efforts of forces dedicated to its acquisition.

In counterespionage, negative intelligence becomes a dynamic and active effort. The purpose of counterespionage is to investigate actual or theoretical violation of the espionage laws, to enforce those laws, and to apprehend any violators, if possible before they succeed in compromising classified information by its delivery to foreign employers. To put it bluntly, the job of counterespionage is to catch spies.

Security intelligence and counterintelligence are essentially intellectual functions. Counterespionage is basically a police function. This fundamental difference is not generally understood, and the failure to understand it leads to confusion and misapprehension. Frequently, agencies charged with counterespionage are accused of failure to apprehend spies before the completion of their missions. Prevention of espionage and sabotage is not the fundamental function of counterespionage, but is properly the responsibility of the other protective services, of security intelligence and counterintelligence at the very source of the information.

Protection at the source is relatively simple. The apprehension of agents at large is a complex and difficult task. "A basic requirement of the secret agent is to disguise himself and his mission," Sir Basil Thomson, chief of Scotland Yard's Criminal Investigation Department, once told me. "Much of his training and basic skill is dedicated to concealment. His organization is supposed to supply him with a foolproof cover story and good documents. He knows how to handle himself because he is a man of exceptional ability, or else he would not be chosen for this intricate job. Because of this, and because the democracies often place more difficulties in the path of counterespionage agents than of the spies themselves, the trapping of the dark intruder is a formidable task."

In 1945, the Royal Canadian Mounted Police, whose assignments include counterespionage, were severely criticized for their failure to apprehend the espionage agents of the Soviet ring operating in Canada. This criticism was only partly justified. Atomic espionage in Canada was carried out between March and September of 1945. Five months is scarcely enough time for even the best counterespionage agency to pursue an investigation to a successful conclusion, unless it obtains information from inside the ring. Most of

204

the Canadians involved in the case were known to the police as Soviet sympathizers, and their names were carried in police suspect files. But a man may be a suspect without being actively engaged in espionage. And he may be immune from prosecution for lack of evidence. Legally, he is not an espionage agent until he is proved one. In democratic countries, counterespionage agencies are bound by the provisions of existing laws. They are permitted to conduct their investigations only by legally sanctioned means. They are allowed to make arrests only when sufficient evidence is on hand, not simply to justify the arrest, but also to make it "stick" in a court of law.

The success of Soviet espionage in Canada was really due to a breakdown of security. A similar breakdown of security was the cause of espionage activity in the United States and Britain. Persons whose alien sympathies were either known or suspected were nevertheless allowed access to sensitive positions and information. Limited as counterespionage agencies are in their funds and personnel, it is physically impossible for them to keep every suspect under surveillance. In view of this, basic security must come from protection and anticipation rather than from counterespionage.

To illustrate this point with a practical example, we may cite the case of a potential "leak" in the United States. In this country, certain aviation maps which contain information useful to an enemy are on public sale. In a country where civilian and private aviation is widespread, such maps cannot be withdrawn from circulation without endangering safety in the air. It is physically impossible to record every purchaser of such maps and then to keep him under surveillance to discover what use he is making of them. Even if a purchaser actually delivered one of these maps to an agent of a foreign power, our counterespionage could do nothing about it. The information is, after all, in the public domain. And as long as a person can openly buy these maps, he can do anything he pleases with them without breaking the espionage laws in any way. Yet, these maps contain tremendously valuable information for any potential enemy of the United States.

The same is true in the case of the publications of the U.S. Government Printing Office and England's Stationery Office. Material printed by them may contain valuable information useful to an opponent, yet as long as it is unclassified it cannot be legally withheld even from spies. In order to protect such information, it must be classified and protected at the source. Arrests can be made only when all legal conditions of this step are clearly evident. The military and naval counterintelligence organs of the United States and Britain do not have the power of arrest or the facilities to conduct broad investigations. They may conduct preliminary inquiries and "shadow" suspects, but in the crucial moment they are not permitted to arrest them. They must call in a law-enforcement agency that has the power of arrest, to make the actual arrest. During the thirties, an American was found by the U.S. Navy to be spying for the Japanese naval attaché in Washington. The Navy's agent shadowed the man when he was known to be in possession of incriminating material and trailed him to a hotel room. The agent burst into the room just as the man was assembling the stolen documents in preparation for the visit of a Japanese officer. The agent had no power to arrest the man, but he did not want to lose him, and so he handcuffed the spy to the bed and went out to call the FBI. When the FBI agents arrived, they perceived that the spy's civil rights had been violated, and they refused to make the arrest. As it happened, the spy continued his surreptitious activities and was eventually arrested under legally proper circumstances.

The best way to hinder enemy espionage is, of course, to restrict the movements of possible agents and make impossible the acquisition of information valuable to an enemy. Although such iron-clad protection is not possible in a democracy, this is exactly what totalitarian regimes do. When the Nazis came into power in Germany all strategic maps were withdrawn from circulation. Picture postcards of aerial photographs were confiscated. The taking of pictures from planes was prohibited, and cameras had to be sealed before their bearers made a flight. Suspects were rounded up and detained in concentration camps.

Even more stringent measures of protection are practiced in the Soviet Union today. Virtually the entire country is off limits to foreigners. Every state paper, even if it contains only production statistics of a non-military plant, is regarded as classified. The exportation of books, newspapers, and periodicals is prohibited. The slightest shadow of doubt suffices to doom anyone suspected of espionage activity.

Similar measures are in force in Spain, Egypt, Syria, Iran, Iraq, Israel, and many other countries, some of which are not usually regarded as dictatorships and which, in fact, have strong democratic traditions. Sweden, for example, bans visitors from the city of Boden, where important military installations are located. Turkey bans unauthorized visitors from parts of Anatolia, and the taking of all photographs is prohibited between the Greek frontier and Istanbul. Similar restrictions exist in the United States, where unauthorized entrance is, for example, forbidden to the several atomic plants. In contrast, no restrictions are placed on visiting the atomic energy center of Norway.

The pattern of protection, therefore, has a clearly defined sequence. Concealment at the source of all "security information" must come first, protection and anticipation next. Action by counterespionage is the final security phase.

This is important to an understanding of the exact position and role of counterespionage in the over-all protection pattern, and to an appreciation of the difference between security intelligence and counterintelligence on the one side and counterespionage on the other. Virtually all countries keep counterintelligence separate from counterespionage in the organizational scheme of protection. Counterintelligence is an important part of the functions assigned to the various intelligence agencies. It is practiced vigorously, not only by Army, Navy, and Air intelligence organizations, but also by the Central Intelligence Agency of the United States. Yet the American law makes it very clear that their jurisdiction in this field is cautiously restricted, and that they are not permitted to perform any one of the police functions associated with counterespionage.

They are by their very nature unequipped to function as counterespionage agencies. They lack the machinery to deal with suspects. They have no technical laboratories needed for scientific detection work, and few of the complex apparatus needed for investigations. Their men cannot arrest suspects. They have no trained staffs to prepare prosecutions for the courts. The facilities needed to clinch a case and carry it to its logical conclusion are left entirely and exclusively in the hands of agencies designated primarily to conduct counterespionage. The security organs and counterintelligence branches of the various intelligence services are largely responsible for precautionary and anticipatory measures that will keep the work of counterespionage at a practicable minimum, but, when precaution and anticipation fail, counterespionage steps in to conclude a case.

In ninety-nine out of a hundred cases, the success of an espionage agent or saboteur is not due to any basic inefficiency of the counterespionage organs of a country, but rather to deficient security measures, especially in the handling of documents and the hiring of personnel. A good example of a protective measure that is inadequate is an American law called the "Foreign Agents Registration Act of 1938, as currently amended." It is the only law of its kind in the world, and it was originally devised to curb German propaganda in the United States. It is designed to set a legal trap for foreign agents, and to punish them for failure to register.

Under this act, "agents of foreign principals" engaged in the distribution of political propaganda must register with the Department of Justice and reveal the nature, sources, and contents of the material they disseminate. In addition, persons who have "knowledge of or have received instructions or assignment in espionage, counterespionage, or sabotage service or tactics of a foreign government or a foreign political party" are also expected to register. Theoretically, the law stipulates that every foreign propagandist and foreign espionage agent check in with the Department of Justice upon arrival in the United States.

In practice, however, the only people who comply with the provisions of the act are those who are not engaged in any surreptitious activity in the United States, or who have effectively severed all connection with foreign espionage organizations. In 1952, for example, a total of thirty-one persons registered as trained espionage agents: eighteen of them former Nazis, six former Soviet agents, one Japanese, two Hungarians trained by Soviet intelligence, one Pole, and one former member each of the Philippine, Danish, and Ukrainian undergrounds. Although it is certain that there are now in the United States at least a few trained British and French espionage agents, none of them is registered. It goes without saying that no practicing Soviet agent is registered, either. The closest this registration law ever came to exposing an espionage agent in the United States was in the case of a man named Hafis Salich, who was apprehended and convicted as a Soviet spy—more than fifteen years ago. While it is doubtful that the Foreign Agents Registration Act will identify many foreign agents by their own voluntary registration under the law, it does provide the legal basis necessary for the prosecution of persons engaging in espionage who have failed to register upon entering this country.

Although the United States is dependent upon such a weak safeguard as the Registration Act, and has outlawed censorship and wiretapping as an invasion of personal liberty, other safety precautions are in force, including internal security measures within government departments, strict screening of personnel in sensitive government and private jobs, and restriction of ingress to sensitive installations.

According to the *Internal Security Manual* published by the Foreign Relations Committee of the U. S. Senate, the

United States has on its statute books something like fifty laws to deal with subversion, sabotage and espionage. They include such major statutes as the Atomic Energy Act of 1946 whose Section 16(a) contains the death penalty for atomic espionage; the Civil Defense Act of 1950; the Communication Act of 1934 as amended; the Emergency Detention Act of 1950 which authorizes the Attorney General to apprehend and detain any person who "will probably engage or conspire to engage in espionage or sabotage" in any "internal security emergency" (as defined by presidential proclamation). In addition, these laws include the Internal Security Act of 1950; the Invention Secrecy Act of 1952; the Logan Act of 1948 which regulates private correspondence with foreign governments; the Magnuson Act of 1950 which controls foreign-flag vessels in American waters; the McCarran-Walter Act of 1952 with its stringent provisions concerning immigration; the National Security Act of 1939 as amended; the Neutrality Act of 1939 as amended; the Subversive Activities Control Act of 1950; and the Trading with the Enemy Act of 1917. Additional pertinent provisions are included in many other laws, such as the Air Force Act of 1942; the Hatch Act of 1939; the Taft-Hartley Act of 1947; the Legislative Reorganization Act of 1946; the Military Justice Code; the Mutual Security Act of 1951 as amended.

Even with this phalanx of protective and punitive laws, the pattern of protection remains incomplete. "Laws and orders are many," Senator Alexander Wiley of Wisconsin wrote in his introduction to the manual, "but effectiveness is uncertain. . . . As any serious student of the problem knows the sheer number of laws on this, or for that matter any other critical subject, is hardly a reliable index for the over-all effectiveness of those laws. . . . Time and again the legal framework in which our society operates and in which the Department of Justice, in particular, operates has unfortunately proven overly restrictive and has militated against the attainment of our national objective of self-preservation. Many laws have served as unnecessary and undesirable shackles and as obstacles to the FBI's and the Department's effectiveness." A democracy like the United States faces a grave dilemma when confronted with the conflict between its traditional civil liberties and the novel problems of defense against secret agents.

What frequently reduces the effectiveness of these laws is duplication in the negative intelligence efforts of the United States. According to Donald Robinson, who examined the problem critically in an informed article written for the

American Legion Magazine, there are as many as twenty-five separate agencies in the United States all involved in the fight for internal security. They often step on each other's toes both literally and figuratively, or cancel out each other's effectiveness.

Among the agencies, the FBI is paramount, but it has to contend with numerous other agencies "muscling in" on its responsibilities. In 1942, for example, the United States was in mortal danger for a fortnight because there were in the country eight skilled and trained German saboteurs with orders to blow up the key aluminum factories of this country and thus bring aircraft production to a standstill. One of the two groups of saboteurs, who came ashore from U-boats off Florida and Long Island, was spotted promptly by a young Coast Guardsman. But his superiors delayed several hours in notifying the FBI. The time that elapsed enabled the invaders to work their way inland and remain at large for two weeks, forcing the FBI to track them down through difficult investigation.

Early in the war an informant notified the FBI that an American scientist would dine with two Soviet consuls in a seafood restaurant on Powell Street in San Francisco. The FBI got ready to set up equipment in the place to monitor their conversation, but found agents of the Army's Counterintelligence Corps already on the spot occupying the only booth where such monitoring appeared possible. "There were more investigators in that restaurant than customers," Robinson remarked. In the resultant confusion both the FBI and CIC proved incapable of getting anything but a jumbled unclear recording. If the conversation had been other than innocent, neither agency would have had recorded proof.

A similar situation exists in Great Britain where at least six separate agencies compete in the field. The Special Branch of Scotland Yard and MI-5 of the War Office share the responsibility for apprehending spies but their preventive work is hampered, both by deficient legislation which allows many loopholes, and by an injudicious distribution of responsibility among the pertinent agencies. There has been in recent years an alarming number of sabotage cases on Her Majesty's ships, but negative intelligence has succeeded neither in stopping the insidious practice nor in locating the culprits. It is known that Soviet atomic espionage had a ring operating in Britain, but to this day it remains unexposed despite clues supplied by Canadian, United States, and Swiss authorities in whose countries other branches of the network operated.

The work of negative intelligence is widely scattered

210

among a number of British agencies. Some of it is assigned to the Home Office which handles immigration and has jurisdiction over narcotics cases, explosives, and civil defense in general. Still other aspects of the work are assigned to the Ministry of Supply which maintains its own security branch combating espionage in atomic energy and guided missile projects. The Foreign Office is involved in internal security through the Passport Office which has several negative intelligence functions, and its own security branch for provision of armed protection for the Queen's Messengers and the diplomatic couriers while traveling in sensitive areas. Naval Intelligence has a negative branch dealing with matters of naval security and the protection of codes. The Air Ministry has its own Security Department handling the security problems of the RAF.

During the Second World War, Britain maintained a small organization called the Council of Three to coordinate all security matters and expedite the work of negative intelligence. It succeeded in streamlining British counterespionage to a remarkable degree. If such a coordinating agency exists today, nothing is known about it, although the current British *Who's Who* lists Sir Percy Sillitoe, formerly head of MI-5, as "director general" of an otherwise unidentified organization called "Security Services."

The existence of coordinating organs in the United States is a matter of public record. There were, in fact, two of them: one, the Interdepartmental Intelligence Conference (ICC), the other the Interdepartmental Committee on Internal Security (ICIS). They were set up by a 1949 directive of the National Security Council. The ICC consists of the director of the FBI; the chief of the Office of Naval Intelligence; the director of the Intelligence Division, Department of the Army; and the director of the Office of Special Investigations, Department of the Air Force. The ICIS is composed of representatives from the Departments of State, Treasury, and Justice, and the National Military Establishment. Both function as special committees of the National Security Council.

While the government of the United States has done everything in its power to insure this country's internal security, it cannot plug all loopholes without sacrificing democratic traditions and institutions. For this reason, the internal security of the United States—and that of the United Kingdom—remains somewhat deficient.

The consequences of this deficiency were illustrated in the case of Harry Gold, one of the Soviet agents engaged in atomic espionage in the United States. Harry Gold was a

211

member of an espionage ring directed by a certain Jacob Golos, one of the chief organizers of Soviet espionage in this country. When Golos' secretary and mistress left the Communist fold in 1945 and supplied information about the Golos ring to the FBI, Harry Gold's name became known to the Bureau. But specific information about his activities was not immediately forthcoming.

In actual fact, Gold was even then the most efficient courier of the Soviet espionage ring operating in the United States. Under the alias "Raymond," he was detailed to act as the ring's cut-out between Anatoli A. Yakovlev, resident director of the ring in New York, and Dr. Klaus Fuchs, a member of Britain's scientific delegation to the United States working on the development of the atomic bomb.

The presence of Fuchs in the British delegation was in itself a case of faulty security. His Communist sympathies were known to British security organs, but this failed to prevent his assignment to one of the most sensitive jobs in the atomic project. Nor were his Communist sympathies communicated to American security organs. In the United States, Fuchs had absolutely no aboveground links with Communists. Harry Gold worked quietly and diligently in a civilian job, and there was nothing in his normal activities to justify surveillance or even suspicion on the part of the FBI.

Yet, underground, both Fuchs and Gold were exceedingly active. They met each other for the first time early in 1944, under the usual cloak of secrecy that Soviet intelligence arranges long in advance of such meetings. Fuchs was directed to go to a street corner on New York's lower East Side at a certain time on a Saturday, carrying a tennis ball in his hand. Gold was instructed to go to the rendezvous with a green-bound book in one hand, wearing gloves, and carrying an additional pair of gloves in his other hand. Contact was made as arranged and then, still following instructions, Gold and Fuchs went by taxi to a restaurant where Fuchs handed over to Gold certain information about the atomic bomb project.

After that, they met regularly, Fuchs giving Gold material in increasing quantities and importance. As soon as Gold left Fuchs, he would go around a corner and meet Yakovlev, handing him the material he had just received from Fuchs. Some of these meetings between Gold and Fuchs and Gold and Yakovlev lasted for less than a minute. During one of them, in the vicinity of the Brooklyn Borough Hall in June, 1944, Fuchs delivered to Gold the actual blueprint of a uranium bomb, a preliminary model of the A-bomb. Later, they met in Boston, where Fuchs supplied details of a plutonium bomb. Whatever information was still needed by the Russians to make a bomb of their own was supplied by Fuchs at 4 P.M. on June 2, 1945, at the Castillo Bridge in Santa Fe, New Mexico. After that meeting, Gold went to Albuquerque and met another spy, David Greenglass, from whom he received drawings of the device that was used to explode the bomb. This single journey was probably the most rewarding trip ever made by any espionage courier in the whole history of the profession.

Up to this point, the spies were strictly on their own. This was entirely positive espionage. Counterespionage had still not come into the act. Although security was strict in the Manhattan Project, nothing was discovered of Fuchs's extra-curricular activities. Then on September 5, 1945, Igor Gouzenko, cipher clerk of the Soviet military attaché in Canada, revealed the existence of the Canadian ring and hinted that parallel rings were operating in the United States and the United Kingdom. On November 8, 1945, Miss Elizabeth Bentley gave corroborating evidence to Thomas J. Donegan, a special agent of the FBI's New York office. From then on, the wheels of counterespionage began to turn, but such is the nature of this delicate work that they could turn only very slowly. Nothing happened for almost two years. Then on May 29, 1947, the paths of the FBI and Gold crossed almost accidentally. The FBI was investigating a man named Brothman whom Miss Bentley had described as a member of the Golos ring. In Brothman's office in Elmhurst, Queens, two special agents of the FBI named Shannon and O'Brien came upon Gold himself.

The agents showed Gold a picture of Golos and Gold identified him promptly as a man for whom he worked. He seemed eager to unburden himself. After a brief conversation in the office, Gold and the two FBI men retired to the agents' car, and there, for two and a half hours, Gold talked. He revealed his real name and his real address in Philadelphia. He gave the details of his association with Golos who, incidentally, was listed in FBI files as an active Soviet espionage agent. Gold even talked of blueprints. "I kept those blueprints in my home in Philadelphia," he said, "and I never did turn them over to Golos."

Although Gold was extremely loquacious, he was also most cautious. He never incriminated himself. He represented his association with Golos as a business connection during which he supplied harmless information that was in the public domain and accessible to anyone. He was careful never even to suggest espionage in general, or atomic espionage in

213

particular. The gist of his words was shrewdly designed to confuse the agents with useless and misleading information, and to divert them from the trail they were following.

At 7 P.M., the agents took Gold back to Brothman's office and typed out Gold's statement. Gold signed it readily. At 9 P.M., the men went their separate ways, the agents to their office and Gold back home to Philadelphia.

Shortly afterwards, two agents from the FBI's Philadelphia office visited Gold at his home. They asked about the blueprints he had mentioned to Shannon and O'Brien, but, when he told them that he had none, the agents left without searching the house. In actual fact, a closet in Gold's basement was full of incriminating material. In July, 1947, Gold was called before a New York grand jury which was following up some of Miss Bentley's leads and bits of material which the FBI investigations had developed. The grand jury took no action against Gold, although he conceded that his actions were at least irregular. The name of Klaus Fuchs was never mentioned. The question of atomic espionage never came up. Gold felt confident that the FBI had little information about his clandestine activities and that the special agents were just fishing.

On February 2, 1950, Klaus Fuchs was arrested in London, on a tip that Scotland Yard received from the FBI. Two FBI agents, Hugh Clegg and Robert Lamphere, were sent to Britain to question Fuchs. They asked him about hundreds of suspects. They finally came around to Gold and showed Fuchs a motion picture they had taken of Gold a short time before. In the meantime, the FBI had searched Gold's house in Philadelphia and found evidence of his trip to Santa Fe in 1944, the meeting that Fuchs described in detail to the FBI agents in England. On May 22, 1950, more than six years after his first contact with Fuchs in Manhattan and three years after his first interrogation by the FBI, Gold confessed and was placed under arrest.

My reason for relating this incident is to demonstrate how tedious and difficult any counterespionage activity is in its concluding stages. Counterespionage agents usually have to work from nothing more than suspicion. There is little they can rely upon, and much that they presume has to be substantiated to be of any value. The weaving of the rope that eventually hangs the espionage agent is a gradual and intricate process in which virtually all the advantages of deception favor the spy.

The Gold case illustrates some of the patterns of protection, but, even more than that, it points up some which were absent. Obviously nothing was known of the clandestine activities of Fuchs, whose own security was a responsibility of the agency for which he worked. Obviously, too, security was deficient at the source. There was no valid or evident reason to suspect Gold of any wrong-doing or to keep him under surveillance.

Yakovlev's assignment at the Soviet Consulate General was known, since his presence there had to be reported to the State Department. But it seems nothing was known of the fact that he was acting as resident director of the New York spy ring, else he would have been under constant surveillance. In turn, such a surveillance would have led the special agents to his contacts and resulted in the exposure of the entire ring. The failure to shadow Yakovlev was a serious omission, since it is an established fact that almost all Soviet nationals among the intelligence personnel work under the cover of diplomatic and trade agencies abroad. If it is not known who in an embassy or consulate is charged with the supervision of espionage, then every member of the Soviet diplomatic staff must be kept under surveillance. This requires a substantial apparatus at the defensive end of the affair, but such an apparatus is needed, no matter how large it may be, if the defenses are to be foolproof.

Thus counterespionage depends on numbers, so to speak, as well as on the efficiency of direct investigations. It will benefit from the false steps an agent occasionally makes, and from the deficiency of his own security. Moreover, it depends on the support that counterespionage receives from a vigilant public.

However, even the best counterespionage agency is bound to fail wherever parts of the protection pattern are omitted, either by inefficiency or incompetence, or by a country's failure to appreciate the danger that lurks in the presence of even a single spy and its refusal to understand the vital need for airtight defenses against what Sir Basil Thomson so aptly called "the dark intruders."

The Evolution of Counterespionage

It is evident that when a country is attacked it must defend itself against the invaders, whether they come in the form of armies or as espionage agents infiltrating a nation from abroad. The recognition that such a defense is needed against spies is not new, but it has taken a long time for nations to organize their special forces against them. For centuries, the task of apprehending spies was assigned to the standing secret services or to the police; and occasionally it was the responsibility of the intelligence services, which were then supposed to conduct negative as well as positive intelligence and espionage.

We meet such a fixed organization for the first time in England in the sixteenth century, when the agents of Sir Francis Walsingham were sent abroad to procure information in Spain, France, and Holland. Agents at home trapped conspirators, both native and foreign, who threatened the person and secrets of Queen Elizabeth. As the conspiracies multiplied, Walsingham enlarged his organization to cope with them, and, then, to justify his existence and to obtain the funds he needed, he invented threats where none existed.

Counterespionage, in the modern sense of the term, came into being with the American Civil War, which pioneered many institutions of the secret war. It was an outgrowth of the turbulence of the election campaign of 1860, and the answer to conspiracies that the bitter advocates of slavery plotted against Abraham Lincoln. Even so, it did not come into existence by the deliberate effort of a government threatened by conspirators. It was, in fact, created in 1861 in Baltimore, Maryland, by the directors of the Philadelphia, Wilmington, and Baltimore Railroad, who were afraid that their investment might suffer irreparable damage in the course of an attempt on the life of Lincoln, the president-elect, on his journey to Washington.

The directors of the P.W.B.R.R. got word that conspirators were planning to assassinate Lincoln on his way to the inauguration, stage a *coup d'état* on the European pattern in Washington, and isolate the capital by blowing up the bridges, tracks, and rolling stock of the railroad. When the directors of the railroad got wind of the plot, they called in Allan Pinkerton to do something about it. Pinkerton was an able Scotsman who had gained nationwide fame for his exploits as a private detective operating his own agency in Chicago.

Pinkerton went about the job in the most accomplished manner of modern-day counterespionage. He arrived in Baltimore under cover, using the alias E. J. Allen. He was accompanied by two of his operatives, Timothy Webster and Harry Davies, the latter turned counterspy after Jesuit training for the clergy. The three men were soon sitting in the bar of Barnum's Hotel, mingling with the conspirators and winning their confidence. Davies was, in fact, present at the meeting

216

in which eight men were chosen by secret ballot to kill Lincoln as he passed through Baltimore. Pinkerton and his men had no power to arrest the conspirators, but they found out enough about the plot to devise a plan of their own that enabled Lincoln to reach Washington safely.

After that, Lincoln invited Pinkerton to organize a "secret service department" on a full-time basis, and the first counterespionage service worthy of the name was set up in a rented house on Eye Street in Washington. But such was the efficiency of the Southern spies, and so lacking was the support Pinkerton received from his own government, that his eventual failure was inevitable. Pinkerton was soon dismissed. But even in failure he pointed the way for others who were to follow.

In 1883, Britain established a "Special Branch" in Scotland Yard, initially to counter the plots of anarchists and nihilists, and subsequently to defend England from Irish Fenians who plotted the assassination of Queen Victoria during her jubilee celebration.

The next country to establish a counterespionage service on a full-time basis was France, in the wake of her disastrous defeat in the Franco-Prussian War of 1870-71. The Prussian campaign had been prepared by Chancellor Otto Bismarck, who employed 40,000 spies at a time when France had virtually none serving her own cause. The lessons of the war induced the French General Staff to build up its own intelligence services and to centralize them under one roof. The so-called Second Bureau was established within the General Staff and charged with both positive intelligence and counterespionage. A department for *Renseignements généraux* (general information) was added to the Directorate General of the *Sûreté Nationale*, the modern successor to the old political police, whose origins dated back to the fourteenth century.

The Second Bureau developed into a hotbed of domestic intrigue. It became best known, not for its successes in catching foreign spies, but for its despicable campaign against one of its own members, Captain Alfred Dreyfus. In that campaign, all the methods and paraphernalia of counterespionage were used to convict an innocent man, a victim of racial prejudice, while persons who actually served the Prussians as secret agents remained at large. The early history of the Second Bureau is a dark chronicle of intrigue and corruption. Its officers were selfish, devious, and callous men who undermined the efficiency of their own organization by treating their informants and agents in a contemptible manner.

Typical of the practices of the Second Bureau in those days was the case of Charles Lucieto, one of the Bureau's most loyal and useful informers. He was hired by the Bureau to serve as a double-agent, to offer his services to the Germans while actually spying for France. Lucieto performed well and loyally for France. But when his payment came due, the Second Bureau arrested him on charges of espionage for Germany to evade the obligation. The history of the Second Bureau abounds in such practices, one of several reasons why it never developed into a truly effective arm of counterespionage, and why France suffered more than any other country from the depredations of spies.

At the turn of the century, Russian spies made their appearance on the international scene and soon were swarming all over Europe. Counterespionage, practiced haphazardly until then, suddenly became an urgent necessity. The need was felt most keenly in Austria, where the Russians deployed their best operatives. In the face of this menace, the Austrians produced an exceptional counterspy in the person of Colonel Alfred Redl of their General Staff.

Although Redl was brilliant in positive intelligence as well, he really distinguished himself in counterespionage. Many methods still used today were originated by him. He was the first to place hidden microphones in rooms to record conversations. He concealed cameras in rooms and photographed suspects. He sprayed metal ashtrays with minium (red lead oxide) to obtain the fingerprints of suspects without their knowledge. He maintained a veritable museum of counterespionage in Vienna in which he exhibited all the tools of the trade and kept a collection of photographs of all the personalities in whom an agency of this nature could have even the remotest interest.

Yet Redl was himself an espionage agent—in the service of the Russians. They blackmailed him by threatening to expose him as a homosexual. Ironically, Redl was trapped in a remarkable coup of counterespionage by the very methods he himself had invented or developed. A clerk at the General Delivery window in the Vienna Central Post Office noticed the regular arrival of mysterious letters and reported the fact to the police. Some of the letters were surreptitiously opened and were discovered to be spy reports. The police set up a day-and-night watch in a precinct station across the street from the Post Office. The General Delivery counter was connected by wire to police station so that the clerk could alert the waiting detectives when anyone asked for mail addressed to "Opera Ball, 13." The police did not have long to wait. One day a man arrived and asked casually for letters addressed, "Opera Ball, 13." The police pounced. The man was Colonel Redl. When he was confronted with the evidence, he shot and killed himself.

The venality of the Second Bureau and the treachery of Redl illustrate some of the pitfalls of counterespionage. Enormous power is usually concentrated in the hands of men who head counterespionage agencies and they do not always use it judiciously. Instead of concentrating on foreign spies, they occasionally become involved in domestic intrigues and use their own conspiratorial apparatus to compound flourishing conspiracies. Such corruption not only jeopardizes their usefulness but actually sets them up as enemies of the countries they are supposed to serve. Necessary though counterespionage is in combating foreign agents, it is nevertheless imperative to circumscribe its powers and curb its chiefs. Otherwise, the services tend to become states within states, a greater menace than the espionage they were formed to counter.

After Redl's downfall the center of gravity shifted from Russia to Germany. Engaged in a bitter naval rearmament race with England, the Germans established an espionage network in the British Isles. There were twenty-two agents in their net, directed by a brilliant but erratic man named Gustav Steinhauer, who dubbed himself "the Kaiser's master spy." He had graduated to positive espionage from the German secret political police and then spent most of his time at the gambling tables of Belgian casinos. It was against such a spymaster and his motley crowd of agents, representing the German intelligence service, that England had to mobilize its own counterespionage forces. The urgent need for such a force was revealed by an accident.

In 1910, the Kaiser visited London to attend the funeral of Edward VII. His retinue included the acting chief of German naval intelligence, an officer well known to Scotland Yard's Special Branch. The officer was shadowed in the hope that he would lead agents of the Special Branch to some of his spies. One night the German left his hotel by a rear entrance and went to a modest house in a working-class district in London. The counterespionage agents trailed him there and established that the captain visited a hairdresser named Karl Gustav Ernst. After that, Ernst was kept under surveillance. It was soon learned that Ernst was receiving bulky letters from Germany. When Scotland Yard opened one of the letters, they found in it several sealed envelopes, addressed to individuals in various parts of Britain, properly franked with

English stamps. Then Ernst was observed mailing the letters one by one. Obviously, the man was a "letterbox." Obviously, too, the addressees were members of the German espionage network.

In due course, Scotland Yard obtained the names and addresses of all the twenty-two German agents in the British Isles and discovered that they were strategically placed in naval ports throughout all of England. It was decided to permit the men to remain at large, thereby initiating a method of counterespionage still used by most agencies today and known as "the long rope system." The term of course, is derived from the apothegm, "Give a man enough rope and he will hang himself."

In the "long rope system" counterespionage accepts the probability that once a spy is unmasked and arrested another one will take his place. Counterespionage is then obliged by a slow and tedious process to ferret out the replacement. Scotland Yard decided that it would be more productive to leave the original spy at his post, keeping him under constant surveillance, watching his mail and his contacts, and arresting him only in an acute emergency. An agent cannot do much harm when closely watched. But he can do his own cause harm if misleading information can be palmed off on him. Furthermore, an unmolested spy can lead watchful counterespionage to his associates and accomplices, and one by one the whole group can be arrested.

The morning after the outbreak of the First World War, Special Branch rounded up these known spies, together with about two hundred of their contacts and accomplices. At the very moment when Germany most needed them, not a single German spy was at large in England. After this brilliant coup, British counterespionage became known, respected, and feared throughout the world. It continued to function brilliantly throughout World War I, owing largely to the skill of Sir Basil Thomson, and to the aid he received from Admiral Reginald Hall, who was then reading the German cables as if they had been his own. One of Thomson and Hall's greatest scoops was the capture of Sir Roger Casement, who had been sent to Ireland by the German secret service to start a revolution in England's back yard.

Between the two world wars espionage flourished, chiefly because counterespionage was permitted to degenerate. An occasional German or Soviet agent was caught in Britain; German spies were caught in Japan; a few Japanese spies were caught in the United States. A cold war of espionage raged in central and eastern Europe, especially in Germany, where an intrepid Polish agent named Sosnovski managed to penetrate to the highest secrets of the German General Staff and obtained the deployment plan it had prepared for a war against Poland. Sosnovski was caught, not because he was incompetent, but rather because he was too good. He came to Berlin in 1934 with excellent credentials, to represent his father, a prominent international lawyer in Warsaw. Frequenting the most exclusive clubs, playing tennis, golf, and polo, he soon became the darling of Britain's highest society.

Before long he was carrying on a number of affairs simultaneously, as if trying to prove that a ladies' man is far more dangerous a spy than an ascetic. Although no one took particular notice of it, every one of his intimate women friends had close connections with the Reichswehr Ministry. At least two of them worked as confidential secretaries in the Ministry's Operations Department, one a middle-aged spinster whose affair with Sosnovski was the first love of an otherwise barren life, the other the nineteen-year-old daughter of a German general. They showed their gratitude by carrying their department's documents to Sosnovski, who copied them overnight and returned them the following morning in time for them to be replaced in the files before the offices opened for the day.

Sosnovski showered expensive gifts on his girl friends. He gave the youngest a fur coat which she paraded at home with the explanation that she had bought it herself with an increase she had received in her salary. Gratified by her daughter's rapid advancement, the girl's mother visited her superior to thank him for the raise. The officer acknowledged her thanks modestly, although he knew that the young fräulein had received no increase from his department. Then he promptly reported the incident to counterespionage, and the girl was placed under surveillance. Within four weeks, Sosnovski's secret was out, but by then Polish intelligence had copies of the German General Staff's highly classified and jealously guarded plans.

Counterespionage Agencies of Today

At the present time, most countries make a strict distinction between their counterintelligence and counterespionage organizations. Counterintelligence is usually assigned to military agencies, while counterespionage is conducted by civilian organizations that are either specially set up for the purpose or attached to existing agencies.

There are, of course, exceptions. In the Soviet Union, the Fourth Bureau of the Red Army General Staff deals exclusively with positive intelligence and has no negative function whatever. Counterespionage is assigned to the Ministry of the Interior, which is charged with all police functions and conducts counterespionage as part of its secret police work. During World War II, a special counterespionage agency was organized to serve in the field. It went by the abbreviated name of "Smersh," the telescoped syllables standing for the Russian words "Death to the spies." The name of the agency indicates the summary manner in which the Soviet Union deals with arrested foreign agents.

In France, the Second Bureau continues to function as the country's central counterespionage service. The General Staff now also has a Fifth Bureau, which handles cases of subversion both at home and in French territories overseas. Both of these bureaus are understaffed, employing between them only a few hundred persons. This shortage of personnel restricts their efficiency tremendously in a country where the danger of espionage, sabotage, and subversion is most acute.

There are no more than fifty detectives employed in that part of the *Sûreté Nationale* which is the counterespionage agency of France, conducting actual investigations on tips received from the Second and Fifth Bureaus and making arrests. The so-called General Information branch of the *Sûreté* is in charge of frontier defense, and, curiously enough, also of horse-racing and gambling. Its chief duty, however, is to collect political information for the heads of the administration and to defend the country from spies, saboteurs, and subversives. It is well equipped for the job so far as technical matters are concerned. The *Sûreté* has several police laboratories in the principal cities and a central laboratory in Lyon which is rated with the best in the world. It also maintains an excellent *Service de l'Identité Judiciaire*, which has on file photographs, fingerprints, and personal descriptions of innumerable espionage suspects.

Even so, counterespionage is hampered in France by the grave domestic difficulties of the country. The agencies are still politically inspired and often corrupt. They depend largely on the antiquated *dossier* system, the keeping of indiscriminate and unevaluated files. The system was inherited, together with its vicious implications, from the secret police of Joseph Fouché, Napoleon's ruthless and shrewd police minister. Some of Fouché's malicious methods still dominate counterespionage in France, although much of his comprehensive efficiency is lacking.

Western Germany, today a hotbed of espionage and the headquarters of innumerable spy rings, now has its own counterespionage agencies within the new *Bundeskriminalamt* (Federal Bureau of Crime Investigation), a relatively small branch of detectives with headquarters in Bonn. Its function is the protection of the president, the cabinet members, and the diplomatic corps, and also the operation of counterespionage. It has limited executive powers, but high technical efficiency.

Excellent counterespionage agencies exist in Switzerland, Italy, Belgium, the Netherlands, and the Scandinavian countries as well as in Israel, India, and Japan. All of these work within their respective police organizations and specialize in political police work and defense against espionage and subversion.

In Britain, the work of counterespionage is distributed between a branch of the War Office Military Intelligence Department, known the world over as MI-5, and the Special Branch of Scotland Yard's Criminal Investigation Department. Considering the tasks assigned to them, they are extremely small organizations. In 1939, when German espionage was at its peak, the Special Branch had only 156 detectives and administrative officers, and MI-5 had only a few investigators under its civilian head, Sir David Petrie. During the war, MI-5 was vastly enlarged to cope with the problems of the war waged on its secret fronts. But the Special Branch never had more than eight hundred employees. Today, MI-5 has only its normal complement of peacetime investigators, while the detectives assigned to the Special Branch number some two hundred. They are stationed at every airport and seaport and also serve as bodyguards for the royal family and prominent personages. Only a relatively small staff is then left to deal with movements regarded as subversive, and to track down espionage and sabotage suspects. Looking at it purely from the size of the organization, Britain's security is definitely limited. However, the numerical inferiority of the various British agencies in the field is compensated by their efficiency and by the exceptional competence of their personnel.

No matter how impressive past British scoops have been in the game of counterespionage, and no matter how elaborate similar organizations of other countries have been, they are all overshadowed by a relative newcomer to the game—the Federal Bureau of Investigation of the United States. Almost from the very first day in 1939 when the FBI joined the spy-hunters of the world as America's central counterespionage agency, it has functioned with unprecedented efficiency, and, what is even more important, with a scrupulous adherence to democratic processes.

In the business of counterespionage, the FBI represents the highest degree of competence. It is today, by any standard, the outstanding example of excellence in this field.

American Counterespionage and the FBI

Americans have every reason to be concerned about their security against conspirators who engage in espionage or sabotage. The safety of this republic was severely threatened by Benedict Arnold, whose subversive activities were calculated to defeat the American Revolution. A British spy named John Henry operated most efficiently in the United States in 1812 and succeeded in undermining the stability of President Madison's administration. Espionage complicated the efforts of the Union to defeat the Confederacy. Saboteurs caused substantial damage in World War I.

In World War II, a code clerk of the American Embassy in London betrayed some of this country's most valuable diplomatic secrets to the Germans and Italians. The espionage activities of native Americans helped the Soviet Union to acquire the atomic secrets of the United States.

Through its history, the United States has been on the receiving end of espionage, the target of positive intelligence. It has suffered considerably from the treachery of native agents and from the insidious activities of foreigners. Counterespionage, therefore, is an important responsibility of the United States government. But although the need has always existed, the recognition of it was rather late in coming.

The freedom with which espionage agents and saboteurs could formerly operate in the United States was only partly a result of the latitude that a democracy provides for such activities. To a far greater extent it was due to the fact that for 163 years of its existence, the United States had no properly organized, permanently functioning, central, counterespionage agency to deal with spies and saboteurs. The U.S. Army and Navy had counterintelligence branches within their intelligence organizations and the Army, in particular, had its own Counter Intelligence Corps and Criminal Investigation

Division. Other government agencies also had certain intelligence functions. But no coordinated effort or central agency existed. Most of the agencies active in the work were hampered by severe legal restrictions placed upon them, or suffered from shortages in funds and personnel. During the First World War, for example, counterespionage was assigned to the Secret Service, which was forced to prosecute this activity in addition to its numerous other commitments.

The result was that by the thirties the United States had become an open hunting preserve for spies. There would have been even more of them, except for the fact that the United States did not practice concealment on an efficient scale, but instead spread out virtually all its confidential affairs for anybody to read or observe. Actually it did not pay foreign countries to maintain extensive espionage organizations in the United States, since most of the information they wanted could be procured without the aid of spies.

Those who did work in America were inferior agents, left over after the better operatives were assigned to more important theaters. And if those who did come to the United States were rarely caught, it was chiefly because hardly an agency existed that could even follow their activities, much less catch them red-handed. Today there is a great deal of talk about belatedly exposed spies of bygone days. But such exposés must be viewed in perspective. It should be borne in mind that those spies were low-level, often untrained, agents, scrambling for largely unconcealed "secrets," and flourishing like mice in the absence of the cat. No serious damage to the United States accrued from their activities, no matter how much their work may now be magnified by self-seeking politicians or by ex-operatives who were themselves merely on the fringes of this espionage carnival.

The situation became serious only in the period beginning in 1938 and 1939 when aggressors in Europe and Asia compelled the United States to flex its own muscles. Then the foreign espionage services began to turn their earnest attention toward the United States. Spy rings of greater professional skill came into existence and began to expand. Better trained and more competent agents were dispatched to the United States. The recruiting of native agents was intensified.

Soviet espionage, in particular, became more interested in the United States. Originally, its only interest was in the so-called industrial "secrets" of this country, but it was quick to discover that most of these "secrets" were on the open market, available through regular commercial channels. They could be obtained simply by the payment of nominal fees at the U.S. Patent Office, or bought at somewhat greater expense from manufacturers themselves, who appeared most eager to do business with the U.S.S.R. These firms sold not only their products but also their secret formulas and special manufacturing processes. During those days, between 1924 and 1933, tanks, guns, planes, and warships were sold to the Soviet Union and exported openly with the proper licenses, issued by the State Department.

An occasional Soviet spy was uncovered in areas other than the industrial field. In 1931-32, an agent procured military data about the Panama Canal from a corporal of the U.S. Army. In 1932-33, another agent was found to be passing $100 Federal Reserve notes counterfeited under the direction of Soviet intelligence. The first espionage ring of any consequence was established in the United States in the mid-thirties by an agent named Gaik Badalovich Ovakimian. He managed to set up a large apparatus but found the pickings rather meager. His greatest achievement was the infiltration of the Justice Department in 1937 and 1938.

In 1938, a small net was discovered on the West Coast through a fortuitous accident. This ring had succeeded in infiltrating a naval district's intelligence office. In addition, a network of political espionage flourished in Washington. It was composed of starry-eyed dupes who held various positions in the United States government and supplied Soviet intelligence with information of such low value that most of it was not accepted by the collectors or, if it was, was never transmitted to Moscow.

The situation changed abruptly in 1938-39 with the appearance of German espionage agents on the scene. They were not particularly well organized and received only half-hearted support from Germany. A jurisdictional dispute raged among the various intelligence services in the Reich about the supervision of these agents. Moreover, because Hitler was anxious to maintain neutrality with the United States, the German Foreign Office opposed the utilization of espionage agents in this country.

Even so, it was left to a German spy to score the outstanding espionage scoop of those years. He was Hermann Lang, a simple technician employed in the Long Island plant of the C. I. Norden Company, which manufactured the famous Norden bombsight. At that time, the bombsight was widely publicized in the press as "America's No. 1 secret." Attracted by this publicity, the intelligence services of the world made energetic efforts to obtain its blueprints and, in the end, all of them did. But Germany was the first to succeed, through the efforts of Hermann Lang. Working at Norden as an expert draftsman and inspector in 1938, Lang memorized the bombsight's details, returned to Germany, and prepared a blueprint of the instrument from memory.

German intelligence was jubilant. The stocky, dark-haired Lang, a naturalized American with bushy eyebrows and sparkling brown eyes, was dined and wined. He was received by Hermann Göring, who thanked him personally for his great scoop and gave him 10,000 marks as a special bonus.

Lang was a member of one of the several German espionage rings that were set up one after another in the United States. They included a strange assortment of people. There were among them a notorious professional spy, several Nazi fanatics, and numerous beautiful women to give the drama its Hollywood touch. Although there is today a tendency to minimize the efficiency and effectiveness of German espionage in the United States shortly before World War II, the fact is that it was both efficient and effective. Every ship entering or leaving the port of New York, every military installation along the eastern seaboard, all fortifications, airfields, naval bases were reported by German agents to Berlin. A permanent card file maintained by one of the rings contained information about United States army camps, disposition of U.S. military forces, troop movements, and arms production. The information was accurate, detailed, and up to the minute. Still others sent data on so-called choke points in the United States to be sabotaged in the event of war. It was from such reports that Dr. Astor, chief of the Western Sabotage Section of German Military Intelligence, selected the targets for the "Pastorius" mission, Hitler's unsuccessful attempt to sabotage American industry with agents who were slipped ashore at night on Long Island and in Florida from German U-boats.

By 1939, the world situation had grown worse. War in Europe was imminent. There were indications that Japan also planned to intensify its espionage activities in the United States, and it was naturally expected that the Soviet Union would replace its amateurs with professional agents. The need for a central counterespionage agency in America was increasingly felt, especially when certain cases got tangled up between various competing agencies that were operating on shoe-string appropriations and with inadequate personnel.

On September 6, 1939, six days after the outbreak of the war in Europe, President Roosevelt issued a special directive in which he took cognizance of the danger and proclaimed the necessity of combating it with greater efficiency than had been shown previously by the scattered agencies. He was determined to end the bickerings and jealousies which interfered with the job. "To this end," the Presidential directive stated, "I request all police officers, sheriffs, and all other law-enforcement officers in the United States promptly to turn over to the nearest representative of the Federal Bureau of Investigation any information obtained by them relating to espionage, counterespionage, sabotage, subversive activities, and violations of the neutrality law." In the words of J. Edgar Hoover, the FBI became "a clearing-house for all matters concerning espionage, sabotage, and subversivism"—America's *central counterintelligence agency* in fact, if not in name.

Until then, the FBI was but one of several agencies engaged in counterespionage. Although normally eventual arrests in espionage and sabotage cases were made by FBI agents, and although the FBI was getting most of the newspaper publicity resulting from those exposés, the Bureau actually did little to develop espionage and sabotage cases. It was somewhat undermanned and far too busy for this extracurricular work. It had charge of "the investigation of all violations of Federal laws" with the exception of counterfeiting, postal violations, customs violations, and internal revenue matters. Even today, the FBI investigates violations of approximately 130 different Federal statutes, of which less than a dozen are concerned with "espionage, sabotage, treason, and other matters pertaining to the internal security of the United States." They include the Federal Kidnaping Statute, the National Bank Act, the White Slave Traffic Act, and the Atomic Energy Act of 1946—and also such statutes as, for example, the Migratory Bird Act.

In the past the FBI and its "G-men" were best known for their campaign against gangsters and racketeers, but today they are chiefly famous for their war against foreign spies. The appearance of the FBI in this specialized field brought an organization into counterespionage the likes of which had never existed before. Compared with its foreign counterparts, it has proved itself to be not only bigger but better, injecting practical, business-like American ideas and efficiency into a profession that in Europe had developed out of the musty past of a predatory secret political police.

With headquarters in Washington, D.C., it has 52 field offices throughout the United States, several training and technical installations and schools, and agents stationed abroad. More than 10,000 persons are permanently employed by the FBI. More than 5,000 of them are special agents, the

228

majority of whom are today engaged in antisubversion work.

At the head of the Bureau, its director, J. Edgar Hoover, has stamped the mark of a remarkable personality not only on law enforcement in general but on counterespionage in particular. He is a dedicated scholar of crime detection. In the words of Alexander Holtzoff, a Washington judge, "Mr. Hoover himself represents the best type of career man in the government." He described Hoover as "a practical idealist," a man of an artistic temperament, and "highly sentimental not only in his own personal circle but also in his relations with all of his subordinates, and even at times in dealing with persons whom he has to arrest." But Hoover is also a strict disciplinarian, an able administrator, and a great educator.

Working under him are specially chosen subordinates who are capable of translating Hoover's theories into practice. The personnel of the FBI is chosen on the basis of careful selection, either for special skills or general aptitude for the job. A man's character and personal habits are dominant factors in selection. The FBI's personnel is not under the control of the civil service but is recruited and managed according to the principles laid down by its director and at his personal discretion. Efficiency methods developed by private enterprise are adopted by the Bureau, in addition to efficient police procedures developed within the organization itself, or imported from other services.

To supplement the work of its personnel the FBI maintains the world's most advanced technical criminal laboratories. Here and in special schools, agents are trained in cryptography, spectroscopic analysis, handwriting identification, fingerprinting methods, document identification, filing and indexing techniques, ballistics and explosives, general disguise and identification methods, communications equipment, photography, search and seizure methods, report writing, and the evaluation of information.

At headquarters, the Bureau maintains a filing system that contains the fingerprints and biographies of millions of people. Along with the data kept on law-abiding government and military personnel in this country as primary security measures, the FBI has at its fingertips similar data on espionage and sabotage suspects and potential alien subversives, both in the United States and abroad. Thanks to these files the FBI was able to round up or keep under constant scrutiny nearly every actual and potential German espionage agent in the United States in December, 1941. So thorough was the list that no effective German spy was left at large, and none showed up for the remainder of the war.

The honesty and integrity of the FBI are legendary. Agents are kept under strict discipline, and the slightest infraction of Bureau regulations may lead to dismissal. The result is that throughout its history this organization has been free of prejudice, corruption, and malfeasance in the course of law enforcement.

The FBI is extremely ethical and democratic. These qualities, naturally taken for granted by Americans as characteristic of any police force, point up a great distinction between the FBI and many foreign espionage agencies. The civil rights of individuals, including those accused of criminal actions, are stringently observed. Special agents are indoctrinated in the need for staying strictly within the law when conducting investigations, even though the law itself may frustrate their primary objective. The idea of a "secret police" or a "political police" is stressed as an abhorrent condition, and the fact that the agency is designed to *defend* democracy is emphasized.

The fact that it is publicly popular is an important element in the over-all efficiency and success of the Bureau. With the exception of Scotland Yard and MI-5, which are also popular with the general public, no other counterespionage agency of the world enjoys as much public confidence and cooperation as the FBI.

When, in September, 1939, the Federal Bureau of Investigation was established as the central counterespionage agency of the United States, it brought to its new task of detecting and trapping spies a wide experience in criminal investigation. The application of certain anticriminal methods to counterespionage is not always effective, and the FBI is striving to develop what Director Hoover himself calls "intelligence methods" to increase the Bureau's efficiency in this particular field. However, counterespionage, as distinct from security intelligence and counterintelligence, is an investigative activity whose methods are not much different from those of criminal investigation. In the final analysis, the spy and saboteur, whatever his motivations may be, is a violator of laws and therefore a criminal. Accordingly, counterespionage has the three phases that characterize modern police science: identification of persons, field work, and laboratory work to examine and analyze clues and traces discovered in the course of investigations.

Like modern criminal investigation, counterespionage also inquires into the methods and techniques the law violator has used in his approach to and perpetration of the crime. It apprehends the criminal, and gathers and collates information

230

on the facts and circumstances necessary for the prosecution of secret agents. The basic methods of finding a fugitive spy are not different from tracing a fugitive criminal. Interrogation has identical techniques in both investigations, as have surveillance and trailing. Like the police, counterespionage agencies also work with informers, plants, confidential informants, and denouncers. Both use the same methods to detect deception, and identical precision instruments for laboratory work. However, although all of this is true, there still remains a vast area of difference between criminal investigation and the detection of secret agents. Criminal investigation invariably begins at the scene of the crime, where it expects to find vital clues. At the same time, it tries to establish specific motives which presumably induced the criminal to his action. In espionage, there is rarely a "scene of the crime." The motive, if any can be found, hardly ever provides a decisive clue.

Even when espionage investigation uses the orthodox methods of criminal investigation, it applies them in its own special way. The three basic methods of counterespionage are identification, shadowing, and what is colloquially called "roping," the criminological jargon for worming oneself into a suspect's confidence, also called penetration or infiltration.

Identification is based on registration work, the maintenance of extensive files on as many potential secret agents as possible, as well as on authorized persons who have access to classified information in their regular daily work. Such files usually include the suspect's fingerprints, his photograph, and whatever biographical data is available. These records are ingeniously cross-indexed and so arranged as to be readily accessible when needed. They provide the basic clues which in routine criminal investigation would be present in a physical form at the scene of the crime. International exchange of information about suspects is designed to facilitate identification still further. Countries linked by mutual interest cooperate closely in the registration and identification of secret agents. This was shown in the case of Klaus Fuchs, who was arrested on a tip from the FBI, while the arrest of a "maildrop" in Scotland during the thirties resulted in the breaking of a German espionage ring in the United States.

Shadowing is the term used to describe the process of following an espionage or sabotage suspect wherever he goes. In a broader sense, this is done to keep him under constant surveillance, either to catch him in an incriminating act, or to uncover other members of his net or ring, as well as to obtain evidence needed for arrest and prosecution. Surveillance of a suspect often includes the tapping of his telephone, although espionage agents nowadays rarely use the phone. When they resort to it at all, they conduct their conversations in code to prevent anyone listening in from obtaining the clues or leads he seeks. It also includes the examination of a suspect's mail and the observation of his contacts. Counterespionage agents often work with concealed cameras and hidden microphones to obtain legally admissible documentation for subsequent prosecution.

Surveillance requires ingenuity and extreme patience. Secret agents are trained in the methods of the enemy and know how to shake off "shadows" and to conceal their activities even from the most ingenious methods of direct observation. Complications that counterespionage agents encounter during surveillance work make their effort a long and tedious process, occasionally enabling secret agents to perpetrate their crimes and to escape even when under active, day-and-night surveillance.

Probably most rewarding among the investigative methods of counterespionage is roping, or the infiltration into the agent's confidence and the penetration of his ring. This may be accomplished by counterespionage agents in disguises but usually is done by special go-betweens, called informers, plants, or double-agents.

The overwhelming majority of cases solved in counterespionage begin with a tip from an informant or plant. When such a tip is received the person denounced is usually put under surveillance. Experience shows that unless an agent himself commits some glaring blunder, counterespionage cannot by itself detect and develop a case absolutely from scratch without outside information. It is therefore ridiculous to detract from the efficiency of Scotland Yard or the FBI by pointing out that their most eminent successes were essentially due to outside efforts, and that they received undeserved publicity for the independent efforts of some other agency or individual. The eventual arrest of a secret agent is usually a long process, starting with the original tip that first brings him to the attention of the counterespionage agency. Enormous and complex effort is needed to prove espionage against a suspect in a democracy.

Even the testing of the initial tip is a serious matter, especially in agencies which receive virtually thousands of these denunciations every year. The weeding-out process is by no means foolproof. Irresponsible accusations consume much of the time of counterespionage agents, while often a tip that proves valuable in the end may appear useless when first received. No counterespionage agency has the staff necessary to track down every tip it receives. Perfunctory investigation and part-time surveillance usually do not yield the results in counterespionage frequently achieved in criminal investigation. During the first ten months of the Second World War, the FBI received 5,246 complaints of sabotage. When these complaints were investigated, it developed that most of them came, as Clyde A. Tolson, assistant director of the FBI, expressed it, "from disgruntled employees, cranks, persons who had grievances." In 1941, for example, the FBI succeeded in convicting 177 persons indicted, but only ten of them were what Tolson described as "actual sabotage cases."

Internal efficiency and technical competence are the two essential attributes of counterespionage. Scotland Yard and the FBI possess both to a high degree. But no matter how efficient and competent a counterespionage agency is, it cannot operate effectively without outside aid. Such cooperation must be forthcoming from all agencies of the government, and in particular from such intelligence and law enforcement agencies as the counterintelligence branches of Army, Navy, and Air Intelligence, the Central Intelligence Agency, regional or local police, and other Federal, state, and municipal law enforcement agencies as the Bureau of Customs, the Bureau of Internal Revenue, the Narcotics Bureau, the Post Office Department, and the Immigration and Naturalization Service.

Of equal, if not greater, importance is the collaboration of an intelligent, enlightened, and patriotic public free of hysteria. In this connection, J. Edgar Hoover once said: "The biggest job facing the American people in their protection of the home is the necessity for the average citizen to do something about his own protection. . . . If his home is safe, it will be safe only when he protects it. This does not mean armed force or physical effort; it implies, however, constant vigilance."

In counterespionage, informants and informers are of exceptional importance. All counterespionage agencies make widespread use of both. An informant is any person who occasionally or regularly reports observations of possible interest to the counterespionage service. An informer is a professional aide of the agency, who may or may not be paid for his services. He is planted under false pretenses within an opponent's organization or where he can deal personally with a suspect.

In addition, counterespionage agents make use of so-called provocateurs and double-agents. The former's job is that of a catalyzing agent, to provoke certain overt acts that will bring the conspiracy into the open and enable the law-enforcement agency to strike. Double-agents are used to give their services to an opponent while in fact they are informing on their activities, contacts, and associations to their own counterintelligence or counterespionage organizations. The job of the informer may not be completely ethical or admirable, but it is essential and often crucial. It may be stated categorically that, without such informers and double-agents, a counterespionage agency would be doomed to failure.

The FBI, in particular, is conscious of the pitfalls involved in the employment of informers, agents provocateurs, and double-agents. It goes to extreme lengths in screening and choosing them. A former Attorney General of the United States once outlined the principles that guide the Department of Justice in the selection and use of its informers. "I have taken personal pains," he said, "to inquire and satisfy myself as to the character, ability, and general worth of every one of the so-called undercover agents of the Department of Justice. . . . They are men of splendid character, of unusual intellectual attainments, and of a wonderfully high order of physical courage . . ."

In the course of its own evolution from a general law-enforcement agency preoccupied with criminal investigation to a central counterespionage agency, the FBI incorporated in its own work all these methods. Today it stands as the outstanding example of a counterespionage service centrally conducted, completely separated from all positive intelligence efforts. The whole complex of counterespionage, then, and in particular the FBI's method of executing it, may be illustrated by a case that typifies counterespionage at its best.

The Case of William G. Sebold

Shortly after World War I, a young veteran of the Kaiser's army came to the United States to escape the turmoil of postwar Germany and to try his fortune. His name was William G. Sebold. A mechanic by profession, he did not find it difficult to get a job. In due course, he became prosperous and established himself as a respected member of the California community in which he lived.

In 1939 he was working for the Consolidated Aircraft Company's San Diego plant and was earning enough to afford a vacation to visit relatives in Germany. He was anxious to go, and he feared that the coming war in Europe would force him to postpone his trip. Sebold's American passport listed his occupation as "airplane mechanic," and the German frontier authorities, who examined the passports of all German-Americans scrupulously, reported his arrival to the Nazi espionage organizations.

A few days after his arrival in Mülheim, his birthplace, Sebold received a visitor. The stranger was suave and polite, but his conversation was very much to the point.

"You are an airplane mechanic," the man said. "We can use men like you, especially in the United States."

"But I'm an American citizen," Sebold countered.

"What difference does that make?" the man said. "You're a German and we expect you to conduct yourself accordingly." The man demanded that Sebold surrender his U.S. passport and departed, leaving the confused German-American to ponder the next step. Sebold was confronted with a dilemma typical in such situations. If he agreed he would forfeit his right to regard himself as an American citizen, and if he refused to cooperate he would not be allowed to return to the United States. He decided to act as an American. He went to Cologne and called on the American consul, telling him everything that had happened. To his surprise, the consul advised him to do as the Germans proposed, to accept the offer and then wait for developments.

Still confused, but somewhat fortified by the assurances he received in Cologne that he would do a great service to his adopted country by spying against it for his native land, Sebold returned to Mülheim to await further instructions from the German espionage agency. He did not have long to wait, and, his acceptance completed, Sebold was sent surreptitiously to an espionage school in Hamburg where he was trained in special photography for the production of microfilm. He was taught codes, telegraphy, the operation of shortwave transmitters, and the use of secret inks. It was obvious that the Germans were training him to serve as the transmitter of a spy ring, the member whose job it is to transmit the information that others collect.

On January 27, 1940, Sebold was called to the office of Nicholas Fritz Ritter, a Gestapo officer who functioned as the principal of the spy school.

"Are you familiar with the Norden plant on Long Island which manufactures the secret American bombsight?" Ritter asked.

"I never heard of it," Sebold said on first impulse, but then

235

corrected himself. "Of course, I could probably find out everything about that bombsight. Perhaps I could even get its blueprints."

"You don't need to exert yourself," Ritter said. "We already have the blueprint. You will work for us in America as a radio operator." He handed Sebold a slip of paper with four names and addresses on it. "These are the collectors for whom you will work," Ritter said. "Here, memorize their names and addresses."

Sebold was then given an American passport made out to "William G. Sawyer," and a cover story to go with the name. He was handed five long documents reduced to the size of postage stamps and told to conceal them in the back of his watchcase. They were instructions for the collectors in New York. He was paid an advance of $1,000 and was told that $5,000 was awaiting him in a Mexican bank. Finally, he was given detailed instructions: "Upon arrival, you will open an office in midtown Manhattan where you will meet the collectors and receive from them their material. You will set up your transmitter in a house somewhere on the Long Island coast and transmit the information by radio."

A few weeks later, traveling on the S.S. *Washington*, Sebold arrived in New York and went to work at once to carry out his instructions. He formed a company he called Diesel Research Company, and rented an office on 42nd Street in New York. In his house in Centerport, Long Island, he installed his short-wave transmitter. Then on May 31, 1940, Sebold locked himself in the room where his radio stood and, at 6 P.M. sharp, prepared the machine to transmit the first information he had received from his collectors.

"CQDXVW-2 calling AOR." Sebold tapped out the prearranged signal.

"Go ahead CQDXVW," an operator at AOR in Germany replied.

"I'm ready to send," Sebold tapped out.

"Splendid," Germany answered, when Sebold had completed his message, and continued with new instructions for the American ring. "Need urgently from all friends data on monthly production of aircraft factories, exports to all countries, especially to England. Number, type, date of delivery by steamer or air. Payment cash-and-carry or credit."

Sebold confirmed the message.

"Rose has money for you," the man in Germany signaled.

Sebold acknowledged and signed off.

For months afterward messages went out from CQDXVW-2 in Centerport, U.S.A., to AOR in Hamburg, Germany, from

Sebold alias Sawyer to Rittler alias Rankin. But there was someone else listening to the signal, too. It was the FBI. From the moment Sebold went to the American consul in Cologne, he was a spy, but only nominally for the Germans. He was what is known as a double-agent, actually a trusted key figure in the American counterespionage network. Sebold was in daily touch with special agents of the FBI. They drafted most of the messages he sent to Hamburg, and his radio was actually operated by communications specialists of the Department of Justice. In his office on 42nd Street, the FBI set up concealed microphones to record the conversation of all his visitors. Cameras were hidden to photograph them. The collectors with whom Sebold worked were placed under surveillance, and the whole ring of German spies was firmly under control.

This game went on for more than a year. Then, on the evening of June 28, 1941, the FBI struck. The entire ring that Sebold serviced with his radio was rounded up. They in turn led the FBI to another ring, and its members were also taken into custody. The Germans were astounded. They had become convinced that their intricate system was invulnerable, and they could not imagine where the leak was. At their trial they got the answer. The FBI produced a witness whose detailed testimony sealed their fate. He was, of course, William G. Sebold.

The Sebold case is a classic example of counterespionage. It proves again the importance of having an informer within a spy ring. It shows how a single informer, if strategically placed, can lead counterespionage agents to a whole ring. It showed, too, how an informer or double-agent serves as a decoy to trap other agents who are not immediately connected with his own network.

The discovery of these rings eliminated virtually all German espionage agents working in the United States in 1941. The period between the arrest of these men and women and the bombing of Pearl Harbor was not great enough to permit their replacement before America imposed wartime counterespionage measures. The action of the FBI in this one major case was manifold in its consequences and, although there occurred isolated cases of espionage and sabotage in the United States during the war, all organized efforts by the enemy to these ends failed.

In wartime, espionage is confronted with added difficulties, one of which is, of course, the intensification of counterespionage. The defensive forces of the battle of espionage are enlarged and broadened, and certain agencies are brought into existence which, in most countries, exist only in wartime to cope with the specific problems of espionage in war. The small counterintelligence forces of the armed forces are expanded. The Army's CIC and CID are given police powers. Naval Intelligence enters the picture more energetically and the Coast Guard also adds its forces to the defensive network of a country organized to combat spies and saboteurs.

Of the agencies specially established or enlarged to cope with the problems of wartime espionage one of the most important is the Office of Censorship. Strictly speaking, censorship is a counterintelligence or security measure, rather than a counterespionage function; it functions preventively, it conducts no investigations of its own. Whenever a suspicious piece of correspondence turns up, censorship forwards it to the proper authorities to determine what is behind it. Even so, censorship is appropriately dealt with here as a counterespionage activity, if only because censorship is regarded as an auxiliary arm of the defensive forces organized against espionage agents.

Censorship

The scope of censorship may be shown by a few figures. During its brief stay in Europe during the First World War, the military censors of the American Expeditionary Force received 30,846,630 letters, of which more than six million pieces were actually examined. Although a secret-ink laboratory was established in France only three months before the war ended, it nevertheless examined 53,658 suspicious documents referred to it by censors. During World War II, the British postal censors had 800,000,000 pieces of mail referred to them, of which more than two million pieces had to be subjected to some kind of scientific analysis in the laboratory. In the First World War, Britain employed more than 5,000 persons in censorship. The number of military censors was more than 10,000 in the Second World War. In the United States, too, thousands worked in the Office of Censorship, examining millions of documents.

A distinction must be made between censorship on the home front and that in the active theaters of operation. The military censor examines mail of overseas personnel, while the home front censor today examines all branches of communication, including the press, radio, and television. Censors work in close cooperation with the security organs and counterespionage agencies of their countries, and receive from them so-called suspect lists, composed of the names and aliases of persons who are suspected of espionage, sabotage, or subversion. Often the names of very highly placed personages appear on suspect lists. In the First World War, for example, the queens of Greece, Sweden, and Spain were included in all Allied suspect lists, as was General Wille, chief of staff of the Swiss Army, known for his pro-German sympathies.

While the democracies maintain censorship bureaus only during war or national emergencies, totalitarian countries maintain them on a permanent basis. The censorship office of Czarist Russia, known as the Black Cabinet, attained conspicuous notoriety. Headed by an infamous double-agent named Karl Ziewert, an Austrian by birth, it examined the correspondence of the political opponents of the czar, and also of his own statesmen, generals, grand dukes, and the czar himself. Ziewert is remembered as an ambitious and ingenious censor, and some of the tools still used in censorship to detect concealed messages were invented by him.

Today censors have delicate instruments which enable them to steam open envelopes and seal them again without leaving a trace. Wax seals can be lifted from envelopes with heated blades or hot wire, and with an intricate little machine originally invented by Ziewert. Censors subject suspicious documents to thermal examination and to chemical or stereoscopic analysis to bring out invisible writings. They also examine certain pieces under ultraviolet or infra-red rays. Censors have means of detecting photographs which have been reduced to microscopic size, simply by enlarging them until they become easily legible.

When a clue is found by censors, it is forwarded to the agencies that conduct counterespionage through investigation. Such clues are extremely useful, since they often contain concrete evidence in the franking and other postmarks, and in the signatures and names of addressees, although the latter are usually concealed mail-drops. These clues enable counterespionage agents to start from a definite premise and, in many cases, help them in tracking down an espionage agent who has compromised his own security by entrusting his message to the mails or other media of open communication.

There is a saying in counterespionage circles that for every spy caught ten remain at large. Some are living on borrowed time, enjoying the temporary benefit of the "long rope." Others are working successfully and without fear of exposure, their identities and missions unknown to the agencies trying to counter them.

If secret agents take risks, so do the countries against which they work so insidiously. Espionage is a game of give and take. Positive espionage is enormously important and no present-day power can afford to neglect it. But for the defense and survival of a country, counterespionage is probably even more important. It is in the truest sense of the word a country's first line of defense.

PART V

Propaganda

What Is Political Warfare?

Intelligence operations frequently transcend the narrower confines of the intelligence service and resort to intrigue in more subtle form, with far greater emphasis on the intellectual potential than in those phases we have previously witnessed. That aspect of intelligence in which information is used aggressively to manipulate opinion or to create special conditions by purely intellectual means is called political warfare. In recent years, political warfare has come to be regarded as a permanent addition to the established forms of human conflict.

According to Sir Robert Bruce Lockhart, wartime director-general of Britain's superbly efficient Political Warfare Executive, this phase of intelligence practices every form of overt and covert attack that can be called political, as distinct from military. It is that form of intelligence operations that uses ideas to influence policies. It deals with opinions and with their communication to others. It is organized persuasion by non-violent means, in contrast to military warfare in which the will of the victor is imposed upon the vanquished by violence or the threat of it.

Political warfare is a British term. In other countries the activity is known by different names. In Germany, for example, it is called *geistige Kriegführung*, intellectual warfare, to stress the fact that it is war waged primarily in the intellectual or spiritual sphere, a contest of ideas. In the Soviet Union where, under the influence of Clausewitz, all warfare is considered political, this particular form of aggression is called propaganda and agitation. In the United States, it is called psychological warfare or morale operations, the former to indicate that it is the application of psychology to the conduct of war, the latter to suggest that it is aimed at the morale of an opponent.

In actual fact, none of these terms expresses the real scope of political warfare. The terms used in the particular countries mentioned above mean chiefly propaganda, the or-

241

ganized effort to influence the attitudes of people on controversial issues. However, political warfare is a more comprehensive concept than that, since in addition to propaganda it may also include diplomatic action and economic moves used in a coordinated manner to attain a nation's ends.

Diplomacy may be used, for example, to persuade nations to enter into alliances or remain neutral; or to break up opposing alliances. It can be applied to terminate wars by negotiations even while military operations continue undiminished. Diplomacy was used in this manner in 1945, when efforts were made to conclude hostilities with Japan in the diplomatic rather than the military sphere.

Aside from diplomacy, political warfare may also involve specific economic moves, the blockading of enemies, the withholding from them of essential raw materials by so-called preclusion buying, the special manipulation of tariffs. In 1935, when Britain endeavored to persuade Italy to refrain from attacking Ethiopia, it exerted diplomatic influence through the League of Nations and also applied to Italy economic pressures in world trade. At the present time, the United States restricts trade with Communist countries, while simultaneously providing lavish economic aid to its allies. This is essentially political warfare. However, both diplomatic and economic warfare are independent activities. They are conducted by special agencies, such as the diplomatic corps or organizations dedicated specifically to economic warfare. They are designed to affect large numbers of people, but they make no direct appeals to those people. Diplomacy in particular is conducted within its own confines, often in secrecy, and without directly approaching the masses.

What Is Propaganda ?

In the sense in which we understand the relation between all intelligence operations, propaganda alone is the major implement of political warfare. The term is used comprehensively here, to include what the British call political warfare, the Germans intellectual warfare, and we in the United States psychological warfare or morale operations. It is the deliberate and organized effort to spread ideas, doctrines, and principles for the distinct purpose of gaining adherents, followers, or allies; to persuade people of the justness and logic of one's cause and the erroneousness and injustice of the opponent's cause; and especially to make others act in a manner advantageous to one side and detrimental to the other.

The ultimate purpose of propaganda is to make others act exactly as we want them to act or to think exactly as we want them to think. It is essentially a totalitarian effort, since it imposes ideas on people without allowing disagreement. In fact, propaganda strives to exclude all opposing arguments, never permitting its objects an alternative. It expects its audience to accept its argument without qualification or equivocation, in contrast to the theory of education and information in which the audience is permitted to study all sides of an issue without bias.

Propaganda is never objective. Although today much is said about "truth in propaganda," the fact is that propaganda is always biased and subjective. Since it is a functional effort with a utilitarian purpose, it is subordinate to selfish design. It goes without saying that propaganda must give the appearance of truthfulness, since mendacity, invented "facts," and palpably spurious arguments are certain to defeat the very purpose of propaganda. However, even the most truthful propaganda is slanted, if only to the extent of the effect of what it leaves unsaid. In the final analysis, propaganda need not be actually truthful as long as it is plausible.

The Germanic theories of warfare and the Communist principles of revolution are strange and repugnant to Americans and Britons, since they do not conform to accepted ideas of moral human conduct. Yet what to us appears as unjustified and barbaric is acceptable to large numbers of people. What may seem false to some may still appear true to others, or, as W. I. Thomas expressed it, "If men define situations as real, they are real in their consequences."

We distinguish between spiritual propaganda, which promotes faith and religious ideologies, and temporal propaganda, which has political designs and aspirations. Spiritual propaganda long preceded temporal propaganda as an organized activity. It was an important instrument of the Roman Catholic Church long before nations used it for their own purposes. The famous sermon in which Pope Urban II called for the First Crusade in November, 1095, at Clermont, France, was a monumental act of propaganda. In 1622, Pope Gregory XV founded what may be called the world's first "propaganda agency," the *Congregatio de propaganda fide*, to propagate the Catholic faith.

Temporal propaganda has become an organized activity of nations only in recent years, but in its primeval form it is as old as man's ability to communicate his ideas. It was used by

243

Gideon when he succeeded in convincing the Midianites that his own force of only three hundred warriors was superior in numbers to their big army. It was utilized by Wang Ming in China and by the Athenian Themistocles, whose shrewd use of propaganda Herodotus described as follows:

"Themistocles, having selected the best sailing ships of the Athenians, went to the place where there was water fit for drinking, and engraved upon the stones inscriptions, which the Ionians, upon arriving the next day at Artemisium, read. The inscriptions were to this effect, 'Men of Ionia, you do wrong in fighting against your fathers and helping to enslave Greece. Rather, therefore, come over to us or, if you cannot do that, withdraw your forces from the contest and entreat the Carians to do the same. But if neither of these things is possible, and you are bound by too strong a necessity, yet in action, when we are engaged, behave ill on purpose, remembering that you are descended from us and that the enmity of the barbarians against us originally sprang from you.'"

In the American War of Independence and again in the Civil War, propaganda played a strong role. In the archives of the Department of the Army there is preserved a long leaflet addressed by "An Old Soldier" to the British redcoats about to embark for the Colonies, pleading with them to lay down their arms; there is a leaflet inviting the British at Bunker Hill to desert. They lie side by side with the famous surrender leaflets of World War II, which were typically short and to the point.

It was not until late in World War I that the potential of the cunningly chosen word was recognized as often superior to the potential of the physical weapon. A German general of infantry wrote: "We expend a lot of costly ammunition trying to destroy the gun in the hands of a soldier. Would it not be cheaper to devise means whereby we might paralyze the fingers that pull the triggers of those guns?"

Propaganda crept into the strategems of World War I until it became a "bluff barrage." Its basic aim was then, and is now, to minimize defeats and magnify victories, to establish one's own cause as just and certain to triumph, and to depreciate the cause of the enemy, doomed to failure.

The first in World War I to lay down this "bluff barrage" were the British. They introduced systematized propaganda as a full-fledged implement of war and assigned Lord Northcliffe, the British newspaper publisher, to organize and conduct it. His work was so effective that the Germans announced, "The enemy has founded a 'Ministry for the Destruction of German Confidence' at the head of which he has put the most thoroughgoing rascal in all the Entente—Lord Northcliffe." The results of British propaganda during World War I were strange indeed. Most of it was aimed at the enemy's troops in the field, yet it served to impair and then crush the morale of the whole German nation. While most often defeatism begins on the home front and then spreads to the troops, it was the other way around in the First World War. Every soldier on leave from the front became an unwitting agent of Northcliffe's. He repeated slogans and assertions of British propaganda and talked of Germany's defeat as if it were an accomplished fact. The German General Staff was scandalized and frightened. "Instances like these," General Erich Ludendorff complained, "drag the honor and respect of the individual and of the whole army into the mud, and have a disastrous effect upon the morale of the people at home."

American propaganda in 1917-18 was confined to the dissemination of the truth everywhere. "You could not keep our people long supporting a war," General Dennis E. Nolan, chief of intelligence of the American Expeditionary Force, said, "unless they knew what was happening." The same method was applied to the enemy. The American chief of staff insisted that public announcement be made regularly of what would normally be regarded as a closely guarded military secret: the number of American soldiers landed in France. He properly expected that such announcements would go far in discouraging the enemy in the sight of this ever-growing force, while his own strength was diminishing by the hour.

The climax of the Allied propaganda effort in World War I was the proclamation of President Woodrow Wilson's Fourteen Points. These promised much to victor and vanquished alike and assured the enemy of humane treatment in defeat. It was not designed as propaganda but evolved from Wilson's humanitarian and civil approach to the whole issue of war and peace. However, it became propaganda in its effect and did speed the end of German resistance.

The Propaganda Effort

Within the propaganda spectrum we distinguish between so-called white, grey, and black propaganda. White propaganda is the open and undisguised activity of a country which clearly identifies itself as the source of the effort. The mass of information going out of the United States today under the auspices of the government's information program is white propaganda.

In grey propaganda the source is clearly identified, but the appeal is slanted to serve a definite propaganda purpose. The operation of Radio Free Europe is in the category of grey propaganda. This is a broadcasting network maintained with private funds by an organization called the National Committee for a Free Europe for beaming appeals to the countries in eastern and southeastern Europe (Poland, Czechoslovakia, Hungary, Rumania, Bulgaria, and Albania) which are under Communist domination. The purpose of these broadcasts is to counter Communist propaganda in those countries, to provide a platform for exiled politicians, and to supply information about events in the free world, the sort of news that is not otherwise available to people living in countries where no freedom of information prevails. Although the source of all material emanating from Radio Free Europe is clearly identified, it uses intelligence in the preparation of its appeals and so slants it as to be most effective in the war of wits. Radio Free Europe is an effective instrument of the cold war, if only because it succeeds in undermining the propaganda monopoly of the Communists in the countries occupied by them, and because it serves as a constant reminder to the listener behind the Iron Curtain that he is neither forgotten nor forsaken. The very existence of this major propaganda instrument indicates to him that Communist occupation in those countries is of a temporary nature and that the free world uses whatever means are available to it to bring about the eventual liberation of oppressed peoples.

A major wartime example of grey propaganda was a campaign run by the mythical Commander Robert Norden of the United States Navy, who talked to officers and men of the German Navy in their own language. It fell into the grey category, despite the fact that its source was clearly identified, chiefly because it depended entirely on intelligence material in the formulation of its appeals, and because it was conducted in support of and in cooperation with conventional military operations. A similar campaign was conducted by Captain Ellis M. Zacharias, of the United States Navy, with the purpose of persuading the Japanese high command to seek peace by unconditional surrender. Captain Zacharias tried to provide arguments for a peace party within Japan's highest echelons and to convince his audience that further resistance was hopeless. Both operations were conducted within an intelligence agency of the United States Navy and were clearly labeled as intelligence operations.

Black propaganda is a fundamental intelligence operation, not only because it uses intelligence material solely as its ammunition, but because it is an independent maneuver conducted in an atmosphere of surreptitiousness. Black propaganda never identifies its real source. It pretends to originate within or close to enemy or enemy-occupied territory, and to be conducted by subversive elements in the enemy's midst. This is a highly secret activity, since its exposure would terminate its usefulness. Today there are several agencies conducting black propaganda on both sides of the Iron Curtain, but they flourish mostly in times of war. Britain is particularly adept at conducting black propaganda. The two most successful such efforts to date were both conducted by British agencies during World War II. One of them was a clandestine radio station called *Geheim Sender Eins* or "Secret Transmitter No. 1," over which the broadcasts of a propagandist called *Der Chef*, The Boss, were beamed. The Boss was a British journalist named Sefton Delmer. He became one of the authentic men of mystery of World War II when he suddenly vanished from sight. Even his name became taboo. His colleagues called him "the Beard," because of the whiskers he cultivated. In the United States, we used to refer to him as "Henry VIII," because this corpulent, bearded, whimsical, quarrelsome Briton reminded some of us of that long-dead king. His skill was universally admired, and today Delmer is regarded as one of the outstanding exponents and practitioners of black propaganda.

On the air, Delmer pretended to be a senior officer of the Wehrmacht with a good record in World War I. He was intensely "patriotic" in a rather petulant German way, but he was against everything. He hated the British, the Jews, the Russians, the Nazis, everybody in the world. This lively combination of boisterous hatred made him irascible and truculent, and soldiers, usually full of beefs of their own, loved to listen to someone who seemed to echo their collective grievances. There was something else that attracted listeners to The Boss. He was the most profane and obscene broadcaster ever to soil the air waves. He bandied about the usual words of trench lingo, but in his scathing delivery they sounded like so many words of endearment.

The Boss went to extreme lengths to gain the confidence of his German audience. At one point he picked a notoriously inefficient German officer whose blunders had resulted

247

in the annihilation of a battalion, and had him denounced on one of the regular "white" B.B.C. broadcasts beamed to Germany. Later he learned that the denunciation had drawn blood. The German High Command had the officer arrested and made him face a court martial. At this stage The Boss decided to intervene. He launched into a bitter denunciation of the German High Command for acting on a tip from the British radio. "Since when are we taking our orders from those confounded British?" he asked with pathos. "Who are they, anyway, to tell us what to do with our own officers? If this goes on, we'll soon have all our officers before court martials—and isn't that exactly what the bloody Englander wants? To err is human, isn't it? Most of our officers err once in a while and they cannot help it if it results in the annihilation of a battalion. Such is war!"

Several times each week the ribald Boss went on the air to hammer at the Germans with his blasphemies, obscenities —and extremely interesting information in which propaganda was shrewdly concealed. He supplied the most intimate details of Hitler's private life. He revealed controversies within the German High Command over operational plans. He mongered gossip and peddled scandal. This, in a sense, was as much a triumph of intelligence as propaganda. It showed the excellence of the intelligence material on which The Boss had based his uncouth, vulgar rantings.

Although the German soldiers listened regularly to *Der Chef*, they rarely doubted the fact that it was an enemy broadcast. Incidentally, until June, 1942, even the U.S. Military Intelligence Service had no positive proof that *Geheim Sender Eins* was where it was. The British let no one in on the secret and conceded their parentage of this fabulous intelligence-propaganda operation only when a couple of American intelligence specialists confronted them with conclusive evidence obtained through a smart piece of detective work the details of which cannot be discussed.

In addition to radio, black propaganda employs a great variety of media. They include underground newspapers which imitate the appearance of well-known dailies. A famous example of this medium was the imitation of the mass-circulation *Soir*, which the Belgian underground published during World War II. Another means of black propaganda is the smuggling of subversive material to specific addressees through the mail. German operations in this field included the sending of letters to French soldiers from their home towns, alleging that their wives were committing adultery. The Nazis sent enormous quantities of their propaganda through the

U.S. mail, and similar material was disseminated by the Japanese, most of it from clandestine sources.

Mass-mailing of propaganda material is practiced with the realization that many of the communications may never reach their addressees. It is still effective however, because it overburdens censorship and ties up the regular mail and thus interferes with morale.

Black leaflets and pamphlets are most effective when properly composed and efficiently distributed. This is an art in which the Communists excel because they were dependent on leaflets and pamphlets as news media for so long before the radio was available for propaganda.

The means of black propaganda are many. Some of them represent bold violations of international law but cause endless embarrassment to the enemy. Among these more violent forms are the counterfeiting of enemy currencies and the forging of ration cards and identification papers. If nothing else is gained, the enemy's bureaucratic apparatus is tied up and his secret police is kept busy conducting investigations. The essence of this, as of all black propaganda, is to confuse the enemy authorities.

The Media of Propaganda

Propaganda—white, grey, and black—depends on established conventional means of communications. Chief among these media is the radio, and the time may not be far off when television will also be used. Although it probably seems as if radio propaganda has been with us always, it is only a little more than twenty-five years old. The Soviet Union was the first and the United States the last to employ radio as a propaganda carrier. Germany began broadcasting propaganda appeals to foreign audiences within a few weeks of Hitler's seizure of power. France responded almost immediately with the establishment of Radio Strasbourg, which beamed propaganda appeals to Germany. It was operated by a few refugees from Nazi persecution.

After that the empire and overseas services of the British Broadcasting Corporation were instituted with a two-fold propaganda aim: to tie the empire closer to the mother country and to serve as an instrument of British foreign policy. Throughout the propaganda contest, in peace and war, the B.B.C. has retained uncontested leadership in this effort, chiefly because it succeeds in concealing the propaganda aim of its broadcasts behind a civilized and seemingly objective form of delivery. The B.B.C. is remarkable for the accuracy of its broadcasts and for their high intellectual level. During the war, it served as Britain's most important link with the world at large. The chief ammunition of B.B.C. propaganda was the news, presented with a conspicuous show of objectivity.

Gradually other countries followed suit, and the United States designated the National Broadcasting Company, the Columbia Broadcasting System, and a firm called the World Wide Broadcasting Foundation to conduct international propaganda by broadcasts. During the Second World War the United States established a Coordinator of Information, later an Office of Facts and Figures, and eventually the Office of War Information, for broadcasting to the world, to both friend and foe. The Coordinator of Inter-American Affairs conducted propaganda to Latin-American countries.

During the Second World War the air waves were overcrowded with propaganda broadcasters operating on both sides of the global front. There was Tokyo Rose, the collective name of a number of Japanese propagandists who specialized in tactical intelligence, often identifying American units which had just arrived in the Pacific to create a sense of superior Japanese intelligence, an important feature of effective propaganda. There was Axis Sally, the Nazi Lorelei, who cooed her way into GI hearts. And Lord Haw Haw, an expatriate Anglo-Irishman named William Joyce who deserted to the Nazis with his chief asset, a thick British accent in which he tried to shake the morale of the British people. The Free French operated a radio station in Brazzaville, on the Congo River in French Equatorial Africa. The Russians conducted their radio propaganda on an enormous scale, using Radio Moscow on innumerable wavelengths, broadcasting in scores of languages.

Next to radio, the printed word is the chief medium of propaganda dissemination. In this category are newspapers and periodicals, books, brochures, and leaflets. Leaflet propaganda in particular is widespread in times of war, and it is used today by the National Committee for a Free Europe which sends leaflets by balloons to the satellite countries of Europe. During the First World War the number of leaflets prepared by the belligerents were dropped by the millions, and in the Second World War the total number of leaflets dropped amounted to billions. During one single week in September, 1951, the National Committee for a Free Europe sent to Czechoslovakia thirteen million leaflets, approximately twenty-five percent of the total number of leaflets the Allies dropped on Germany in World War I.

The motion picture is another medium of propaganda dissemination, and today both the United States and the Soviet Union make the most of it. According to C. D. Jackson, one of the foremost proponents of American propaganda, "more people see American films in Europe and in the rest of the world than at home." Audiences totaling 110,000,000 people see American movies abroad every week, while the total weekly audience at home is 90,000,000. Behind the Iron Curtain, much of the Soviet propaganda appeal is carried by motion pictures, since all movies made in Communist countries must carry propaganda messages.

Propaganda Manipulations

Whatever media are used, propaganda must be painstakingly prepared with seven specific principles in mind. The basic principle requires that whenever it is used aggressively it must be aimed at personalities rather than issues. Concentration on personalities simplifies the problem, since underlying issues are usually complex and cannot be handled with the simplicity that propaganda basically requires to be effective and widely understood. It is generally accepted in the newspaper world that "names make news"; the same principle prevails in propaganda.

Second, it must be carefully camouflaged so as not to appear as propaganda. Conducted in the name of propaganda it is bound to fail. It cannot be conducted in a detached manner.

Third, propaganda must be based on intelligence and knowledge, on evaluated information, and especially on a close familiarity with the political, intellectual, military, economic, and emotional trends of the country and the people to which it is directed. A fluent knowledge of the language in which the propaganda is conducted is a prime condition, since audiences resent the misuse of their native tongue by foreign speakers.

Fourth, propaganda must never appear to create issues, but instead must recognize existing issues and treat them in a manner most advantageous to the propaganda cause. Communist propaganda rarely uses Communism as an issue, but

251

concentrates instead on issues prevalent in the target countries, such as unemployment, internal dissension, or political unrest. It exploits the issues by twisting them. It then bases its argument on the twisted interpretation.

Fifth, propaganda must never be rigid or stationary, but must be adaptable to daily developments, always prepared to shift its interpretation of an issue to conform to a changing scene.

Sixth, propaganda cannot be conducted by remote control. While directives and instructions may come from a central propaganda authority, the actual tenor of propaganda material must be left to the discretion of the men who disseminate it.

Seventh, propaganda must utilize all existing facilities, especially the citizens of the countries to which the propaganda is directed, by winning them over to function as its unwitting carriers.

In developing a propaganda plan, it must be borne in mind that it must be simple and repetitious, without being monotonous, harping on the same ideas over and over again. While it is sometimes aimed at reason, it is usually directed at the emotions. In emotional appeals propaganda pits love against hatred, justice against injustice, truth against lies. In order to enhance the effectiveness of a propaganda theme, it should be boiled down to a slogan, which then is repeated relentlessly. A brutal quality is frequently regarded as an important element of good propaganda, not only because it shows strength, but because it is provocative and is most likely to attract attention. "Propaganda and terror are not opposites," the German expert Eugen Hadamovsky wrote. "Violence, in fact, can be an integral part of propaganda." The role of violence, he added, is "the lightning-like effect of exciting attention and manipulating it at the propagandist's will."

According to the best qualified experts, the most effective propaganda is the show of power and success. Victory is infinitely more effective than the promise of victory. When the aim of propaganda is to promote peace, it is by no means sufficient only to talk about peace; it is necessary to put forward some concrete plan designed to promote peace. If the aim is to terrorize, threats are insufficient in effective propaganda; there must be actual terrible deeds to exploit.

Propaganda does not try to make direct converts to the doctrine it is designed to propagate. It is only supposed to undermine resistance to the acceptance of new ideas by using whatever argument is most likely to influence those to whom it is addressed. In good radio advertising, the merchant rarely describes his product in physical detail but instead stresses the advantages it provides. Soviet propaganda rarely advertises in terms of Communist theories, but endeavors to win adherents by promising the solution of economic and social inequalities and the improvement of unpopular conditions.

Rumor as a Propaganda Weapon

Word-of-mouth spreading of news and rumor is a widely recognized and effective channel of propaganda. There are those who believe that rumor has almost as great an influence on public opinion as the radio or press. Rumor can be used positively to enhance the position of those who spread it, or to promote favor for their claims. Negatively, it can be used to drive a wedge between the people and their government, to make them doubt the justness of their cause, and especially to influence them against the claims of the opposition.

The spreading of rumor is a part of human nature, and this peculiarity of man is frequently intentionally exploited by what are called "directed rumors." The generals of Genghis Khan, for example, employed this technique to exaggerate their strength and confuse their enemies. They planted spies in the headquarters of their foes where they reported that the armies of Genghis Khan "seemed like grasshoppers, impossible to count." Other spies warned, "They breathe nothing but war and blood, and show so great an impatience to fight that their generals can scarcely moderate them." As a result of such rumors the frightened Europeans described the Khan's cavalry as "a numberless horde," although in reality it was numerically far inferior to their own forces.

"How much of human history, we may reasonably ask, can be regarded as the reactions of important groups of people to current rumor?" This question was posed by Professor Gordon W. Allport of Harvard University, one of the great rumor experts of the world. And he himself answered it, "A great deal, we suspect, for until very recent times the inhabitants of the world had little to rely on other than rumored information." But, despite the increased circulation of newspapers, despite the invention of the telegraph, telephone, radio, and television, the net role of rumor in molding public opinion is even greater in our time than ever before.

Rumor became a problem of grave national concern during the years of 1942 and 1943. Within six weeks of Pearl Harbor malicious rumors flew so thick and fast that President Roosevelt had to repudiate them in a special "fireside chat." Even then they did not subside. During the summer of 1942 Dr. R. H. Knapp of Harvard University collected some thousand different rumors then current throughout the country. Most of them (65.9 percent) were "wedge-driving" rumors which tried to pit people against each other within the United States. They promoted anti-Semitism, and fanned distrust of the Army, the Navy, and the Red Cross. They tried to stimulate draft evasion, suspicion of the Roosevelt administration, opposition to the purchase of war bonds, anything that weakened the war effort.

Many of them (25.4 percent) were "fear" rumors, which distorted or magnified our initial military setbacks, invented tales about fifth-column activities and sabotage, exaggerated the enemy's strength and cunning, invented atrocities, and stressed our shipping losses.

A few of them were "pipe-dream" rumors about the imminence of peace, the discovery of destroyed enemy submarines all along our coasts, or unscored victories. Wedge-driving rumors were prevalent in the Middle West, fear rumors in the South, "pipe-dream" rumors along the Atlantic seaboard, possibly reflecting the attitudes and sentiments of the population of those regions.

The rumors which Dr. Knapp found most widespread were about the Navy dumping three carloads of coffee into New York harbor and the Army destroying whole sides of good beef. Another insisted that the Russians were getting most of our butter and using it for the lubrication of their guns. In another, the Red Cross was accused of charging soldiers in Iceland outrageous prices for sweaters knit at home.

Political Warfare and the Cold War

After 1943 when victory seemed more certain and more information could be broadcast about the actual conduct of the war, the deluge of rumors subsided.

When the Second World War was followed by the cold war, intelligence operations suddenly came into their own. There is nothing remarkable in this sequence. The cold war is merely a synonym for intelligence operations. Military means are used only occasionally, and then at the periphery of the conflict. In a large measure, diplomats and propagandists are used to wage its hottest battles.

For the Russians the coming of the cold war represented no problem, since they did not have to create new agencies to wage it. They had only to revive a few old ones. The place of the Comintern was taken by the Communist Information Bureau, the Cominform. The Amsterdam-Pleyel peace movement was revived almost without change in the organization called "Partisans of Peace." Radio Moscow, the first to engage in the propaganda war of the air, never ceased to exert its subtle influence on the listening world.

In the United States, Britain, and France, new offensive and defensive networks had to be organized almost overnight. This is how the Central Intelligence Agency came into being. This is why the Voice of America was changed from an information to a propaganda organ, as was the B.B.C. in Britain to some extent, and the international radio services of France, Turkey, Yugoslavia, and Spain. Special cold war agencies were formed, including Radio Free Europe, Radio Liberation (beamed to the Soviet Union), and Radio Free Asia.

Despite the fact that the cold war is nothing but an intelligence operation on a monumental scale, the West is still reluctant to regard the conflict as a war of wits and to shift operations from the military to the intellectual field. Emphasis remained on conventional military means, on rearmament revolving largely about the Air Force and atomic and thermonuclear weapons. This failure to place emphasis on intelligence operations led to the loss of China, to the consolidation of Soviet rule in eastern and south-eastern Europe, and to the prolongation of peripheral wars in Indochina, Malaya, and Korea.

After a number of skirmishes, the cold war reached a climax on June 17, 1953, when rebellions flared up against the Soviet Union in Czechoslovakia, Poland, and on an impressive scale in Eastern Germany, especially in the Soviet zone of Berlin. As they had on July 20, 1944, in rising against Nazism, the Germans again acted on their own initiative, and without foreign aid. In both revolts, they rose against the power of greatest resistance, against 'the entrenched security forces of a totalitarian regime. Throughout eastern Europe the 1953 risings were spontaneous. They were engineered by workers. The forces of an unorganized populace were thrown against the tightly organized security forces of the oppressor.

The intelligence operations listed in this book represent certain definite patterns of non-military warfare as it is waged in our own days. Each has its own motivations, strategies and tactics, weapons, special local characteristics.

Different though these operations are, there is something common to all of them. They represent a new form of warfare, and common to all of them is a new force that propels these conspiracies. It is a force that wages war without military means.

For what is war? It is merely the continuation of a nation's policy by physical means, or, as Clausewitz defined it, "an act of violence designed to compel our opponent to fulfil our will." Although Clausewitz's theories of total military destruction of an enemy influenced many nations and led to the increased use of violence in war, an old concept that conflict need not be violent at all is beginning to manifest itself in the foreign policies of some nations today.

"The popular idea that war is a mere matter of brute force, redeemed only by valor and discipline," wrote George F. R. Henderson, "is responsible for a greater evil than the complacency of the amateur. It binds both the people and its representatives to their bounden duties. War is something more than a mere outgrowth of politics. It is a political act, initiated and controlled by the government, and it is an act in which the issues are far more momentous than any other."

Clausewitz formulated his famous tenet at the beginning of the nineteenth century. Those were interesting years in the life of mankind. Thinkers were puzzled by the direction in which society was moving and tried to apply the lessons of this evolution to the age-old problems of war.

At the start of the last century, wars were no longer what they used to be. Neither was man any longer the helpless automaton that circumstances had compelled him to be for centuries. After the dark ages of oppression, the citizen began to emerge as Aristotle envisaged him, the possessor of political power. He began to sit on juries and in assemblies. The oligarchs, monarchs, and tyrants found that their influence was waning as the influence of their subjects grew. Gradually the old order was broken, in England by political philosophers, in America by indignant patriots, and then in France by the mob whose way to the Tuilleries was led by intellectuals. It was obvious that after centuries of helpless obscurity the people could no longer be ignored, much less oppressed. They themselves were the dominant factors when it came to the molding of their own destinies.

Before Clausewitz had established himself as a military theorist, a strange figure appeared in Prussia. He was Dietrich Heinrich von Bülow, black sheep of a famous Prussian family of high officials and generals, younger brother of a field marshal. He had been in turn soldier, writer, actor, trader, and adventurer, and had proved a failure at everything.

Yet this apparently worthless scion of a famous family occupies a far more important role in the history of conflict than his successful brother or some of the celebrated generals whose names survive in the annals. For Heinrich von Bülow was the first to define the enormous influence that the gradual change of society exercised on war. He became the originator of the concept that today finds its way into all thinking dedicated to the problems of human conflict.

Bülow regarded war as "organized disorder" in which organization was vastly overstressed while the nature of the disorder was overlooked. He thought that war itself, the actual clash of arms, was far less important than the "friction" that preceded and caused it. Years before Clausewitz came to his conclusion that war is never an isolated act but rather the continuation of policy by other means, Bülow maintained that military strategy was but a subordinate instrument in human conflict, the extension and not the substance of political strategy and action.

Bülow examined closely the nature of frictions and then sought their solution, not in the mobilization of the obtuse and regimented mass, but in the manipulation of the sensitive and informed individual. He went further than that. He regarded man as fully capable of solving the problems created by "frictions" by intellectual rather than military means.

To be sure, the power of intellect was never completely neglected in war. But while former wars had shown the value of a trained general, the wars of the new era began to show the value of an educated army and an educated people. The people have gained a direct influence on war, not only on its conduct, but also on the events which precede it. The progress of enlightenment suggested alternatives to the solution of frictions. War was but one of the alternatives. Diplomacy was another.

Bülow spelled out his ideas in his major work, which he called *The Spirit of a New System of War*. They were brilliant ideas but, when he first proclaimed them in 1799, they were far too original and far too premature for his times. His principles shocked his contemporaries steeped in the traditions of warfare, for Bülow was contemptuous of the callous military system of Frederick the Great, and he thought little of Napoleon's aggressive military strategy. He advocated the humanization and intellectualization of war, and suggested that it be waged in the political rather than military sphere.

Many observers of our own contemporary scene have stated in so many words that human conflicts need not necessarily be resolved by the violence of armed action. They have recognized the intellectual progress of mankind, the spread of knowledge and information, the growing participation of the masses in public affairs.

They have recognized the gradual growth of political thinking which has enabled man to devise alternatives to the customary traditional solution of conflicts by arms. They have pointed out the mental poverty of the political philosophers and military scientists who see in war the only agent for social and political change, and they have concluded that man is capable of imposing his will on others by outsmarting or outthinking rather than outgunning his opponent.

What we have called intelligence operations represent a long step on the road that leads gradually away from the old-fashioned war to a resolution of differences in the intellectual sphere. Today we begin to see that wars can be waged without actually sending armies into the field. We call it cold war. It is conflict, yes. But it is directed by statesmen and diplomats rather than generals. It is waged by intelligence specialists and propagandists rather than soldiers.

But even as we witness this evolution, we still fail to recognize the cold war for what it is, a war of wits. And since we fail to recognize it, we continue to spend billions on arms. Between 1776 and 1781, George Washington spent approximately eleven percent of his entire military budget on intelligence operations. The fact that today we spend less than one percent of our peacetime military budget on these same activities shows how little the function of intelligence is appreciated and supported, how little effort is being made to solve the "friction" by intellectual means rather than brute force.

The Roman Seneca was sensible to the degradation of man when he exclaimed that only men wage wars—no beasts ever do. Since his time, every age has merely improved the art and instruments of rage.

Now for the first time, man is exploring the means of waging war without resorting to violence. Instead of flexing his muscles, he is trying to use his head. It is not to be expected that all nations will recognize the efficacy of this philosophy simultaneously, for indeed they will not. However, this fact does not minimize the responsibility of those who do see it for making a relentless effort to replace physical conflict with the war of wits. To this end intelligence activities occupy a position of tremendous importance and can contribute immeasurably.

Source Notes and References

These notes and references are offered as documentation of the material presented in the text. The starred titles are suggested as a selective bibliography of the subject. The figures to the left designate the pages and lines of text to which the notes refer.

6:46   Henderson, G. F. R. H., "War," in *Encyclopaedia Britannica*, 11th ed., 1911, v. 28, p. 305.

7:9   Ludendorff, E., *Kriegführung and Politik*, (Berlin), 1922, pp. 320-342.

7:24   Blau, A., *Geistige Kriegführung*, (Potsdam), 1938; Münzenberg, W., *Propaganda als Waffe*, (Paris), 1934.

7:35   *Aston, Sir G., *Secret Service*, (London), 1931, p. 29.

8:11   New York *Times*, 1954, March 5, p. 7.

8:25   For definitions of the term "intelligence" in its social scientific connotation, see Young K., *Sociology*, (New York), 1942, p. 355.

8:32   *Kent, S., *Strategic Intelligence for American World Policy*, (Princeton), 1949, pp. 3-10, 209-211; *Pettee, S. G., *The Future of American Secret Intelligence*, (Washington), 1946, pp. 95, 102-108.

8:45   *Department of the Army Appropriations for 1955*, Hearings, (Washington), 1954, p. 47.

9:16   Spaulding, O. L., Nickerson, H., Wright, J. W., *Warfare*, (Washington), 1937, p. 7.

9:27   In his preface to Hoy, H. C., *40 O.B.*, (London), 1926.

9:30   13 Numbers 1-33.

9:35   Frontinus, Sextus Julius, *Strategematica*, (London), 1816.

9:36   Saxe, Maurice de, *Reveries on the Art of War*.

10:6   Muir, Sir W., *Life of Mahomet*, (London), 1861, v. 4.

10:10   Mohammed ibn Omar al-Waqidi, *Mohammed in Medina*, abr. tr. by Wüstenfeld, (Berlin), 1882.

10:12   The battle of Badr was fought on Ramadan 19 in the second year of the Hegira, usually made to synchronize with March 17, 624. In the *Koran*, the date is called the "Day of Deliverance."

10:22   Wells, H. G., *The Outline of History*, (New York), 1931, pp. 606-607.

11:4   The overwhelming importance of meteorological information is presented dramatically in Eisenhower, D. D., *Crusade in Europe*, (New York), 1948, pp. 116, 239, 248-250, 253, 261-263.

11:28   According to A. W. Dulles, about 20 percent of total intelligence handled by CIA is economic information; the rest is political, military, psychological, scientific and technical intelligence. See interview in *U.S. News and World Report*, 1954, March 19, pp. 62-68.

11:35   *Sweeney, W. C., *Military Intelligence. A New Weapon of War*, (New York), 1924, pp. 13-29.

12:27   *Ibid.*, pp. 146-149.

13:2   Elmer, A., *Napoleons Leibspion, Karl Ludwig Schulmeister*, (Berlin), 1931, p. 107.

13:4   Urbanski, A. V., "Aufmarschpläne," in *Lettow-Vorbeck, P. V., *Die Weltkriegsspionage*, (München), 1931, pp. 85-88.

13:8   *Thompson, J. W., Padover, S. K., *Secret Diplomacy. A Record of Espionage and Double-Dealing,* (London), 1937, pp. 42-50.

13:19   Breasted, J. H., "The Battle of Kadesh," *Decennial Publications,* University of Chicago, 1904, First Series, v. 5, pp. 81-126; Erman, A., *Life of Ancient Egypt,* (London), 1894, pp. 41-46, 526.

13:36   Aston, *op. cit.*

13:46   *Dept. of the Army Appropriations for 1955,* (q.v.,) p. 323.

14:15   *Ibid.,* p. 323.

14:22   *Department of the Navy Appropriations for 1955,* Hearings, (Washington), 1954, p. 893.

14:45   *Zacharias, E. M., *Secret Missions,* (New York), 1946, pp. 334-335. Also see his "The Inside Story of Yalta," *United Nations World,* 1949, v. 3, no. 1, pp. 12-18, where he wrote: "My estimate . . . was based on an extremely careful study of Japan's conscription system, including draft statistics, physical fitness reports, and on intelligence reports revealing the rapidly increasing manpower difficulties of the Japanese Imperial Army." The study mentioned above was conducted by the present writer.

15:24   London, K., *How Foreign Policy is Made,* (New York), 1949, pp. 16-36, 39-74, 99-130, 140-150, 155-165.

15:33   Nicolson, H., *Diplomacy,* (London), 1939, pp. 3-27.

15:35   Maskelyne, J., *White Magic. The Story of the Maskelynes,* (London), 1936, pp. 83-86.

16:4   It was the present writer who, in December 1945, called the attention of Mr. Byrnes to certain pertinent passages in V.v.I. Lenin's *Collected Works,* (Russian Edition), v. 27, pp. 84-85, reprinted in *Strategy and Tactics of the Proletarian Revolution,* (New York), 1936, pp. 57-61.

16:8   For the Soviet's use of diplomacy in intelligence operations, see Stalin, J. V., "Report on the immediate tasks of the Party in connection with the national problem," printed in *Marxism and the National Question,* (New York), 1942, pp. 98-110, where Stalin said: "The whole purpose of the existence of the People's Commissariat of Foreign Affairs is to take account of these controversies [between the imperialist states], to use them as a point of departure, and to maneuver within these contradictions."

16:13   Goltz, H. V. D., "Politische Spionage," in *Die Weltkriegsspionage,* (q.v.), pp. 153-157; Kent, *op. cit.,* pp. 35, 49.

16:27   *Nazi Conspiracy and Aggression,* (Washington), 1946, v. 3, pp. 19-27, 32-35.

16:45   Jones E., "The psychology of quislingism," *International Journal of Psychoanalysis,* 1941, v. 22, no. 1, pp. 1-6.

17:18   Possony, S. T., *Strategic Airpower,* (Washington), 1949, pp. 116-118.

17:26   Calkins, C., *Spy Overhead. The Story of Industrial Espionage,* (New York), 1937.

17:27   *Enc. Brit.,* (q.v.), pp. 492-493.

17:44   Goldenberg, H., "Das Wissen vom Gegner," *Soldatentum,* (Berlin), 1938, pp. 259-263.

18:3   Blau, *op. cit.,* pp. 43-57; Farago, L. (ed.), *German Psy-*

18:13   *chological Warfare*, (New York), 1942, pp. 264-270.

18:13   Beck, W., "Amerikanisches Soldatentum," *Soldatentum*, 1936, pp. 137-141.

18:41   Keilhacker, M., "Grundzüge des englischen Volkscharakters, etc.," *Beihefte, Zeitschrift für angewandte Psychologie*, (Berlin), 1938, v. 79, pp. 187-208.

19:15   Sayers, M., Kahn, A. E., *Sabotage*, (New York), 1942, pp. 16, 26, 28-30, 32-34, 41, 121.

19:35   Goudsmit, S. A., *Alsos*, (New York), 1947, pp. 14-25.

19:43   *Ibid.*, pp. 50-56.

20:15   *Miksche, F. O., *Secret Forces*, (London), 1950, pp. 134, 138-142.

20:35   Eisenhower, *op. cit.*, pp. 233, 296.

21:41   Erfurth, W., *Surprise*, (Harrisburg), 1943, p. 195.

22:21   The events related here are described on the basis of the author's first-hand experience. Also see, Stimson, H. L., Bundy, McG., *On Active Service in Peace and War*, (New York), 1948, pp. 617-633; Baldwin, H. W., *Great Mistakes of the War*, (New York), 1949, pp. 88-108.

23:3   Statement of W. Averell Harriman, Hearings, *Military Situation in the Far East*, (Washington), 1951, v. 5, pp. 3328-3342.

23:16   Zacharias, *Secret Missions* (q.v.), pp. 332-341.

23:27   Zacharias, E. M., "The A-Bomb Was Not Needed," *United Nations World*, 1949, v. 3, no. 8.

24:3   Zacharias, *Secret Missions*, (q.v.), pp. 332-350. For General Marshall's attitude to non-military operations, see Carroll, W., *Persuade or Perish*, (Boston), 1948, p. 385: "General George C. Marshall, the wartime Chief of Staff, had been as responsible as anyone for the obsession with military ends which put the United States in such an unfavorable position for the post-war political struggle."

25:23   The incident was related to the author by its participants. *Cf.*, Cant, G., *The Great Pacific Victory*, (New York), 1946, pp. 118, 125, 162-163.

27:3   Farago, *op. cit.*, pp. 153-155; London, *op. cit.*, pp. 81-89.

27:34   For a typical sample of such an official biographical study prepared by an intelligence agency, see the estimate of Malenkov's personality, *Ostprobleme*, 1953, April.

27:42   Perkins, F., *The Roosevelt I Knew*, (New York), 1946, pp. 82-84. Upon the sudden death of President Roosevelt in 1945, the chancelleries of the world were flooded with "biographical estimates" of the new President, Harry S. Truman. On April 16, 1945, Lord Halifax, the British Ambassador in Washington, cabled Mr. Churchill: "It may be of interest that Truman's hobby is history of military strategy, of which he is reported to have read widely. He certainly betrayed surprising knowledge of Hannibal's campaigns one night here. He venerates Marshall." Churchill. W. S., *Triumph and Tragedy*. (Boston), 1953, p. 481. On the same day, Foreign Secretary Anthony Eden cabled to the Prime Minister: "My impression from the interview is that the new President is honest and friendly. He is conscious of but not overwhelmed by his new responsibilities. His references to you could not have been warmer." *Ibid.*, p. 484.

28:44   *The Report of the Royal [Canadian] Commission, (Ottawa), 1946, pp. 123-161.

29:24   *Soviet Atomic Espionage, (Washington), 1951, pp. 13-59.

30:31   Activities of Soviet Secret Service, Hearing, (Washington), 1954, pp. 24-25.

30:37   Foreign Office List, (London), 1946.

30:44   Kent, op. cit., pp. 58-61.

31:10   Wells, op. cit., pp. 958-959.

31:27   *Nicolai, W., Geheime Mächte, (Berlin), 1921, pp. 10-11.

31:30   *Pinkerton, A., The Spy of the Rebellion, (New York), 1883.

32:4   *Rowan, R. W., The Story of Secret Service, (New York), 1938, pp. 274-283.

32:14   Enc. Brit., (q.v.), v. 4, pp. 791-792.

32:19   Aston, op. cit., pp. 13-42, 293-300. The War Office Intelligence Branch was established in 1873 in the office of the Adjutant General of the Forces, as a result of the lessons learned in the Crimea where blunders and hardships were largely due to a woeful lack of information about the enemy. The first "MI" was housed in an abandoned coach house on Adelphi Terrace. Later it was moved to a secluded and shuttered house at Queen Ann's Gate which for decades became the hush-hush center of British secret intelligence.

32:21   When the huge new Admiralty Building was erected off Trafalgar Square, the planners allocated only two small rooms to accommodate the budding intelligence department.

32:32   *Mashbir, S., "What is intelligence," in I Was an American Spy, (New York), 1953, pp. 41-56.

33:4   *Cookridge, E. H., Secrets of the British Secret Service, (London), 1948, pp. 1-9; Firmin, S., They Came to Spy, (London), 1946, pp. 144-150.

33:8   *Hagen, W., (pseudonym of Dr. Wilhelm Höttl), Die geheime Front, (Linz), 1950, pp. 9-12.

33:15   *Willoughby, C. A., Shanghai Conspiracy, (New York), 1952, pp. 170-172.

33:43   Hearings, Subcommittee of the Committee on Appropriations, House of Representatives, 81st Congress, 2nd Session, part 1, (January 9, 1950), pp. 1-15; Phillips, C., "The supercabinet for our security," New York Times Magazine, 1954, April 4, pp. 14-15, 60-63.

34:12   United States Government Organization Manual 1953-1954, (Washington), 1953, pp. 62-63.

34:34   *Baldwin, H. W., The Price of Power, (New York), 1947, pp. 203-219; Pettee, op. cit., pp. 102-118.

35:1   Hagen, op. cit., p. 12.

35:4   Görlitz, W., Der deutsche Generalstab, (Frankfurt), 1950, p. 427.

35:8   Congressional Record, 83rd Congress, 2nd Session, (1954), v. 100, part 45, pp. 2811 ff.

35:19   Seid, A., "Der englische Geheimdienst," Schriften des Deutschen Instituts für Aussenpolitische Forschung, (Berlin), 1940, no. 23.

35:21   For the public part of PID's table of organization, see the 1946 edition of the *Foreign Office List*. In the 1954 list, Political Intelligence appears as part of Research and Library, headed by Ernest James Passant as Director of Research and Air Commodore K. C. Buss as Deputy Director. Mr. Passant is an eminent historian who taught at Cambridge and served in Naval Intelligence, combining erudition with practical experience.

35:23   The actual director of PID, or more accurately, of Her Majesty's Secret Service, is shielded from the public by ironclad secrecy. In *The Fourth Seal*, Sir Samuel Hoare called him "the nameless spyking of the British Secret Service Organization." Sir Paul Dukes recalled with some awe: "It was eighteen months before I was allowed to know his real name and title, and even then I was careful never to use it." Sir George Aston remarked: "He wears many well-earned decorations, few people know how well. His name is—shall we say 'X,' the Unknown Quantity.'"

35:28   Cookridge, *op. cit.*, pp. 4-7.

35:45   *Whitaker's Almanac*, 82nd Annual Volume, (London), 1950, p. 370.

36:11   Testimony of Ismail Ege (Colonel Ismail Gusseynovich Akhmedoff), former chief of Soviet Intelligence's Fourth (Technological) Section, before the Senate Internal Security Subcommittee, on October 28-29, 1953. Also see Richard Sorge's description of the organization in Willoughby, *op. cit.*, pp. 171-172.

36:13   *Rep. R.* [*Can.*] *Com.*, (q.v.), pp. 20, 26-27, 733.

36:21   The "Center" has four major branches: Operations, Information, Training, Auxiliaries. Within its Operations Branch, it maintains eight "strategic intelligence sections." Section 3 is concerned with the United States. Section 4 collects technical and scientific data. Section 5 conducts intelligence operations, organizes terroristic acts, kidnapings, assassinations, uprisings. Section 6 handles such technical details as authentication, the development of special intelligence weapons and instruments. Section 7 is charged with tactical military intelligence and Section 8 with cryptography and cryptanalysis. The Navy has its own intelligence administration, a far smaller, but reputedly efficient service.

36:35   *Alsop, S., Braden, T., *Sub Rosa. The OSS and American Espionage*, (New York), 1946, p. 9-26.

37:9   *MacDonald, E. P., *Undercover Girl*, (New York), 1947, pp. 5-36.

37:19   "The CIA: Who Watches the Watchdog," Richmond (Va.) *News Leader*, 1953, March 30; "About Which You Actually Know Nothing," *ibid.*, 1953, July 17.

37:26   According to A. L. Miller, *Congr. Rec.*, 81st Congress, 1st Sess., v. 95, part 13, pp. A1663-A1664.

37:38   The table of organization presented here is the author's idea of an efficient secret service. It is not based on any existing tables of organization, certainly not on that of the CIA.

39:27   Zacharias, *Secret Missions*, (q.v.), pp. 302-316.

40:16 Urbanski, A. V., "Was kostet die Spionage," in *Die Welt-kriegsspionage* (q.v.), pp. 165-166; "Battle Order of Espionage," *United Nations World*, 1949, v. 3, no. 6; *ibid.*, 1949, v. 3, no. 7.

40:20 *Enc. Brit.*, (q.v.), v. 28, pp. 293-294.

40:31 According to Dr. Mynors Bright's researches in the Pepysian Library, Magdalene College, Cambridge, *cf.*, Rowan, *op. cit.*, p. 104.

40:40 *Hansard*, 1954, pp. 1307-1308.

41:7 Farago, L., "England's secret government," *Ken* magazine, 1938, v. 1, no. 1, (April 7), pp. 46-48.

41:11 Cookridge, *op. cit.*, p. 5.

41:22 Rowan, *op. cit.*, pp. 489, 712.

41:36 Kisch, E. E., *Der Fall des Generalstabschefs Redl*, (Berlin), 1924.

41:39 Foote, A., *Handbook for Spies*, (New York), 1950; *Neue Zürcher Zeitung*, 1953, November, 3, 4, 5, 6.

41:43 *Rep. R.* [*Can.*] *Comm.*, (q.v.), p. 68.

42:9 Army Appropriations, (q.v.), pp. 317-346.

42:19 According to *The Reporter* magazine, the National Security Agency, "known until recently as the Armed Forces Security Agency is . . . believed to have somewhere between four and eight thousand employees, engaged, it has been said, in breaking foreign codes." v. 10, no. 13, June 22, 1954, p. 23.

42:22 *Congr. Rec.*, 83rd Congress, 2nd Sess., v. 100, part 45, p. 2814.

42:27 *Ibid.*, pp. 2811-2813.

42.46 Sweeney, *op. cit.*, pp. 141-161.

43:6 Pratt, F., "That real spy, the researcher," New York *Times Magazine*, 1948, August 15, p. 10.

43:13 Baldwin, *op. cit.*, p. 204.

43:22 London, *op. cit.*, pp. 85-88.

44:16 Pettee, *op cit.*, pp. 39-46; Kent, *op. cit.*, pp. 9, 157, 164-168.

45:9 New York *Times*, 1935, March 21, September 19, 23. The account of Herr Jacob's adventure is related here on the basis of the author's on-the-spot investigations at the time of the incident.

48:44 Alsop and Braden, *op cit.*, pp. 17-18.

49:12 Zimmermann, J. L., *The Guadalcanal Campaign*, (Washington), 1949, pp. 14-19.

49:19 Cookridge, *op. cit.*, pp. 19-36.

50:3 Interview with A. W. Dulles, *U.S. News and World Report*, 1954, March 19, pp. 62-70.

50:11 Zacharias, E. M., "What is wrong with our spy system," *Real* magazine, 1953, v. 2, no. 2, pp. 14-17, 78-81.

50:32 *World Almanac*, (New York), 1954, pp. 724-734.

50:45 Sweeney, *op. cit.*, p. 86.

51:3 For a typical question concerning Her Majesty's Secret Service, see *Hansard*, 1950, 480, pp. 1166-1167.

51:39 Information supplied by the editors of the *Current Digest of the Soviet Press*.

52:33 Speier, H., Kris, E., *German Radio Propaganda*, (New York), 1942, pp. 103-107, 289-325.

53:9 Hoy, H. C., *op cit.*, pp. 21, 181-184, 192.

54:29   Cookridge, *op. cit.*, pp. 19-21.
55:11   Aston, *op. cit.*, pp. 28-38.
56:15   MacDonald, *op. cit.*, pp. 248-251.
57:18   The system of personal observations by professional intelligence officers was introduced into the British secret service by General Sir Henry Wilson when he was commandant of the Camberley Staff College. He encouraged his aides to make "holidays trips" to the Continent. On one of his own bicycle tours, Sir Henry succeeded in obtaining information from which he deduced the basic details of the Schlieffen Plan.
57:20   Görlitz, *op. cit.*, p. 453.
57:27   Bismarck, B. V., "Der Militärattache im Nachrichtendienst," in *Die Weltkriegsspionage*, (q.v.), pp. 104-110; Beauvais, A. P., *Attaches Militaires, Attaches Navales et Attaches de l'Air*, (Paris), 1937; Schweppenburg, G. V., *Erinnerungen eines Militärattaches*, (London) 1933-1937, (Stuttgart), 1949, pp. 9-25.
57:35   Nicolai, *op. cit.*
57:41   Zimmermann, *op. cit.*, pp. 14-16; Pratt, F., *The Marines' War*, (New York), 1948, pp. 3-30.
58:36   *Ibid.*, pp. 8, 9-10, 38.
58:41   *Feldt, E. A., *The Coast Watchers*, (New York), 1946, pp. 78-103.
59:29   Cant, *op. cit.*, p. 138.
60:12   Spaulding, Nickerson, Wright, *op. cit.*, pp. 14-16.
60:40   Schwien, E. E., *Combat Intelligence. Its Acquisition and Transmission.* (Washington), 1936, pp. 57-60; *Thomas, S., *S-2 in Action*, (Harrisburg), 1940.
61:6   *World Almanac*, 1954, p. 732. The grand total of all mobilized forces in the First World War was 65,038,810 officers and men. Of the 7,995 U.S. combatants reported as missing in Korea, 4,631 prisoners of war were returned by October 23, 1953. The Republic of Korea reported 459,429 as missing. Of them only 7,848 prisoners of war were returned.
61:21   For the emotional trends among prisoners of war, see Strong T., (ed.), *We Prisoners of War*, (New York), 1942, pp. 32-37, 38-40, 78-83.
61:24   *Enc. Brit.* (q.v.), v. 32 (1922), pp. 150-162.
61:39   Moorehead, A., Montgomery, (New York), 1946, pp. 143-144.
62:7   "Information obtained from prisoners should be priced at the right value; a soldier sees nothing beyond his company, and the officer at most can give an account of the movements and position of the division to which his regiment belongs. The general in command should not consider confessions torn from prisoners, except when they square with reports of the outposts, to justify his conjectures as to the position the enemy occupies." Sweeney, *op. cit.*, p. 162.
62:20   Einsiedel, H., *Tagebuch der Versuchung*, (Berlin-Stuttgart), 1950, pp. 17-78; Hahn, A., *Ich Spreche die Wahrheit*. (Esslingen), 1951, pp. 14-29, 130-136.
62:23   Liddell Hart, B. H., *The German Generals Talk*, (New York), 1948.

62:29   *The Battle of the Atlantic. The Official Account of the Fight Against the U-Boats 1939-1945*, (London), 1946, p. 57.

63:2   The incident was related to the author by the officer who conducted the interrogation.

64:12   Schwien, *op. cit.*, pp. 59-60.

64:33   *The Confidential Records of the French General Staff*, (Berlin), 1940.

65:7   Pratt, *op. cit.*, pp. 44-46.

66:2   *Documents on German Foreign Policy 1918-1945*, (Washington), 1949, *cf.* General Introduction, pp. VII-XIII, where the editors state: "Never had three victorious powers set out to establish the full record of the diplomacy of a vanquished power from captured archives 'on the basis of the highest scholarly objectivity.'" The captured archives went back to 1867. Similarly, the papers of the German Army, Navy and Air Force were captured and published. Martienssen, A., *Hitler and His Admirals*, (New York), 1949. According to Martienssen, "during the final stages of the Second World War, enemy State documents were captured on a scale which was unique in history." The largest haul of documents was made at Schloss Tambach, near Coburg, where some 60,000 files of the German naval archives were captured, relating to the German Navy from 1868 until the date of their capture, April 1945.

66:29   This incident was related to the author by one of the persons directly involved in the capture and exploitation of the order.

66:36   Wilmot, C., *The Struggle for Europe*, (New York), 1952, pp. 18-34.

68:15   Arnold, H. H. and Eaker, I. C., *Winged Warfare*, (New York), 1941, pp. 128-130.

68:45   Bley, W., "Luftspionage und Fernzerstoerung," in *Die Weltkriegsspionage*, (q.v.), pp. 140-152; Urbanski, A. V., "Flugzeug und Spionage," *ibid.*, pp. 635-647.

69:24   Rowan, R. W., "Something German in Denmark," in *Spy Secrets*, (New York), 1946, pp. 89-92.

69:34   Dornberger, W. R., *V2 Der Schuss ins Weltall*, (Esslingen), 1952, pp. 263-271; Churchill, W. S., *op. cit.*, pp. 50-53.

70:32   Sweeney, *op. cit.*, pp. 162-187; Fell, H. W., "Die Auswärtung und das Ergebnis der Agentennachrichten," in *Die Weltkriegsspionage*, (q.v.), pp. 158-164; Pettee, *op. cit.*, pp. 25-38; Schwien, *op. cit.*, pp. 61-67.

71:10   Kent, *op. cit.*, pp. 170, 172-173. Letters to and including "F" may be used to indicate the trustworthiness of a source, and numerals up to six to rate the probability of information. Material from the public domain is similarly rated or marked with the word "Documentary."

71:40   Churchill, W. S., *The Grand Alliance*, (Boston), 1950, pp. 355-356.

72:35   *Military Situation in the Far East*, Hearings, (Washington), 1951, pp. 18, 84-86, 122, 157, 239-241, 350, 436, 545, 639, 758, 1035, 1190, 1429, 1436, 1778, 1832, 1859, 1990, 2113, 2267, 2273, 2583, 2629, 2914, 3581.

72:45   Dulles, A. W., New York *Herald-Tribune Book Review*, 1950, October 29, p. 5.

73:18   Baldwin, *op. cit.*, p. 210.

73:25   Sweeney, *op. cit.*, pp. 188-205.

74:1   *Executive Order 10501* of November 5, 1953 (18 F.R. 7049), safeguarding official information. It established various classification categories; limited authority to classify; regulated declassification, downgrading and upgrading; and the storage, transmission, disposal and destruction of classified documents. Also see *Atomic Energy Act* of 1946 as amended, Section 10.

74:9   Ingersoll, R., *Top Secret*, (New York), 1946, p. 104.

75:20   Based on the author's personal experience.

75:46   The material in this section reflects the author's own concepts and theories. Part of the nomenclature developed here is original.

76:14   Farago, L., *Axis Grand Strategy*, (New York), 1942, p. 60.

76:39   Lasswell, H. D., "Policy and the intelligence function," in *The Analysis of Political Behavior*, (New York), 1947, pp. 120-131.

77:5   The evolution of the policy of His Majesty's Government between 1935 and 1939 is described on the basis of Wilmot, *op. cit.*, pp. 34-40, 49, 53-54.

77:10   *Nazi Conspiracy and Aggression*, (q.v.), v. 3, pp. 11-13.

79:29   Sontag, R. J., Beddie, J. S. (eds.), *Nazi-Soviet Relations 1939-1941*, (New York), 1948, pp. V-VIII.

79:44   *Ibid.*, pp. 217-254, 258-259; Rossi, A., (pseudonym of Jean-Ange Tasca), *Deux ans d'alliance Germano-Sovietique*, (Paris), 1949, pp. 166-180.

80:37   *Assistance to Greece and Turkey*, Hearings, (Washington), 1947, p. 11; Acheson, D. G., *The Pattern of Responsibility*, (Boston), 1952, pp. 139-144.

82:8   See note 91:23, v. 4, pp. 2668-2677.

82:37   Zacharias, "The Inside Story of Yalta," (p.v.), pp. 12-16, based on the present writer's source material.

82:44   Sherwood, R. E., *Roosevelt and Hopkins*, (New York), 1948, pp. 843-845.

83:29   Stettinius, E. R., Jr., *Roosevelt and the Russians. The Yalta Conference*, (New York), 1949, pp. 90-91.

83:37   Harriman, *op. cit.* On pages 3338-3340 of the document, several pertinent memoranda prepared by the Joint Chiefs of Staff are reproduced verbatim. Also see, Byrnes, J., *op. cit.*, pp. 42-43, 92, 205-207, 208-213, 263. *The Forrestal Diaries*, (q.v.), pp. 57-58.

83:39   Deane, J. R., *The Strange Alliance*, (New York), 1946, pp. 47, 60, 107, 223.

84:12   "Most of the Japanese troops [defeated on Saipan and Tinian] were veterans of the Manchurian campaign," Karig, W., Harris, R. L., Manson, F. A., *Battle Report. The End of an Empire*, (New York), 1948, pp. 261-262, 272. The 18th Infantry Division under Lieutenant General Renya Matagushi, including the crack 114th Regiment, was annihilated in New Guinea, the 5th Imperial Guards and the 24th Division were destroyed elsewhere. They

formerly formed part of the Kwantung Army and were
carried as such in the Order of Battle.

85:5   Forrestal, *op. cit.*, p. 31.
85:20   *Ibid.*, p. 70. Also see Leahy, W. D., *I Was There*, (New
        York), 1950.
86:39   Stimson, Bundy, *op. cit.*, pp. 617-618, 624.
87:4   Schwien, *op. cit.*, pp. 27-40.
87:12   Baldwin, *op. cit.*, p. 206.
87:36   Gilbert, V., *The Romance of the Last Crusade*. (New
        York), 1923, pp. 183-185.
89:25   Baldwin, *op. cit.*, p. 206.
90:34   Reid, O. R., Bird, R. S., "Are we inviting disaster?",
        Congr. Rec., 81st Congress, 2nd Sess., v. 96, part 16, pp.
        A5623-A5624.
91:15   Forrestal, *op. cit.*, p. 360.
91:25   *Congr. Rec.*, 81st Congress, 2nd Sess., v. 96, part 8, p.
        10086.
92:4   Washington *Evening Star*, 1951, May 10.
92:36   Entry dated November 7, 1942, *The Ciano Diaries, 1939-
        1943*, (New York), 1946, p. 540.
93:14   Reid and Bird, *op. cit.*
94:33   *Ibid.*
95:9   Taylor, T., "To improve our intelligence system," New
        York *Times Magazine*, 1951, May 27, p. 12.
96:28   Sulzberger, C. L., in New York *Times*, 1950, April 10,
        November 4.
97:9   Marshall, *op. cit.*, pp. 13, 15, 45-47; Lüdecke, *op. cit.*, p.
        89; °Baden-Powell, R. S. S., *My Adventures as a Spy*,
        (London), 1915; Dukes, P., *The Story of ST-25*, (Lon-
        don), 1938; Lawrence, T. E., *Seven Pillars of Wisdom*,
        (New York), 1935.
97:15   Sweeney, *op. cit.*, pp. 248-259.
98:6   Thompson and Padover, *op. cit.*, pp. 46-50, 83-85, 93;
        Enc. Brit., (q.v.), v. 26, pp. 902-903.
98:22   °Abshagen, K., *Canaris, Patriot und Weltbürger*. (Stutt-
        gart), 1949; Colvin, I., *Chief of Intelligence*, (London),
        1951.
98:23   Willoughby, *op. cit.*, pp. 166-167; Deane, *op. cit.*, pp. 56-
        63; °Kriwitsky, W., *In Stalin's Secret Service*, (New
        York), 1940.
98:39   Pennypacker, M., *General Washington's Spies on Long
        Island and in New York* (Brooklyn), 1939.
98:41   *Time* magazine, 1953, August 3, pp. 13-14.
98:46   Alsop and Braden, *op. cit.*, pp. 9-13.
99:24   Hendrick, B. J., *The Life and Letters of Walter H. Page*,
        (New York), 1925, v. 3, pp. 360-384; also Hoy, *op. cit.*
99:35   °Thomson, Sir B., *My Experiences at Scotland Yard*,
        (London), 1923.
100:3   Bardanne, J., *Le colonel Nicolai, espion de genie*, (Paris),
        1947; °Nicolai, W., *Nachrichtendienst, Presse und Volks-
        stimmung*, (Berlin), 1920.
100:21 "Time to re-examine CIA leadership," *Christian Century*,
        1952, v. 67, November 12, p. 1308.
100:39 Baldwin, *op. cit.*, pp. 203-219.
101:6   Sweeney, *op. cit.*, pp. 120-140, 248-259.

102:27 MacDonald, *op. cit.*, pp. 246-261. Also see, E.7, *Women Spies I Have Known*, (London), 1939.

103:10 Picker, H. (ed.), *Hitler's Tischgespräche in Führerhauptquartier 1941-1942*, (Bonn), 1951, p. 327.

103:17 New York *Times*, 1934, June 17-21.

103:23 Zacharias, *Secret Missions*, (q.v.), pp. 4-5.

103:28 Nicolai, *op. cit.*

104:9 Schmidt, D. A., *Anatomy of a Satellite*, (Boston), 1952, p. 52.

104:26 New York *World-Telegram*, December 11, 1941.

104:33 *Busch T. (pseudonym of Arthur Schütz, *Entlarvter Gehemdienst*, (Zürich), 1946, p. 456.

105:15 *Ibid.*, pp. 456-457.

105:25 Donovan, W. J., "Military intelligence," in *Enc. Brit.*, (1952), v. 12, pp. 459-462.

105:28 Dodd, M., *Through Embassy Eyes*, (New York), 1939, pp. 96-129.

105:36 New York *Times*, 1953, March 5, p. 2.

106:13 *Memoirs of M. de Blowitz*, (London), n.d.; Sir William Howard Russell of The [London] *Times* rendered equal service in military intelligence, *cf.* Woodham-Smith, C., *The Reason Why*, (New York), 1954, pp. 148, 172, 187-189, 265, 270.

106:19 Hesse, F., *Das Spiel um Deutschland*, (München), 1953, pp. 38, 59, 81, 203.

107:19 *Maclean, F., *Escape to Adventure*, (Boston), 1950.

108:15 About "the clever young men at the British universities," see Wells, H. G., *op. cit.*, p. 1062.

109:26 Marshall, *op. cit.*, pp. 17-18, 26-27, 37, 41-48, 50-62, 85, 91, 93-100.

109:32 Farago, L., "The murder that shocked the world," in *Real* magazine, 1953, v. 2, no. 3, pp. 68-71.

110:23 Alsop and Braden, *op. cit.*, pp. 18-26.

110:29 Mashbir, *op. cit.*, pp. 53-56.

110:41 In a speech to the American Legion, New York *Herald-Tribune*, 1953, June 17, p. 1.

111:3 Coffin, T., "America has ace spies, too," *Coronet* magazine, 1951, v. 30, August, pp. 37-41.

111:14 Mitchell, W. A., *Outlines of the World's Military History*, (Harrisburg), 1940, p. 203.

111:28 Baldwin, *op. cit.*, pp. 204-205; Pratt, F., "How not to run a spy system," *Harper's* magazine, 1947, pp. 195, 241-246.

113:26 General Marshall said: "It is a rather touchy subject, particularly because it takes a long time to develop an effective intelligence service such as we intend for the CIA under General Smith, and one of our great difficulties as I see it is the amount of public discussion in regard to it, because all of that detracts against it. I think those special agencies, notably Great Britain and others, you never hear of them, I doubt if you even know the designation of the unit. It is just kept entirely out of discussion, comment, and we have a long way to go to reach the point where we have more authoritative sources." During the MacArthur hearings, see note 91:23, v. 1, p. 640.

114:41 Vansittart, Lord, *Lessons of My Life*, (New York), 1943.

115:14 Davis, F., "The secret history of a surrender," *Saturday*

Evening Post, 1945, September 22, pp. 9-11; 29, p. 17.

116:1 °Ronge, M., *Kriegs und Industriespionage*, (Zurich), 1930.

122:9 Lettow-Vorbeck, P. V., *Die Weltkriegsspionage*, (q.v.), a monumental anthology. No comparable work exists in the English language.

122:10 Bullock, A., *Hitler. A Study in Tyranny*, (New York), 1954, pp. 572-598. The Barbarossa operation order was issued on December 13, 1940, as Führer Directive No. 21. It is available as Document no. 446-PS among the Nuremberg papers (q.v.).

122:15 The significant episode is presented here on the basis of material supplied by Dr. Wilhelm Höttl, a former high official of Germany's wartime secret service. Further documentation came from Flicke, W. F., *Agenten Funken Nach Moskau*, (Kreuzlingen), 1954, pp. 47-61, and Foote, *op. cit.*

123:17 Flicke, W. F., *Spionagegruppe Rote Kapelle*, (Kreuzlingen), 1953, part 3, pp. 191-261.

123:22 Stalin's fantastic refusal to accept the corroborated intelligence of his own secret service was described in dramatic detail by Colonel I. G. Akhmedoff, an eyewitness. According to Akhmedoff, on April 17, 1941, the section of Military Intelligence (RU) which he then headed received a report from one of its chief sources in Czechoslovakia, a vice president of the Skoda Works named Shkvor, that "the Germans are concentrating their troops on the Soviet frontiers and that the German High Command [had] stopped all Soviet military orders in the Skoda plant." Akhmedoff regarded this as the most important report ever received by RU. Because of its importance, the report was taken immediately to Stalin by Major General Panfilov, deputy director of Military Intelligence. That same night, Panfilov showed Akhmedoff the original report, with Stalin's handwritten marginal note which read: "This information is English provocation. Find out who is behind this provocation and punish him." Colonel Akhmedoff was sent to Germany to track down the provocateur. After that, reports continued to pour in, including the two explicit ones mentioned in the text. But Stalin persisted in dismissing them as "English provocations." Then, on June 21, 1941, while still in Germany, Colonel Akhmedoff received information that the Wehrmacht would begin operations against the Soviet Union on June 22. He presented the report to Ambassador Vladimir G. Dekanosov, who was at that time Stalin's right-hand man. (He was liquidated in the great Beria purge in 1953-54.) Dekanosov refused to believe the information and continued preparations for an Embassy outing he was arranging for next day, a Sunday. "But that picnic did not take place," Akhmedoff concluded, "because at 3 A.M., Sunday morning, Dekanosov was called to von Ribbentrop and delivered the note about the declaration of war by Germany." Cf., *Interlocking Subversion in Government Departments*, Part 15, (Washington), 1953, pp. 1005-1006.

124:2   Kaledin, V. K., *The Moscow-Berlin Secret Service*, (London), 1940, by an agent who worked in both.

124:21   *Maugham, W. S., *Ashenden or the British Agent*, (London), 1927.

124:28   Tolstoi, L. N., *War and Peace*, tr. Louise and Aylmer Maude, (New York), 1942, p. 709.

124:43   Lüdecke, *op. cit.*, pp. 119-170.

125:11   This section is based in part on the author's conversations with former high-ranking officials of the Soviet secret service who escaped to the West; also on Richard Sorge's memoirs, printed in Willoughby, *op. cit.*, pp. 134-230, one of the most important documents of intelligence literature; *Gouzenko, I., *The Iron Curtain*, (New York), 1948, pp. 102-118; *Foote, A., *Handbook for Spies*, (New York), 1949, pp. 61-91; the *Report of the Royal Canadian Commission*, (Ottawa), 1946; and on exhaustive firsthand information supplied by Colonel Issmail Gusseynovich Akhmedoff, former chief of Section IV of the Military Intelligence Department of the Red Army General Staff.

127:31   Willoughby, *op. cit.*, pp. 23-132.

128:13   *Rep. R. Can. Com.*, (q.v.), pp. 12-13.

128:16   Foote, *op. cit.*, pp. 48-60.

128:38   Massing, *op. cit.*, pp. 163-180, 206-211.

129:10   *Hirsch, R., *The Soviet Spies*, (New York), 1947.

130:42   *Rep. R. Can. Com.*, (q.v.), pp. 447-458.

131:16   Such dependence on espionage is by no means exclusive with the Communists in Russia. During the First World War, for example, Austrian espionage succeeded in apprehending only a single French spy, two British agents, and a total of 16 Italian operatives, while catching as many as 323 Russian spies. *Cf.*, Ronge, *op. cit.*, p. 393.

132:9   Knebel, F., "Red spies. The inside story of the people who betrayed their country," *Look* magazine, 1951, vol. 15, no. 13, (June 19), pp. 31-37.

132:27   "Der Ostspionagefall vor dem Bundesstrafgericht," *Neue Zürcher Zeitung*, 1953, November 5, Section 7, Also, *ibid.*, no. 2576, a summarization of the charges against Rudolph Roessler and Dr. Xavier Schnieper.

132:36   Based on a tabulation of espionage cases reported in the New York *Times* between 1917 and 1954.

132:40   Burnham, J., *The Web of Subversion*, (New York), 1954.

133:26   Picker, *op. cit.*, pp. 87, 139.

134:3   Roscoe, J., *The Ethics of War*, (London), 1914.

134:10   Maugham, *op cit.*, p. 4.

134:17   Mennevee, R., *L'espionnage international en temps de paix*, (Paris), 1929, two vols.

135:7   For examples of such operations instruction, see Marshall, *op. cit.*, pp. 19, 49; for a characteristic operational scheme of an espionage network, see Foote, *op. cit.*, pp. 63, 81; and Landau, H., *All's Fair*, (New York), 1934, pp. 48-57.

135:20   Sweeney, *op. cit.*, pp. 206-208.

135:42   Cookridge, *op. cit.*

136:4   Churchill, W. S., *Triumph and Tragedy*, (Boston), 1953, p. 49.

136:14   *Rep. R. Can. Com.*, (q.v.), pp. 15, 20-21.

137:17 Gouzenko, *op. cit.*, pp. 181-195, 262-279.

137:29 Foote, *op. cit.*, pp. 80-91.

138:3 Willoughby, *op. cit.*, pp. 25, 33-38, 45, 78-79, 90-92, 108-110, 117, 120-124.

138:19 Turrou, L. G., *Nazi Spies in America*, (New York), 1938, pp. 3-30, 275-299; Hynd, A., *Betrayal from the East*, (New York), 1943, throughout.

138:29 °Best, S. P., *The Venlo Incident*, (London), 1950; Hagen, W., *Die geheime Front*, (q.v.), pp. 43-44. Additional information was supplied by Mr. H. B. Gisevius, a prominent member of the German anti-Nazi underground.

138:45 Sweeney, *op. cit.*

139:11 Mashbir, *op. cit.*, pp. 127-150, 188-208. The only recorded attempt at direct espionage by the United States prior to the Second World War was the mission of Lieutenant Colonel Peter Ellis of the Marine Corps to a closed Japanese island in the Pacific. Colonel Charles E. Burnett, American Military Attache in Tokyo, made this comment to Mashbir on Colonel Ellis' impending journey: "Colonel Ellis here, after many years of study, has suddenly conceived an intense and irrepressible desire to study the flora and fauna of the island of Jaluit. Now undoubtedly the Ambassador is being deceived by this, and I am being completely deceived by this, but the question is: Do you think it will also fool the Japanese." Ellis died mysteriously during the journey. (*Cf.*, Mashbir, *op. cit.*, pp. 103-104.)

139:23 Based on the author's examination of pertinent documents.

139:35 Willoughby, *op. cit.*, p. 116.

140:10 Weisenborn, G., *Der lautlose Aufstand*, (Hamburg), 1953, pp. 203-217, an authoritative and authentic account.

140:18 Gisevius, H. B., *To the Bitter End*, (Boston), 1947, pp. 480-483; Hagen, *op. cit.*, pp. 455-458.

140:28 Dulles, A. W., *Germany's Underground*, (New York), 1947, pp. XI-XII.

141:10 Sweeney, *op. cit.*, pp. 211-212.

141:31 The "Müller" incident is based on an unpublished wartime narrative.

142:30 Altmann, L., "Zur Psychologie des Spions," in *Die Weltkriegsspionage*, (q.v.), pp. 37-52.

143:13 The most famous homosexual espionage case was that of Colonel Alfred Redl of the Austro-Hungarian General Staff, (*Cf.*, Kisch, E. E., *Prager Pitaval*, (Berlin), 1928, pp. 67-108). The other was that of the 18th century French diplomatic agent, Chevalier d'Eon de Beaumont; (*cf.*, Rowan, *op. cit.*, pp. 128-137).

144:17 °*Assessment of Men. Selection of Personnel for the Office of Strategic Services*, (New York), 1948, pp. 230-315, 450-493; MacDonald, *op cit.*, pp. 39-52.

145:23 For the unhappy ending of espionage missions, see Baumann, F., "Wie sie starben," in *Die Weltkriegsspionage*, (q.v.), pp. 53-61; Ott, K. A., *Der Mensch vor dem Standgericht*, (Hamburg), 1948; Pölchau, H., *Die letzten Stunden*, (Berlin), 1949.

146:2 Tickell, J., *Odette*, (London), 1939, pp. 102-117.

146:8 °Churchill, P., *Of Their Own Choice*, (London), 1951. No human activity has as many occupational hazards as the game of espionage. A study of the case histories of sixty Allied agents who operated in France during World War II showed that only 24 managed to escape the hunters. Six died in action, eleven by execution. Of the 60 agents, 30 were captured.

147:31   *Assessment of Men*, (q.v.), pp. 58-63.
148:40   *Ibid.*, pp. 63-202.
149:4   *Ibid.*, pp. 91-92, 310-311, 343-344.
149:16   *Ibid.*, pp. 133-138.
150:12   Urbanski, A. V., "Spionageschulen," in *Die Weltgriegsspionage*, pp. 99-103.
150:12   Sweeney, *op. cit.*, pp. 255-260.
151:28   Dioneo, "The republic of spies. How Soviet 'shadowers' and 'scouts' are taught their work," *New Russia*, 1920, v. 3, pp. 175-178.
151:40   Zacharias, E. M., Farago, L., *Behind Closed Doors*, (New York), 1950, pp. 96-98; *House Report No. 1920*, p. 71. *Hearings*, Special Committee on Un-American Activities, 1939, v. 9, pp. 6984-7025.
152:19   Snowden, N. (Pseudonym of Miklos Soltesz), *Memoirs of a Spy*, (New York), 1933, pp. 1-9.
152:22   For the only reliable account of Dr. Schragmüller's activities, see Rowan, *op. cit.*, pp. 557-564.
154:20   MacDonald, *op. cit.*, pp. 37-52; Ford, C., MacBain, A., *Cloak and Dagger. The Secret Story of the OSS*, (New York), 1946.
154:45   *Ibid.*
155:21   Gouzenko, *op. cit.*, pp. 168-180.
156:11   Lüdecke, *op. cit.*, pp. 15-16.
156:18   *Ibid.*, pp. 17-18.
156:36   Baden-Powell, *op. cit.*, pp. 61-69.
160:16   Chambers, W., *Witness*, (New York), 1942, pp. 319, 724.
160:26   For a classic example of such an operation, see Moyzisch, L. C., *Operation Cicero*, (New York), 1950, pp. 48-64.
161:10   Chambers, *op. cit.*, pp. 422-423.
161:44   *Rep. R. [Can.] Comm.*, (q.v.), pp. 120, 125.
162:8   *Ibid.*, p. 14.
162:15   *Ibid.*, pp. 454-455.
163:8   Willoughby, *op. cit.*, pp. 179-180, 194-199.
163:42   *Weyl, N., *The Battle Against Disloyalty*, (New York), 1951, pp. 209-212, 214-216.
164:1   Willoughby, *op. cit.*, pp. 231-242; Lüdecke, *op. cit.*, pp. 19-21.
164:18   Sweeney, *op. cit.*, pp. 159-161.
164:24   Lüdecke, *op. cit.*, pp. 19-21.
164:42   *Koop, T., *Weapon of Silence*, (Chicago), 1946.
165:4   Hoover, J. E. "Enemy's masterpiece of espionage," *Reader's Digest*, 1946, April, v. 48, pp. 1-6.
165:6   Rowan, *op. cit.*, pp. 636-642; Busch, *op. cit.*, pp. 111-118.
165:23   Sayers and Kahn, *op. cit.*, pp. 32-34.
165:38   Silber, J. C., *The Invisible Weapon*, (New York), 1926.
166:8   Foote, *op. cit.*, pp. 61-79.
166:38   Firmin, *op. cit.*, pp. 62-68, 123-129.
167:7   Foote, *op. cit.*, pp. 48-60.
167:32   Miksche, *op. cit.*, pp. 30-41, 119.

167:42 *Schreider, J., *Das War das Englandspiel*, (München), 1950, pp. 61-68, 149-161, 212-225.

168:38 Willoughby, *op. cit.*, pp. 62-63, 73.

169:11 *Ibid.*, pp. 117-120.

169:13 *Enc. Brit.*, 1911, (q.v.), v. 7, pp. 565-566.

169:32 Busch, *op. cit.*, pp. 176-192.

171:31 Pratt, F., *Secret and Urgent*, (Indianapolis), 1939.

172:42 Count Ciano noted in his diary: "You never know with cipher. We are reading everything the British send—are we to believe that other people are less good at the game than we are?" In *Ciano's Hidden Diary 1937-1938*, (New York), 1953, p. 49.

173:7 Rowan, *op. cit.*, pp. 601-603.

173:12 Levine, I. D., "Execution of Stalin's spy in the Tower of London," *Plain Talk*, 1948, v. 3, no. 2, (November), pp. 21-25.

173:32 *Yardley, H. O., *The American Black Chamber*, (Indianapolis), 1931.

173:33 Hoy, *op. cit.*, pp. 23-107.

174:8 Zacharias, *Secret Missions*, (q.v.), pp. 84-89, 97-98.

174:27 For a description of the agencies mentioned in this section, see Theobald, R. A., *The Big Secret of Pearl Harbor*, as reprinted in *U.S. News and World Report*, 1954, April 2, pp. 59, 67.

174:30 Rowan, R. W., *Spy Secrets*, (New York), 1946, pp. 110-112.

174:45 Aston, *op. cit.*; Busch, *op. cit.*, pp. 193-195.

175:27 New York *Times*, 1945, September 10, p. 6; 12, p. 1, 2; 13, p. 5; 16, p. 36.

178:23 Busch, *op. cit.*, pp. 239, 260-264; Firmin, *op. cit.*, pp. 36-38.

180:2 Busch, *op. cit.*, pp. 474-475.

180:28 *Moorhouse, A., *The Traitors*, (New York), 1952, p. 1.

181:1 Smith, W. C., *Sabotage. Its History, Philosophy, Function*, (Spokane), 1913.

181:15 Tompkins, D. C., *Sabotage and its Prevention*, (Berkeley), 1942, a comprehensive annotated bibliography. Also see, Söderman, H., O'Connell, *Modern Criminal Investigation*, (New York), 1952, pp. 436-444.

181:21 Miksche, *op. cit.*, pp. 124-125.

181:28 Trautman, W. E., *Direct Action and Sabotage*, (Pittsburgh), 1912.

181:34 Saunders, H. A. St. G., *The Green Beret*, (London), 1950.

181:36 Lenin, V. I., "Partisan warfare," in *Proletariat*, 1906, October 13. Skorzeny, O., *Geheimkommando Skorzeny*, (Hamburg), 1949.

182:4 Söderman and O'Connell, *op. cit.*, pp. 408-435, Farren, H. D., *Industrial Guard's Manual*, (New York), 1942, pp. 55-64; Sayers and Kahn, *op. cit.*, pp. 3-7, 99-105, 110-119.

182:21 Merker, P., *Revolutionäre Gewerkschaftsstrategie*, (Hamburg), 1929; Miksche, *op. cit.*, p. 127; Flynn, E. G., *Sabotage. The Conscious Withdrawal of the Workers' Industrial Efficiency*, (Chicago), 1916.

182:39 Busch, V., *Modern Arms and Free Men*, (New York), 1949, pp. 149-150.

274

183:3   Farren, H. D., *Sabotage,* (New York), 1941.
183:14 Miksche, *op. cit.,* pp. 134-135; Rowan, *op. cit.,* pp. 520-524.
183:15 Valtin, J., *Out of the Night,* (New York), 1941, pp. 121-137, 209-226, 233, 344-374.
183:39 Rowan, *op. cit.,* pp. 518-525, 715-716.
184:8   Palat, E. B., *La Ruee sur Verdun,* (Paris), 1921.
184:21 *Rintelen, F. V., *The Dark Invader,* (New York), 1931; Hall, W. R., Peaslee, A., *Three Wars With Germany,* (New York), 1944, pp. 71-194; Papen, F. V., *Memoirs,* (New York), 1952, pp. 29-52.
184:32 "Im Rücken des Feindes," *Die Wehrmacht,* 1939, April 26.
184:34 *Nazi Conspiracy and Aggression,* (q.v.), v. 2, pp. 264-265, 390, v. 5, pp. 390-392.
184:42 *Ibid.,* v. 3, p. 320.
185:25 *Ibid.,* v. 5, pp. 507-508.
185:29 Abshagen, *op. cit.,* chapter called "Sabotage der Sabotage," pp. 286-301.
185:31 Skorzeny, *op. cit.,* pp. 219-256.
185:39 Marshall, *op. cit.,* p. 13.
186:6   *Kovpak, S. A., *Our Partisan Course,* (London), 1947; Ignatov, P. K., *Partisans of Kuban,* (London), 1945; Vinogradskaya, Y. A., *A Woman Behind the German Lines,* (London), 1944.
186:17 The incident in Israel was related to the author by Major Lou Lennart who served as chief of staff to the Israeli officer in charge of the operation.
186:23 Pearlman, M., *The Army of Israel,* (New York), 1950, pp. 129-133.
187:43 Yerxa, F., Reid, O. R., *The Threat of Red Sabotage,* (New York), 1950.
188:21 Miksche, *op. cit.,* pp. 129-142.
189:5   *Ibid.,* p. 142.
190:7   Alsop and Braden, *op. cit.,* pp. 116-225.
190:9   Abshagen, *op. cit.,* pp. 273-285; Erhardt, A., *Kleinkrieg,* (Potsdam), 1944.
190:12 Marshall, *op. cit.,* pp. 12-16; Davidson, B., *Partisan Picture,* (Bedford), 1946.
190:17 *Guerilla Warfare in the Occupied Parts of the Soviet Union,* (Moscow), 1943.
190:30 Charts in Miksche, *op. cit.,* pp. 81, 110, 112, 117.
191:19 Lawrence, *op. cit.,* pp. 188-196; Garnett, D. (ed.), *The Letters of T. E. Lawrence,* (New York), 1938, pp. 181-258.
191:21 Buckmaster, M. J., *Specially Employed. The Story of British Aid to French Patriots of the Resistance,* (London), 1952.
192:14 Miksche, *op. cit.,* pp. 85, 142-156; *Kompani Linge,* (Oslo), 1948, pp. 37-116; *Assessment of Men,* (q.v.), pp. 268-279, 372.
192:27 Rintelen, *op. cit.;* Papen, *op. cit.*
192:37 Firmin, S., *op. cit.,* pp. 96-100.
192:41 Miksche, *op. cit.,* pp. 103-105.
193:33 As quoted, *ibid.,* pp. 14-15.

194:1   *Kompani Linge*, (q.v.), v. 1, pp. 169-193; Laurence, W. L., *Dawn Over Zero*, (New York), 1946, pp. 94-112.

199:25   Yerxa, Reid, *op. cit.*, pp. 3-5.

200:1   Valtin, *op. cit.*, pp. 230-232, 235, 558-565.

200:30   Plivier, T., *Des Kaisers Kulis*, (Berlin), 1930.

200:44   Valtin, *op. cit.*, pp. 358-368.

201:23   Stowe, L., *Conquest by Terror*, (New York), 1952, pp. 265-266.

201:27   The narrative of the Hungarian sabotage operation is based on the private report of "Pete."

203:1   Kent, in *op. cit.*, pp. 209-210, regards "security intelligence" as the foundation on which all intelligence functions rest and from which positive intelligence evolves. His is a novel and interesting approach, fully justified by the realities of today's intelligence complex. My own approach to this present discussion of negative intelligence was stimulated by Kent's premise. The subdivision of negative intelligence as proposed in this section is an original attempt to introduce specialization into what used to be a monolithic structure. The idea of such specialization developed from a careful study of the over-all security problem in the face of internal subversion and the mass attack of espionage agents.

203:10   For the problems of internal security, see Weyl, N., *The Battle Against Disloyalty*, (New York), 1952, pp. 179-197, 339-342; Barth, A., *The Loyalty of Free Men*, (New York), 1952, pp. 99-136, 137-153; *Report of the President's Temporary Commission on Employee Loyalty*, (mimeographed release), 1947, March 22; Nikoloric, L. D., "The government loyalty program," in *The American Scholar*, 1950, Summer.

203:24   Koop, *op. cit.*, pp. 16-30, 47-58; for press censorship, Thomson, G. P., *Blue Pencil Admiral*, (London), 1947; for radio censorship, Saerchinger, C., "Radio, censorship and neutrality," *Foreign Affairs*, 1940, 18, pp. 337-349.

204:6   Heinz "Spionageabwehr," *Jahrb. d. deutschen Heeres*, (Leipzig), 1938, pp. 129-127; Ronge's classic work, (q.v.); and Sulliotti, I., *L'armata del silenzio*. (Milano), 1931.

206:7   Zacharias, *Secret Missions*, (q.v.), pp. 166-172.

207:20   Section 102 (d) 3 of the *National Security Act* (Public Law 253, 80th Congress).

207:25   Thomson, Sir B., *The Story of Scotland Yard*, (New York), 1937, pp. 225-234.

207:44   *Report of the Attorney General*, (mimeographed), 1953, May, pp. 1-11, 119-120.

208:45   "Provisions of Federal Statutes, Executive Orders, and Congressional Resolutions relating to the internal security of the United States," (Washington), 1953.

209:26   *Ibid.*, pp. 3-4.

209:44   Robinson, D., "Our comic-opera spy set-up," *American Legion Magazine*, 1951, February.

210:8   Thorwald, J., *Der Fall Pastorius*, (Stuttgart), 1953, pp. 8-18.

210:20   Robinson, *op. cit.*

211:15   Firmin, *op. cit.*, pp. 55-61.

211:44   Moorehouse, A., *op. cit.*, pp. 87, 90-92, 94-95, 98-99, 203; *Soviet Atomic Espionage*, (q.v.), pp. 3-4, 145-152; *The Shameful Years*, (Washington), 1951, pp. 67-70.

213:14   Gouzenko, *op. cit.*; *Interlocking Subversion in Government Departments*, (Washington), 1953, pp. 1-3, 17-19.

213:23   *Pilat, O., *The Atom Spies*, (New York), 1952, pp. 57-78.

214:22   Moorehouse, *op. cit.*, pp. 144-145, 155-156.

215:6   Pilat, *op. cit.*, pp. 43-47, 80-82, 174-176, 280-281.

216:9   *Enc. Brit.*, (q.v.), v. 28, pp. 293-295.

216:17   Rowan, *op. cit.*, pp. 276-277.

216:38   Pinkerton, A., "History and evidence of the passage of Abraham Lincoln from Harrisburgh, Pa., to Washington, D.C. on the 22nd of February, 1861," (Chicago), 1891.

217:6   Pinkerton, *The Spy of the Rebellion*, (q.v.).

217:14   Moylan, Sir J., *Scotland Yard*, (London), 1935; Prothero, M., *The History of the C.I.D.*, (London), 1934.

217:19   Rowan, *op. cit.*, pp. 326-335, 349-353.

217:36   Steinthal, W., *Dreyfus*, (Berlin), 1928.

217:44   Lucieto, C., *On Special Missions*, (London), 1924.

218:20   Redl, A., *Organisation der Auskundschaftung fremder Militärverhältnisse und die Abwehr fremder Spionage im Inlande*, (Wien), 1903.

218:33   Renwick, G. "The Story of Colonel Redl," in Nicolai, W., *The German Secret Service*, (London), 1931.

219:23   Steinhauer, G., Felstead, S. T., *Steinhauer. The Kaiser's Master Spy*, (London), 1924.

220:32   Hoy, *op. cit.*

221:1   Steele, J. in New York *Times*, 1935, February 18, p. 1; 19, p. 5.

222:6   *Activities of Soviet Secret Service*, (Washington), 1954: the testimony of Captain Nikolai Evgenyevich Khokhlov before the Senate Internal Security Subcommittee, on May 21, 1954. According to Khokhlov, domestic counterespionage is the job of the First Chief Directorate of the Ministry of the Interior (MVD); while counterespionage abroad, including infiltration of enemy espionage organizations is assigned to the Second Chief Directorate whose Section 9 is charged with terroristic action, kidnapings, and the assassinations of enemy agents.

222:9   *Sinevirskii, N., *Smersh*, (New York), 1950.

222:23   Söderman and O'Connell, *op. cit.*, pp. 15-17; Belin, J., *Secrets of the Surete*, (New York), 1950, pp. 88-110, 166-178, 223-240, 258-277.

223:11   Political counterespionage was assigned to a special agency called Federal Bureau for the Protection of the Constitution. In July 1954, this Bureau attained notoriety when its chief, Dr. Otto John, deserted to the Communists. Cf. *Die Zeit*, (Hamburg), v. 9, no. 30, 1954, July 29, pp. 1-3, for an authoritative account of the strange case.

223:18   Cookridge, *op. cit*; Firmin, *op. cit.*

224:11   Van Doren, C., *Secret History of the American Revolution*, (New York), 1941, pp. 143 ff.

224:13   "Documents of Henry, the British Spy," in Singer, K., *Three Thousand Years of Espionage*, (New York), 1948, pp. 76-87.

224:16 Rowan, *op. cit.*, pp. 252-258.
224:19 Busch, *op. cit.*, pp. 274-289.
225:13 "It was my impression that, at that time—I mean before
the war—when I was in the Soviet Union, the Soviet Intelligence was more interested not in the United States of
America, but in Japan and other countries which were in
direct conflict with the Soviet Union." Testimony of Colonel Igor Bogolepov, reprinted in *Institute of Pacific Relations*, Hearings, (Washington), 1952, part 13, p. 4590.
226:8   *The Shameful Years*, (q.v.), pp. 5-21.
226:20 Zacharias, *op. cit.*, pp. 203-205.
226:25 Chambers, *op. cit.*, pp. 425-426. "The volume of production was high . . . But Bykov was continuously exasperated
by their material and distrustful of them. . . . At times
Bykov convinced himself that he was being cheated. . . .
Yet I was in the curious position of agreeing with Bykov
about the value of the material, but for different reasons.
. . . I concluded that political espionage was a magnificent
waste of time and effort—not because the sources were
holding back; they were pathetically eager to help—but
because the secrets of foreign offices are notoriously
overrated."
226:37 Sayer and Kahn, *op. cit.*, p. 26.
227:27 Thorwald, *op. cit.*, pp. 18-22.
227:35 Zacharias, *op. cit.*, pp. 147-212.
227:43 *Annual Report of the United States Attorney General*,
1939, p. 153; p. 152; Hoover, J. E., "Stamping out the
spies," *The American* magazine, 1940.
228:13 Lysing, H., *Men Against Crime*, (New York), 1938, pp.
9-20, 123-136, 145-196.
228:24 *United States Government Organization Manual 1953-54*,
(Washington), 1953, pp. 180-181; interviews with J.
Edgar Hoover, *U.S. News and World Report*, 1950,
August 11, pp. 30-33; 1951, March 30, pp. 32-37.
228:32 *Collins, F. L., The FBI in Peace and War*, (New York),
1940.
229:4   *Congr. Rec.*, 87th Congress, pp. A2466-A2472.
229:14 *The Story of the FBI, Look* magazine, (New York),
1947.
230:24 I am indebted to Dr. Harry Söderman for invaluable advice in the preparation of this section.
233:5   N.Y. *Times*, 1942, June 9.
233:9   Schwarzwalder, J., *We Caught Spies*, (New York), 1946;
Spingarn, S. J., Lehman, M., "How we caught spies in
World War II," *Saturday Evening Post*, 1948, November
27, pp. 214-216; December 4, pp. 42-43; December 11,
p. 28.
233:28 Quoted in Lysing, *op. cit.*, p. 242.
234:13 *Hearings*, House of Representatives, Committee on Rules,
66th Congress, 2nd Sess., 1920, v. 1, p. 49; v. 2, p. 212.
234:32 Sayers and Kahn, *op. cit.*, pp. 23-34.
238:20 Koop. *op. cit.*, pp. 16-30, 47-58; Busch, *op. cit.*, pp. 636-
642.
239:13 Rowan, *op. cit.*, p. 486.
241:1   *Lerner, D., Propaganda in War and Crisis*, (New York),
1951.

241:3   Lasswell, H. D., "The rise of the propagandist," in *The Analysis of Political Behavior*, (q.v.), pp. 173-179.

241:11   *Lockhart, Sir R. H. B., *Comes the Reckoning*, (London), 1948, pp. 125-224.

241:21   Speier, H., "Psychological warfare reconsidered," in *The Policy Sciences*, (Stanford), 1952.

241:25   Farago, L., "Soviet propaganda," *United Nations World*, 1948, v. 2, no. 8, pp. 18-24.

241:33   Lasswell, H. D., "Political and psychological warfare," in *Propaganda in War and Crisis*, (q.v.), pp. 264-266.

242:36   Doob, L., *Propaganda. Its Psychology and Technique*, (New York), 1944, pp. 71-154.

243:23   Young, K. in *German Psychological Warfare*, (q.v.), pp. XV-XXII.

243:37   According to Carlton Hayes (*Enc. Brit.*, q.v., v. 27, p. 790), "it is well established that Urban preached the sermon which gave the impetus to the crusade." The sermon was written out by Bishop Baudry. It can be found in J. M. Watterich's *Pontif. Roman. Vitae.*

243:39   See Ranke's *Popes*, v. 2, pp. 468 ff.

243:41   De Martinis, *Juris pontificii de Propaganda Fide*, (Rome), 1888. In 1627, Urban VIII founded the College of Propaganda for the education of missionaries and the printing of polyglot press.

243:43   *Linebarger, P. M. A., *Psychological Warfare*, (Washington), 1948, p. 3.

244:3   *Ibid.*, p. 7.

244:20   Davidson, P., *Propaganda and the American Revolution*, (Chapel Hill), 1941.

244:21   Linebarger, *op. cit.*, p. 20.

244:31   Geyer, H., "Uber die Zeitdauer von Angriffsgefechten," *Militärwissenschaftliche Rundschau*, 1939, v. 4, no. 4, pp. 179-186.

244:35   Rowan, *op. cit.*, pp. 643-646.

244:42   Fyfe, H., *Northcliffe. An Intimate Biography*, (New York), 1930, pp. 238-256.

245:30   Wellesley, Sir V., *Diplomacy in Fetters*, (London), 1944, pp. 9, 30, 42, 54.

245:39   Kris, E., Leites, N., "Trends in Twentieth Century propaganda," *Psychoanalysis and the Social Sciences*, (New York), 1947, v. 1.

245:40   *Overseas Information Programs of the United States*. Part 1: Report of the Committee on Foreign Relations; part 2: Hearings, (Washington), 1953.

246:7   Stowe, L., *op. cit.*, pp. 85, 141, 259, 281, 284-287, 289; Barrett, E. W., *Truth is Our Weapon*, (New York), 1953, pp. 96, 214, 276-277, 281.

246:33   Zacharias, *op. cit.*, pp. 307-311; Barrett, *op. cit.*, pp. 9-10; Carroll, *op. cit.*, p. 366.

246:41   Zacharias, *op. cit.*, pp. 332-383.

247:3   Linebarger, *op. cit.*, pp. 44, 88-89.

247:15   Farago, L., "British propaganda," *United Nations World*, 1948, v. 2, no. 9, pp. 22-25. Lochner, L. P., *What About Germany?*, (New York), 1942, pp. 234-235. Mr. Lochner, long-time AP correspondent in Germany, accepted "the Boss" as a genuine representative of the German anti-

Nazi movement, but appeared scandalized by his obscenities.

247:17 The other effective British clandestine radio operation was the so-called *Soldatensender Calais*, transmitting black propaganda virtually around the clock.

248:35 Linebarger, *op. cit.*, p. 206.

249:12 Warburg, J. P., *Unwritten Treaty*, (New York), 1946, pp. 151-161.

249:22 Siepmann, C. A., *Radio, Television and Society*, (New York), 1950, pp. 117-154, 292-316.

249:29 Sington, D., Weidenfeld, A., *The Goebbels Experiment*, (New Haven), 1943, pp. 139-140, 149, 181-193.

249:34 Katz, D., "Britain speaks," in Childs, H. L., Whitton, J. B., *Propaganda by Short Wave*, (Princeton), 1943, pp. 109-150.

250:12 Thomson, C. A. H., *Overseas Information Service of the United States Government*, (Washington), 1948, pp. 17-192.

250:19 Ettlinger, H., *The Axis on the Air*, (Indianapolis), 1943; Linebarger, *op. cit.*, pp. 81-88.

250:38 Herz, M. F., "Some lessons from leaflet propaganda," *Public Opinion Quarterly*, 1949, Fall.

251:6 Jackson, C. D., "Assignment for the press," in Markel, L. (ed.), *Public Opinion and Foreign Policy*, (New York), 1949, pp. 180-187.

251:15 Stern-Rubarth, E., *Propaganda als politisches Instrument*, (Berlin), 1921.

252:29 Hadamovsky, E., *Propaganda und nationale Macht*, (Oldenburg), 1933.

253:6 Allport, G. W., Postman, L., *The Psychology of Rumor*, (New York), 1947.

253:29 *Ibid.*, p. 161.

254:2 Knapp, R. H., "A psychology of rumor," *Public Opinion Quarterly*, 1944, pp. 22-37.

254:32 Stone, S., "Chart of the cold war," in Markel, *op. cit.*, pp. 143-155; Carroll, *op. cit.*, pp. 371-392; Barrett, *op. cit.*, pp. 219-300.

255:1 Barghorn, F. C., *The Soviet Image of the United States*, (New York), 1950, pp. 3-38, 103-290.

255:29 Riess, C., *Der siebzehnte Juni*, (Berlin), 1954.

255:34 Zeller, B., *Geist der Freiheit*, (München), 1952; Görlitz, *op. cit.*, pp. 647-672.

256:8 Clausewitz, C. V., *On War*, (London), 1940, v. 1, pp. 2-3.

256:16 *Enc. Brit.*, (q.v.), v. 28, p. 306.

256:44 *Ibid.*, v. 4, pp. 794-795.

257:2 Bülow, P. V., *Familienbuch der v. Bülow*, (Berlin), 1859.

257:12 Cämmerer, V., *Development of Strategical Sciences*, (London), 1905.

258:1 Mannheim, K., *Man and Society in an Age of Reconstruction*, (London), 1940. Also see, Kennan, G. F., *American Diplomacy 1900-1950*, (Chicago), 1951, pp. 58-62; Lippmann, W., *The Cold War*, (New York), 1947, pp. 58-62; Werfel, F., *Star of the Unborn*, (New York), 1946, a utopian novel in which conflict is transferred into what Werfel called "man's astromental sphere."

258:25 Rowan, *op. cit.*, p. 682.

Index of Names